TRAITORS' GATE

BOOKS BY KATE ELLIOTT

Crossroads
*Book I: *Spirit Gate*
*Book II: *Shadow Gate*
*Book III: *Traitors' Gate*

The Novels of the Jaran
Jaran
An Earthly Crown
His Conquering Sword
The Law of Becoming

Crown of Stars
King's Dragon
Prince of Dogs
The Burning Stone
Child of Flame
The Gathering Storm
In the Ruins
Crown of Stars

The Golden Key (with Melanie Rawn and Jennifer Roberson)

WRITING AS ALIS S. RASMUSSEN

The Labyrinth Gate

The Highroad Trilogy
I: *A Passage of Stars*
II: *Revolution's Shore*
III: *The Price of Ransom*

*A Tor Book

TRAITORS' GATE

BOOK THREE OF CROSSROADS

Kate Elliott

TOR®

A Tom Doherty Associates Book
New York

TRAITORS' GATE: BOOK THREE OF CROSSROADS

Edited by James Frenkel

Map by Elizabeth Danforth

A Tor Book
Published by Tom Doherty Associates, LLC
175 Fifth Avenue
New York, NY 10010

www.tor-forge.com

Tor® is a registered trademark of Tom Doherty Associates, LLC.

Library of Congress Cataloging-in-Publication Data

Elliott, Kate.
    Traitors' gate / Kate Elliott.—1st ed.
        p. cm.
    "A Tom Doherty Associates book."
    ISBN-13: 978-0-7653-1057-6
    ISBN-10: 0-7653-1057-0
    I. Title.
    PS3555.L5917T73 2009
    813'.54—dc22
                                        2009012929

First Edition: August 2009

Printed in the United States of America

0 9 8 7 6 5 4 3 2 1

This novel is affectionately dedicated to
Ruth Perzley Silverstein,
surely the world's most generous and loving mother-in-law.

ACKNOWLEDGMENTS

FIRST, I MUST particularly thank my son Alexander, who dutifully read early sections and offered useful feedback and who also helped me strategize.

Second, a special shout-out to William-James McEnerney, LT, USN, who, in the course of spending a couple of hours talking with me one evening, made me rethink certain aspects of the story; I'm sure it's his fault the book is so long.

Third, to my LiveJournal communitarians: Thanks! They came up with the title for the book; it was a subtle but meaningful change from my working title of *Traitor's Gate* to the final title of *Traitors' Gate*.

Finally, thanks to the usual suspects: Constance Ash, Katharine Kerr, Sherwood Smith, and Michelle Sagara West, who answered when I called; James Frenkel, my exceedingly patient editor, and his minions, especially his assistant in Madison, Alan Rubsam; Flatiron people Liz Gorinsky and Steven Padnick, and intern Emily Attwood; copy editor extraordinaire Terry McGarry; the supportive Orbit crew; Paul Emanovsky, for forensic advice (mostly for *Shadow Gate*, but I forgot to thank him then); Russ Galen, as always; and my other two children and long-suffering spouse, who put up with me.

AUTHOR'S NOTE

IN THE HUNDRED, any and every set and sequence of patterns is seen as having cosmological significance. Every number has multiple associations. For instance, the number 3 is associated with the Three Noble Towers present in every major town or city (Watch Tower, Assizes Tower, and Sorrowing [or Silence] Tower); with the Three States of Mind (Resting, Wakened, and Transcendent); with the Three Languages; and with the Three-Part Anatomy of every person's soul (Mind, Hands, and Heart). The number 7 is associated with the Seven Gods, the Seven Gems, the Seven Directions, and the Seven Treasures.

Folk in the Hundred measure the passing of time not via year dates set from a year zero, but rather through the cyclical passage of time. The standard repeating twelve-year cycle is named after animals, in the following order: Eagle, Deer, Crane, Ox, Snake, Lion, Ibex, Fox, Goat, Horse, Wolf, Rat. However, this year cycle is meshed with the properties of the Nine Colors to create a larger cycle of one hundred and eight years. A clerk of Sapanasu, or anyone else who can do this kind of accounting, could thereby identify how long ago an event happened, or how old a person is, depending on the color of animal year in which he or she was born.

Each animal or color, having its own particular and peculiar associations, lends to all events in that year and to people birthed therein specific characteristics. Therefore, Keshad, born in the Year of the Gold Goat, combines Goat characteristics of cleverness, vanity, strong will, jealousy, pride, a deep sense of purpose contrasted with instability of shallow purpose, and a talent for seeking wealth, with Gold qualities like energy, intellect, intensity, dishonesty, envy, and aloofness.

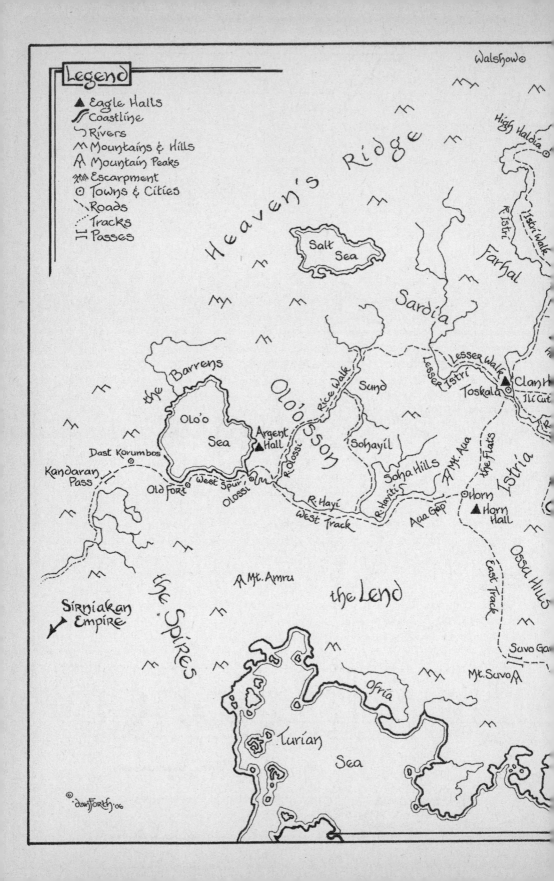

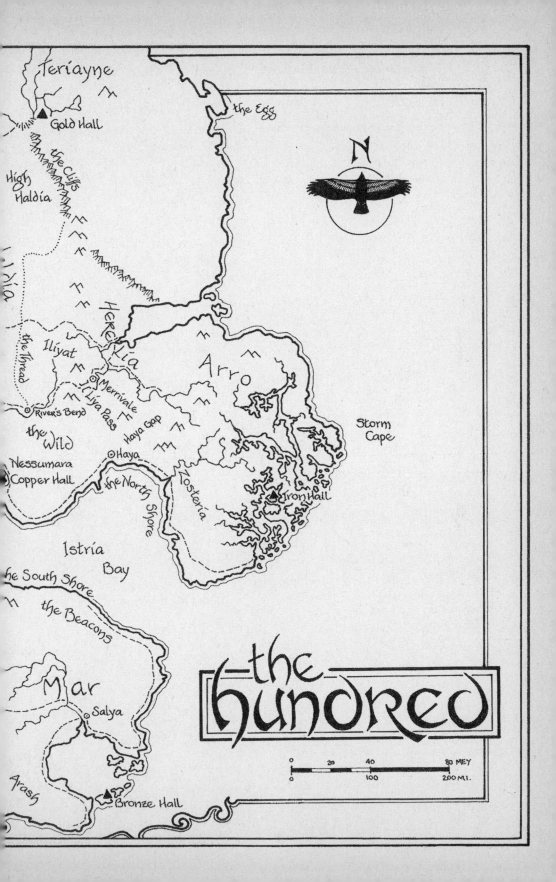

Teriayne

the Egg

N

Gold Hall

the Cliffs

High
Haldia

Ilixia

Heredia

Iliyat

the Thread

Arro

Merrivale

Liya Pass

River's Bend

Haya Gap

the Wild

Haya

Storm
Cape

Nessumara
Copper Hall

the North Shore

Zosteria

Iron Hall

Istria
Bay

the South Shore

the Beacons

Mar

Salya

the
Hundred

Arash

Bronze Hall

0   20   40   80 MEY
0   100   200 MI.

TRAITORS' GATE

PART ONE: FOREIGNERS

1

LATE AT NIGHT a fight broke out beyond the compound's high walls.

Keshad sat up in darkness. At first he thought himself in the Hundred, in the city of Olossi, still bound as a debt slave to Master Feden. Then he smelled the rancid aroma of the harsh local oil used for cooking. He heard shouts, jabbering words he could not understand.

He wasn't in the Hundred. He was in the Sirniakan Empire.

He groped for the short sword he had stashed under the cot.

"Eh? Keshad?" A bleary voice murmured on the other side of the curtain.

"Quiet. There's trouble."

The cloth rippled as Eliar wrestled with clothing, or his turban, or whatever the hells the Silvers were so cursed prudish about. Bracelets jangled. There came a curse, a rattle, and a thump as the cot tipped over.

"Where's the lamp?"

"Hush." Kesh wrapped his kilt around his waist, approached the door, and, leaning against it, pressed an ear to the crack. All quiet.

"Nothing to do with us," he whispered. "Yet."

The cot scraped, being righted. "The Sirniakan officials have locked us in the compound, won't let us trade, and hand over a scant portion of rice and millet once a day so we don't starve. One of their priests told you the emperor is dead, killed in battle by his cousin. They've locked down Sardia and are restricting all movement. These troubles have *everything* to do with us. We have to get out of here, return to Olossi, and report these developments to Captain Anji."

"Say it a bit louder, perhaps. That will help us, neh? If everyone figures out we're spies?"

"No need to constantly criticize me—"

Aui! No matter how much he disliked Eliar, he had to make this expedition work or he'd never get what he wanted. And to get what he wanted, he had to stay on Eliar's good side.

"I beg your pardon. It's hateful to be stuck in this cursed compound day and night."

Eliar grunted in acknowledgment of the apology, which Kesh knew was gracelessly delivered. "We've got to do *something*."

Kesh jiggered the latch and cracked the door. It was strange to deal with hinges instead of proper doors that slid, but in the empire things were done one way or not at all, and if you didn't like it, the priests would condemn you to the fire. In the courtyard, a lamp hanging from a bracket illuminated the storehouse gates, but the far walls with their set-back doors into other storerooms and sleeping cells remained hidden in shadows. Trumpets, shouting, and clash of weapons swelled in the distance, well away from the restricted market district where foreign merchants were required to reside and carry out all their trade. A whiff of burning oil stung his nose as a flame flared behind him.

"Pinch that down, you fool!" he whispered. "We don't want anyone to know we're awake." Nothing stirred in the courtyard. If anyone had seen that flare of light, they weren't acting on it. "Listen, Eliar, you stay here. Make sure no one goes after our trade goods. I'm going to the gate to see what the guards will tell me."

"The guards never tell us a cursed thing."

"They talk to me because I worship at the Beltak temple."

That shut Eliar up.

Keshad sheathed his sword and slung the sword belt over his back. He eased into the courtyard and padded cautiously past the open inner gate to the forecourt. The double gates had been barred for eight days, since the night when trumpets and horns had disturbed the peace and all the markets had been closed. Several figures huddled by the ranks of handcarts. One raised a lamp.

"Master Keshad? Maybe you can get these cursed guards to talk to you, since they favor you so much."

The other Hundred merchants didn't like him any better than he liked them. They thought him a traitor for abandoning the gods of his birth for the empire's god, but what did it matter to them what god he chose to worship or what benefit that worship brought him? There were a pair of outlanders as well, a man out of the Mariha princedoms and one from the western desert whose slaves, languishing in the slave pens, he hadn't seen for days. For that matter, the drivers and guardsmen he and Eliar had hired in Olossi were confined in different quarters altogether, and he'd had no contact with them since the citywide curfew was imposed.

He rang the bell at the guardhouse. A guard in one of the watch platforms above turned to look down into the forecourt. Bars scraped and locks rattled. The guardhouse door opened and the sergeant pushed into the forecourt, a pair of armed guards at his back and another guard holding high a lamp.

"Get inside!"

His angry words drove the merchants back into the main courtyard.

Keshad held his ground. "Honored one, may I ask if we are in danger here?"

The sergeant's expression softened. "I know nothing. Men have broken curfew. Best you get inside until the storm passes."

The storm roared closer. A clatter of running feet in a nearby street was followed by a chorus of shouts so loud the sergeant flinched. Kesh took a step back from the double gates. The distinctive clamor of clashing swords and spears hammered the night, the skirmish racing as though one group was chasing another. The guards drew their swords; a fifth man popped out of the guardhouse.

"All ranks at the ready," snarled the sergeant, and the man vanished back into the tower. "They may try to break in."

The skirmish flowed along the street outside as Kesh gripped his sword so tightly he was shaking. The noise reached a pitch and abruptly subsided.

The sergeant exhaled. He spoke to his guards in the local language, but Kesh was too rattled to catch more than a word here and there. Foreigners. Market. Fire. Traitors to the emperor.

Kesh glanced through the open door into the guardhouse, which snaked through the compound wall; there was a small gate for the guard unit on the street side because the guards watched both ways, keeping locals out and foreigners in.

As though slapped by a giant hand, the gates shuddered. The sergeant swore, signaled to his men, and bolted inside, swinging the door shut. A struggle erupted outside. Several merchants came running from the main courtyard, but Kesh shoved past them and ran to his cell, where Eliar waited by the door.

"These gods-rotted empire laws have us caged like beasts," Kesh snapped, "not a chance to get in or out nor anywhere to hide or escape to. Curse them."

"Maybe we can get out over the roofs. I've had plenty of practice getting in and out of tight places in Olossi. My friends and I, we smuggled goods over the river."

In the forecourt, merchants shouted, "Block the gate!" "Block the guardhouse door!"

Kesh began to laugh, because there wasn't anything else to find funny in their situation. "The hells! Were you part of that gang the Greater Houses were constantly chasing?"

He felt the sting of Eliar's smile as though he could touch it. "I was."

"Aui! You didn't really get up on the roof, did you?"

"I did. One night when you were sleeping. I used rope tied around the lamp brackets. But there's a walkway around the entire roof. They patrol it all night."

"Keeping us in, or others out. Grab rope. And whatever you can carry that's too valuable to leave behind."

"Climbing out of the compound is easy. But how can we get out of the city without being killed?"

"The hells!" Kesh collected the pouches of local spices, best-quality braid, and polished gems he'd brought south from the Hundred; he slung them over his back, buckling tight the straps so the pouches wouldn't shift as he moved. Then he grabbed rope coiled against the door that led into a small storeroom accessible only from this chamber. None of the goods he and Eliar had stored in there were worth his life.

"I'm ready," said the Ri Amarah from the door.

Eliar's bulging packs brushed Kesh's arm. "What in the hells are you carrying?"

"All the oil of naya."

"Aui! Don't drop it by a flame."

Kesh shouldered past and led Eliar to the archway of the inner gate. A few merchants were frantically shoving carts and benches in front of the closed double gates, but the rest were hiding in the storerooms. A struggle raged within the gatehouse, and outside the gates a crowd screamed words Kesh was pretty sure meant something like "Kill the foreigners! Kill the traitors!"

"They haven't given us up," said Kesh suddenly.

"What do you mean?"

"The sergeant and his guards could let that mob in. But they're defending us. Eiya! We'll need oil of naya."

He expected Eliar to protest, but the other man swung down his bulky packs. Keshad ran to the cistern in the middle of the courtyard and climbed up.

"Heya! Heya! Get your weapons! Move! Our guards are defending us against a mob that wants to kill us. If we don't help them, we're all dead. I need rags. Anything that will burn easily. Hurry, you cursed fools!"

He ran to the forecourt. The guards had abandoned the watch platforms that flanked the gates. Access to the platforms and the wall walk was from inside the guardhouse, now being fought over.

Merchants came running with weapons, with rags, one dragging a thin pallet. Two carried lamps. Eliar brought three leather bottles. Muffled crashes and shouts came from the guardhouse. Someone was taking a beating.

Keshad indicated the platforms above. "We'll splash oil of naya over the crowd, light rags, and throw them down on top. That should drive them away."

"Heh. Just like the battle over Olossi," said one man.

"I'll go up," said Eliar immediately.

As Kesh slung a bottle over his shoulder he called the other merchants closer. "Those who can fight, brace yourselves. Form up around the inner gate. Tip carts over, under the arch, to make a bottleneck. One of you roust out the cowards. We need everyone. Now, hoist me up."

Kesh and another man climbed up on a cart. The man laced his fingers together and, when Kesh set a foot into the makeshift stirrup, raised him up so he could throw rope around one of the poles making the scaffolding of the platform. He clambered up and crouched on the platform as Eliar was helped up on the other side. The mob below hadn't yet spotted them. Men surged past the guardhouse door, pushing inside only to be cut down by the armed guardsmen. But the mob was growing, howling and barking like animals, or so it seemed to his ears. Workingmen who had, Kesh supposed, filled up with fear and now had to take it out on someone else, they were armed with torches, sticks, tools, and other such humble implements. None seemed to have bows. He licked his lips, tasted smoke. Elsewhere in the market district, compounds were burning.

The top of the twinned gates was broad enough to walk across if you didn't mind the height. Eliar hauled up a basket and crouched beside it, lifting out a burning lantern. Below, within the mob, a face looked up. Down along the street about ten men came running carrying ladders.

Keshad unsealed the first bottle. This was the dangerous part! He shook the vessel, oil spraying on the men crowded up below. Eliar set fire to a rag and flung it outward, but it fell to the ground and was stamped out. Men threw sticks and debris up at them. The first ladder was pushed up against the gate. Keshad emptied the first vessel on top of the men at the base of the ladder. He unsealed the second and ran out along the top of the gate, flinging oil out as far away as he could. Men cursed at him, wiping away the oil that splashed on their faces. Spreading it. A second flaming rag fluttered down, and a third—

Fire touched oil on skin.

Shrieking, the man staggered, slamming into the men around him, half of whom had been splashed by oil of naya. The conflagration spread. The mob disintegrated as men fled in terror. The stench was horrible, and the screams were worse. But the street was clearing fast.

Keshad ran back to the platform, swung his legs over, and paid out the rope to let himself down to the forecourt. When he touched earth, his legs gave out. He pitched forward as the merchants babbled and cried.

Eliar bent over him. "Keshad? Are you hurt?"

"Neh." His speech was gone. His limbs were weak. He still heard screams.

"That saved us," added Eliar.

"For now."

"Clever of you to think of it. Just like at Olossi."

The door to the guardhouse scraped open and the sergeant stumbled out, blood splashed all over him. Seen past the sergeant, a whitewashed room looked like a slaughterhouse, with tumbled corpses, the hazy smoke of torches, and a guardsman kneeling beside a fallen comrade.

"What do you? What do you?" The sergeant loomed over him, swiping smears of blood from his beard with his left hand while he extended the right. "Good, good."

Hesitantly, Keshad reached out, and the man clasped elbows in the grasp of kinship seen in the market among believers but never extended to foreigners.

SOON AFTER DAWN, a squad of mounted soldiers resplendent in green sashes and helmets trimmed with gold ribbons clattered up to the closed gates. Smoke drifted over the rooftops. The merchants who had sat the rest of the night on watch on the roofs hastily clambered down as the gates were opened.

The sergeant genuflected before the squad's captain. As the sergeant kept his head bowed, they exchanged a running jabber in their own language. An older merchant murmured a translation.

"There was trouble all across the market district last night. There is to be an inquiry anywhere local men were killed."

"Against the mob, or against us?" Kesh muttered.

Worry creased the sergeant's face as he surveyed the merchants. The captain snapped a command that made the sergeant wince. With an apologetic grimace he pointed—quite rudely, as outlanders always did, using the fingers—at Keshad.

"Bring him." The captain's gaze paused on Eliar, with his butter-yellow turban. "You come, also."

Eliar took an obedient step toward the squad, but Keshad held his ground.

"What about our trade goods? What surety do we have they'll not be stolen while we're not here to guard them ourselves?"

The captain raised a hand, and soldiers drew their swords. "You come. Or I kill you."

Keshad wiped sweat from his eyes as his throat closed over a pointless protest. He shrugged, pretending calm. Eliar looked as if he'd been struck.

They walked under the market district gate and into the main city, a place no foreign merchant was ever allowed to enter. The empty streets were broad and clean-swept, walled on both sides, with gates opening at intervals into compounds. The hooves of the horses echoed in an eerie silence. Once Kesh saw a face peeping over a wall, dropping out of sight when their gazes met. Their procession wound inward and upward as the sun rose, and just when it was beginning to get really hot they arrived at a vast gate that opened into a grand courtyard lined with pillared colonnades carved of finest white marble.

The captain indicated a bench in the shade. "Sit there."

They sat. Four soldiers settled into guard positions while the captain rode into a farther courtyard glimpsed through a magnificently carved archway.

"Look at the figures carved on the arch," whispered Eliar. "There is the sun in splendor, the moon veiled, and the stars assembled in ranks to acknowledge the suzerainty of the god they worship here."

" 'The god they worship here'? That kind of talk will get you burned."

Eliar shrugged. "I'm saying it to you. Not to them. What would they do? Force me to worship at their god's temple?"

"How naïve are you? Don't you know anything about the empire? They could tell you to say the prayers to Beltak, or suffer the punishment meted out to those who don't believe. Who in the Hundred could do a cursed thing if they killed you, eh?"

Eliar's smug smile infuriated Kesh. "I am a faithful son of the Hidden One. That is all that matters. Look there!"

Kesh looked up and their guards came alert, then relaxed, tossing remarks to each other as he sank back on the bench. Eliar had just been pointing to a different section of the arch.

"There, the different officers of the court pay homage before the emperor's throne."

"There's no one sitting in the throne."

"He is holy, like the god, not to be pictured."

"How do you know?"

"I read it! I know most of you in the Hundred don't read—"

" 'You in the Hundred'! I thought you Silvers keep claiming you are simply humble Hundred folk just like the rest of us."

"That's not what I meant—"

"If the emperor's not to be pictured, then why is there a statue of the emperor in the marketplace?"

"That's not the emperor. It's a statue of a male figure representing Commerce, richly clad and adorned with gilt paint to remind all those in the marketplace that through trade the empire becomes wealthy."

Kesh puzzled over the vacant throne. Sure enough, there were the officers of the court attended by an array of half-sized men, meant perhaps to represent their underlings, and certain animals that evidently had some significance to each officer's mandate. At the height of the arch, above sun and moon and stars, was carved an elaborate crown ornamented by wavy lines most likely representing fire.

Mounted soldiers clattered in and passed through the open gates. Their garments were splashed with blood, and they looked grim.

"Did you really learn all this from books?" Kesh asked finally. "How can you know it's true?"

Deep in Eliar's answering smile rose a glimpse of the sister, seen once and never ever to be forgotten: a reckless, bold spirit, unquenchable. "Of course I can't know it's true. Someone thought it was, but that doesn't mean the one who wrote it was correct, does it? The person might have been wrong. Or might be right."

"How do you Silvers—" As Eliar's mouth twisted in disapproval, Kesh caught himself and changed course. "How comes it that you Ri Amarah possess books with so much detail about the empire?"

"Many of our houses—our clans—lived here for six generations, as it says in the prophecy, until they were driven out by the Beltak priests for not worshipping the empire's god. It's said in our histories that some among us renounced the Hidden One and stayed in the empire, because they prospered here, but I don't believe that."

"You don't believe they prospered here? That any foreigner could?"

"I don't believe they renounced the Hidden One. How is it possible to renounce the truth?"

Keshad laughed. The guards turned, and he clamped his mouth shut.

Eliar fulminated. "Are you laughing at me?"

"You've never been a slave. People renounce the truth all the time if it will give them an advantage. Then they convince themselves that what they wish to be true is the truth. Think of Master Feden, who once owned my debt. How could he have allied himself with that cruel army out of the north? He told himself he was doing the right thing even when everything he saw must have told him otherwise. Olossi is fortunate he's dead and that the army was driven away. Otherwise, where would you and I be?"

As soon as the words left Kesh's mouth, he was sorry he had spoken them, and yet not for Eliar's sake. Where would he be now? He and his sister Zubaidit would be somewhere in the north, starting over as free people unencumbered by debt slavery or obligation to the temple. If the defenders of Olossi had lost the battle, then they would not have been able to track down him and Bai and haul them back to stand before the Hieros of Ushara's temple in Olossi. There, Kesh had been condemned for a theft he had committed without knowing what he was doing was a crime.

Folk claimed a man could expect to be rewarded for good deeds and punished for bad ones if he made the proper offerings. The temples said so, and the Beltak priests said so, and no doubt the Hidden One said so. The only god he'd run into who didn't seem to say so was Mai's god, the Merciful One, who offered shelter in times of trouble, of which there were plenty. Yet had the gods cared for him and Zubaidit after their parents had died?

And yet. And yet. If it all had not fallen out as it did, he would never have seen Miravia.

A man dressed in a red jacket hurried toward them. The four guards kneeled. There was an extended consultation in the local jabber so quick Kesh could not pick out words. The red-jacket guard gave an order and gestured at Kesh and Eliar in trade sign: *Rise.*

They followed him into a courtyard bustling with movement as soldiers assembled in ranks while others, dismounting, handed their horses over to grooms. The red-jacket guard led them through a second pair of gates into a dusty square where several hundred riders loitered beside saddled mounts, with a train of laden pack-horses and a herd of spare mounts besides.

"You go." The red-jacket guard indicated two sturdy geldings before moving away to exchange words with a young captain resplendent in green jacket, helmet adorned with gold plumes.

"Where are we going?" Eliar whispered, but Kesh shrugged. What use to speculate?

And yet he could not stop wondering, thinking, sorting. They rode out through the city on a wide avenue empty of traffic and thence out a handsome stone gate into the patternwork countryside, everything tidy, nothing out of order.

Only the empire was not truly in order. The emperor had been killed in battle by his own cousin as they fought over the throne. Which faction had taken them prisoner? What did they mean to do with them? Because there was another thing blazingly obvious about the soldiers who escorted them. Half wore green jackets to mark them as underlings of the gold-plumed captain, a man who did not over the course of that first day speak a single word to Kesh or Eliar. But the rest were Qin, with their phlegmatic expressions, unadorned armor, and scruffy little horses that were nothing much to look at but as tough as any creatures Kesh had ever encountered. And that raised a cursed uncomfortable question, didn't it? Where had these Qin soldiers come from, and why were they riding in company with Sirniakan troops?

2

"HEYA, KESH!" ELIAR called to him from a nearby campfire where he sat with a gaggle of junior officers, all quaffing from brass cups. "This poocha's so strong it'll make your eyes water. Come try some?"

The junior officers looked nervously toward Kesh, and then, politely, back at their cups. How like Eliar not to notice their discomfort, although it pranced right in front of his face. Keshad glared, but the cursed Silver could not see him well enough in the dusk to be properly stung and instead went back to his drinking and chatting and laughing, although how he could understand half of what the locals jawed on about Kesh could not imagine.

"You do not approve of your companion."

Kesh jumped to his feet. "Captain Jushahosh."

A slave opened a camp stool, and the captain sat.

"I have no wine or poocha to offer you, Captain." Kesh sat likewise.

Slaves approached bearing trays laden with cups, pitchers, eating utensils, and platters that they placed on a camp table. The captain murmured a blessing over food and drink before continuing. "As you are my prisoner, I cannot expect you to offer hospitality. I see, Master Keshad, that you have remained aloof these ten days from the junior officers, who are merely warrior-born. Your companion seems easy with them. He is one of the heretics, is he not?"

"I'm not sure what you mean."

"There is a story taught to educated men of a tribe of men who came by sea out of the east to settle in the empire. In our own tongue they were given the name, the men with silver arms. They lived with proper comportment for six generations, as it says in the holy books, but then their error was revealed and the priests were shown the truth of their hidden ways, that they spat upon the commands of the Shining One inside the walls of their own compounds. Out of respect for a kindness shown to the emperor by one of their number—or, as I consider more likely, because of a massive bribe paid to the temple—they were allowed to depart the empire without molestation, leaving behind all they could not carry. This they did. Some went north over the mountains and some west into the desert and some south into the forest of choking vines, but none sailed back east over the ocean to the place they had come from. You are a believer. You pray with us morning and night. Do you trust this man Eliar, with his silver arms?"

The captain stabbed a slice of spiced meat and popped it into his mouth. Keshad copied him, gaining a respite while he chewed and swallowed. The meat was moist and peppery.

"Have you some reason not to trust him that I should know of?"

The captain was sleek in all aspects; dressed and shod well, he carried a fine sword and rode a string of beautiful horses with roan coats like enough in texture and color that Kesh supposed them bred out of the same stable. "He might be a spy."

"So might I, then, as we are business partners."

"One partner may not always know what the other plots in the shadows."

"True enough. Eliar is decent enough, for a Silver."

"A Silver?"

"That's what we call them in the Hundred, Captain. For the silver bracelets they wear on their arms. It seems your chroniclers called them the same."

"He's like a creature out of a story walking into your father's palace. Does he have horns?"

The captain looked very young, and Kesh realized they were of an age but separated not by their lives as men of different countries but rather by the circumstances of their birth. Kesh was born to a humble clan whose kin had seen fit to sell him and his sister into slavery when their parents died; Jushahosh was born into a palace, son of a noble lord with many wives and slave women and therefore many such lesser sons.

"I don't know," Kesh said confidingly, leaning closer, "for he clings to his privacy, as his people do. I've never seen him without the turban covering his head."

They shared a complicit smile.

A prisoner who is a foreigner pretending to be a legitimate merchant only while being in truth secretly a spy and who fears he is being taken south to be burned as a spy must yet attempt to gather information, in case he gets out of his current situation alive.

"Strange to see the Qin soldiers here," he added, nodding toward the circle of fires where the Qin had set up their own encampment. "Are they under your command? Do they take your orders? Don't they speak a different language?"

"Their chief can talk the trade language, just as I can. What they jabber about otherwise I don't know, but I suppose they mostly talk about sheep and horses." He flashed a grin, and Kesh laughed. "You're familiar with the Qin, eh? Seen them up in the Hundred?"

Sheh! Caught at his own game.

"I've heard of them, all right. Did I tell you the story of the journey I made into the Mariha princedoms? Two years ago, it was. I never saw so many strange creatures as out on the desert's borderlands. Didn't think I'd make it home. The Qin were the least of it!"

"What did you see?"

Kesh could embellish a story as well as anyone, for tales were the breath of the Hundred, exhaled with the beat of the heart and a lift of the hand. "Demons, for one thing. Maybe you call them something else here."

"No." His gaze flicked, side to side, as he twisted his cup in his hands. "What did they look like?"

"Ah. One was a woman—"

"Of course!"

"Her skin was as pale as that of a ghost. And her hair was the color of straw."

"Truly a demon, then!"

"Her eyes were blue."

The captain had just taken a mouthful of poocha. He spat it out, coughing and choking, as Kesh sat rigid. But the man waved away his slaves and laughed through his coughing. "Horrible to look upon! Go on."

Kesh dropped his voice to a murmur as the captain bent closer yet. "She was enveloped in an enchanted cloak of demon weave, like cloth woven out of spider's silk. And beneath that cloak . . . she was unclothed. That was the other way I knew she was a demon."

The captain's eyes flared with shame and heat; a flush stained his cheeks. "What did she looked like, underneath?"

"Exalted Captain!" A junior officer, wearing his watch duty sash over his green jacket, came running up, his face slicked with a sheen of sweat although the evening was only moderately humid and warm. "There's a company of men upon the road. Imperial guards."

A blast from a horn brought the captain to his feet. He strode off toward the lines, where lamps bobbed along the length of the road. In his wake, slaves gathered up tray and stool with the same swift grace they'd shown in setting it up. Kesh speared meat off the platter before they could whisk it out of his reach, and a slave waited impassively until he'd gulped down the strips before taking the eating knife away from him and following the others to the captain's tent. The junior officers set down their cups and charged off, chattering excitedly. Kesh hurried over to the fire and plopped down beside Eliar.

"Is there anything left to eat or drink here?"

Eliar rose, stepping away from him as if he bore a stench. He stared toward the lights half seen along the distant road. "Do you think there might be a skirmish? How can you possibly think of eating when—?"

"You eat when there's food. No telling when you'll get more." He hooked a triangle of flat bread off the common platter and crammed it in his mouth. He managed to down more bread and a crispy slice of a white vegetable, still moist and a little peppery, before servants descended to collect the trays and cups. Eliar was bouncing on his toes as if movement would help him see over the ranks of soldiers gathering amid the tents. Out by the road, men shouted, so much tension in their tone that Kesh rose likewise to stand beside Eliar.

"If they start fighting, make for our tent. We might have to run for it . . ."

Eliar grabbed Kesh's forearm, the touch so unexpected that Kesh flinched. "I know you don't like me, but promise me this. If we die here, you'll tell the truth of it to my family." He released him.

"If I'm dead, I can't tell anyone the truth, can I?"

"You seem like the kind of person who can get out of anything," said Eliar, his voice as hoarse as if he'd been running. "Even if it means abandoning others to do so."

"At least I know what you truly think of me. You think I've got no cursed honor, don't you?"

Eliar shook his head stubbornly. "If I die, Kesh, don't let them sell my sister into marriage with the Haf Ke Pir house in Nessumara. Promise me."

From the road, the voices continued. The Qin soldiers had melted away to their horse lines.

"Don't you think it's too late? By the time we get back, won't they already have delivered her to Nessumara?"

"How could they? The roads aren't safe."

"Reeves could fly her there! Or did that never occur to you?"

Eliar groaned. "Aui! But no. Reeves aren't carters."

"Is there one single thing in this world that isn't for sale if enough coin is offered? And if you get back safely and she's still at your home? Will you escort her yourself to Nessumara, to her new husband? The one she doesn't want to go to? It'll be all right then, knowing you've had your adventure?" Kesh knew how the words must sound, greasy with sarcasm, but cursed if Eliar was too caught up in his own writhing discontent to notice.

"If I die, I'll have cast her into misery for nothing. She in her cage, I to be burned. What have I done—"

What charged the air Kesh did not know, but before Eliar could draw another breath everything changed, as if lightning had struck. A trio of Qin soldiers, swords drawn, trotted out of the darkness masking the horse lines. Screams and shouts broke from the road. A flame—one of the lamps—arced high into the night sky as if flung heavenward, and then an arrow shattered it. The horn stuttered, answered by a call from down the road, a triple *blat blat blat*, and cursing and shouting and swords clattering like hooves in their staccato rhythm.

Kesh grabbed Eliar's wrist. "Let's go!" He tugged, and yet Eliar would stand there like a dumbstruck lackwit gazing on the dance of festival lights.

Suddenly, that trio of Qin soldiers trotted up beside them with the unsmiling but not precisely unfriendly expressions of men come to do their duty. One hooked a thumb to indicate they should move away from the altercation. Kesh yanked harder until Eliar stumbled after him, gaze turned toward the skirmish whose color and sound made the camp seem as bright as day and twice as fearsome. Kesh's heart was galloping, like distant horses. Orders rang in a voice remarkably like Captain Jushahosh's, lilting high as with fright. A rumble spilled an undercurrent through the clash of arms. A woman's scream cut through the tumult.

As Kesh sucked in a startled breath, the world fell silent. For one breath there were neither questions nor answers, only the shock of hearing a female voice where none belonged.

The fighting broke out anew, redoubled in intensity. The Qin soldiers pressed them toward their tent. Eliar was so pale Kesh wondered if he would faint, while meanwhile he was himself looking in every direction, trying to figure out how and where he could run, how far he could get, and if it was worth trying to get the Silver to move with him lest he have otherwise to explain to Eliar's beautiful sister how Eliar had gotten abandoned with their enemies. And yet, how thoroughly impossible it was to hope for escape through a countryside where he would be known for a foreigner at first glance.

A swirl of Qin soldiers appeared out of the darkness, carrying on a running commentary with their fellows, words like the scraping of saws, all burrs and edges. They ran with choppy strides and corraled Kesh and Eliar. Movement roiled through the camp, a second wave of black-clad Qin soldiers driving the enemy before them like so many sheep.

Captain Jushahosh limped, his face smeared with blood and his sword mottled.

"Hei! Hei!" he cried. The Qin soldiers stepped away from their flock as more green-jacket guards streamed in and two aides brought forward lanterns. Four men had fallen to their knees, faces pressed into the dirt. The other figure was veiled, and she clasped a small body against her own, shielding it as the captain approached her. He gestured, and one of the junior officers stepped forward, grasped the little child, and ripped it out of her arms.

Her silence was worse than a scream would have been.

The Qin soldiers stared like dumb beasts as the junior officer cut the silk wrap off the child to reveal his sex. The child could not have made more than two years, a plump, healthy-looking boy with a strong voice exploding into a terrified howl.

The captain gestured. The junior officer slapped the child so hard he was stunned, splayed his body on the ground, and stepped back. The veiled woman flung herself forward, but before she reached the child, the captain hacked off the boy's head. She scrambled on hands and knees, a keening sound rising, and as she crawled to the body her veil and outer robes were wrenched into disarray, split to reveal an underrobe heavily embroidered with gold and silver thread. Her head, exposed as the veil ripped away under her crabbed hands, was that of a young woman of exceptional beauty; her eyes were dark, wide with stunned grief, and her hair, falling loose from its pins and clasps, was as thick and black as a river of silk.

The Qin soldiers shook their heads, frowning.

The captain raised his sword again.

The Qin chief stepped forward, a man of easy competence who reminded Kesh of the scout Tohon. "Captain Jushahosh. No need to waste this young woman. I will take her as a wife if you do not want her."

But the motion was already complete, her fortune long since sealed. The cut drove deep into her neck, and she slumped forward, twitching, not yet dead, mewling and moaning. As the captain stepped back with a look of dazed shock, as if he'd thought to kill her in one blow, the Qin chief calmly finished her off but with a wry smile that Kesh took at first for cruel amusement. A murmur swept through the Qin soldiers like breeze through trees, but the Qin chief raised a hand and all sound ceased. The chief turned his back on the dead as a look of pure disgust flashed in the twist of his mouth and the crease made by narrowed eyes. Then he caught Kesh watching him, and his expression smoothed into the solemn look the Qin normally wore, as colorless as their black tunics.

Perhaps the captain had seen. "A woman of the palace! She can have no honor left, her face exposed in such a manner. And her hair, seen by every man here, even by barbarians! Death honors her, although she disgraced herself."

"She's dead now," said the Qin chief, facing him with the same deadly smooth expression unchanged. "Why kill the child?"

"That was one of the sons of the Emperor Farazadihosh."

"A boy can be raised as a soldier, useful to his kinsmen."

Servants brought canvas and silk to wrap the bodies. "Why do you think we found a palace woman on the road at all? Escorted by a contingent of palace guards? With Farazadihosh's death in battle, the palace women who have borne sons of his seed have scattered. If even one survives, a standard can be raised against the new emperor. With a few such deaths, we bring peace. Isn't peace to be preferred to war?"

"This seems settled then," said the Qin chief. "Are these slaves to be killed also?"

"Slaves belong to the palace, not to the emperor. They obey those who rule them." He handed his sword to an aide, who wiped it clean. "Master Keshad, will you continue our meal?"

Eliar stumbled away, collapsing to all fours as he heaved. Kesh looked away from the bodies being rolled up, from the slaves awaiting their fate. He studied the Qin chief, but the man's gaze made him nervous, like staring down a wolf who might be hungry and thinking of you as his next meal or might recently have fed and finds you merely a curiosity. It was not that the Qin were merciful, but rather that they valued their loyalty to their kinsmen above all. For that, Kesh admired them.

But he was in the Sirniakan Empire now, and the Qin were, presumably, mere mercenaries. He turned to Captain Jushahosh.

"Yes, certainly, Captain. I hadn't finished my story, had I?"

They walked back through camp to the fire where they had first sat. Here, the slaves had already set out folding table, tray, cups, a fortifying wine warmed with spices. The white-robed Beltak priest who accompanied their troop was being helped by a pair of underlings toward the road, his priest's bowl hanging by a strap from his right wrist.

"The skirmish did not last long," remarked Kesh as he settled onto a folding stool opened for him. The stool marked, he thought, new status in their eyes.

"They were desperate, but few in number. Still, there are dead, and the priest must oversee the proper rites. Those who fought must be cleansed at the next temple."

"You're wounded? I saw you were limping."

"No, not a scratch." His grin was lopsided, a little embarrassed. "Turned my ankle jumping out of the way of a man trying to stab me." He sipped at the wine, and made a face. "Eh. It tastes of blood."

It tasted perfectly fine to Kesh, and when the captain had not the stomach to eat, Kesh finished off the spiced meat and freshly cooked flat bread. Slaves never knew when they would next eat. Not even the smell of blood and the memory of the little boy's headless corpse could put him off a good meal like this one. Anyway, ten days from now, or tomorrow, he might be dead, and it seemed a cursed waste not to enjoy such pleasures when offered.

The captain sighed. "I wish I had your stomach, eh? I admit, that's the first battle I've been in. We missed all the action before."

"You've never killed a man before?"

He waved a hand. "I've had to kill disobedient slaves on my estate. But that's more like killing animals."

"Ah." Kesh swallowed bile. A man in a position as precarious as his must not risk offending his jailkeeper. "How is it you come to this duty? Your house was an ally of the new emperor?"

"That's right. My grandfather went to the palace school with the younger brother of Farutanihosh for two seasons. They never cut that bond, the two men, even through all the years that followed. And of course the Emperor Farutanihosh never had his younger brother killed, as he ought to have done. It's always a disruption of God's order to raise the flags of war, but everyone knows that a woman who has birthed a son born of the emperor's seed will rouse her relatives to war on that son's behalf even though war is evil. That Farutanihosh did not foresee and prevent this by killing his younger brother was a sign of moral weakness, one that would be passed into his sons. Therefore, his sons must be corrupted by his failure and unworthy for the throne."

"Yet now Farutanihosh's son Farazadihosh is dead, and it is his nephew, the son of the brother he left alive, who will become emperor."

"That's right. Ujarihosh will be seated on the gold throne in the eight-gated palace, and the priests of Beltak will anoint him as Farujarihosh, he who has gained the favor of the King of Kings, the Lord of Lords, the Shining One who rules alone."

"How far are we riding?" Kesh asked, wanting to lick his fingers but taking a fine linen cloth from a slave to wipe his hands instead.

"I'm not sure." Jushahosh glanced toward the road, not visible from here, although they could hear the talk of men at the grisly task of clearing the road and the singsong chant of the priest. "Until we meet the one who has summoned you."

"Who is that?"

The captain sipped at his wine. "I'm only a messenger. The truth is, I don't know any more than you do."

WITH EACH DAY they rode deeper into the heart of the empire, traveling south through countryside so densely populated there was always at least one village within view, and more commonly three or four. Farmers laboring in their fields paused in their work, bent with hands on knees, heads bowed, as the company passed. Kesh wasn't sure if they were showing obedience, or praying that the beast would ignore them rather than ravage them. But the captain and his soldiers took no notice of the common folk. Life went on unmolested. Whatever war had been fought between the noble heirs of the imperial house did not affect those who must bring in the crops. Not like in the Hundred, where the strife had precisely ripped through the houses and fields of the humblest.

"We'll never see home again," said Eliar every morning as they made ready to mount and go on their way.

"Speak of your own end, not mine," replied Kesh every day, and every day he found a way to fall in beside Captain Jushahosh, because Eliar's morose company had become unbearable. To risk so much and then grouse about it! Death was a small price, compared with his betrayal of his sister!

But Jushahosh was a man like Eliar in many ways: son of a wealthy house, one of many such sons accustomed to a life of sumptuous clothing and platters piled high with food, who in his life had seen little enough hardship and so craved the excitement he kept missing out on. A civil war! How exciting! Yet his company, backing the eventual winner, had seen no action beyond that encounter on the road, which was nothing to be boasted of although they had pickled the heads of the woman and the child in a barrel of wine so the new exalted administrator of the women's palace could make an accounting of who was dead and who, therefore, missing. He never tired of hearing Keshad's tales of his travels. It seemed never to occur to the captain that a man could embroider a small tale and turn it into a large one. Kesh found him lacking in imagination.

At night, in the privacy of their tent, Kesh forced Eliar to go over and over the basic tale of their partnership, their trade, their expedition south. "So they can't catch us out in contradictions and decide to burn us."

"Maybe I'd be better dead," whispered Eliar.

"Maybe so, but I wouldn't. I intend to survive this interview, give a good account of myself, and go home with a decent profit."

"Yet if we fail—eiya!—when I close my eyes I see that poor little child with his head sliced off. And that woman—his poor mother—cut down like a beast. Doesn't it haunt you, Kesh? Are you so unfeeling?"

"Yes, I am. There's nothing I can do for them. They're dead. I concern myself with the living."

The living—like Eliar's sister. The woman he could never discuss, whose face he ought never to have seen. That face—her glance—haunted his nights and his days.

They rode ten days after the skirmish on a road marked at intervals with distance markers, just as in the Hundred, only the empire measured not in meys but in a measure known as a cali, about half the distance of a mey. Kesh was careful to count off their distance, and every night he had Eliar record the cali traveled in the accounts book Eliar had brought.

"It's a good thing you're useful for something," Kesh said, watching the young Silver slash marks by lamplight. "Did you make note of the two crossroads we passed and at what distance we reached them?"

"Do you think I'm a fool?"

Kesh did not answer.

"Yes, you do. I did note them. I noted the letters marking the posts. They indicate which towns and cities lie along that road. I also recorded the number and density of villages we passed today, and the water wheels and forges that I could be sure of. All in a script which no one but the Ri Amarah can read, so we can't be caught out if my book is taken from me. Unless, of course, the act of writing in a book is seen as suspicious, which I must suppose it will be."

"What are those?" Kesh asked, pointing to a secondary column of odd squiggles falling on the left-hand side of the page.

"I'm recording the words and sounds of the Sirniakan language. Why do you think I talk so much with the officers? They're not particularly interesting. We have in our archives a record of the language from our time of exile here, but we no longer know how to pronounce things properly and what certain words truly mean. That's what you don't understand, Kesh. All you can think about is how much coin you'll get from this expedition. If we survive it, which I doubt. But there are more valuable things than coin. There is knowledge."

"Information to be sold—"

"No. Knowledge in itself— Why do I bother?" He broke off and cleaned the brush and without speaking another word boxed his writing tools and lay down on his blankets with his back to Kesh.

Kesh wondered what would happen if he grasped the cloth of Eliar's turban and ripped the coiled cloth from his head. His hands twitched. With a laugh, he crawled out and paced to the central watch fire, where he found Captain Jushahosh still awake and conferring with an officer in a red jacket holding a fancy stick like a reeve's baton, plated as in gold.

The captain looked up sharply at Kesh's approach, and without interrupting his flow of words to the other man, lifted his left hand and gestured with a flick of the fingers that seemed to say *go away*. Kesh stepped back, then took himself over to the pits as if that was where he'd been heading all along. He lingered, hearing scraps delivered too quickly for him to sort out what words he knew. In time, the stranger made his courtesies, and Jushahosh his own in response, and the man strode away. Kesh crept back toward the central watch fire and was rewarded with a cup of the spiced wine that was the only thing in the empire he had come to love.

"In the morning, you'll ride with Captain Sharahosh," said Jushahosh. "We part here, for I'm sent on a new assignment, hunting down another infant son of Farazadihosh, if you must know. No glory there." He sighed. "I was hoping for battle, but it seems most of the troops loyal to Farazadihosh have surrendered. There will likely be no more fighting. I was hoping for at least one battle."

"It seems the southern prince had more support than expected. He won quickly, did he not?"

"The Lord of Lords, King of Kings, has showered His favor on the deserving. Now we will have peace." He sketched the gesture signifying obedience to the god's will, and Kesh copied it. The captain smiled, an odd light in his eyes that Kesh recognized, after a moment's doubt, as admiration. "I thought all barbarians were brawling drunks with hot tempers, ready to fight at any excuse, like those Qin riders."

"Do the Qin get drunk and brawl? I've never seen—ah, one of these—lose his temper."

"Maybe not these, since they are under our command, but you know how barbarians are. Still, you're different from the others, I suppose because you are a believer. You've walked fearlessly into the wilderness, stalked the desert's edge, battled with naked demons, ridden over the snow-choked pass, bargained with deadly— what did you call them?—with deadly lilu. Is it true they have the bodies of women and the skin of snakes?"

"Oh. Eh. Some of them."

"Whew!" The captain grinned. "I wish I had your cool. Having seen such sights as you have, and survived such dangers! My thanks to you, truly, for being generous enough to dine and drink with me. You being such an important man in your part of the world."

"Yes. Eh. And my thanks to you, Captain, for sharing your food and drink. You've shown me hospitality. I won't forget it."

The awkward parting accomplished, Kesh took his leave.

In the morning, he rose to find Captain Sharahosh in command with a new troop of Sirniakan cavalry. Captain Jushahosh and his troop were gone. The Qin company remained.

Captain Sharahosh was an older man uninterested in conversation, and he held his soldiers aloof from prisoners and Qin alike. They rode for another day, follow-

ing a road so wide that four wagons might roll abreast. Fields, vineyards, and orchards crowded the landscape, no scrap of land unmarked by human industry. The
next morning a vast wall rose out of the earth. They entered a city through gates
sheeted with brass and rode down an avenue bounded by high walls. At intervals,
bridges crossed over the avenue, but Kesh never ascertained any traffic above, although he heard and smelled the sounds of men out and about in the streets beyond
the walls. The rounded dome of the city's temple grew larger as they rode into the
heart of the city.

The sun rose to its zenith before they reached a second gate, which opened into a
courtyard lined with a colonnade, pillars hewn out of rose granite. The structure resembled in every detail the palace court in Sarida where he and Eliar had first been
taken into custody. There was even a farther gate into a farther courtyard, spanned
by an archway carved with reliefs celebrating the reign of the emperor: the officers of
the court approaching an empty throne, the sun and moon and stars in attendance on
the crown of glory that represented the suzerainty of Beltak. The temple dome could
be glimpsed to the right, the sun glinting off its bronze skin. Maybe it was the same in
every cursed Sirniakan city, the palace supported by the temple and the temple supported by the palace, one unable to exist without the architecture of the other.

"Sit here," said Captain Sharahosh, perhaps the tenth and eleventh words he had
spoken to them in their days together. He dismissed his soldiers but left the Qin riders waiting in the hot sun in the dusty courtyard as he vanished beyond a more
humble gate.

In the Hundred, of course, the temples of the seven gods were the pillars that supported the land, and the tales wove the land into a single cloth. Or so the priests of
the seven gods would say. And they had to say so. They had to believe, just as the
priests of Beltak had to believe. What were they, after all, if the gods meant nothing?

Kesh had all along prayed at dawn and at night with the empire men while Eliar
and the Qin soldiers had stood aside in silence. But he did not believe, and Beltak
did not strike him down, and the priest accompanying the soldiers did not see into
his heart and know he was lying.

"Do you think they will kill us now?" Eliar muttered.

"They could have killed us before, if they meant to kill us. Anyway, we are simply
merchants, traveled to Sarida to turn a profit."

Eliar wiped sweat from his forehead. "You're right."

"Right about what?"

"Don't you recall what you said when we were waiting in the courtyard in Sarida?
It looked exactly like this one, didn't it?"

Would the cursed man never stop chattering about his own gods-rotted fears?

"You said people will renounce the truth if it will give them an advantage to do
so. And then they convince themselves that what they wish to be true is the truth."
He twisted his silver bracelets as though twisting his thoughts around and around.
"Folk tell themselves what they want to hear. I traded my sister's happiness for my
own—or what I thought would be my own happiness. Now I'm ashamed."

The tone of his voice seared Keshad. If they could join together and find some
way to free her from the unwanted marriage, then surely they would be allies, not
enemies. "Eliar," he began, but faltered, not knowing what to say or how to say it.

Eliar brushed at his eyes with a hand.

In the shadows off to the right, tucked away in an alcove unnoticed until now, a door opened. Captain Sharahosh beckoned, his face impassive. Kesh cast a glance toward the Qin soldiers. He had a crazy idea of calling to them for help. Surely if he invoked Captain Anji's name and lineage—the nephew of your var!—they would sweep him and Eliar up and gallop away to safety.

But these were not Anji's men. These men belonged to someone else, perhaps to the var, who had according to Captain Anji's account tried to have his nephew murdered over a year ago. That very plot had precipitated Anji's journey to the Hundred.

Over a year ago, the Sirniakan civil war had not quite yet begun, although surely it was then brewing. The Qin var, it seemed, had chosen to back Farazadihosh. But that being so, then why was a Qin company riding like allies beside troops loyal to Farujarihosh, the prince who had rebelled against and killed his cousin, wresting from him the imperial throne?

"At once," said the captain.

They crossed under the lintel into darkness. A lamp flared. By its light, they descended a long flight of stone steps and, reaching the limit of the lamp's illumination, halted. The lamp sputtered and died, and a second lamp bloomed ahead. They walked down a corridor, lamps flaring and dying at intervals. Blackness unrelieved by daylight dogged them before and behind. The walls were painted in an elaborate hunting scene, but Kesh glimpsed only snatches of color, of a white hare, a gold lion, a red deer, and a green bird, each transfixed by an arrow. They walked thus a full ten lamps of distance. Captain Sharahosh uttered no words, nor did he deem it necessary to defend himself against them or even once look back to make sure they were following. After all, what could they do? If they drew their swords and cut him down, they were still trapped in the midst of—or underneath!—a building so vast Kesh could not visualize its proportions. Anyway, there might be traps. He tried to observe what he could see of the long scene, perhaps a representation of a tale unfolding along the walls, yet his thoughts turned and turned Eliar's words. How deep ran Eliar's regret? Could Keshad suggest to Eliar that his precious sister might be released from the marriage into which she had been forced? That they could work together to save her?

Or was Eliar one of those who spoke words of regret but didn't really mean them if it meant he had to give up the privilege that came from another's sacrifice?

A line of light appeared ahead like a beacon. They crossed under a lintel and into a round chamber faced with marble. Kesh looked up into a dome whose height made him dizzy. A balcony rimmed the transition from chamber to dome; red-jacketed soldiers stood at guard beneath lamps hung from iron brackets. The amount of oil hissing as it burned made it seem as if a hundred traitorous voices were whispering in the heavens.

A person dressed in a plain white-silk jacket and the loose belled trousers common to wealthy empire men sat in a chair carved of ebony. He was a man, but odd in his lineaments, his face looking not so much clean-shaven as soft like a woman's, unable to bear the youthful burden of a beard. Yet his posture was strong, not weak, and his hands had a wiry strength, as if he'd throttled his enemies without aid of a garrote.

He said, in the trade talk, to the soldier in the red jacket, "These are the two?"

"Yes, Your Excellency."

His voice was a strangely weightless tenor, but his words rang with the expectation of authority. "I've interrogated four others already this morning, and they were not the ones I am seeking."

The captain frowned in a measuring way, not an angry one. "What are your names?"

Eliar opened his mouth, and Kesh trod on his foot.

The soldier smiled, just a little.

The man in the chair spoke. "You are perhaps called Keshad? Sent to spy in the empire at the order of my cousin Anjihosh, son of Farutanihosh out of the barbarian princess?"

All the market training in the world, all those years as a slave, had not prepared Kesh for being called out deep in the bowels of an imperial palace by a man he did not know but who was, evidently, one of Captain Anji's royal cousins.

His surprise and silence was its own answer, even as his thoughts caught up with his shock and he cursed himself for a fool. He'd been warned about the empire's secret soldiers, known as the red hounds, fierce assassins and spies in their own right. Anji had warned him, yet it appeared their intelligence gathering was more formidable than anyone suspected.

Too late now.

When cornered, you can choose submission and surrender, or you can leap to the attack and hope the fierceness of your resistance will give you an opening for escape.

"Begging your pardon, Your Excellency. But if you and your brother have only recently defeated the Emperor Farazadihosh in battle, how comes it that you are privy so suddenly to the secrets that could have been brought south only by agents of the red hounds? Who are sworn to serve the emperor? Not his rivals."

"An interesting question," agreed the man, with a nod of acknowledgment.

"And furthermore," continued Keshad, feeling really borne up now on a high tide of reckless anger at being trapped so cleanly and easily, all his hopes wrecked, "if it is true that the cousin of Farazadihosh has taken the throne, and therefore the right to be named as emperor, through victory on the field of battle, then how comes it that a brother of that man—as you imply yourself to be—remains alive? The heir of the ruling emperor has all his brothers and half brothers killed in order that none shall contest his right to the throne."

Captain Sharahosh made a gesture, and four of the guardsmen on the balcony raised bows with arrows nocked. "You are imprudent in your speech," said the captain, "more bold than is fitting."

"Nay, let him speak," said his master. "I would like to know how a man posing as a simple foreign merchant knows of the existence of the red hounds. For surely they are only known to those raised in the palace, and those who oversee the temple."

"What is it worth to you?"

The prince's smile was brief and brutal. "What makes you think it is worth anything to me? It might be worth something to you." His gaze flicked to Eliar. "These questions are meaningless, because a Ri Amrah walks beside you."

"Ri Amarah," said Eliar.

"Ri Amrahah? Ama-ra-ah? A-ma-rah. Ah. Is that the way your own people speak the word? It is recorded otherwise in our chronicles. Is it true you have horns? And sorcerous powers brought with you from over the seas beyond which lies your original home, from which you are now exiled? Is it true the women of your people keep your accounts books, which as you must know goes against the will of the Shining One Who Rules Alone?"

"We do not worship that god."

"There is only Beltak, King of Kings, Lord of Lords, the Shining One Who Rules Alone."

"So you say."

The prince's amusement reminded Keshad startlingly of Captain Anji's way of smiling: he was not one bit flustered by those who contradicted him. "I do not 'say so.' I am repeating the truth."

"Why on earth," demanded Kesh, "would it be against the will of God for women to keep accounts? Women keep accounts as well, or as badly, as men do. How can anyone imagine otherwise?"

The prince clucked softly, still deigning to look amused. "No wonder the Hundred is in chaos. Can it be otherwise, with the rightful order turned on its head, and what should be forward facing backward?" He turned his gaze back to Eliar. "Unwrap your turban."

"I will not!"

The prince gestured, and the other eight guardsmen raised their bows, targeting Eliar. "Unwrap your turban so I may satisfy my curiosity, or I will have you killed."

Keshad wanted to take a step away, but he feared exposing himself as a coward.

"No." Eliar lifted his chin, jaw clenched. "Kill me if you must. When I am dead you can assuage your curiosity, if the Hidden One allows it."

The prince laughed, and the guardsmen lowered their bows. "You are the ones I seek. You are Keshad, without patronymic to identify your lineage, and you are Eliar, a son of the Ri Amarah, son of Isar, son of Bethen, son of Gever. Sent as spies into the empire, which is ruled by the rightful heir, my elder brother, Farujarihosh, may his reign be blessed by the glory of the King of Kings who rules over us."

There followed a moment of complete silence, punctuated once by a drifting lilt of some kind of stringed music, cut off as quickly as if a door had closed. The prince studied them. Eliar wiped his brow. Kesh was panting. How could it be he had come so far and risked so much, only to have it all snatched out of his hands?

Aui! Captain Anji had warned him. He'd understood the empire better than anyone, because he had spent his boyhood in the palace. He'd been willing to gamble with the lives of Keshad and Eliar, and the drovers and guardsmen, because it cost him nothing personally to make the attempt should it fail, and offered him benefit if they succeeded.

Fair enough. Kesh had accepted the bargain. No use blaming anyone now that disaster sat in a serviceable chair and stared him in the face, mulling over how best to use him.

To use him, not to kill him.

The prince nodded. "I am not the enemy of my cousin Anjihosh. His mother made plain her intent to remove him from the battles over the throne when she smuggled him out of the palace and sent him west to his uncle, the Qin var, the year Anjihosh gained twelve years of age. But that does not mean my brother and I can pretend he does not live and breathe. He remains the son of an emperor. You may see that this presents a problem for us. Yet we are peaceable men, seeking order, not war. Our father taught us that it is better to be prosperous than to quarrel. Thus, when my brother sired a son, I accepted the place foreordained for me, so that we could work together rather than sunder what would otherwise be strong."

"You've been cut," said Eliar, going pale about the month. "I've read such stories, but I didn't think—"

Cut? What on earth did that mean?

The prince whitened about the mouth but spoke mildly enough that Kesh wondered if he were a man trained never to show overt anger. "We do not use such a crude term."

"I beg your pardon, Your Excellency," said Eliar. "I know no other. There is no word in the Hundred that describes . . ." He blushed.

"In the trade talk they might say gelded, but we have a more honorable term in our own language, which is more sophisticated than the crude jabber used in the marketplace."

Gelded! Kesh had to actually stop his own hand from reaching down to pat his own privates, to reassure himself they were intact. "Captain Anji isn't the kind of man to accept a knife cut so as to live."

"We have something else in mind. And you, Keshad of no patronymic and Eliar son of Isar of the Ri Amarah, are the ones who will deliver our offer to our cousin. You will accept the assignment?"

Kesh looked at Eliar. Eliar lifted a shoulder in a half shrug.

"What choice do we have?" Kesh said.

The prince lifted both hands. "You can be brought before the priests and accused and convicted of being spies. It is a choice. An honorable one in its own way, since an honorable man speaks truth at all times."

"What punishment would we then face?" Kesh asked.

"A merciful one. A swift execution, rather than burning such as heretics and nonbelievers suffer. You, Keshad, in any case. I am not sure how the Ri Amarah would fare as those of his people who lived in these lands were banished from the empire one hundred and eighteen years ago because of their heretical beliefs. He might merit burning."

"Yours is a cruel law," said Eliar.

"Hsst!" Keshad kicked him.

"Men are cruel," observed the prince without heat. "The law binds them in order to mitigate their cruelty. Such is the wisdom of Beltak." He folded his hands on his lap. He was as sleek and well groomed as any treasured gelding, a strong workhorse, and a handsome person in his own way, better-looking than Anji if measured by symmetry alone. "So. I have found you, and made my proposal. Do you accept? You two, to carry our offer of peace across the Kandaran Pass to our cousin in the Hundred."

"This is no trick, no hidden poison or sorcery meant to kill him?"

"No trick, no poison or sorcery meant to kill him. It is an honest offer, the best one he will get."

"What else can we do?" muttered Eliar.

Kesh had spent too much time as a debt slave to trust masters and merchants who, given a monopoly, did not exploit their advantage. But that didn't mean a clever man couldn't gain advantage for himself on the sidelines as the powerful wrestled. "Very well, Your Excellency, we'll take your offer to the captain. What is it?"

The prince nodded at the captain, who gestured. The guardsmen on the balcony backed up out of sight. The captain crossed to a door set on the far side of the chamber. He opened it and went through, leaving the prince—apparently unarmed—with Kesh and Eliar and their swords.

"So do you have horns?" asked the prince in a pleasant voice. "I've always wondered."

Eliar flushed.

The door opened and a woman entered the room. She was veiled, perceived mostly as cloth obscuring both face and form, yet she walked with confidence and carried a short lacquered stick with a heavy iron knob weighting one end. She was short and, it seemed, a bit stout, but vital and energetic. As soon as the door was shut behind her by an unseen hand, she pulled off the veil that concealed her face and tucked it carelessly through her belt.

The hells!

She was an older woman, not yet elderly, and she had a face so distinctively Qin that Keshad at once felt he was back riding with Qin soldiers. She circled the two young men as a wolf circles a pair of trapped bucks as it decides whether it is hungry enough to go to the bother of killing them. Then she turned on the prince.

"These are fearsome spies?" The trade talk fell easily from her lips.

"An exaggeration, I admit," the prince said with a careless smile that had something of a scorpion's sting at its tip. "Do not trouble me with your contentious nature."

"You will be glad to be rid of me."

"I need have nothing to do with you. From what I hear, the women's quarter will be glad to be rid of you after all these years. My brother has thankfully decreed there are to be no more foreign brides, only civilized women, admitted to the palace quarter."

"He says so now. But wait until your brother, or his heir, or that heir's son, sees benefit in contracting a foreign alliance. When the gold, or the land, or the horses, are too tempting to refuse. Then your words will change and your hearts will turn, and some poor young woman will be ripped from her family's hearth and thrust into a cage, as I was."

Eliar gasped, as if the words had been aimed at him.

The prince rose, his eyes so tightened at the corners that Kesh supposed him to be very angry. But he spoke in the blandest of voices, addressing Kesh and Eliar. "This woman carries our offer to Anjihosh. You will escort her and those attendants she brings with her. Be assured that agents of my choosing will ride with you over the Kandaran Pass. If you do not deliver her safely, they will kill you."

Kesh looked at Eliar; the young Silver was his only ally. "Yes, Your Excellency. Can you tell me who we have the honor of escorting?"

"And idiots, too, in the bargain," she said. She walked to the door, rapped on it with the iron knob of the stick, and, as soon as it was opened, vanished within.

"You claim to be a believer," said the prince, "because of which I will offer you a piece of advice. That woman is a serpent, with a poisoned tongue and a barbarian's lack of honor. Do not trust her."

"That's Captain Anji's mother, isn't it?" As soon as Eliar spoke the words, Keshad realized she could be no one else.

"The palace is rid of her at last," said the prince. "As for you two, should either of you set foot in the empire again, you'll find your lives swiftly forfeit." He clapped his hands thrice.

The door opened, and the captain strode swiftly out, posture erect and shoulders squared, like a man about to take his place in the talking line and perform one of the tales, a martial story told with defiance and bold gestures. These people knew what they were doing, entirely unlike Kesh and Eliar, their expedition begun as a toss of the sticks and exposed so easily Kesh felt the shame of it. Now they were delegated to be mere escorts to a bellicose woman being returned in disgrace to her son.

The prince sat in his chair as the captain led them away. Yet as they walked the length of the underground corridor with its hunting stories faded in the dim light, Kesh considered the last time he had brought a woman north over the Kandaran Pass into the Hundred. He'd believed one thing about her, but he'd been entirely wrong; Cornflower had turned out to be quite different from what he originally thought she was, not a helpless mute slave at all but rather a terrible demon bent on vengeance. Aui! There was really no telling what would happen when Captain Anji's mother arrived in the Hundred, was there?

PART TWO: ENCOUNTERS

In the Year of the Red Goat

3

DON'T OPEN THE GATE.

Those were the last words Nekkar had said to the apprentices before he had slipped out of the temple to get a look at the army that had occupied Toskala eight days ago. Reflecting back on their frightened faces and anxious tears, he knew that leaving them had been a gods-rotted foolish thing to do. He should have stayed in the temple grounds to keep some order in the place. Make sure none of the young ones panicked.

Aui! Too late now to fret over what he couldn't change.

He had reached the front of the line.

A sergeant caressing a long knife finished his interrogation of a thin man, a farmer by the look of his humble knee-length linen jacket and bare legs. "So you admit you are a refugee, come to Toskala from the country in the last six months?"

"We had to flee our village because of the trouble—"

"No refugees allowed in Toskala. You'll be marched to the gates and released. Return to your village."

A bored soldier beckoned to Nekkar, a gesture meaning *You next.*

The farmer didn't budge. "I've children waiting in the alleys. I have to get them."

"You should have thought of that before you left your gods-rotted village." The sergeant nodded, and soldiers grabbed the man by either arm. As he'd done numerous times before, seen by everyone standing in line, the sergeant sliced three shallow cuts into the man's left forearm. "We cleanse those who sneak back into the city after they've been marked."

"But they'll starve!" The man's voice rose shrilly as his desperation mounted and the pain of the cuts stung into tears. "Their mother is dead. We lost track of our clan—"

The soldiers dragged him out by a different door. Aui! The refugees who had flooded into Toskala over the last year had put a strain on the resources of the city and caused a great deal of hard feeling, but to separate a man from his children in such a way was beyond cruel. Yet none dared protest. Soldiers lined the main room; an inn called the Thirsty Saw had been cleared of customers and set aside for their use. Many more folk besides him waited in line, some wringing their hands or rubbing unmarked forearms, others weeping. Most stood in silent, bitter dread. Eight days ago, on the cusp between the days of Wakened Ox and Transcendent Snake, their good city had been overthrown by treachery and fallen into the hands of thieves and criminals.

The bored soldier's voice sharpened. "I said, *You next.*"

Nekkar limped forward.

The sergeant looked him up and down without smile or frown. "What's your name?"

"I'm called Nekkar."

"What's your clan?"

"I'm temple-sworn." As any tupping idiot could see by his blue cloak with its white stripe sewn over each shoulder! Those who wore the blue cloak marking them as servants of Ilu the Herald, patron of travelers and bringer of news, became accustomed to being addressed as "Holy One." That the sergeant had not used the customary honorific was a deliberate slight. He swallowed angry words as he glanced uneasily around the chamber. The other detainees, swept up like so much detritus by the soldiers now patrolling Toskala's streets, stared, trying to gauge what questions they might be asked and what answers would serve them best.

"What clan in Toskala marks your kinfolk?" The sergeant's impatience edged his tone. He wore a silver chain from which hung an eight-pointed tin star, a cheap medallion compared with the finely wrought chain likely obtained in the first frenzy of looting.

"Why, no clan in Toskala!" he replied, surprised. "Why should it? I was sent to Fifth Quarter's temple at sixteen as an apprentice and transferred five years later as an envoy to Stone Quarter's temple. I have lived here in the city the last thirty years, and never regretted one moment of it." *Until today.* "My kin are hill people from the Liya Pass, if you must know, a day's walk from the town of Stragglewood on the Ili Cutoff."

"I know the place. Go on."

Faced with the soldier's unrelenting gaze, he cleared his throat nervously and went on. "Most of my people follow the carters' or woodsmen's trade. Easy to work together, then, you see, cousin hauling logs for cousin. Never had a badge, like they do here in the city. Honest country folk don't." The sergeant didn't blink at that jab, nor rise to the bait, nor touch his own ugly star badge, if that was what it was. "I haven't been back there for over twenty years. My life is here in the city now."

"What clan?" the sergeant repeated.

He wiped sweat from his brow with a hand made grimy when the soldiers who had cornered him had shoved him to the ground. His wrist hurt, and his twisted ankle was swelling. "Tumble Creek lands, mostly. Some granddaughter branches that range the roads and paths, as carters do. We're a daughter branch long split from the Green Sun, call ourselves Tumble Sun, if you must know."

The sergeant blinked, as if the names meant something to him.

Dread opened its maw and swallowed Nekkar in one gulp. He had the horrible feeling he had just betrayed his entire clan, who had never done one wrong thing to him even for all he had been thrilled to leave the quiet hills for the glories of the finest city in all the Hundred.

The sergeant pointed to the white trim on his cloak. "You're wearing an ostiary's stripes."

"Yes, I'm ostiary over the temple of Ilu that's located here in Stone Quarter. We're well known as the most minor of the five temples dedicated to Ilu in Toskala."

"An ambitious person raised to a high position might feel slighted to be called 'minor.' Maybe you were hoping for a better place."

He was very irritating, and Nekkar was anxious about his charges and sick of seeing unoffending refugees cut like debt slaves and dragged away. Standing in line half the day with hands and ankle throbbing and without food or drink had made him light-headed enough to kick him into incautious speech, that sarcastic way he had of lecturing youth when they were being idiots. "I'm perfectly happy with an orderly, unambitious existence. Keeping to my place and serving the gods as I am sworn, and leaving others to go about their lawful business. In peace."

The soldier's hand flicked up. A gasp voiced behind was his only warning. A blow cracked him across the shoulders and he dropped to his knees, too stunned to cry out. His gaze hazed; lights danced. He sobbed, then caught a tangle of prayer and chanted under his breath to take his mind off the pain blossoming across his back and the fear sparking in his mind.

"Hold him for questioning." The sergeant's voice faded.

They dragged him out to the back and dumped him on the ground. Pain paralyzed him. He tried to imagine what Vassa might be cooking for dinner tonight, but his parched mouth tasted only of sand. It was easier to let go and close his eyes.

HE CAME TO with a start, his back throbbing as if a herd of dray beasts had stampeded over his body. Voices staggered back and forth, fading, growing louder, and fading in a slide that made him dizzy although he was flat on his stomach and sucking in dust with each nauseated breath.

"Just these two outlanders in the last eight days?" a woman asked. "That's all you've rounded up, Sergeant Tomash?"

"My apologies, Holy One. I have been searching according to the orders given out by the Lord Commander Radas and Commander Hetti, Holy One. Every household and guild is required to open their compound to my soldiers and present a census of their household members and their wealth. These two slaves are the only outlanders I've found in Stone Quarter."

Someone was weeping, desperate and afraid.

"Release them, or kill them, as you wish. They are useless to me."

"My apologies, Holy One." The sergeant, whose contemptuous tone inside the inn had made folk cringe, sounded as near to tears as a whining boy dumped by uncaring relatives on the auction block. "I've been diligent. I am interviewing compound by compound throughout this quarter, just as I was ordered. Anyone unlawfully on the streets is brought before me. These folk I had dragged out here all need further examination, Holy One."

"Look at me!"

The sergeant whimpered.

Nekkar opened the eye that wasn't jammed up against the ground. At first he thought his vision was ruined; his open eye scratched as if scoured by sand, and when he blinked, it hurt to open and close. Then he realized that actually it was dusk, and also that a few paces from his head floated a cloak of rippling fabric like the night sky speckled by stars.

A person in travel-worn sandals wrapped over dusty feet was standing not three steps from his nose; it was this person who wore the cloak.

"You've spoken the truth about the outlanders," said the cloak.

The sergeant sobbed with a gasp of relief. "Yes, Holy One."

"You've done as well as anyone could."

"My thanks, Holy One."

"Bring the prisoners before me one at a time." She moved away to a trellis.

Nekkar eased up onto his side. He was lying in the inner courtyard of the Thirsty Saw, where he and other folk in Stone Quarter often drank under the shade of an awning green with vines. Soldiers lined the compound wall, staring at their boots. Prisoners were tied to the posts that supported the massive trellis, and more were stuffed doubled over and in evident pain into livestock cages. Many had soiled themselves from being confined for so long, their reek mixing with the sour stench of spilled wine.

The sergeant designated a pair of reluctant soldiers to haul the prisoners forward one at a time. The first man had been beaten so badly he could barely walk, and his head swayed on his neck as if he were not quite conscious.

The woman held a writing brush and a neatly trimmed sheet of mulberry paper. Her cloak's hood was thrown back to reveal a nondescript face, pleasant enough in its lineaments and near in age to Nekkar, who had at the turn of the year made forty-seven and counted his thirtieth year in service to Ilu, the Herald. The prisoner's gaze was forced to meet hers.

She marked on the paper like a clerk. "Veron, son of the Ten Chains clan of Toskala. You have committed a terrible crime."

The man collapsed. After a moment, it became apparent he was dead. Just like that. His spirit had fled through the Gate, leaving its husk.

A soldier retched. Two others grabbed the dead man's ankles and dragged him out of sight as another prisoner was shoved forward. This one, a woman Nekkar knew by sight from the market square, sobbed noisily as she confessed that her clan had hidden its gold beneath the planks of their weaving house.

"Were you not commanded to reveal all coin and stores in your household's possession, as well as provide a full census of household members including any outlanders or gods-touched residing there?" asked the cloak, her tone calm. "Why do you not obey when you know there will be a punishment?"

"We cleanse them who disobey our orders so flagrantly, Holy One," said Sergeant Tomash. "As an example."

The woman began to scream, pleas for mercy, anything but to be hung by her arms from a post until she died of exposure and thirst, but the cloak gestured and she was dragged away. Another was hauled forward in her place.

So went the weary round. The sergeant was a cunning man in his own way; every person here had triggered his suspicion, and every one now confessed either to some petty crime or to concealing valuables or in one case an outlander slave. A merchant babbled about how he cheated on his rice measures. All were condemned to the post.

One frail old fellow fell to his knees as he begged her pardon for having killed another laborer back in his youth.

"You killed him? You confess it?" She lifted her brush, touched it to the rice paper.

He croaked a gasp, or perhaps it was meant to be a word, but like the first man he tumbled forward onto his face. Dead.

Nekkar shut his eyes as the corpse was dragged away.

"This man turned himself in to spare his clan," the sergeant said. "He confessed to hoarding nai—"

"Look at me," said the cloak. "Sergeant, lift his chin—"

Nekkar opened his eyes just as the sergeant wrenched the man's chin up. The prisoner was young, hale, and with the thick arms and powerful legs of a laborer. He struggled, keeping his head down, but his eyes flicked up anyway, as though gauging his distance.

She took a step back. "Kill him."

As soldiers drew their swords, the young man fought free and tugged a knife from his boot; he leaped toward the cloak, but spears pinned him before he reached her.

"He concealed no nai." Her tone remained even as she watched him thrashing, still fighting forward despite flesh pierced and his blood flowing. "He came to attack me. That is why he hid his gaze."

"No heart can be hidden from you, Holy One," murmured the sergeant. "Cut his throat."

The young man screamed; his failure was worse than the pain, no doubt. At least this one had fought back instead of waiting passively, too fearful or too shamed to stand up.

"Enough," Nekkar said aloud.

What a gods-rotted fool he was, knowing he was responsible for the temple and yet staggering to his feet because he could not bear to watch this perverse assizes any longer. He straightened, grimacing at the stabbing pains in his abused body.

"Heya!" barked the sergeant. "Stop, or you'll be cut down likewise."

Nekkar faced the woman in the cloak. "Enough! Why do you do this? Are you not a Guardian? For by your look, and your power, you seem to be one of those who wear Taru's cloak and wield the second heart and the third eye to judge those who have broken the law. The orphaned girl prayed to the gods to bring peace to the land, not cleansing."

"Does cleansing not bring about peace?"

"As well argue that fear and terror bring about peace. Guardians are meant to establish justice. Is that what you call this? *Justice?*"

"Stay your hand," said the cloaked woman before the soldiers could rain blows down upon him. She captured his gaze.

Aui! There it all tumbled as she spun the threads out of his heart: the mistakes he had made, the harsh words he had spoken, his youthful temper and rashness and the fights he'd gotten into, breaking one man's nose and another's arm, the girl he'd impregnated the month before he had entered the temple for his apprenticeship year. He had afterward lied outright, saying it wasn't his seed, to avoid marrying her, and afterward taken seven years of temple service to make sure they couldn't force him, although many years later after being humbled and honed by the discipline of envoyship, he had made restitution to her clan. And what of his twenty years bedding Vassa? Yet what had he and Vassa to be ashamed of, he an ostiary forbidden to marry and she a young widow who had preferred her widowhood to a second marriage arranged by her clan? They did nothing wrong by sharing a pallet; he served the temple as he had done for thirty years and she cooked in her family's neighboring compound as she had done her entire life.

Enough! The cloak's gaze pierced him, but it did not cripple him. He had made peace with his mistakes and his faults.

She regarded him with a sharp frown. "The gods enjoined the Guardians to seek justice. People suffer or die through a recognition of their own crimes, in their own hearts."

"It looks to me like you kill them. Or hand them over to your lackeys to be cleansed. If you believe that to be justice, then you are no Guardian!"

The sergeant snarled. The soldiers hissed with fear.

"You are bold in your honesty, Ostiary Nekkar," she said, having gleaned his name from his thoughts. "You provided a census of your temple to the authorities, I see. Know you of outlanders in this city? Know you of any man or woman, outlander or Hundred folk, who can see ghosts, as the gods-touched are said to do?"

He did not want to tell her, but his thoughts spilled their secrets and she lapped them up however he struggled to conceal what he knew of Stone Quarter's clans and compounds. He wept furiously, hating how he betrayed them: He knew of eight outlanders who were slaves in Stone Quarter, and he'd glimpsed others in Flag, Bell, Wolf, and Fifth Quarters as well. They came from foreign lands and usually served out their days with the clan who had purchased them. There was a young envoy stationed in Flag Quarter known to be gods-touched. Some years ago he'd met another at the Ilu temple up on the Ili Cutoff, an older man. A pair of gods-touched mendicants were said to wander the tracks and back roads of lower Haldia, aiding troubled ghosts in crossing away under Spirit Gate. Shouldn't such holy ones be left in peace to do what the gods commanded?

She released him by looking away to pinion the sergeant. "Sergeant Tomash, you will accompany me to Flag Quarter. I must search out this young gods-touched envoy. After that, I have a new assignment for you. Collect all the census records. I want a hostage taken from every compound and handed over to the army."

"But my work in Stone Quarter, Holy One?"

"Is no longer your concern. There are two cohorts marching down from High Haldia to take over administrative duties here once the army marches on Nessumara. You will report directly to the main command as my personal adjutant, with your rank raised to that of captain. I'll call on you and your company as I have need of them."

"You honor me, Holy One. Shall we cleanse the ostiary, Holy One?"

"No. The gods will dispose of an honest ostiary as they see fit. Come. My errand is urgent. The gods-touched are our enemies. All must be brought before me."

The soldiers shrank back as she skirted the bodies of the fallen to reach a gate that led into the alley separating this compound from an adjoining emporium. She opened the gate and walked through.

The new captain paused under the lintel, a malicious smile slashing his face as he contemplated his enhanced authority. "Dump that one in Scavengers' Alley like the rubbish he is. Then we'll see how the gods choose to dispose of an honest ostiary."

The blow took Nekkar from behind. A second smashed into his shoulders as laughter hammered in his ears. Distantly, a man sobbed. He toppled dazedly to the dirt, wondering why there was a salty taste in his mouth. What had Vassa cooked tonight for supper?

With the third blow came oblivion.

4

HOW TO DESCRIBE what you grew up never having words for? Nallo had been born and raised in the rugged Soha Hills, where a person might stand on a ridge path and survey higher slopes where rock broke the surface of the soil like old bones, and deeper gullies where streams ran white. But to fly! To hang in the harness below an eagle as the land unrolled beneath you like so many bolts of multicolored cloth!

That was something.

She had never seen a river so wide that a shout might not carry across it. To the north, forest tangled the earth. To the south, on the far side of the river, neat rectangles marked densely packed fields, and every village boasted a flagpole and one or two small temples, each one easily identifiable from the air. There lay a quartered square, a temple built for Kotaru the Thunderer, the god she had served for one year as an apprentice. Here rose the three-tiered gates holy to Ilu the Herald. Roofs thatched with fanned leaves from the thatch-oil tree covered altars raised to Taru the Witherer, their bright green color withering as the rains faded. She spotted a walled garden sacred to Ushara the Merciless One, a few people loitering in the forecourt, too tiny to distinguish male from female; in the Devourer's garden, such distinctions did not matter as long as you brought clean desire to the act of worship.

She glanced toward her companion reeves. Kesta led while Pil flew the west flank. Ahead lay the ocean, a seething expanse of water that fell into the sky far to the east.

Tumna chirped, jerking Nallo's attention to a discoloration lying athwart land and ocean dead ahead. It was hard to fathom until the eyes began to identify the multitudinous strands of water plaiting the land and the rank upon rank of wood and stone buildings rising on islands within the delta as though they were a crop of stone being raised out of the earth. Was that Nessumara, the jewel of the sea, the city of bridges, the largest city in the Hundred?

I'm just a hill girl born to goat herders! I'll never get used to this!

Following Kesta's eagle, Arkest, Tumna dropped toward one island among many within the branching arms of the great river. Nallo laughed with the blend of fear and thrill she'd not yet gotten used to. The wind rumbled in her ears. The city flew up to meet her, and Tumna banked to overfly the largest parade ground, where Kesta and Arkest were just setting down. Nallo counted four parade grounds, separated by a maze of walls and lofts, as Tumna veered toward an empty one. Jessed eagles concealed in lofts called out in challenge, but Tumna ignored them. Extending her wings to their greatest extent, she raised her talons to make a perfect landing on a massive wooden log set horizontal to the ground.

"Whoop!" Nallo shouted. Tumna chuffed, shaking herself as Nallo unhooked from the harness and dropped to the ground. Two fawkners jogged out from the lofts.

"Heya! I'm Nallo, out of Clan Hall. Greetings of the day."

"Yeh, yeh, you're new, aren't you? Your eagle did all the work, that's for sure. What's your eagle's name? Anything we should know?"

The brusque voice brought her up short. "She's called Tumna, and"—she paused to get their attention—"she ripped off the head of her last reeve."

"Deserved, no doubt," said the stouter one, who did all the talking. The wiry one nodded with a sneering grin.

They were experienced fawkners and she a novice reeve, not even yet able to steer her eagle properly. Sparring with them was not a battle she could win. "We're here to pick up rice and nai for the siege."

"So we heard. You can't possibly ferry enough sacks of rice and nai by eagle flight to feed Toskala."

"We're not feeding Toskala, only the defenders up on Law Rock."

"Why stay in Clan Hall at all? Why not evacuate? Copper Hall could use reinforcements at our main hall on the Haya shore. And Horn Hall is abandoned."

"We can't abandon Law Rock and Justice Square to those who mean to overthrow the law."

The fawkner shook her head. "Maybe not. But we're overrun with refugees from Istria and Haldia. We're starting to see hungry and sick refugees out of Toskala, and for sure there are more to come, eh? Our reeves are buried under fights and altercations all along the roads, even with the militia out patrolling."

The wiry fellow spoke up for the first time. "Seems selfish of you Clan Hall reeves not to disperse to reinforce the other halls. Work together. Be of some use."

"We're not giving up Law Rock," snapped Nallo. "Now, can you show me where we're to pick up the grain? I hope the merchants of Nessumara are more polite than you."

"Whoof! Don't cross this one, eh, Arvi?" said the woman before she hawked and spat on the dirt. Hostility was easy to see in the creases of her mouth. "You've got that godsrotted old Silver to bargain with. He'll suck you dry." As one, they took a step back as Sweet pulled up neat as you please to land on the other side of the parade ground. "The hells! We heard rumor an outlander had jessed, but we didn't believe it. Is he human?"

"As human as I am," Nallo retorted. "Although I wonder about you two, not even giving a proper greeting and then speaking ill of some old man I've never even met."

"Whew! My ears are burning!" They sauntered away to get a look at Pil.

She turned back to Tumna, awkward with the hand signals. "Remain" was easy enough, a sweep and clutch sketched in the air. Then she ran after the fawkners. "Heya! Where am I supposed to go?"

Copper Hall's island was larger than Argent Hall. To make it all more confusing, this parade ground was rimmed on all sides by buildings, lofts, barracks, storehouses, even a smithy roiling with smoke and noisy with beaten strokes, *wang wang wang*! Her head hurt already, and in addition to the iron sting wafting from the smithy, there crept into her nostrils a slimy fragrance that dwelt in the air the same way a winter byre full of goats has a smell as much texture as scent.

"To the docks," they shouted back before they approached Pil. He had climbed up the ladder to the fawkner's board just below the perch to examine Sweet's wings. Sweet was a good-tempered bird, less territorial than most not so much because she was friendlier but because she seemed bored of going to the trouble of posturing over each least perch. Nallo suspected that things wouldn't go so smoothly if you really crossed the old bird.

Pil satisfied himself on the matter of the wing feathers—how he fussed over that eagle!—and descended the ladder. His exchange with the fawkners was briefer than hers had been; then he jogged to meet her, gesturing toward a gap between the smithy and a warehouse.

"That way," he said.

The experienced reeves assured her she'd eventually get the hang of retracing, on earth, ground she'd flown over. Pil could already backtrack easily. She hurried after him, the fawkners staying with the raptors.

He stopped short, and she barreled into his back.

"Oof! Aui, Pil, what's—?"

Few things surprised Pil, but right now he was gaping like a dumbstruck child. A *creature*, human in shape but stout and hairless, had backed out of the enclosed smithy to slop a bucket of steaming water over the paving stones. Its skin, like coals, was charred black and broken with veins of fiery red.

"A demon!" murmured Pil.

With the clamor hammering within the smithy and the distance between them, no ears should have been able to catch that muttered comment, but the creature swiveled its head as if identifying distance and direction.

"Heya! Are you two the other reeves from Clan Hall?" A steward came running down the alley between smithy and warehouse. She wheezed to a stop beside them, bent to rest hands on thighs as she caught her breath. "Hunh! Eie! Your other reeve . . ." A spate of coughing calmed her. "She needs a hand there at the dock. Old Iron-goat-shanks is in full spout." Excitement gave air to her voice. "Despicable man! We hear a rumor he's getting a new bride from Olossi. Poor lass. They're already running bets in the hall over how long she'll survive his beatings. Two years, maybe; five if she's strong. I'm Ju'urda, by the way. I hope those cursed fawkners Arvi and Offina weren't rude. My apologies on behalf of the hall."

"What is that?" Nallo gestured toward the smithy.

"Eh?" She looked around in the manner of someone who can't see anything except what she expects to see. "What?"

"That, uh, that—oh, the hells!" Cursed if the creature wasn't already looking in their direction as if it could hear every word over the boom and hammer coming from inside the confines of the smoky forge. "It's a delving, isn't it? Just like in the tales."

"A delving?" asked Pil.

"Country cousins, eh?" Ju'urda laughed in a way that stung, but immediately she tipped back her head and spoke past them, not shouting as a normal person would have to, to have a hope of being heard above the racket. "Heya, Be. These are reeves visiting from another hall. One's an outlander and the other has never seen your kind before. Their apologies."

It raised an arm to acknowledge her speech and glided back inside the smithy carrying the empty bucket.

"The delvings can be cursed touchy, not that I blame them," said the steward. "It doesn't pay to insult them. Your grandchildren might find themselves with a ban still held against them when they least expect it."

"What is a delving?" asked Pil.

"No time." She glanced at Nallo. "How in the hells did an outlander get to be a reeve?"

"No time," said Nallo with a grin meant to have an edge, but Ju'urda laughed with real amusement, then set off at a trot, leading them down the alley. Nallo could see nothing of the hall grounds or the city beyond because they were hemmed in by buildings, none more than two stories tall and all with railings along the flat roofs and canvas set up over bare roof beams as if folk lived up there, too.

Ju'urda was soon flagging, although the jog seemed easy enough to Nallo. Pil, of course, was as tough as any man she'd ever met. Born, raised, and trained as a Qin soldier, he would die rather than show weakness.

Which made it all the more curious, Nallo supposed, that when he saw a creature he did not recognize, he immediately identified it as a fearful demon. Maybe they had more demons in the lands outside the Hundred. The gods had ordered the Hundred; naturally they had desired variety, for weren't there three languages spoken in the Hundred, and weren't there Four Mothers, and eight "children"—thinking creatures— shaped by the Mothers? Weren't there five feasts, six reeve halls, and seven gods?

That's what made this marauding army all the worse. They all wore a medallion they called the Star of Life. They didn't respect the gods. They burned altars and ransacked temples, and worst of all, they flouted the law on which the Hundred was built. It was like digging out your foundation from under your house without concern for what would happen afterward.

They emerged onto a clear area of docks emplaced along a channel of murky gray water. The slimy stench made Nallo flinch. The water heaved with sludge and garbage. On the far side of the channel, buildings crammed the far bank. Boats and barges and slender canoes clogged the waterway.

A barge lodged at the dock had disgorged a pair of men wearing the distinctive wrapped turbans that marked them as Silvers. The elder was arguing with a furious Kesta.

"—bare-faced and parading around half naked—" The Silver was very old but vigorous despite the wrinkle of years on his face. He spoke in the loud voice Nallo associated with people who, having lost their own hearing, assume no one else can hear well.

"You might as well throw swill in my face," said Kesta, a flush darkening her cheeks. "How dare you speak to a reeve—?"

"Throw swill I would, for it's the only fitting punishment for a woman who flaunts herself—"

"Here, now, Grandfather," said the weedy grandson with a fluttering gesture.

The old man whacked him across the back with his cane. "Shut your mouth, pup!" He looked up, seeing Pil. "Here, now, ver. You're one of those Qin outlanders I've heard story of, aren't you?" The women might as well not have existed. "I brought rice and nai to feed one hundred adults for one month, a generous allotment, if I must say so myself. Five cheyt for the lot. To be delivered in an even split of unhusked rice and whole nai. Nai flour will spoil, so you'll have to pound your own."

Pil looked at Kesta, but she was too choked with anger to speak. He looked at Nallo and lifted a hand, palm up: *What do I do?*

Nallo was no clerk of Sapanasu, to add up such staggeringly large numbers in her head; she had never even seen a gold cheyt coin, not once in her twenty years of living. But she'd fed a household. In the village, a tey of rice sold for ten vey and was enough to feed one adult for one day. Nai was more filling, and cost less. Sixty vey equaled one leya, and sixty leya one cheyt. . . . "It seems like a fair price."

"I-It's—cursed—generous," huffed Ju'urda in a low voice. "Just—cursed—clasp—agreement—so—his—hirelings—can—unload."

Pil looked uncomfortable as he addressed the old man. "It is agreed to be a fair price, ver."

"It's not a fair price! It's a bargain, a steal, a quarter of what I could get on the open market, and no doubt in these dire times I could raise my prices to gouge the desperate if it weren't forbidden to make a profit from the suffering of others."

"Yes, Grandfather, you're as generous as the sun. Everyone knows it. Especially since you're expecting a favor from the reeves in return." Silver bracelets ringed the grandson's forearm halfway to the elbow as he extended the arm.

As senior reeve, Kesta took a step forward in response.

The old man's forearms were entirely bound in silver rings, jangling and flashing every time he shifted, as he did now, thwapping the lad on the rump. "Touch her, and you'll never be allowed to marry, stupid pup. I'll toss you out the door and you'll have to live on the street."

Nallo nudged Pil from behind, the movement unseen by the older man but in clear sight of the younger, who had the grace to look embarrassed. Pil knew how to obey orders. He and the other young man exchanged the traditional clasp of agreement.

"It's no wonder this unholy army is stampeding across the Hundred," shouted the old man, stabbing at the air with his cane. "Where are all the men, if they are not in their proper place?"

He stomped to the barge and shouted across the gangplank. Laborers swarmed up, hauling sacks off the boat and dumping them on the dock.

The young Silver released Pil's hand and blushed, easy to see on his paler skin. "The old goat is in a particularly foul mood. My apologies."

"What gives him leave to think he can talk to a reeve that way?" Kesta said.

"He calls it an affront for women to stand in authority in public," said the youth.

"An affront to women, you mean! Him talking like that!"

"He's gotten worse as the gout has ailed him, and his hearing has gotten very bad, so he tightens his hold on his memories of the past, although I admit to you I'm sure the old days weren't as he pretends to recall them."

Ju'urda pressed a hand on Kesta's arm. "No use digging into this wound, eh? Say nothing more of it, Yeshen. It's a cursed generous offer, well under market value."

Kesta whistled. "It'll take us some time to haul it all north, one sack per eagle."

"What will happen now the commander of Clan Hall is dead?" asked Ju'urda. "There's no one in charge."

"We've sent messengers to the other halls." Kesta's gaze drifted to the sacks piling up in rows. The hirelings worked efficiently despite the old man throwing comments like knives.

"Don't drop that, you clumsy nit! Aren't you strong enough? Move faster!"

Kesta shook her head. "Is that scrap of coin all he really wants? Hard to see him as generous."

Yeshen frowned. "He's got an affianced bride in Olossi he wants flown up here."

"Reeves aren't carters whose services can be purchased with coin!" objected Kesta.

He shrugged. "I'm just telling you what he expects. Anyhow, verea, three houses of Ri Amarah in High Haldia were killed, every man, woman, and child they got their hands on, and their holdings looted and compounds burned. A few escaped to Nessumara to tell of it. Whatever else, he knows what will happen to us if Nessumara falls." He rubbed a sweaty forehead with the back of a hand as if that could wipe away the fear. "Even so, I don't see how the enemy can hold High Haldia, Toskala, and the countryside, *and* attack Nessumara as well. No one can have that big an army. Can they?"

Nallo snorted. What a gods-rotted pampered youth he was!

He flushed.

Ju'urda flashed an annoyed glance at Nallo. "It does seem impossible, doesn't it? But we've got every reeve out on patrol and our hirelings detailed to build barriers and strengthen the gates on the causeway. Better to be prepared than taken by surprise, eh?" She nodded at Kesta. "So it falls to me and you to deal with old goat-shanks besides."

"His ill temper is worth enduring to get these provisions. I've dealt with worse-tempered mules." Kesta considered the sacks. "We'll need to store these in your warehouses until we can haul them north."

The young Silver gestured. "My hirelings will move them wherever you'd like, verea."

"My thanks." Ju'urda left with a hireling to show him the warehouse, while the young Silver retreated to the boat and the shadow of his glowering grandfather.

Kesta stalked over to Nallo and Pil. "Grab a sack and let's get moving."

"There's more than five hundred people trapped on Law Rock," said Nallo. "Is there any chance we'll lift some of them off to get them out of the way?"

"It's not my decision to make," said Kesta. "There's a hundred children, and another two hundred adults useless for defense and hard to feed. We need a *commander*, but Peddo and the other messengers aren't back yet." She loosed a glare at the back of the old man, for all the good it did. Then she grinned. "You kept your mouth shut tight, Nallo. That's a wonder!"

"I was too shocked to say anything. I just kept wondering if he has horns under that turban! Seems like he would, doesn't it?"

Kesta snorted.

"Anyway, Pil and I, we saw a delving. It was working in the smithy."

The news did not cause Kesta to gasp or goggle. "Copper Hall has a dispensation from the delving assizes, as repayment for an ancient favor done to aid the delvings. I think it's in one of the tales. They get seasonal work from a chain of delvings out of Arro— Here now, why am I babbling on? Grab a sack, you loafers. You've got the hauling harness with your eagles. Make sure it's bundled tightly. Let's move."

As Nallo shouldered one of the heavy sacks, she caught a glimpse of the old man looking her way with a grimace so ugly a spark of anger flared and she found herself taking a step toward him. There was a man who needed a few blunt words shouted in his griping face.

"Nallo," said Pil in his soft way.

With a sigh, she followed him. Toskala could not wait. He was just one cranky, selfish, old, and very rich man. Maybe all Silvers were like him, or maybe he was an unpleasant old coot whose wealth had purchased him the right to bully those within reach of his cane. She'd been mean to those in her care a time or two, just because she let her temper and her resentment get the better of her. Who was to say she couldn't become like him, if she wasn't careful?

It was a sobering thought.

UP!

Nessumara and the delta fell away behind and below as streaming air wicked away the stench of brackish water and too many people crammed onto too many islets. The smithy had smelled a cursed lot fresher, nothing fetid or decomposing where metal was forged. Nallo kept seeing the delving in her mind's eye, the way its head had turned at the sound of their voices. You could tell if someone was looking at you across a distance; eyes had a way of holding and meeting, or maybe it was just the way bodies tensed and shoulders straightened or dropped. It had heard every word.

About forty mey separated Nessumara from Toskala, as the eagle flew. It was difficult to get used to flying in half a day a journey that by river or road might take as many as eight days. The huge river wound a convoluted course, with the wide roadbed of Istri Walk cutting a course more or less parallel to the main channel of the river. The road below was clogged with traffic: people in wagons, pushing carts, trudging with children hoisted on their shoulders. Folk were fleeing from the army that had betrayed and conquered Toskala.

At the sight of those cursed helpless refugees, it was as if a hand reached right into her heart and squeezed until tears like blood oozed up out of her eyes, she who prided herself on being too tough to cry no matter what was thrown at her. She'd had plenty of cause to cry, growing up as a daughter more tolerated than liked in a large clan that couldn't afford to keep so many children, especially one burdened with such a foul temper. They'd been thrilled to marry her off to a much older man she'd never met. For her part, she felt the gods had been kind in sending her to a gentle man whose patience had been as wide as sky and as steady as earth. Her clan hadn't cared what manner of man he was; they'd gotten a better bride-price than they expected.

Now he was dead, killed by the Star of Life army, and she was a reeve, safe up here while others trudged vulnerably down there, not knowing who might clatter up from behind and rip the breath out of their bodies. Wasn't the entire point of being a reeve to be able to help those in need? In the tale, hadn't the orphaned girl begged the gods for a way to restore justice?

The hells! She'd lost track of both Kesta and Pil. She didn't know how to hasten Tumna along, and the cursed lumpy sack of nai was bumping her knees to bruises. Tumna did not like the extra weight, and she was not a raptor to cooperate when she was disgruntled.

As they got closer to Toskala, the traffic fell off to a trickle. Soon, no movement stirred at all, although hamlets and villages lay everywhere on this rich land. Paddies lay close to harvest, untended. No one was turning the fallow fields for the dry season.

An orange flag flashed to her left. Pil and Sweet hung above the river. She tugged on a jess—the wrong one—and cursed as she corrected. Tumna beat in a long curve toward the river. As they flashed over the muddy gray-green current, a barge was being poled away from the west bank while a gang of men pursued it along the shore with swords and bows. Cargo in tidy rows took up much of the barge, and passengers—children!—cowered among the sacks, barrels, and chests as arrows rained over them.

The river fell behind as she overshot. She tugged until Tumna with the greatest reluctance began a sweep back around while Nallo could not even twist to get a look because of the heavy sack of nai. By the time she got the river back in view, Pil had vanished. But then Sweet appeared from downriver, beating straight up the central current. Pil was loosing arrows, and at least one man on the bank went down. The barge had caught the current; men on its deck had their own bows at ready. A man clad all in black loosed, his arrow flew, and a man on the shore staggered and fell into the river, the waters taking him as his companions grabbed hopelessly after him.

Pil and Sweet cut hard around as the black-clad man, below, raised a hand in acknowledgment. The enemy dropped away, no longer a threat. Tumna set her head north, following the river and, perhaps, Kesta's Arkest, by now out of Nallo's sight.

"Cursed bird," muttered Nallo, but it wasn't Tumna she was angry at. She knew what it was like to flee on the roads as a refugee. Months ago she'd walked homeless and hungry and scared, and sold herself into debt slavery besides in order to get a meal. She had rejected the reeves once, but in the end, as that cursed handsome Marshal Joss had warned her, the eagle had gotten what it wanted: it had wanted Nallo. She had come to Clan Hall to be trained as a reeve, but there'd been no time or thought for arms training in the confused days after Toskala's fall. Without training, she was useless.

"You're going to have to help me out, you ill-tempered beast." Her knuckles were white as she gripped her baton, surveying the earth for any sign of enemy whether on the march or sent out as strike forces to harry the countryside south of Toskala. Maybe they saw her from their hiding places; she did not spot them.

This region of lower Haldia was rolling plain, and soon the distinctive rock marking the prow of Toskala like an upthrust fist came into view and grew until it loomed huge as Tumna glided in, extended her wings, and pulled up short for the landing. The sack whumped down so hard Nallo feared it might burst, but it had been bound with heavy leather belts in a doubled sacking.

Fawkners came running together with stewards to carry the sack to the storehouse, but as soon as her harness was shucked, Tumna warbled her wings and walked in her clumsy way over to a rope-wrapped perch to preen, ignoring the fawkners.

"I like the bloom on her feathers," said one of the fawkners. "She's beginning to grow out those fret marks. Have you coped her beak? Or talons?"

"I have not. I don't know how to do anything!"

"Aui! No need to snap at me! It was just a question."

"My apologies. I'm hungry."

"If you're sharp set, then go eat."

Still no sign of Pil. The promontory of Law Rock was an astounding physical formation, with its sheer cliffs and flat crown wide enough for an assizes court, a militia and firefighters barracks and administration compound, and four grain store-houses and the city rations office. Clan Hall was built along the northern rim. Beyond the reeve hall lay a tumble of boulders surrounding a string of ponds running the curve of the northeastern rim, where raptors liked to bowse and feak.

Law Rock, the actual stele, stood near the prow under a humble thatched-roof shelter. The rest of the space was dusty, open ground suitable for drilling, assemblies, festival games, or eagles landing in waves. Four new perches had been erected in the last eight days, the logs hauled up from distant forest by the most experienced reeves and strongest eagles. The fresh-cut smell, the litter of wood chips from shaping and sawing, lingered as Nallo raced past the newest one and headed for the promontory's prow, where she could scan for Pil.

"Heya!"

Nallo turned as Kesta ran up.

"Where's Pil?" the other reeve asked, wiping sweat from her neck and brow.

"He must have turned back. I saw soldiers—an enemy strike force—attacking a barge. It was so far behind the main flow of refugees that I'm thinking they were folk who escaped Toskala after the siege was set. There was a Qin soldier on that barge."

"What would a Qin soldier be doing all the way here? They're all with their captain in Olossi, aren't they?"

"Except for Pil."

"Pil's a reeve. He's no longer one of them."

A reeve who knew what he was doing. Who could sweep and turn and yank on the right jess to go the right direction; who could shoot arrows and kill men from harness. Who could actually *do* something.

"What's wrong?" asked Kesta, grasping Nallo's wrist and leaning toward her with lips parted in alarm.

This close, Nallo saw clearly the scar on her chin and another on her neck, as if she'd caught an arrow or blade in the flesh. Trembling, she thought, *I should kiss her.*

Eyes flaring, Kesta said, "Nallo?" But her gaze skipped up from Nallo's face to the sky, and whatever else she meant to say was obliterated by a grin of relief. "Cursed outlander. Look at him come down at such an angle!"

Pil and Sweet plummeted down over them. Shrieks of alarm were followed by whoops of laughter as the old raptor came down with a flourish right out in the open rather than in the more isolated parade ground.

"For such a quiet lad, he's turning into a bit of a show-off, eh?" Kesta hadn't released Nallo's arm. "What's troubling you?"

Nallo had never before had trouble speaking her mind. Indeed, it had been the thing people had liked least about her. But a horrible swell of uncertainty—about being a reeve, about Kesta, about their hopes for succeeding stranded up here—strangled her tongue. "I'm just hungry."

She shook free of Kesta and hurried to meet Pil, while Kesta dogged her steps in a most annoying way. Yet the other reeve said nothing as they greeted Pil; as they checked in with the fawkners; as they sat down over an afternoon bowl of rice flavored with the last of the dill weed as Pil described in his endearingly awkward accent the brief battle on the river shore.

"It was Tohon," he said. "The Qin scout."

"The hells," muttered Kesta. "So that's what Volias was on about. Why would folk from Olossi risk sending scouts up here, when they know if they're captured they'll just be interrogated and executed?"

"They prepare an attack by scouting ahead into the territory," said Pil with a shrug, as if the answer was obvious to him.

Kesta's laugh was edged with a despairing anger. "We think the enemy may have as many as ten cohorts spread along the River Istri. That would be six thousand men. As good as the Qin may be, they have—what?—two hundred men? There is no army to save us!"

"Not yet," said Pil, scooping up more rice.

"We don't *have* to be useless!" snapped Nallo.

"What's eating you?" Kesta waved her spoon.

Nallo leaped up and strode away as other reeves stared. She found a shaded corner deep in the compound, slammed her back against a wall, and stood there breathing and trembling for a while. It was the cursed sense of helpless uselessness that ate at her.

After a while Pil walked around the corner and leaned back beside her, settling in as though he meant to wait all night if need be. In truth, it was getting dark.

"Ah, the hells!" she said with a bitter laugh. "Let's go look at the cursed city, eh?"

Silence was assent. He walked companionably, saying nothing as usual, until they reached the big balcony that jutted over the cliff face. Off to the right sat the huge winches for the provisions baskets, safely roped up. A wooden barrier fenced off the stairs so no idiot child could go climbing down and get trapped in the rubble that blocked the steps.

The sun had already set as they leaned on the railing and stared over the city turning to shadow below. Before, twilight had been a bright and busy time in Toskala, lamps bobbing along the avenues as carters and porters made their final deliveries, the night markets coming to life as the day died. Now the city lay dark except for the army camp beyond the outer walls where campfires flickered, and lanterns that lighted the sentry and curfew stations in the main squares and central thoroughfares.

With Pil she could say what she wanted without being judged.

"How can I be a proper reeve when I hardly know how to fly, can barely handle my raptor, and haven't the least idea what to do in a fight? I lost sight of Kesta and you. I would have been lost except for the river. I came to Clan Hall to get training. Now there isn't time. At least you know how to fight."

"The commander makes this decision, how to train new reeves."

His calm words smoothed the turbulence in her heart. Someone would have to take charge, and then things would change. "Flying provisions up from Nessumara might not seem like much, but it's something. As long as we hold Law Rock, the people of Toskala have a hope that we can overcome the enemy. That matters, doesn't it?"

Since she expected no answer, she was content to lean on the railing as stars came out between the patchwork clouds. The voice of the river blended with the steady wind in her ears. After a while, a lantern bobbed toward them, and Kesta walked up.

"I wondered where you had gotten to." She hooked the lantern over a post and leaned on the railing next to Nallo. "Did you ever figure out what's troubling you?"

"I just feel cursed useless, that's all, but maybe once the halls choose a new commander we can get some kind of order and routine restored."

"So we can hope." Her hand was curled invitingly close to Nallo's on the railing. Nallo sucked in a sharp breath.

Pil took a step back. "Fire!"

One moment it was like a lantern's light flaring in a distant quarter; the next, flames rippled skyward.

"That's in Stone Quarter!" Kesta ran to the fire bell, grabbed the rope, and swung the clacker back and forth.

The noise rose skyward like the blaze, and a cadre of firefighters came running from the barracks to crowd on the balcony and watch, but of course there wasn't a cursed thing they could do except to wonder what in the hells was going on in the occupied city.

*   *   *

THE TOUCH OF a hand roused Nekkar, and he flinched.

"I'm here to help you, Holy One," said a female voice softly. She spoke with an odd way of rounding her *e*'s, and she stank so badly he gagged. "Can you move?"

A horrible taste coated his mouth. But when he twitched his feet, his legs, his hands, his shoulders, nothing seemed broken, although shifting the twisted ankle made his eyes tear.

"I think I can walk. Was I beaten?"

"Alas, you were, Holy One. I saw it all from the rooftop. But then they were called off to some other task before they could finish the job, fortunately for you."

"Who are you, verea?"

"Let's get you out of this rubbish."

The ground slid beneath them as she hauled him out of a pile of stinking garbage. He could barely put weight on his left ankle; pain ripped through his shoulders with each movement. She led him to a ladder propped in the gap between gutter and eaves and, after looping a rope around his midsection, supported him up to the roof of a low storehouse. There he sprawled, spread-eagled and fearful he'd slide and plunge over, back into the rubbish heap. She pulled up the ladder.

"We've got to move you away from this alley, Holy One, before the soldiers come back looking for you. Can you move?"

The pain made tears flow. "Yes."

She patted his forearm. "You've got courage, Holy One. Follow me."

They wedged the ladder into a higher set of eaves to get from the storehouse up onto the warehouse roof proper. He tried not to let his weight drag on the rope, but as they bellied up to the peak of the roof, he slipped twice and she dug in her toes and halted his fall. Once at the peak it was easier to move sideways to the far end of the warehouse.

Like the other quarters, Stone Quarter was laid out in blocks, each block made up of compounds, one vast architecture of roofs crammed in against each other except for the occasional courtyards associated with artisans' and guild workshops and the six temple grounds. Tonight, not even one paper lantern was hung out under eaves to illuminate the walkways below. No street vendors sold noodles or soup; no apprentices staggered drunkenly down the avenues roaring popular melodies.

They reached the warehouse's edge just above an archway whose span bridged the avenue below to reach the roofs on the other side of the street. "Hold on, ver. This part is tricky."

"We're going across?"

"We are. I'm taking you to your temple. But you'll have to help me find it once we get down on the streets."

"The soldiers will arrest us for being out after curfew. You're not local, I can hear it. They'll cleanse you."

"They won't catch us."

She let herself down the pitch, then helped him negotiate a pair of drops that brought them to the span. It was a festival arch, sturdy enough. In daylight it would be seen to be painted a brilliant yellow, but the shadows were kind and it was not difficult to scoot across with a leg on either side of the peak. They were about halfway across when the woman slumped against the tiles. Feet shuffled and slapped on the street below. He flattened himself as lantern light bobbed into view. Soldiers drove a mob of folk down the avenue. Many of the prisoners were sobbing; others trudged silently, heads bowed. A few called out.

"At least allow us to gather our belongings before you expel us! We never did anything wrong!"

"Please let me return and get my children! They'll starve. You can't be so heartless."

"Sheh!" The swaggering man at the front barked a laugh. "They break curfew, and yet they complain about *us*!"

"They could have stayed in their villages instead of running to the city, eh?" agreed another soldier. "Makes 'em look like they have something to hide, I reckon."

A man broke, making a dash toward the alley snaking away behind the warehouse compound. While the forward contingent of soldiers pressed the rest of the group onward, three others went running after the fleeing man. So no one looked up as the crowd passed under the arch and down the avenue into a night illuminated only by the lanterns carried by the soldiers.

From the alley, a man's screams rose, then failed abruptly.

After a moment, the three soldiers trotted out of the alley and hurried under the arch after the others, chortling and boasting as if they hadn't just killed a man.

"So I said, 'You've not fattened up that veal yet.' Heh. That's when I called you two over. We'd have given that foreign slave something to trim his pinched face, eh? Thinking he had the right to say no to us, eh! If sergeant hadn't called up formation just right then, I'd've bust him down."

A comrade answered. "You report him? That you saw an outlander, I mean?"

"Sure I did, but I got no coin because their tent wasn't there no more when I led the captain over that way. I wonder what happened to that lot of young whores."

"If they tried to set up in the city, they'll just be thrown out, neh? Like the rest of these gods-rotted refugees."

Their laughter faded into the gloom.

His shoulders throbbed and his ankle burned, and he was furious and shaking, but he crept after his companion to the next roof and after that to another, the huge rations warehouse overlooking Terta Square. There, arms hugging the roof ridgeline, they rested.

The square was lit by lanterns fixed on poles. Directly opposite, the temple dedicated to Kotaru was flanked on one side by a militia barracks brimful with enemy soldiers and on the other by a fire station left without a night guard except for its loyal dog. The rest of the square's frontage was taken up by several large inns and substantial emporia now shuttered and dark. There were four wells sunk into the center, guarded by a contingent of soldiers. A long line of people still waited outside the Thirsty Saw, guarded by yet more soldiers. Several shuffled in through the door while, from the alley that led into the back courtyard of the inn where he had seen the Guardian, ten or more hapless folk came staggering out into the square clutching their left forearms. These refugees were prodded into line. Over in the gloom by the alley entrance lay a pair of discarded bodies.

"How do we get to your temple from here? Which street?"

"Lumber Avenue. Who are you?"

"I am a spy. Not from around here."

"That I can hear in your speech. Yet there are people who sell information or their services to the army, in exchange for coin or preference or safety."

"True enough, Holy One. But I'm not one of them." He sensed a smile from her tone. "I need something from you I can't get from the army."

"This reminds me of an episode from a tale, verea. Cruel soldiers. A chatty, attractive spy. A decrepit man of middling years."

"How do you know I'm attractive, Holy One?"

"You've held me close a time or two as we've made our way here. I know the feel of a shapely female body. I'm not dead. Yet."

Her body shook with suppressed laughter. "Then we'll hope for a happy ending as in the tale, eh?"

He smiled but could not sustain it. "How can I trust you?"

"How can any of us trust, in days like these with an army rampaging down the length of the River Istri, burning and killing as they go? Just like in ancient days, as it says in the Tale of the Guardians: 'Long ago, in the time of chaos, a bitter series of wars, feuds, and reprisals denuded the countryside and impoverished the lords and guildsmen and farmers and artisans of the Hundred.'"

Nekkar mumbled the next line reflexively, overcome with bitter memory of the Guardian he had met. "'In the worst of days, an orphaned girl knelt at the shore of the lake sacred to the gods and prayed that peace might return to her land.'"

Below, soldiers whipped the detainees out of the square as those in line watched helplessly, unable to flee or to fight.

"I'm a hierodule," whispered the spy. "An assassin, sent from the south. I mean to kill Lord Radas, who walks in the guise of a Guardian wearing a cloak of sun. He commands this army. If we can cut off its head, then we can hope the body will die. Will you and your people help me?"

Her words struck him harder than the blows that had felled him. "Is this even possible? Guardians can reach into your mind and heart and know what it is you intend. I have faced one. I could hide nothing from her."

"I will do it, because I must."

She was so sure of herself! Not in a boasting way, but in the way master carpenters surveyed roofs and made pronouncements about what it would take to fix them.

"And when Lord Radas is dead, the soldiers and their captains and sergeants will run away and we'll go back to how it was before?" he asked wryly.

For a while, the assassin remained silent. When she spoke, her words weighed heavily in the humid night air.

"There comes a time when change overtakes the traveler, as it says in the Tale of Change. Hard to say what lies beyond the next threshold. We must be ready for anything." She brushed her fingers over his hand as a young woman might greet her uncle, not sexually but affectionately. "I'm called Zubaidit."

The gesture sealed his heart. "Very well, Zubaidit. Our resources are limited, but if you can get me back to the temple alive, I'll do what I can to help you."

"My thanks. Tell me one thing, Holy One. Have you heard they are searching particularly for anyone?"

"Indeed, yes. I heard it from the mouth of a Guardian, wearing a cloak of night. She seeks the gods-touched, and outlanders."

Her body tensed. "Would you hide a gods-touched outlander, Holy One? If I brought such a one to you?"

He thought of the man killed in the alley because he had tried to run away to find his children. He thought of the dead in the courtyard of the Thirsty Saw and those being dragged away for cleansing. He considered his apprentices and envoys, whom he must protect. The army would come round and take a hostage soon enough. But his temple had no protection if they thought to trust to the whims of those who held the whips.

"I will do what I can. That's all I can offer. I'm Nekkar, by the way. We can't climb roofs all the way to the temple. How do you mean to get me home when I can barely limp along?"

"Wait here for as long as it takes to chant the episode of Foolish Jothinin from the tale of the Silk Slippers. After that, move down to the alley behind this warehouse. You keep the rope. Stay on the lowest roof. Do you see it, there?"

"Yes."

"Be ready to move."

She slid backward. Nekkar heard faint scrapes, and even that slight noise faded beneath the buzz of soldiers chatting and folk shifting and coughing and crying in despair. A guard slapped a kneeling woman until she struggled to her feet. From off over in another quarter of the city, dogs started barking, and an outcry rose into the night like so many wildings on a howl, as it said in the tales. Soldiers tensed. A man trotted out of the inn and cast his gaze toward the sky, but not—thank the Herald!—toward the rations-warehouse roof.

After an intense shower of noise, the storm of distant trouble quieted, the soldiers relaxed, and the man shook his head and strode back inside as the people in line extended hands toward him like beggars hoping for a handout. His soldiers used the hafts of spears to push them back.

The tale! He murmured the chant under his breath. Wind breathed over the square, marred by a tincture of smoke.

The brigands raged in,
they confronted the peaceful company seated at their dinner,
they demanded that the girl be handed over to them.

All feared them. All looked away.
Except foolish Jothinin, light-minded Jothinin,
he was the only one who stood up to face them,
he was the only one who said, "No."

It was one of his favorite episodes, even if it took place in the city of Nessumara, which claimed to be most important of cities in the Hundred when everyone knew Toskala was the holy crossroads of the land, keeper of Law Rock itself. All those apprenticed to Ilu loved the tale, since Jothinin had been an envoy of Ilu, although not a very good one. His hands twitched, wanting to sketch the tale as the words flowed, but he dared not move, not even at the dramatic conclusion when Jothinin's brave stand was all that prevented the innocent girl from being slain as, with his lengthy speech, the envoy roused the populace into the revolt that would overthrow the rule of brigands and restore the law. His final silence, the gaps in the chant where his words would have gone were he not dying from stab wounds, always made Nekkar's eyes mist over.

The wind turned. He licked his lips, feeling the greasy taste of scorched oil on the air. What was he thinking, to put the apprentices and envoys at risk? How could this self-confessed "assassin" possibly get him back to the temple with the city under curfew?

Screams burst as fire blazed up in the upper story of the closed emporium on the opposite side of the square. He stared in awe and horror as the people in the square cried out, as soldiers grabbed buckets stored in the fire station. Stone Quarter could burn down! Everyone was running, most for the fire station, setting up lines at the wells, while others dashed away into the darkness of back streets, escaping while they had the chance. The fire bell atop Law Rock clanged in the distance.

Obviously this was a diversion! Time to go.

He scraped palms as he scrabbled for purchase on the tiles, jamming his right leg as he barely caught the gutter instead of tumbling over the drop. Pain stabbed through his left ankle, blinding him. Then he breathed out of it and found the strength to heave himself onto the lower roof and roll to lie precariously along the edge.

"Holy One?" Her voice drifted up from the alley below him.

His anger blazed. "It could burn down the entire quarter. What of the poor folk who own that shop, whose entire livelihood is going up in flames?"

"Their goods had already been looted." The assassin's voice was staggering in its calm intensity. "Anyway, that fire is nothing to what I've seen this army do, and what worse things they'll do if they're not stopped. Now is the time to go, if you mean to come with me, Holy One."

She was right.

When he threw his legs over and eased himself down, bruised arms and shoulders screaming at the effort, she caught him. He showed her the way, and she supported him through the empty night streets as the fire drew the attention of the army. Past Lele Square, they reached the temple gate, locked and barred, but the dogs whined to alert the night guard and the small gate was cracked open to allow him in.

She waved him on.

"You're not coming in?"

"Neh. I must retrieve my comrade. We'll return tomorrow night or the next. Watch for us, Holy One."

Then she was gone into the night, and the gate was closed and barred behind him. As he limped into the dark courtyard, all the envoys and every apprentice flooded out of the sleeping house, crowding him, touching him, weeping with relief, until he thought he would faint for needing to sit down. He was bereft of speech. The fire bell had ceased ringing. Smoke scented the air. One of the night guards called down from the sentry post: "Looks like it's stopped spreading!"

Vassa pushed her way through the acolytes with sharper words than he had ever heard from one who was always gentle. When she shone lamplight in his face, everyone gasped.

"Gather a few things and sit out here in the courtyard until we know the danger is passed," she said to the envoys and apprentices. "Kellas, haul out the litter in case we must carry the ostiary."

"I can walk—" Nekkar croaked, and put his weight on his twisted ankle. The light hazed. The world spun. Many arms took hold of him and lifted him.

"You'll take a wash and some poultices for your injuries, some food and tea, and then you'll lie down."

"I must talk to you—"

"Yes," Vassa agreed, and he realized in a distant way that she was trying not to cry. "Here, you lads, carry him."

He was too weary and too much in pain to struggle. Tomorrow or the next night, the assassin had said. Tomorrow would be soon enough to see what trouble he had called down on the temple. They had to be ready for anything.

5

DON'T OPEN THE GATE.

That was the last thing Zubaidit had said to Shai before leaving on her spying expedition yesterday. Now it was dawn, Bai hadn't returned, and someone was rapping hard on the nailed-together planks set against a gap in the abandoned storeroom in which he had slept.

"Open up!"

"The whole compound looks abandoned to me."

"The dog thinks otherwise."

A dog snuffled along the exterior of the planks. Shai tucked his sword along his torso and slid a hiltless knife into a sheath cut into the leather of his boots just as the soldiers kicked down the planks. Shards splintered.

He pretended he was just waking up. He'd successfully played stupid before. "Eh, ver. Eh. You frightened me."

Burly soldiers prodded spears in his direction. "Heya, Sergeant! Got an outlander here. Whew! He stinks."

"That's because we're in an old tanning yard, you imbecile," came the reply. "Bring him out."

"Out!" They treated him as they might a dog whose temperament was chancy.

"Eh, ver, Mistress told me to wait here for her. She'll whip me if I leave."

"Our orders are to kill anyone who disobeys."

"Maybe he can't understand you," said the second man.

Shai had already cut a hiding place for his sword into the foundation. He rolled over the sword, shoved it into the gap, and covered it as he kept talking. "Please don't hurt me, ver. My mistress, she said she would whip me. Please don't."

He crawled on hands and knees, feeling the points of the spears like stinging scorpions along his back, but once he got outside into the colorless dawn, the soldiers drew a step back and let him stand. He shook out his loose trousers, flicked dust from the sleeveless leather vest that covered his chest, and wiped a smear of dust from his lips. This tannery compound hadn't been used for some time, and lay far enough away from Toskala that Bai had thought it safe to use as a hiding place. But every structure in this entire area where the camp followers had set up days ago was being searched and their occupants driven outside and rounded up. Women were arguing, children crying, old men fumbling as they tried to keep their bundled possessions slung over thin shoulders.

As they came into the disrupted camp, a sergeant trotted over to look him up and down. "An outlander, all right! Look at those arms!"

"Mistress said to wait for her here, ver."

"And where is she, your mistress, eh?" demanded the sergeant.

"Out in the camp, ver. She always goes out at night."

"A whore, eh?" cackled one of the soldiers. "I wonder what she wants a slave for, if she can get men to pay for it?"

The other soldier poked Shai with the haft of his spear. "He's got no slave mark. What if he's concealing a weapon beneath that vest or trousers."

"Fancy a look, do you, Milas?" said the first soldier.

"Shut it," barked the sergeant. "Milas is right. Get that vest off."

In the Hundred, folk walked about with a great deal of skin uncovered, while Shai still felt awkward about his bare arms. So his embarrassment made him slow, and the soldiers got more threatening, others circling in, attracted by the commotion. The light rose from gray to a pearly pink. Overhead, clouds chased the wind north.

Shai was strong from years of carpentry, and lean from the recent weeks of privation. He kept his head bent, knowing he was blushing as he stripped off the vest.

"Sheh! Reason enough, neh?" Milas laughed once Shai stood with with vest hanging from his right hand. "Cursed if those camp women aren't staring and licking their lips. You want us to strip him all the way, Sergeant? A nice show for the lasses and such lads as are fashioned that way, neh?"

The sergeant had already turned away. "This is taking too long. A cloak will sort this out. Bring him." He raised his voice. "Let's get this camp cleared."

Shai pulled on the vest as he shuffled over to join the rest of the detainees. He kept his head deferentially lowered as he scanned the encampment: canvas tents and lean-tos, tiny huts precariously assembled out of scraps of wood. A few abandoned structures like the old tannery in which he had slept gave the temporary camp a look of ruined permanence, and the clotheslines where rags flapped and the stink of the crudely dug refuse pits reminded him of certain neighborhoods in faraway Kartu

Town where the outcast and the poor had barely scraped by living in their own filth. The Qin conquerors had forced gangs of townspeople to raze such compounds and build blocks of more sanitary housing, easy to police and control.

But he had left Kartu Town. He no longer lived under the suzerainty of the Qin. He had come to the Hundred together with a troop of exiled Qin soldiers only to find himself in the middle of a chaotic internal war. He and Zubaidit had been sent north with five others to spy out the enemy, and now, *of course*, he'd gotten himself captured.

Again.

The soldiers herded the group along a barrier of wagons that marked off the edge of the army's main camp. An early wind teased trampled ground where draft beasts and horses grazed. In the days since Toskala had fallen, much of the army had taken up stations within the city, leaving the camp followers to starve because the soldiers could get food and miscellaneous goods as well as repair work done elsewhere. Some had drifted away into the countryside. Now, it seemed, the commanders of the army meant to sweep up and dispose of the rest.

"Heya! I walked all the way from Walshow, feeding the army. What am I to do?" called a man hauling a cart laden with the pans and tripods of a movable kitchen. Beside him, a boy bent double under the weight of a bundle of goods, his left eye scarred with the mark of a debt slave.

A young woman, red-eyed from weeping, kept trying to get the attention of a pair of soldiers who resolutely refused to look her way. She held an infant wrapped in a decent piece of cloth that matched the green scarf she had wrapped around her hair. "Where's Joran? Why hasn't he come back for me and the baby, like he promised?"

Shai hung back until he was at the tail of the crowd, the dust kicked up by their feet smearing his tongue. After months of regular rain, it had not rained in three days, and the churned-up ground had dried. Off to the left sprawled the city, too big to comprehend in one glance. It was marked most obviously by a huge rock outcropping thrust up where the River Istri and the Lesser Istri had their confluence. There, during the day, the giant eagles ridden by reeves landed and took off. A pillar of smoke drifted above one quarter of the city, losing coherence as the wind tore at it.

"Keep moving!" A soldier prodded Shai while speaking to his own comrade. "Milas says this one's got muscles like you wouldn't believe. A real woodchopper!" They both laughed, as if the word meant something different.

"Where's the outlander?" Shai recognized the sergeant's voice. "Move him out separate."

"What are we doing with the rest of them, Sergeant? That poor lass. Joran did promise to take care of her and the baby, but I hear he got assigned guard duty at the lord commander's headquarters."

"Not our problem. Our orders is to clear the camp and cleanse those who give us trouble. Anyway, the girl was stupid for leaving her village to follow him. She can walk home. If Joran cares about her, he'll fetch her when the campaign is over."

By now the detained camp followers numbered in the hundreds, and those at the front began wailing as they neared the road. Poles lined the road up to the city gates, bodies strung up by their arms on at least a third of them. Living people, some still struggling as they tried to relieve the pressure on their arms, some with broken legs unable to carry any weight. Flies swarmed on the faces of hanging folk helpless to swipe them away.

Hu! Not even the Qin conquerors were that cruel. They had executed criminals and traitors and, indeed, anyone they deemed a threat for whatever reason they cared to name, but they killed them first and hung their bodies out as a warning after.

A captain rode his horse along the road, surveying the poles, both the unadorned and those ornamented with the dying and the dead. Shai could not help but criticize his uneasy seat in the saddle, a man come late to riding to whom the gelding was merely a badge of authority. He lacked the Qin grace on horseback. He preened, relishing his power, as he looked over the frightened faces gazing up at him.

"Orders have come down from the commanders," he shouted, his voice raspy. No doubt a captain of an army that is imposing its control over a hostile city had good reason to go hoarse from shouting. Shai held his position at the back of the crowd, but the sergeant kept staring right at him. "You lot are to return to your homes. The army has no more need of you."

A chorus of protests rose: "You can't dump us—!" "We walked all that way with you—" "How are we to live—?"

The captain rode to the front of the crowd, drew his sword as folk shrieked and pressed back, and cut down the lass with the infant. She died without a sound, collapsing into a heap with the baby in her arms. Her ghost emerged with startling swiftness as a mist exhaled from her nostrils. Her ghostly fingers plucked at the squalling baby as she cried in a voice only Shai could hear.

"Help my baby, please! I beg you!"

Ghosts may be warned by senses other than sight and hearing. With a terrible shriek she flung her essence uselessly at the captain as he casually leaned down and stabbed the infant, like piercing a haunch of uncooked meat once, twice, and a third time.

Folk scattered away, screaming, but the soldiers drove them back together like so many stampeding sheep rounded up and confined before slaughter. The cursed sergeant grabbed Shai's arm, his smile that of a man who has seen his dinner waiting and knows it'll be tasty.

"Don't try to run, ver."

"Silence!" shouted the captain. Soldiers plied the flats of their swords like clubs until the crowd huddled in submissive fear. Many had dropped their goods, leavings scattered: a ladle here and a sieve there, a tangle of leather cords crushed into the dirt, and a forlorn dog cowering. In the turmoil, the ghosts had vanished.

"You were allowed to follow the army from Walshow on sufferance. Now you are no longer needed. Go home. Any found by day's end within sight of the city will be cleansed, I promise you."

He reined aside as the soldiers formed a barrier between the city and the crowd and waited sullenly for the camp followers to accept the inevitable and start moving off.

The sergeant hailed the captain. "Captain Dessheyi, we found an outlander."

The captain rode over, the horse skittish with the crowd seething so close by. "So I see, Sergeant. Good work. I'll take him."

"There's a reward for outlanders, Captain. If I might say so. I found him."

"Did you? Or did some of your men roust him out, and now you take credit for it? Very well. There's a cloak at the city gates. Take him there."

He should have run at the first sign of trouble. Now it was too late. Some called the cloaks "Guardians," saying they were holy guardians of justice sent to the Hundred by the gods long ago. But Shai figured they were demons. Of the four he had encountered, one was a horrible pervert. Another had taken on the form and face of a dead slave girl Shai had once owned, and she had easily killed an entire cadre of the enemy before allowing Shai and the children he was caring for to walk free. The third had seemed harmless enough, a middle-aged man dressed in a blue cloak who talked too much. The fourth had been his dead brother Hari's ghost.

The commander of this army, Lord Radas, was one of these demons, the very man Zubaidit had been sent north to assassinate. So this was Shai's chance to be more than the least and last of seven brothers, the least and last of the Qin tailmen. This was his chance to prove himself.

"Glad it's not me has to face a cloak," muttered Milas as the cadre marched Shai up onto the road toward Toskala. Outside the city walls, houses rose in village blocks linked by paths to the city, although the folk who lived there had fled. Every patch of ground was cultivated, rice fields, vineyards, vegetable gardens, wheat. Mulberry trees lined the irrigation ditches that crossed the area. Farther out along the Lesser Istri spread compounds like the abandoned tannery he had hidden in, anything that stank too much to be allowed within the environs of the city.

Gangs of workers tended the fields under guard by cadres from the army. Ten heavily laden wagons rolled past. A steady stream of people trudged out of the city on footpaths, more refugees to join the banished camp followers. It was a pleasant morning for walking, as long as you didn't think about the dead and dying people hanging from posts.

When their cadre reached the gate, they found a line of detainees waiting beyond the gatehouse under the supervision of bored soldiers.

"Heya!" called the sergeant, seeking out the captain in charge. "I've got an outlander. Can I take him forward?"

This captain had a lean, watchful face and enough arrogance to make you blink. "Get in line with the rest."

"These lot aren't outlanders!"

"I'm pleased you can tell the difference. Everyone here has to be judged for one reason or another, so get in line. You're not the only one who's brought in an outlander. I'll call you forward in due time."

They waited the rest of the morning. Shai measured the height of the walls, the speed and frequency of traffic—all as Tohon had taught him—but after a while he began to think his efforts pointless. The soldiers stood, or sat, or went to relieve themselves; two mounted an expedition for food and returned some time later with a heaping bowl of noodles that they shared out between them. Shai got nothing. His stomach rumbled with hunger, but he'd endured worse and, even so, he had never suffered the abuses forced on the children he'd been held captive with for many weeks. Had Eridit and the others found Tohon? Had their party reached Nessumara safely? He murmured a prayer to the Merciful One: *Shower mercy over them;*

protect them; grant them refuge. But he had no offering gift except the pain and fear and grief in his heart.

Clouds gave intermittent protection from the sun. It was not as steamy as it had been earlier in the year. The season was changing. Having grown up in a distant land where the round of the year was utterly predictable, he could not hope to know what this new season would bring. He considered the knife concealed within his boot and offered a brief prayer to the Merciful One: *Let them not search me.*

Was Lord Radas himself conducting interrogations?

"Heya!" The familiar voice jolted him. "What are you lot doing with my slave, eh?" Zubaidit strolled up in her tight sleeveless vest, her kilt swinging with each twitch of her shapely hips.

"So you're the whore," said the sergeant with a laugh.

"I'll thank you not to use that insulting word, Sergeant. I'm an honest merchant."

"Taking coin for sex is not honest work," said Milas with a sneer.

She looked him up and down until he blushed. "Like you never paid? Just how long have you been marching with the army, ver? Or do you sharpen your tool yourself?" His comrades laughed. "You lot scorn the Devouring temples, so I figure that gives us something in common." A medallion in the shape of an eight-pointed star hung by a leather thong around her neck, just like the ones worn by all the soldiers. "Can I have my slave back? I'll make it worth your while."

The sergeant placed himself between her and Shai. "Listen, verea. You look like a tasty morsel, that's for sure. You've got the look of a hierodule."

"I was a hierodule, truly, until I left, because the old bitch of a hieros kicked me out." She was a bold woman who knew how to attract the eye, but Shai recognized the strength in her shoulders and the taut muscular grace of her legs, signs the soldiers ignored in favor of the sexual charms she flaunted to put them off their guard.

The sergeant grinned in reply. "Well, lass, I don't like to be the one bearing bad news, but all you camp followers have been told to get out. Any one of you found within sight of the city by day's end will be cleansed." With a jerk of his chin, he indicated the poles lining the road, an avenue of death.

Zubaidit did not even look at the suffering. "Whew! That's cold comfort for those who served the army all this way. You lot figuring to settle in here? Else who will help you on your further campaigns?"

"Not my problem. It may be those bed warmers who have pleased the officers get dispensation to stay with the army, but I wouldn't take my chances even on that. We saw a soldier's favorite lass with a baby born of his getting, cut down by Captain Dessheyi just for being in his way. Why don't you get on, then? No cause to get yourself in trouble, eh?"

She regarded him with a quizzical look, a moment of sympathy, perhaps, or something more complicated. Then the expression vanished, and the mocking smile reappeared. "I'll just take my slave and get out of here."

"Neh, can't let you do that. How'd you afford a brawny lad like this, anyway?"

"He was cheap. He's dumb as an ox. That's what I call him, anyway. Ox."

Shai took the hint. "Mistress, I waited for you. Then they made me go. They're taking me to see some fancy cloth. I tried to wait, Mistress. Please don't whip me."

The soldiers snickered.

Bai's smile was its own whip. "Are you sure it's worth wasting the time of your interrogator, Sergeant? You see what I mean."

"There's a reward if we bring in outlanders."

"Eiya! I thought no one cared for outlanders here. I've been trying to hire him out for the novelty of it, but he's too cursed stupid to know what to do with women, or with men, for that matter. I think he can only tup sheep."

That got them roaring. Shai was just grateful there were no sheep around, lest they amuse themselves by suggesting he perform.

"Heya!" The captain in charge of the line beckoned. "Sergeant! Come."

"You can't just steal him from me like that," objected Bai.

"Go back to your village and get yourself a respectable shop or a respectable husband," said the sergeant in a manner meant to be kindly. "You don't want to find yourself like that lass and her infant babe who are dead."

Bai did not protest as they led him away. She could not. Anyway, they both knew he had to take a chance at the cloak.

At the gatehouse, coin changed hands, and the sergeant and his cadre took off, happy to be rid of him. He was shoved down a corridor and fetched up in a spacious courtyard between high walls where a horse grazed on a patch of grass. Cloth had been strung along rope to conceal one half of the courtyard. The sun's light revealed three figures against the cloth: one kneeling abjectly and one waiting with a soldier's alert posture over to the side, half turned away. The third man stood with a slumped tilt to broad shoulders Shai thought he recognized.

"Please, I beg you." By the motion of clasped hands, Shai guessed it was the kneeling figure who spoke. It was painful to hear a man reduced to such wretched sobs. "You've seen into my very heart, you know all my secrets. It wasn't my choice to hide those barrels of wine, nor the ale. It was my sister. It was her idea!"

The third man slapped a hand to its head in an exaggerated gesture Shai had seen before. "Of all things, I detest folk who betray their own to protect themselves. Sniveling, selfish bastard."

The sound of that voice knifed into Shai's heart.

"I might have seen fit to show mercy to a merchant who, not unreasonably, sought to salvage some of his goods rather than see them looted. But to blame your own sister, when you and I know perfectly well that you told her to do it—sheh!"

The Hundred word—for shame!—fell easily from those lips, and Shai shuddered as, his strength failing him, he dropped to his knees.

"Captain Arras, take this one away for cleansing. Quickly. He stinks."

"Can't we just execute him, my lord?"

"I have to throw them a few bones, you know that. He disgusts me. Just take him."

The condemned man shrieked and struggled as soldiers entered from the other side and dragged him out past Shai. Past the briefly opened curtain, Shai saw a trim man of military bearing, the same watchful captain from the line. The captain lifted hands to shield his face, turning to face the third figure, still concealed as the cloth slithered down to seal away the area.

"They've brought the outlander, as you commanded, my lord."

"Ah."

A brown hand pulled aside the cloth. A man emerged from behind the curtain, dressed in the local fashion and wearing a cloak for the rains. Shai had been little more than a boy when, six years ago, his favorite brother had been marched in chains out of Kartu Town, a prisoner of the Qin conquerors.

Hari was dead. Yet here he stood, looking at Shai with a well-known and much-loved sardonic smile on his blessedly familiar face.

"Hello, little brother," Hari's ghost said, smile lingering. "You've grown up."

*　　*　　*

NEKKAR WAS SLUMBERING fitfully when Vassa woke him, her worried expression illuminated by the lamp she carried.

"She's here."

A deep bruise in his right hip made it difficult to stand, even leaning on a crutch, the effect made worse because his swollen left ankle throbbed if he rested any weight on it. But he limped out to the porch to find one of the night guards standing nervously behind the assassin. She was younger than he had imagined.

"Zubaidit."

"Holy One." She assisted him with strong arms to settle onto a pillow.

Vassa sat down on his other side, smiling in a way he knew meant she was reserving judgment. She set down the lamp on the planks. "Kellas, bring what remains of the warmed khaif."

The lad, hovering since Nekkar had fainted the night before, ran off.

"A humble cottage for an ostiary," remarked the assassin pleasantly as they waited. "Another person of your rank might insist on more ostentation."

Vassa snorted, but she unbent slightly.

"I serve Ilu. Not wealth and the fickle opinion of those who care about such displays."

She chuckled in a way he found endearing. "An honest acolyte! Not as common a treasure in these days as we might hope."

"That's as may be, verea. We could chatter on in this vein for half the night and would be considered polite for doing so. I beg your pardon. You said you had an associate. A gods-touched outlander. Where he is?"

"Taken prisoner." Her words were clipped.

"How did it happen?" asked Vassa sharply.

"I blame myself. I should have sent him away when I had the chance, because he lacks training, but he is gods-touched and therefore I thought I could use him to fulfill my mission. While I was here exploring Toskala, the army decided to send away the camp followers. He was caught in the sweep."

"Saving me, you lost him."

She shrugged with an angry lift of her chin. "We can't know it would have fallen out differently had I not saved you, Holy One."

Kellas appeared out of the darkness with a tray. Vassa served the spy with her own hands, a courtesy Nekkar observed with interest. Something in the woman's confession had earned Vassa's sympathy, and he trusted his lover's instincts for people more than his own.

He took his cup, sipped at the pungent sludge that had come from the bottom of the pot, and set it down with a grimace. "We have seen many troubling and terrible things in recent days."

She drained her own cup without answering.

"Bring nai porridge as well, whatever's left in the pot," said Vassa to the lad, "and make sure Odra keeps the rest of the apprentices down on their pallets."

"Yes, Auntie." Kellas trotted off. The night guard remained out of sight in the darkness.

"What will you do?" Nekkar asked.

"Go on with the mission. I waited as long as I could by the city gate after they took him inside, but I never saw him brought out and hanged. So maybe he is dead by other means. Or maybe he has succeeded beyond my expectations. I may never know. Such is war."

"What do you want of us?" Vassa asked, and in her tone Nekkar heard a tincture of weariness: It got so tiring to have to be suspicious of everyone. Sometimes you had to trust as an act of hope.

"Is there any possible way you can get me up to the reeves on the rock and back down again without being caught?"

"Up to Law Rock and Justice Square?" The words startled him. "No. The thousand steps are blocked by a rockfall. If you don't have wings, there's no other route beyond the provisions baskets, and I'm sure they're winched safely up top. The army must have a blockade at the base of both routes—basket and steps—to guard against folk down here sending weapons or food up in aid of the reeves."

Vassa folded her arms over her chest. "What message have you for the reeves? Or for us, for that matter? We're forced to abide by curfews. We're promised the markets will be allowed to open under strict supervision if we obey. Yet this morning word came by street crier that every house, clan, and guild compound will be required to give up coin and storehouse goods to the army, and a hostage as well, one from each household, clan, guild, and even the temples."

"Just as the Guardian commanded," murmured Nekkar.

Zubaidit whistled. "That's a heavy tax."

"Theft can be weathered, if one is willing to tighten one's belt through the lean months to come." Vassa broke off as Kellas hurried up with a covered bowl, set it down in front of the assassin, and retreated. Zubaidit set a hand on the cover and, trembling, drew it back.

"Go on," said Vassa, voice gentling. As a cook, she could not bear to see people suffer from hunger.

"My thanks, verea." She dug in with a will, devouring half the porridge before she forced herself to stop and let it settle. "My apologies."

"How long has it been since you've eaten?" demanded Vassa.

"It doesn't matter. Listen, Holy One. Verea." She gestured with the spoon in the direction of the gates. The wick whispered as it consumed the reservoir of oil. "The army intends to march downriver and attack Nessumara. They'll leave a garrison to defend their interests in the city."

"We could fight them if there are only a few!" cried Kellas from the end of the porch.

"Apprentice, it will be bed for you if you can't keep silence," said Nekkar, although it was difficult not to chuckle at the lad's enthusiasm. Her words likewise set his own heart hammering. He turned to the assassin. "Could we fight?"

"It is a risk to leave Toskala with only a garrison to control it. That must be why they are taking hostages to march south with the main army. Such hostages can be cleansed if anyone in Toskala rebels."

"The hells!" murmured Vassa.

The pain in his body swelled tenfold, as if he were thrown once again into the courtyard of the Thirsty Saw to face the Guardian's penetrating gaze. "Of course no one will dare attack the garrison if they fear for the lives of their kinsfolk. Aui!"

"I need to let my allies know of this, as well as other observations I've made. Can you get me up the rock?" She looked at Vassa. "For I think you know something, verea, that you're not saying."

"Vassa?" he said, indignantly. "Do you know something you've not shared with me?"

She patted him on the knee. "You are not my husband, to be privy to my clan's secrets. Nor are you local, Nekkar. You've only lived in Toskala thirty years. I was born here." She leaned forward to regard the assassin with a stare from which the other woman did not flinch. "To help you puts us in deadly danger. We must live here while you will leave."

"A fair concern, verea," replied the spy, "so I'll offer you a trade. Help me get a message to the reeves. When it comes time for your clan, or this temple, to hand over a hostage to the army, I'll go in place of one of your own. If I can't reach Lord Radas here, I have to go with the army. This is my chance. What do you say, verea?"

"Eat the rest of that porridge before it congeals," said Vassa, in that way she took with the apprentices, to whom she was devoted although she lived in the compound next door and spent most of her day cooking for her clan of mat makers.

Zubaidit ate slowly with an effort that made it clear she was starving.

"They'll notice her southern way of talking at once," said Nekkar, not sure whether to laugh at the thought of sticking one in the eye of the army, or weep at the chance of disaster that might engulf them were they to be caught.

"I served Hasibal for my apprentice year with a troupe of festival entertainers," Vassa said with a sweep of uplifted chin that captured their attention. Nekkar smiled to see her brightness come alive after so many days smothered in anguish. "We'd have to stage it, like actors do over in Bell Quarter. My clan could let her pose as the southern bride of my nephew, gotten in a trade deal. We'd hold her back when the army comes round, make it seem like he and all of us are besotted. Get them to choose you as if against our will. It would be tricky. Not least due to his charms. He's a handsome lad."

"I'll take that risk, if I must." Zubaidit grinned in a way that made Nekkar laugh softly.

"A hierodule, indeed," he murmured.

"I serve the Merciless One," she agreed. "And the reeves?"

"I'll talk to my people," said Vassa. "And they'll talk to other people. It's dangerous, with this curfew, but there is one hidden path. Can you be patient, verea?"

"I can be as patient as I must be."

6

STUCK ALL DAY up on Law Rock because Tumna was out on her hunting day, Nallo had had enough.

"Sit your stinking ass down and keep your mouth closed, ver." The snap in her voice made the cursed merchant take a startled step backward, out of her face. "I'm tired of hearing you complain, and so is everyone else, neh? You'll have your turn to get your rations and make your complaints when it comes to you."

"I'm a respected guildsman! You've no right to talk to me in that way, some village girl thinking she's as good as me just because—"

"Just because I have an eagle that can rip your head off? End of the line, ver."

Nallo signaled to the firefighters who made up what passed for a militia atop the rock. Using their fire hooks as prods, the young men chivvied the furious merchant out of his place and to the back as he protested in an obnoxious voice while onlookers smirked. He'd made no friends with his demands for special treatment.

She surveyed the folk waiting in line for their daily rations. "We mean to hold Law Rock. So you've got to bide your time, do your part, accept your rations, keep calm. Those of you who can train to fight, will train. Those who are hoping for a lift off the rock will have to wait your turn."

At the head of the line, on the long porch fronting the militia barracks where many of the stranded people slept, a shaven-headed clerk sworn to Sapanasu the Lantern made a mark in her accounts book as the fire captain ladled out a ration of rice porridge to a woman with two children hanging on to her taloos. The clerk called for the next person in line, and bent forward to hear his name.

We're Toskala's last defenders, Nallo thought, *and a sad herd of bleating goats we're proving to be.*

The cadre sergeant beckoned. "Heya, Nallo! You're called to a reeve's meeting."

"Hold the line," she said to him. "Anyone who bawls out of turn gets sent to the back like that one. Better we had a sack of mildewed nai than him. At least we could dump the rotten nai on anyone trying to clear the steps."

"Heh, that's a good one." The firefighters liked her irritable temper and sharp tongue, although few others she'd known in her twenty years had appreciated it. "Wish I'd seen your eagle rip the head off those men who killed the two eagles on Traitors' Night."

But Nallo remembered how her friend Volias had dropped dead beside her in the instant his own eagle had expired. That her own eagle, Tumna, had slaughtered the murderers didn't make her feel better. "I'd have ripped off the heads of those gods-rotted, hells-bound traitors if I'd gotten to them first."

"Aui! I'll bet you would have!"

She trotted over to the gate that led into the reeve compound, where she found Pil waiting. She paced beside him into Clan Hall, an impressive complex with its skeletal watchtowers where eagles could perch, the two vast lofts for shelter, a long, narrow parade ground for training, and a sheltered garden tucked away behind it all near the edge of the cliff where the commander of Clan Hall had her office and chamber. The commander was dead, of course, murdered with so many others on the night they were all now calling "Traitors' Night." Odash, the old reeve who had acted for years as hall steward because he was too crippled to fly, had taken the cote's porch for his headquarters as he tried to keep Clan Hall functioning.

The forty-eight reeves remaining, not counting the four who were on patrol and the thirty-three who were in some stage of flying individual refugees down to Nessumara and returning with sacks of rice and nai, gathered in the commander's courtyard. Seventy-two fawkners, stewards, hirelings, and slaves were also stuck up on the rock. Odash sat on a three-legged stool, looking as exhausted as ever.

He raised a hand and everyone quieted. "We've held this rock ten days. We're helpless to stop the murders going on below. However, we've now established communications with the city, via the auxiliary basket on the north cliff. Yesterday a message was left in the basket. Here's the news: There's been extensive looting. The army is forcing all refugees to leave the city. Anyone who speaks out against the army, and people who have ties with militia or specific clans are executed immediately. A governing headquarters has been set up in Flag Quarter. Taxes are being levied compound by compound. Wherever weapons are found, they are confiscated. A curfew's been established. The markets are closed, and people are hungry."

Pil made a gesture that caught Odash's notice.

"What is it, Pil?"

It wasn't easy for Pil to speak up, but he managed to force out words. "The army wants to rule the city. If people have hunger and have fright, they then will obey the ones who rule, if they fear them."

"That something your people used to do, out in foreign lands?" demanded one of the older reeves, a man named Vekess. He eyed Pil with suspicion.

"It is an effective method."

Some of the reeves hissed, but Kesta moved closer to slap Pil on the shoulder. "Cursed glad you're here with us, Pil. Gives us some insight into what these gods-rotted criminals might be doing." She bent her fierce gaze on Odash.

The old reeve made a business of clearing his throat to focus attention back on himself. "My contacts want to send a person up here to meet with us."

"Could be a trap," said Vekess.

"Cursed well could be, but there's little danger for us if we haul the contact up in the auxiliary basket. The one in the basket and those who must set him there are the ones who might be caught."

"That's fair to let them take the risk," said Vekess. "They're more expendable than eagles."

"Reeve Vekess is right," said Pil unexpectedly. "There are few eagles, and many people."

At Vekess's flush, some chuckled. Pil's mouth quirked, as it did when he was practicing archery and scored a solid stream of bull's-eyes.

"It's a fair argument," agreed Odash. "I'll give the signal. Expect someone to come up in the basket tonight."

The meeting dissolved into the usual chorus of indignant comments and exchanges of angry recriminations, not for any of the assembled reeves, of course, but for the army, the traitors in Toskala who had opened the city gates to let in the enemy without a fight, the other reeve halls that had not responded to their pleas for help. The general disorganization of it all. A wind wafted the smell of rotting waste off the city; as the breeze turned, Nallo caught the sweet scent of the late-blooming vine roses growing in the troughs that rimmed the commander's cote. The sliding doors were closed tight. Odash slept on a pallet on the covered porch, like a dog waiting for its master to return. She couldn't decide whether she found it touching, or idiotic. Sheh! What was she thinking? He was doing his best, accustomed to carrying out the orders of a leader who had been horribly murdered just ten days ago.

"Heya!" Simultaneous shouts rose from the watchtowers. "Eagles coming in."

Reeves ran for the parade ground.

Kesta said, "That's Peddo and Jabi. Aui! There's Scar!"

The eagles came in with wings outstretched and talons lifted, thumping onto the big perches in the middle of the parade ground. Unhooking, the reeves dropped from their harness and stepped out from under the shadow of the eagles.

Peddonon, grinning as usual, called out. "Heya, Kesta! How'd you fare at Copper Hall?"

Her shrug was a negative. "They arranged for us to get supplies off the local merchants. But they wanted *us* to retreat from here and reinforce *them*. So, we're on our own."

"Iron Hall? Gold? Bronze? Are the reeves who flew there back yet?"

"Bronze Hall wouldn't even let our messenger meet with the marshal, just said they'd consider sending a legate, typical brush-off. Iron and Gold said they were too overstretched to spare even a single reeve to meet with us—but we're welcome to keep them up to date on our situation."

Peddonon's grin widened. "So I win! I told you he would come himself. What do you owe me?"

"A kick in the ass, just like always."

The reeve sauntering forward beside Peddonon Nallo knew well enough, for he'd been the one who had first tried to coerce her into becoming a reeve, back when she'd been a refugee out on the roads. She had not understood then that no person chosen by an eagle had a choice about becoming a reeve. Nevertheless, he had handled it poorly, for all his charm.

He made a big show of greeting everyone, and truly everyone did know him; he'd left a posting at this hall to become marshal of Argent Hall in the southern Hundred less than a year ago.

"How are you faring?" He strolled up to her with an irritating smile on his handsome face. How she hated people who assumed you would be happy to see them just because they were so good-looking, even a man as old as he was, fully forty years if he was a day. "It's Avisha, isn't it?"

"It's Nallo. Avisha is my stepdaughter. The pretty one."

He blinked. "That's right." He laughed at his awkward words. "I meant, that's right that you're Nallo and she's Avisha. She got married."

Nallo flushed, thinking of poor Avisha, orphaned and kinless with two small siblings to protect and thereby having no better option than to marry one of the Qin soldiers because they were rich and without wives. "I hope he'll treat her well."

Pil said, "Who chose her?"

"It doesn't work quite that way," said the reeve, scratching his clean-shaven, noble chin. "I've forgotten your name."

"It's Pil, Marshal."

"Pil. That's right. Men can offer, but it's the woman who must accept or refuse."

"How likely is it that a woman will refuse if her entire clan insists," asked Nallo curtly. "How much of a choice does a poor woman have if she has only one offer?"

Marshal Joss's glance at her was keen. "That's right. In this case, your pretty stepdaughter had more than one suitor. One was Chief Tuvi."

Pil whistled under his breath, but said nothing.

"However, she chose a tailman. A decent fellow, everyone says."

"Jagi," said Pil, and an unexpected grin flashed.

Joss shrugged. "I don't recall the name." He smiled winningly again and walked over to greet Odash. The two men moved down the alley between barracks and storehouse toward the commander's cote, and most of the reeves followed in a shuffling, uncertain crowd, not sure what to expect or what to do now that help had come from the south in the form of a single reeve known to be a drunk and a womanizer. Nallo walked to the gate, Pil pacing alongside her.

"Will he treat her and the children well?"

"He will." The certainty in his tone brought tears to her eyes.

"Good, then. Good."

She settled against one of the gateposts and, crossing her arms, stared out at Justice Square. The rations line had gotten shorter; about forty people, including the fuming merchant, waited to receive their portion. Others had retreated to the porches to sit in the shade. From the direction of the militia barracks came the call and clap of drill.

"Heya, Pil." Kesta smiled, and settled in beside Nallo. "They want you to report on the incident you observed on the river."

"Now?"

"Now." Her smile collapsed into a brooding frown as Pil strode off toward the commander's garden. She looked at Nallo. "So here we stand, surrounded by countless enemies, plagued by self-important merchants, and hoping we can fly in enough food to keep us going while we stick it out here more for the show of the thing than for any purpose. Does Clan Hall even serve a purpose? Do the reeve halls want to work together to battle this army, or are they only going to look after themselves?"

"If they do that," said Nallo, "we'll fall one by one."

"You don't need to tell me that. When the commander and senior reeves were murdered on Traitors' Night, I felt like the reeve halls were murdered, too. She did her best for all these years to be a fair and effective commander. Yet who now listens to Clan Hall? Why should they? We're as barren as a woman without a basket, as impotent as a man with no plow."

"There has to be something we can do!" But in swiping strands of hair off her sweaty forehead, Nallo measured the fragility of her words, how they might penetrate the air with seeming force only to dissipate as if they had never been uttered. "Maybe Marshal Joss can do something."

Kesta mopped her own brow as in imitation of Nallo. "So here we all wait to see what *Joss* will say and what *Joss* will do! Eiya! I don't know whether to laugh or to cry."

*   *   *

"WE'VE BEEN FORTUNATE so far with the provisions from Nessumara," Odash was saying as Joss picked up his cup of rice wine and, with a grimace, set it down without drinking. "But it can't go on forever. We'll need another source of rice and nai. We've flown off forty-eight refugees, mostly children, but that still leaves us with one hundred and fifty-seven in the reeve hall, ninety-eight firefighters, militiamen, and ordinands, thirty-eight clerks of Sapanasu, and four hundred and sixty-three refugees from Toskala of whom two hundred and three have stated they are able and willing to join the defense of the rock."

Joss turned the cup around. "I'm not sure reprovisioning is our biggest problem. We can continue to delegate less experienced reeves to fly supply and take off the remaining refugees. As long as we are careful to ration the food strictly and control what numbers we allow to remain up here, we can hold the rock. The cisterns and the deep well will supply water indefinitely."

"What do you think is our biggest problem?" Peddonon's earnest expression reflected all their worries.

"The top leadership and all their years of experience were wiped out ten days ago. Not to mention Volias dying like that. He may have been a prick, but he knew what he was doing." He downed the rice wine in one gulp, feeling the burn, then wiped his mouth. "That's one thing. The other is that the army took Toskala through treachery. We don't know who we can trust. Finally, setting aside the matter of what the enemy intends to do next, these demons who call themselves Guardians can fly onto this rock and kill any of us."

"Do you think they're demons?" Odash asked.

"Captain Anji does. He's the outlander captain who saved Olossi. But I'm not sure he means the same thing by the word as we do. For myself, I don't know what to think."

"It was swords killed all the men and women in the council hall on Traitors' Night," said Odash.

"You're sure? In the tales it's said Guardians can kill with a word and a look alone."

"The only survivor of the massacre was one of the traitors. She said the cloaks promised order and wealth to anyone who aided them. Afterward, the cloaks turned on the traitors who had done the dirty work of actually murdering the council, and killed them—with a look and a word, like in the tales."

"Used and discarded! So the question is, why didn't the cloaks kill the council themselves? Can I interview this survivor?"

As Odash hesitated, all the others drained their cups. "She threw herself off the promontory."

"Eihi! Just like in the tale. What did she tell you?"

"Nothing but how if she'd known otherwise she wouldn't have done it, useless apologies, if you take my meaning. All I know is that she's from the Green Sun clan, and they all cleared out before the attack. If we can get more information from the city about what other clans cleared out, we might know who betrayed us."

"We'll send that message as a warning to Nessumara," said Joss as folk nodded.

"Why, just so!" cried Odash as the others looked at Joss and then at their empty cups. "That's why we need a new commander."

"Commander of Clan Hall? Over all the reeve halls? Are you asking *me*?"

Odash bent a baleful glare on Peddonon. "Surely Peddo mentioned—"

"I thought he was *joking*!"

"We didn't know who else to turn to," added Odash.

"I'm the only one who answered the call?" He rested his forehead on fists, his head so heavy he thought he might never again raise it. "Let me sleep on it. I'm cursed tired from the journey and everything we've had to deal with down south."

"Allies from Toskala are sending up a messenger tonight."

"All the more reason to sleep now."

Peddonon hung back after the others had gone. "I wasn't joking. We need you, Joss."

"Let me sleep first!"

Peddonon grinned. "Can't keep your looks without enough rest, my friend. Wise of you."

"I wouldn't want to end up looking like you, true enough. Say, how are the two recruits doing? The young Qin reeve gave an excellent account of the encounter on the river."

Yet he wondered: Had Zubaidit been on that barge Pil had seen on the river? Was she still alive?

"He's exceptional, it's true." Peddonon scratched his chin. "What's his story? Can we trust him?"

"Eh?" Joss slapped a hand down on the table so hard Peddonon startled. "Has he caused trouble?"

"Not at all!"

"Neh, I meant nothing bad by it. I just wondered because Captain Anji specifically asked me to move him north to get him away from the other Qin soldiers. I'm not sure if it's considered ill luck that he was chosen by an eagle . . . or a disgrace . . . or if Anji means him to serve as a spy in our midst—"

"Think you so?"

"Does he behave suspiciously?"

Peddonon grinned in the way Joss had come to associate with his admiration of certain firefighters. "No. He's cursed good with his weapons and his eagle, and he's very shy. That Nallo is like his older sister, always ready to tear your head off if you even look sidewise in the wrong way at him."

"Is that how it is? What way have you been looking at him?"

Peddonon sat down again. "He's fashioned like me, not like you, I'm sure of it."

"You're usually right."

"In this matter, I'm always right. But—"

"I knew there was a but." Joss stifled a yawn. "No luck there, I take it."

"Maybe I'm feeling cheated out of a bit of flirting, but I think it's more than that. A young person is shy about these things. That's to be expected. That's what Ushara's temples are for. But he's of age, plenty old enough."

"The Qin aren't like us, that's true. Captain Anji has forbidden any Devouring

temple to be built out at his settlement in the Barrens west of the Olo'o Sea. Maybe
it's just inexperience, as you say."

"Sheh! Maybe. Yet I wonder if there's more to it. It's almost as if he's ashamed of
looking at a man, and he sure as the hells never looks at women in that way."

This time when the yawn rose, Joss could not hold it in. He raised both hands in
apology. "I don't know. Keep an eye on him. Report anything suspicious. Otherwise,
we have to assume he's just what he is, a young outlander suddenly harnessed to an
eagle and torn from the company of his familiar comrades. Fortunate for him he has
Nallo, eh?"

Peddonon laughed. "She scares me!"

"That Tumna chose true, neh? Listen, post a steward to wake me when we get the
signal."

Peddonon slid the door closed behind him. With some trepidation, Joss ventured
into the sleeping chamber behind a screen of doors. He'd known the commander of
Clan Hall for many years; they'd been lovers for a short time, not that she'd gone any
easier on him for it afterward. Exploring the sparsely furnished room now, he wasn't
sure if Odash and the hall steward had already cleaned out her belongings or if she
simply had never accumulated anything. The pallet was rolled up along one wall.
The shelf held two neatly folded jackets of the kind that could be wrapped around
any size body and a pair of loose trousers. An alcove in which an ornament appropriate to the season might be displayed sat empty. A pitcher had been recently filled
with water and placed beside a bronze basin. He poured water, then washed his face
and hands. Afterward, he unrolled the pallet and lay down on top of the coverlet in
his clothes.

Yet he could not relax. Zubaidit's scorching gaze and shapely form kept intrud-
ing. Pil had seen Tohon. Tohon had ridden out with Zubaidit. The last time he'd
seen her, she had slapped him. Aui! Why should that memory arouse him so?

He fell from uneasy waking into unsteady sleep, sinking into an old dream whose
contours had become an achingly familiar landscape: A woman wearing a bone-
white cloak walks away into a veil of mist, and he cannot help but run after her although he knows he will never catch her.

Twenty years Marit had been dead, and yet she still walked and spoke in his
dreams. She called herself a Guardian now, although he could not understand why
his dreaming mind, or the gods, made her do so. Yet strangely, her warnings to him
in dreamtime always bore fruit.

"Marit!" he called after her fading form. "What should I do?"

"Joss."

He startled awake to find Peddonon jostling his shoulder, a lamp shining behind
his broad body. "Heya, Joss. You're mumbling in your sleep. Signal's come."

Reeves learned the knack of waking to alertness. Joss rolled up to his feet as Peddonon stepped back, and they hurried outside, slipped on sandals, and followed the
steward and his lamp through the darkness. Clan Hall had been built along pretty
much the entire northern rim of the rock, with various launching points over the
drop from bare scaffoldings that also served as secondary watchtowers. Where
clouds parted, a half-moon appeared low in the west. They hurried along the wall
walk. Fires glimmered where the enemy had set up guard stations along the Istri

Walk. They descended a ladder into a pit hewn out of the rock, musty with damp and mold. A gate was set ajar.

The steward halted. "I can't go out on the ledge with the lamp. Be careful."

Joss and Peddonon paced along a stone-walled corridor, the echo of the river's voice murmuring around them. They emerged cautiously onto a ledge with the wind tearing along the cliff face to their left, upriver. Downstream and curving away to the right, the prow rose to its peak. A pair of burning lamps marked the humble shelter protecting the stele for which the promontory was named. Four reeves lowered a big basket over the edge and eased out the ropes.

The ledge was a sheer drop to the water many hundred baton-lengths below, where a sliver of rocky shoreline was hidden behind broken boulders. The shoreline was pretty much impossible to reach, since you either had to battle the nasty shoreline current in a boat and cut a treacherous angle in among the rocks, or climb out along the lower face of the cliff.

Of course there were folk so reckless and stupid as to enjoy the challenge; he'd been one back when he was young. One time he'd dared a particularly fabulously defiant lass, a banner clan girl, to meet him there at sunset. That had truly been a memorable night.

"Thinking of that banner clan girl?" Peddonon whispered.

"Aui! How'd you know about that?"

"Everyone knows all about your adventures. They're famous in Clan Hall. They'll make a cycle of stories from them someday, the tale of the Handsome Reeve."

"A comic tale, no doubt."

Peddonon snickered.

The reeves handling the rope tensed. "Got it. Hauling up."

Peddonon grabbed the safety rope and braced himself against a pair of stakes hammered diagonally into the rock face. Joss stayed out of the way, rubbing his chin, enjoying the feel of the bristles. He needed a shave. How in the hells could he sort out the complications that dogged him?

Last year, a huge army had swept down out of the northern wilderness under the command of Lord Radas. The army had overwhelmed cities and villages across Haldia and now Istria, throwing the land into chaos; they'd even sent a second army south to attack the city of Olossi. In the south, Captain Anji's outlander Qin soldiers had, with the aid of the reeves of Argent Hall, defeated that second army. At the behest of Olossi's new council, the captain was training an expanded militia to protect the entire region of Olo'osson. Meanwhile his soldiers were beginning to marry local women under the supervision of his beautiful and extremely clever wife, Mai. Who had ten days ago given birth to a boy child over whom Joss now stood as uncle.

Aui!

The reeves and eagles of Horn Hall had vanished. Folk claimed to see Guardians walking abroad, while others called them demons or cloaks and identified them with the leaders of the marauding army. His own work as marshal at Argent Hall had become complicated by the arrival of numerous unjessed eagles seeking new reeves, so many that they'd had to establish a secondary training hall. Naya Hall had been raised on the western shore of the Olo'o Sea near the settlement founded by Captain Anji on land deeded to him and his wife as part of their payment for aiding

Olossi. Elsewhere in the Hundred, folk burned out of their villages wandered the roads. Children went hungry. Half the people Joss met while on patrol no longer trusted reeves. And now the desperate reeves of Clan Hall, blindsided by the murder of their most experienced reeves, wanted him to sit as commander over all the reeve halls. Yet the other reeve halls were beleaguered and uncooperative. Why should they agree to a new commander, much less Joss? He rubbed his head, wondering if he was going to get a headache.

It was difficult to imagine how his life could become more tangled.

"Here we are," muttered a male voice.

They heaved the basket up over the edge and dragged it back from the brink. A single person sat inside.

"Eh, that was a ride, I'll tell you," she said as she clambered out. "I thought I was going to pitch right over and fall to my death. And I'll tell you—that path out along the rock isn't a path at all! It's not even a goat track. I slipped into the river twice. I'm soaking wet."

Joss sagged against the rock as his pulse hammered in his ears.

"Best we know who you are first." Peddonon stepped out from the wall.

She chuckled, as Joss knew she would. "I'm called Zubaidit. I convinced some brave clan folk within Toskala to get me up here. I've a message from them. But truly, I come from the south, from Olo'osson, at the behest of the Olossi council and their allies. I have news to pass back to Olossi, if you reeves will carry it."

"Do you know about this, Joss?" Peddonon asked.

"Surely not Marshal Joss of Argent Hall?"

"The same," Joss said, surprised at how smoothly his voice came out, not much of a croak at all. "Well met, Zubaidit. What of the other scouts?"

"I'd be happy to give my report. But must I stand here in these wet clothes, with the wind chilling me?" she asked, the curl of her voice such a blatant tease that his ears burned. "Or is there somewhere I can take them off?"

Cursed if every gods-rotted reeve standing there didn't start snickering, trying to hide the sound beneath hands clapped over mouths.

Smothering his own laughter, Peddonon said, "It seems you two know each other. But if you don't mind, can we get off this cursed ledge before one of us falls to his death? I mean, the one who hasn't already taken the plunge."

Snorting and chortling, the other reeves hurried away through the arch and down the corridor, leaving Joss to follow Peddonon and Zubaidit. The glow of the steward's lamp illuminated the assassin as she looked over her shoulder at him.

It wasn't that he'd seen her so cursed many times in his life, since that first day less than a year ago when she had flirted with him and afterward tried to kill him. It was just that he remembered so well every curve, the way her hips tilted as she walked, the lift of her chin. The way you knew she knew how to use her body, trained in Ushara's temple as the most deadly of assassins. Her vest and kilt were soaked, the cloth clinging to her like a second skin. Whew!

She grinned.

He was like a man staggering after a blow to the head.

"You're the messenger?" asked the steward, drawing her attention.

"I am."

"You fell in the river?" Neffi asked with an appreciative grin. "I did that once, climbing the same route."

"Does every local in this city know it?"

"We here in the reeve halls do, obviously. We try to keep quiet about it." He winked past her, at Joss. "Some managed better than others."

The reeves clambering up the ladder were laughing, bolder now inside, where there was no chance they'd be spotted by the enemy. "Trust Joss to know every adventuresome female . . ." one was saying as his voice broke into guffaws.

"Let's get on with this," said Joss curtly. "Neffi, can you get her dry clothes?"

"I was joking about the clothes." The jesting tease molted right out of her tone. Her brows drew down as Neffi, frowning in confusion, lowered the lamp. "Best I deliver my report right here and then you lot lower me back down to my contact so I can return to the city before daybreak."

Peddonon called to the reeves. "Heya, boys. Go get Odash and the other seniors. Then get back here yourselves, or get fresh muscle. Move!"

"We can fly you back to Olossi," said Joss.

She shook her head. "I haven't completed my mission."

He leaned against the wall and crossed his arms over his chest, trying to look nonchalant. "Go on. What of the other scouts?"

"What other scouts?" Peddonon asked.

"Seven scouts walked out of Olo'osson. We were delayed by lendings for a few days and lost our horses to them, but carried on, on foot. One of your reeves spotted us outside Horn and flew down to deliver a message to Shai. Now I don't know if it was him coming down with that cursed eagle, or if we had already been seen anyway, but a cadre of outlaws attacked our encampment on his heels. They killed Edard and captured Shai."

"Edard was the censor."

"That's right. One of Kotaru's Thunderers. Pretty cursed useless, if you ask me, but Tohon and I managed despite his clumsy attempts at leadership. Anyway, our lad Shai was captured and we had to follow that cadre lest they hand him over to one of those cloaks. As it turned out, we weren't the ones who rescued him. The outlander demon the reeve came to warn us about, an ugly pale girl with demon-blue eyes, she killed the whole cursed cadre with her magic and left us with Shai and the children the cadre had taken as slaves."

Peddonon whistled, and the steward shook his head.

"Those children were badly misused." Her expression darkened until she looked as if she'd have been happy to cut the throats of every one of those outlaws. Which, no doubt, she'd have done, given the opportunity. "I'll cut the rest of that tale short. Eridit, the two militiamen, and Tohon went south with the children to Nessumara, which we thought would be safe."

"They were spotted, safe on the river."

She smiled, then lifted her gaze as her smile faded. "As you know, I was given another mission."

"A mission that will almost certainly lead to your death. Why go on?"

"Because I'll die anyway, whether today, or tomorrow, or when I've reached the venerable age of eighty-four, having seen seven rounds of the year cycle. It's necessary to take the risk to achieve the ends. Things are worse than you know. The news I bring from Toskala tonight is that the army is marching south on Nessumara."

"The hells!" exclaimed Peddonon and Neffi in unison.

"They're driving out all the refugees from Toskala. They've ruthlessly cut loose all the camp followers who marched with them from Walshow and sent them away. They intend to take hostages from every clan and family and guild compound in Toskala. Those hostages will serve the army on the march through Istria. The hostages also will stand as surety for the good behavior of the Toskalans. The army will leave a garrison behind, but the threat to the hostages will be what keeps the population in order. I hope to go with the army as a hostage. Once with the army, I'll keep my eyes open, and strike when opportunity arises."

"A dangerous venture," said Peddonon with an admiring whistle.

"What do you think, Marshal?" Her gaze challenged him.

He wasn't about to show how much it bothered him to think of her risking herself like that. "What about the seventh scout? What did you say his name is?"

"Shai?"

"Isn't he the uncle of the captain's wife? He's an outlander, but not Qin."

Her lips quirked. "Those outlanders all look alike to me, Marshal." But she didn't mean it; she was just goading him, because sometimes a person took you that way, that you had to constantly be poking at them to get a reaction. It was not quite, and not only, lust, and it wasn't truly love; sometimes two bodies just fell out that way, impossible to explain why.

They'd had no chance to act.

Maybe they never would.

"It's gotten cursed hot in here," muttered Peddonon.

Neffi said, without anger, "Oh, shut up, Peddo. This is cursed serious, you idiot."

Joss pushed away from the wall as he heard voices. Odash, Kesta, a fawkner, and another senior reeve climbed down the ladder. A flurry of questions filled the dark chamber. Zubaidit restated her news about Toskala. He could not look away from her as she talked in that forceful, silky voice.

"What help do you want from us?" he asked when she was done.

"I was told the commander of Clan Hall is a woman. Where is she?"

Haltingly, Odash relayed the tale of Traitors' Night, and as he related the story of betrayal and the murder of Toskala's council and all the senior reeves, her gaze flicked from Joss's face to each shadowed face of the others listening.

When Odash had finished, Zubaidit looked at Joss. "So. All the witnesses counted six cloaks departing from the rock after the murders. It seems the ghost girl has joined their ranks. Some call them Guardians, and they ride winged horses, as it says in the tale. But I also hear people call them demons. What are they?"

Witnesses had reported that one of the demons seen in Justice Square wore a cloak that gleamed in the night like polished bone; it could not have been Marit. She walked in his dreams, not on earth. Yet the strange words she spoke in his dreams haunted him: *I see with my third eye and I understand with my second heart that they are corrupted, so I dare not approach them. They will destroy me if they find me.*

A person can be destroyed in many ways, not just through death.

His clenched jaw was going to bring on another gods-rotted headache. "How can any of us know what a Guardian is? Or what they want. A cloaked man called Lord Radas commands this army, that I am sure of."

"Lord Radas is the one I mean to kill, but if Clan Hall's commander is dead, then who stands as commander over all the reeve halls now?"

All looked at Joss.

"You?" she demanded.

He sighed.

She made a noise rather like a chuckle and something like a cough of disdain. "Have you any plan other than holding out up here as kind of a stick poking them in the eye?"

"Heya!" objected Kesta furiously. "If we hold this rock, then we give hope to others."

Zubaidit's grin caused Kesta to settle. "It's a brave choice, and the right one. But you'll need a plan."

"What do you suggest?" drawled Joss, annoyed at her way of blowing in like a strong wind and expecting everything to bend before her. "Since you seem so cursed sure of yourself."

Her grin sharpened as with anger before it curved into a frown. "I don't know what's to be done in Toskala, with hostages being taken and none to stop it. If the city folk rebel, their relatives will be killed in retaliation. I don't know what you here on the rock plan to do, and I'll thank you not to tell me in case I'm caught out and forced to stand before one of the cloaks. For you know they can see into our hearts with their third eye."

"That's what it says in the tales," said Joss. "But what does it really mean?"

"It means what it says. They can see into our hearts. You can feel them walk into your mind." She shuddered, the movement so subtle he stepped forward, thinking to reassure her with a touch, but he stopped himself and wiped his brow instead.

"Don't try to face them," she added. "You've no shield. Not even the strongest of you."

Yet Anji had faced one of the cloaked demons and not flinched. Anji's soldiers had suffered the same reaction described by Zubaidit, and Joss had taken the testimony of numerous other witnesses from the day the ghost girl had invaded the Qin compound in Olossi and killed two men there; her demon's gaze had brought even Chief Tuvi to his knees. Why was Anji not affected, if everyone else, even other outlanders, had no protection against the third eye and the second heart?

"Locate Tohon, and fly him back to Olossi," she went on. "He has valuable information for Captain Anji. He's surveyed the land and the army. His report is crucial. Get Eridit, Ladon, Veras, and the young ones out if you can, too, lest they betray my purpose if they are captured when the army takes Nessumara."

"You think the army will defeat Nessumara?" Joss asked.

"How can they not? We in the Hundred have no militia that can stand against such an organized force."

"They're a formidable enemy, but surely they can be defeated, as their secondary army was at Olossi."

"The soldiers sent to Olossi were the dregs. These are real soldiers. Not so easy to defeat. You've seen how many there are."

"Is there anything else we need to know? Or that you need from us?" Joss asked her.

She shut her eyes, thinking it through. "The demons are looking for outlanders and the gods-touched in particular, taking them into custody. The army shows little respect for the gods, and there's a cursed lot of talk among the soldiers about how the cloaks have defeated death. The soldiers fear the cloaks, but they also want what they believe the cloaks can give them: wealth, life, land, power. Sex." When she opened her eyes, her hot gaze seemed to burn him to ash.

Peddonon said, "Heya, Kesta, get this lot out to ready the basket, will you? Odash, we'll need to assign someone to go after these scouts that went to Nessumara. Warn the other halls about this business with the gods-touched and outlanders. And the Green Sun clan, the traitors." He grabbed the lamp out of the steward's hand. "You go, too, Neffi. You're getting cursed old. You need your sleep, neh? I'll keep the light until she's down safely."

"Eh, yes, Peddo. Right away."

They went, Kesta down the corridor with the other four reeves while Odash and Neffi climbed the ladder.

"I've got to take a piss," added Peddonon, setting the lamp on the floor. "Be right back." He scrambled up the ladder.

Joss hadn't known that stone breathed, but he swore he could hear its exhalations in the silence that followed, or maybe it was his own breathing gotten cursed irregular as he became exceedingly aware of how very alone they were, caught within the glow of light and with folk busying themselves nearby but out of sight.

"Are these soldiers really our enemy, or only the worst reflection of our own selves?" she asked in a low voice. "We made them. We have to unmake them, not just defeat or kill them."

"What do you mean?"

She shrugged, looking angry. "It seems to me that when an army can recruit so many discontented men and convince so many of them to act in ways they would once have considered criminal, then it is only building with bricks already formed and baked by others. Why do so many men march with the army? Spit on the gods? Steal what they could earn by their own labor? Rape when they can walk into Ushara's temples and worship? Why didn't they just stay home in their villages and towns, marry, tithe, and sire children? The Hundred has let itself rot from within. Now the contagion of discontent and anger is spread by those greedy enough to encourage the worst in those too weak to resist."

"Harsh words," he said.

"True words. We must all take responsibility for the troubles that engulf us."

He did not know what to say because every word seemed meaningless compared with her presence as she stood there with wet cloth stuck to her skin and her body balanced with deadly grace. Her glare forced him a step back, and he bumped against unyielding stone. He was trembling with the effort of staying where he was, as his pulse throbbed and his breath caught in his throat.

She shook her head, no smile, no frown. "A woman can look a long time before she finds a man who can really take his time."

"A woman can look a long time if she never pauses long enough to try this man."

She laughed.

"Aui!" He pushed away from the wall.

She met him, and for a glorious moment he held her as they kissed, and kissed. And kissed.

Just when he thought they might have to do something very reckless despite knowing how close all those other reeves were in the covering darkness, a discreet cough interrupted them.

She broke away. Riven of contact, he swayed, and as Peddonon caught his arm to steady him, she vanished down the corridor toward the ledge.

"You've got it bad, my friend," murmured Peddonon.

Joss brought a palm to his face. "Am I crazy?"

Peddonon snorted.

"She's leaving!" He pulled out of Peddonon's grasp and stumbled after her.

"Don't go over the edge, Joss."

Too late. She was sworn to the goddess, a trained assassin, fixed on her mission. She'd already been lowered over the cliff, the reeves letting out the rope hand over hand. He stayed out there in the night and the wind until they received the three tugs that indicated she'd gotten down safely. Until they hauled up the empty basket and stowed it under the overhang where it couldn't be spotted in daylight by an enemy patrolling the far shore. Until they'd all gone away, leaving Peddonon and Kesta waiting for him in a patient silence that hurt more than the hollow feeling in his gut.

The cooling breeze off the water reminded him that the dry season lay ahead. He rubbed his arms, but the ache did not go away.

"Heya," said Kesta softly. "Come on, Joss. Let's go have a drink, eh? We've missed you these past months. It's not the same without you here at Clan Hall."

"I might never see her again."

Peddonon whistled under his breath. Kesta sighed. The river rushed toward the distant sea, just as the army would, marching south through fertile and heavily populated Istria toward Nessumara, said in the tales to be the second-oldest inhabited place in the Hundred and certainly its largest city now. He must do what was required of him, just as she would.

"The first thing we must do," he said, "is warn Nessumara's council and Copper Hall to seek traitors in their midst. And get Tohon and his group out of there."

Only then, as he turned to go with his companions, did he realize she had never said what had happened to the outlander, Shai.

7

"YOU'RE NOT THE boy I remember, Shai."

Hari lounged on a silk-covered couch, the kind of furniture found in the houses of the rich in Kartu Town. The florid couch looked out of place inside a campaign tent otherwise furnished with only two rugs, a folding table holding a pair of cups and a ceramic bottle with an unbroken seal, and a single lit lamp. Two objects rested on the table: the Mei clan wolf ring and wolf belt buckle Hari had been wearing the day he'd been marched out of Kartu Town as a prisoner of their Qin overlords.

Shai pointed to them. "I went through terrible things to get that ring and buckle back. Will you put on your ring?"

"No. I'm no longer a son of the Mei clan."

Shai displayed the wolf ring he wore as a child of the Mei clan, although his ring wasn't anything like as fine a quality as the one that had been given to Hari by Grandmother when Hari had reached manhood. After all, Hari was the favored third son, while Shai was merely the excess seventh. "Who are you, if not a son of the Mei clan? Father Mei sent me to bring your bones back to the clan for proper burial."

As a boy, Hari had perfected the ability to raise a single eyebrow; he could mock you while looking so exceedingly clever that you found yourself smiling in sympathy, wanting him to approve of you. "Here I am."

Today, Shai wasn't smiling. "You're dead."

"Harsh words, little brother. Yet you would know, you who can see ghosts."

Shai flushed. "Have you forgotten that in Kartu Town, they burn people who see ghosts?"

"I never told anyone you could see ghosts. I would never have betrayed you."

"Yet here I am, your prisoner." He walked to the tent flap and twitched the entrance curtain aside to stare over the camp, where soldiers worked into the dusk breaking down tents and loading gear into wagons in preparation for a dawn departure. Guards surrounded the tent.

Behind him, Hari sighed. "You're not my prisoner. I'm sheltering you. Don't you trust me? You used to."

Shai let the cloth fall as he turned. "You were the best of my brothers, it's true."

"As if that's saying much!"

"It's why I came all this way to find a dead man. Yet you're no ghost. You live and breathe."

"Maybe it just seems to you that I live and I breathe. Maybe I am a ghost. The soldiers call us cloaks. A few whisper that we're lilu. Some name us as Guardians, the ones who bring justice." His crooked smile made his expression bitter.

"This army brings no justice."

"I never said it did."

"Yet you ride with murderers and rapists and thieves. You command them."

"I am a prisoner of those who command *me*."

Furious, Shai walked over to the couch. "You don't look like a prisoner! You look like a lord, who with a gesture of his hand marks who will live and who will die. You sent a man to be hanged from the pole. How can you do it, knowing what he will suffer?"

Hari shrugged, his expression masked. "I'm not the brother you think you remember."

"You can't have changed that much! You were the bold one, the bright one, the one who always spoke his mind!"

"Maybe you didn't know me that well. You were young. You saw what you wanted to see. Maybe I was the drunk one, the stupid one, the dissatisfied one. Maybe I pushed our Qin overlords too hard not out of a sense of righteous anger, but as a prank. Or on a dare. Or because I was bored. Or wanted to impress my reckless idiot friends."

"I don't believe it!"

"You want to believe I am something I never was. Now listen, little brother. We've got to get you out of here before Night or Lord Radas discover you—"

Shai grabbed one of his brother's wrists and squeezed it; it was shocking to feel he might overpower the older brother who had once been able to sling him over a shoulder, run down to the pond, and toss him into the water howling and laughing. He tightened his grip until Hari winced. "How did you get to the Hundred?"

Hari lifted his chin defiantly but in the end looked away. He addressed words to the sloped end of the couch, the fabric a saturated dark purple similar to the hue of the cloak he wore carelessly flung over his shoulders. "Will you let go?"

Shai let go.

Hari rubbed the wrist. His forehead was beaded with sweat. "I'm done speaking of it. What use is there in me speaking? All my words are tainted, because I'm a demon."

The tone of self-loathing hit Shai hardest. The Hari he knew had never hated himself. "You aren't a demon."

Hari grasped Shai's shoulders. Years ago, Hari had grabbed him so, stared into his eyes, and scolded him: *Stand up for yourself, Shai. Speak up, Shai!*

Best of brothers!

But now he looked leached at the edges, as if sickness had drained his vitality.

"Aren't I? I can't see into your heart to know what you really think of me. What if you scorn me, and I would never know?"

"I would tell you what I think."

"People say so, but they never do." Hari laughed mockingly. "People say what they think you want to hear. But now, their hearts and thoughts are laid bare to me, and I can see what's true. All their pain and greed and rage and selfish lust cuts me, just as it cuts them. I can't rest for thinking of all the horrible things I've seen in people's hearts. And yet I can't look away. I want their secrets and their shame. Then I don't have to think about my own."

"Stop it!"

"Why are you hidden from me, Shai? No one else is, except the other cloaks. And you're not a cloak."

Shai clasped his hands. "I'm just your brother, Hari. We'll go home together. It's what we're meant to do."

Hari broke free and leaped to his feet, pacing to the entrance and back again. "I can't go home! Night will hunt me down, or Lord Radas will. If I don't obey them, they hurt me. And since I can't die, then I just suffer and it hurts so badly. We've got to get you out of here. If they know I have you, they'll force me to betray you. And I'll do it, because I'm a useless selfish coward. I've always been one. What do you think I've been running from all my life?"

Voices from outside startled them both. Shai began to stand, but Hari grabbed his arm and shoved him down on one of the rugs, gesturing for him to lie flat. He rolled Shai up inside the rug. From within the stifling confines, Shai heard Hari plop down on the couch as several people entered.

"Aren't you ready to go yet?" demanded a coarse voice bleeding with raw rage. "You're such a cursed lazy ass, Hari."

"Yordenas, control yourself." The other voice was also male, as sharp as poison. "Harishil, I expected you to be ready to depart. There are slaves who can collect these furnishings."

"I thought I was going back to Walshow with the camp followers to make sure they disperse," said Hari, his voice more like a sullen lad's than a grown man's. "And then afterward set up as commander over the northern region based in High Haldia with Captain Arras as my administrator. That's what you promised me."

"That's what Night promised you," sneered the one called Yordenas. "Because she favors your sorry, rotten hide despite you running the second army into disaster at Olossi."

"Yordenas!"

"My apologies, my lord." The cringing tone sounded real enough, as slimy as scummed water. "I would have done better, had I been given the chance. I was a reeve. Marshal of a reeve hall. I know how to command."

"You are to be given your chance now, Yordenas. As for you, Harishil, may I remind you that promises are not coin, they are contingencies. Our plans have changed. We've pulled most of the forces out of the far north and Haldia in order to quickly subdue Nessumara and the delta region. Surely you understand that under the circumstances, given your complete failure to direct the southern expedition against Olossi, you will have to prove yourself to us before we can possibly allow you a new command."

The other man sniggered.

"Furthermore, there is the matter of the woman wearing Death's cloak, the one called Marit. You may not have betrayed us, precisely, but we can't be sure you are reliable. You may have mixed loyalties. I would be rid of you if it were up to me. Yet Night has insisted you be given a second chance. Therefore, I have a special assignment for you."

"I should have had it," groused the one called Yordenas. "I wanted to go."

"I thought you wanted to command an army," said Hari. "But if you can't make up your mind, you're welcome to take my new assignment, whatever it is."

"Don't be hasty, Harishil," said the poisonous voice.

"What is it you want, Lord Radas?"

"Neh, what is it *you* want? Do you want your staff?"

Felt even through the muffling layers of thick carpet, a shift of tension tightened the air like the taste of a coming storm. Weight pressed on Shai's left hip as one of the men rested his foot heavily there.

"Maybe I do," mumbled Hari. "Maybe I don't care. Maybe I don't want to judge people, as you do."

The poisonous voice grew silkier, killing with a sweeter flavor. "You know Night wishes to interview all the gods-touched, but we're seeking in particular an outlander Bevard captured not far west of here, a young man who was veiled to his sight. He should have reached the army by now."

"He'll talk when I get my hands on him!" Yordenas had a mean edge to his voice that Shai imagined was accompanied by a grin, rather as Shai's awful brother Girish had giggled when he contemplated the nasty things he could do to helpless children.

"Sure he'll talk," drawled Hari, "after one whiff of your foul breath, Yordenas. What's to say the cursed outlander isn't dead already? Or fled? Or that Bevard wasn't so drunk that he mistook his vomit for a man?"

The pressure of the foot eased abruptly. The sounds of a scuffle ended with Yordenas's yelp.

"Harishil, you do not amuse me," said Lord Radas. "That such an outlander exists I do not doubt, nor should you. Now and again a rare individual is gods-touched, able to see ghosts. Such individuals are veiled to the sight of Guardians. Therefore dangerous. Able to commit crimes and lie about it."

The dust in the carpet made Shai's eyes itch, or perhaps it was the memory of ghosts that stung.

"Dangerous to justice," Hari asked, "or merely dangerous because we can't bully them by ripping out their hearts and fears and shames?"

"Your gods-rotted outlander ass is just waiting to get itself whipped, isn't it?" said Yordenas.

"You're one who loves to bully, aren't you, Yordenas?"

"Enough!" The voice of Lord Radas cut deep. The weight of the foot returned, pinching Shai's skin, but he sucked in the pain and did not move. "As it happens, Bevard encountered another such outlander, at Westcott. A man veiled to his sight. Do you suppose all outlanders can see ghosts and are therefore veiled, Harishil?"

"I wouldn't know. I'm not 'all outlanders.'"

"Be respectful, you ass."

"Quiet, Yordenas. Harishil, I want you to track down this outlander captain Bevard encountered at Westcott. We have reason to believe he may be related to, or the same man as, the one who captained Olossi's militia to victory."

"What about Yordenas and Bevard? What will they be doing?"

"Their duties are not yours to inquire after, but as it happens, I am willing to tell you so you can see what rewards you can expect if you succeed. Bevard will accompany the camp followers to Walshow and afterward take temporary command of the northern region and assizes. He'll be scouting Haldia for signs of the two cloaks who ran from us—obviously we can't trust *you* with that task given your relationship with the woman called Marit. Yordenas will take part in the attack on Nessumara, to improve his command skills."

"I'd rather go to Walshow," said Hari.

Yordenas snorted. "I'm surprised they're letting you go off on your own at all. They don't trust you, Hari. Nor should they, you being a cursed outlander and all."

"Then why don't they release me?" retorted Hari in a voice Shai would once have heard as bold and forthright and now recognized as angry with reckless despair.

The pressure of the foot lifted. Shai let out breath, sucked in, and almost choked on a lungful of dust and a stray wisp of straw that caught in his throat.

"I can call a soldier in," said Lord Radas as calmly as if he were suggesting a tray of tea, "and have him stick his sword in your guts. Once. Twice. A third time."

"No. No. No. I'll go, as you command."

"Coward," said Yordenas.

Hari said nothing.

Shai gritted his teeth and swallowed a sneeze.

"Be ready to leave at dawn on your new mission." Lord Radas's footfalls moved toward the entrance. "Bring me the head of this outlander captain who Bevard says is veiled."

"How am I to bring you his head if I have no weapon? Give me my staff, and I might manage it."

"Your weapon is your ability to command others to kill him. You've yet to prove yourself to us. Do so, and I will give you your staff and a chance at a new command. One other thing. I was given a report that you interviewed an outlander today."

"I interviewed more than one," said Hari so easily that Shai's gut relaxed. Maybe Hari wouldn't betray him. "Slaves, craven and weeping. Their hearts revealed nothing more than the misery of being torn from their homeland and forced to endure the lash of cruel masters. I let them go. Their masters were waiting. Just as mine do."

"I wonder if you are telling the truth," said Lord Radas.

It seemed to Shai he could actually feel like the brush of fingers the man probing the tent, seeking what was hidden.

Hari said, "You think it might have been more merciful to have them cleansed and thus released from servitude? I suppose so."

"Don't tempt me," said Lord Radas. The touch of poison eased; vanished. The man had left.

"You'll never manage to kill that outlander captain," said Yordenas. "You're a gods-rotted coward and a stinking outlander. I hate you."

"Do you, truly? I don't care enough about you to hate you. Mosquitoes gripe me more. Run after the one whose boots you lick, eh?"

"You'll regret speaking this way to me."

Hari laughed.

Yordenas's hot presence stamped out of the tent, and then it was cool and quiet and Hari whispered, "Don't move, don't speak. We can hear better than you know."

He apparently went outside, because it was silent for some time. Shai thought maybe he was getting a rash on his forehead where the coarse fibers were pressed against the skin. An outlander captain veiled to the sight of the demons. A man who could, like Shai, see ghosts. Obviously, they meant Hari to hunt down and kill Captain Anji.

With a shove, Shai was tumbled around and over and rolled gasping out of the carpet. Hari tugged him up to his feet, and Shai turned away to sneeze, three times. He wiped streaming eyes with the back of a hand. He had been so close to Lord Radas, and he had not acted. Yet how had he intended to strike?

"When they find out you're veiled, they'll kill you." Hari grasped Shai's arm and pulled him around to face him. Hari's gaze bored deep, but Shai matched him until Hari shook his head in frustration. "We have to get you out of camp before they find you. And they will find you. Someone will betray you. I'll betray you. Hu! How did you even get to the Hundred?"

"Father Mei sent me to bring back your bones."

"You can't have walked all this way yourself!" His bitter laugh cracked. "Those Qin soldiers I saw on the road with you months ago. They pinned me with arrows. The bastards! Did the Qin make you a soldier and slave, as they did me?"

Thinking of Mai, Shai shook his head. "I am not soldier or slave. How can I kill Lord Radas?"

Hari flung himself away, walking again to the entrance and peering out as if he was sure Shai's words had carried outside the tent wall. Then he strode back. "You can't."

"Lord Radas threatened to have you killed."

"No, only punished. He has a soldier stab me until I'm dead, but since I can't die, I live through the agony of dying and then I heal through pain worse than that of dying. Don't you remember how your Qin soldiers shot me full of arrows? How do you think I survived that?"

"Yet here you stand. A ghost, who yet lives." He touched Hari's arm, but his brother jerked away. "Didn't you ask him to release you?"

"Only a cloak can destroy a cloak. Five Guardians can judge one. You who are not prisoners of the cloak cannot kill us." Tears shone in his eyes. "Do not pity me."

"I don't pity you! You pity yourself!"

Hari raised a hand to strike, then flung himself away, pressing that hand to the clasp that hooked his cloak around his throat.

"You don't have to be their prisoner! Just take it off!" Shai dogged Hari's steps, reaching for the cloak's elaborate clasp, but Hari shoved him so hard he fell onto the plush upholstery of the couch.

"It will burn you, kill you, if you touch it. You think I haven't seen Yordenas torture people? He forces them to touch his clasp until their flesh burns away to the bone!"

"Then release yourself!"

Hari's smile lit him with a flash of his old charm, but the reckless glint was twisted and bitter. "Once started down this path, no one is ever content, little brother. Do you know why I'm their prisoner? I hate what I am, and yet I embrace it, because I fear the shadows that lie beyond the gate. Now that I am dead, I fear death more than anything. Just as she does."

"She?"

"The cloak of Night. The one who woke me and taught me to know what I am. She fears death, too. We all fear death, who have suffered it. That's why we are what we are and why we do what we do."

This could not be Harishil, best of brothers. This was his shell, inhabited by a demon.

The cloak ran a hand over his head, face creased, eyes tight, other hand in a fist. "You must have come to the Hundred with the Qin. What do you know about an outlander captain? One who might be veiled?"

Shai looked the demon in the eye. His heart sang with grief, even as his mouth opened and his voice emerged with astonishing evenness, the lie as easy as breathing. "Nothing. If you'll give me safe passage out of camp, I'll accept it with thanks."

*   *   *

"CAPTAIN ARRAS."

Lord Twilight stood with his back to the captain. A single lamp burned, the flame's wavering light rippling across the fabric of his cloak.

"What brings you to Toskala, Captain? I'll admit, I enjoyed our time together in High Haldia. I had been looking forward to a quiet retirement up there in the north with you as my congenial colleague."

"My lord." If it were possible to feel comfortable around a cloak, then Arras felt comfortable with this man, but he knew better than to believe they could ever be comrades. "Two weeks ago I received orders that a new administrator would be taking over the occupation of High Haldia. I've been reassigned with my three companies to serve at the whim of the governor of Toskala."

"Are you glad to come to Toskala?" The cloak kept his back to Arras.

"Presiding over an occupation does not suit my temperament. I'm trained to fight, not hang people up from poles just for the pleasure of watching them die."

"Some in this army gain too much pleasure out of the suffering of the vanquished."

"It's better to kill rebels, criminals, and traitors cleanly and at once, and move on with the real work."

"What if I were to use my influence to make sure you got reassigned in support of the army marching south on Nessumara? Do you trust me, Captain?"

They were alone, no one in earshot as long as they spoke quietly. The tent's furnishings had been hauled away; all that was left were a pair of rolled-up rugs.

"Yes, my lord. I trust you."

"As much as you trust any of us, eh?" said the cloak with a laugh that made Arras grin.

"I return what is given. You trust me enough not to demand my compliance through eating out my heart. It's a courtesy I appreciate."

A smile creased the cloak's profile. "Then we understand each other. I am required to depart immediately, leaving unfinished business here in camp."

"The outlander?"

"You can see the problem this presents me. I'm asking you to disobey orders. You could betray me to Lord Radas and I wouldn't fault you for it. Or you can help me. If we both survive this war, I'll have reason to be grateful to you. Although I can't promise my gratitude is worth much."

"Are you asking me to betray Lord Commander Radas, my lord?"

"No. I just need to get a single individual to safety in Nessumara without him getting caught and turned over to Night. Without anyone except you and me knowing or suspecting what's being done. A tactical challenge, if you will." Still, the cloak did not turn to use his third eye and second heart to expose Arras's intentions. "Will you help me, Captain?"

Trust can never be offered lightly, nor lightly refused. In the army, Arras was just one ambitious captain from the uplands of Teriayne, with no means for advancement except distinguishing himself and his companies in battle. He'd been left behind in High Haldia despite fighting well and taking the brunt of the initial attack, while better-connected men who'd done less had received promotions and moved on.

"Get me assigned to the attack against Nessumara, my lord. If you do, I can help you."

*   *   *

JOSS LEFT CLAN Hall at dawn, alone, guiding Scar downstream toward Nessumara. Eagles he had ordered out on patrol sweeps soared in the distance. It was easy from this height to perceive the land as if it were at peace, until you recognized how many villages bore the scars of battle: burned houses, freshly built scaffolding on which to lay the dead, empty paths and roads. A crude encampment lay hidden within woodland, but he dared not land to see who they were. It seemed almost cruel to grab bites of rice cake and swigs of cordial from the pouch of provisions lashed to his harness while wondering if those refugees were starving.

He caught up with the enemy midmorning. Three eagles floated above, observing. He knew the reeves by their eagles: Peddonon, Vekess, and Disi. The soldiers marched in orderly ranks, cohorts spaced at intervals. Clearly they did not expect to be attacked. The vanguard had taken control of the town at Skerru, where the River Istri split. The deep channel cut west along an ancient ridgeline. Copper Hall reeves flew patrol over Istria, and by Scar's attention, others soared too far away for him to see but not so for the raptor with its exceptional vision. Downstream, many small channels braided into a vast delta.

Two causeways spanned the wetlands, linking the city to the mainland. The northern causeway, a raised roadway from Skerru that pushed into the delta through a swamp forest, was already blocked by barriers. An eagle preened in the sun on a massive log off to one side. The eastern causeway linking the trading town of Saltow to the docks and markets of Nessumara was packed with refugees fleeing *into* the delta. A pair of reeves had set down in the midst of the traffic where a knot of confusion had brought movement to a halt. Boats bobbed within the marshy hinterlands; others were being rowed or poled along the narrow channels of the inner delta where the flow of water was regulated by a complicated scheme of locks, dikes, canals, and holding pools.

With the sun at zenith, he and Scar dropped over Nessumara, a city sprawled across a hundred greater and smaller islands. Copper Hall's four watchtowers beckoned. He flagged—*and received no answer.*

The hells! No one was manning the watchtowers. Where was everyone?

Scar skimmed low south to the swirling confluence of land and sea while Joss scanned the landscape. The hive of activity might be better described as chaos. The entire place was coming apart.

There were a hells lot of boats and ships out in the bay; the harbor of Ankeno was crowded with vessels. Any one who could afford passage was running before the tide. Where in the hells did they all mean to go? And how keep themselves once they were there? The countryside crawled with folk in motion. More reeves down there betrayed even more trouble and confusion. Was it possible for reeves to police this kind of upheaval, much less maintain order at their own hall?

Scar found an updraft and they spiraled up, then began a long descent toward what was now the main compound of Copper Hall, where the marshal had his cote. The eagle seemed eager, recalling his home perch, the place he had jessed Joss. The shores of the Haya coast unfolded below. Surf rolled against sand beaches, or sprayed where rockier ground met the water. The wide North Shore Road had a cursed lot of traffic on it, folk trudging east toward the Haya Gap and Zosteria. Reeves were out in force.

Late in the afternoon he spotted the familiar watchtowers. It was here Joss had trained; here he had met Marit; here he had flung his reckless defiance into the face of Marshal Masar one too many times until the marshal had forced him to transfer to Clan Hall just to be rid of him. Looking back, Joss supposed he would have done the same in Masar's place. What a gods-rotted rebel he'd been! There'd been no purpose to his troublemaking beyond the frustration of a young man who had had something he craved torn from him. He was older now. It was easy to see the pattern.

He flagged the tower and received permission to come in.

Scar landed with feathers fanned out and talons forward, almost vertical. He grasped a perch, and Joss, swinging gently, unhooked and dropped. The raptor chirped eagerly as he inspected his surroundings. He knew where he was, of course. He'd called Copper Hall home for longer than Joss had been alive.

A murmur of activity came from the main compound, yet in the empty quiet of the visitors' ground, you might think the place deserted. Joss inspected Scar, waiting for fawkners, but spotted only a lad skulking in the entrance to a loft.

"Where are the fawkners?" Joss called.

The lad shrugged.

"Can you fetch someone for me?"

The lad scratched his short hair, then ran for the gate. Joss swore under his breath as he attended to Scar's needs. The visitors' lofts were empty, so Scar lumbered into the closest loft and found an open perch, settling in to preen. The afternoon light falling through the open doors shone gold onto Scar's glorious feathers.

Joss jessed him and went out. In the main compound, smoke was rising from the kitchens, two women squabbled, wagons piled with bags of rice rumbled up to one of the storehouses. The forge boiled with heat and noise, hammers ringing.

No one took notice of Joss. He walked down the alleyway between storehouses and fawkners' barracks that led to the marshal's garden. Long ago, during Joss's days as a novice, Marshal Alard had lovingly tended beds of bright flowers just for their beauty, but now every plant here had its use: culinary herbs, lavender, woundwort, wiry desert tea, peony, ginseng with its tapered leaves.

The door into the marshal's cote stood open. Joss climbed the steps into the shade of the porch. In the marshal's audience room, an elderly man sat behind a low writing desk, forehead propped on a hand, back bent. An old map, frayed and ripped at the edges, lay unrolled, its corners held down by cups. Smears of ink blotted the sheet; one spot, near the center, had been rubbed so many times it was worn through.

"It doesn't matter what emergency you bring word of," said the marshal to the desk. "I've got no more reeves to send out."

"I'm not here—"

The man looked up. "*Joss?* The hells!"

"Masar? I thought you retired—there was a new marshal—"

The old reeve's cheeks were hollow with age and exhaustion. "There was. Why are you here? Aren't you marshal of Argent Hall?"

No niceties. No wine. Masar gestured with the *quick-hurry-up* known to all.

"Clan Hall's council has asked me to step in as commander. As a temporary—"

"No need to ask my permission, if that's why you came. I don't see how Clan Hall's administrative juggling affects us here."

Joss coughed into a hand. "Well, as commander of the reeve halls—"

Masar's curt laugh silenced him. "All right, then, Commander. We're over-whelmed. Have you brought supplies? Come with brilliant ideas on how to beat back this cursed army?"

"I have to order things at Argent Hall, get a sense of what is going on at the different halls, find out what happened to Horn Hall—"

"Yes, and after you've managed all that, *then* you can come back and offer me and mine aid. Is that what you're saying? Fine. I heard you. Good-bye." He looked past Joss. A rare smile graced his stern face. "Jenna! There you are."

A pretty young woman wrapped in a bright orange taloos climbed the steps carrying a covered dish. Behind her trotted a lad not much younger but clearly her sibling. As she paused to kick off her sandals, she looked at Joss with a pretty smile.

"None of that!" scolded Masar. "He's too old for you."

"I never said a word!" protested Joss, burned by Masar's scorn. She was a pretty enough lass, but so cursed young.

Masar's frown lowered like a threat. "These are my grandchildren, Jenna and Kedri."

"Reeve Joss!" The lad's cheeks flushed as he stared. "I've heard so many stories—"

"Enough!" snapped Masar. The lad ducked his head as his sister flicked fingers on his arm to silence him. "Clan Hall can call you their commander if they will—and I suppose you'll do no worse than anyone else given the chaos—but it's cursed meaningless to us. My own daughter is missing and her husband dead, these two of their five children fled to me. And they aren't the only refugees sheltering here."

"I'm cursed sorry, Masar," Joss said, raising his hands to show he'd no weapon and no excuse. "That's a terrible thing for a parent to suffer. I really did come seeking what information you have to tell me. To let you know the situation at Clan Hall. And to pass on vital information about the army and certain clans in Nessumara who may be plotting to betray the city."

Masar nodded at his grandchildren, and Jenna hurried off, dragging her hero-struck brother behind with a parting smile for Joss. "My apologies. I'm no worse off than many, and more fortunate than some. Sit down. Let's talk as reeves do. What are we up against?"

AND HEAR JOSS did, so much so that at dawn he felt he might never sleep if he tried to right all the wrongs afflicting the Hundred. The list was endless, and it only began with the recent death of the marshal who had replaced Masar when he had retired from active duty. Joss flew north toward the southernmost spur of the Liya Hills, where twenty years ago he'd often rendezvoused with Marit. How distant those halcyon times seemed now! The Haya Gap could be seen to the north; south lay the vast tangled forest known as the Wild, a refuge of the mysterious wildings. The eagle followed the north-leading ridge of the hills. At last, Joss caught sight of the ragged notch in the hills that marked the Liya Pass.

He tugged on the jesses without conscious thought, and soon enough Scar pulled in to land on the stony height of Candle Rock. The towering rock was deserted; without wings, no man or woman could reach this spot. He scouted the environs, the fire pit, the hollow where eagles roosted, an overhang where the remnants of a wood stack moldered beside an even older axe held together by hope and twine. The decaying wood had been tossed into a jumble while the wood still solid enough for a good burn had been stacked in one place. Some reeve had been up here in the last few months. And why not? It was an unassailable position, overlooking the road below.

He found a log, not yet split and half shot through with rot, and dragged it over to Scar. The eagle was delighted, pouncing on the log and squeezing it with his talons. Joss set to work on the fire pit, restacking the rocks where they had shifted and come loose. He layered a few to create a tiny crevice, where stones painted to mark the phrases of the moon could be left for the next reeve: Meet here when the moon is full. By the time he was done Scar had reduced the log to splinters and settled in, extending his wings to sunbathe.

Joss settled as well. The wind streamed over the crags and the afternoon sun beat down on his back. Twenty years ago, reeves had patrolled these lands regularly. Over the years, mey by mey, village by village, they had retreated. Given up ground as a new commander had claimed their territory.

The abandoned patrol stations needed to be put back into use as observation posts and havens. It was the kind of thing the commander of the reeve halls could order done.

He lifted his gaze east to the ridge held by the hierarchs to be sacred to the Lady of Beasts. The distinctive spire called Ammadit's Tit loomed, but he had no desire today to scout the Guardian's altar where he and Marit had made their fateful discovery over twenty years ago. That's where it had all started to go so terribly wrong.

It was time to head south toward Argent Hall. He whistled Scar down and hooked in. Wind buffeted them as Scar plunged into a powerful updraft. They climbed until the air he sucked into his lungs seemed as thin as his memories of the past, falling away below. His eyes watered, but surely that was the wind.

8

ROLLED UP IN a carpet Shai endured, sucking at such air as he could pull in. The carpet was carried for some ways and then deposited, he guessed, in a wagon. In Kartu Town he'd heard a story about the Qin: rather than shed the blood of Qin nobles deemed rebellious by the Qin var, the offending personages were rolled up so tightly in carpets that they suffocated. He calmed himself by focusing on the scrape of wheels.

How long they traveled he did not know. He dozed, and startled awake when they halted. The carpet, and other goods, changed hands as coin clinked. The carpet was lodged in another vehicle with Shai wedged uncomfortably as a scream crawled up his throat. His mouth and tongue were so dry he could not even moisten his chapped lips. But he could not die now. He must survive and escape to warn Captain Anji before Hari found him. The rumbling journey went on and on as Shai's thoughts churned. His favorite brother Hari would never kill Anji. But the creature Hari had become, would.

They stopped. A hard drop to the ground winded him. A shove unrolled the carpet. He lay gasping on his back as a shod foot prodded him.

"The hells! This one's an outlander."

He rolled over, fixed trembling arms under his body, and shoved up to hands and knees, heaving as the dust coating his mouth gagged him. A sharp point pressed into his back.

"Here, now, my friend. Give us no trouble, and we'll give you none."

"Heya, Laukas! What've you got there?"

"A cursed outlander!"

Shai raised his head. Two other carpets, unrolled, had sheltered two women, just now twisting to rise as about ten armed men and women gathered around, all as ragged as bandits and twice as surly. The older of the newcomers made a gesture with her right hand, middle fingers bent in, thumb and little finger raised. Seeing it, folk relaxed.

Cautiously, Shai sat on his heels, aware of a bristling circle of spears, staves, and sharpened sticks surrounding him. His neck hurt, his head ached, but he was breathing fresh air in a clearing surrounded by trees.

"I need to get to the nearest reeve hall," he croaked. "Can you help me?"

They laughed.

"That's right," said the stocky young man called Laukas. "You say you want to reach Copper Hall, but you'll drop out of sight the moment our backs are turned and go running back to give your master a full accounting of our numbers and disposition."

"I need to get to a reeve hall. I am not—" In truth he *was* a spy, and if he got back to Olossi he would certainly give Captain Anji an accounting of the numbers and disposition of even such a ragtag group. "I am not from the army. I am fleeing the army. They want to kill me because I am an outlander."

A shout of joy cut through his stumbling words and Laukas's skeptical expression. A man pushed through the circle of spears to embrace the older of the women. When they parted, she introduced the other refugee, a young woman wearing the blue cloak of an envoy of Ilu.

"The Ilu priests asked us to get Navita out of the city. She's gods-touched, and all the gods-touched and outlanders are being hauled in for interrogation." She indicated Shai. "Although I've never seen that one before. Maybe a kind master wanted to spare his life, eh? He's not bad-looking."

"Eiya! You've not changed," retorted her exasperated brother. "Now he's seen us, we can't leave him. Place a guard on him at all times, Laukas. Let's move."

They rolled up the carpets and slung them into the back of carts, which were hitched to mules. Laukas and another man helped him up, not kindly but not roughly.

"Who are you?" Shai asked.

"Who do you think we are?" asked Laukas with a barked laugh. "We're the cursed resistance, aren't we? We're all that stands between Haldia and that cursed army."

"It's enough to make a strong man weep," remarked his companion.

"That explains why you're not crying."

"Sheh! Who was it won our last arm-wrestling contest?"

"Only because you had Geda shoving down on your hand, eh? Two against one, and her with her tits in my face, distracting me."

"Piss-head, you'll face me again, or I'll have the whole camp calling you an ass-licking coward."

"Depends on whose ass. Geda's been giving me the look—" With a laugh, Laukas dodged a swipe of the other man's spear.

"And when I tell Geda what you've been saying, she'll chop off your eggs with that axe of hers and cook them for her supper."

"Now, *that* I would believe."

They followed the carts along a rutted track into tangled forest where shadows lay heavy even with the sun shining overhead. Four men trailed their party, sweeping away such tracks as they could, scattering leaves across the path to make it look as if no one had passed this way recently. After some time, the track by now barely wide enough to accommodate the wagons and increasingly uneven, they halted and with practiced ease unhitched the mules, loaded them with the goods, and concealed the carts beneath undergrowth. On they walked. Laukas and his friend Ketti kept so casual a guard on Shai that he began to wonder if they were hoping he would bolt just so they could have a bit of excitement chasing him down. The leader dropped back to walk beside them.

"Greetings of the day. I'm Tomen."

"I'm called Shai."

"Shayi?"

"Shai."

Laukas shrugged. "These outlanders have cursed strange names."

Ketti murmured the name a couple of times, trying to get the vowels right.

"Who was willing to take the risk of smuggling you out?" Tomen asked. "You'll understand we have to be suspicious of anyone we don't know."

Shai considered his options.

With a tight smile, Tomen went on. "While you're thinking up a likely story, try making it an entertaining one."

They trudged in silence but for the weight of feet and hooves on the trail. It was cool under the leaves; with only a vest and trousers, Shai found himself suppressing a shiver. Mud coated his bare feet. His toes were cold.

"I am a scout," he said finally. "But not for the army. I am spying *on* them. I was pretending to be a slave. Then the call came that all outlanders must be interrogated by the cloaks. So I had to get away."

"Not a very colorful account," observed Tomen.

"No fights, no devouring, no wine," agreed Laukas.

"I've heard my little sister make up better tales," added Ketti.

"Who are you spying for?" Tomen continued. "How did you contact the smugglers? Why did they agree to help you? You can see these are questions we'll need answers for."

"If you're captured, anything I tell you can be taken from you." He coughed the last bit of dust out of his throat. "By the Guardians who command the army."

"I've heard it said the commanders of the army wear cloaks and call themselves Guardians. But Laukas here could wear a cloak and call himself a Guardian."

"Still wouldn't help him get women to sleep with him," added Ketti. "Him with that—problem—he has."

"You wish you had my problem," said Laukas with a laugh, slapping Ketti on the ass. "They're all afraid of me because I have such a masterful tool."

"Call them demons, then," said Shai, over the banter. "They look into your heart and eat your memories."

That made them frown. Tomen strode ahead to talk to his sister and the young envoy. They walked along casually enough, but Ketti looked over his shoulder whenever the men walking as rearguard fell out of sight behind a bend. Some of the group carried regular weapons, spears with iron points, short swords, but the rest made do with hunting bows, scythes, axes, or stout walking staffs with one end sharpened to a point. He might outrun them, Shai thought, but then he'd be lost, weaponless, and without food or shelter. They hadn't killed him yet. He still had a chance to enlist their help.

Through the afternoon they stopped twice to water the mules and drink from leather bottles filled with a sour-sharp juice that made Shai's mouth pucker as Laukas and Ketti laughed.

Late in the day Tomen dropped back with his sister, who had a roving eye that took in Shai's form from toe to head, lingering on his hips and chest in a way that made him blush.

"It could be true," she said. "He could be a scout come to spy on the army. I never saw any outlanders marching with the cursed occupiers. Still, there's a tale in the street that a second army was sent to Olo'osson but got whipped and its remnants sent crawling home. That might be a story people tell to themselves to gather hope where there is none, or it might be true. What do you say, Shayi?"

"Let us say I tell you who I am and where I come from. Let us say you are captured. Then if they take you in front of one of the cloaks, all the things I tell you, the cloaks will come to know. Better I keep silence."

"Can these cloaks eat our hearts?" Tomen asked his sister.

"Folk are terrified of them, that's certain. I never faced one. Let's see what the honored ones say."

They camped that night on the edge of open ground, sleeping among the bushes with guards set over Shai. At dawn, two strangers were led blindfolded into the encampment. Coin changed hands, and the two men led away the mules, the carpets, and certain of the heavier encumbrances, while the remaining baggage was distributed among the group.

"I can take more," Shai said, after they'd burdened him with bolts of cloth lashed together, an awkward bundle whose weight drove down his back.

"Wsst! Look at him, showing off," said Laukas.

Ketti snorted.

"Quiet," said Tomen.

All morning they slunk along the verge of cleared fields, neat orchards, a small lake with shores grown heavy with rushes and several wooden piers built out into the shallows, a cluster of villages ringed by carefully husbanded woodlots. About midday, they crept through the abandoned ruins of an old waterwheel housing half-collapsed over a stream. A spur of woodland had grown into decaying outbuildings that had been left to rot long years ago. Moving away from the stream's splashing chatter, they picked their way through underbrush toward a massive tree of a kind Shai did not recognize. Below branches thick as roof beams, a path had been cleared, hard to see unless you were right on it but well maintained along its twisting length. Now they picked up the pace, stopping twice to take swigs of the juice which was only growing more sour as time passed. After a while they left the path and splashed down a stream until Shai thought his feet would freeze.

"You're tough, I'll give you that," Laukas said when they climbed onto a sliver of trail. "Not one word of complaint."

Birds whistled in the canopy as they followed the trail through branches and dragging vines as likely to slap you in the face as part gracefully at your passing. When twigs snapped or leaves rustled, he could not see what had made the noise. His bundle got caught several times in vines or limbs, forcing him to wait for someone to chop him free. It was as if the forest were clutching at him.

At last he stumbled into a clearing overtopped by trees whose canopies spread like roofs. A fire burned in a brick hearth, two big blackened pots hanging over coals and meat sizzling on a spit. Hammocks swung from the lower branches of trees, while canvas roofs were slung higher up where huge limbs branched and boards had been hammered between to make platforms.

He had expected a larger group, but once he sorted out the faces he already knew from the unfamiliar ones, he counted only thirty-seven fighters. They greeted each other with jostling, hugging, and kissing while he stood in their midst with all that weight on his shoulders, forgotten except for Laukas with an eyebrow cocked toward him. Ketti had his arms full with a tall lass.

She looked over his shoulder at Shai. "What's this? A new mule?"

"Ouch," remarked Laukas to Shai. "You must admit I've been hells more polite to you, eh? That's Geda. Tongue like a dagger."

"What else it's good for you'll never know," she retorted, releasing Ketti and circling Shai with the same hungry look Tomen's sister had used, the one that made color rise to his cheeks. Women in Kartu Town never looked at men like that. "Well built, I must say."

"Heya!" said Ketti. "You're my girl."

"I'm not your girl. I'm just sleeping with you." She dismissed all three men with a shrug and walked over to greet Tomen and his sister.

Laukas helped Shai out of the straps. "Poor Ketti. Oof! That's heavier than I thought."

An elderly woman took charge of the goods with the measuring gaze of an experienced merchant. In the clearing, logs made benches, and folk settled with pleasure to take a meal. Someone with plenty of time on her hands had carved trenchers enough for every two or three to share, using carved spoons to scoop nai porridge and sticks to pluck scraps of meat sliced from the haunch. To Shai's surprise, there was plenty. He ate until he was full, and they begrudged him none of it even as Laukas kept a seat to one side and Ketti to the other. Talk poured like rain; Shai, exhausted, had trouble following it. There fell laughter and songs, and afterward as he nodded in and out of a sitting doze, men pulled out a table and set it on flat ground. The arm-wrestling began, first among the women—Geda won this tournament—and afterward the men took turns in a complicated system he was too tired to sort out.

Laukas pulled on his arm. "Up, Shayi. It's your turn."

"My turn?" He rubbed his face. "But—"

They steered him to the table and sat him cross-legged in the local way. They'd pitted him against a weedy young man who was no struggle, a pop down to the table, which made them roar with laughter and sit down another volunteer. He demolished nine before Ketti sat down with a good-natured smile that tightened at the corners of his eyes to betray a man who did not like to lose. It occurred to Shai that he needed to shake off his wool-headedness. An odd scent tickled his nostrils as if in a stinging wind off the sandy desert; he could not identify what it was. Branches swayed, but he felt no wind.

He fixed hand to hand with Ketti. Geda was bent so far over to watch that her breasts seemed likely to pop out of her tightly laced vest right in his face.

Laukas, standing as referee with a hand resting atop their clasped ones, laughed. "Careful, Shayi. If you win, then you have to sleep with Geda. Enough to suck away a man's strength, eh?"

"I don't have to sleep with anyone," said Shai, thinking of Eridit.

That set them whooping and laughing. Laukas released their hands.

Eihi!

One thing Shai was, was stubborn. Ketti was as strong, but he'd never learned to focus in and endure. To wait for the opening.

At a wavering in Ketti's grip, Shai pushed, and Ketti's arm sank backward. Catching the tipping point, Shai slammed Ketti's hand onto the table top to a chorus of hollering and clapping and jeering.

The noise ceased between one breath and the next.

Ketti released Shai's hands and sat back, swiping sweat off his forehead as he looked nervously to his left. Folk melted back as a creature glided through the gathering and halted by the table. Ketti scrambled up, and the creature settled into the vacant place. The creature set its right elbow on the table, hand up, with the left lying beneath. Laukas backed away.

Naked to the waist except for its leather forearm guards, it was quite obviously female, although its broad shoulders and muscled chest made its small breasts seem insignificant in contrast. He forced his gaze up to the face. Although it had lips, nose, and face molded in a familiar form, it was not human. Its skin had the color of leaves, a downy growth of hair also tinted green, and yet as he cautiously grasped its hands, its palms felt exactly like human palms. Its hair dangled in vine-like ropes, as though its head sprouted a garden rather than hair. Its ears were tufted and set slightly away from the human-shaped head. Its eyes were not ordinary eyes: they were many-faceted. When it blinked, a sheer inner lid flicked down; a second more ordinary eyelid flashed and opened. Its eyes had changed: what stared at him now shone black, like polished jet. As he recoiled, it tightened its grip on his left hand.

None in the assembly spoke. No one moved.

Its smell had a humid savor, like the forest.

Hu! The others did not fear it, although their silence implied respect. He shifted his seat to ground himself. It grinned to display a remarkably human set of teeth.

"He's done for now," whispered Laukas, dropping a hand over their clasped hands and, after a count, releasing.

Shai braced, but was driven down, the press against him. The creature was simply so much stronger that he might have been a child testing its strength against a patient adult, one who didn't want to smash his hand down lest it wound his pride.

He was a fist's-breadth away from defeat.

Its ears flicked.

It released him and rose so quickly that one blink it was braced before him and the next was leaping into the trees as a faintly heard and very low rumble trembled in the air: a horn.

Tomen pushed through the group with a stream of orders: "Laukas, ten on the path. Archers, to the trees. Ketti, pull the elder back to the cave. Geda, have your slings and nets ready."

They moved.

Tomen grabbed Shai's vest, hauling him up. He was strong, maybe not strong enough to defeat Shai arm-wrestling but with enough strength to make his will known. "If you're a spy who has betrayed us, you'll die."

"I have not betrayed you. I'm just trying to get to Nessumara."

A whistle pierced the air, followed by a scatter of cries like flocking birds. With weapons in hand, folk faced the track. A bare-legged and bare-footed youth raced into the clearing, a skinny child not more than twelve or thirteen years of age clothed in a dirty linen jacket belted at the waist and reaching its knees.

"Soldiers . . . attacking . . . Upperpool . . . village . . . no quarter . . . help . . ." Words gave way to a hacking cough and a spew of bile.

"Arm up, all hands," said Tomen as everyone listened, poised and tense and eager.

"Action at last," murmured Laukas.

"Anyone who wants to stay back with the elder can help her move the supplies to the cave," added Tomen.

No one wanted to stay back. They assembled with such weapons and armor— thick leather coats—as they possessed, while Tomen coaxed information out of the youth.

"Lots of them. More than twenty? I didn't see. Upperpool burning. We can see the flames from Lowerpool. My cousin got away. There were others running."

"Lowerpool will be hit next." Tomen raised a hand to gain the attention of his fighters. "These strikes on villages are the same, a cadre of bullies with good weapons using surprise and intimidation to overtake resistance. We've talked over the drill. We're equal in numbers. They're better armed. We'll use archers and ambush to pick them off, then we close and kill the rest. No prisoners. Laukas, you'll take lookout."

"The hells! I want to fight—"

"You'll take lookout. It's time for us to make known we don't intend to let this army burn and pillage at will. Tonight our weapons will be our voice, a bold cry against the invaders!"

The company cheered.

"Uh. Might I ask a question? If you don't actually know how many there are—?" Shai's voice fell unheeded as they scrambled for the track, those still gathering their gear swearing as they hurried so as not to be left behind. He was left behind as the clearing emptied.

"What are you?" the youth asked, looking alarmed as he saw Shai. "An outlander!"

Branches pitched as though in the grip of a mighty wind. A figure dropped from tree to earth, not six paces from the youth, who tripped and sprawled backward. Shaking, he displayed his hands palms up, then sketched a familiar gesture of meeting as he stood.

"Greetings of the day, honored one."

It blinked, black-eyed, before copying the hand gesture so perfectly that Shai expected it to continue into some extended tale told through song and gesture. It was a male, its slim hips and legs clothed in leggings.

"I have to go, honored one." The child ran down the track after the fighters, and the creature loped after it.

The noise of their passage faded.

"Here, mule," said the elder, beckoning to Shai. "Help me and Navita carry things."

Was it better to run now while he was unguarded, to head south alone and easily marked as an outlander, knowing everyone he met would be suspicious of him? Or should he stay here, hoping to earn their trust and help? The elder and the young envoy watched him, surely needing no third eye or second heart to interpret his thoughts.

He shrugged. "Show me what you need carried, verea."

He hauled from the clearing along a track and over a streamlet and through rockier ground where trees struggled for a foothold. They reached an escarpment thrust so abruptly out of the ground it was like walking into a wall. Vines obscured the face of the cliff. He pushed through a tangle of ropy vegetation to deposit the basket on a dirt floor in the gloom. The cave smelled of dirt and tasted of the forge.

As they came out, the young envoy smiled anxiously at him, as if she had decided to treat him as a comrade. "My ostiary said I had to get out of town because I was being hunted. I've never been outside the city before today. I don't like the forest. It smells funny. Anything might be creeping up on you!"

"Heya!" called the elder.

Shai and the envoy, sharing a complicit glance, hurried after. They hauled supplies as the afternoon lengthened into dusk. When it got too dark to see, the elder lit a lantern. Eventually they paused for a rest in the abandoned clearing.

"You're a hard worker, Shayi," the elder said, "I'll give you that. You might have bashed me over the head and taken a run for it, although you'd not escape the wildings, would you, eh?"

"The wildings?"

As if the word were a summons, the male dropped out of the trees. In lamplight, it sketched gestures with its hands.

The old woman became rigid with disbelief. "Ambushed at the waterwheel? No survivors? Soldiers coming this way?"

The wilding gestured toward Navita and indicated that the young woman should climb onto its back. *Hurry! Hurry!*

The breeze waned to stillness. A distant shout hung in the air, and then it was drowned by an odd sound shuddering within the trees, a spill like falling rain. A rippling shadow descended out of darkness: a woman cloaked in night, riding a winged horse. Soldiers emerged out of the forest, surrounding them.

The cloaked woman reined in the horse, raising a hand. "Child of the Four Mothers," she said to the wilding. "I will not harm you because of the ancient law binding my kind to that of the other children of the Hundred. Out of the same blood and bone and thread we were created."

It hesitated, an arm extended to indicate the trembling young envoy.

"You think to save her, but no action you take can save her from my scrutiny. Go. I may not kill you, but that does not mean my soldiers may not grow impatient and strike."

It showed its teeth in a grin of furious despair but retreated, vanishing into the trees.

"Aui!" called one of the soldiers. "Was that a *wilding*? It's cursed bad luck to kill any of the other children. Curses ten times down the generations."

"Shut up," said the captain in charge. "Holy One, this girl is the Flag Quarter envoy we've been seeking, I'm sure of it."

"Look at me," said the cloaked woman pleasantly.

Meeting that gaze, the elder staggered and clutched at her heart as she dropped the lantern, which hit square and did not tip. Two soldiers hauled Navita forward to face the cloak.

"Veiled to my sight!" said the cloak, more a murmur of disappointment. "You are a seventh daughter, perhaps?"

The girl maintained her dignity with remarkable self-possession. "I am, Holy One. Seventh of eight girls born to my good mother. I am gods-touched, and according to the law will serve out my days as a servant of the gods. I was dedicated to Ilu the Herald three years ago."

"Still young," said the cloak, signaling to the captain, who moved up behind the young woman with his drawn sword. "But gods-cursed, not gods-touched."

The man stabbed Navita in the back, up under the ribs. Her grunt was all that betrayed her surprise. The elder collapsed, sobbing, to her knees, as the captain cut Navita's throat. Her death was swift, and her ghost, twisting out of her body, cast a surprised look at Shai.

"You're gods-touched, too!" the ghost cried. "Hurry, Shayi! Save yourself!"

Then her spirit fled, crossing under the Gate.

"Are you the veiled outlander Bevard spoke of?" the cloak asked.

"I don't have to tell you," said Shai. "What harm did Navita ever do to you?"

"Those who are veiled are dangerous because they can lie without fear. They are demons with human faces. It was not the intention of the gods that any stand veiled before us. Captain?"

The captain moved up behind Shai, sword still wet with blood.

"You don't want to kill me," said Shai.

The cloak sighed a mournful smile. "Why not?"

"I came to the Hundred looking for my brother. You know him. His name is Harishil, and he wears one of the cloaks."

The captain whistled. "There is a resemblance between him and Lord Twilight."

"Harishil's brother." The cloak's gaze was as smooth as a polished stone and just as unfathomable. "Captain, take him to Wedrewe. I'll join you after I have tracked down the gods-touched mendicants so many have spoken of."

"To Wedrewe! Holy One, that's a cursed long way!"

"Are you a captain, or do you wish to be a sergeant again?"

"Of course, Holy One. It will be done exactly as you wish." He prodded Shai with the bloody point of his sword. "Pick up the lantern, and let's get the hells out of this cursed woodland and to a decent road."

Not dead yet: at this point, that seemed to be the most Shai could ask for. He picked up the lantern and starting walking.

9

THE ENEMY CREPT cautiously out of the forest's edge, watching for the glare of fire in the distance where villages burned. Captain Arras had set his ambush carefully: four lines of attack, trip wires, and a gauntlet of spearmen to sweep around from behind so no stragglers could escape back into the trees. The fighting was short, sharp, and efficient; not one of his men was killed, although ten sustained wounds and two were so badly hurt they'd likely be crippled. Ten of the enemy survived the main attack on their feet and refused to surrender, preferring to fight to the death, so he had them taken down with arrows. Three of the enemy were mortally wounded but still breathing; he cut their throats himself, as a mercy.

At dawn, he commanded the men to drag the bodies into the open clearing behind the ruined waterwheel, where he paced out the measure of the dead, his sandaled feet moistened with dew as he counted thirty-four men and women, two short of a full cadre. Too bad they'd joined up with the wrong side; he could have used such bold, hard fighters, molded them into something more than a ragtag poorly led herd of frustrated rebels.

Sergeant Giyara herded the shivering child forward and, at his gesture, moved away to the perimeter. No one could overhear them now.

"You did as you were told," he said to the child: he wasn't sure if it was a homely boy or a brawny girl. "How many were left at camp?"

The child was weeping, tears smearing lines through its filthy face. "Dunno. A few. Not fighters."

"Any outlanders?"

"I saw one." Its voice trembled as it contemplated the ashes of its triumph. Under Arras's steady gaze it found its tongue and spoke in a whisper. "You won't kill my family?"

"First, you'll lead us to the clearing." The captain fastened a hand over the neck of the child's jacket.

The raid on the villages was well in hand, according to the runners who came in from his other companies to report. He called in the men, had the wounded set up a perimeter within the ruins to await his return, and settled the rest into files, making sure his strongest, most stubborn fighters were concentrated in the van and at the rearguard. The dogs and their handlers were sprinkled throughout the line in case of attack while they were strung out and vulnerable on a forest track. This was the dangerous part of the operation, so he took point with a pair of trusted men, put the child on a rope, and sent him ahead like a dog. They trotted at good speed along the track.

A mind, surely, was like this forest, tangled and overgrown, its reaches hidden to the common eye. What the cloaks possessed was something like the path they marched along, a way to punch into what you otherwise could not penetrate. What if there was a way to let your thoughts grow over and hide from the cloaks?

The enemy hadn't been entirely stupid. They'd emplaced a lookout, but the person had fled, the only survivor. They'd tried to cover their tracks, keep their base hidden. His company had to wade up a stream, a good technique for throwing off dogs on a scent, and take a second track yet deeper into the forest. But in the end they found the clearing with its canvas structures still strung up. The fire was ashes. Platters were scattered around logs set out as benches; small animals had been feeding on the leavings. Wind bellied the canvas awnings. Birds fluttered away through high branches. Two corpses cooled: an elderly woman and a lass wearing the blue cloak of an envoy of Ilu.

He had an itch on his shoulders, that gods-rotted feeling he was being watched, but although he paced the edge of the clearing and peered into the foliage, he saw not even a bold crow. There! The bright flash revealed birds with red and yellow plumage.

"Track over here, Captain," called Sergeant Giyara.

"Secure the site," said Arras to her. "Search for weapons, supplies, and coin. You twenty, come with me."

They followed the second trail through more forest, over rockier ground, only to have it give way at a rocky spine thrust out of the earth and covered with hanging vines and low-growing shrubs nestled in its crevices. There was an actual cave inhabited by a scatter of ancient debris, rotting leaves blown in through the vines that screened the entrance, and a jumbled pile of animal bones scored with tooth marks.

"A predator's nest," said one of the men nervously.

"Nothing's lived here for a long while," observed the captain, "and I see no sign they were storing anything here either."

They lit a pair of torches, but the cave's ceiling lowered in the back until they'd have had to crawl to get in any farther, and there was an odd smell like rotten eggs that made the man in the front cough and choke until he couldn't speak, so Arras called them back. They searched the vicinity but found only a scumble of tracks.

"I think we've flushed out what's left of this nest of rats." He took no pleasure in killing; it's just it had to be done and he liked doing what he was good at. Yet he still had that prickling feeling on the back of his neck: someone watching. "We'll gather up the other units and march on."

"We going back to Toskala, Captain?" asked one of the newcomers assigned to his command by Toskala's governor along with seventeen other untested men. Arras had spread them out, three to each cadre, keeping them isolated from each other so they'd bond with the soldiers he knew and trusted.

"No." His strong voice carried. "We're marching on Nessumara to join the army there, as we were commanded to by Lord Twilight himself. There's fighting ahead, and plenty of coin and loot to be had after the city falls."

The three newcomers whooped, then fell silent as the veterans yawned and scratched, pretending to ignore the novices' enthusiasm.

The cadre retraced their steps to the clearing, where the pathetic items swept up from the remains of the camp were neatly laid out under Sergeant Giyara's supervision. Arras liked a woman with a tidy mind; Giyara was tough-minded and effective. She was attractive as well, but he knew better than to indulge that itch with a valued subordinate.

To the men he said, "Divvy up what's portable in even lots."

Giyara had already divided out the food: ten small sacks of rice, nai, turnips, bundled herbs, and a substantial store of smoked venison. The durable trenchers were easy to store in their travel packs. The canvas was good quality.

"We'll meet up with our other companies and continue south to Nessumara," he said, again, his voice ringing beneath the canopy. "According to our orders from Lord Twilight. We're expected to make good time, so let's hustle."

The sergeant called out, "Line up!"

The child looked like a beaten dog, all mournful eyes and drooping head. "Are you leaving? What about my family?"

"Your family has not been harmed." As the men began to march out, he realized he could still make use of the child. "A word of warning. The other survivors will begin to suspect your family's curious luck in escaping with no injuries. And although your family may be grateful now, they'll come to hate you later. Your kinsfolk's resentment may be worse than the anger of your neighbors. If I were you, I'd leave, and find a new place to make your way."

He fell in with the rearguard.

No doubt it would straggle home bawling, yet wasn't it better to die than be a traitor? The angry ghosts of its dead would haunt it for the rest of its life, however long that would prove to be in these disordered times. He wondered if he felt kinship or disgust for the child.

"Captain?" Sergeant Giyara had fallen back. "Sure you don't want that child's kinsfolk cleansed? Traitors ought to be punished."

"Neh, we made them, so leave them be. Anyway, if I were a wagering man, I'd bet you the child will follow us and before five days are out be begging to let it join the company."

"You think so?"

This was how you obscured your trail. "I do."

He scanned the forest. He was used to high-elevation trees, ones that could survive frost and a seasonal dusting of the snow never seen down here. These lowland hothouse woodlands creeped him, for sure, so dense and moist it was like being inside a vast sensate beast. Branches were swaying although the breeze wasn't strong enough to send them rocking like that.

At the ruins of the waterwheel, they carted up their wounded and called in the other companies, leaving behind half-pillaged villages with corpses and burned houses scattered like chaff. There was a decent north-south road here, running roughly parallel to but rather more inland than the famed Istri Walk, the major road that ran on high ground on both banks alongside the magnificent River Istri, whose humble headwaters he had grown up fishing.

Strange where life took an insignificant ordinand. He'd never imagined in his youth that he'd find himself living in a time where he could become a true soldier, just like those who were more reviled than admired in the tales.

By midafternoon they could no longer smell the smoke of their raid, and in the villages they marched through they paused only long enough to demand coin. In one village, a pair of rambunctious cousins begged leave to join them, and he allowed them to sign on as hirelings mostly because their clansmen were clearly horrified at this desertion. Later, when he halted to allow his men to wet their throats at an inn, a rough-looking traveler named Laukas asked for a hire, saying he'd tend to horses or boots, anything for a meal and a chance at learning how to fight properly. The new men worked hard that evening when they set up camp; they'd either grow tired of the labor, or they wouldn't. Only time would tell.

He made a circuit of the sentry lines and returned to his own fire to eat nai porridge and smoked meat. The sergeants gave their reports, and afterward he dismissed all except Giyara.

"I'm thinking of that child," Arras said, as if the thought had just leaped upon him and wrestled him to the ground. "Maybe you could leave a parcel of food and drink out beyond the sentry lines, something the child might stumble upon if indeed it is following us."

Giyara cocked her head, examining him as if he were crazy. "As you wish, Captain."

"I just have a feeling," he repeated, and shook his head, sensing he was overdoing it. "What have you heard about the eighteen new recruits we were saddled with?"

She'd known he would want to hear the gossip, so she had already done her talking with the company subcaptains and cadre sergeants. Her analysis was succinct: Fifteen would likely work out, one had died in the raid through sheer idiocy, and the other two were troublemakers he'd need to deal with soon.

"Just kill them," he said. "Rid us of the problem immediately rather than let it drag on. You can slot those three new men in, but be sure to split up the cousins."

He dismissed her, then considered the flames, the pleasant noises of an orderly camp settling down for the night, and the distant scream of a rabbit caught in the dusk by a predator.

"Captain."

"The hells!" He sprang up, hand on his sword hilt, but it was already too late. A woman cloaked in night walked out of the darkness and captured him, her voice the hook and her eyes the spear. Down he tumbled, his heart and mind laid open to her sight, all his secrets revealed.

He liked Lord Twilight, truth to tell, although he knew a humble soldier like him hadn't the right to feel any sense of comradeship with a cloak, who was either a holy Guardian or an unholy lilu or some hells-brewed stew of both. Anyway, you couldn't say no to a cloak, even if—especially if—the cloak's orders were likely to get you strung up on a pole.

So he would cover his tracks as well as he could. He would play the game of misdirection. He had crushed a nest of bandits. Nothing suspicious in that. Meanwhile, he would send Sergeant Giyara out with parcels of food every night, ostensibly for a child who might be brash enough to follow, although he deemed that particular child unlikely to have the courage. That was the kind of child who stuck it out in a bad situation, too afraid to bolt, and got itself whipped and eventually, when its own people had come to despise it enough, butchered. Rotten, they would call it, and then they'd fling its spiritless flesh into the woods to be scoured by the Lady's beasts and pretend it had never existed. Every night someone other than him would take out those parcels for a child who probably wasn't following them, while he would hope that a fugitive outlander seeking safe passage to Nessumara had actually been hiding in the forest within hearing of his voice.

She released him.

He fell forward, barely catching himself on his hands, his nose brushing the dirt. "Do you mean to have me cleansed, Holy One?"

She spoke without anger or sorrow. "Captain Arras, I followed you because I was curious why three companies stumbled onto the very same bandits I did. It seemed unlikely it was a coincidence. Nor was it. I have a better insight into events now. Yet I do not fault you for obeying Lord Twilight's order. I appreciate your loyalty and your cleverness. You attempt to protect your soldiers as well as yourself. Very commendable."

"How may I serve you, Holy One?" he said, keeping his head bowed and straining his will to empty his mind. Maybe he had a chance of surviving this.

"Fight well with the army, Captain. When Lord Twilight returns, when he seeks you out, as he will, tell him I have his brother."

*   *   *

"GREETINGS OF THE day, verea. Nice the markets are open again, eh?"

Ostiary Nekkar examined a tray of withered caul petals as he crouched on his haunches beside an old woman selling remnants from her garden.

"Generous of you to say so, Holy One. Only from second bell to fourth bell, and then us chased back into our homes." She was very wrinkled, with many teeth missing, but she had a vigorous heart and was willing to speak her mind.

"Where's your granddaughter, verea? I miss her cheerful face."

"As if we'd risk her in the marketplace in days like these." She indicated two soldiers leaning on their spears and two others strolling as they looked over the merchandise. Usually, one bell after dawn, the main market of Stone Quarter was alive with chatter and gossip and laughter. Nekkar never tired of observing people: the blazing health and innocent beauty of the young, the nagging and hopefully jovial complaints of those who, like him, were mature without being elderly, and the enduring strength of folk like Gazara, twice widowed but a great-grandmother, the pillar of her poor but proud clan of day laborers, men and women who dug ditches, cleared canals, and worked on the road beds.

He nodded. "Is there work for your people? How are you managing?"

She bent over the caul petals to separate the merely withered from the desiccated. "The soldiers pay coin to anyone who brings them information, so I hear."

"I remember," said Nekkar carefully, "that your clan took in two families of distant cousins some months ago."

She wiped her mouth with the back of a hand and spoke in a whisper. "They're with us still, Holy One. We're keeping it quiet, for fear they'll get themselves expelled and us hanged."

"A dreadful thing, truly. Verea, before the main army marched downriver on Nessumara, I was interrogated, because I went out scouting one day while the curfew was still on. This has been my first chance to get out."

She measured him. "You've a few bruises, like fallen fruit."

"I'm asking around the market for a particular reason." She looked up, alarmed, but he smiled in what he hoped was a reassuring way. "When I was roughed up, there was a refugee in the line ahead of me. He was killed later, trying to get back to whatever alley he'd left his children in."

"Orphans," she muttered gloomily.

"I'm asking around, if anyone has heard tell of three children being swept up or driven out, or taken in, or glimpsed in the alleys."

"Those village children were always gawking at the silks and the noodle sellers." She cracked a reluctant smile, but it fled quickly. "The soldiers have been cleaning out the alleys. They've worked through the entire quarter riverside of our compound."

"And the canal-side neighborhoods over by the temple," he said.

"I'm sorry to say my lads have been forced to take hire building out that burned merchant's hall in Terta Square, that one they're turning into a fortified garrison headquarters. I heard them remark just last evening there are still neighborhoods over by the masons' courts with refugees hanging on in nooks and crannies. Eiya! It was better when those refugees weren't here, for they ate up the rations we need now, but it's a cursed terrible thing the army is doing—"

"Hush, my friend," he said in a low voice, seeing the soldiers approach from her blind side. He went on loudly. "I can't pay that ridiculous price, verea. I'm surprised you even suggest it!"

"For shame, Holy One! How can I feed my grandchildren if I can't sell my produce for a pair of vey, eh?"

The young men sauntered up behind her. "Eh, look at those withered caul petals! My grandmother would have been too proud to demand coin for what she'd feed to her pigs."

The old woman bent her head to hide the spark of anger.

Nekkar smiled blandly up at them. "Greetings of the day, my nephews. A fine day, eh? The sun is very lively today, good weather ahead."

"We've got our eye on you, uncle," said the taller soldier. "You can't trust those cursed envoys of Ilu, that's what Sergeant Tomash told us before he got reassigned. Always sneaking around, gossiping, getting into the business of others."

"Where did you serve your apprenticeship, nephew?"

"Thinks he's got the right to ask, eh?" said the shorter to the taller, guffawing as at a merry joke. They sauntered over to a woman selling plums and took the nicest off her tray without paying.

"They call that 'tithing,' " muttered Gazara. "Cursed thieves."

"The young have sharp hearing," he said mildly.

The soldiers glanced over and gestured as if to say, "Don't think to escape us."

"I thank you for the tidings, verea," he added, knees popping as he straightened.

"Don't get into trouble, Holy One. We here in Stone Quarter rely on you for your honesty and good temper."

"I wish there was more I could do. For now, we must keep our heads down and try to survive."

No matter how much he wanted to go haring off toward the masons' courts immediately, he loitered in the market, purchasing three honey-sesame cakes and tucking them in his sleeve as he made his way along the main thoroughfare toward the square where he had faced interrogation ten days earlier. The army had swept up ransom and hostages, and departed, and Nekkar was cursed sure that the garrison left behind to guard Toskala were the worst of the lot, bullies and thieves who took whatever they fancied just because they had the power to do so.

A pair of soldiers—likely the same ones by their mismatched height—trailed him at a distance, but he knew the neighborhoods better than they did. Behind Astarda's Arch, he cut into a nook where, according to temple history, there had once stood an age-blackened statue of Kotaru the Thunderer, a relic of an earlier era. He heard the startled cries of the men tailing him and the patter of their footsteps as they raced down the street in pursuit. He hurried back the way he had come and made his way into the warren of alleys behind the masons' courts.

He surprised a couple of locals scavenging through canvas shelters still strung from walls. Crude pallets had been cut open. A ripped and muddied doll lay in the street—it seemed there must always be a doll torn from the grip of some poor sobbing child. A dead dog had gone rigid, feet pointing up; at least it did not yet stink. He hurried past, but heard a scrape and turned back. A ragged child had grasped the hind legs of the dog and was dragging it into the shadows.

"Child," he said softly, holding out the honey-sesame cakes.

The child froze. Its posture, as rigid in its own way as the dog's, betrayed the intensity of its fear and hunger. For a few breaths, they watched each other. Then Nekkar allowed his gaze to probe the shadows. A half-closed-up drain was tucked away under the two-story building leaning out over the alley. A face wavered in the opening. He could not be sure these were the children of the murdered man whose pleas had gone unheard by all except Nekkar, but truly, it did not matter.

"That's one very dead dog, neh? Not even the firelings as in the tales could heal it, eh?"

The child quivered but did not let go of the legs.

"You're right to be cautious. You are protecting the ones hiding in the drain. I'm an ostiary, not one of the soldiers. I've come at your father's request to take you to the temple, where you'll be safe."

"We gotta wait 'til he come back," said the child in a raspy voice. Impossible to say if this filthy scrap was male or female, and it was certainly no more than ten.

"Yes, truly you do, but aren't the little ones hungry?"

Its gaze flicked toward the shadows and away, fearful of giving up its secrets.

"I tell you what. You come with me now, and we'll wait at the temple until your father comes."

The child relinquished its hold on the dog's legs. It scratched the rash blooming across its exposed neck. "He said to wait."

"And so you have. But he's had to go out of the city, and now he needs you to come with me to the temple. How long has it been since you've seen him?"

The child answered with a shrug.

"Meanwhile, the little ones are hungry. And need a bath. By the honor of Ilu, child, I promise to care for you."

Aui! Let the child be not so stubborn!

The sag in its shoulders acknowledged its weary defeat. It turned to face the shadows and called. "Heya! We're goin' to the Ilu temple and get fed."

A smaller child crawled out from the hole, its body smeared with mud, followed by an even smaller child who wore only a scrap of linen tied over one shoulder, like a mockery of a cloak, and was therefore exposed as a boy-child. Both children were little more than sticks with joints that bent and eyes that blinked.

"You sure?" asked the middle one, who was clutching a bundle.

"You wanna eat this dog?" asked the eldest.

"We best hurry," Nekkar said, "lest soldiers come. They were here before, neh?"

"We hid," said the eldest.

The middle one raised a hand. "I hear them coming," it whispered in a voice rubbed raw.

The eldest cocked its head as its eyes flared. "We gotta hide, Holy One."

Too late Nekkar heard the smack of footfalls and the conversational rise and fall of young male voices fading and growing as they turned an unseen corner that brought them closer.

"Hide," he said.

He ducked down and slid on his belly through a stinking muck that slopped on his neck. The drain was stone on all sides, damp and fetid. The two little ones scrambled in behind, but the eldest darted back to grab at the dead dog.

Soldiers shouted. The child ran the other way to draw their attention away from the drain. They sprinted past, and their shouts of triumph told the rest of the tale. Then back they came, dragging the child, and the littlest one scrabbled out through the hole after his sibling and the middle one followed as his muddy foot slipped through Nekkar's grasp.

The hells! He was not so young and so fit as he had once been, and his tunic snagged and he had to rip it loose, gods-rotted nail! By the time he crawled out they were gone around the bend although he heard voices well enough:

"I knew we'd missed a few of these stinking roaches, eh!"

He hurried after them. As he bolted out from the alley into the street he ran straight into the soldiers who had been following him.

"Whew! You stink!" That was Shorter speaking with a cheerful grin. "What, Holy One, you scavenging from what those refugees left behind? Aui! I thought better of an ostiary."

"Them thinking they're better than us," added Taller, grasping Nekkar with a cursed strong hand and towing him away from the direction in which the children had been taken. "Yet they do tax and tithe and claim to be pure as new milk when they're just gods-rotted thieves without a scrap of shame, thinking it's owed to them."

"I—I—"

"Eh? Eh?" They mocked him, his flushed face, his trembling hands, his ragged breathing. "Are those honey-sesame cakes?" They ripped the cakes from his grasp and ate them.

"I need to see the sergent for Stone Quarter. There were some orphans given over to the temple I was meant to take possession of, but because of the curfew I couldn't get out to leash them in until today—"

"Slave takers, too," said Shorter, and all at once Nekkar realized the young man had a debt scar scored into his face, by his left eye. "Cursed temples take our labor and work us and then discard us. How I hate them!" Like lightning, he backhanded Nekkar so hard across the face the ostiary stumbled to his knees on the street, so much pain he couldn't stand at first even as they shoved and then punched and then kicked him until he staggered up half blinded by tears.

"I need to see the sergeant." His voice sounded like that young child's, scoured raw.

They hauled him to the inn after all, punctuating the long walk with a running commentary about what the sergeant would do to him, fingers broken, eyes gouged out, toes cut off, cleansed on the pole. They were enjoying the conversation because they knew he could do nothing to stop their chatter. Their talk was like a winding chain, winching them tight and tighter.

The inn was empty but for three young women serving ale to ten off-duty soldiers. His pair traded jests with their comrades before prodding him upstairs. There he waited in the corridor, pain jabbing in his ribs. After a while, another man, soberly dressed and moving as slowly as if he were recovering from a severe beating, invited him into a long chamber overlooking the square.

The sergeant seated in the chamber had a lass to pour his wine, a couch to lounge on, and a pair of writing desks set against the wall where two shaven-headed clerks hunched over accounts books. As Nekkar entered they glanced up and looked down at once, as if expecting to be hit.

The sergeant had a knife in one hand, coring an apple. "What trouble are you causing? Be quick about it."

If he talked fast, he didn't have to imagine what it would feel like to be hanged on the pole.

"Sergeant, I'm Nekkar, ostiary at the Ilu temple here in Stone Quarter. Three orphans were consigned to my care some days ago, and I've only just now been able to collect them. But your soldiers took them away. So if I can just fetch them from wherever they've been hauled off to, then I'll take them off your hands and the temple will provide—"

"They're probably being taken to the brickyards."

"The brickyards!"

"We've a fair lot of building to do. Fire damage to fix. Defensive walls to reinforce. Small hands can work in the brickyards."

"They're very young, the smallest not more than four—"

"I'm done with this conversation. You know, ostiary, I might well send soldiers by your temple if I've need of your novices' labor. Best you take care of your own, and be careful you don't displease me further. Indeed, I'll thank you to come by every morning after second bell and give me a report on Stone Quarter's doings. Now, get out!" He popped a slice of apple into his mouth, then offered one to the lass, who glanced at the ostiary before she took it and devoured it.

He was shaking. "Sergeant, if I may—"

The sergeant whistled, and the two soldiers entered the room, their grins fading as they took in the sergeant's grim frown. "Get this cursed ostiary out of my sight. But don't be beating on him, you gods-rotted fools!"

They were strong with youth's surety. They marched him through streets empty-
ing of traffic as the fourth bell tolled the curfew hour, although the laborers working
on the army's projects would hammer and haul until dusk. They shoved him to the
closed gates of the temple, and waited until the watch let him in past the growling
dogs.

He shut the door in their faces. It was all he could do.

"Holy One?" asked the envoy on watch, looking worried. The novices came to the
porch of the learning hall, staring but saying nothing. "Shall we haul water for a
bath?"

He shook his head roughly. "I'll haul the water myself."

So he did, each bucket spilling into the bronze tub along with his tears.

And when he poured the last bucketful in, the water splashed, rippled, lapped,
and stilled to become a mirror. His own filthy, bruised face stared up at him, the ordinary face of a man who has done his duty and lived as decently as he could manage according to the precepts of the gods. No special craft, no exceptional skills, no
particular ambition.

"I will fight," he said to his reflection, to his hidden spirit, perhaps, or to the gods.
"Let me be a messenger, as befits my calling. Let me be an envoy, to carry resolve
where it is needed. There must be a way to defeat them. We must find a way."

PART THREE: DEMANDS

10

TWENTY-FIVE DAYS AGO, Mai had taken refuge in a valley entirely wild, its soil untrammeled by human feet and its bounty unharvested by human hands, a place so high and isolated in the mountains it could only be reached only by eagles. Here, in a cave behind a waterfall, she had given birth to a son.

At dawn on the day called Resting Ibex, Atani's hungry fussing woke her. She nursed him from the comfort of her sleeping mat. She slept under a framework of poles raised two steps off the earth with canvas hung for walls and roof. A second structure housed the reeves and hirelings and guards brought in to assure the baby's comfort and safety. Their stores of rice and grain rested in a storehouse raised on stilts.

After Atani's demands were satisfied, she tucked the infant in a sling, slipped into her sandals, and stepped out. Sprawling jabi bushes fenced in the clearing; the stream burbling down from the waterfall higher up in the vale chased into the trees beyond. She greeted the sentries and, with them pacing behind her, followed a track downstream beside trees whose branches drooped, so heavily laden were they with sunfruit and mamey and mango.

The mountain escarpment rose on three sides, all bold peaks and daring angles. On the fourth side, the stream that welled out of the sacred pool upstream spilled over a rocky ledge at the edge of a mighty cliff overlooking a wilderness of rugged foothills. In the right light at the right time of day, rainbows glittered in the spray below, and if the last gasping breath of a high-mountain storm sprinkled out of the Spires from the heights behind you, you might see rainbows above and below.

Surely the Merciful One favored this place. From this vista a person might hope to see into the future, or recall the past.

How long ago had Mai been carried away from her family and childhood in Kartu Town by the Qin captain and his troop? One year? Two? It seemed like half her life ago. Far more had happened to her in that short span of time than in the seventeen years previous: she had been married off to a man she did not know, had embarked on a long overland journey, had sealed a merchant's bargain on which her life and fortune and that of many others depended, had made a dear friend, had supervised the building and expansion of a settlement, had survived battles and assassins, and borne her first child.

"Mistress?"

She turned. "Greetings of the day, Priya. I'm coming."

Together, she and her attendants walked back to the clearing and onward up a path twisting through the foliage toward the heights. Mai carried whatever small offering took her fancy. This morning she plucked a bouquet of red-and-yellow fall-of-joy with its swoony scent. Each morning more attendants followed, most no doubt out of curiosity, some in the hope of currying favor, and a few with perhaps a bud of faith. Even Sheyshi accompanied them, although poor Sheyshi could still barely recite the most basic of prayers, stumbling over the same words every time.

Not that the Merciful One was a jealous or critical god, demanding fearful obedience or exacting perfection. Far from it! The Merciful One was a pilgrim who had wandered far from home, finding a resting place wherever folk raised an altar. The procession—fully eighteen people today including all six off-duty Qin guardsmen as well as the three on-duty ones—climbed to the rocky clearing around the pool. The waterfall boomed, which meant rains had fallen higher up in the Spires beyond sight and sound of the valley. The churning waters hid movement beneath the foam, but she never quite glimpsed an actual living creature swimming there.

She led the way through low walls that marked an ancient ruin. The walls had once entirely rimmed the pool, but now they were as broken and worn as the teeth of an elder. They entered the cave in single file along a ledge, cliff wall on the right and the waterfall's curtain on the left.

Two lamps burned within the cave. A slab had been set across the birthing stones where Mai had labored to create a humble altar covered with a red cloth. Here she laid today's offering of flowers as Priya intoned the first prayers.

" 'The Merciful One is my lamp and my refuge.' "

The others settled, the most interested kneeling at the front behind Sheyshi, the merely curious to the back. Four had not come in at all, loitering in the ruins beside the pool hoping to catch a glimpse of the mysterious creature that lived within what all now called "the birthing pool" in honor of Atani.

Yet as Priya chanted the Three Refuges, the Four Undertakings, and the Five Rewards, as Mai repeated the responses and joined in where she knew the longer threads, she tasted an iron tang on her lips and felt the tingling in her bones that betrayed the presence of unseen others. The lamps burned, flames hissing softly, but she did not need oil's light to see within the cave's dim enclosure. Threads glittered along the ceiling of the cave. This morning, twenty-five days since she had given birth, less than a full month according to the calendar of Sapanasu but a full turn of the moon, fewer threads netted the ceiling than had been there yesterday, or the day before. That these threads were themselves living creatures she did not doubt. She had felt their touch while in the throes of labor; their net of light had clothed her when she was naked. When she entered the precinct of the sacred pool now, she still heard an echo of voices whose speech—if it was speech—she did not comprehend.

She did not fear them, nor did they fear her.

" 'Merciful One, your wisdom is boundless. Excuse me for the transgressions I have made through thoughtlessness, through neglect, through fear.' "

Human voices whispered, their changed timbre causing her to turn. Did the glimmering threads brighten? Or was it only her own heart and eyes that caught fire as Anji ducked into the cave? He kneeled at the back of the group, asking for no special precedence; he bowed his head in the same manner as everyone else.

" 'May the rains come at the proper time. May the harvest be abundant. May the world prosper, and justice be served. Accept my prayers out of compassion. Peace.' "

Priya's attention never wavered from the altar, but as soon as she finished, she efficiently herded the others out of the cave, leaving Mai and the baby alone with Anji. Mai rose. While once she might have grasped for Anji immediately, seeking solace, protection, strength, and reassurance, now she waited, watching him.

"Well, Mai," he said with that slight upward twist of the lips that signified his satisfaction. "You are looking more beautiful even than before. By all reports—which I naturally have been receiving daily—the child remains healthy." He glanced up at the threads gleaming on the ceiling, and a frown bruised his expression so briefly that in the instant after it cleared she thought she must have imagined it. "Let's go outside."

"It's been a full turn of the moon since I gave birth. I admit, I was expecting you to arrive yesterday or today. Yet I had hoped for a more private reunion."

His answering smile was sharp with desire; she felt it in her own flesh; maybe the air sang it. The baby stirred.

"Patience, Mai." He grasped her wrist as his gaze swept along the ceiling with the look of a man deciding whether or not to commit his troops to battle. "Not here. This valley puzzles me, and I don't like puzzles. I've come to take you home."

"Back to the Barrens?" She sighed, thinking of how much dried fish she had eaten in the settlement in the Barrens. Atani woke with an exploratory mewl of discomfort. "Am I going to be exiled to the Barrens forever?"

After all, he was teasing her. "Home to Olossi."

He was so close!

After a full turn of the moon, it was no longer forbidden. She could not resist.

She kissed him, and he caught her close, and they forgot to say the formal words in which the father greets the mother of his child and the child itself, who have survived for a full turn of the month without demons finding and devouring spirits made vulnerable by the precious and difficult passage known as birth.

He let her go and stepped back. "Hu! This is not the place!" He wiped his brow. "I have been considering the situation. As we have seen, the red hounds can track me anywhere. So it is better to accept the risk and attack in its turn that which we *can* alter. I'm making changes in how traffic is secured on the roads. Folk can still cross wilderness on deer tracks—we'll never be able to stop that—but we can place controls on the roads and gates that will alert us to anyone who does not belong."

"Even so, we can never know what lies inside a man's mind," she said. "People can be bought, or coerced to act at another's command. And we never know until it's too late."

"It's said the Guardians of old could know what secrets lay hidden inside a mind." He scratched at his jaw thoughtfully. "Such Guardians would be valuable allies."

"Until they saw into your thoughts! I haven't forgotten the ghost girl who took the form of Cornflower and killed those soldiers! When she looked at me, it was like she tore my heart out!"

"Demons are a different matter. They must be killed." He touched Atani's coarse black hair. "Let's go outside. I'd like to look at the baby, where I can see him properly."

The change in his voice stiffened her shoulders. He walked out, and she followed. The sun had risen high enough to flood the open area with its light. Only Qin soldiers remained in the clearing; Priya and Sheyshi had gone down with the others. Chief Tuvi hastened over as Mai lifted the baby out of the sling and presented him to his father with the words traditional in Kartu Town.

"Here is your son. Son of your seed, son of your blood, son of your bone. Let the ancestors favor him and strengthen him. Let him bring honor to your name."

The baby's black eyes were open, and he stared gravely at his father, making no sound. Anji took him from Mai as Tuvi waited beside her. Anji's personal guards, Sengel and Toughid, and other senior soldiers filed up behind. Anji placed the baby on a smooth stretch of wall and began to unwrap the swaddling. He glanced up at Mai, who felt unaccountably nervous. What if the baby was not perfect? He was so silent, rarely crying, often sleeping. He was so small! Tuvi set a hand on her shoulder, grasping firmly as if to hold her still.

"Mai," Anji said. "I've news from the north. Shai is alive."

Her legs gave way. She groped for a place to seat herself. As Anji laid bare the infant and examined him, head, genitals, torso, and limbs, she wept.

"A healthy boy," said Chief Tuvi.

Only after all the senior men had admired the naked baby, nodded their agreement, and offered polite blessings to the mother did Tuvi remove his hand from her shoulder.

TWENTY NOVICE REEVES were detailed to fly her retinue out of the valley. They could have flown all the way to the settlement, but for the last mey of the journey, Anji insisted they mount well-groomed horses ornamented with ribbons and silver-studded harness and ride in ranks appropriate to the occasion.

It was how the Qin did things.

At the gates, they were greeted with song punctuated by rhythmic clapping, for that was what folk did in the Hundred.

Enter, enter, we welcome you.

That you walk here is like flowers blooming.

The Qin soldiers had prepared a feast surely offered only to a prince among the Qin. Vats full of sheep's-head soup bubbled over massive hearths. There was plenty of rice and nai, but also special wheat cakes made in squares, sweetened curds, and a fermented milk so strong it made your eyes water. Mai and Anji sat on pillows on the porch of their house with the baby displayed in a cot between them, festively decked out in a gold cap and a red sash. First the senior Qin soldiers—and their wives, if they had them—and then the middle rank of Qin soldiers—with their wives, if they had them—and finally the lowest rank of Qin soldiers and the tailmen and the grooms—with their wives, if they had them—approached the porch and spoke rote greetings to the newborn and offered fealty to father and son and honored mother.

Afterward, the townsfolk brought the local customary gifts of nuts, fruits, and sweets.

"I feel a little uneasy," Mai whispered as she leaned into Anji's shoulder, savoring the feel of the length of his arm along her own. "I remember how our last festival turned out."

"We slaughtered every one of the red hounds who attacked the settlement that day." Anji shifted away from her, not liking to touch in public.

"Surely there are red hounds—spies—in hiding." Mai scanned the crowd, seeing only faces smiling with approval and excitement.

"We scoured the settlement." From the porch of the captain's house at the crest of the hill, you could see down over the settlement, past the half-built wall, and all the way over the parade ground to the fan of darker earth where an underground channel, still being constructed, would bring rainwater down from the mountains. He indicated an untidy sprawl of tents and shacks raised away from the settlement on dry ground; it had grown up in the twenty-five days she had been away. "Now we admit through the gates only those who have a license for trade granted by the clerks of Sapasanu."

"I'm not a coward, Anji. But you must admit it was frightening when the red hounds rode out of the wilderness like that. So many of them! I don't worry about myself so much. Well, maybe I do. It's natural to be scared after seeing such a thing. But—" She brushed a hand over the baby's cap. He had gone to sleep, his sweet face calm in repose. "This little one, I worry for."

His gaze followed the stroke of her hand. "You can be sure I will not put my son at risk. Here is Mistress Behara."

Behara's noodle business had flourished so greatly in the last six months that she had brought in a number of clan members to increase production. She presented a tray containing balls of sweetened rice paste, admired the baby, and addressed Mai.

"Verea, I am sent as a representative for the merchants in the town. Most of the women who live here today came to this place at your behest, hopeful to make a decent marriage or because you offered seed money for them to engage in a business of their own. While you bided here with us, you were accustomed to listen to those disputes that arose between various of our number and offer a judgment."

"Were you?" asked Anji.

"I did listen when folk had grievances," said Mai. "Usually, once folk talked things over, they sorted things out for themselves."

The noodle maker sketched a gesture of respect toward Anji, prudent toward those carrying swords, but she turned back to Mai. "It's said you are returning to Olossi. Would you preside over an assizes tomorrow? There are several cases that have arisen that would benefit from your clear head, and all have agreed to respect your judgment. In addition, there is talk that perhaps Astafero—"

"Astafero?"

"That is what folk are calling the settlement now." Behara sketched a phrase with her hands. " 'The shore burned,' the night those red hounds attacked. What I mean to say, verea, is that because it was your coin and the captain's victory that established this settlement, some say we must ask your permission before voting in a council to oversee the administration of the settlement."

Mai glanced at Anji, but he opened his hands to say: This is not my purview.

After all, how could it be? Beyond the Hundred, west of the border of the Sirniakan Empire in the Mariha princedoms and along the Golden Road, Qin armies under the var ruled as conquerors, but Anji had been forced to flee into exile with two hundred soldiers, his wife, and their grooms and slaves.

Mai turned back to Behara, who had, by the flickering of her gaze, noted this silent exchange. "Every city and village in the Hundred has a council, does it not? Why should it be different here? An assizes tomorrow. We will convene at dawn."

"The gods' blessings upon you and your child, verea. Captain." Behara made her courtesies and retreated.

Behara, coming last, had brought the heaviest request. The celebration spilled down into town, where folk ate and drank and sang, as folk would do, given the opportunity. Anji nursed a wheat cake, having nibbled half of it, and drank cups of the harsh milk as his men called out praise for the child's beauty, his strength, and his quiet uncomplaining nature, seen as a sign of excellent character among the Qin. Mai devoured three balls of sweetened rice and a pair of wheat cakes and an entire bowl of nai.

"I expected to see Avisha," she said, when the edge of hunger was dulled.

"Who is Avisha?" Anji shaded his eyes to survey the Qin soldiers sitting close by with swords at the ready, drinking deeply and eating well, laughing and talking with such open smiles and with such a clamor that she might have mistaken them for other people entirely, not the stolid Qin soldiers to whom she had grown accustomed. Some of the men with local wives had already gone down to join the celebration below.

Mai looked at Tuvi. He had stiffened slightly, maybe even blushing a little, remembering his ignoble defeat.

Anji saw Tuvi's expression and sighed. "Ah. The one who knew herbs and flowers."

"She was not right for you, Chief Tuvi," said Mai tartly. "You did not truly love her. You were only taken in by her pretty face. Beauty flies quickly." She rapped his forearm with her closed fan. "You would have gotten bored of her."

The chief relaxed. "I admit, I did not expect to be rebuked in such a manner. Refusing to eat my rice! But a man does get lonely. Perhaps you will choose for me, Mistress?"

Anji raised an eyebrow.

"I will keep my eyes open. For you, Tuvi-lo, someone special only."

And it was true, she thought, as the chief chuckled with Anji, that Chief Tuvi had felt the rejection more than the loss. Tuvi had not loved or even particularly respected Avisha, who was a pleasant young woman Mai's own age and knowledgeable about plants, as Anji had naturally recalled because he always remembered any fact that might be of possible use to him, but she was not a deep spirit, not like Mai's dear Miravia, who was lost to her now, trapped in a cage of her clan's making.

"What did become of the lass?" asked Anji. "I seem to recall . . . Jagi, wasn't it?"

Tuvi nodded, expression determinedly bland.

To have lost the girl to a mere tailman! How it must sting.

"Ah, yes, you recommended Jagi, Tuvi-lo, did you not?" Anji turned to Mai. "We have set up training camps in different parts of Olo'osson. We've assigned Qin troopers to stand as sergeants over companies drawn from local men. They've got to train fast and hard, become cohesive units. We don't know how soon we'll have to fight."

"Jagi is good with the locals." Wth a wry smile, Tuvi gestured toward the square of benches seen below that marked the spot where marriages were finalized. "He's patient with them. They like him. The troop of local lads he was training here consistently won in trials, so we sent him and his troop and his wife and the two children to Dast Welling. If all goes well, he'll be training an entire cohort."

"That's a substantial responsibility," said Mai. "I'm pleased for Avisha's sake."

"You were fond of her?" Anji asked. "Women feel most comfortable with women around them. Maybe you are lonely for the company of other women?"

"I have Priya, of course."

"Of course. She is an educated woman. A priestess of the Merciful One. You are fortunate to have such an exceptional woman in your household."

"I am. She is the greatest comfort to me. But it is true—" Only Tuvi stood close enough to listen. Even Anji's two bodyguards, Sengel and Toughid, had relaxed enough to walk away out of earshot, although not eyeshot, to suck down ladles of fermented milk. "I miss my dear friend Miravia. Do you suppose you could talk to her father and uncles? You might be able to persuade them to allow me to visit her again. I have accepted she will never again be allowed to visit in our own compound, after that terrible incident. After men not of her kin saw her face—"

His expression closed. "The Ri Amarah run their own houses by their own laws. We do not meddle with those who have treated us as guests and given us aid. That is all I have to say."

She knew that look. She had grown up in the Mei clan, where Father Mei ruled all and must be consulted in all matters except the most trivial. It was what she had expected in her own marriage. But in matters of business and marriage, Anji had let go of the reins; she was in charge, and he never meddled because he assumed she knew what she was doing and that she would do what benefited them. It was a potent brew, going straight to the head like too much sweet cordial.

But there was a line, and on the other side of that line, he commanded.

As the baby gurgled, he smiled and lifted up Atani to dandle him. The matter was closed to him; he would not think of it any longer, but she had not that facility. She would think of Miravia and Miravia's troubles, and mourn the loss not of a friendship, for they could write one to another, but for the voice and smile and touch that had come to mean so much to her in so short a time. To lose the intimacy of their friendship was a grief so sharp it was like a wound.

"Mai?" His smile faded as he watched her.

She sealed her sorrow as in a cask and set it away beside her fear for Shai. *Alive*, Anji had said; not *coming home*.

"What other news?" she said, more brightly than she intended. "What of the reeves? Have you heard from Marshal Joss? Reeve Miyara told me he was called away to the north."

Anji's eyes narrowed as if he were looking into the sun. He shifted the baby more firmly into his grasp. "From the north, the news is bad. Are you sure you wish to hear an accounting on such a pleasant day?"

"I do not wish to hide from the truth, if that's what you're asking."

"Very well, then. The news from the north."

11

JOSS SHIFTED HIS seat on his pillow in the audience room of the commander's cote in Argent Hall. He'd arrived midday from the north with his thoughts in a tumult at everything he must try to accomplish. Facing the senior fawkners, he began to doubt he could change a cursed thing.

"You want to name a fawkner to act as marshal over Argent Hall so you can go be commander at Clan Hall." Askar rubbed his grizzled chin. He was missing two fingers on his right hand, but the injury never seemed to hamper his fawkner's work, or his strong opinions. "It can't work."

"It's true that a fawkner has never stood as marshal," said Verena thoughtfully, "but in the Tale of Fortune, an ordinand stands in for Marshal Foragerda at Horn Hall for two years while the marshal searches for her mother. And in the tale of the Swift Horse—"

"A comic tale, in which folk are ridiculed," remarked Askar.

"It's the reeve hall that's being ridiculed, and then it turns out a hieros and his hierodules and kalos restore order in the hall when none of the reeves who stepped up to the task could manage it."

"Are you saying you're willing to stand as marshal of Argent Hall, Verena?" Joss asked. "You'd be a good marshal."

"And be accused of having slept with you to get the preference? Askar would be a better choice."

Askar yelped. "Neh, I won't do it! I don't want the aggravation."

Joss turned to the third fawkner, who watched with a calm gaze. "Geddi? You're well liked. Folk confide in you."

"Because they know he never opens his mouth to tattle their secrets!" Verena smiled affectionately at the man, who was thirteen years younger, a Violet Eagle with all that meant: honest, respectful, an especially hard worker, and known to have kept out of the quarrels and cruelties that had plagued the hall during the months of misrule by Marshal Yordenas and his cronies.

Geddi ran a hand over his close-cropped hair.

"You've a lot of friends among the younger reeves," added Joss. "They trust your judgment."

"I'm not the right one," said Geddi. "If it's a temporary measure, Verena should do it. Everyone respects her and Askar for sticking it out in the bad years, keeping true to the eagles. Besides"—he had the grin of a man who likes wicked gossip—"talk in the hall is not that you slept with the marshal to get *preference*, Rena."

Joss flushed. The hells! They'd only slept together once, and that at Verena's instigation.

Verena's glower would have curdled milk. "What *do* they say behind my back, then?"

"That you were the only one bold enough to act on what the rest were wishing for."

Joss groaned and hid his face behind a hand.

Askar said, "No doubt he's grinning behind there, eh?"

"And that you only bothered the one time, so maybe that sends a message to the younger women who might have thought of strutting after him otherwise."

"Ouch," said Joss.

Verena chuckled in the confident way mature women can have, the ones who can't be rattled. He'd seen the terrible scars on her torso; he knew how tough she was. "Were you wondering why no one else in the hall tried to seduce you, Marshal?"

Joss rested his hand on his hands. He was vain of his looks, it was true; he took for granted that women would find him attractive.

"They're just jesting with you," said Askar.

Joss raised his head. "Neh, I surely deserve it. Anyway, you're all honest enough to speak your minds, a precious thing. Verena, will you take the authority of marshal?" He indicated the chamber, neatly organized by a clerk brought in from Olossi to manage the marshal's correspondence and the hall's accounts books. "The sleeping room's a bit messy . . ."

Askar sighed.

Geddi snorted, laughing.

"It's nothing I asked for," said Verena, "nor do I want it. But I love this hall. I gave my clan three children who survived to adulthood, and now I'm free to do the work I care for most. Argent Hall is barely recovered from the rot introduced by Yordenas. We've got to heal if we want to recover our strength. We've got the training hall to oversee as well—Naya Hall must have strong leadership, too. How do you propose we manage all this?"

"If we don't unite the halls, then we'll all go down to defeat by the northern army. Do you know what happened to Horn Hall?"

"They vanished," said Askar. "No one has heard a word of them for over a year."

"And what of those corrupt reeves who were here at Argent Hall, obeying Yordenas, the ones who fled we know not where?" Joss pressed his point. "What if Lord Radas is already at work corrupting other reeves? Other halls? We have to do something different from what we were doing before—*which was nothing*—as the Star of Life rose to swallow so much land. All that time we ignored the changes taking place around us. Yet there comes a time when change overtakes the traveler, as it says in the tale. We can't know what may happen next. We must be ready for anything."

He'd first heard such words from Zubaidit. At the time, he'd protested mightily. But after the events of the intervening months and the power displayed by an army commanded by cloaks claiming to be Guardians, he had come to believe she was right. And not just because mere days ago she had kissed him in a way that still troubled his dreams and daylight hours—

"You're passionate today," said Geddi. "The tone you use is very persuasive, Commander. It's true the reports from Haldia and Istria and Toskala and the north are enough to scald one's ears. It's like we're living in a tale, not chanting one. Cursed uncomfortable, if you ask me. I liked it quiet the way it used to be back when I was a lad."

"Yet you've told me many a time how you came from a quarrelsome family!" said Verena with a laugh.

"True enough! That's why I find the eagles so restful. They're more honest than humankind. They don't take sides."

Verena gestured for silence. "If these Guardians fly about on winged horses and can command those who kill for them to kill each other in turn, as you say happened in Toskala, how can anyone be safe?"

"No one is," said Joss. "I'm not yet sure how reeves can be best used, but we can't merely patrol the roads, stand at assizes, and haul in criminals for trial."

"You think we have to become soldiers," said Geddi.

"Every hall has records going back many generations. The stewards and fawkners and senior reeves know which eagles are from family groups, which tolerate each other, which have to be kept well apart. We already send out reeves to patrol in pairs and threes. The first thing I want is a roster of how—if—we can create larger patrol units."

Askar grunted, looking skeptical. "What good will larger patrol units do? Anyhow, eagles won't fly in pretty ranks the way those Qin soldiers ride. Nor are they dogs to fetch and run at their master's will."

Geddi said nothing.

Verena nodded. "A roster can be written up. What's the second thing you want?"

"Make sure we identify and restock every way station and haven reeves can shelter at in Argent Hall's territory. Especially ones rarely visited."

Verena whistled. "You don't ask for much. Anything else?"

The writing desk behind which Joss sat had been cleared of paper, everything in its place. No wonder the commander at Clan Hall had kept her cote sparsely furnished and neatly ordered: no matter how much of a morass she was wading through, she could always close the doors and enjoy a moment of serenity in a place where there was no mess.

He smiled crookedly. "I'm making this up as I go along."

The bell announcing dinner rang three times. A man shouted in the distance, the sound followed by bright laughter.

Joss rose. "Marshal Verena, Argent Hall is yours. I'll announce it in the hall over the evening meal."

"What do you mean to do next, Commander?" she asked.

It seemed that between one breath and the next, Joss found himself answering to a rank he had never aspired to. Commander of the reeve halls. Aui! Life took strange turns.

"The only thing I can do. Gather my allies and make a plan."

*   *   *

FROM THE COUNCIL square in the port town of Ankeno, which was situated on a bluff overlooking the Bay of Istria, Captain Arras studied the green landscape on the horizon: the delta of the River Istri.

"How do you propose to attack a city protected by a powerful river channel on one side and a vast mire on the other?" he asked. As he looked around the outdoor gathering of some thirty or more company subcaptains and cohort captains, he recognized that his question had irritated half of them and made the other half uncomfortable.

"Captain Arras, is it?" Captain Dessheyi's badge designated him as captain of First Cohort, which meant he was a man with connections to Lord Radas. Whether he was militarily up to the task remained to be seen.

"That's right."

"And you command—?"

"I'm here with three companies, the remnants of Sixth Cohort. We took heavy casualties in High Haldia. After the siege, we were assigned to garrison High Haldia and regroup. I had to reorganize six undermanned companies into three complete ones and rid myself of a few cripples and incompetents while I was at it. For a few months I was chief administrative governor over High Haldia, under the command of Lord Twilight."

"Lord Twilight is the cloak who commanded the failed expedition to Olossi, is he not?"

The cursed man was trying to needle him. Arras bit down a retort. "I follow orders, Captain Dessheyi. My company was reassigned here. Since we reached the lower Istri, we've been assigned to pacify villages between here and the Wild, just a few skirmishes and a few rebels running into the deep forest."

"Where they'll be slaughtered by wildings and have their heads pinned to racks as a warning to the rest of us. How come you here today, Captain?"

"Commander Hetti ordered my companies to report to you for assignment. He told me you're still setting a perimeter around the delta." He did not mean the statement to sound critical, but by the twitch of Captain Dessheyi's eyes, the fellow had taken it that way.

"Setting a perimeter in this region is not like building a fence to corral your sheep in an upland valley, Captain, where all you have to do is collect rocks and stack them in a circle. This cursed delta runs ten or twelve mey in length from the river's main branching at Skerru south to the bay, and it's almost as wide. If you know how to stretch ten cohorts to fence in that much territory when we also have to patrol the restless countryside and outfit enough boats to oversee traffic in the bay, I'd be pleased to hear your suggestions."

The others—some of whom he recognized from the attack on High Haldia and some he'd never seen before—looked over to see how Arras would respond.

He wasn't daunted. "How do the Nessumara folk themselves patrol their territory? Given that they're famous in the Hundred as traders and merchants, always after a deal, known to be as rich as Sarrelya, they must have lines of communication we can exploit."

"They do, indeed," said Dessheyi with the sort of condescending smile Arras distrusted in any man. "That's why our commanders have already sealed bargains with certain clans in Nessumara who will deliver the city into our hands in the same manner we took Toskala. As we did here in Ankeno." He indicated the deserted streets of the port town.

"They'll betray their own, in return for personal gain and clan power." Arras nodded, although the prospect wearied him. "Seems cowardly to me, and it's a sad day when no fighting is involved, but it's certainly easier on the troops than a full-out battle. My soldiers took heavy casualties on the High Haldia campaign."

"As you mentioned before," replied Dessheyi. "But there's fighting yet to be had. Olo'osson certainly has shown they mean to resist."

"I'll look forward to marching to Olossi, then."

"I am sure you will, but not today. Today, we're considering how we will defend Nessumara after our allies deliver the city to us."

"If there are any left who will dare oppose Lord Commander Radas," remarked Arras, wondering if the rest were as mutely passive as they looked. A person who feared that every least word might get him bitten could no more command in battle than he could train a belligerent dog.

Captain Dessheyi nodded, as much answer as Arras was going to get, and resumed his speech. "The western channel of the River Istri can't be forded. It's simply too powerful. There is only one bridge—a rope and plank bridge—that spans it, at Halting Reach. It's been reeled in by the defenders. So, once we take control of Nessumara, we'll have no trouble maintaining the western perimeter."

It was a brilliantly clear day, no haze off the water at all and no clouds in the sky. The vast bay lay tranquil, more green than blue except where streaks of muddy-colored water flowed out from the delta's hidden channels. Ships and boats plied the waters, but he couldn't be sure if they were fisher folk about their usual toil or refugees fleeing Nessumara. He was pretty sure the army did not have a fleet of ships to patrol the Bay of Istria, but he supposed they would soon commandeer boats and crews.

"That leaves us with two areas to defend once the city is in our hands: the network of canals across the inner delta, and the two causeways that bridge the mires."

Shifting into a patch of shade, Arras found himself looking downslope through a gap between houses to a lower courtyard, evidently the square training yard of one of Kotaru's temples. About ten people, stripped naked, kneeled with heads bowed and arms lashed behind their backs as guardsmen stood at attention. There was something utterly humiliating in the way the prisoners were being forced to wait with bodies fully exposed; no matter how little clothing folk wore in the hottest weather, a kilt or cotton taloos gave a man or woman dignity. It was too brutal to watch folk so deliberately demeaned. He raised his gaze.

Captain Dessheyi was oblivious of the scene unfolding out of his sight. "There are few places in the Hundred as well defended by natural obstacles alone. There's certainly no city as important to hold if we mean to rule the Hundred."

It was difficult to tell if the shoreline Arras was looking at was islands or mainland, swamp or dry ground made impenetrable by dense growth. "Where is Nessumara? Isn't the city's port here on the bay, like this town?"

They laughed; he'd as good as stumbled, revealing his ignorance, and he noted their expressions. Not everyone was hostile. Some merely looked relieved that another had voiced a question they needed an answer to.

Captain Dessheyi scratched his chin. "Nessumara lies on islands deep within that delta. Weren't you listening, Captain?"

Arras knew better than to answer the question. He shaded his eyes from the sun as he examined the distant shoreline. It was impossible to identify any distinct rivers emerging from the tangle, whose vivid color reminded him of the skirts of the Wild, the ancient forest in whose depths any trespassers would meet their death at the hands of the mute wildings. Born and raised in the north, he wasn't used to vegetation growing so thick it was like a breathing beast waiting to strangle the unsuspecting. He had a cursed good idea that the folk who lived in the delta knew the wetlands landscape as well as he had known the escarpments and ravines of the uplands where he'd grown up. He spotted three eagles soaring overhead.

"Even if the city is betrayed from within, what's to stop a local resistance from taking refuge within the swamp?" he asked. "Striking at will? Aided and abetted by the reeves?"

Captain Dessheyi smiled as a wolf bares its teeth. "A good question, Captain Arras. I'm assigning your companies to explore the land around the eastern causeway and probe the barriers raised there while we await the signal to advance. I'll expect a thorough report."

The other men chuckled, relieved to have another man bear the brunt of Dessheyi's ill humor. As the captain went on to discuss assignments for foraging expeditions, Arras again glanced down into the Thunderer's courtyard.

A woman stood in front of the row of cowering prisoners. A cloak of night enveloped her, and she was lecturing as a teacher might, brandishing a writing brush. Each time its tip touched paper, one of the sobbing prisoners collapsed like a puppet whose strings have been cut; like a body whose spirit has been severed from the flesh.

Arras recoiled a step, shuddering as terror stabbed deep: *So she could have done to me, that evening by the fire.*

Where Guardians walked, people must obey. There was no other choice.

12

AT ARGENT HALL they told Joss that Captain Anji had last been seen at Storos-on-the-Water, where a training camp had been set up. At Storos-on-the-Water they told him Anji had ridden back to Olossi, to his main encampment, and here Joss and Scar flew. It was difficult for Joss to make sense of all the new building around Olossi, especially since the lower town had been so badly damaged in last year's battle. More walls were going up beyond the inner city, like the rings of an onion, and beyond the reconstructed Crow's Gate there was yet a new walled neighborhood, men and women raising walls and gates. Farther afield, West Track was spanned by staggered checkpoints out to the limit of Joss's vision.

Two mey from the city, fields formerly used as pasture had been walled off and divided into quarters like one of Kotaru's enclosures, two lined with neat rows of tents for barracks and storehouses and two wide-open fields for training. Joss circled as men paced through drills below. Dust puffed under their feet. Their enthusiastic shouts filled the air. They were two cohorts at least, and he spotted a third cohort riding a mey away to the south along the skirts of the Lend, on some kind of training race. How had Anji gotten so many horses? A watchtower sentry flagged him, and he pulled an answering flag and sent Scar down.

A sergeant—the Qin called them "chiefs"—came out to greet him respectfully, a sober man whose name he could not recall. "Captain Anji went to fetch the mistress out in the Barrens. A full turn of the moon has passed since the birth. He can safely greet the baby, make sure it's healthy, not tainted by demons."

Joss blinked. "Newborn babies can be tainted by demons?"

"Hu! Surely you Hundred folk know that, Marshal! Demons leave a particular kind of blemish, sickliness, deformities. Don't you rid yourselves of demons?"

"Rid ourselves?"

"Kill them. They're a danger to the tribe."

The word did not at first register; then Joss lifted a hand in a warding gesture, surprised to find himself trembling. *Kill?* "I should have been present, for I stand as uncle to the child. Best I go quickly."

If not too late.

He flew to the Barrens, but in the settlement now being called Astafero, he learned that the captain's party had taken ship. It was not until his questioning elicited a great deal of commentary about the darling baby and how the captain had carried the child his very own self onto the boat that the edge of anxiety softened. Weariness hammered him; he staggered to Naya Hall and commandeered a cot in the darkest corner of a tent barracks. Of course Anji would have done no such horrible thing. Nor would Mai ever have allowed it!

How long he slept he did not know, but he was roused by Siras sticking his head past the curtain slung up to give privacy.

"Greetings of the day, Marshal. I mean, I should say, *Commander*. A bold and bright Wakened Wolf it is, even if you look more like a resting-day festival cake the worse for being nibbled raw by hungry mice."

Joss rubbed sandy eyes. "What in the hells are you doing here, Siras? You don't even have an eagle." The young man grinned so wide that Joss blinked, thinking there was too much light in this dim corner. "She came back, did she?"

"While you were flown north to Clan Hall, Commander. They sent me here to Naya Hall to get a bit of retraining, me not having been in harness for over a year."

Joss sat up, blankets twisting around his torso. He'd had the sense to strip before falling onto the cot, although he had no clear memory of having done so. His clothes were, as usual, scattered every which way on the ground. "Aui! My mouth is like a swamp. How early is it?"

"Midday. You slept an entire night and half the day. There's a dram of cordial waiting for you in the mess tent along with porridge, if you want it."

"Aren't you on duty?"

"Arda assigned me to you."

"Seeing as you know how to handle me."

Siras's grin popped again. "Something like that. Let me shake out your clothes, Commander. There are scorpions around here. No one leaves their gear on the ground." He tossed him a clean kilt. "There's a trough out back, if you want to wash."

Joss wrapped the kilt and found his way to a roofless enclosure where a trough was filled with clean water. The enclosure was rigged with canvas for a modicum of privacy. He dipped in a bucket and dumped its contents over his head. The cold braced him for a second round. This time, as the water gushed down his bare chest, from behind came a burst of giggling. He spun to discover four women of varying ages peering in where there was a gap in the canvas walls. Two wore reeve leathers, and the other two—the hells!—there were four others, each carrying a basket or buckets.

Cursed if the oldest didn't start singing a famous line from the tale of the Reckless Farmer—*she could not help but admire his plough so straight and strong*—and one of the reeves, because unencumbered, sketched the accompanying gestures with her hands, nothing fancy in her execution but everyone knew them and, truly, the entire song was so obscene . . .

"Heya! No loitering!" The reeves and hirelings scurried away, chortling and singing snatches of song. He was scorched he was blushing so hard as that gods-rotted trainer Arda sauntered up to the gap and looked in.

She rolled her eyes. "I should have known it would be you."

"The hells, Arda!"

She laughed as he checked to make sure that the kilt, now damp and clinging to his hips, thighs, and groin, had not slipped. "Don't pretend you don't enjoy it. So. You've become acting commander of Clan Hall. If you can bear to get dressed, Kesta's here. She brought a Qin soldier found at Copper Hall. You know anything about a Qin scout gotten all the way to Nessumara?"

"That'll be Tohon." His embarrassment sloughed off as quickly as the desert air sucked away the moisture on his skin. "That's unexpectedly good news."

Siras appeared with his clothes, and he dressed and met Kesta and Tohon in the mess hall. The reeve and the scout were talking like old comrades as they measured cups of cordial.

"Careful, Tohon," he said as he came up. "Kesta can outdrink every reeve I know."

The scout rose to greet him in the Qin manner, forearm clapped to forearm, like two rams bashing.

"Ouch," said Kesta.

Joss winced and sat, rubbing his arm, as Tohon grinned. Siras set down a tray laden with cordial and porridge and slid in beside Joss, staring wide-eyed at the Qin scout.

"So they found you, eh?" Joss asked.

"So they did," said Tohon with a friendly nod at Kesta. "Picked me up at Copper Hall. Hu! That was a thing to see, I'll tell you, the way that river got so wide and then split into so many tiny channels. I've never seen—what is it you call it?"

"Ocean," said Kesta.

"Plains of water. What a sight! Then we flew a few circuits around the delta, to observe the army's positions. I'd say they mean to attack along the two causeways. Not sure that's wise, myself. Good archers—or reeves from the air—could pick them off as they march."

"What of the others who were with you, Tohon?"

Kesta replied. "We were able to strike a deal with that gods-rotted festering old Silver to place the other people from Tohon's party and the children they'd rescued on one of his vessels, sailing for Zosteria." Her glare resembled that of an eagle. "It's a cursed dangerous thing for reeves to be owing favors like that. Not just to a Silver. To anyone."

"Does he want something besides coin?"

"He wants a lass from Olossi," Kesta said sourly. "I'm supposed to haul her to Nessumara."

"I wasn't consulted about this!"

"Copper Hall agreed. Then told me to do it, since I was flying down here anyway. Can we refuse?"

"Eiya! I suppose we're committed now. What the Ri Amarah do is no business of ours, and he did help us get Tohon's party out of the reach of the army."

"Where does the Star of Life army come from?" asked Tohon.

"Walshow," said Kesta.

Joss shook his head. "I think it started in Iliyat with Lord Radas, who expanded his influence north into Herelia first and then expanded into Teriayne and the highlands and set up a major base in Walshow. You don't know this, Tohon, but the region of Herelia has been closed to us reeves for twenty years. We no longer know what goes on there. It's all of a piece, isn't it?" He shook his head as that troublesome pain began its familiar throb in his temples. "Bit by bit Radas has been placing his traps, eating the land, and surrounding us. And us never noticing because it came on so slow. What fools we've been!"

His voice had raised, but only a pair of hirelings loitering at the big tent's entrance turned to look as he grabbed his cup and downed the cordial in a gulp.

"It's strong," warned Kesta.

As the taste stung in his throat, he started to hack. "Too . . . late!"

"Best you eat some porridge, Commander," said Siras. Cursed if the lad didn't sound like an old auntie cajoling a stubborn child.

Tohon regarded Joss steadily. The Qin scout was perhaps ten years older than Joss, and his years had weathered him more. "I'd like to reach Captain Anji, Commander, and so would you, I wager. He's gone by ship for Olossi."

"I need to meet with Arda and the senior reeves, and then I'll fly you over the water. We'll wait for the captain in Olossi."

"That would suit me."

"It would suit me as well, for Scar will need a hunt and a rest."

"Joss," said Kesta, "I want to see that Arkest gets released for a hunt. Do you need me?"

"No. I'll fill you in on the rest when we are back at Clan Hall."

She left.

Joss set into the porridge, so hungry he thought he would faint if he did not eat, and his head was swimming from the effects of the cordial. "Siras, find Arda and the senior reeves."

"Yes, Commander!" The young man chased away the hirelings who had lingered by the entrance to stare.

This time of day, it was warm under the canvas even though the changing season brought a cooler tinge to the air. Tohon calmly ate his nai porridge as Joss dug into a second bowl. Hitting bottom, he sat back.

"Tohon, is it true the Qin kill any newborn babies among them who are tainted by demons?"

"Hu! A strange question to ask."

"I beg your pardon. Perhaps I'm being rude."

"It is something we don't commonly speak of, that's true, although it's known to all. Demons are dangerous creatures. Still, my youngest son never rode as a soldier for having a twisted foot that he was born with. The elders of our clan said at his birth that he was demon-tainted. We ought to have killed him, but he was such a beautiful child, quite the most beautiful of any born to my wife and me. She loved him for that twisted foot, because she knew it meant he would have to stay close by her. Not that he can't ride as well as anyone, it's just walking that he'll always do with a limp. In the end we lost one boy to the wars and another rides in the east with the army still, so it's hard to say if he'll live or die, if he'll ever marry and sire children. And our daughter, of course, her we lost to the water spirits and my poor wife of grief soon after. So I'm not sorry for having taken the risk of sparing the other one."

Abruptly he looked up at Joss, his gaze steady. "You saw Zubaidit, Kesta says, but what about Shai?"

Joss shrugged. "She said he walked with her into the army's encampment. That's all I know."

Like most of the Qin, Tohon was not a demonstrative man. He merely nodded, but Joss suspected deeper currents ran beneath.

Arda walked briskly into the mess tent, followed by Miyara, the reeve who, with Joss, had witnessed the birth of Mai's child.

He greeted both women, then turned to Miyara. "The baby got off safely?"

"Atani?" Her smile lit her face. "A sweet child, very small, mind you, but healthy. He was feted with a feast and songs, very proper, although done in the Qin manner. I don't mind saying that they eat terribly strange food." She glanced at Tohon. "Begging your pardon, ver. Just not what we are accustomed to."

Tohon had a genial smile. "Hard to offend me, verea. Food is food, different in different lands. As long as I'm not hungry, I'm content."

Both the women studied him with that look women got, Joss had observed, when a man surprised them in a way that pleased them. It was different from an admiring stare for good looks or an attractive body.

An older male reeve hurried in, puffing as though he'd been running. "Heya, Arda! I got the flag. Marshal Joss!"

"Etad. Greetings of the day to you. Please sit down."

"I will. You're back from the north. What news?"

Siras entered with more cups and a pitcher of cordial. After he'd poured around, Joss leaned forward on his elbows. "I've agreed to stand as commander over Clan Hall until the emergency has passed—"

"Or we're all dead," said Arda with a snort.

"Or we're all dead," agreed Joss, "or some other calamity befalls us. In any case, I'm asking you three as representatives of Naya Hall if you'll accept Verena as acting marshal of Argent Hall for now, and with you, Arda, and Miyara and Etad to stand for Naya Hall as a daughter hall to Argent Hall."

"That goes against tradition," said Miyara, "although in the tales—"

"Yes," said Joss, "we already discussed appointing an ordinand or a hieros."

Miyara chuckled. "There's some appeal in the latter. Yet in days like this, with that which ought to face upward facing downward, maybe a fawkner as marshal is not such a bad thing."

Etad nodded. "Rena stuck it out through the months we suffered under Yordenas. She never truckled to him or his lackeys. Yet neither did she beat herself bloody trying to go against them when it would have done no good."

Joss knew Arda cursed well because of all the years they'd served together at Clan Hall. He could see a grin forming on her face.

"And also—" she began, "—since your mention of a hieros naturally brought devouring to mind—"

"Don't say it!"

She laughed and did not say one word about who had tumbled whom and what had transpired after. He plunged into a discussion of how soon the Naya Hall reeves should start being sent out on patrol with more experienced reeves, and how else they might be used to free up experienced reeves for more difficult tasks, and how Clan Hall was going to attempt to create larger units for coordinated ventures.

"Reeves were never meant to be soldiers," said Joss, "nor is it anything I wish for, but we can't exactly ask that army's leave to come stand for judgment at our assizes. Nor can we stand aside and do nothing."

They were thoughtful. They had good ideas, and they laid them out sensibly. They understood how bad things were in the north, and how what was bad would overflow to flood them. He was relieved when they had said all there was to say for the moment. He and Tohon went to the parade ground and he whistled down Scar and got him harnessed while the Qin soldier watched. Joss was restless; he needed to do something, to do more.

Zubaidit had walked into danger just as Marit had that day more than twenty years ago when she'd been killed by outlaws. It was the Hieros and Captain Anji who had loosed Bai on this impossible mission to kill Lord Radas. Aui! She'd gone gladly enough. She wasn't his to fret over. Even so, he could not stop thinking of how sweet she was to hold in his arms. Yet when he remembered kissing her, he fell also into erratic flashes of memory of nights fireside with Marit, only a blanket between them and the earth. Had he really been so young once? Such a cursed innocent fool? Would he ever stop dreaming of her, seeing her trapped in the body she'd worn then, the body and spirit he had loved in a way he could never hope to find again?

Scar chirped interrogatively, catching his mood. Joss tugged on the last hook and buckle and stepped out to join Tohon.

"You're brooding," said the scout.

"So I am. I like to be aloft."

"Hard to stand and watch," agreed Tohon. "A man gets used to riding on at the break of day. Comes to think that movement and noise is where life is, when after all there's life in stillness and quiet, too."

"Wise words, my friend. Listen. We'll have a pair of days to wait, and I am sure you will want to report immediately to whichever chief commands the militia camp, but if you don't have to go there straightaway I might as well let you know I'm thinking of taking a turn out to the temple of the Merciless One first."

Tohon grinned. "Don't mind if I do. No hurry for me. I don't belong to the captain's regular troop."

"You don't?"

"No. I was transferred over to Captain Anji's command in the Mariha princedoms. Before that, I served Commander Beje."

"Ah." There was a useful piece of information, all unwittingly spilled. But after all, did a man as canny as Tohon ever reveal anything he did not mean to? Hard to know.

"Need we bring gifts or fripperies or coin to the temple?" Tohon continued.

"Neh. It's shameful to offer coin for what's freely given."

"Then how do they live, there in the temple?"

"Folk offer tithes to all the temples. Every young person who has celebrated the feast of their Youth's Crown serves a year as apprentice in one temple or another, and their family pays a tithe to feed and clothe them. A few serve longer, in the manner of debt slaves. A very few serve their entire lives."

"Like Zubaidit," observed Tohon.

"Why do you say so?" asked Joss sharply. "Her contract was bought out."

Tohon stroked the straggle of hairs that served him as a beard. "That part of the contract paid for in coin. But surely it's easier to count sheep on a distant hill grown dense with snowflower bushes than to measure the extent of a person's service to a god." His gaze was easy but his understanding keen. "She's already taken, my friend."

Joss flushed. "I didn't say—"

Tohon chuckled. "Not in words. But I can judge the lay of the land pretty well."

Joss scratched behind an ear, a nervous habit he thought he'd lost as a child. "You traveled with her a fair way. Did she ever—ah—" The hells! He sounded like a love-struck youth! Wheedling after any mention of the object of desire. And her almost young enough to be his own daughter had he married and begotten a child by the age of twenty, as most folk did. As Tohon no doubt had done.

"It's true we talked about many things and many people. She's a cursed interesting woman to talk to. But she never once mentioned you."

"I'm put in my place."

"Maybe. But I thought it strange."

"You thought what strange?"

"That she never once mentioned you, for you're an important man whose acts all of Olossi has reason to be grateful for. It either means she never thought of you at all, or that she thought of you enough to deliberately not speak of you."

*   *   *

AFTER THREE DAYS slogging in the mire—he lost two men to sand traps and one to snakebite—Arras pulled his men back to the main encampment at Saltow and left them to clean their filthy gear while he and Sergeant Giyara, in all their mud, reported to Commander Hetti.

"We probed as well as we could." He stood in the sun, because he dared not smear with mud the commander's fancy rug. "Barriers have been erected on the eastern causeway in four spots."

"That won't be a problem." Hetti lounged on a field couch under an awning. "The question before us is how are we to defend the perimeter once the city is ours? How impenetrable are the wetlands?"

"We didn't penetrate to the worst areas. Where you think there's firm ground there's a sucking mire, and where it looks unstable might well be the only safe path. I lost three men, in a cautious foray against no resistance. We have no local cooperators, but we'll need guides to be effective. Or we'll need to kill any locals who do not cooperate with us, so they can't use their knowledge against us. Still, it could be impossible to track them if they retreat into the swamps."

"Dirty, too." The commander was a stout man no longer in fighting trim. He had a bottle of wine on hand and no cups, nor did he offer drink to Arras or the sergeant. His attendants were sour-looking men content with their idleness. There were a pair of painted women, too, of the kind who trade sex for jewels and coin. "We'll take command of the locals in the same way we took command of Toskala. Assign hostages to every company. That'll keep the rest in order."

"Toskalan hostages?" Arras glanced around the bustling camp, with folk he had thought were camp followers or hirelings hard at work: cleaning harness, husking rice, pounding nai, braiding rope, hauling water and wood; the endless round of tasks necessary to keeping a soldier ready to move.

"You were assigned none?"

"We were not. We do everything ourselves."

"Ah. Your companies reached Toskala late. You've what—? Three hundred men?"

"Three companies, Commander. We're slightly understrength, having only three hundred and nineteen. I could absorb new recruits."

"I've only myself to offer as a swordsman," said the commander with a genial laugh as his gaze flashed to the young women, who pretended to smile. No doubt Commander Hetti had fallen prey to the aging man's need to see himself as a youthful contender in the other ancient art of swordcraft.

"Have you made any attempts to recruit dissatisfied locals, Commander?"

"Eiya! We've enough trouble with them scuttling in at night and stealing our chickens!"

"Have you? We've recorded no such depredations in our encampment."

"I suspect those cursed Toskalan hostages are turning a blind eye to the pilfering or even helping it along, if you take my meaning. We haven't been able to catch them at it, nor will they squeal on each other. They're a gods-rotted sullen lot."

Since Arras could think of no reason why a hostage ought to be cheerful, he said nothing. Sergeant Giyara scratched at a welted hand, where in the mire a clinging vine had scraped its barbed tendrils over her skin. He flicked a glance skyward: as always, an eagle floated very high up, keeping an eye on the camp and their movements. Only dusk drove the reeves down to their halls.

"I'll have my clerk assign a cadre of hostages to your command," Commander Hetti went on. "See they're not killed. If they're dead, they're no use to us, eh?" The commander laughed at his own joke, and his attendants and the two young women laughed with him.

"I have a more extensive report to give, Commander. And maps we've drawn of the land we reconnoitered. Some thoughts—"

"I'll send a sergeant to take your report. Meanwhile, take two days' rest for refitting. Expect to move out at dawn on Wakened Ox."

"Isn't Wakened Ox the same day the gates were opened in Toskala, last month?"

"Good fortune, don't you think? Lord Radas likes that day. Meanwhile, keep your eyes open for outlanders and gods-touched, as before."

"Why this interest in outlanders and gods-touched?"

"Cursed if I know or am likely to ask. If you find any, even slaves, bring them immediately to me. Also, I'm looking for a cadre of volunteers—"

A shriek lit the air like fire. Shouting rose from one corner of camp, and men rushed to see what was happening.

Commander Hetti fluttered his hands in the direction of his attendants. "It's those cursed thieves again, I'm sure of it. Go see—" His words were drowned out by a larger outbreak of noise, a real brawl breaking out.

Arras had no desire to have any of his men volunteered for whatever task Commander Hetti had in mind, so he cocked an eye at Giyara, and she nodded.

"At once, Commander!" he said, loudly enough for the words to penetrate. He and the sergeant moved off. It seemed half the soldiers were running in that direction, maybe bored from having sat in camp for too long awaiting the knife in the dark whose blade would open Nessumara for them. Now he heard voices shouting wagers, and encouragement.

"Ten vey on the fat one!"

"Eiya! Don't give up, you wine-sodden wretch! Keep pushing!"

"Think they're betting on a fist fight?" Giyara muttered, with the twisted grin she used when she found any situation darkly amusing.

He pushed through the crowd, men giving way when they saw the lime-whitened horsetail epaulets marking his rank. A circle had formed around open space where two men, one beginning to spread into corpulence and one trimmer but clearly drunk, were grappling, locked in a swaying attempt to topple the other man. There was a woman, *of course*, egging them on in the way of the vain woman who likes to see men fight over her. She was tall and lean and not the handsomest female he'd ever seen. . . .

Then she moved, dropping into a crouch to look not at the fight but at something going on lower to the ground. He marked the supple way her body flowed, her complete command of her limbs. Whew! There was a woman worth grappling with.

He nudged Giyara and with a flick of his chin got her looking in the same direction; she caught his intention at once.

"Trained fighter, but not my type. I can see she might be yours, though. She's not outfitted as a soldier."

"Hostage? Hireling?"

"Spy?"

He pushed Giyara into the second rank of the crowd so he could watch without being spied. There the woman went, shifting backward until he lost sight of her.

He tapped the sergeant's arm. "You stay here."

He circled around until he saw, in the gloom, the ranks of wagons piled with poultry cages, all the birds asquawk as if a fox had come raiding. It was easy to miss the noise beneath the roar of the agitated crowd; easy to ignore a pair of dark shapes lifting a pair of cages from the rearmost wagon.

He strolled up. "You've got permission to secure those, eh?"

One of the figures—a thin youth clad in nothing more than a kilt—shrank back, but *she* turned to confront him as bold as you please, having set the two cages on the ground at her feet.

"Who are you to ask?" Her voice was low and assured.

He grinned. "I'm called Captain Arras. You're not a soldier."

"I'm not."

"A spy, perhaps?" He set a hand on his sword hilt.

She rubbed her chin, head cocked to one side. "It's sure I'd admit it if I were."

"Heh. I'd say you were one of the hostages out of Toskala, but you don't talk like them."

"I don't, it's true. Not that it's any of your business, but I was married into one of the mat-making clans in Toskala. I'm from the south. I guess the army thought my husband would miss me if they hauled me away."

"Do you miss your husband?"

She spoke with the posture of her body, playing to his obvious interest. "He's young and energetic. I have no complaints of how he's treated me since we were wed."

"But some complaints of the army, I take it. Why are you stealing chickens?"

"Do you suppose our masters feed us properly?"

"You could get whipped for stealing."

"So I could, but I don't like to see my comrades suffering."

"You're young to take on so much responsibility, knowing you'll take the brunt of the punishment. Where'd you serve your apprentice year?"

"Where do you think?"

He laughed, lifting his chin to make the question a command. "What's your name?"

"Zubaidit."

"Tell you what, Zubaidit. You collect a cadre of hostages, hard workers and decent folk, and bring them along to my company. I'll see you and your people are decently fed and cared for as long as you do your work and cause me and my soldiers no trouble."

"That's a generous offer, of its kind. What will you ask for in return?"

"It's true I like a good workout at the Devourer's temple, same as any person, but I'm not one of those who uses the power he has to coerce folk into sex. I like that you're not afraid to talk to me, although I've caught you in the act of stealing, for which I could certainly see you and the lad whipped had I a mind to it. Or force you into my bed to spare you the welts."

"So you'll pull me along to work for your company and hope to persuade me by other means? I've a husband, as I've mentioned."

"Many a woman has a husband, and many a man a wife, and the tales repeat what observation tells us: that the Devourer acts as she wills, and folk will find pleasure as they are driven by her will acting within them. What's your point? If you're worried you might conceive a child for his clan not of his breeding, then there are ways to make sure no child is sown in fertile ground. As every hierodule in the Devourer's temple knows."

"You've made your plan of attack plain!" She laughed, and he wasn't quite sure whether she found him attractive or ridiculous, but anyway she wasn't recoiling. "How do you know I'm fashioned that way?"

"I know how you're fashioned."

Behind them, the fight was breaking up. She set a fist on one hip, the angle emphasizing her shapely torso, the fit of her sleeveless vest, the curve of her hip over loose trousers belted up so the hem lapped just above her ankles. She knew he knew. It was just the first skirmish in a longer battle.

"Put those chickens back," he added, "and I'll speak with the captain you're assigned to right now."

She gestured, and the youth set the cages back on the wagon. Out of the darkening night, a pair of soldiers strolled up on camp duty.

"Got a problem here, Captain? The hostages are forbidden from congregating around the supply wagons. They're all gods-rotted thieves."

"There's no problem," said Arras.

After looking over the young woman and her mute companion, the soldiers walked on up the line of wagons.

She gestured after them. "So we are at your command, Captain Arras."

"There's one thing," he added, stepping up close enough to let his muscle speak. "Don't ever mock me."

She didn't shift at all. "I don't mock, Captain. I'll tell you straight to your face what I think of you."

He liked a dangerous, confident woman who wasn't afraid of him, and he was cursed curious about so young a woman married into a humble mat-making clan, come so far from her own people's home. What gave some folk that sense of confidence? Discipline. Training. And a more intangible quality, gifted to them from the gods.

Later, after he'd detached twenty-six hostages of her choosing from the cohort to which they'd been assigned, he went to speak to the quartermaster in charge of the provisions wagons. It was well into night by this time, but the quartermaster was still awake, supervising six clerks working by lamplight as they administered the flow of provisions and supplies into companies refitting in preparation for the fall of Nessumara in four days.

"How can I help you, Captain?" the woman asked, looking him up and down to let him know she found him attractive. She was full-figured, about his age, competent and confident, but although he appreciated her interest, he could only think about Zubaidit. Aui! Where's there an itch, you must scratch. He could not tell if, like Nessumara, Zubaidit had already fallen and was just holding out for a few more days to prepare the ground properly, or if he'd have to endure a longer campaign.

"Captain?"

"A favor, if you will. You've records for the poultry wagons?"

"I do." Clearly, she was the kind who kept accurate records. "I've taken my day count earlier. I do another count at dawn, and then allocate birds according to those companies that have reached their week's turn for a meat ration. I can't change your company's ration, if that's what you're after."

"I'm just curious. Any chance you could do another count?"

"Now?"

"Now."

Sure enough, the count came up one cage short, a cage pilfered from the middle wagons, well away from the rear of the line where he'd been kept busy. Thoughtful, he strolled back to camp under a cloudless sky, swatting away the bugs, whistling under his breath. The stars shone like jewels cast across the heavens, as it said in the tale. He carried a lamp to guide his feet. One did need a lamp. It was so easy to stumble.

He grinned.

He had soldiers to drill, to make ready for Wakened Ox, because they would need rigid discipline even if all went smoothly, as such things rarely did. That first, then. He was a patient man. After the fall of Nessumara, he would have plenty of time to unravel the mystery of his hostage. One task at a time.

A whisper of wind stirred the air as a shadow passed over him. A horse, wings spread so wide they blotted out a length of sky, galloped low, dropping to earth. The cloak of the rider billowed behind, and Arras ducked without meaning to, feeling as if the sweep of that rider's eyes was a spear-thrust that caught him in the back. Fear ripped away the strength of his legs, and he dropped to his knees, panting.

How angry would Lord Twilight be when he returned to discover that Night had captured the outlander Arras had been tasked to protect? What if Lord Radas questioned him and chose to punish him for disobedience, even though he'd only been obeying Twilight's orders? How was an ordinary man to balance walking this edge, when it was not even his choice to do so?

He picked himself up, wiped off his knees. The day of Wakened Ox could not dawn soon enough. After Nessumara fell, he would ask to be sent forward with his cohort into the next assault of the campaign. Battle was a cursed sight simpler to deal with than Guardians.

13

SOMEHOW, JOSS COULD not be rid of folk speaking of Zubaidit. Late that afternoon he reclined on pillows in the pavilion of Ushara's temple as the Hieros poured rice wine into cups and with her own hands offered one to Joss and one to Tohon. The old woman and the two men sat alone under a roof wreathed with harvest flowers from jabi bushes. The scent was overwhelmed by the tart aroma of tsi berries being cooked down as they were every year in this season. A pair of older women—like Captain Anji's personal guards—hovered within sight but out of earshot, and there was a lad lurking in the bushes.

"Strange," the Hieros was saying, indicating two ginny lizards who had crawled up onto the pavilion floor and were sizing up Joss with mouths gapped to show teeth. "I'm not sure they like you, Commander."

"Aren't those the pair that traveled with Zubaidit?" asked Tohon.

The old woman terrified Joss, but the smile she turned on Tohon would have melted a block of ice. She'd been stunning in her youth, no doubt of it, and was still handsome in the way of women who have kept their vigor along with fine bone structure.

"So they are. Most folk can't tell the difference, but ginnies are as unlike as any one person is from the next. What news of my hierodule, Tohon?"

The scout packed information into a comprehensive review of all he had said and done and seen. "If you don't mind my asking, Holy One," he finished, "do you think we can buy horses from the lendings? They had good breeding stock."

"It would be difficult. They never come out of the Lend, and we do not enter for fear of falling afoul of their boundaries. I'm surprised you made it out."

"The lendings took *our* horses," said Tohon with a laugh.

The Hieros sipped thoughtfully. She was so different a person seen in this light that Joss was amazed. Like this particular rice wine, she had a pleasing disposition, slightly sweet and markedly elegant. "If you are serious, you'd best inquire at Atiratu's temple. The mendicants sworn to the Lady of Beasts journey out that way seeking various medicinal plants that grow only in the Lend. They know how to make an arrangement with the tribes."

"What of Zubaidit?" asked Joss impatiently as the conversation wandered away from the subject that interested him most. "Can she and Shai possibly succeed?"

"She will do as she must," said the Hieros coolly, unmoved by his passionate words. "As you did, in agreeing to stand as commander over the reeve halls, a position I believe you did not seek nor are eager to assume."

"True-spoken."

"Yet you will do as you must. So tell me, are you come today to embrace the Merciless One?"

The hells! Was she trying to get him out of the way? "I'm feeling restless, it's true." Tohon smiled sweetly at him.

Joss laughed, half shocked to realize the two of them were clearly intending to sleep together.

The Hieros gestured, and the lad dashed out from under cover of the dense vegetation. "Take the commander to the Heart Garden," she said to the boy.

Joss went obediently, while Tohon remained behind.

"I remember you," said the lad. "I've never seen Bai go after a man the way she did you."

"What's your name? Have we met?"

He had a sly grin, a real troublemaker. "I'm called Kass." But his expression drew taut as he sighed. "Will we ever see her again?"

Joss didn't know whether he braced himself or the youth with the pointlessly optimistic words that emerged from his lips. "If anyone can succeed, she can."

They crossed through white gates into the Heart Garden, where men and women were seated on benches among the flowers. Here folk would linger before being called to enter the gates, but Kass led him straight to the gold gate and tugged on a rope that jangled a bell on the other side. The inner door within the double gates opened, and a young man who might have seen twenty years peered out. Joss smiled at him as the kalos sized him up appreciatively.

"Come in." The kalos flicked a hand to shoo Kass away. "I'll see if there are any women wandering free who might find you of interest, not that I can see why they wouldn't. You have any brothers?"

"As it happens, I don't. I was the only boy among more sisters and female cousins than I could count."

The kalos laughed as he beckoned Joss under the threshold and latched the door behind them. They walked into the outer precincts of the inner garden, an open area paved with flagstones and moss and ringed with trees, bushes, and carefully constructed screens that concealed the greater part of the garden. To the right, a roof topped a bathing pavilion where four men were chatting companionably as they washed themselves while waiting for acolytes to come look them over. Their clothes were draped over benches. Pipes brought water for the rinsing buckets. There was a wooden tub as well, steam rising like breath. Set farther back, half hidden, were a few shelters for private bathing.

"I get the impression you've visited temples aplenty and need no instruction." The kalos walked over to the pavilion and hitched up on a bench near to one man, starting a conversation.

Ushara's temple contained, like desire, an outer facing and an inner fire. To enter the outer court through the gate was to ask permission to worship. If granted, then within the central court you might loiter while you decided whether you truly wanted to approach, and by subtle signs you were shown whether any within would be likely to grant your petition. Only then did you cross under one of the gates—silver for women and gold for men. Past these gates waited hierodules and kalos, who might approach you according to how you were fashioned, if they so pleased. Water cleansed you.

Beyond that, the inner garden lay bathed in equal parts light and darkness, impossible to discern because of many warrens and walls. There rose an undercurrent of noise something like a constant wind in the branches that made his skin prickle with anticipation. As well as private bowers in the grass, there were rooms and closets and attics in the farther buildings. Joss was pretty sure that in his time he had experienced pretty much everything the Merciless One's temples had to offer.

Yet even so, never once had he embraced the Devourer without thinking of Marit.

Aui! Wasn't it Zubaidit he'd just been thinking and talking of? He rubbed his forehead, wondering why he had come.

Two young women fetchingly dressed in taloos appeared with empty buckets resting on their hips. They slowed down as they passed the bathing pavilion and looked the men over; then one saw Joss and nudged the other, and they strolled over while the men under the pavilion made laughing complaints about being abandoned for a newcomer.

They looked him up and down, and they looked at each other and smiled.

Whew!

The splash of water startled him so much he looked away from the tight wrap of their taloos and their cocky grins, the vital young who expect admiration. Over by the bathing pavilion, a woman was pouring water into a bronze tub. She was a woman probably in her thirties, maybe one of those who served a shorter second apprenticeship later in life as an offering, or to break the monotony of their own lives, or to escape a difficult clan for a few months, or just because they'd enjoyed the service in their younger days and wanted to remember what it was like. She might have been dedicated to serve her whole life long. She might even have been a debt slave, although she had no debt mark by her left eye. But she walked nothing like Zubaidit; she looked and acted nothing like Marit; she looked comfortable and lush. From the distance she took her time looking him over as hierodules did, for in the measuring they decided whether they'd any interest. Indeed, the act of measuring was its own provocative delight.

For an instant, it was just like the first time he had entered Ushara's temple: Would she find him attractive?

She laughed, as if she could see right into his thoughts, and with empty bucket in hand she sauntered over. The two young women shook their heads as if scolding him for turning down a bite of sweet cake, but they walked back to the men waiting at the bathing pavilion.

The woman halted before him, bucket hanging from one hand and the other hand set akimbo on the curve of a hip. "You're the best-looking man I've seen this month, mayhap this year, not that you'll not have heard that line before. Do you need some help finding the garden where the young hierodules sit? Like those two." She gestured with her chin.

He took the bucket from her hand as she smiled. "My thanks, verea, but no. I've found what I'm looking for."

"COMMANDER JOSS?"

He hadn't known he was so tired. He woke on a pallet set on the porch in the outer court of the temple, suitable for worshipers too exhausted to make it home in one evening. He had a vague memory of stumbling out here late, the worse for drink but otherwise well satisfied.

He cracked open an eye to see a youthful face looking down on him. "Kesh, right?"

"Kass. There's a boat waiting. Tohon says the captain's ship came in. We can see all the ship traffic off the sea, you know."

The temple had kindly lent Joss a kilt to sleep in. He dressed quickly and slung his kit bag over a shoulder. Dawn had scarcely risen; the captain's ship must have rowed up the channel the instant there was light enough to see. Kass led him to the docks, so furiously not asking questions Joss supposed the lad had plenty of questions he wanted asked.

"How comes it she entrusts you to stand around at all her private councils?" Joss asked as they crunched down the path.

The lad had the wicked grin of a favored child who gets away with plenty of mischief but whose nature hasn't been spoilt to souring. "I'm her great-grandson. Her daughter chose the path of a mendicant. *Her* son—my father—offered at the Witherer's altar and was able to marry into a farming clan. I'm in the middle of eight children, too many to feed. They sent me here when I was five. I'm not a kalos, you know, even though I'm old enough."

"Do you serve the Merciless One?"

"I haven't served my temple year yet. I haven't discovered which god I'm best suited to serve."

Joss laughed. "And to think you've got that hard-hearted old woman keeping you here in luxury while you take your time making up your mind."

The lad sobered as they approached the docks where Tohon waited. Mist rose off the waters. A heron flapped across ripples. In the shipping channel, merchant boats sailed downstream for the sea, oars dipping in the placid water where the current broke into a dozen smaller channels. The River Olo's estuary was but a tiny spray of channels and islets compared with the vast delta in which Nessumara nestled.

"You'll send word of Bai, won't you?" Kass asked in a low voice.

"If I can. The Hieros will hear as soon as anyone."

Tohon greeted him, and they settled into the boat as the oarsmen shoved away from the pier. The oarsmen worked upstream to Dast Olo through a backwater channel. Red-caps flitted among the reeds. A fish's silver back parted the surface. The oarsmen worked in silence, and Tohon seemed content to watch the banks slide past under the early-morning sun.

"Have a good night?" Joss asked finally, rubbing the last of the muzz out of his eyes.

Tohon tugged on an ear as the boat rocked under them and waves slapped the side. He didn't reply.

"Sorry. How'd you hear about Captain Anji arriving?"

"I saw the ship pass at dawn. There's a tongue of land at the point of the island, out behind the buildings. You can see where the river meets the sea."

"They made a quick journey of it."

"The captain has that habit."

A woman knee-deep in mud, pulling a trap out of the shallows, lifted her gaze to watch them go by. She waved gnats away from her face as she stared at the Qin soldier, then shrugged and went back to work. Huts clustered on hummocks and racks of drying fish marked the edge of the village.

In Dast Olo they rented horses for the ride to Olossi. Joss offered the usual deposit to the stablemaster, to be marked and returned at Crow's Gate by one of Sapanasu's clerks.

"Neh." The man waved away the coin, indicating Tohon. "The Qin are honest. If you say the horses will get turned in to my agent at Crow's Gate, it'll be done. I'll tell you, things are changing for the better. Two years ago I'd have had to send a gang of armed men with my stock to Old Fort or Candra Crossing. Now I'm hiring stock up the pass and all the way to Storos-on-the-Water. I sent my own daughter and two hirelings to Old Fort with a wagon and pair on delivery for men hauling oil of naya out of the Barrens. Plenty of guards and checkpoints on the road against mischief. I call that new militia commander good for business, even if he is an outlander."

Joss thanked him. Tohon offered a calm nod, as if he was used to hearing his captain praised for making the roads safe.

"Didn't think you'd know how to ride, being a reeve," Tohon said after they'd paced awhile.

"I served my apprenticeship to Ilu the Herald, riding messages along the North Shore Road. I'm out of practice, though."

Tohon grinned. "What say we race? To that pole." He pointed to a distant vertical line that Joss had to squint to recognize as a pole.

With a challenge like that, it had to be done. Joss lost horribly, but he didn't disgrace himself by falling off. The two men chatted easily about inconsequential things as they made good time the rest of the way to the militia encampment beyond the outer city.

The local militiamen standing guard at the outer gates waved them through. The captain's pennant rippled in a midday breeze. The black cloth was worked with a silver-white stitchery outlining the head of a wolf: a black wolf running in a black night.

Tohon handed the horses over to a groom and instructed him to rub them down, water them, and return them to Crow's Gate. A pair of Qin soldiers greeted the scout as the two men crossed the central drill ground, empty at this hour.

Chief Tuvi stood on a porch that ran all the way around the raised platform, built of planks and covered by a canvas roof, that served as the captain's office. Mai's younger slave sat on the steps staring vacantly at the sky. The chief was chatting with the older slave, who held a baby swaddled in a length of best-quality linen. As Joss and Tohon stepped onto the porch to be greeted by Tuvi, the baby opened its eyes and to Joss's shock fixed a black stare on him as if it recognized him.

"Here is your uncle," said Priya to the infant, although it was obviously too young to understand. "Do you want to hold Atani, Commander?"

News of his new rank had reached here before him. How did Anji get his information? But when he took the baby, the tiny creature was so comfortable in his arm that he forgot all else. What were those faint blue gleams shot through its irises? It had a wise gaze, as newborns did, a remnant of the memories it had left behind the Spirit Gate in its passage into this world. He smiled, hoping to evoke a similar expression, but the dark eyes just sucked him in until, disconcerted, he glanced up.

He stood with his back to the others, who were talking. Priya's voice was smooth in contrast to the rumble of the two soldiers. The inner and outer walls of the captain's office were cloth that could be tied up into any configuration depending on the time of day, the rays of the sun, and the direction of the wind. Though weighted at the hems, the walls fluttered, caught in a stray gust, and for an instant he saw through a series of parting gaps into the innermost chamber where two people stood closely entwined.

Aui!

Certain kisses are not meant to be seen by others. Flushing, he jerked his gaze down to the baby, who had closed his eyes and, apparently, fallen asleep. The child's face was so peaceful that at length Joss's flush faded. He was content to hold the little one as kinfolk were meant to do, providing arms for shelter. Would Anji really have slaughtered a helpless infant? Surely not.

"Commander!" The captain pushed through cloth to emerge onto the porch, looking trim and composed. "Here you are, elevated in rank."

"Yes. I'm an uncle now."

Anji glanced back as the cloth walls parted again. Mai stepped into view while patting her thick black hair, all bound up on her head. Her color was high and her beauty as powerful as sunlight.

Seeing Joss, she smiled as a flower blooms. "Marshal! Ah! I must call you by another title. Commander! Will you have to grow a beard now?" She halted beside him, whatever perfume she wore as heady as the scent of the Hieros's garden. "It suits you, that traveling look, as if you've not had time to pause and tidy yourself."

"Here I've been so careful all these years to keep myself neat." It was cursed impossible not to admire her in her carefully wrapped silk taloos, best quality, the color a somber green that handsomely set off her black hair and dark eyes and dusky, flawless complexion. She had filled out with nursing. He vividly recalled that he'd been present in the cave when she had given birth. The hells! He'd glimpsed her when she was naked.

A becoming flush crept up her cheeks, and she shifted to less volatile ground. "You're very comfortable with Atani."

"He's a lovely boy." He caught Anji watching him. Aui! That narrowed gaze made him cursed uncomfortable.

The captain pointedly looked at Tuvi and raised his chin. Tuvi nodded and clattered away down the porch.

"He sleeps a lot," said Mai, her expression sweetly tender as she examined the precious face. She seemed content to watch Joss hold the baby, and he had to admit it was a pleasant sensation, child and woman both.

"You've brought Tohon, as I hoped," said Anji. "Will you join me to hear his report?"

The words dragged him back to earth. "Of course."

"Mai, Tuvi's gone to bring horses. You and Atani and Priya and Sheyshi can go immediately to the compound. I'll come later."

Tohon pulled on an ear, twisting the tip between thumb and forefinger. Priya retrieved the sleeping infant from Joss.

"Will we see you soon, Commander?" Mai asked as she paused beside Sheyshi on the steps.

"I'll be returning to Toskala as soon as I can."

"Even reeves must eat."

"As my eagle does today, while I am trapped on earth."

She looked at Anji. "Bring Joss with you. It would be a fitting gesture to feast our return to a favored house. Guests bring honor to a feast."

"And the day is Wakened Ox," Joss said with a laugh. "An auspicious day for two born in the Year of the Ox to meet again, neh?"

Her smile was glorious. She glanced skyward. "It's a little late, but there will still be decent pickings at the market."

"A generous offer," said Anji in an odd tone.

She glanced at him, looking surprised, and then at Joss. "I hope we will see you later today."

Priya touched her arm and they went down, followed by Sheyshi.

Joss had to force himself to address the captain rather than Mai's lovely backside. "Don't you worry about the red hounds striking again? Mai returning to Olossi? Going out in the market again?"

"Of course I do." Anji watched her intently as she reached Tuvi, bound the baby tightly in a sling against her back, and mounted, clearly comfortable in the saddle. "But I have put substantial measures in place on the roads and at the gates into Olossi, and additional patrols. There's also now a separate camp outside the walls to house foreign caravan guards and merchants, who for the time being aren't allowed to enter the city. If we control the traffic, then we have some control over what elements move in and out of our lands. The alternative is to let fear shackle us. If you're afraid, don't do it. If you do it, don't be afraid." He drew aside cloth, indicating they should enter. "Tohon? Joss?"

Joss felt the ghost of the baby's weight on his arm. He shut his eyes, but the vision of Mai's passionate embrace of her husband burned there, an intrusion he was very very glad no one had noticed him seeing. Like the child, the moment did not belong to him.

"Out on the Lend I saw the most magnificent horses," Tohon was saying. "Perfect for breeding stock, if we can get some. We need to talk to Atiratu's mendicants."

Shaking himself free of the mire of cursed useless thoughts, Joss followed them in. When they reached the visual privacy of the innermost chamber and its fluttering walls, Tohon delivered a brutally concise description of the desperate situation in Toskala and Nessumara and the regions along the River Istri.

Anji listened with a stillness Joss admired, and nodded when Tohon finished. "If they consolidate power in Haldia and Istria and impress unwilling soldiers into their army, then what chance have we when—and it will be when, not if—they turn their gaze again toward Olo'osson?"

"They won't make the mistake a second time of thinking Olossi an easy target," said Joss.

"No, they won't." Anji walked to his low writing desk and looked down on the paper unrolled there, with lines and hatch marks sketching a map of the Hundred, although it had more blank than detail. Tohon examined it from the opposite side of the desk, arms crossed. "People want to live at peace, undisturbed. They want to raise healthy children to adulthood, eat every day, do their work, attend their festivals. If their gods grant them fortune, they hope to live to see grandchildren and a measure of prosperity. Why should Hundred folk be any different?"

"I don't believe they are," said Joss.

"People in the north surely hate and fear Lord Radas's army. Yet I have seen folk hate and fear the Qin, although you must not imagine the Qin behave in any way like these ones who call themselves the Star of Life. Still, if order is imposed through fear or privation, folk will in the end settle into that order, not wanting to risk more disruption, more fear, more dying."

"What are you saying, Captain?"

Anji grabbed his riding whip off the desk and tapped the map, then traced a line from Olossi to Toskala. "Before such deadly order is imposed and folk become accustomed to its relative peace, we must act. We have to hit them before they become too powerful."

"I agree. But we're badly outnumbered, and they have years of fighting experience and wagonloads of weapons to use against us. This will be a far harder fight even than the battle we waged here in Olossi."

Anji drew his whip through his fingers, his gaze so sharp Joss was startled. "Surely the new commander of the reeve halls will begin by commanding the halls to act in concert against this threat."

Joss raised a hand, as if fending off a challenge. Anji's intensity disconcerted him; it was almost as though Anji was angry at him for something else. "I've already begun to do so. But every hall is autonomous. Clan Hall holds a supervisory position only. So for the other halls to undertake to institute any changes I propose—"

"There's a saying among the Qin. One arrow is easily snapped in half, but bundle many arrows together and they cannot easily be broken."

"I understand that, truly I do." He was momentarily irritated, but an outlander like Anji could not be expected to comprehend the ways of the Hundred, so Joss smiled an easy smile and tried out a more charming, soothing voice. "I'm just telling you that the reeve halls may take some while to come around. People don't like change, especially not when they are settled in their old ways of doing things, and we in the Hundred do love our traditions. We have to be patient and work at them."

Abruptly, the captain relaxed. "Just as some people will flirt the same as they will breathe, having become accustomed to handling people in that manner."

Joss grinned. "I beg your pardon."

It was difficult to tell if Anji was jesting, or if he was serious. "It's your job to persuade them, something at which it is obvious you have plenty of practice. The question is not whether they will change, because they will have to. The question is, will they agree to do so before it is too late?"

14

HOME. HOME. HOME.

Everything was as Mai had left it months ago, dusted and tidied, and alive with voices as hirelings sang and chattered in the gardens and rooms of her utterly wonderful compound in the fabulous city of Olossi. She smiled as she walked into the chamber at the heart of the complex, where she and her husband slept. Priya opened up a tiny cot, and Mai lowered the sleeping infant into its confines. Atani slept and suckled and eliminated, a placid baby, easy to care for despite his too-early birth.

"I want to see the counting rooms!" said Mai. "And the crane room. And the rat screens—my favorite! And the gardens. So lovely! All that green!"

"You are glad to return, Mistress," said Priya with a gentle smile.

Mai laughed, feeling giddy. "After all those months in the Barrens, I should think so. I thought I would be forced to live there forever. Then we had to bide a month trapped in the valley after the baby was born. A beautiful place, to be sure. A perfect setting for a tale, where the handsome bandit hides his treasure, but still—"

Priya's furrowed brow caught Mai short.

"What is it, Priya?" She knelt beside the baby, but his little face remained peaceful and his eyes closed.

"The valley was a merciful place, and well guarded. A safe haven from the red hounds. But creatures live there we do not understand. Like demons, such creatures have their own desires and demands, different from our own. We are fortunate they did not trouble us more than they did."

Mai brushed the baby's black hair. Fearing for herself was one thing, but when she looked at her vulnerable son, a new and horrible realm of terror opened an abyss before her. If anything happened to him, she would—as her long-lost and much-missed sister Ti would have said—*die die die*. "Do you think it was a bad omen when they wrapped themselves around the baby? They were so bright. It's hard to imagine them as malevolent."

"Beautiful things can cause harm as well as dull ones. Yet we had no choice but to take refuge in the valley. The Merciful One watches over the faithful. What you cannot change, let go."

"And what you can change, grasp with both hands, neh?" With a tenuous smile, Mai rose. "Sheyshi?"

Mai had brought three slaves with her across the desert and over the mountains. Her father had sent the big man, O'eki, to watch over her physically. Priya Mai had herself chosen off the auction block in Kartu Town many years ago; over time, she had come to rely on Priya's wisdom and affection more than that of her own mother and aunt.

Sheyshi was a different matter. A Qin general named Commander Beje had warned Anji that Anji's own uncle, who was his mother's brother and also the var—ruler—of the nomadic Qin, had agreed to deliver Anji into the hands of Anji's half brother. That half brother was the newly anointed emperor seated on the Sirniakan throne, and he intended to kill all of his living brothers and half brothers so they could not contest his right to rule. To live, Anji had to die by riding into exile, taking his retainers with him. Yet he wasn't the only one whose life had been saved by their long journey into the Hundred. Sheyshi had served khaif at the meeting between Anji and Beje. Because she had therefore overheard a conversation which could incriminate Beje in the eyes of his var, she was, being a mere slave, expendable. Mai had taken her to save her.

It seemed Sheyshi could scarcely bear to stand more than a stone's throw away from Mai, or Anji, at all anymore, as if she feared what would happen to her if she lost sight of them.

She had been kneeling just outside the door, and at Mai's call she padded in, head bowed. "I am here, Mistress."

"Sit with the baby, Sheyshi."

"Yes, Mistress." She sank down beside the cot, staring after Mai in a possessive way that made Mai uncomfortable.

Away from the chamber, Mai said to Priya, "Do you think we should marry off Sheyshi? Maybe she would like that."

"To a Qin husband? Have any of them expressed any interest in her?"

"Now that I think of it, they have not. Isn't that odd?"

"Maybe not, if they believe she serves you."

They wandered through the compound to reacquaint themselves with its chambers: here, the crane room, with its painted screens showing cranes through the seasons; there, the rat room, decorated with screens depicting rats in jackets or taloos flying kites and playing hooks-and-ropes. The outer garden was lush with flowers and late-ripening fruit. The large inner garden with its pools and gazebo lay cool and green in these last days of the rainy season. In the back court, women who were washing laundry greeted her cheerfully as she addressed each one by name. The smell of nai porridge and steaming fish rose from the kitchens.

"Priya, will you come with me to the market?"

"Best you not go today, Mistress."

"You are still worried about the red hounds?"

"Chief Tuvi will want a few days to establish a watch, assign guardsmen, send your escorts into the market to look it over before you go down. Then they'll know if there are any unexpected changes precipitated by your arrival."

"You've thought this through!"

"I have consulted with the chief and O'eki, it is true." Priya's gaze was always full with the affection woven between them, but she was also clear-sighted and willing to speak her mind. "Don't push too fast now you have been allowed to return, Mistress. It cannot have been easy for the captain to place you at risk, knowing he can protect you better—or so a soldier might think—by confining you in a cage as the Sirniakans do to their women. Let those who seek to protect you and the baby feel they have some control."

"But the red hounds could strike again."

"Perhaps they will. Do you wish to return to the merciful valley? There, at least, only those ferried in by reeves can enter."

"No. I don't want to live there. I would rather take the risk. Anji will do everything he can, and I am sure that the Hieros has her own agents seeking word of spies from the empire. I'll send someone from the kitchen staff to the markets, and bide here patiently. For now."

Priya kissed her on the cheek. "You are naturally a little tired as well. Also, it may be you will wish to feel refreshed when the captain returns."

Mai flushed, thinking of those few private moments she and Anji had stolen behind the curtains in the militia camp. Anji had been seasick crossing the Olo'o Sea; water did not agree with him. They had not yet celebrated their reunion as she yearned to do. "I'll bathe."

Priya smiled and let her go. Mai spoke to the kitchen women while Priya arranged for a tub to be filled in the small courtyard at the heart of the compound, off the private rooms. Mai, after checking on Atani, who was still asleep, joined her. Hot water steamed out of the tub, set on flagstones beneath the roof of a little pavilion. The splintered doors had been repaired; there was no sign any demon attack had occurred.

"I sat with Miravia just there," Mai said. "I wonder if I'll ever be allowed to see her again. Her family is so very angry. We insulted their honor."

"It wasn't your fault, Mistress. No one could have known the demon would attack and kill those soldiers on any day, much less the day when Miravia visited you."

"No one could have known," Mai repeated, as if saying the words again would make the memories of that day less painful. But they did not. She might well lose the dear friend she had made, a young woman of the same age and with the special connection that sometimes sparks between two people, as if they had known and touched each other before birth in the mists beyond the Spirit Gate where souls reside. "She lives in a cage."

"The Ri Amarah have been good friends to us, Mistress."

"I know they have. It just seems—" It was better simply to strip off her taloos and sit in the warm water and scrub, and let Priya wash her hair. Later, she would take a cadre of women and go to the real baths. Ah!

Then the baby had to be nursed, and afterward she busied herself in the kitchens with the other women. But at dusk came a message that Anji would not be coming home. He had gone away with Tohon on urgent business to do with horses. He might be gone several days; hard to say. Reeve Joss was gone with him, having sent his regrets at not being able to attend the feast. No guests after all.

She wept, and it seemed she was more tired than she had realized, because when she lay down to nurse the baby, she fell into a heavy sleep and remembered no dreams.

*   *   *

ABOUT MIDDAY, CAPTAIN Arras and his three companies, mockingly referred to as Half-the-Asses-They-Should-Have Cohort by the rest of the army, marched past the dismantled remains of a fourth barrier. They followed First Cohort's six companies, who had been given pride of place in the van of the approach over the eastern causeway. Because the eastern causeway was the shorter passage into the city, First Cohort would be first to enter Nessumara's famed Council Square and therefore get to fly their banner from the Assizes Tower.

Four cohorts—First, Seventh, Eighth, and Arras's remnant Sixth—had set out in staggered ranks just after dawn. They had made excellent time because the causeway was an excellent piece of construction: raised out of the wetlands like a dike, it was wide enough that two wagons might pass. Not that there was any traffic today. Beside the army tromping briskly into the delta and birds fluttering among reeds and shallows, the world seemed utterly empty. The mire glistened to either side. A boat skulked in the reeds; was that a fishing line stretched taut from the prow? The cursed eagles floated overhead, eyes on everything.

A runner loped along the causeway from the front, a youth with hair tied back and a quilted jacket wrapped around his torso. He sighted for the company banners and, reaching them, marked the horsetail epaulets that identified his quarry.

"Captain Arras? Message from Captain Dessheyi."

"Go on."

The lad pulled up beside him and began to talk. "First Cohort has crossed the first bridge, Captain. It's a plank bridge. Single wide, one wagon at a time, easy for counting toll and controlling traffic. Looked to me like you could remove the middle planks and block it. The front ranks are crossing the island beyond it now, toward a second bridge."

"What is the island like?"

"Storehouses, courtyards, a threshing ground, gardens and orchards. It's deserted."

"Interesting. What are my orders?"

"Cross the first bridge. First Cohort will move forward over the second bridge, while Sixth holds position on the island until the cohort behind yours reaches the first bridge. Then you'll cross the second bridge in support of First Cohort."

"Each cleared space taken possession of immediately. I see. Anything else?"

"I'm to continue on to give my message to Seventh Cohort, commanded by Captain Daron."

"Very well. Follow me."

He signaled Sergeant Giyara to maintain control of his personal staff and, with the runner in tow, dropped back from the front of his unit. He passed the first-strike infantrymen, his heaviest shields. Behind them marched a cadre of guards walling in the hostages, followed by five cadres of proven infantry with new soldiers mixed in among the veterans. Next in line came the wagoners with their six wagons rumbling along without incident, archers pacing them with bows ready. He reached the rearguard, where his toughest men were wiping their brows and eyeing the distance opening between them and Seventh Cohort, its vanguard barely in sight behind them. The youth took a swig from his flask, then sprinted off as Arras followed his swift progress with an approving gaze.

"Anything?" he asked Subcaptain Orli after he had relayed First Cohort's orders.

"No, Captain. Seventh Cohort is maintaining distance, according to plan. As for the mire, cursed if I know. I saw a boat."

"So did I. Stay alert. Betrayal seems cursed simple, but something could easily go wrong."

The runner reached the vanguard of Seventh Cohort. Arras worked his way back up through the unit to the wedge that surrounded their twenty-eight hostages, all of whom looked frightened and weary.

All but one.

The other hostages watched what she did, listened for what she said, adjusted their stride to match her pace. They were cowed hostages who knew they were alive only on the sufferance of their captors. She was not cowed. Interesting.

She offered him something that wasn't a smile as much as a challenge. "Captain Arras. How nice of you to come explain yourself."

"Explain myself? I'm still trying to figure what you did with those chickens." He clasped his hands behind his back as he fell into step beside her.

"We didn't do anything with the chickens. We had to put the cage back. You saw the whole thing."

"The other chickens. The ones you successfully stole via misdirection."

"I did nothing but what you saw me do, Captain. I'm sorry you believe otherwise."

It was a discussion they'd had four times in the last four days; he was no nearer to figuring if the hostages had managed to cook the birds without him knowing or to trade them without being caught, and in the latter case for what items in exchange? He had the hostages' bundles searched every night for weapons and contraband, but nothing ever showed up beyond the usual gear: a spoon, a bowl, a flask, a hat and cloak to keep off rain and sun, a spare linen jacket, soap, a comb, a towel, and a mat to unroll on the ground.

"I meant to say," she went on, "I'm surprised you didn't leave us back in camp instead of forcing us to march into battle with you. Won't we just get in the way?"

"Only if there's trouble."

Her lips curved into a mocking smile. "Traitors opened the gates of Toskala. Nessumaran traitors can easily tear down barriers that block causeways. They'll let you take the city without a fight. It's the same day, is it not? Wakened Ox."

"It's better this way. For the Nessumarans."

"Not for you?"

"Fighting threshes the weak from the useful. Helps me get to know my soldiers."

She walked in silence, strides of her long legs matched to his. She was thinking over his words, or hoping he would go away; he wasn't sure which. He was pretty sure she wasn't afraid of him, as she ought to be. It was a cursed admirable trait, to be so cool and confident.

"Captain!" His attendant, a decent young man named Navi, had slipped back along the causeway. "Sergeant Giyara sends her respects, Captain. Our vanguard has started across the bridge."

"I'll come right up."

"It's cursed strange, though, Captain." The young man swiped a hand over his left shoulder in a nervous gesture he had, the kind of thing that could get to irritating a man if the youth weren't so stolid otherwise.

"What's that?"

"Just that the channel we're crossing is running so strong, Captain. You'd think they'd control the flow of water better. With dams and locks and flood barriers."

"What good would that do? I'm uplands born and bred myself."

"I'm Istria born, Captain. There's plenty you can do by diverting a strong river current into irrigation channels and canals. I'd have thought they'd divert a side channel into a series of canals that would make haulage and transportation easy within the inner delta and the city, that's what I'd—"

He seemed likely to chatter on, made enthusiastic by knowing something his captain did not. Arras cut him off. "Well observed. We'll see what to make of it when we come to know the city better, as we will—"

Light glinted on the water, a flash repeated twice. Arras raised a hand to shade his eyes, staring over the flat expanse marred here and there by a bright explosion of greener brush or tenacious trees grown on hummocks.

Zubaidit lifted an elbow to point up. "That came from the sky. The reeves are signaling to someone out there in the swamp."

"Why would they be—?"

Once before in his life, as a youth training as an ordinand, out on a field expedition with eleven others like him, he'd heard a sound before he realized he'd heard it. His action, back then, had saved his own life although it hadn't saved the lives of the other young ordinands he was with. He'd not been captain of their merry little band. Indeed, he'd been youngest and least experienced among them, but the slaughter had taught him a lesson he would never forget: Don't act for yourself alone; you are responsible for your comrades.

"Shields up!" he shouted as he grabbed Navi's arm and yanked him behind the cover of the nearest infantryman.

Streaks darkened the sky as shapes rose out of the water, but his soldiers had already obeyed. Arrows rained down on the causeway, thwacking stone, thudding on upraised shields, but no one was hit. Hostages sobbed with fear.

"Get down!" cried Zubaidit to the Toskalans. She dropped, and the others followed like wheat mowed down as a second flight of arrows rose into the sky from the wetlands and clattered down. A man among the hostages screamed and thrashed.

"I'm hit!" cried one of the soldiers, without panic, just letting everyone know.

"Heh, trying to grow a second tool from your ass, Tendri?" laughed one of his comrades.

Arras heard the clamor of battle joined far ahead, whose first tremors in the air had warned him before he fully recognized what he was hearing.

"Tortoise!" he cried. The soldiers shifted seamlessly, forming a barrier with their shields. Movement flurried through the ranks as Sergeant Giyara pushed back to join him. For an instant he stood above the turtling backs of the shields, above the cowering hostages, and scanned the entire prospect: the deadly mire, the exposed bridge and the solid island beyond, the enemy in the swamp, boats slipping into view with more archers within, a chaos of dust and hammering action ahead where the vanguard boiled with action against the haze and smoke raised by the commotion. Impossible to see what they were up against.

"Captain Arras," said Zubaidit from the ground. Her grin was so cocky that he wanted to kick her. "I think your betrayers have either betrayed you, or been betrayed in their turn and had their plan exposed."

She was right, curse her.

Seventh Cohort's captain acted at last: Figures, small at this distance, broke off in clusters from the cohort behind his and plunged into the water toward the half-hidden archers, only to flounder into traps and sinkholes.

"Captain!" Sergeant Giyara yanked him under a shield as a new shower of arrows fell. His people were too cursed exposed, and they were taking hits.

Zubaidit grabbed his arm. "Captain! I beg you. Can the hostages hide under the wagons? I've got five hit already."

He shook her off. "Sound the drum! Push over the bridge and get onto land! Move! Move!"

Arrows flew. Men staggered. Some fell, and were dragged by their fellows as the companies pressed forward, pushing hard to get off the causeway. One man spun away over the edge of the causeway and tumbled into the shallows, facedown in the muddy water. Behind, Seventh Cohort was retreating, cursed fools; they had three mey of causeway to cover to get back to dry land; they'd be picked off.

"Sergeant!" he called, having lost Giyara in the forward surge. He took a sharp blow to his head. An arrow slid down his body, and he stepped on it, snapping it in half. The hells! He swiped a hand over his helmet, but the arrow hadn't dislodged anything.

He snagged a pair of unbroken arrows. "Pick up every arrow you can find. Toss them in the wagons. Keep moving!"

The soldiers on the outside had their shields wedged well together to cover legs and torsos. The line inside had lifted shields to cover the heads of the outer rank. They marched in pace with the drum. The wagons rumbled. Arrows thudded into the gravel, or were swept up by a spare hand and tossed into the wagons. A driver grunted as an arrow sprouted in his side, but he kept driving, hunched over. Zubaidit leaped up on the bench and yanked the reins from the man's hands. Where were those cursed hostages? If they were getting in the way of his troops, he'd slit their throats himself. But they had boxed themselves in between the wagons, hauling their injured. A young woman went down in a fresh shower of deadly arrows. He felt the kiss of death brushing past, but nothing hit him; instead, he stepped over a limp body, a young soldier shot in the eye. Dead instantly, no doubt. Unfortunate. He grabbed the fellow's sword and kept moving. Looking back, he saw one of the hostages—an older woman with her hair tightly wrapped in a scarf—wrench the shield from the soldier's slack hand.

The gravel of the causeway surface gave way to wood planking, the crunch of his footsteps turning to a scrape as he moved over the bridge in the midst of his personal staff. The current in the channel ran swiftly beneath, a purling sound so loud it muffled the roar of confusion coming from up ahead where First Cohort was fighting a foe of unknown size, ferocity, and skill.

The bridge went on and on, as arrows rained down, but although one man and then a second and then a third slumped against the railings, the drummer did not cease her steady beat, the wagons rolled, the men held. The Toskalan hostages grabbed wounded men and slung them on the backs of wagons.

They marched out onto dry ground where he got a quick impression of plenty of dangerous open space and scattered abandoned carts and wagons and hitching gear plus boats drawn up and overturned by the river wall. There were warehouses, trees in planted rows, low brick walls surrounding several conjoined garden plots, a long brick row house with porch and multiple doors, many left open, the place clearly deserted in haste. The island was small, with a lane piercing straight through to a distant bridge, where a mob of fighting churned and boiled, dust thick in the air.

He pushed forward to find the vanguard setting up a quick and dirty perimeter using a pair of storehouses as their cornerstone.

"We're not stopping. We push up to support First Cohort—"

A massive *crack* made everyone flinch. Out of the chaos ahead, men screamed; shouts rang as the enemy cried aloud in triumph. Arras ran out beyond the perimeter: the distant clot of First Cohort's rearguard was falling back in confusion, completely out of order. Smoke billowed from the vicinity of the bridge and the unseen ground beyond it. Flames licked, running high. A horrible screaming yammer— maybe no more than ten men—caught in those flames on the bridge, but their agony stabbed panic into the rest. Arras had seen men break and run. He knew what would happen next; he'd witnessed the death of his comrades before, because once you are routed, you are easy prey.

"Heya! New orders!" The rain of arrows had abated now that they were on the island, but he knew their enemy out in the mire was merely taking this chance to regroup, or was pursuing Seventh Cohort down the causeway. "We're fixing a perimeter on this island. Move to those garden walls."

"There's good cover, Captain, in these warehouses—" cried one of his vanguard sergeants.

"Neh. They'll burn us out of wooden structures. That thatch will go up in a heartbeat. Set up an outer perimeter along the warehouse line. Everyone else back to the brick walls. Sergeant Giyara!"

"Captain!"

"I want sweep teams through every abandoned building while we're free of archery fire. Strip any provisions, supplies, everything. I'll need another cadre to drag in all the wagons and boats. We'll break them up and build shelters, arrow breaks, barriers. If we can manage it in staggered units, break down that row house for bricks to strengthen our perimeter. We'll make the three walled garden plots our main defensive hold, build it up as we can, and I want to include that mulberry orchard, too, so we have range of motion and some protection from that direction. We'll need forward outposts, and banners torn up to form signal flags. Cadre sergeants—"

"I'll assign them, Captain," said Giyara, as he'd known she would.

"Captain!" Subcaptain Orli's runner came panting up, face streaked with mud. "There's trouble on the first bridge. Burning arrows, Captain."

"Get back to Subcaptain Orli. I want everyone over and the main central planks pulled out. We must control access to the bridge, stop their reinforcements from marching up over the causeway."

"They can still land boats, Captain—"

"One thing at a time! Get those men over and close down that bridge."

His soldiers fell to their tasks with the discipline he'd drilled into them, but as he scanned the shape of the island—too big a slab of ground to encompass easily but not so large that it offered a range of environment—remnants of First Cohort came fleeing down the road with shields slamming on their backs in rhythm to their pounding steps. Their faces were tight with bewilderment and unthinking fear.

He grabbed a company banner ripped by arrow shot and placed himself in the center of the road with the pole held horizontal to block their headlong flight.

"Halt, you gods-rotted cowards!"

He'd trained all his youth with an ordinand's staff; of all weapons, a strong staff still felt most comfortable in his hands. He lashed out now, thumping the men in the front with a flurry of blows that knocked them back or sent them to their knees.

"Halt!"

The second rank slowed, men responding to his voice in the shaken manner of people coming awake abruptly. The soldiers behind them had to stutter step to avoid smashing into those before them, and this shift altered the entire momentum of their collapse.

"Get in your cadres! Form up!"

Folk who feel helpless desire order just as the starving desire food, or the falling man grasps at any object that will stop his fall.

"You!" He grabbed a soldier who was moving too slowly and backhanded him. Others skipped into ranks, startled by the blow.

The young man he had hit reeled sideways, then caught himself and snapped upright. "Captain?" he squeaked.

"Where's your sergeant?" Arras roared

Men looked around, seeking sergeants. "Captain! I don't know, Captain!"

"Move your group off the road. Stay in formation!" The mass began to seethe as the press behind them thickened. "You there!" He pointed at another man. "Where's your sergeant? Eiya! Move your group off the road, to the other side. Stay in formation!" He whistled, and one of his runners jumped up beside him. "I need Subcaptain Piri and his company."

By the time Piri arrived, Arras had two cadres sorted out.

"Captain!"

"Piri, take your company to the forward bridge. Make sure it's blocked, then hold the perimeter. I'm sending these two cadres with you."

"Captain?"

"If we're stuck on this island, we'll claim all the ground and place our perimeter on the shoreline. Dig in."

"Captain!"

As Piri and his company pushed through First Cohort's retreat, Arras cracked the whip of discipline over the fleeing men, separating out more cadres, sending them with runners to reinforce: this cadre to Orli at the eastern bridge; three cadres to Giyara to break up wagons, but not boats, so his own troops could be released to set a shoreline perimeter. With the remains of First Cohort, he might have enough to hold the island.

Yet every time he looked skyward, those cursed eagles circled, spying out his every move. A sweating runner sprinted into view.

"Subcaptain Piri's compliments, Captain. The bridge approach is secure. Any intact planks on our side are pulled back for later use if we choose to push forward. We'll need more planks. We've set up a strong archery screen so they can't completely dismantle the railings on the far side. First Cohort's forward companies on the far side look pretty well slaughtered. There are bodies in the channel, but they're getting swept downstream by the current into the swamp. Orders, Captain?"

Arras looked him over, a stocky young man with a fresh cut on his chin. "You're one of the new recruits. Laukas, isn't it?"

"Yes, Captain." The young man didn't smile as some new recruits did, when the captain honored them by recalling their names. He wasn't a friendly sort like Navi. "Orders, Captain?"

"Escort this sorry-looking cadre to Piri. Have him split them out among his own company. I want a secure perimeter. I'll be up soon to get a look."

"Yes, Captain." No nonsense there. He ran back to the front.

Arras beckoned to the lone sergeant wearing First Cohort's spear-and-star tabard. "What's your name, Sergeant?"

The man looked gray about the eyes, as ashamed as he should be. "I'm called Eddo, Captain."

"Take your cadre and secure every boat you can find on this cursed island. We'll need them all, half placed at each bridge. Then break down the planks in those warehouses. In case we need to build a floating bridge."

The man stared at him, not responding.

For a moment Arras thought he was addled, or an imbecile. "Sergeant Eddo?"

There's a look men get when they have lost hope and then, unexpectedly, find a spark they can feed with the kindling of resolve. "Yes, Captain!" He briskly took charge of his men.

Arras rubbed his throat, and then his forehead. When had he gotten so sweaty? His hand came away smeared and dirty, as though his face had been rubbed in the earth by a bully, and he realized he was grinning.

Two First Cohort cadres—both lacking a full complement—waited alongside the road, watching him as if he were insane, or gods-touched. Waiting for orders. How many cursed companies did he now command? He'd not had time to count. He whistled over a runner and sent the lass to scout out Giyara, with an order to make an accounting and assign out the new cadres into the commands of his three subcaptains.

"Neh, neh," he said, calling the lass back. "Tell Sergeant Giyara to attach as many cadres as she needs to her own staff, specifically for laboring. Got it?"

"Yes, Captain." Off she ran, braided black hair tailing out from her boiled leather helmet.

He examined the two cadres left to him, one at half strength and looking completely demoralized and both missing their commanding sergeant, as if the enemy had specifically targeted sergeants as a way to break down and panic units. A smart tactic, if it wasn't just by chance. He pulled the man standing straightest out of the larger cadre. "Your name?"

"Fossad, Captain."

"You're acting sergeant now, promotion to be reviewed according to performance. Your task is to find shovels, anything you can use, and start digging. We'll be throwing up earth ramparts all around this island."

"Yes, Captain!"

He turned to the final group, the sorriest-looking ragtag bunch he'd seen, scratched, limping, streaked with smoke, many with faces and arms reddened from burns.

"You lot were on the bridge?"

After a moment, the oldest among them spoke up. "Yes, Captain."

"Get your wounded under cover in one of those warehouses. As for the rest of you, we'll need a steady source of water. You make a survey of the island, you dig within the gardens if you have to, or you collect buckets and start hauling to fill cisterns. You're in charge, Sergeant—"

"I'm not the sergeant—"

"You are now. Your name?"

"Segri, Captain."

"Sergeant Segri, you're in charge, under my personal command. Get moving!"

That was the last of them. Without looking, he could hear and sense the focused activity of his troops around him, and he thought too that he felt a stammer of hesitation among the enemy. They'd launched their attack, but he had responded, fenced off his own people as well as he could. They must decide how to answer. He called in his personal staff and trotted west to the forward bridge. The causeway, in a sense, cut straight across the island; the bridge lay at the same elevation, no ramp leading up, merely a continuation of the roadway.

Subcaptain Piri met him with runners in tow and they surveyed the rushing channel, the stalwart reeds that could conceal an enemy, more flat islands beyond. The militiamen who milled about on the far shore shook spears and swords in their direction; they paced among the fallen, dragging their wounded and dead free and stabbing any wearing the tabards of First Cohort's companies. Like the other cohorts, First had brought along a number of Toskalan hostages, but he had no idea what had happened to them; he'd marked none among the survivors who had reached him.

Above, the sun had passed the zenith and begun its steady descent. Eagles sailed, sharp-eyed reeves dangling beneath in their clever harnesses, waving flags to send messages each to the others and to their allies on the ground.

"Hard to win a war when they've got the eyes," he remarked to Piri as the two runners listened. "Good thing the reeve halls are split as they are, no one liking to take orders from the next."

"Lord Commander Radas had the reeve commander executed in Toskala. That's cut off their head."

"If only we could kill the rest of the cursed reeves. Or unite them to work for us. I wonder who in Nessumara betrayed our plan."

Piri laughed scornfully. He was an older man, his face pitted with scars and his back scored with the marks of many whips long since healed. He'd been one of the first soldiers assigned to Arras's first command, a man with a reputation, nothing good, but he'd been steady and true for the last eight years. Tough as stone, steady as an Ox, which he was. "I can't cry for those willing to betray their own when they're betrayed in their turn, Captain. It just leaves us in a worse situation than we expected."

"I did not want to be ambushed today," said Arras with a laugh that made those around him chuckle nervously, attempting bravado. All but that young man, Laukas, who just watched, thin-lipped and serious. "But here we are. First Cohort is a loss. We'll absorb their cadres into our own companies. It's strange, though. They lost cohesion so thoroughly."

"They were hit hard and fast." Piri shaded a hand to survey the militia gathered across the rushing channel, their hurried councils as they tried to decide what to do next. "The militia killed a cursed lot of the sergeants. There's not one captain left standing, like they were targeted specifically. Maybe you and I should tear off these horsetails, Captain."

"Neh, we're made of stronger stuff. The thing that concerns me is we've got no means to communicate with the other cohorts. Listen, Piri. Blood Cloak—Lord Yordenas—was marching in the front with First Cohort, wasn't he? Leading the advance?"

"I saw him."

"Yet no sign of him now. Do you think—" The idea did not bear voicing aloud, but the situation required it. "Do you think they *killed* him?"

"The cloaks can't die, Captain."

But if he'd been in the lead, and he wasn't dead, then was he taken prisoner? Impossible. Had he fled? Abandoned them? Arras shook his head.

"Captain?" asked Piri.

"Neh, it's nothing."

"What do we do now, Captain?"

Arras surveyed the island, the sky and its spying reeves, the rushing water that would, he hoped, make boat travel on the channels more difficult for the defenders. They had too much daylight left, with reeves watching their every action. Later, night would cover the movements of their enemy, who knew the channels and mires as he and his people did not.

"We dig in."

Across the way, a man approached the channel's bank waving a strip of cloth, an offer to parley.

Arras grinned. "I know what they're going to say. If we retreat in order along the causeway all peaceable like, they won't let our sleeves get dirty."

"Cursed liars." Piri snorted.

"My thought, too." He whistled for a runner. "No, not you, Laukas. I've got a more difficult job for you, if you'll take it."

The young soldier did not flinch or even look excited. "I will, Captain."

"You. Lati, isn't it? Get back to the gardens. Send Navi up to me. Also, I need a pair of sergeant's badges. Any will do. I want all the Toskalan hostages bound and confined in one of the warehouses. Find me among the hostages the woman who calls herself Zubaidit, and bring her here. If she won't be of use to me one way, then she can be in another."

"What do you mean to do, Captain?" asked Piri.

"I'll give her sergeant's badges so if they kill her, we won't have lost one of our own. She can do the parley knowing the safety of the hostages depends on her coming back. And Navi and Laukas can keep an eye on her, while getting a chance to prove themselves. What do you think of that, Laukas? Willing to take the chance, going over to walk among the enemy?"

His expression did not change. He nodded obediently, like a good soldier ought. "Yes, Captain."

*   *   *

HAVING SLEPT PAST midday after several interruptions to nurse, Mai felt better. She nursed the baby, rose and washed, and ate crunchy stalks of pipe-stem slip-fried with steamed fish.

"Sheyshi, you'll watch the baby. Come and fetch me if he cries. Priya and I will be in the counting room."

A fair amount of rebuilding and fortification had taken place in the compound in the months she had been gone. The main house's entrance porch had a newly rein-forced gate leading into the entrance courtyard; she heard horses, wagons, voices raised as the Qin guardsmen went about their morning duties on the other side of the high wall. The door to the counting room was on the left, and while before it had simply slid open and closed like all the other doors in this part of the world, now those doors had been replaced by a locked and barred door that opened on hinges like a gate. One of the soldiers standing guard lifted away the bars so Mai and Priya could cross into the office. As the door was opened, Mai heard O'eki scolding a young clerk.

"This is the accounts book we use for all shipments pertaining to the building of the mistress's household in Astafero. *This* is the accounts book used for expenses pertaining to this compound. The two compounds are accounted separately, not to-gether! Now, you'll have to go back over the entire last month and divide the ex-penses out properly. Hu!"

The big slave nodded to acknowledge their presence.

The scolded clerk murmured a barely audible greeting.

Another clerk, even younger, blushed and stammered. "G-G-Greetings of the day, Mistress." Hu! The poor girl's head was shaven, and her thin face would have bene-fited from the softening ornament of hair.

"Sit down," Mai said, hoping she sounded gracious as the clerk brushed at the stubble on her head as if she had guessed Mai's thoughts. Eiya! Judging a young woman by looks alone was the kind of thing her mother and aunt would have done! Beauty was all very well, but Mai was painfully aware that if Anji had been a cruel man, then her beauty would have brought her tears rather than joy. She attempted a smile; the clerk groped for her brush and, having picked it up, set it down again im-mediately, thoroughly intimidated. Mai sighed. "O'eki, show me the books."

Three lamps burned although it was day; there were only two windows that could be opened in the long room, one at each end and both set with grilles. The door into the warehouse was closed, but they received light through the porch door, which had been left propped open because the captain's wife was inside. The customers' door, leading into the warehouse, was closed and locked. So much was closed and locked!

The scolded clerk hunched his shoulders as Mai looked over his shoulder.

"Those are very clear entries," she said. "Very readable."

O'eki grunted impatiently. "Yes, but not all in the right place. You see this lumber, marked to this account when it should be here, while the settlement account has been debited with this purchase of dye stuffs." He pulled a counting frame over and flicked wooden beads so quickly their colors blurred. "Just on this page alone you have two hundred and forty leya misaccounted."

"Are you going to send me back to the temple?" The clerk looked so young! Although, Mai thought, he was probably no younger than she was herself.

"If you fix this properly and make no further mistakes, I'll know you are learning," said O'eki. The lad nodded gratefully as the other clerk looked on, with her face pulled into an almost comically anxious expression. "Lass, you double-check the spare ledgers against the main set."

As the clerks bent back to their labors, Mai drew O'eki aside, over to the long drawers where Anji kept a set of maps. She opened the top drawer, in which lay a detailed drawing of the city of Olossi, how it nestled on bedrock in a bend in the river, how its streets climbed the hill toward Fortune Square, how its inner and outer walls separated the city into an upper and lower town.

"Where did these two clerks come from?" she whispered.

"The temple of Sapanasu. It's the only place I can hire clerks, Mistress. It's the custom here, to hire your accounts keepers from the temple. But these two are very inexperienced."

"Their numbers and ideograms are very readable."

He laughed, and both young clerks, startled, looked up from their books and self-consciously down again. "One thing I will say for that Keshad. He might have been arrogant and temperamental, but he kept excellent accounts."

Mai closed the drawer and opened the one below it, whose lines described the region surrounding the Olo'o Sea, as much as the Qin scouts and Anji could describe of it. Past the town of Old Fort the road pushed into the foothills and thence higher up into the mountains here called the Spires. Precise handwriting that she recognized as Anji's had inscribed "Kandaran Pass" above the village named Dast Korumbos; at the edge of the map where the pass sloped away south and west, the same hand had written "Sirniaka."

That way lay the empire, whose red hounds still hunted Anji. He would always be in danger from that direction.

"I wonder how Keshad is doing," Mai murmured. "Will he and Eliar be able to spy out information in the empire?"

Priya had come up beside them. "I wonder if they are still alive."

"The empire is a terrible place," murmured Mai. "If Anji's half brother is now emperor, and has killed all his other brothers and half brothers, then he will not want Anji alive, even if Anji has no intention of claiming the Sirniakan throne. And there are other claimants, too. These cousins, sons of Anji's father's younger brother. How can I keep track of them all?" A few tears ran down her cheeks. She wiped them away. "How clever of Anji to label his maps with a script no one in the Hundred but he and Priya can read."

"You are reading it now, Mistress," said Priya with the smile she offered only to Mai or O'eki.

"I am learning." She gestured toward a table. "I'll sit here for a while. O'eki, maybe that young woman will sit with me and review the ideograms. I want to be able to write my own accounts book in the Hundred style."

The girl's name was Adit, and she had been born in the Year of the Ox, just like Mai, but she was a timid creature, hard to draw out, so after a while Mai concentrated on forming and memorizing the ideograms. Priya and O'eki had seated themselves together at a writing desk, heads bent intimately together as they discussed an unknown matter in low voices, hands touching.

A guard stepped in, glanced around, and stepped out. Sheyshi entered, carrying a fussing Atani.

"I'll nurse him over here," said Mai as she took the baby to the far end of the room where pillows were stacked for visitors. Atani was an efficient eater, very hungry but not one to dawdle. When he was done and she had burped him, Adit crept over and shyly asked if she could hold him, for it transpired she had left a beloved infant brother at home when she went to the temple. So then she could be coaxed to speak of her home and her family in northern Olo'osson, and when Mai at length had Sheyshi take the infant out, she and Adit settled back to work companionably, trading comments, chuckling over an awkward stroke, asking and answering questions. Eventually the lad rose and, in the course of stretching and straightening his already neat jacket, paused by the table where the two young women worked.

"That's just the basic work," he said in the tone lads got when they were showing off for girls. "Those ideograms are the old way of recording. Anyone can do that. That's why the clerks of Sapanasu keep them around, because even merchants who didn't apprentice with the Lantern can tally with numbers and ideograms. Writing is much harder."

"Don't try to boast, Wori," said Adit in a low voice. "It makes you look stupid."

"I would like to learn this other writing of the Hundred," said Mai.

"If you didn't apprentice with the Lantern, you can't," he said, tweaking his sleeves.

Adit hid her flushed face behind a hand.

"Why not?" Mai asked.

"Because you can't," he repeated stubbornly. She suspected he now felt trapped by her attention and Adit's embarrassment. "No one does."

"Not doing it is not the same as not being able to do it. For one thing, surely the Ri Amarah did not apprentice with the Lantern and yet they know how to write in the temple script—"

"Eiya! Well! Them!"

"What does that mean? *Them*."

He shrugged. "They're outlanders. They don't even worship properly."

"I'm an outlander."

"Do you make offerings at the seven temples?"

"I don't. I have a shrine to the Merciful One. That's where I pray."

"That's the Merci*less* One," he said with a smug smile.

"No, it isn't," said Adit suddenly. "I've talked to the women who work here, and they told me it's the Merciful One. Full of mercy. There's a prayer they say, 'I go to the Merciful One for refuge. I go to the Truth for refuge. I go to the Awakened for refuge.' "

To hear these words flow from the girl's lips surprised Mai. She had thought the local women who worked for her only came to listen to Priya lead the service in order to be polite to the employer who paid them. "Why, that's right. That's part of the prayer."

Wori said, "Who ever says a thing like that? 'I go to the truth for refuge.' That doesn't mean anything."

Voices raised outside: men were speaking vehemently in the warehouse. There came a shout, and then a hammering on the warehouse door. Chief Tuvi called out an order; footsteps pounded like a cloudburst as men raced across the entrance courtyard.

She rose, her own heart at a driving run. Would she never be free of the red hounds?

Priya hurried over and grasped her elbow. "Quickly. Come farther inside."

Soldiers appeared in the office door leading to the porch. "Quickly, Mistress. Come inside."

"Will this never end?" she cried angrily.

A rhythm rapped on the warehouse door, the signal giving the all-clear.

"Seren," she said, more sharply than she intended. "Open the door."

The young soldier limped over to the door. His comrade drew his sword as Seren slid back the iron eye panel.

"Clear to open," said Tuvi's voice from the other side.

Seren undid the bolts and bars, braced his crippled leg, then swung the door open. Chief Tuvi entered first, marking the occupants with his sharp gaze. An older man wearing the turban of the Ri Amarah strode in behind him.

"Master Isar!" said Mai. "I am honored at your visit, but I admit I did not expect you—"

"Have you seen my daughter?"

She flinched, for his tone reminded her exactly of Father Mei in one of his tempers. So many months had passed since a man had spoken to her in that way she had almost forgotten how it felt, but of course she would never truly forget because it was the male voice she had grown up with. It angered her now more than it scared her. She cooled her voice to a pitch of such sincere graciousness that she hoped her demeanor would scare *him*.

"Ver, will you sit? Priya, might you bring wine? Here is a pillow."

He paced the length of the room and back again. She waited. Chief Tuvi watched through narrowed eyes. The two soldiers shut the door to the warehouse and stood with backs against it. O'eki loomed, and the clerks retreated to the cabinets.

Isar was a good-looking man somewhat older than Father Mei, a man of considerable influence and wealth, accustomed to deference. Because he was Ri Amarah— outlanders who had settled in the Hundred about a hundred years ago and yet had never come around to worshiping the Hundred's gods—he was also, it seemed, accustomed to being distrusted.

Still pacing, he spoke without looking at Mai directly. "I have come to you, verea, because of your friendship with my daughter, whose name we do not speak in public spaces. This trouble began when she was allowed to visit you in this compound. Not that I fault you, verea, for certainly you cannot understand our customs. But she has become unruly and disobedient since that day—"

Mai wanted to protest that Miravia had spoken discontentedly of her fate and the restrictions placed on her on the very first day the two young women had met, many months ago, but she knew better than to try to stop his flow of bitter words.

"—and now it appears she has utterly cast all honor and duty and sense of propriety into the dirt and *run away from home*."

Chief Tuvi looked at Mai, and she wasn't sure whether he was shocked, or ready to burst out laughing. Isar stared around the office.

"Must all these strangers stand here and listen?" he demanded.

Mai gestured. "Adit. Wori. You are released for the day. We will see you at dawn tomorrow, neh?"

With relieved nods, they hurried out.

"Seren. Valan. Bolt the door, and wait outside on the porch for my signal."

As the two soldiers left, Mai turned to Isar. "Chief Tuvi and my advisors stay."

"Your advisors? Your slaves, you mean!"

"Master Isar, surely you did not come to insult me, since you know perfectly well that my husband has supported your people. Your customs are not our customs."

"My apologies, verea. I am distraught."

"What has happened to Mi—to your daughter?" She was truly becoming anxious now, as dusk settled outside and the chamber darkened.

"She was to leave tomorrow morning."

"Leave for where?"

"Leave for her wedding. To take her place in her new home."

His words shocked her. "To Nessumara? You can't possibly be sending her on the roads, Master Isar. Captain Anji has secured the roads in Olo'osson, but you know better than most that beyond Olo'osson the roads are not safe, not even for an armed caravan."

"It has been arranged that a reeve will fly her there. A female reeve, I might add." Surely his complexion was pallid more with anger than concern. Did he truly care for his daughter, or was she merely a piece of merchandise he could trade to benefit his family's wealth and position?

"The reeves aren't carters, hauling cargo for money. They enforce the law!"

"Master Esaf has repeatedly supplied foodstuffs for Clan Hall at no profit. Given transport to refugees likewise. He asked for one favor in return. Even a very pious man yearns for a wife when he has been without one for some time."

As lecherous old goats lust after lovely young brides they've bought like animals at the market! she thought.

Something in her thoughts must have communicated to Master Isar, because he plunged on. "It's a substantial sum that he's forgone."

As if coin answered all objections!

Yet, were Isar and his relatives any different from her own family? Anji had seen her at the market, and because he was a Qin officer in a town conquered by the Qin army, he had gone to her father to purchase her.

"I'm sure Master Esaf's wealth is considerable, ver. But this is your daughter. Toskala has been overrun by a marauding army. They are marching on Nessumara."

"I have not forgotten the army's trail of bitter conquests," he said, jaw tight.

"I should hope not! An army that burned High Haldia and laid siege to Toskala. Your own people have died!"

He wasn't willing to meet her gaze directly. "You are remarkably well informed, verea."

"Captain Anji makes sure I receive daily reports." She tried to remember her market voice and her market face, but she could not hold on to them. "Surely you can't intend to send your daughter into a city soon to be attacked? The young scholar she was originally engaged to was killed in the attack on High Haldia, wasn't he? Do you want to expose her to such risk just for coin and better trade opportunities?"

He was by now quite red in the face. "What do you think your husband would say, to hear you speak such words to a man of the same age as your own father? Are you challenging our right to do what we must? What we know is right for our house? Are you so lacking in respect? A mere chit of a girl, accustomed to getting her way because folk pet her for her beauty which is exposed in the most unseemly manner—?"

Chief Tuvi interposed himself between Mai and the Ri Amarah merchant. "I beg your pardon, ver," he said in a voice the more threatening because he had not raised it.

In the silence, O'eki set down a sheaf of papers he had been holding all this time, its rustling like that of eavesdropping mice scattering away under the floorboards.

Isar swallowed. "I am not myself, verea. I beg your pardon. I will return another time."

He went to the door. Tuvi drew back the bolts. As Isar vanished into the warehouse, Tuvi glanced back with an evocative shrug as if to say *Men! Daughters! Outlanders! How does one make sense of them!* Then he went out after the merchant, and Seren came back inside and bolted the door after him.

Mai drew in a shuddering breath.

"Those in desperate need of coin will do what they must to get it," said Priya softly, still standing at her side. "Even sell their beloved daughter to the temple of the Merciful One. We must learn to forgive and let go when we see that their hearts are trapped in despair."

"I should never have lost control like that," murmured Mai, afraid her voice would crack and she would start weeping. "Said those things to him." She sank down onto a pillow and rested her head in her hands.

"Mistress?" One of the women peered in through the open door to the porch. "Sheyshi sent me, Mistress. The baby is awake."

It was a relief to fuss over tiny Atani, as cranky as she was herself until he latched on and nursed. She dozed off as he suckled, and started awake when Priya gently disengaged the baby from her breast and burped him. Mai settled him in a sling, and she and Priya lit lamps in the altar room. An image of the Merciful One gazed kindly on them, one hand upraised to signify awakening and the other cupped at the belly to signify comfort. One of the kitchen women hurried in carrying a mass of flowers, their fragrance filling the room.

"Mistress, I knew you would want an offering," she said, bringing forward the bouquet. "We got these at the market before it closed."

"Why, Utara, I thank you! Will you make the offering?" As the words left her mouth, she winced. Had she overstepped?

But the hireling smiled, color rising. "I would do so gladly."

Trembling, she placed the flowers on the offering platter as Priya began the prayers.

"I offer these flowers at the feet of the Merciful One. Through the merit of offering may I walk the path of awakening. The color and fragrance of flowers fade, so does the body wither and disintegrate. Receive this with compassion."

Other members of the household gathered, some murmuring the responses and others watching, rather like the infant, whose eyes were open, taking everything in.

The short evening service, and her nap, restored Mai somewhat.

"I'll work in the office," she said.

"Do you want me to take the baby, Mistress?" asked Sheyshi eagerly.

"No. I'll shift him to my other hip. As long as he is quiet, I can work."

Priya attended her, guards at each door, while around them the compound grew quiet as the rest of the household settled to sleep. Mai set a sheet of rice paper on the writing table and practiced her brushstrokes.

"Better," said Priya with a smile.

"How do I write out the prayers?" Mai asked. "Maybe that would help my mind grow quiet. Anji is always out on militia business. I know he's good about sending me word. I don't expect anything else. And truly I am grateful to be in Olossi again. Yet what if he decides it's too much of a risk. No one can control every least goat track! I'll end up living in a stone tower, trapped within high walls!"

"You are troubled indeed, Mistress."

"Thinking of poor Miravia makes me weep."

Priya said nothing. Lamp flames hissed.

"She must have been desperate."

Priya took her hand, meaning to comfort.

Mai clung to her. "But she's no different from me, is she? When Anji made it clear he wanted me, my father could not have said no to a Qin officer. At least he bargained hard to get a high price for me! That shows he cared!"

"We cannot know under what constraints the Ri Amarah labor. They are still seen as outlanders despite living in this land for a hundred years or more."

"It's just I thought maybe because the women of her people do all their accounting, and seem to whisper of some kind of magic that causes them to know all kinds of things, like Atani would be a boy, that it would be different for their daughters. Was it any different for you, Priya? Sold to the temple in your own land, and then taken away over the mountains by raiders to be a slave in a strange country? Isn't Master Isar right? That I can ignore all these things because I have always been petted and made a favorite?"

She shook off Priya's hand and crossed to the drawer of maps. She opened the third drawer, that contained an incomplete map of the Hundred.

Anji spent considerable time working on his maps. He had engaged the services of a draftsman out of the temple of Ilu, because the envoys of Ilu were messengers who, in more peaceful times, walked everywhere. The temples possessed maps, so it was said, but they guarded their knowledge jealously.

Anji did not let that stop him.

The map was limned in loving detail in the regions he had himself traversed, and she supposed she could trace his travels over the last year. Farther afield lay regions marked in traceries of charcoal pencil, ready to be erased and redrawn if necessary. The map had the look of a thing still in motion, as if it needed simply a strong hand to set the brushstrokes that would confine it.

Here was south, here north, here east, and here west, roads and rivers laid as lace-work across the land. Here stood the crossroads city of Toskala along the River Istri, and downstream on a delta at the sea lay Nessumara, where they would take Miravia and confine her in a house from which she could never after set foot in the world beyond without her husband's permission. All ordered and tidy, lines drawn on a map.

"It's late, Mistress," said Priya quietly.

The baby smacked his lips, stirring restlessly as his infant thoughts turned to hunger.

"Of course. I am tired."

They went back to her chambers, and she nursed the baby and Sheyshi brought water for her to wash and rolled out the pallet and unfolded the bedding. The slaves went to their own pallets; Mai snuffed the lamp flame and lay down on the pallet with Atani tucked in beside her, his soft breaths like a flame on her heart. She had no name for what she felt for him. It wasn't any emotion she had known before.

He breathed. She slept.

"Mistress."

She startled up, but Atani slept peacefully. A hand touched her shoulder. A flame flickered in the darkness.

"Priya! What is it?"

"Mistress, come. Sheyshi, stay with the baby."

Mai wrapped a taloos around her body, tucking it in loosely as she followed Priya and her lamp. In the courtyard outside, a dawn-chat pipped. Because Priya said nothing, Mai remained silent. Chief Tuvi met them on the porch, fully dressed.

"Mistress, come," he said in a low voice.

Her heart plunged. Had they news of Anji? Terrible news? But Tuvi led her into the office where the warehouse door stood open into the utter darkness of the building beyond.

A figure concealed beneath a long hooded cloak the color of twilight stood in the doorway, half in and half out as if unsure of its welcome. In this warm country, folk wore short cloaks to protect against the rain, and only the envoys of Ilu wore long traveling cloaks like this one. Or that demon girl who had ridden into this very house and killed two Qin soldiers with her demon's magic.

Mai had learned in the market how to turn a bland face to any situation. Never let them know what your real price is, or how desperate you are.

"Who are you?" she asked in her coolest voice.

The figure tipped back its hood to reveal a face that Mai stared at, at first unable to recognize one she did not expect to see standing so boldly like any ordinary person in the door of her residence.

The figure spoke.

"Mai. I've run away."

By wearing no veil in a public room with others looking on, Miravia made plain her determination to break utterly from her family. She dropped to her knees and raised her hands, as might a supplicant begging for her life or a desperate woman come to pray at an altar.

"Will you help me?"

15

ARRAS HAD GROWN up in the highlands, where ridges and hills and peaks cut into the sky. Here in the delta, as night pressed down over the mire, the flat land troubled him. How did you distinguish sky from land, or land from water? Divisions ought to be clear; that which was blurred was untrustworthy. Here the only consistent element was the humid, musty smell of water and vegetation like a two-finger porridge coating his tongue.

But as he gazed upward at the stars and strands of cloud streaking the moonless sky, he smiled. No reeves out spying. Night was a good time.

"They're coming back over the bridge, Captain," said Giyara, who was standing beside him.

A lantern detached from the enemy lines and swayed in a cautious journey over the dismantled span. Subcaptain Piri walked forward with a detachment to meet the negotiators, but he brought back to Arras only Zubaidit in her tabard with its sergeant's badge and young Navi, the runner.

"Where's Laukas?" Arras asked.

"They took him," blurted out Navi.

"What do you mean, they took him?" He fixed his gaze on Zubaidit. "Give me your report, *Sergeant*."

He thought she'd been about to smile, but at his tone her brows furrowed. "Navi and Laukas and I were taken to meet with their captain. He's an old fellow, walks with a cane and a limp. He made the offer you expected: He'll call his people off if you'll turn your men around and march back to the mainland and leave Nessumara alone."

"He could have shouted that offer over the channel. Why did he keep you there so long?"

"He took us on a tour of the militia awaiting us on the island. Wanted to make sure we saw how many armed men were waiting to hammer us should we not agree to retreat."

Arras scratched his chin. "How many?"

"About five hundred, that I counted."

"And Laukas?"

Zubaidit smiled almost mockingly. "I guessed you sent the lads to spy on me as much as to pretend to be my personal runners, make it seem I was a real sergeant. Now you'll never know if I meant to betray your secrets to the Nessumarans." Her gaze sharpened as her amusement faded. "Because it seems that your lad Laukas was a traitor. I'm not sure what signal he gave, because he never spoke one word out of our hearing. But all at once the captain signaled and a pair of guards hustled him away. I'll bet he's spilling his guts right now, telling them everything."

Arras glanced at Navi. "They never separated us," the youth said. "It's just as she says."

"The strange thing is," Arras added, "that I still can't know what you would have done if it weren't for me threatening to kill the other Toskalan hostages if you didn't return."

"Then I won't waste my words trying to convince you of what I know is true."

He grunted, lips twisting into half a smile. "Laukas seemed so competent, willing to work hard to prove himself. Ambitious, even. That will teach me to trust new recruits before they've proven their loyalty."

"They could attack tonight," she said.

"It's what I would do. But they'll see we're digging in. They may hesitate. They may have only five hundred men, and no more. Anything else?"

"I need a stick to mark with—" Arras handed her his dagger. She cocked an appreciative smile as she handled it, getting its weight and balance, then crouched and began scoring lines in the dirt: a double line for the causeway that ran into a double line crossed by vertical lines to suggest the bridge joining the two islands; the buildings and structures and paths she had seen on the second island; the pattern of their troop disposition. "Note how they are massed here along the road. They expected First Cohort to push all the way over, so perhaps their counterattack was more successful than they expected. They're city militia, not as disciplined as your men. Also, I saw heaps of dead—piled here, and here—so it's impossible for me to know how many Nessumarans were killed and wounded by First Cohort before the First collapsed."

"You're observant, Zubaidit. Not a common skill."

"I had an excellent teacher."

"What of the farther portion of the island, its connections to what lies beyond?"

"This is all we saw. Navi will corroborate my report."

"I feel sure he will." He gestured, and Giyara and Piri pulled back with all the attendants to leave him standing within the hazy pool of light splashed on the ground by the lamp. She was painted a rich golden brown in its light, lustrous and compelling. She wore her hair twisted up atop her head and pinned tightly back, but tendrils brushed her shoulders. Had they shaken loose accidentally, or did she wear them that way on purpose, to distract the men she was dealing with?

Her smile irritated him. "Captain, you'd like to devour me, that's certain. You're a good figure of a man, and I have no objection to the act, as long as you acquit yourself well, but you must know I'd not be doing it because I'm enamored of you but because you are of me."

The words stung, but they made him laugh, too. "That's honestly spoken. You've hit me where I'm vain. I'm not likely to press you now."

"Another man might."

"I'm not another man. I won't come begging. I hope your husband is to your taste, for you'd be a fearful woman to be wed to if he weren't. Better your scorn than your indifference."

"He was an unexpected pleasure, I admit," she said with the same half-absent flicker to her gaze as when she'd talked about the unknown "teacher" who had trained her to be an excellent scout. "Just as charming as his aunt warned me he'd be."

"And yet you are torn from him." He shook his head. "A sad tale."

"There speaks a man who is captain in the army that took hostages in Toskala in order to force Toskala to bide quietly under its hand. And hung other innocent folk up on poles to die from pain and thirst."

"Only the Guardians can truly know who is innocent and who a criminal."

She rose angrily. "It's true," she said, the words clipped in a way that suggested she was forcing down what she really wanted to say, "that few are truly innocent in any meaningful way."

"I'd be surprised if any were, beyond children too young and those gods-touched too simpleminded to know what is right from what is wrong. Anyway, isn't it better for the Toskalans to bide quietly than lose hundreds or thousands more as happened in High Haldia?"

Her frown fell as swift as the night-wing's call. This close to the bridge he heard the steady waters slushing along in the nearby channel; a splash plopped farther out, but he didn't understand the sounds here: it might be a thrown rock, a fish, a merling, a man; it might be the Water Mother's afterthought, a tear from her left eye. Lamps glimmered on the far shore while his own people worked in darkness. Curse that gods-rotted Laukas, and himself for being careless and overconfident.

Her voice spilled low across the undercurrent of night noises, trembling in much the same way water surges when too much is forced through too small a channel. "My husband is well enough—he's far better than what I might have found myself bound to—but what choice had I in the matter? I'm obedient to those who rule me. I have no power of my own. It chafes me. . . ."

Her words trailed off. She seemed ashamed, if folk could be ashamed of wanting what they had always been told they should not desire. Was a man wrong to like the discipline of battle? The tales of the Hundred did not speak kindly of war, and yet Arras had never tired of hearing over and over again those episodes elaborating the clash of weapons, the daring of stalwart soldiers, the courage of those who sought to resolve disputes with clean force.

"I refused to marry the woman my clan wished to bind me to," he said at last, "so they cast me out for my rebellious nature. I found comfort in the Thunderer's cohort as an ordinand, but it was not until I was recruited to this army that I have found true satisfaction. The cruelty they practice, which they call cleansing—the hanging from the pole—is pointless, but it is not my army to command."

"Do you wish it was?"

He laughed. "I'm content to fight, as long as they respect me. For in the end, Zubaidit, we must all bow our heads before the cloaks."

"Captain!" Two runners pounded up, one holding a lamp, the other bending double as he heaved out and sucked in air and came up talking.

Giyara ran up in their wake. "Captain Arras. Ten boats are coming in to the shore twenty paces north of the eastern causeway."

"How came I not to hear any sounds of fighting?"

"Subcaptain Orli had screens set up to conceal spearmen in the shallows and men in the water to tip others overboard. We killed about thirty so fast the rest fled. Runners are tracking their movements along the channel downstream. Of the rest, we've taken four living prisoners and six boats."

"Excellent! If the others come to shore, kill them. Otherwise, waste no arrows in the dark. Their report to their commanders will give the enemy pause. They'll not attack again so quickly. Is there aught else?"

"No, Captain. Your orders?"

"Just as I've told you."

"Yes, Captain." The youth nodded at his comrade holding the lamp and after taking a pair of slow breaths, more pushed out than pulled in, he set out at a run.

"Good lad," said Arras. "But I don't recognize him."

"Maybe you couldn't see it from your angle, Captain," said Giyara, "but he's wearing a First Cohort badge. Orli must have detached him from his old unit—"

From the far shore came a burst of shouting, a frantic call for archers.

"The hells!" said Arras, raising a hand to signal. "Do they mean to attack—?"

The sky swept low. A brush of smothering wings and sullen dread doubled him over before he realized he was groveling. Hating himself for his weakness, he straightened. The winged horse trotted to earth on the graveled roadway. The man dismounted stiffly. He walked stiffly, favoring his right leg, and held his left shoulder at an odd angle.

Arras made the obeisance at once, open hands hiding his eyes. "Lord Yordenas."

"Who is in command?"

"I am, lord. I'm Arras, captain of the Sixth Cohort."

"Took heavy losses at High Haldia, did you not?" The cloak's tone was surly. Arras dared not look up to gauge his temper, but anger and resentment swept off the cloak so strongly it was like keeping one's balance in a winter gale.

"So we did, lord. We regrouped into three companies, half strength, and more recently were ordered to join the main army for the assault on Nessumara. We have taken positions on this island and absorbed the remains of First Cohort."

"You did not retreat?"

"I saw Seventh Cohort in trouble on the causeway from archers, lord. I deemed it better to push forward to a strong defensive position than to retreat under heavy fire from an enemy whose position we could not penetrate."

"First Cohort fell apart," said the cloak with the petty disgust of a child who'd had his favorite toy snatched out of his hands. "Captains dead, cadres routed. We were supposed to march into Council Square in triumph! The cursed Nessumarans betrayed us!"

Arras thought it prudent not to remind the cloak that the only traitors in this case were the folk who had been prevented from allowing the army to enter the city unopposed. "Yes, lord. What of the two cohorts caught out on the causeway?"

"I don't know! I haven't reached the main camp in Saltow. I've galloped all the way to the northern causeway and back. Heavy woodland, sunken into this cursed marsh. They didn't take the barriers down at all on the northern causeway, as they said they would! Instead, there came archery fire out of the woods. Traps dug into the mire around the causeway. Snakes and snappers in the water and among the twisting roots of the cursed trees! Our cohorts had to retreat despite Lord Radas's best efforts at keeping them in line and moving forward. Now what will we do?"

The cursed man was throwing a temper tantrum! And that, gods rot him, after he had abandoned the troops he was supposed to be leading.

Arras kept his voice mild, his shoulders bowed, and his gaze fixed on the ground.

"My cohort is intact, lord. I have the remnants of First Cohort well in hand as reinforcements for my own soldiers. If we can learn the disposition and number of the local troops, we can determine our best course of action. Has the city militia sent its entire strength out to the causeways? Have they milked themselves dry in setting up this ambush? If we strike hard and push past now, will we meet concentrated resistance? Or are these troops all they have? If so, we can still take the city today."

"What do you recommend, Captain?"

The cursed cloak did not know what in the hells to do. That the gods had endowed him with such power had not made him wise or clever. He had no more understanding and discernment than he'd ever had—and that clearly was not much—yet he was meanwhile able to reach right into your heart and kill you.

Even so, a single cloak could not conquer a city alone.

"To come up with a plan, Lord Yordenas, I need information about the number and disposition of troops and barriers and skirmishers within Nessumara and the surrounding region."

The cloak's anger stung like wounds. "So you have already said. Don't lecture me!"

"My apologies, lord, for speaking out of turn." Arras kept his head down, knowing an incautious glance would betray his secrets. "I only mention it because you, my lord, are best suited to reconnoiter."

"I am a holy Guardian! Not a scout!"

"My lord, I'm only pointing out what I am sure has already occurred to you. If you scout ahead now, when no reeves can fly, it would allow us to know whether it's best to retreat, or to attack."

"It was flying ahead of the lines that got me stuck with arrows. Cursed archers! We must wait for Lord Commander Radas. He'll meet us at Saltow."

"But my lord, the more time they have to regroup and recover and retrench—" .

"I command you to retreat to Saltow! Do you defy me, Captain?"

"No, my lord."

With that, the cloak was content. His passing left Arras shaking so hard it took him many breaths to calm himself. When he rose, only Giyara remained. All the others, even Zubaidit, had fled from the cloak's brutal presence.

"Captain?" A shout caused Giyara to take a step back, looking for the source of the noise. She kicked the lamp, but with quick reflexes caught it on her boot and tipped it back upright before much oil spilled. Fire flared on the ground, eating the oil as it hissed smoke.

They listened but heard no further alarm.

He shook his head. "We can hide from the eyes of the reeves beneath a forest canopy, or inside buildings, or underground like the delvings. Out in this flat land, it's impossible. They'll always know where we are, except at night. What a waste. The only way to make this work is to overrun Nessumara's defenses quickly, burn down Copper Hall, and drive out the reeves. One setback is not a defeat. An attack might still have worked—"

"We're going to retreat?"

He whistled, venting anger. "You heard the order. We retreat at dawn."

16

AS MIRAVIA SLEPT, Mai sat on the porch overlooking the tiny garden at the heart of the compound, her private retreat. A night wren chirped, but the taste of the air was already growing sweeter with the promise of a rising sun.

"There is a man loitering outside our gates," said Chief Tuvi. "I suspect he is an agent hired by the Ri Amarah. If he knew for certain she was here, then likely he would have fetched Master Isar already. That he has not suggests he suspects she is here but has yet no proof. So, if I give a word to him, he'll run—"

"No!" The forceful word spoiled the delicate hush.

"Of course she must be returned to her father. I am sorry if that answer displeases you, Mistress. You have a kind heart. But Captain Anji will insist."

O'eki and Priya said nothing, but the gazes they bent on her were like the pressure of a hand checking impetuous speech. Did they want her to say one thing and expect her to say another? Yet her heart was determined. In the chamber behind, glimpsed through a partially open door, Miravia lay sprawled on the pallet; she had been so exhausted she had collapsed soon after Mai had drawn her inside. The baby's cot was tucked into the corner. Sheyshi, snoring lightly on a pallet just outside the sleeping chamber, had not even awakened.

"How did Miravia get inside?" Mai asked.

"I let her in."

"Do you ever sleep, Tuvi?"

"I was restless, Mistress. Thinking of things. Hard to sleep then, eh?"

Certainly, as exhausted as Mai had felt earlier, she was wide awake now. "I can't do it, Tuvi. I can't betray her."

"She belongs to her father, Mistress. You accepted such a marriage. You were wiser than she was."

"Maybe I was just fortunate!" she snapped. "Hu! I beg your pardon, Chief. I know you are only telling me what everyone else will tell me, but I cannot do it."

"I'll do it, Mistress. A word to the suspicious agent outside or a messenger sent directly to the compound, if you wish. The Ri Amarah will thank us, and Captain Anji will return home to a peaceful house, just as he likes it."

His calm words decided her. Rising, she found her market face. "Of course you are right, Tuvi. Never let it be said I turned my back on a distasteful task and let another perform it in my place. I'll go myself to the Ri Amarah house. But I must sleep first, for I'm very tired."

He nodded. "You are an honorable person, Mistress. Now, if you will, I want to settle the dawn rounds."

She released him, a courtesy he extended to her, for although she ran the household and all of the business arrangements and dealings, he commanded the security measures in Anji's absence. Just as he would never question any negotiation she entered into or any contract she sealed, she knew where her authority ended and where Anji's began.

She slipped inside the door, Priya behind her. O'eki remained standing on the porch. From the bushes, the first dawn songs were trilled. The sky was still black, stars blazing.

Priya touched her elbow. "In the Mei household folk often called you stupid, or light-minded, or simpering, or precious. But I know these words describe what they see, not what is there. If you show a calm face to the world, it is not because you are without passion. If you do not challenge those who command you, it is not because you are too placid to protest. If you are obedient, it is not because you obey thought-lessly, knowing no other course of action. I hear defiance in your voice, even if I am surprised Chief Tuvi did not. What are you planning?"

"I'll need help from you and O'eki to get out of the compound and the city. No one else must know. Can you do it?"

From the porch, O'eki spoke as if he had already guessed her intentions and run through several plans. "It's possible to get out the back gate if you are willing to hide cramped in a chest, Mistress. I will need another hireling to help me carry it. Priya will have to stay here to guard the chamber and say you are sleeping. It will be easy enough to hire a covered palanquin down by Crow's Gate. Even so, our movements can be traced."

"There lies the risk. I'll have to take Atani in case he wants nursing."

"Chief Tuvi is right," said Priya. "Captain Anji will tell you to return her to her father."

With trembling hands, she grasped Priya's fingers. "I know." She swallowed a sob, like drinking down sorrow. "But I will never forgive myself if I do nothing. Never never never."

Miravia stirred. Abruptly, she sat bolt upright. "Mai?" she croaked.

Mai released Priya's warm hands and knelt beside Miravia, whose hands were cold. "Hush, my sister. You must wake now. We're going to leave right away."

"Where are we going?"

A pallor had lightened the shroud of night to a gleam neither night nor day which is called twilight for partaking of both and yet sustaining neither. Priya watched Mai, expression quiet in the gloom. O'eki waited on the porch, big body blocking her view of the garden.

"The only place we can go," said Mai.

*   *   *

SOON AFTER DAWN, Arras gave the order and his cohort moved out, shields tor-toised and wagons crammed with wounded and provisions. He forced the hostages to walk outside the shields. If the Nessumaran militia broke the truce and attacked, they would kill unarmed civilians first. It's what he would do, in their position: he'd shoot down the civilians and break through the shield wall, because a cohort stuck out on an unprotected causeway was too easy to pass up. But he doubted the local militia had the stomach for such slaughter.

He hung back with the rearguard until the last soldiers cleared the bridge. Four sorry-looking hostages, the most truculent of the crew, trotted at the end, tied by long ropes to the rearmost wagon so they couldn't bolt. He moved up alongside the unit, marking their brisk pace and even footfalls, their confident gazes, their energy.

The other hostages stared over the mire more than they watched their feet, although no one tried to run. If the enemy did not kill them, his people would shoot them in the back as they splashed into the swamp.

"Captain!" Zubaidit hailed him. "Must I walk out here with the rest? Didn't I prove my loyalty by walking in among the enemy last night to take your message?"

He kept striding along with his attendants streaming behind. He thought he heard a few among the hostages hiss at her words, but that sound might also have been the flutter and flurry of wings as waterfowl rose in numbers off their tranquil feeding ground, disturbed by the tread of feet. Boats bobbed out of his reach. The rising sun glinted on stretches of water. Reeds swayed in the morning breeze.

They reached the front of the cohort. The causeway speared straight over the mire; he could not yet see the solid earth of the mainland, only the blur of gray-blue water and green reeds.

"Captain?" Sergeant Giyara gestured up.

Eagles soared overhead; those gods-rotted reeves would never let up. Then gold winked, like a spark of sunlight detached from the spreading rays. He squinted, shaded his eyes, tilted his head and tried to find that trick of the light again, but it was lost in the gleam.

"The hells!" swore Giyara.

The cloak trotted to earth on the causeway before them, and the soldiers dropped to their knees, bowing their heads.

Lord Radas himself had come. His cloak—almost as bright in its golden splendor as the sun itself—rippled as in an unfelt breeze. Arras felt fear as a knife in his ribs, but he walked forward anyway, because he must. He was captain; he was responsible. He knelt on one knee and raised both hands to shield his gaze obediently.

"Lord Radas. What is your will?"

"What is your name?"

"Captain Arras, of the Sixth Cohort. I have with me remnants of the First Cohort."

"You are retreating rather than holding the forward position. When Lord Yordenas spoke to you last night, you were encamped farther out, on an island."

When thrown off balance, it was best to right yourself by throwing a punch. "Lord Yordenas ordered the retreat, my lord. I suggested we hold the forward position and asked Lord Yordenas to undertake a reconnaissance to estimate the true strength of the Nessumaran militia."

"We were betrayed." Lord Radas had a mild voice, nothing odd in it, only its tone had a timbre that made a man shudder even to hear simple words spoken in a seemingly reasonable manner. A madman might speak so as he was cutting your throat. "Look at me, Captain."

Aui! A man in his line of work could never know, never plan for, and must never dwell on when death might arrive to carry him to the Spirit Gate.

No sense waiting.

He looked up.

The man had youthful features but did not seem young; rather, he appeared rather unsettlingly *well-preserved*. He had deep-set eyes and broad cheekbones set off by a mustache and beard; no dashingly handsome man, as in the tales, but an ordinary fellow if not for the eyes, which were a weapon cutting you open so your guts spilled out.

Here it is, all of it:

Lord Twilight told me to arrange for an outlander to be conveyed out of camp without the other lord commanders knowing of it and by chance I was able in addition to use the outlander's trail to track down a nest of bandits and kill them. Kill me for it if you must; I obeyed the cloak, as I am required to do. I didn't know who the outlander was, but then Night tracked me down to say she had captured him. She said he was Lord Twilight's brother.

I don't enjoy killing or savor its power. I don't mind it, either, and if it has to be done I'll do it, as I have done since the day I left my village forever. Nothing against my clan or anyone else there; it just wasn't a life or a bride I was willing to accept. I like battle, because it tests the mind and the body and it tests your resolve, your reactions, your reserves.

As for Captain Dessheyi of the First Cohort—even in an ambush he ought not to have allowed his soldiers to break ranks and lose cohesion like that; he ought to have had a decent chain of command in place. But some of these men are cursed better at oiling up their superiors to grab for rank than they are at actually doing the work of fighting.

Lord Radas laughed, the sound so startling Arras flinched. "So Harishil and Night are playing a game of hooks-and-ropes. He'll not survive her displeasure. Perhaps she means to replace one outlander with the other."

Shaking, Arras brought his hands up to cover his eyes. He was on both knees, sweat streaming, hands moist.

"Keep the remnants of First Cohort as your own," said Lord Radas as easily as if he were handing him a cup of cooked rice for his supper. "You have a full cohort now. It's up to you to mold them into a cohesive unit. There will be a full war council in Saltow on Wakened Horse. I will be sure to consult your opinion at that time. I expect you to have a plan of action to present, that can be considered along with other strategies. We have underestimated the Nessumarans. Now we must defeat them." He began to rein his horse around.

"Lord Radas! If I may be permitted to speak."

The horse sidestepped as the cloak twisted in the saddle and Arras ducked his head to avoid that gaze. "It's the reeves, Lord Radas. They see everything we do. As long as they have that advantage, we'll struggle."

"Be sure we are not finished with the reeves," said the cloak over his shoulder before he urged his mount onward.

The wings unfurled, their span almost as wide as the causeway and so bright and powerful Arras forgot to fear and simply gazed in awe. In a transition he could not measure or mark, the horse ran off the causeway and up into the sky as if the roadway split and it had merely taken a path he could not see. The man and his billowing cloak seemed almost an afterthought to the magnificence of the beast's wings and graceful form.

"Heya!"

Arras leaped up, whipping round to see a soldier racing up on the heels of Zubaidit. She staggered to a halt as she stared after the rippling sheen of the gold cloak falling away like rays off the rising sun. Her expression was unfathomable, mouth slightly parted, eyes narrowed. Is that what she would look like in the arms of the Devourer? Whew! He'd completely forgotten about her in the face of Lord Radas's gaze.

"Cursed hostage took off running, Captain," said the panting soldier. "Everyone was staring at the cloak." He aimed the haft of his spear at her, taking a halfhearted swipe, and she turned on Arras.

"You cursed ingrate! I only went on that cursed negotiating expedition for you because you said you'd kill the other hostages if I did not. Now they're all spitting on me and calling me a traitor."

He dusted off the dirt on his trousers and, straightening, shook off the muzz afflicting his thoughts. "That would seem to make them the ingrates, not me."

Her gaze flicked eastward toward the mainland, taking in the mire and the gods-rotted honking waterfowl dotting the sheets of water. Already the cloak had vanished from view.

"I'm tired of being strung along as on a rope," she said. "First my clan marries me off north to a man I've never met. Not that I've any complaint of him, mind you. It's just I had no choice. I've never had a choice." Her tone hardened as old grievances bubbled to the surface. He saw that look in a lot of the young men who came to him. "Seems to me you lot have more choice in what happens in your life. I want to join your cohort as a soldier."

"What's in it for me?"

She snorted. "Do you ask that of every recruit?"

"I might have asked it of that cursed traitor Laukas. What's to say you won't betray us, as he did?"

"What's to say anyone won't? I'm one person, Captain. Not that difficult to keep an eye on."

"Indeed not. I might have to keep you close by me, just to be sure."

Her lips twitched, reminding him abruptly of a hook used to catch a fish. "Do you want me to play that game, Captain? I shouldn't think your men will respect you for it." She looked around, because of course everyone within earshot was listening openly, and no doubt those cursed boats bobbing off shore, out of arrow-shot, were also wondering what in the hells was going on.

"Tortoise up!" he shouted, angry at his lapse. The entire cohort could have been shot to pieces while he gaped like a lust-struck moonwit. "March!"

He fell behind the front rank of shields, and although the soldier who had chased her queried him with a gesture, he waved him off. She did not drop back to walk with the other hostages, nor did he make her go. Hadn't he already decided?

"You'll plague me until you get what you want, won't you?"

"Yes." She matched her stride to his.

"I won't have it said I enlisted any soldier in my cohort in exchange for sex." He glanced at Sergeant Giyara, who had dropped into step on his other side. She'd no doubt have an opinion to share with him in private, later. "That's not the kind of unit I run."

Zubaidit flashed that handsome smile. "That's why I respect you, Captain."

They walked in silence except for the tread of feet. The causeway stretched to the horizon.

"Captain," said Giyara at length, as if she'd been chewing for a while and had finally swallowed, "does that mean Lord Radas thinks we did the right thing by giv-ing up our forward position?"

"Surely he knows I couldn't refuse a direct order. He told me to present a plan at the war council on Wakened Horse. I've a few ideas. Spread into the countryside. Confiscate the harvest, all flocks and horses, take wagons and tools. We can cut off every land route into Nessumara. Field boats out of Ankeno and do damage to their shipping as well, cut off the flow of refugees fleeing the city. Trap them in the delta like rats. They have fields and storehouses, but surely not enough to feed all the refugees. And the dry season is coming. Maybe this cursed mire will dry out and we can advance across a longer front, off the causeway. Maybe we can set fire to the is-lands and drive forward under the cover of smoke, to hide from the reeves."

Giyara whistled. "Fire is a two-edged sword. It can't be controlled."

"War is a fire, isn't it? If we burned the grand and glorious city of Nessumara to ruins, what a message we'd send to any other people who think to resist us, eh?"

Zubaidit sucked in a sharply audible breath. Then she laughed, tossing her head.

"You find that funny?" he asked.

She lifted both hands, palms up, the well-known gesture of the-child-asking-an-obvious-question in any of the tales. "If you burn Nessumara, Captain, then what do you possess afterward?"

"Victory. What else matters?"

*   *   *

THIS TIME OF year, as the rains faded to a whisper, the winds drew cooler drier air out of the northwest. You could taste the change, the locals said, see the shift in the color of the vegetation, hear the altered voice of the river announcing the advent of the dry season.

Mai peeked out through a slit in the curtains she'd opened with her fingers. Where the River Olossi met the Olo'o Sea, a green sway of reeds carpeted the shallows while blue sky melded with blue-green sea out beyond the last channels. She licked her lips, but all she tasted was her own anxiety. She let the cloth close.

"You're out early, ver," said the boatman, speaking to the hirelings as they set the curtained palanquin on the dock. "Your mistress or master can't wait, eh?"

"Don't ask me," said one of the hirelings brusquely. "We were hired to carry the palanquin at Crow's Gate and were told to deliver it to the boat and wait to deliver it back to Crow's Gate. Can we get going? Cursed cold out here by the water. We want to go wait in an inn."

Mai had a shawl wrapped around her shoulders, but not for the cold; it was for a covering should she need to conceal her face. Miravia sat on the narrow bench op-posite, clutching the baby beneath her long cloak. She had looked so fragile at the beginning of this journey, and therefore Mai had handed Atani over to her as soon as they were hidden inside the curtains of the palanquin. Holding a baby gave one a measure of stability.

The palanquin was heaved up, pitched right and then left, and settled into the boat. Coins changed hands with a clink of vey counted out in pairs. The boatman grunted as he poled away from the dock. He made no attempt to converse. The boat rolled as they hit choppy waters, and then they glided through a long calm stretch and at last bumped up against another pier. The tang of salt was now flavored with a brush of bitter incense. A whisper of bells chimed an ornament to the hiss of wind and water in reeds. She heard the slap of feet running down to meet the boat.

"Eh, this isn't our early day, ver. What were you thinking?" The voice was cheerful, followed by laughter from others on the shore.

Mai slipped a folded piece of paper through the curtains. "Take this to the Hieros, I beg you. I assure you, she will want to read it."

A person wrenched the message from her fingers.

After a moment, the first voice said, "Go!" and footsteps raced away. "Bring the palanquin onto the dock. Quickly, you clod-foots."

With much pitching, the palanquin got hoisted out of the boat and set on mercifully firm ground. Mai rubbed legs and arms sore from the journey smuggled in the chest. Miravia shut her eyes.

"Eh, that was a good game, the last of the hooks-and-ropes tournament," said the boatman, determined to make the time pass by visiting with the unseen loiterers. "You see it?"

"You think we get a festival day off? Wasn't there a new team competing?"

"A militia team, yeh. I was impressed. They'd only been practicing together for four months, at the order of the commander, and yet they came in third at the stakes. They'll win next year."

A new voice chimed in, older and female. "You see all the checkpoints and such they're setting up? I'm not sure I like it!"

The boatman snorted. "I don't mind! Better than fearing bandits and criminals, neh?"

Outside, the voices argued about the new road regulations. The curtains stirred, and a tooth-filled snout poked into the palanquin. A scaly shape shimmied in so fast Miravia shrieked, and Mai gasped, and the baby woke and began to cry.

Outside, the temple folk laughed.

Inside, a ginny lizard nudged Miravia's leg and tried to crawl up onto the bench beside her.

Mai snatched Atani from Miravia as her friend smothered laughter and crying beneath a hand clapped over her own mouth. "I—I—I never thought I would see one," she whispered. "I read about them in books."

Mai was struggling with her taloos and at last got the crying baby latched on. He began sucking noisily. The ginny backed down from Miravia and spun so quickly it seemed it had levitated, turning with a whip of its long tail. It nosed at Mai's feet, showed the merest edge of teeth, and tried to climb up on Mai's lap.

"You will not!" she said indignantly.

Its crest lifted, and a spasm like faintly glimmering threads of blue traced its knobbly spine. Atani let go of the breast, milk squirting his round face as he turned his head. Almost as if he knew it was there.

A voice called. "Heya! The Hieros says to bring up the palanquin *right away*!"

The ginny scrambled out, curtains swaying in its wake. The palanquin rose; they rocked. The baby burped and burbled and, like any newborn, complained as he rooted, seeking the breast. Their bearers were less experienced than the hirelings who had carried them smoothly from Crow's Gate to Dast Olo's docks; Mai could not get a moment of stillness to let the poor little one fasten on, and by the time they were dropped roughly to solid ground, he was wailing, inconsolable.

Miravia twitched aside a lip of curtain to peer outside. Her eyes widened. "It's a lovely garden!"

If joy had a fragrance, it might be something like this: flowers exhaling, the sun shedding warmth, the earth sighing, the air braced by a light breeze off the salty inland sea. Atani got hold again and began suckling. Mai sighed as the milk flowed, and a tingle of well-being, the breath of the Merciful One that penetrates all living things, coursed through her.

Miravia opened the curtain a little wider. "There's a pavilion here. How pretty! But I don't see anyone, just plants. Musk vine. Both orange *and* yellow proudhorn. Heaven-kiss. Look at those falls of purple muzz! I've never seen so thick a flowering!"

"What if we're not supposed to see onto sacred ground—?"

"You say that now?"

Their gazes met. They both began to giggle, then to laugh, the anxiety and tension like water overtopping a cup, pouring over the lip, coursing everywhere.

"Are you coming out?" The voice was old, strong, and not kind. But it wasn't angry. Like Anji, it expected to be obeyed.

Miravia grasped and released Mai's hand before pushing aside the curtain. Mai tucked Atani into the crook of an arm and followed.

The Hieros sat on a low couch under the pavilion's roof. Miravia and Mai kicked off their sandals and climbed three steps to kneel on pillows in front of her. For a while there was silence as Atani nursed contentedly. A spectacular taloos wrapped the old woman's slender form: silk of the most delicate sea-green hue. Woven with an inner pattern of scallops like waves, it might have been an actual layer of water skinned off the surface of the deeps of the inland sea and spun into fabric.

The baby let go of the breast, smacked his tiny, perfect lips. As soon as Mai burped him he closed his eyes and sighed into a doze. She adjusted her taloos and shifted him to the other arm.

"I admit," said the Hieros, examining first Mai and then Miravia with a cool gaze, "that I did not expect to see the wife of the outlander captain enter the precincts of the holy temple, not after he expressed so strongly to me on a separate occasion that his wife would never set foot in Ushara's temple. Yet even less did I expect ever to see the face of a Ri Amarah woman."

Miravia glanced at Mai, and Mai nodded. "I am named Miravia, ken Haf Gi Ri, daughter of Isar and his wife, whose name I am not free to mention."

The Hieros looked at Mai. "Why have you come?"

"We have come, Holy One, to ask you to give refuge to this woman."

"You have not come—one newly a mother and the other soon to be married, so it is rumored, to a rich man of poor reputation in Nessumara—to gain some pleasure in our gardens?"

"No!" said Mai, genuinely shocked.

The Hieros's expression darkened as a storm front occludes the horizon.

Mai plunged on. "I beg you, Holy One, listen to my petition. Miravia has run away from her family. She does not want to marry the man they've chosen for her."

"Does not want to marry? Is she asking to dedicate herself as a hierodule at the temple?" She surveyed Miravia with a look that made the girl blush to a sodden red.

"I am not, begging your pardon, Holy One," Miravia said hoarsely. "Meaning no disrespect. It's just—" She gulped out words between sobs. "Oh, what good will it do, Mai? No one will help us! Everyone will just tell me to accept the marriage for the honor of my clan! I would have been better off to sell myself as a debt slave!"

"Do you believe you would be better treated as a debt slave, you who are Ri Amarah and scorn all those who sell their bodies and their labor?" asked the Hieros coldly.

"Yes! It would be better! My life in Nessumara will be like living in one of the hells. But maybe I should just let that reeve fly me there. If the Star of Life invades Nessumara and overruns it, then I can hope to be raped and killed and that would still be better than living in a prison with a wicked old man who abuses those he controls!"

The Hieros clapped her hands. An attendant, an older woman with a sharp gaze and a curious eye, appeared on a path shrouded by flowering plants.

"Tea," said the Hieros, and the attendant nodded and vanished. The Hieros turned to Mai. "Does your husband know you are here?"

"No." Mai tucked her chin, her body remembering the lessons learned in the Mei clan, when you kept your gaze down and shoulders bowed as Father Mei or Grandmother addressed you in that scolding way. But then she remembered she was mistress of her own household. She was a good businesswoman. She had overseen the birth of a new settlement. She had blessed the marriages of more than forty local women and Qin soldiers, bonds that would carry them into the years to come, that would bind them to the land. She lifted her chin and looked the Hieros in the eye. "He is away on militia business. I have taken this action on my own."

"Ah."

"I did not know who else to turn to. Can you shelter her?"

"The Ri Amarah will take me to the assizes once they know she is here. They'll demand her return, according to their laws, by whose measure she is still a child because not married. How old are you, Miravia?"

"I was born in the Year of the Deer."

Her frown deepened. "Twenty. Far too old to be called a child." The attendant walked up the steps, set a tray on a low table, and poured three cups of steaming tea. Birds called from the trees, and a ginny lizard—maybe the same one who had nosed into the palanquin—ambled into a patch of sun and settled to its full length.

"However, few love the Ri Amarah," added the Hieros. "Fewer will support them in a dispute against the temples. What will Captain Anji recommend?"

Mai nodded as the old woman examined her. "You already know. That is a magnificent length of silk, Holy One."

The compliment drew a smile. "A fine bolt of first quality out of Sirniaka. No one else produces such exquisite silk. Miravia, you will hand out the cups."

Miravia took them one at a time, each one cupped in her palms, offering the first to the Hieros, settling the second in Mai's free hand, and sitting back on her heels with the third held close to her mouth as she inhaled the scent. "You've put in a tincture of rice-grain-flower."

"The Ri Amarah women are known for their herbal knowledge." The old woman sipped, and Mai sipped, and Miravia sipped and smiled her approval.

In silence, they finished drinking.

"As I said," continued the Hieros, "the displeasure of the Ri Amarah I can weather. They do not enter or tithe to the temples. But I am not as eager to set myself against Captain Anji. We negotiate difficult times. We are beset with creatures wearing the cloaks of Guardians who have raised an army that can be turned against us at any time, and no doubt will be if they gain control of the north, as they seem likely to do. Am I willing to offend a competent commander who may be key to our ability to withstand the storm? His ability to organize others into an effective force makes him valuable. He himself knows this. What if he were to change loyalties? To ride north and offer his services to the army in the north because we offended him here?"

"He would not!" Mai cried.

"Why not? Are you saying Qin soldiers did not conquer territory in lands far away from the Hundred? Is it not true that you grew up in a town they conquered? That you are yourself a prize for a victorious warrior?"

All the words she wanted to say—to protest that Anji would never ally himself with folk who burned and raped and killed—died in her throat. Her tongue was dry, and her hands had gotten cold.

"It's all true," she said in a low voice, never dropping her gaze from the Hieros's fierce glare. "Beyond the Hundred, the Qin are conquerors. You could say I am a prize taken in war. But we came here as exiles. I speak because I have done my best to find willing and honest wives for the Qin soldiers. To encourage women to marry men they might not otherwise look at because they began their lives as outlanders."

"There's been much discussion about how you encouraged young women and Qin men to make their own choices. In this country, clans and elders arrange marriages. That is the proper way to do things. Youth is not celebrated for its wisdom. Lust is a slender reed on which to build a house. We recognize the power of the Merciless One. We do not construct homes on her body."

"That's also how it was arranged in Kartu Town, where I grew up. Yet it seems to me, Holy One, that people did not treat each other very well in the house where I grew up. I sold produce in the market for several years and I heard plenty about the misery folk endured in their households. Maybe people could have at the least the right to say no to an arrangement. Then maybe more would treat each other decently and fewer fall into abuse."

"Spoken passionately, verea. And with some understanding of human nature, rare to see in one so young as you. Yet you must know, having seen the ceremony of binding, that we do not force young women to accept a marriage. She doesn't have to eat the rice."

"There are other means of coercion."

"Those who truly fear the arrangement made by their clans are not required to suffer. The temples can always serve as their refuge."

Mai lifted her chin, sensing victory in those words. "Miravia is not fortunate, she is not willing, and yet she cannot say no. Folk will say she went willingly, when the truth of her heart speaks otherwise. I believe her when she says she will suffer abuse in that house in Nessumara. If I can do something to stop it, then it is dishonorable of me not to try!"

Miravia hid tears behind a hand.

The ginny thumped its tail once, then lapsed back into stillness. A small bird with a red-feathered cap and white-tipped wings fluttered in under the pavilion roof, landed beside the tea tray, and looked them over with sharp black eyes.

"You may suffer for this act today," said the Hieros.

"I know," said Mai. "But I can't do anything else."

The old woman bent her head, as if considering whether to make one more attempt to bargain Mai down. Her hair was entirely silver except for a few strands of black. It was bound up and pinned in place by lacquered hairsticks like those Mai herself used. Once, Mai supposed, it had been luxuriantly thick hair. Now, of course, age had thinned it.

She raised her head and looked at Mai. "Do you trust me?"

"I came to you for help, Holy One."

"Very well. I'll help you. But she'll have to leave Olo'osson immediately. Today."

"There is another way, Holy One," said Miravia. She sucked in a breath as for courage and spoke again. "I could enter the garden."

"Mira!" Mai grasped her arm. "You can't—"

"Not as a hierodule. No offense to you, Holy One. I have no place in the temples as an acolyte. But merely as a—a—a—" She shook off Mai's touch, not in an angry way but in the manner of a person who knows she must walk the next stretch of the road alone. "Once I enter the garden—and do what is done there—my family can no longer marry me off."

"You can't possibly—" Mai cried.

"No clan among the Ri Amarah would ever accept me," said Miravia calmly. "They will say I am no daughter of theirs. They will say I am dead."

The old woman had features honed by age; in them you could see the ghost of her youth, and yet Mai could not imagine her young. "Who are we, daughter, if we have no clan? We are a fish hooked out of the water that sustains us and left to die on the shore. Do not be so eager to embrace this form of death."

"I do not want never to see my mother and brothers again. But it is still better than what awaits me in Nessumara. Can you imagine sending one of your own daughters into such danger?"

The Hieros smiled. "Certain of my daughters are trained to walk into danger, and they do, and I will likely never see them again. But you are desperate, indeed, Miravia. Is this truly what you wish?"

"Doesn't anyone ever think I also might be curious? That I might want to—" She stammered. "Don't all the tales say it brings pleasure? I see in the blush on your cheek, Mai, when you speak of Captain Anji. Why shouldn't I be allowed to experience what every girl born into the Hundred expects she can have simply by walking to the temple after she has celebrated the feast of her Youth's Crown?"

"I am not one who will argue this point with you," said the Hieros. "Enter if you wish. If you feel apprehension natural to one coming from your circumstances, be aware that certain of the hierodules and kalos are trained specifically to— Well, it should be obvious we are accustomed to every temperament and wish a person might have, entering Ushara's holy precincts."

"Miravia," whispered Mai, "it would be—with someone you don't even know, or—" Humiliated, she looked away.

"All are allowed to enter who have not offended the goddess," said the Hieros. "You, too, may enter if you wish, Mai."

"I would not! Anji would—!"

"Does he own your body, as a master owns the debt of a slave?" asked the Hieros.

She could not find a safe place to fix her gaze. "It would be shameful. I couldn't."

Miravia grasped her free hand. "Oh, Mai. Do you think less of me?"

"Never!" She burst into tears. "I just want you not to suffer what I grew up with! That hateful house! Grandmother Mei's spite. My father's temper, and how it made everyone walk with their heads down for fear of looking him in the eye and getting punished for it. He beat my brother, Younger Mei—my dearest, twin to me—because he wasn't strong and angry like Father. And now my dearest twin doesn't even have me to protect him or hold his hand. But I always knew I would have to leave the house. That's the way of it, that the girls must leave to join their husbands' households, where they bide at the mercy of those who may treat them well or ill. Bad enough I should have to leave. I couldn't bear to think of you, Miravia—"

"It will be well." Miravia kissed her and stroked her. "Once my family casts me out, we'll find another way."

"I'll gift you with so much coin," sobbed Mai, "you can set up your own stall selling herbs and ointments." She sucked in breath and wiped her cheeks.

They embraced.

Mai pulled away. "Best I go quickly, Holy One."

"You came in secret, did you?" said the old woman with a faint smile, perhaps of disapproval. "Now we will see what colors this thread layers in the cloth."

"I don't want you to get into trouble," said Miravia in a husky voice.

One last embrace. Maybe their last one.

Mai walked out of the garden with the palanquin carried behind her by silent but clearly curious folk. They did not attempt to speak to her.

It will be well, she thought fiercely.

The baby woke, and as she crossed under the white gates, ginny lizards peered down upon them from the trees and tall bushes. Atani turned his head as if trying to track them. As she passed under the outer gates and beyond the temple's outer wall, the sun had risen a hand's breadth above the estuary. The path down to dockside gritted under her feet. The force of all she had said and done overtook her in a rush of feeling that made her tremble. What would Anji say?

The boatman stared at her as the acolytes jostled the boat while getting the palanquin fixed across the board, but mercifully he said nothing except "You'll have to sit inside, verea, for there's no place otherwise."

He balanced the boat deftly as she clambered aboard, tightening her grip on the baby until he squawked in protest. She settled onto the bench inside the curtains as the boatman poled away from the dock. She kissed Atani's sweet face for comfort.

The water had gentled, and the easy slap of water in the back channels lulled her. Smells and sounds rose from the channel: musty molding thatch; the dry rustle of reeds; the whit-whoo of a bird calling after its mate. Soon she heard the rumble of wheels, a hammer pounding a steady rhythm, a burst of laughter cut short. A boy's voice lilted: "There is it, Seri! Go get the porters!"

What would she tell Tuvi? She'd not thought that far ahead.

The boat bumped the dock. An odd spill of silence emanated from the dockside where she might have expected the lively sounds of commerce.

"No need for such a look, ver," said a voice she recognized as that of one of the hirelings. "We just took the coin like any hire."

The palanquin thumped hard to the boards. Weren't the hirelings going to pick her up and start back to the city? She bit her lip and reached for the curtain, to tell them, kindly but firmly, that they had to go right away.

"I beg your pardon, ver, but them who hires the palanquins have to be able to expect privacy—"

The curtain was abruptly pulled back. She looked into Chief Tuvi's face, his expression so blank she thought it hid a deeper emotion. His mouth quirked, as if he had a wish to speak but could not. At a movement behind him, he flipped the curtain up over the roof of the palanquin and stepped out of the way.

There stood Anji, his riding whip clenched in his left hand and his normally neat topknot as frayed as if he'd bound his hair up in haste. To come riding after her.

Her breath caught in her chest; her fingers went cold; her cheeks flushed hot.

But not this cringing. One sharp breath she took in, and then with her market face as bland as ever she could make it, she stepped out of the palanquin with the baby in her arms and smiled with blander politeness at him, facing it out with pleasant words in the tone with which she would greet a treasured acquaintance.

."Anji, I was just—"

He slapped her, the back of his hand to her cheek, the blow so sharp and unexpected that all grounding in time and place fell away for forever and one instant as she fell and she drowned

he's furious

he's reaching for his sword

he's going to kill me now

Merciful One, please give me the strength to endure this

She was too stunned to react when instead of cutting her down he took the baby out of her arms and turned his back on her. Then he paused, shoulders tense like coiled steel, and turned halfway back.

"Bring her," he said to Tuvi.

He walked to his horse, mounted, and rode away.

"Hu!" Tuvi sighed, and as through a haze Mai saw him take his hand off his sword's hilt. Her cheek was stinging.

All kinds of people were staring, old and young and laborers and merchants and debt slaves and girls at their harborside slip-fry pans with mouths dropped open. Everyone was staring, except the Qin soldiers detailed to escort her, who were carefully looking elsewhere. The river churned behind her.

"Follow my lead, Mistress," Tuvi said in a low voice. "It's best if you ride, so they can see you are still honored among us. Do not let them see you cry. You've nothing to feel shame over." He paused, fingering his wisp of beard as he studied her. "Do you?"

Her face was really hurting now, a throb that reached to her left eye. "It wasn't wrong to help Miravia." Her voice was a scrape over tears held in. "Are you angry with me, Tuvi? I couldn't bear that on top of the . . . other."

He shook his head, as if she'd given the wrong answer. "Ride with me, Mistress."

She had no more of a choice than the day Anji had approached her father and proposed that Father Mei might be interested in marrying his daughter to a Qin officer, a polite way of saying: I'm taking her. He could have hauled her out of the marketplace where she had sold produce, and done whatever he wanted; no one could or would have stopped him. The family would then have taken her back in shame, or left her to make her own way as a whore. It happened to women all the time, didn't it? Only the old stories and songs made it seem glamorous.

She struggled to gather calm as she turned to the porters. "The second half of your payment is waiting at Crow's Gate when you return the palanquin, as was agreed." She followed Tuvi to the waiting soldiers.

But of course it was impossible to ride in a taloos. Trembling and embarrassed, she had after all to call the bearers and return to Crow's Gate sitting within the palanquin as the Qin soldiers plodded before and after like jailers. She wept once and then wiped her eyes. Her cheek hurt if she touched it, so probably it was going to bruise, and then she wept again, and after that she thought of what Tuvi had said and she was done with weeping. She had done nothing wrong! Even if everyone said otherwise—that of course a young person must marry according to the wishes of the clan—she could not stand aside while her beloved friend was handed over to a man who had already killed three wives.

They arrived at Crow's Gate. The line at the gate moved slowly, and when she peeked out from behind the curtains, it was to see sober young militiamen interviewing each incoming party and clerks of Sapanasu checking accounts books. She leaned out, but did not see Anji among those waiting in line.

"Set me down, please." The bearers did so, and she climbed out and walked over to Chief Tuvi. "How long will this take, Chief? Don't they let Qin soldiers through?"

"They do not, on orders of the captain. If the locals must endure these delays in order to make the roads safe, then so must we when we are about the ordinary business of the day. Lest we appear as outlanders in their eyes, taking privileges we deny to them."

"No, of course Anji is right." She looked away, pretending that her bracelets must be turned. Her breasts were beginning to ache, a sense of fullness that anticipated a feeding, for although Atani did not take much at any one time, he nursed frequently.

Tuvi dismounted and handed his reins to one of the soldiers. "You four escort us, two before and two behind. The rest of you wait your turn and be sure that the bearers and palanquin owners are properly paid."

"Tuvi, are you sure—?"

"Do you want to stay in the palanquin, Mistress? I can engage its services to return you to the compound."

"I'd rather walk." To delay returning home to face Anji's anger. To feel the sun on her face, to pray for the grace of the Merciful One to cover her heartache.

He led their little cadre up to the gate and invoked captain's privilege to pass them through ahead of others.

"That's the outlander, the captain's wife," someone said in the crowd.

Another called out, "Greetings of the day to you, verea! You brought good fortune to my cousin's husband's sister, who married one of the soldiers after her own husband was killed on West Track. She'd have had to sell herself into debt slavery otherwise."

"Council members say you're the one bargained those cursed Greater Houses down until they begged for mercy." This comment brought general raucous laughter. "Thanks to you, verea. They say it's thanks to you the Qin soldiers fought at all."

"Out Dast Olo way, eh? Getting a taste at the temple? For sure you've earned it."

A flush rose in her cheeks, maybe enough to hide the red mark.

Folk made pretty greetings as Tuvi inexorably led her forward. She spoke words of greeting in return, nodding and smiling at every person who nodded and smiled at her, but all she could see was Anji's face in the instant after he had struck her, a man she did not recognize.

They worked free of the crowd and walked up the road to the inner gate. People were too busy going about their business to pay any mind to Qin soldiers; it was nothing they didn't see every day.

"Hard to know where to start," said Tuvi. "Let me tell you a story. One time, you see, there was a boy named Anjihosh, the son by the Sirni emperor sired on a Qin princess, who was herself sister of the Qin var. The Qin var had handed his very own sister over to the emperor to seal a treaty. That's the way of things."

"I know, but Miravia—"

"Best to let me speak," he continued in a soft voice that as good as cut her throat. "For a while the Qin princess was much in favor with the emperor because she was not like any of the other women in his household, and be assured that he had many women in his household, confined to a special palace reserved for the emperor's women into which only the emperor or his cut-men—eunuchs—could enter. Now I suppose most of those women were slaves, chosen for their beauty or some special skill like weaving or herb knowledge or cooking. But a few were wives according to the Sirni way, that is, they were the daughters and sisters of powerful men of noble families. So it could not have sat well with these wives, and their fathers and brothers, that the emperor should shower so much favor on an outlander, and more especially, on the son she had borne him. For you can be sure that Anjihosh was as a child well-spoken and attractive in temperament, quick at his lessons, and naturally the best among the young princes at riding and archery and weapons. His enemies whispered that he was the emperor's favorite among his sons, a threat to the worthy noble families of pure Sirni blood. What the emperor thought of this we cannot truly know.

"There came a time when one among the wives decided to act. Her son was older than Anjihosh and had for many years been considered the likely heir. Among the Sirni, only one man rules as emperor, although the emperor has many sons. It is common for the mothers of the sons of the emperor to fight a war within the women's palace from which only one emerges victorious." He offered an arm to help her over a gouge in the street cut by the wet-season rains. "Hard to imagine wasting so many good soldiers, lads who could be trained up as captains and commanders. It's no wonder these people are weak."

"If they're weak, why haven't the Qin conquered them?"

His smile was a tip of the lips, a thought held to itself. "The empire is very large. But it so happened that the Qin princess found herself alone and despised in the women's palace with no one to support her while meanwhile her greatest rival had called in her powerful family to put pressure on Emperor Farutanihosh to name her son Azadihosh as heir after him. Which naturally would mean that any other boy sired by Emperor Farutanihosh would have to be killed. So the Qin princess found a way to smuggle her boy out of the palace. Through one means and another, she got him to a border post, and thence into the hands of Qin clans willing to bring the boy back to his uncle, who must raise him or be seen to be dishonorable in the eyes of all the Qin. For it is shameful to kill one's own relatives, is it not? Naturally the head of a clan must make sure that the line remains untainted by weakness, but any child let live becomes the charge of all his clansmen."

"So the boy and his mother returned to the Qin."

"Eh? No, Mistress. The boy did indeed arrive at his uncle's tent. But his mother could not escape the women's palace. Nor could she hope to journey through the empire without raising the alarm, for as you recall, women do not travel openly on their roads. I suppose, if she still lives, she remains in the palace still."

Mai's fingers tightened on Tuvi's arm. "Surely you see that I couldn't allow Miravia to walk into a prison like that?"

"Let me finish, Mistress. That is not the end of the story. The boy Anjihosh was raised by certain of his uncle's retainers, who were assigned to take charge of him. Without exception they became his kinsmen of the heart, because he grew to be that kind of man, who inspires such trust and loyalty."

"That's you!"

Seren, hearing the chief's voice fall silent, looked back to make sure nothing was amiss, but Tuvi nodded at him and they trudged on. It was a warm day but mercifully not hot, yet each step dragged, harder than the last. Her legs were as heavy as sacks of rice; her belly ached; her cheek was a stab of flame. But if she concentrated on Tuvi's voice, then she didn't notice these pains so much.

"In time Anjihosh came of age to ride in the Qin army. A wife was proposed from among the daughters of the var's high command. It was a good marriage with Commander Beje's girl. Has Anji ever spoken to you of his first wife?"

She flushed. "Neh. I just remember, that time we met Commander Beje, that the commander said she was a headstrong girl. 'Precisely her charm,' that's what Anji said in reply. But Commander Beje also said Anji could have shamed the commander's entire clan in front of the var because of what she did. Yet Anji did not. That's why Commander Beje helped Anji. Because Anji had acted honorably in the matter of his daughter. Anyway, I thought she must be dead."

They had come to the gate into the inner city, another checkpoint with militiamen making their painstaking interviews and folk waiting with remarkable patience, bred no doubt from the still-fresh memories of the siege and from the years before that when the roads had not been safe.

They waited in silence, people glancing at them but holding their tongues. When they reached the front of the line, the guards recognized Tuvi and waved them through.

Only after they crossed Assizes Court and started up the hill did Tuvi start talking again, his voice so low Mai strained to hear. "She was seduced by one of the western demons, the ones with ghost hair and ghost faces and blue eyes. Like that slave Shai had."

"Cornflower."

"A demon very like that slave girl, yes," said Tuvi. "She rode away with the demon into the west. So that is the same as being dead, actually. If you walk into demon land, then you are dead, aren't you?"

"Did she hate Anji? Hard to see how anyone could hate him, but maybe she was forced to marry him. That can breed resentment."

"Naturally the elders of a clan consider marriage prospects and make suggestions, and negotiate terms. And of course in the matter of secondary wives and concubines taken by men in the army, that is naturally done by their preference. But within the Qin clans themselves, it would be very bad to force two young people who did not like each other to marry because then if one mistreated the other, the clans would get involved, and there would be a feud, so as you can imagine clans wish to avoid such an outcome. Generally a proposal is made, and the two meet and decide if they can cooperate. If they and the families agree, he offers her a banner sewn especially for the marriage. They race, and if he can catch her, then it is destined that they wed." His shrug came and went like a brief smile. "Of course, a woman may choose under such circumstances to allow a man to catch her."

"That's how they do it here, too," said Mai, "only with the bowl of rice offered and accepted, or offered and refused."

Was that a tinge of color in his cheek?

"I'm sorry about Avisha, but she wasn't right for you, Tuvi-lo. Anyway, even here, even if people say girls have the right not to eat the rice, to refuse the man who courts them, or if a lad wants one girl but is told to marry another for the benefit of his clan, there are other ways to coerce a person to marry by making it seem you'll be disappointed or you need the treaty or you must have the coin lest the entire clan be ruined . . . and what about the Qin var? Did the var's sister, Anji's mother, *want* to go to the empire as the seal on a treaty?"

"You're not listening to me, Mistress. Anjihosh was loyal to his first wife, but she was not loyal to him. Where did he find you today?"

"I don't understand what you're trying to say."

He grinned in that lively way the Qin had, and shook his head as at the antics of a child innocent in its charm. "Mai, I expected you to help Miravia leave the city."

"You did?" Her voice rose to a squeak. The soldiers glanced at her, and hurriedly away. "No, no, of course you must have. Of course we couldn't possibly get out of the compound without you knowing of it. What an idiot I was to believe otherwise! Why didn't you just help me, then?"

"I obeyed what I knew would be Anji's command in the matter. Also, I could therefore afterward speak the truth with a straight face to the Ri Amarah and their agent—that one loitering at the gate hoping to catch a hint of her whereabouts—that I had advised the girl be returned to her family, as Anji would have done, had he been there."

Having nothing to say, she walked in silence. Had Anji been there, she would never have dared defy him.

"Not much farther to go," she murmured, feeling the pain in her cheek magnified.

"But I did not think, Mistress, that you would take her to the whore's temple."

"It's Ushara's temple, Tuvi! We must speak of it with respect, because we are Hundred folk now."

"And you went with her, to partake of what is offered in the garden?"

She stumbled over her own feet, and he caught her arm and kept her walking as she covered her bruised cheek with a hand. "Can that be how it looked to him? I went with her to plead her case to the Hieros!"

"His father betrayed him. His half brother betrayed him. His mother sent him away alone, to be raised among people he did not know. Then his wife betrayed him, and finally his uncle the var betrayed him, for he sent Anji east to the frontier to be killed, as we discovered only because Commander Beje felt obligated to repay Anji for the dishonor shown to him by the commander's own daughter. Now he wonders if *you* have betrayed him."

"I would never! I only went there because I hoped the Hieros could help me. . . . You haven't even asked what happened to Miravia."

"Best I don't know, Mistress. Here we are." He stopped her with a hand on her elbow as they reached the familiar gates of their compound. She smelled meat roasting, and the savory tang of a big kettle of spiced caul-petal soup. "Take my advice, Mistress. Don't go to him. I'll have Priya bring you the child, for nursing."

Her milk had let down, twin spots darkening the front of her taloos. She crossed her arms over her chest. "Can we go in?"

"Don't go to him," Tuvi repeated. "Bathe yourself. Make yourself particularly beautiful, as you can, and preside over the supper table as if you are the queen and he a humble captain honored to be seated at your table. If you have nothing to apologize for, then do not apologize out of fear. Qin do not respect those who are afraid."

"If you do it, don't be afraid," she murmured.

"If you're afraid, don't do it. You have offended him, Mistress, but I know you, and I know you went to the temple with no thought for anything except the other woman. Yours is a generous heart. Do not be generous with your apologies. And if I must say so . . ." He twisted his beard hairs again, frowning. "Do not ever under any circumstances go again into a temple dedicated to the Merciless One. Let the Hundred folk have their ways, as they must. No Qin woman would ever do such a thing. In this matter, the captain will never ever change."

17

FROM THE HEIGHT, Joss marked the many humble fishing villages strung along the wide curve of Messalia Bay like so many variegated beads on a vast necklace. Folk were busy on the paths and beaches, about their end of the day business. Fish dried on racks; kelp marinated in vats; children got in a final round of hooks-and-ropes on a dusty field with the oval scraped out of the sandy dirt. Every council square—some as humble as a stone wall and not even a sheltering thatched roof—had been decorated with ribbons in the color of the season, the faded blues and dried out greens marking the Whisper Rains.

At the mouth of the River Messali, he and Scar flew over a substantial port town where every compound flew ribbons or banners in the old custom that Joss's mother and aunts had often talked about but which had fallen out of favor in his own life-time. Leaving its wharves and markets behind, reeve and eagle skimmed over the water toward the band of islands and islets that beaded the mouth of the bay. The shallows and deeps of Messalia Bay were easily discerned as distinct shades of blue, sand pale beneath. If only people were as easily mapped. It was high tide and so the bay was full, lapping on white sands. The golden light of the late-afternoon sun glimmered on the flat water; no storms today.

At length, he caught sight of a watchtower on a stony islet. He flagged the sentry, who replied with a burst of activity, flagging Joss the "clear" and then bending to shout unheard words to his fellows as Joss guided Scar to the outer landing islet of Bronze Hall, on the bayward side of the much larger island that housed the main hall and grounds.

A pair of fawkners approached, holding batons painted in the grandfather patterns, very old-fashioned. They tapped and gestured the full, wordless greeting of hall to visitor, which he'd learned in training but never had done since. Cursed if he could recall what he was supposed to do in reply.

They finished and stepped back, waiting.

"Greetings of the dusk," he began, but he faltered when he heard how thin the market words sounded in the silence left by their formality.

Scar dipped his big head. He had watched it all with keen attention, and now he chirped in a distinct greeting and settled immediately despite being in a hall he barely knew.

Joss walked to the waiting fawkners. Four men, armed like ordinands, loitered by the archway that led to the bridge.

"If you please," Joss said, "could you let Marshal Nedo know I'd like a meeting with her. I'm Joss, commander at Clan Hall."

The older fawkner began to laugh. The younger cast Joss a startled look and trotted over to the loitering ordinands; two took off as Joss frowned. "Aui! Did I say something laughable?"

"Neh, sorry," said the fawkner, wiping his eyes. "Just never thought I'd see the day when a reeve would fly in here and call himself commander of Clan Hall and not even know the proper forms, eh? Not to say we haven't been warned. I'm Kagard and that is Lenni. Let's look at your eagle, then. Anything I need know, besides that he knows the old forms better than his reeve does?"

The words rankled, but Joss kept his temper jessed. "Scar's calm, if you're calm. I'd appreciate your opinion on these two wing feathers."

Scar accepted their attention, and flirted a little with the younger fawkner when he approached with a pair of files. Joss coped the one trouble spot on Scar's beak, and when they were finished he allowed Kagard to direct him and Scar to an empty loft, where a haunch of deer was brought in and tossed to the eagle after Joss had leashed him to his night's perch.

They walked outside onto the landing ground, now entirely in shadow. Lenni called an assistant out of a storehouse to pull closed the barred gate.

"It's been years since I've been at Bronze Hall," said Joss. "I go out the archway and over the bridge to the main island, neh?"

Kagard touched him on the elbow in a friendly way, and smiled in a friendly way, and spoke in a friendly way. "Best you wait here for marshal's people to give the go-ahead, eh? It shouldn't take long for them to get back."

"For the go-ahead? Is there some kind of trouble?"

"Hasn't been any trouble since marshal instituted the new measures and talked to all the town councils in Mar."

"Was there trouble before?"

"Trouble in the Beacons and in the Ossu Hills. But we've culled out most of that trouble."

"What manner of trouble are you talking about?" Joss asked, feeling increasingly uneasy as he looked around the expanse of ground. The islet was a rocky outcropping artificially leveled to create the landing ground for visiting eagles; there was a good launching point at the prow of the islet. The place housed a dozen separate small lofts and a storehouse and barracks and, as he recalled, stairs cut into the rock beyond the archway that led down to a stone pier where supplies could be paddled in. The folk here did a lot of fishing, too.

"Not for me to say," observed Kagard.

Joss knew a dismissal when he heard one. He licked the taste of salt off his lips, remembering his own childhood on the coast near Haya. "Fish for dinner tonight, I'm hoping," he said, and got a laugh from them, as he had hoped. They weren't thawing, though. They kept a formal stance. "Your eagles here, you've got more known family groups than any of the other halls, neh?"

"We do," agreed Kagard.

Lenni was more voluble, perhaps seeing an opening to show off his youthful knowledge under the gaze of his seniors. "We've got cursed good records of family groupings. They say that Bronze Hall eagles cooperate better than those of any other hall. That's why we keep visitors out here. Fewer tangles."

"Good to hear."

A pair of ordinands and a reeve trotted into sight under the archway. One of the lads carried a lamp. Joss strode over to meet them.

"Marshal Orhon will see you now," said the reeve.

"Orhon?" Joss had no image of any such reeve. Not that he expected to know every gods-rotted reeve in the Hundred—obviously that was impossible—but after his years at Clan Hall he usually knew the names, at least, of the senior reeves at various halls because the legates of each hall did talk about the goings-on at their home compound. But an Orhon, out of Bronze Hall? Nothing.

How idiotic had he been to come here alone? A cursed headstrong fool, as always, acting on impulse instead of thinking. The Commander would never have acted so, but she was dead, wasn't she? So far, he was still alive.

He hefted his pack to his back and noted that they did not ask him to give up either short sword or baton as they crossed under the archway and out into the odd stillness of dusk exposed on the high rock cliff of the islet. The water swirled in white foam still visible in the gloom. Stars bloomed. There was no moon. Their footfalls made an erratic rhythm on the plank bridge. A bell tolled in the distance, ringing the last fishermen home.

On the far side of the bridge, the trail divided. They followed a track to the left, set along a cliff and lit by lamps hanging from iron posts. As they came around the headland the wind off the ocean rushed in his face, but even in the last gasp of day crossing into night it was beautiful. Far out, the ocean rolled, billows drawing white-caps in and out of the dusk.

A cottage was set alone in the midst of low-growing seawort and clumps of berry-wax bushes. Lamps hung from the eaves. They clumped up onto the porch, where Joss pulled off his boots. The reeve, who had not introduced herself, rapped on the door. A hand bell chimed. The reeve indicated that Joss should let himself in. With a startled shrug, he slid open the door, stepped through onto mat, and closed the door.

The ocean's breathing and the wind's thrum beat in his ears as he stared at the man sitting cross-legged on a pillow in a chamber otherwise empty except for two flat pillows resting to the right of the door.

"I am Marshal Orhon." The man had a shiny red blotch sprayed across the right half of his face. The left side of his face drooped, that eye fused shut, the skull shaved to stubble, the ear not much more than a twisted nub. His jaw didn't work properly; that accounted for his soft voice.

"Where is Marshal Nedo?" Joss asked.

If Orhon's expression changed, Joss could not interpret it. His voice's timbre did not alter. "Her eagle was killed."

"*Was* killed."

"Deliberately killed. By raiders in the Beacons. They mutilated both bodies. To send a message."

"We never heard—" Something in the twist of Orhon's scarred mouth cut Joss so hard he closed his lips over the rest of the pointless words he'd been about to utter.

"There is a great deal Clan Hall does not know, if indeed you are from Clan Hall as you claim. Yet you cannot even respond to the formal greeting, the one passed down through generations of reeves. One which, according to report, your eagle recognized."

"Everyone says Scar is smarter than me, and I see no reason not to believe them on that score."

"Sit down," said the marshal, and Joss wondered if his voice softened. Had he found the comment amusing? The confession humbling enough?

He grabbed a pillow and sat. Voices murmured on the porch; feet thumped; the door slid open.

"Sidya!"

Sidya, once Bronze Hall's legate at Clan Hall, nodded at the marshal, not meeting Joss's eye. "Yes, I know him. His name is Joss. He was legate from Copper Hall, in all kinds of trouble because he kept insisting on honesty and holding to the laws. He got sent off on an expedition to find out about some trouble on the roads. Last I heard before we were called back here was that he'd been named marshal of Argent Hall to try to clean the place up. As for the commander of Clan Hall, I know nothing about that, only the word we got a few weeks ago about a massacre in Toskala where the old commander was murdered. As for his claim to be the new commander—well—any reeve can name himself 'commander' but that doesn't make it so."

Orhon did not move. It was eerie, as if he were not a living man at all but disfigured skin stretched over the wooden frame of a man.

"Do you vouch for him, Sidya? Do you think he's telling the truth?"

As the silence drew out, Joss grimaced. "The hells! I thought we parted on amiable terms. That was three years ago, Sidya."

The comment cracked a laugh out of her, and he glimpsed the enthusiastic woman he'd shared a bed with for about half a year. She reached for the other pillow, tossed it down next to Joss, and sat beside him. "I've no complaints of you, Joss. Anyhow, I broke it off, not you. I'm just—" She looked at the silent Orhon, whose one good eye did not shift focus. "These are troubled times. I don't know who to trust, but I guess I'd trust Joss as much as anyone. I've never known Joss to be anything but honest." She looked back at him. "But why in the hells are you come here calling yourself commander of Clan Hall?"

"Because I'm the last person you'd think the Clan Hall council would elect?"

She grinned. "True enough." Her smile flattened. "But if enough of their senior reeves were murdered . . ."

"There wasn't much left to choose from," he admitted. "I've gained experience as marshal at Argent Hall. Together with the militia there, and an outlander captain and his soldiers, we defeated an army that attacked Olossi. So I suppose that makes some folks think I might be able to protect the rest of the Hundred. I accepted the post and the responsibility because someone has to fight."

"Why are you here?" Orhon asked him. "Bronze Hall has recalled its legate and attendant reeves from Clan Hall. We don't intend to send them back, especially now that Toskala has fallen into the hands of a creature called Lord Radas."

The words were not spoken in anger, simply as a statement of fact, the more chilling for its even temper.

"Surely you see we must stand together or fall separately. We've got to institute new practices. Reorganize. Work in concert with the forces assembling to fight Lord Radas's army."

"You want us to change. To give up our gods-given charge of enforcing the law and become soldiers instead?"

"I don't *want* it. But we have come to that crossroads where we must choose the path of change."

"So you say. But Clan Hall has failed the reeve halls. They've let the old formalities lapse. The old disciplines are not followed. Where the old order decays, then what is new has crept in with its rot."

It was hard to hear because his voice was so soft, but Joss at last got a handle on the odd cadences in the man's speech. "You're not from Mar."

"I fled Herelia fifteen years ago after my village was burned because we refused to submit to the rule of Lord Radas's archons." His good eye flickered as at a memory. "After years as a beggar and itinerant laborer on the roads, I washed up half-starved in Salya, here in Mar, where I found work in the marsh cutting reeds. Then an eagle chose me."

"How did you come by these injuries? In the line of duty?"

"Neh. These I got the day my village in Herelia burned, when I tried to rescue my mother and aunts and the other children from the flames."

"And an eagle chose you despite—!" Sidya cast an accusatory glance, and Joss broke off, flushing. "I beg your pardon, Marshal. But eagles choose—"

"Eagles choose men and women who are whole and healthy and strong, not those who are crippled. Why did Stessa choose me? Because the gods made it known to me through the eagle's calling that I must restore the proper forms, the proper discipline, the old ways. Adherence to tradition is the only way to defeat the pollution that breeds these troubles. It is the only way to defeat an army whose adherents wear the gods-corrupted Star of Life. Until Clan Hall recognizes this truth, we cannot support her. Or you."

*   *   *

IN THE QIN style, the baby's cot was placed beside the table as Mai spooned soup into bowls. In Kartu Town, children did not dine in company with the master, but the Qin did not consider a meal to be a meal if there were not children and kinfolk present. Food taken on campaign, among soldiers, took a different word, akin to horses and sheep grazing.

Horses and sheep would have been better company.

Mai had overheard Tuvi telling Anji that it would look bad to the men if he did not eat the homecoming meal with his wife and child. So there Anji sat, formally dressed, not a hair out of place. None of the senior officers were present today, although the doors were slid open so that anyone passing by could look in. The cooks had outdone themselves with dishes spiced both hot and subtle. Anji did not eat. He did not speak. He simply sat there, not looking at her. His silence made of the meal a mockery.

She would not succumb. It might seem that a hundred knives pricked her, so nervous was she, but she kept her hands steady as she ate. Even her dark mood could not kill her appetite. Also, handling spoon and eating knife gave her something to do as Anji did not talk and did not eat and did not look.

At length she finished, and called for Sheyshi to take away the dishes. As soon as Sheyshi had placed the dishes on a tray and carried them out, Anji rose. He caught up Atani and carried the baby to the door.

"Really," said Mai in a voice that made him pause, back to her, at the threshold, "it shows no respect to those who have cooked, taking particular care to make special dishes, to refuse to eat this food simply because you are angry not at them but at another person."

He said, in a lower voice, addressing the door, "The Ri Amarah showed us hospitality in every way openhearted and generous. That we have succeeded here is in great part due to their aid. Now you repay that hospitality by betraying them. Leaving me to make apologies and restitution, if any can be made given the enormity of the dishonor."

He banged the door shut behind.

Mai rested her forearms on the table and her head on clasped hands. So had Father Mei sounded as he scolded one or another of his wives or brothers: never able to be satisfied.

Well. Anji could kill her. That would be painful, certainly, but then it would be over. Surely if he had meant to beat her he'd have done it already. Anji's was a contained rage, and she supposed he might continue on in this horrible way for days or months or years.

What if he did? Her heart would weep, but hearts endure years of unhappiness all the time. She had probably breathed more happiness in this last year than Grandmother Mei had inhaled in her entire life. After all, she had always told herself that the only place to find happiness is inside. That was the lesson she had learned growing up in the Mei clan.

Yes, it would be difficult. Yes, she would cry. But she had a healthy son. She had a fine compound. She had plenty of coin, a house to run, a settlement to administer where folk praised her and asked for her to listen to their disputes and sit in judgment over them even though she was young. She could conduct trade in her own person and with her own collateral. She was learning to figure a proper accounts book and actually to write and read.

"Mistress?" Priya slid the door open just enough to slip through. "The captain has gone out, with the baby." Her frown creased her forehead.

Mai opened her mouth to speak but no word came out. A hammer had smashed her heart, leaving her breathless. Priya sat down beside her and took her hand.

At length, Mai whispered, "I need something to do, Priya."

"Yes, Mistress. We'll sweep. Best to change out of that good silk, though."

They swept the porches and the flagstone pavements, then raked the garden walkways in neat patterns until dusk make it impossible to continue and she had the beginnings of a blister on her right forefinger. She washed face and hands and feet, put aside her clothing, took down her hair, and lay down on the pallet unrolled by Sheyshi. But although she was exhausted she could not sleep. At length, she heard voices and the hiccoughing wails of the baby.

Priya crept in, holding the boy. Mai put him to her breast and his nursing calmed her and made all ill things seem, for the moment, too distant to matter. Male voices conversed nearby, tense but muted, and even their rumble faded as her eyes closed and she dropped away. . . .

To wake.

She was still alone in the bed, of course, a single coverlet nesting her and Atani. A light shone through the rice-paper squares set into the door. She settled the baby in his cot. Her sleeping robe, pale as silver, seemed poured over the chest set on one side of the room. She slipped her arms through the sleeves, bound it around her waist, fumbling the knot. She tried to open the door quietly, but he—still dressed, his hair still caught up in its topknot, and seated cross-legged on a pillow as though he meant to bide there all night—looked up at once as she paused in the opening, darkness behind her, the lamp's flame dividing her from him.

His expression was as unforgiving as stone. "If you betray me, I will kill you."

After everything, this was too much.

"When did I ever betray you? When have I ever given you reason to question my honor? You bought me from my father, did you not? Surely that gave me reason enough to feel I was nothing more than your slave. I could have resented you. I could have nursed sorrow. But I held my tongue in the early days. I hoped for something— I don't know—perhaps just those tales and songs I grew up with that you think are so silly, the bandit and the merchant's daughter, like the tale of the Silk Slippers that they tell here in the Hundred where the girl escapes all those who are hunting her and marries the carter's son. Maybe it was foolish of me to dream of those tales as if they could ever have been true. But I wanted to make a decent life for myself out of what had been forced on me. Isn't that what any of us want? Less pain and more joy? I wanted to love you. I wanted—"

The sharp movement of his head, as though she had just slapped him, caught her short.

The flame hissed. He lifted his chin, voice scarcely more than a breath of terrible yearning. "Do you love me, Mai?"

"Of course I love you. Has there ever been a stupider question heard in all the annals of the world than whether I love you? How can you even doubt it?"

"I see how you talk to other men. You smile at them exactly as you smile at me. Like that reeve."

"Joss?"

"Of course you would think of him first!"

"Besides Miyara, he's the only reeve with whom I've ever exchanged more than ten words. He's personable, it's true. And he's an Ox, like me, and naturally those who are born in the Year of the Ox feel a particular affinity each for the others, because of the particular attributes of our character. Because we are hardworking and pragmatic, with a dreamer hidden inside."

"The heart of an Ox leaps to the heavens, where it seeks the soul that fulfills it. For the Ox is very beautiful. Is he not?"

"Handsome, certainly, but very old!" she retorted tartly.

"Not too old to father a child."

"Anji!" For an instant she was too scalded by fury to see, and then as the haze boiled away she stepped fully into the chamber and grabbed the first thing that came to hand: a ceramic cup off a tray. "All you think about is if I have dishonored *you*. What makes you think I would ever dishonor myself?"

She flung it at him, flung herself back into the sleeping chamber, and slammed the door so hard shut its reverberation startled the baby in his sleep, a flinch heard more than seen, and then he cooed within his baby dreams and settled.

Strangely, the cup had not shattered. Surely she had thrown it hard enough!

She fingered open the door, easing it back just enough to peer through. There stood Anji, in lamplight, holding the cup in one hand and staring at it as if its existence, such an object as a cup that could hold liquid that might please the tongue and warm, or cool, the throat, puzzled him.

Then he smiled, an expression touched by a whisper as of doubt throttled. He tossed the cup into the air and caught it in the same hand. He crossed toward the door, and Mai scuttled back and collapsed to her knees beside the mattress.

He slid the door open with a foot and came in carrying the tray with its two ceramic cups and a matching ceramic bottle, sealed with a cap, and the lamp, still burning. He set the tray on the chest and poured out rice wine into each cup. Offering her one cup, he sat cross-legged on the matted floor and drank the other down in one gulp. She sipped cautiously, watching him.

He undressed, and when he was in his robe he sat down on a pillow at the end of the mattress and handed her a comb, merely gesturing to his topknot, which it was her right and indeed duty as his wife to unbind and comb out.

His black hair was not as coarse and straight as that of the other Qin, but had a lustrous glow she never tired of. She stroked for a long time, enjoying the peaceful rhythm because it eased her heart. She knew they would have to discuss Miravia, but not now. In truth, she wanted desperately to lean into his back, to kiss the nape of his neck, to entwine him in an embrace that would cause him to turn and caress her, but she remembered what Chief Tuvi had said. She must not seem to be apologizing. Helping Miravia would cause trouble for them, but she could not have done otherwise and still lived with herself; she would accept the consequences. As for the other—going to the temple, and that ridiculous accusation thrown out against Reeve Joss—she had nothing to be ashamed of. *He* ought to be ashamed, for even thinking it.

He shifted, and she thought he was about to speak, but he did not. Yet he did turn, easing the comb from her hand, and turned her to face away from him. He gathered her unbound hair and started working through it with the comb from the top of her head down to its ends, which brushed the floor. It was impossible to concentrate on anything except the warmth of his breath on her neck, the way his fingers brushed against her back, or her arms, or the lobe of her ear. This state of suspension, him brushing and her sitting so still lest she utter his name or throw herself into his arms, was almost painful, and yet she dared not move for fear of breaking the connection. Anji was a patient man, very disciplined, and she began to wonder if he meant to comb her hair all night just to see who would break first. And because she was so very tired, and wrung tight, and aching with misery and hope, she began to laugh, a little hysterically perhaps, but laughter all the same even if there were sobs caught in it.

He set the comb on the tray.

"Enough, Mai," he said, his voice husky with desire, perhaps with satisfaction, perhaps with anger still simmering. He embraced her, pulling her close. "Enough."

MUCH LATER, A sharp voice jostled her awake. Anji was already rising, drawing on his sleeping robe. He grabbed his sword and slid open a door that led onto the covered porch overlooking their small private garden. The light of a Basket Moon, somewhat past the full, gave a faint sheen to the outlines of the room: the square corners of the chest, the rectangular paper screens of the doors, the puddle of Anji's clothing where he had let it fall on the matted floor. He slid the door closed with his foot, cutting off the light and her view.

The baby was stirring in his cot, and Mai's breasts were heavy with milk. She pulled on her own robe, letting it hang open as she lifted Atani out. As she nursed him, reclining first on her right side and then switching to her left, she listened to low voices in an extended discussion on the porch outside although she could not quite pick out words.

The door scraped open. Anji slipped inside and sank down on the mattress beside her. Atani smacked and gurgled.

"What is it?" Mai whispered.

"One of the guards thought he saw a demon flying overhead, a winged horse, but Sengel has the night watch searching the compound and they have found nothing. The tailman who saw it is one of those who was present when the demon invaded the house."

She nodded, remembering the evening when the demon in the shape of the dead slave girl, Cornflower, had flown into the compound riding a winged horse and killed two Qin soldiers with sorcery.

"Sometimes, on watch at night, you sink into a place that is neither dream nor sleep. It's a world demons haunt."

"Maybe he was dreaming."

"Maybe." He tucked his sword alongside the mattress. "Where is your knife?"

The baby released the nipple and exhaled a tiny burp.

"Don't move," whispered Anji, drawing his sword as one of the doors into the interior slid open. A figure paused on the threshold between the rooms, half in and half out. Its face was concealed beneath a long hooded cloak of a substance that, although dark in color, remained distinguishable from the shadows. Anji rose. Mai tucked the baby against her, using her body to shield the infant.

The figure raised its hands to pull back the hood to reveal its face. "Mai?" it said hoarsely.

By the light that glowed from its right hand, Mai stared into the face of a man she had never thought to see again. "Uncle Hari?" she whispered. "We thought you were dead."

His gaze opened a well of memory, a shaft down which she plunged. Best of uncles! He had always teased the little ones in that smiling way that made them feel they weren't just a nuisance meant only to stand in silence around the grim adults. He carried them on his back, horse to their Qin warrior, a game played only in the privacy of their own courtyard, for the Qin had forbidden all people of Kartu Town to ride. He could sing a merry tune, and he knew all the best tales, the ones in which the swooning maiden was carried away by the handsome bandit only to discover the bandit was really a prince, the ones in which the villains fought and died, and those in which the prince triumphed and died anyway. After Father Mei had forbidden him from speaking out against the Qin within the Mei compound, he had spent more time away from home and perhaps inevitably had gotten involved in a foolish, doomed scheme which no one had ever had the courtesy to explain to her, only that he had disgraced the family and they were fortunate they weren't all executed because of his rash actions. The Qin had decreed that every man, woman, child, and slave must witness the punishment of the rebels who had dared speak out against those who governed them. Sixty or more young men had been marched in chains out of Kartu Town into the east. Not a single one had ever been seen or heard from again.

Then Hari averted his gaze, as if it was too painful to look on her, and she was back in her sleeping chamber with Anji poised motionless beside her. Hari brushed fingers along his forehead as if it ached.

"Uncle Hari!" She rushed forward with the baby in her arms and flung her free arm around him. "Eihi!" She flinched back, skin stinging where it had pressed against the cloak. "Does that cloth have barbs in it?"

"Mai," said Anji. "The baby."

The baby! "Uncle Hari, do you see? You have a great nephew, this fine young lad. His name is Atani, after his grandfather. It's a water-born name, here in the Hundred. As yours would be—neh, it would not be, would it? For you're really Harishil." She took a step back to display the child, and another step back, which was far enough to see past Hari's body into the chamber behind, where Tuvi, Sengel, and Toughid were edging in through the open doors.

"I won't harm the baby," said Hari, turning his gaze to Anji and, after a moment, wrinkling his forehead as in puzzlement. "Call off your men, Captain. Mai, why is this man in your bed?"

"He is my husband! Father Mei married me to him."

"You were supposed to marry the Gandi-li boy. The sheepherder's clan."

"So I was. But then Captain Anji wanted to marry me."

"Naturally my brother would not say no to a Qin officer, even in the matter of his favorite child," said Hari drily. "He gave them anything they asked for, hoping to remain in their favor. But what he never understood was that they would treat him favorably only so long as they had a use for him. That was their nature, to take what they could use. What they had no use for, they discarded or ignored." He glanced over his shoulder, his gaze sweeping the dark room behind him, and the soldiers actually cringed away from him. Sengel grunted as if he'd been slugged in the belly, and dropped to his knees.

"Stay where you are," said Anji in a louder voice, meant to reach his men. Although he wore a fine silk sleeping robe tied with a embroidered ribbon and had his fine black hair falling loose halfway down his back, he could not be mistaken as anything except a soldier. "If I may ask, Uncle Hari," he went on carefully, "why have you entered this compound without seeking permission at the gate? You can be sure any relative of Mai's would be greeted hospitably."

Hari's ironic smile flashed just as she remembered it, enough to make you smile and frown together as his glib tongue entertained you. "Mai and your soldiers reveal all that is in their hearts to my gaze, as it must be. And who could not wish a glimpse into Mai's heart, truly? Your soldiers have not quite such generosity in their souls although they seem clean enough in their hearts despite being soldiers whose job it is to kill. Yet you are exactly the puzzle that pervert Bevard said you would be. I admit I would not have believed any person could stand veiled before me if I hadn't met Shai. By any chance, can you see ghosts?"

"Shai!" Mai took a step toward him, caught Anji's curt gesture, and halted. "How did you meet Shai? Hari, you must tell me."

He would not meet her eye, and yet he watched Anji closely. "Shai is in the north. He wanted to stay with the army for some reason he would not tell me, but I forced him to leave. In doing so, I saved his life, because Lord Radas has ordered all outlanders to be interrogated. Bevard told Radas he'd encountered two outlanders veiled to his sight. Naturally, we must find them. I suppose, Captain, that you know Shai's purpose in being in the north better than I do. I admit, he seems changed from the lad I used to thrash when I was trying to get him to show some spirit. He impressed me. But the chances are still that they'll catch him and kill him before he can make his way to safety."

"Uncle Hari! How could you not have found a way to get Shai out of danger?"

"I risked enough doing what I did do! I had no other chance to help him. You have no idea what goes on with the army, what they want, what they intend."

"What do they intend?" asked Anji. "Why are you here?"

"To kill you, Captain, as I've been commanded."

The words fell like stones. But Mai would not be crushed. She stepped between Hari and Anji. "He's the father of my child. I won't let you kill him!"

Hari laughed. "I think those are lines from the tale of the merchant's daughter and the fox bandit, are they not?"

She flushed. "Don't ridicule me, Hari. Girish used to do that."

"Whew! That's a deadly thrust."

Anji did not move or relax his guard. "Who wants me dead? Besides the ones I already know about?"

"Lord Radas wants you dead. He suspects you are the one who led the successful defense of Olossi. Who destroyed that cohort of soldiers Bevard was trying to lead out of Olo'osson. Lord Radas wants no competent commander leading a rebellion against him."

"I'm leading no rebellion," said Anji. "The people of Olo'osson do not want to be conquered by his army. That's all."

"No more did the people of Kartu Town wish to be conquered by the Qin. That did not stop the Qin armies from overtaking us, did it?"

"And you support Lord Radas's plan to rule the Hundred with an army that, by all accounts, burns villages, rapes women, enslaves children, hangs innocent people from posts to frighten the rest of the population, and destroys the councils through which cities and towns and villages in the Hundred are ruled?"

"As a Qin officer, surely you see the irony of your criticism of Lord Radas's methods of conquest."

"The Qin army keeps villages and towns intact as long as they do not rebel. What use is a town if it has no markets, no herds, no fields, no artisans producing goods for sale? The Qin governors are harsh toward criminals, but in return those who obey the law live in an orderly and peaceful way, undisturbed by crime."

"Lord Radas promises much the same thing. Perhaps he needs to complete his conquest of the Hundred before he can impose his orderly and peaceful ways."

"Enough!" cried Mai. Both men, startled, shifted to look at her. "Chief Tuvi, tell Priya to brew tea. We are going to drink tea and discuss this as civilized people do. Hari, you must be aware that if you mean to kill Anji you will have to kill me first. Anyway, you have neither sword nor knife, so it is not at all clear how you mean to kill him."

"Demons kill with sorcery," said Anji.

"If that's true, then I fail to see how a sword can parry sorcery. Can you go in the adjoining chamber and wait, Hari? And close the door. I need to—make myself presentable."

He chuckled, stepped into the chamber behind, completely vulnerable to the swords of the Qin, and slid the door shut.

Mai walked to the table, snapped spark to flint, and lit the lamp.

Anji lowered his sword. "Mai, he's a demon. He's not your uncle."

"Maybe he isn't my uncle. It's possible. But here in the Hundred, they count demons as a civilized race, like the other children of the Four Mothers. So even demons must be treated with the hospitality due to guests."

"He came here to kill me. He says so honestly enough."

"Did it never occur to you, Anji, that we might make an attempt to change his mind? No, of course it did not. You are a soldier. But I am a merchant. We can't fight sorcery with swords. Did you see that light in his hand? That light did not burn from oil. Here, take Atani."

She offered him the child. He kept his sword in his right hand but settled the infant in his left arm. The baby was awake, perfectly calm, and as soon as he was in Anji's arms, his dark gaze fixed on his father's face. Anji smiled down at the baby as Mai tugged her robe tightly closed, tied it with a sash, and tugged on a jacket over it as a second layer. She grabbed a pair of hairsticks off the side table and twisted her hair up behind her, pinioning it in place. Then she stepped behind Anji and bound his hair up in something resembling the topknot he normally wore.

"You look well enough for a man awakened in the middle of the night," she said as she measured him. "What of me?"

He sighed.

"What does that mean?"

"The question need not be asked. I don't like this situation."

She picked up the lamp, opened the door, and went into the other chamber. Hari stood in the middle of the chamber, not looking at Sengel or Toughid, who stood ready to strike. The far door slid open and Chief Tuvi entered, marking Hari without looking him in the face. He got out of the way to allow Priya to enter bearing a tray with three cups and a ceramic pot. The slave's gaze flashed toward the cloaked man. She faltered for a breath, then with an effort continued to the table and set down the tray.

Mai settled on a pillow and placed the lit lamp on the table. "Uncle Hari, if you'll sit, I'll serve you tea in the proper fashion. Anji?"

Anji handed the baby to Priya, then sat next to Mai, his sword still in his hand. The three soldiers kept their silent study. No one looked directly at Hari except Anji and Mai, and even she found it difficult to meet his gaze because such startling and uncomfortable memories churned into life when she did so, things she did not want to share with anyone: Uncle Girish's constant pinching and the way he had leered at her until Father Mei had beaten him so badly that he had finally left alone the children of the house; the vomit and diarrhea that had poured out of her in the first leg of her journey away from Kartu with the Qin, when she had thought she would die of sickness; the desert stars, so bold and bright they seemed close enough to touch, like hope; Anji's kisses; Miravia's whispered confidences and warm embrace; the dusty market lane in Astafero with its women working so very hard to make a new life for themselves out of the unexpected fortune tossed their way by the Qin outlanders; Tuvi's flush as Avisha rejected him; the tingling charge that had permeated the air during Atani's birth, blue threads like living silk clinging to her and then to the baby as if through touch they sought to communicate, or to infest his flesh—

"Mai." Anji touched her arm, a jolt like fire.

Hari touched his fingers to his eyes. The light that had shone from his hand had vanished. Looking like a perfectly normal person, he sank down cross-legged onto a pillow opposite Mai, the table a polished surface between them.

"Let me pour the tea," she said, out of breath.

In Kartu Town you poured tea one way for visitors—their tea must be poured and served first, each cup separately according to importance—and another for family. She set out the cups and poured all first, then considered her dilemma. Anji was her husband, yet Hari was her uncle.

She picked up a cup with each hand and set them before the two men at the same time, then raised the third one for herself and spoke the conventional words: "The gods give us tea for our health, we drink with their blessings."

She sipped first, to show she trusted the brew. Anji watched her, then picked up his cup with his free hand and waited, pointedly, for Hari to pick up the cup that sat before him. Both men drank. Mai poured a second cup.

"Uncle Hari, please do not let me sit here wondering. How did you reach the Hundred? Why are you still here? And why have you come, as you say, to kill my husband, when truly you would be better off to stand beside us, not against us? Those who are kin should not battle each other. We should be allies."

Hari kept his gaze fixed on his cup, but his words were directed at her. "You are changed, Mai. Yet it seems you are very much the same. How can that be?"

"Perhaps you would like something to eat? Our cook makes very good sweet rice cakes. There are some left over from yesterday, are there not, Priya?"

"Yes, Mistress," she said in a barely audible mumble. "I'll go right away, Mistress." The door slid open and then closed.

"The baby has escaped," said Hari. "Not that I would have harmed an infant."

"Plenty of babies died when Lord Radas's army invaded Olo'osson last year," retorted Mai. "Or were orphaned, which amounts to the same thing, for if they do not then die, they will likely be sold into slavery if there are no kinfolk to take them in, or if their kinfolk have not the means to support extra mouths. That is why we must stand with our kinfolk."

The lamp's light glowed on the surface of the table. It was odd how the light was absorbed into the fabric of his cloak, whose color Mai could not define. She thought there was something more there, threads that reminded her of the twisting blue filaments in the valley, but then she would blink and see nothing but a silken cloth saturated with the sinking dusky purple of twilight.

"I am not what you think I am, Mai."

"Maybe not, but that does not make you any less my beloved Uncle Hari. For you can't deny you are him, can you?"

"I can't deny it. I am him, and I am not him. He is dead. What I am is a shell. A ghost. Perhaps I am a demon." He raised his eyes to challenge Anji's stare.

Anji, who could look right at him and not flinch.

"Even ghosts and demons have kin," said Mai briskly. "Would you like more tea?"

When he did not reply, she poured again and signaled to Tuvi. "More tea, Chief, if you will. Perhaps Sengel and Toughid can fetch it."

The chief looked startled. He flashed a look at Anji, who considered the wall with an expression that meant thoughts were boiling in his head that he wanted to sort into tidy ranks. He signaled with a hand, and Tuvi gestured, and all three soldiers left the chamber. Mai felt their presence on the other side, but here in the antechamber, she and Anji and Hari now sat alone.

"Why do you take such a risk, Mai, when I have already confessed that I come here to kill the man who sits beside you?" asked Hari.

"You have already said the soldiers cannot kill you. So their presence does not advance our situation, nor does it protect us. I saw what happened when the ghost girl invaded my house. How did you come to the Hundred, Hari?"

His frown was like a scar. She was not sure he would speak. When he did, words poured from his lips in a rush. "You watched me being marched away by the Qin as a slave. You. The entire Mei clan. Every person who lived in Kartu Town. Later, I was sold to be a mercenary. The Qin make soldiers of slaves. Or maybe that was the Mariha princes. I'm not quite sure who sold those of us who survived the desert crossing. My new master took a chancy hire out of greed, and we were marched north over frightful high mountains as escort to a trading caravan. I talked the master into it, if you must know, stupid as I was. The caravan master's tale of injustice caught my attention, or maybe it was only his beautiful daughter. But once we reached the Hundred, we were ambushed. We fought a stupid battle, in the cursed blowing rain, I might add. The girl died defending herself with a paltry knife while I was busy slipping like a clumsy calf, and afterward I got a sword thrust up under the ribs. It's a tiresomely unheroic story."

"Maybe you only think it must be, because you are angry at yourself for surviving when she died."

"If you call this survival."

"If it is not survival, then what is it, Uncle?"

His hand gripped the cup. "They call it 'awakening.' The blow should have killed me, yet later I woke, weak but recovering. Wearing this cloak. Surrounded by creatures who laughed at my misery. Anyway, ghosts are like mist, aren't they?" He looked at Anji.

"Ghosts can't be touched," agreed Anji. "Nor can they drink tea. That I have ever seen."

"So after all, it seems I'm not dead." He gulped down the tea and set the cup down hard. "Lord Radas is not even your worst enemy. The cloak of Night is far more dangerous to you. She seeks any who are gods-touched—that is, those who can see ghosts, who are veiled to the sight of Guardians—and she kills them. She and Lord Radas know you are one of them, Captain, because you foolishly revealed it to that pervert Bevard. You are dangerous to us, because we cannot control you. Therefore, you must be eliminated."

Anji made no show of reacting; even Mai could not guess what was going on in his mind. In the harsh silence, she reached across the table and touched her uncle's hand, a fleeting brush. When no snap of power pricked her, she wrapped her fingers around his wrist and held on.

"Uncle Hari, you don't have to go back to them. I know a place you can go, where they won't find you."

"There is no place—"

"You have heard no voice but your own voice, and their voices, for so long you can't hear any other words. Stop listening to them! You weren't the one who scraped the dirt before Grandmother Mei and my father. You were the one who talked back. So why crawl now?"

"You cannot understand how—"

"Is pain all they can inflict on you?"

"Isn't pain enough?"

"Bad enough, of course. But I don't think that's what you fear the most."

"What do you think I fear the most, Mai?" He turned the cup over, a single drop pooling on the surface of the table, and then he lifted one edge of the cup and placed it over that smear of liquid, trapping it.

"I think you fear yourself. You have disappointed yourself, and now you are afraid to be anything except a disappointment. It's true, you might try to break away from them and fail. That would be bitter, indeed. But you might break away, and succeed. You might have to make a new place for yourself. You might have to walk into an unknown country without knowing what will happen when you get there."

He scrambled to his feet, and Anji shifted to get his legs under him, but Mai grabbed Anji's wrist and squeezed until he stilled. Hari had only begun to pace, his cloak belling and sagging with the measure of his turns.

"Even if you think you know," she went on, "even if you think everything is determined, that the Gandi-li boy will become your husband because it has been talked of for two years and the contract is next to sealed, you can never know. Even if you think it's likely you will lose a battle to a numerically superior enemy, you can never know. Even if you think your dearest friend will be forced to marry a cruel old man who will abuse her, you can never know."

"Even if you think your wife will naturally obey what she knows to be your wishes," said Anji in a soft voice, "you can never know."

Hari's steps ceased. That smothered sound might have been a chuckle. He stood with his back to them. Lamplight rippled in the threads of his cloak like a living creature caught in the weave. "And in this secret place you recommend, what would I be? A creature living in solitude? A prisoner? A crippled man trapped in the corner of a house until he fades into blessed oblivion?"

"I'll come visit you," said Mai, "but you must wait and be patient, for it's possible I won't be able to visit often. It's a beautiful place. You'll find the waterfall and cave of particular interest."

"Why not? What can they do to me they haven't already done?" He raised one arm, elbow rising sideways as though he was wiping away tears. "You haven't changed, Mai. I suppose you still sneak peaches out of the basket and hand them to orphaned beggar children and pathetic slaves, and then overcharge the spiteful who have riches to make up the difference."

"How did you know—!"

"She overcharged me," said Anji. "Looked me in the face and named double the asking price. I respected a woman bold enough to cheat a Qin officer. That's why I married her."

"It's not cheating," said Mai, "to name a price. I'd be a poor merchant had I not tried to increase my profit. You could have bargained."

"I did," said Anji more quietly still. He was not smiling.

The words stung in a way she did not expect, and as she looked down at her hands, one lying flat on the table and the other curled around her cup, she had to blink back tears.

Anji kept speaking. "Where the River Olossi meets the Olo'o Sea, there's a low island where eagles and sea birds perch. I'll send a message to Argent Hall to have Reeve Miyara meet you there, this coming evening, just before sunset. I'll send her with a wolf banner, so you know she came from me. Do not go directly to Argent Hall and display yourself. The fewer people who know where you are, the less likely you are to be found by those hunting you."

Hari walked to the door. "It's true enough I must hide. I'll find this islet, and wait there until a reeve named Miyara arrives to guide me to a valley where I can shelter without fear of being discovered by Lord Radas or by Night."

"What you tell us about their plans could help us defeat them," added Anji.

"I'll talk to none but Mai, and certainly not to the hated Qin. That's the price of my cooperation."

He slid the door open and walked out past the Qin soldiers; they looked away as he strode past them. Even the Qin must fear a creature who could reach into your heart and steal your secrets.

"Anji," she began.

He shook his head. They waited as the Qin soldiers followed Hari.

At length, Chief Tuvi returned. "I'm not sure how he came in without anyone seeing him, Captain, but he's gone now. He mounted a winged horse and flew out over the wall. Shall I set a doubled guard?"

"Do it, but I think it unlikely he'll return unless he has allies waiting to attack us, which I doubt. Surely he could have killed me, if he'd meant to, and yet he stayed his hand. Meanwhile, alert the reeve on duty to send a message to Argent Hall. Reeve Miyara must come at once."

Tuvi left.

Anji crossed back to the table. "It's too dangerous for you to see him again."

"What's to stop him coming back here to see me, for one thing? And for another, Uncle Hari trusts me. If I reject him, he will despair, and despair will lead him back to them. Isn't despair one of the things that turns people into demons?"

"If they were people before. Usually demons are demons."

"Hari wasn't born a demon."

"He might have been born with a human face and body, and no one to know better or ever suspect."

"I might be a demon, then!"

He studied her as the flame hissed, its light spilling over the polished surface of the lacquered table. "You just might be." Then he kissed her, and she was suddenly so weary that she sagged against him, letting his embrace support her. "If he was born as human as you or I but has become a demon, it must be because corruption has eaten his heart. So you must be doubly cautious, Mai. I suppose I'll let you visit him, as it seems I must if we are to get any information out of him. That's information we desperately need. We can take Miravia with us. She may have some special sorcery to challenge his—"

"Miravia!" She pushed out of his arms and stared at him, but he was not a man who teased for the pleasure of seeing you squirm. "She can't stay in the temple."

"Ah. I went to the Ri Amarah last night."

"When you were still angry with me."

He smiled crookedly. His dimple flashed. "I went to offer them a larger share of the oil of naya we put on the market."

"Anji! The oil of naya is the foundation of our wealth. If we unconditionally offer the Ri Amarah a larger share of what we put on the market, then we're cutting into our own profit—"

"I was still angry with you. Hear me out. I never got that far. The entire household was in an uproar. The Hieros had sent word that Miravia had entered the temple. Master Isar told me the entire tale. He had no idea you were involved in any way with her escape. Or that I might already know where she was."

"Tuvi said they'd hired an agent. A man was watching our gates. If he saw her, or me—"

"The agent will no longer trouble us."

"But—"

"He'll tell the Ri Amarah nothing."

Something about his clipped tone made her shy away from further comment. "Yet so many people saw you, and me, at the docks in Dast Olo—"

Anji shook his head curtly. "It's unlikely anyone in Olossi will pass on stories from the street to the Ri Amarah. Or that Master Isar would believe such gossip if he heard it."

"Every merchant listens to the word on the street."

"Certainly. But they have no proof to connect your visit to the temple with Miravia's flight there. Without such proof, I am too valuable an ally for them to cast aside on hearsay. What matters to us is that they now consider Miravia to be dead."

"Dead! Poor Miravia." She blinked, but no tears flowed. "Yet that means she is free."

"Orphans who have no protection and nowhere to shelter are not 'free.' They are vulnerable and inclined to end up dead. However, we can adopt Miravia. It would be valuable to us to have such a person in our household who may interpret Ri Amarah customs and their secret language. The source of their wealth. Their sorcery, if they possess sorcery."

"Don't you trust the Ri Amarah?"

"As much as I trust anyone. Also, you'll be leaving Olossi for a month or more. You and Atani will ride with me on a circuit of the training camps and militia forts in Olo'osson. You'll talk to the local councils and merchants while I'm about militia business. Miravia will be company for you on the road."

"When will we see Uncle Hari?"

"We'll come to Astafero as part of the circuit. That will be time enough for him to make a decision about where he intends to stand. I have it all worked out, Mai. It will do very well."

PART FOUR: GUARDIANS

18

BEFORE DAWN ON the second day of the Month of the Ibex, in the Year of the Red Goat, a storm boiled up from the east over the mountains of Heaven's Ridge to break over a high salt sea and a vast escarpment that overlooked the western desert far below. Marit left her companions and the horses under the shelter of an overhang and walked into the downpour. If she stood out here long enough, would the rain pummel her into droplets that would pour over the jagged edge and plunge down cliffs too tall to measure until they shattered into nothing and were gone beyond redemption? Just as the life she had once led—Reeve Marit, who partnered with her eagle, Flirt—could never be regained.

Over twenty years ago she had been murdered, but instead of crossing under the Spirit Gate, she'd awakened as a Guardian, wearing the bone-white cloak of Death.

Marit had never feared storms. As a child she had sneaked out at night to see how close lightning would strike or if the blue spark of a fireling had left glittering in its wake a tangible mark of its passing, a ropy thread fine like spider's silk but as strong as iron. At such times her father would drag her in and slap her, and afterward hang fresh amulets over the doors and shuttered windows to prevent demons from creeping in on the trail his thoughtless daughter had left open. Her mother would scold her for upsetting her father and waking the others in the compound, but her mother never bothered with amulets and wards. She made offerings to the seven gods and expected the gods to deliver justice through the day-to-day work of the reeves and through the assizes presided over by the gods' holy representatives, the Guardians. That Marit's mother had never herself seen a Guardian did not shake her faith in their holy purpose.

Lightning chased across the sky, leaping from cloud to cloud. Storm scent prickled Marit's skin. Along the distant southern shore of the inland sea, a dance of firelings lit the horizon, winking into flame, flicking out, and popping again into life. She wept at their beauty.

Were the firelings not like the spirits of humankind? It is so easy to cut the breath out of a living, breathing person, to send the spirit fleeing past Spirit Gate, and yet again and again spirits will kindle. The drive to live, to flower, to grow, is unquenchable; the kiss of the Four Mothers breathes it into the world and even the least of things—a patch of lichen on stony rocks, a frail sparrow battered in stormy winds, an unloved child—will suck in that strength and struggle to stay alive.

Whatever living might be.

She trudged across the pale mud into the shelter where her companions waited: two people who, like her, wore the cloaks of Guardians, and the three winged mares they rode, who were named Seeing, Telling, and Warning.

Jothinin smiled with relief. "Not much to see in such weather, neh?"

"I saw firelings."

His pleasant smile widened into something more heartfelt. "Seldom glimpsed and therefore always welcomed. Among their gifts are said to be healing, and a filament as fine as spider's silk yet as strong as iron."

"What is a fireling?" asked the girl where she crouched by the fire, turning a spit on which she had skewered five conies trapped among the rocks.

Jothinin settled down cross-legged with a satisfied grin.

"We're about to hear a tale," said Marit with a laugh as she sat down.

"So quickly you understand me." He pretended indignation, but he was a man who wore lightheartedness as easily as the sky-blue cloak that swathed him. Yet Marit did not think him light. "It happened in ancient days when the Four Mothers ordered the Hundred. They gave pattern and form as weft and warp. The tales weave the fabric of the land, and within the tales lies the Hundred count."

"What is the Hundred count?" the girl asked. She never left off asking questions.

"The hidden order of things. The Hundred count is the skeleton beneath the flesh. In the Hundred count we comprehend the architecture of the land. Just as we count numbers, so can we count the frame of the Hundred. The Hundred is many, yet it is also one. The Hundred is the one crossroads at which many roads meet. Yet it is also two: female and male; night and day; wet and dry; life and death. We who live and think possess three parts: the mind, the hands, and the heart, and three states of mind: resting, wakened, and transcendent. Every town and city builds three noble towers, and within the Hundred three languages are spoken. The Four Mothers created us out of water, fire, earth, and air. The Five Feasts delineate our lives. There are six reeve halls," he nodded at Marit, "and seven gods, seven treasures, seven holy gems. Seven directions."

"How can there be seven directions?" demanded the girl.

Marit hissed, for it was very rude to interrupt a tale, but Jothinin smiled with the calmness of a man who has faced the worst in himself and come to the conclusion that he can see very little after that to unsettle him.

"Nine Guardians and nine colors, the hues of their cloaks. Ten Tales of Founding."

"What about eight?" cried the girl.

"Naturally, I was hoping you would ask," Jothinin said.

Kirit laughed, the sound so unexpected it made the dreary day brighter. Thunder rumbled in the distance, and outside first light glimmered over the sodden ground and restless waters.

" 'These are the eight children, the dragonlings, the firelings, the delvings, the wildings, the lendings, the merlings, the demons, and we who call ourselves humankind.' There's your answer, Kirit. Firelings are one of the eight children—you might call them tribes or clans—of the Mothers."

"That is no answer."

"Lendings live in the grass, wildings in the high forest canopy, merlings in the ocean, and delvings in the stone. Firelings live in storms. They're seen most often in mountainous regions. They are blue, and sometimes red, and they appear to our vision for a moment only, as if they can slip into this world and out through the Spirit Gate, inhabiting both that place and this one. There are also tales of how firelings have saved lives of dying children, chased wandering goats home, and aided women in childbirth when they had no midwife to attend them. As the tale says, 'the spark of the living spirit is the spark of the fireling.' That which lives draws them."

"What of us, Jothinin?" Marit asked as the fire streamed heat and smoke over her damp cloak and wet hair. "We are met here, we three. You called us 'the last of our kind.' But the Guardians are spirits arisen out of the pool at Indiyabu in ancient days, raised by the gods in answer to a plea. As it says in the tale: 'In the worst of days, an orphaned girl knelt at the shore of the lake sacred to the gods and prayed that peace might return to her land.' Are we truly Guardians if we did not rise out of the pool at Indiyabu? For it seems to me that the others—Lord Radas, Night, Yordenas, Bevard—have crossed under the Shadow Gate into corruption. They sow the fields not with justice but with discord, hate, and cruelty."

"They are demons," said Kirit.

"Demons are one of the eight children of the Mothers," objected Jothinin. "They, too, are sheltered by the Mothers' protection. I would not call demon any human who does wrong just on account of that wrongdoing. In older days, the gods-touched were said to be demon-born."

"You forgot Hari," said Kirit, stubbornly sticking to the main point. "He's one of them."

"Hari is not like the others," said Marit quickly.

"You hope he is not," said Jothinin. "But if he has become their creature, then they have five. Five Guardians can kill one."

"As the cloak of Night tried to do to me in Toskala on that night when the army attacked. But Hari wasn't there. It was Kirit who refused to cooperate with them. She saved me. For which I hope I have thanked her enough."

Kirit frowned, her brows drawing down. To look at her with her colorless hair and her demon-blue eyes and her ghost-pale skin was to remember she was an outlander. Easy to call her a demon, since she looked nothing like a person. Yet what was a demon, really? Marit's father had feared demons, while her mother, like Jothinin, had believed they were no more dangerous than any other of the children of the Hundred, having merely their own ways and customs. Her mother always said humankind were the most perilous of all.

"If we are to fight them," said Marit, "then we must find Hari and convince him to join us. We must seek out as well the cloak of Earth. Then *we* will have five, and they will be four, too few to hunt us down and kill us."

He scratched behind an ear like a man trying to sort out the solution to a difficult bit of accounting. "Cloak of Earth vanished long before any of the rest of us understood that corruption was eating into the Guardians' council."

"She deserted you, instead of warning you!" cried Marit. "Don't you think that's wrong?"

"It is what it is. I am the last to judge."

"The gods created the Guardians to judge. As it says in the tale, 'Let Guardians walk the lands, in order to establish justice if they can.'"

"To establish justice. To restore peace. Do you ever suppose, Marit, that the gods never meant for the Guardians to become the final measure of judgment in the land? Of course they traveled from assizes to assizes and stood in judgment over the most intractable cases, able to see into the hidden heart of those they judged. But over time folk trusted their own courts less and began to speak as if only the Guardians could bring justice. And then perhaps the Guardians came to believe it, also. I am not so sure things have fallen out as the gods intended."

" 'Who can be trusted with this burden?' " she said, echoing the Tale of the Guardians. "The burden of justice."

" 'Only the dead can be trusted,' " he answered in the cadence used in the tale. "We three died fighting for justice, in one way or another. You were an honest reeve. Kirit took many opportunities to help folk more unfortunate even than she was, and it is difficult to imagine, I think, people who have endured as much as she did."

"I found a cloak," said the girl, her voice barely audible above the patter of rain that had started up again outside. The cloak that bound her was as pale as mist, barely visible in the gloom. "I unbound this cloak from her dead body. Was that justice?"

The words rocked Marit. "No living person can unbind a cloak. Hari told me so."

Jothinin watched the girl, his expression creased by a fissure of doubt. "A Guardian can seem dead but merely be at rest in a healing trance."

Marit nodded slowly. "I saw Hari in such a stupor, after he was—stabbed—punished by one of Lord Radas's soldiers. I suspect I have fallen two or three times into such a stupor, after I was murdered, and then awakened afterward without understanding what had happened. How are we healed, Jothinin?"

He shrugged. "The land heals us."

"In other words, you don't know. Kirit, how did you unbind the cloak?"

She spoke in her raw scrape of a voice. "I was out hunting and found the body. We were a very poor tribe. The silken cloth of the cloak she was wearing was very rich, something I could trade with. When I touched the clasp, the metal burned me. So I wrapped my hands in cloth and undid the clasp. Then I wrapped the cloak up and carried it with my belt. I got blisters on my skin. The blisters healed after a few days. I thought she was dead."

Jothinin frowned, fingering his clean-shaven chin, which Marit had not, in fact, observed him shaving. Just as her own hair never grew out, his beard never grew in. "The cloak would have to be in a stupor, spirit poised on the threshold of the Spirit Gate. Otherwise no person could remove the cloak without destroying herself. The cloak protects the one who wears it."

"I thought the spirits within the cloaks never changed. Now you tell me it is the cloak that remains and the spirit that changes?"

"Yes. That must be obvious to you, who wear the cloak of Death, which was worn by others before you. Of the cloaks who stood in the Guardians' council when I was first awakened, only cloak of Night remains for certain, unless Eyasad, she who wore the cloak of Earth, still walks somewhere in the Hundred. All the others, and some many more times than once, are new faces. New spirits."

"It's like the cloaks *jess* us? Like we're new reeves, chosen by old eagles."

He chuckled. "I hadn't thought of it that way, but it's as good an explanation as any."

She paced to the edge of the overhang. As the first kiss of dawn lightened the sea and wide plateau beyond the overhang, a vista opened toward the south where rugged spires and crowns appeared in such distinct relief they seemed close enough to touch. Like answers.

Turning back, she paused beside Kirit, who was still turning the spit with admirable patience. "Jothinin, tell me again how the cloak of Mist came to be walking in a far distant land beyond the Hundred."

He nodded. "Here is the tale. Nine Guardians walk the land, presiding over assizes, establishing justice. Together, they constitute the Guardians' council. The gods understood that all creatures are susceptible to corruption—so it was explained to me—so within the council it was possible for five Guardians to raise their staffs to execute one. That way, if one Guardian became rogue, the council could eliminate that one."

"And the cloak would pass to an uncorrupted spirit," said Marit.

"Yes. But when the cloak of Night became corrupted, she concealed her corruption. She subverted four other Guardians and persuaded them to eliminate those she felt would not support her. Ashaya, the cloak of Mist, realized too late she had become corrupted and then used to murder holy Guardians. She fled the council and the Hundred."

"She was a coward," said Kirit fiercely. "Running away."

"Was she?" he asked gently.

"Why did she leave the Hundred?" Marit asked, crouching beside him.

He rested a hand on hers, for Guardians could touch each other, offer comfort they could no longer endure from other people. They could gaze into another Guardian's face without being overwhelmed by the emotions and thoughts of that person. "It is possible for the spirit held within a cloak to grow weary of the task and desire oblivion. To lie down and let your spirit pass away."

"To die?"

"To release yourself. It is possible, but it takes courage to embrace the second death if you have become accustomed to surviving beyond death." He caught Kirit's eye and held it until the girl frowned. "So Guardians have done before. Released themselves and let the cloak pass to a new spirit who might have more vigor for the task. So Ashaya meant to do. But once the cloak left her, she would have no control over what spirit the cloak would choose when it was ready to claim a new spirit. She did not want Night to have a chance of reaching that new cloak and poisoning its spirit, as she had poisoned so many others. So Ashaya walked out of the Hundred, hoping to release the cloak in a place so far away that Night could never reach her." He removed his hand from Marit's and, with a wry smile, indicated Kirit. "It seems the gods had other ideas. For by one means and another, the cloak returned to the Hundred."

Marit rose. "I think the gods chose well," she said, trying to coax a smile from the serious girl, but Kirit kept turning the spit. "Yet had the cloak of Night succeeded in having me executed by five Guardians in Toskala, she could not pass my cloak on to whatever person she wanted it to go to, could she? You said cloaks choose, just as eagles choose reeves. Otherwise you could turn any criminal into a demon with the power to kill but not be killed. So if the cloaks wrap spirits at the behest of the gods, how could any corruptible person become a Guardian?"

"Is there an incorruptible person, Marit?"

"Aui!" she murmured, with a weary smile to answer his. "Of course there is not. At best, some are less corruptible than others. For instance, what of you, Jothinin? You are a man who strikes me as having little arrogance or vanity, and a cursed gentle way of laughing at yourself, and yet it seems you have walked as a Guardian for so long that a story from your youth has become one of the ancient tales we chant at festival time.

> "*The brigands raged in,*
> *they confronted the peaceful company seated at their dinner,*
> *they demanded that the girl be handed over to them.*
> *All feared them. All looked away.*
> *Except foolish Jothinin, light-minded Jothinin,*
> *he was the only one who stood up to face them,*
> *he was the only one who said, 'No.'*"

He flicked a hand up in a gesture that softly mocked himself. "I am sure I cannot understand what I ever did beyond drinking and gossiping and gaming. None could have been more surprised than I, after the brigands killed me for refusing to hand her over, to awaken and find myself wrapped by a Guardian's cloak. I was always the most frivolous of men." He studied her. "Where are you going with this, Marit? You hunt like a reeve. Your questions quarter the ground as you seek your prey."

"Is that not the best way to proceed?" she asked, surprised, and then realized he was laughing at her, as he laughed at everything. Perhaps it was the way he had managed to thwart corruption all these years. "Listen. When Lord Radas punished Hari, he had a guardsman stab him. He did not do it himself. Why not?"

"The cloak of Sun wields a staff shaped as an arrow, but its point does not pierce physical substance. Because we are ghosts, in a way, we cannot wield a blade against living flesh. Our staffs—your sword, my staff, Kirit's mirror—sever spirits from flesh, it's true. But we can only judge humankind and then only when guilt is laid plain. We cannot judge the other children of the Hundred, who are veiled to us. Therefore, we cannot ourselves strike or kill another Guardian. Not alone."

"We can kill another Guardian if a majority of the Guardians' council agrees. And *we* can be hurt by the swords and arrows of others. It's just that our cloaks—or the land—will heal us if we are injured. Isn't that right?"

He seemed about to reply but she raised a hand as thoughts cascaded. Too agitated to stand still, she ran to the shore of the sea, where water drowsed along the flats. She kneeled at the edge to pull a hand through fingers of salty foam left where the waves had receded after the turbulence of the night's storm.

The cloak of Night had always been present at the Guardians' council, so Jothinin claimed, and if he was indeed the Jothinin sung of in the tale of the Silk Slippers, then he was unimaginably old. Yet the first time Reeve Marit had met Lord Radas in Iliyat, he had been a man. He had passed judgment on criminals as fairly as he might; possibly he had striven for justice and mercy. The second time, when he had ordered his men to kill her and Flirt, he wore a cloak. He was already corrupted.

Night had traveled for a few days with Marit, testing her—Marit saw that now—to see if Marit, too, might be corrupted. In a way, it was good to know Night had preferred to see her killed. Which meant the cloak of Night had waited, great round of years by great round of years, probing to seek awakened hearts she could corrupt: Radas, Yordenas, Bevard. Even Hari.

The sun rose over the salty inland sea. Beyond the rim of the high plateau lay a vast gulf of air. Shimmering into the west stretched the endless desert, an outlander country where no human could live. Into that wilderness the cloak of Mist, then named Ashaya, had walked, and an outlander girl with demon-blue eyes had found what she thought was a dead body and stripped the cloak from it, hoping to help her tribe survive. The girl had not died then. She died much later, in a sandstorm, on a southern desert. Somehow the cloak had found and claimed her. In time, it brought her to the Hundred.

Marit walked back to the overhang, where Kirit was teasing the conies off the spit and splitting them with her knife. She had a neat, practiced hand. She licked her fingers and looked up at Marit. She ventured a quirk of the lips that was, perhaps, an attempt at a smile. Not friendly, precisely, but inclusive.

"The cloak of Night. Do you know her name?" Marit asked.

Jothinin shook his head. "I never did. She was best loved, you know. Always pleasant. Always helpful. Always cheerful. I never would have thought she would walk into the shadows."

Marit smiled as she might at a child she wanted to reassure. He had that quality, that she wanted him not to fret, even if she knew he would. "Sometimes those who seem strong prove to be weakest. And those who seem weak or light-minded and foolish, are in truth strongest of all."

He shrugged away the compliment.

"How did you discover the plot to corrupt the Guardians?"

He looked at the irregular rock wall and the shadows and light that spilled in ripples along it. "To my shame, I did not. I walked from assizes to assizes, pleased to bring justice to the Hundred. I was oblivious to the signs of trouble among the other Guardians. Ashaya was the one who warned me, before she fled."

"How did Night corrupt the others?"

"All I know is what Ashaya told me: false words and exaggerated suspicions. Whispers that some Guardians were not doing the work of the gods and must therefore be eliminated. Too late she realized she had herself become as corrupt as those she thought to guard against. She fled the Guardians' council, warned me, and left the Hundred. After that, I disguised myself as an envoy of Ilu and avoided the altars and my winged horse. An envoy of Ilu is a humble man, easy to overlook. I blame myself for not seeing sooner what was going on." He sighed, shoulders drooping.

Kirit said, "Are you hungry, uncle? Here is meat." Then, after a hesitation, "And for you, Marit." She set down her knife and popped a strip of meat into her mouth, chewed, swallowed, and considered. "A little tough. Not bad."

Jothinin straightened as he forced a smile. He tore meat from a steaming carcass, watching Marit. "You have a plan. I see it in your face."

"Why did the cloak of Night turn against the Guardians? Why then destroy the other Guardians? Does she truly want chaos? Murder? Rapine? Villages burned and children orphaned? It seems unlikely, shortsighted, messy. I talked with her, traveled with her for a hand of days. She did not strike me as shortsighted or messy."

"We must judge them," said Kirit unexpectedly, "not by their words but by what they allow to be done under their authority. The headwoman of a tribe who shows hospitality and generosity is pouring those qualities into the heart of the tribe over which she sits in authority. Likewise, a headwoman who is greedy, who is already rich but allows her people to steal from those who are weak and poor, who steals children and sells them into the hands of demons, she will poison her tribe long before they become aware that a sickness has overtaken them and ruined their herds and children."

"I may wear a Guardian's cloak," said Marit, "but in my heart I'm still a reeve. I'm going to Iliyat and Herelia to investigate. To see if I can find out who Night is, and what she wants. If we understand her, we may be able to figure out how to defeat her. Also, I must find Hari, and convince him to join us."

"Is it wise to split up?" asked Jothinin.

"I won't leave you, uncle," said Kirit.

"Lord Radas is busy conquering Haldia," said Marit, "so it's unlikely they have more than one or two cloaks out searching for us. Meanwhile, *you* must find the cloak of Earth. It will be easier for me to convince Hari to join us if he is sure he is on a side that can win."

"I am pretty sure the cloak of Night holds his staff," said Jothinin. "The spear of Twilight, which penetrates from day into night and from night into day. Even if he joins us, we still cannot pass judgment if he does not hold his staff. Consider this, Marit. Once we begin to pass judgment in the Guardians' council, we are then doing to the other Guardians exactly what the cloak of Night did to those who came before us."

"What choice do we have?" she retorted bitterly.

"We have to fight," said Kirit. "It is worse not to fight."

Surprised at this unexpected support, Marit smiled at her, but the girl had fixed her gaze on the man. Grotesque she might be, with that ghastly pallid complexion and those demon-blue eyes and the serious frown of a youth who has forgotten how to play, but there was something reassuring in the way she watched Jothinin.

She is trying to remember how to be human. She thinks he can teach her how.

"How can I possibly find the cloak of Earth?" he added. "A woman named Eyasad wore Earth's cloak when I last saw it. A young woman, small, vibrantly plump. With black hair like silk spun by the wildings out of forest spiders' soft webbing. Easy to become entangled in." His expression softened as his gaze turned inward toward memory.

"And did you become entangled?"

"Eiya! I would have liked to have done, but she was not fashioned that way. Anyhow, why should she trust me now? I suspect, with the exceptional hindsight I possess, that Eyasad perceived the threat before the other cloaks believed it might be possible Night could have fallen so far into the shadows despite honey smiles and generous gestures. That was a great round of years or more ago. Twelve rounds of twelve years, a very long time. Her cloak may have passed to another, or she may be in hiding still. So how am I to find her if, after all this time, I have not already done so wandering the Hundred as an envoy of Ilu?"

"Because you have a reeve as your ally," said Marit with a grin. "A cursed observant reeve, if I may say so. You said one time that the cloak of Earth carries a staff which is also a snake. I now understand I spent many years awakening, wandering on the paths between death and life. Early on, before I comprehended what was happening to me, I encountered a shepherd boy in the mountains south of here. It was near an altar set into a ledge on a black cliff face, rising out of the wooded hill."

"In Heaven's Ridge? These western mountains? Above the altar where lies only rock, and the cliff ends in jagged teeth?"

"That sounds right."

"You must be speaking of Crags. What has that to do with Earth?"

"I saw into the boy's heart. I didn't know at the time what I was seeing, but he and his village had a measure of protection set over them. He thought of a snake."

"I've seen her staff appear as a hooded cobra."

Marit shuddered. "I'd have remembered seeing a venomous snake."

"But it appears also more benignly as a garden snake, if those who come before her for judgment have committed no serious crime."

"It is worth seeking, is it not? Just as Hari may be willing to listen to me because we shared— Aui!—" She blushed, recalling Hari's grin, his attractive body. Jothinin waved away smoke, trying not to laugh, and it made her happy to see his melancholia slide away. "We shared what two lonely people who find each other attractive may share. He will at least listen to me."

Then he did laugh. "As a man, I can assure you, he will. If you call that listening." He wiped grease from his lips, and looked at Kirit. The outlander in her cloak of Mist nodded at his unspoken question. "Very well. Kirit and I will go south, to Crags, and see what we can find. Is that the whole of your plan, Marit?"

Marit sat on the rock and, suddenly voracious, ripped apart a coney.

Kirit said, "Tell a story, Uncle."

"A difficult task for a water-born Blue Rat, who loves nothing more than to talk," he said, smiling. "Give me a moment to think. Hmm."

"Tell me again the story of how this wide salty lake up here was made," Kirit said.

The morning sun lanced over the waters and the rocky ridge that rimmed the plateau, which the delvings, according to the tale, had built as a vast salty prison for a merling they had taken captive. In the gulf beyond the ridge, scraps of cloud floated so close it seemed to Marit that she might comb out cloud-silk from which to weave a pillow for a lover. Why must she think of Joss? She imagined him young and vibrantly alive as he had been twenty years ago, and then older and still handsome, as he was now. She had seen into Joss's heart, and she did not want to look there again because she did not want to know: that he had loved her, so long ago his memories of her were a tangle of regret and nostalgia overlaid with years of fleeting relationships with other women and a cursed lot of cordial and rice wine. It was his life, not hers. It could never be hers.

She realized Jothinin had fallen silent when he grasped her forearm as an uncle might, to comfort a distraught niece. She had to choke down the taste of dreams, the life she had once thought she would have.

Let it go.

"Uncle," she said.

He released her arm. "What is the rest of the plan?"

"You'll seek Earth. I'll look for Hari. I'll seek what information I can about Night. We'll meet here at the end of the year. If we gain a majority on the council, it may be possible to resolve this without killing. But we must have a second plan, if this one does not work."

Kirit pulled her bow into her lap. Jothinin shut his eyes.

"Lord Radas commanded a guardsman to stab Hari. To inflict a mortal wound, knowing Hari would suffer as he died and healed. So that means if that guardsman could do it, others could as well. A Guardian could be mortally wounded, if taken by surprise, and their cloak stripped off when they fall into the healing trance. As Kirit did. If we can't kill them, someone else will have to."

The fire popped. A puff of ashes rose and settled.

He opened his eyes. "Do you believe there are any who can be trusted with this knowledge? To kill for us? On our behalf? And not turn against us afterward, once they know it can be done?"

"One man might."

19

FOR THE QIN, the pace of travel from training camp to militia fort and on around the wide plain of Olo'osson was slow. For poor Miravia, who had never before ridden a horse, it was brutal. They arrived at Candra Crossing in the rain six days after they departed Olossi, a pace of about six mey each day. The folk busy thinning burgeoning rice and nai fields ignored them, but once in town people emerged onto the porches of the shops and inns and warehouses to gesture a welcome. The river crossing, glimpsed through gaps between buildings, was lined with sodden flags; a flat-bottomed ferry crammed with wagons and livestock was being winched across toward people huddled beneath a shelter on the far shore.

"Was this place attacked?" Miravia asked as they approached the center of town.

"The temples and council house were damaged," said Anji, "and a few buildings burned, but otherwise the enemy pushed through here so quickly they hadn't time to do permanent harm."

He rode ahead to the militia encampment east of town, leaving the women and their escort, commanded by Chief Tuvi, at the council hall. They dismounted in a courtyard flanked by two wings, one braced with scaffolding. Men set down planking for a floor. A trio of council members greeted the party and showed Mai onto a porch out of the rain and thence into a suite of rooms in the travelers' wing.

"It's small," said their escort, "but the other rooms are occupied."

The outer room was floored only with refurbished planks but the two sleeping rooms had fresh floor mats. The walls were washed white, as stark as the furnishings: pallets rolled up along one wall, a long low table, a stack of pillows, and an unlit brazier set in a corner next to a covered bucket.

"Will this suit you, verea?" asked the eldest, a woman so old that her back was bent, although her walk was spry. "We haven't the fine furnishings and silks rich folk in Olossi can afford."

"It's very pleasant," said Mai with a smile. "You have my thanks. If we might have water to wash in?"

"There's good baths in town, verea." The old woman's gaze strayed to Miravia, and a frown flickered and vanished.

"If there is time, I'll go gladly to the baths," said Mai, "but for now, a basin of water to wash off the worst of the dirt would be much appreciated. And kama or sunfruit juice, if you've any. Khaif, perhaps? What is the market price here?"

"Neh, verea. The council will feed and house you. Without Captain Anji's militia, we'd not be back in our homes. Do you see how folk work in the fields? Carts and wagons on the roads? The ferry carrying again? To feed and house you is a small enough tithe in exchange. If there's anything else you need?"

"I would gladly meet with the council and indeed any merchant."

"Do you represent the Olossi council, verea?"

"I have a seat on the council as a merchant, although I do not come today as an official member. Yet I would gladly ask what problems and questions folk here may have regarding the security of the roads and the safety of trade within the region. I can discuss supplies of various oils, which I sell. Also, as you may have heard, we are still looking for women willing to consider marrying the Qin soldiers. Over the last six months I know of forty-nine marriages between Qin soldiers and local women. We hope to arrange more. So if you'll just give us time to wash and rest and eat something—"

A meeting was arranged, and the women hurried away to spread the word in town. Miravia had stood all this time not saying one word, but as soon as they were alone she limped into one of the sleeping chambers, eased down to her knees, and tugged open one of the pallets. She collapsed forward across it.

Mai took a basin of water brought by a curious pair of girls and carried it into the sleeping chamber while Priya and Sheyshi shook out their rain cloaks, hung them from rods set along the porch, and rinsed the mud off the outdoor shoes.

"Let me wash your hands and face," said Mai. "Is the ache better?"

"It's less worse." Miravia's groan was half a laugh. "Will I ever stop hurting?"

"Yes." Mai bathed her hands and face as Miravia relaxed, the grimace of pain smoothing away.

Priya brought in a tray of juice and some rice cakes flavored with red berry, very tart, but restorative enough that Miravia sat up.

"Eiya! I never imagined it would hurt to ride. Where is Atani?"

"Anji took him to the encampment."

"How he loves to display that baby! Not that Atani is not a fat and handsome boy, well worth showing off to everyone."

"Best you walk around before you stiffen up."

"Of course."

She insisted on walking with Sheyshi to the well to help haul water. Tuvi had seen to the horses and to setting up guards around the compound. He paused on the porch beside Mai to watch Miravia and Sheyshi set off out the open gate toward the town well.

"She doesn't complain," he said.

"No, she does not," agreed Mai, carefully examining his face. But he was not looking after Miravia with the smiling sigh of a hopeful lover; he was just stating what he observed, as the Qin did.

The door to another room along the long porch slid open, and a woman and child peeked out. The child shrieked as the woman quickly shut the door.

"Refugees from the north," said the chief. "There's a steady stream of them coming through who've heard there's safety to be found in Olo'osson. Some are folk ferried down here by reeves, people who were stuck up on a rock in Toskala."

"Toskala was attacked almost three months ago. That's a long time to be stuck on a rock."

"Maybe they ran out of food. Best you remain inside the compound, Mistress. No running out into the market until the captain returns. Just as a precaution."

Already locals were trickling in through the gate in twos and fours to take a seat on the council benches under an open-sided shelter. Mai knew better than to argue with Tuvi on such grounds. She went back into the outer room, washed her own face and hands and tidied her dress and hair; drank and nibbled, to refresh herself; sat cross-legged on the matted floor and shut her eyes for as long as it took to recite the Ten Blessings under her breath. Miravia and Sheyshi returned, lugging water for the barrel in a corner of the room.

"I'll just lie down," said Miravia, and promptly fell asleep on a pallet.

Mai went outside and approached the council benches. "Greetings of the day."

"Sit," they said, offering her a place.

Names, markets, goods, gossip, grievances. Mai had grown up in the marketplace; she knew this talk to her bones. The merchants and businessfolk of Candra Crossing had nothing but praise for the militia, but they were angry about the middlemen charging exorbitant rates to cart goods along the West Track from Olossi. Two clans who used to cart goods in this region had taken heavy losses in the attacks of last year; no one was willing to set up in their place out of respect for tradition, because those two clans had always been the local carters. Meanwhile, with their equipment stolen by the invaders and never recovered, the clans hadn't the wherewithal to regroup.

"Young women from those clans might consider marrying Qin soldiers stationed out here. We'll settle a fair price on such alliances, for we've a wish to see the men peacefully housed and connected with local families."

"Are you trying to buy brides, verea?"

"Aren't most alliances settled with goods and coin, and a mutually beneficial agreement? Do you act otherwise when it comes time to marry your own children out of the clan?"

They did not, of course. No one did. And when she mentioned the trade in oil of naya, and the possibilities for business and herding and irrigation farming in the Barrens, folk listened more closely and asked more questions.

The council had absorbed the costs of housing refugees from Toskala, as well, people who must be fed and sent on their way with nai bread for the journey downriver to Olossi.

"They brought no coin with them from Toskala?" Mai asked.

Though traveling merchants and guildsmen certainly paid to stay at inns, a destitute or holy traveler was never charged, in honor of Hasibal the Pilgrim. At Mai's innocent question, a debate caught fire over the proper designation of refugees. Were they a kind of pilgrim, able therefore to ask for the gods' tithe to be fed and sheltered for a night or two before they moved on? Or were they properly to be treated as paying customers because they were going to set up a new life elsewhere?

"What do you think, verea?"

"Surely not every instance is the same. A young woman who comes to my gate asking for refuge and a chance to consider marrying one of the Qin soldiers because her village has been burned down and her family is dead and she has nothing but the clothes on her back must be treated differently than I was myself treated on reaching Olossi. I had coin, a husband, a clan if you will call a troop of soldiers and grooms and servants a clan. For me, it would have seemed shameful to receive the gods' tithes not because I would consider it shameful to take food and shelter from the gods but because it might be better used to help those who truly have nothing. So if a refugee comes from Toskala with his sleeves full of strings of leya and a heavy chest of gold cheyt, then I would treat him differently from a poor woman and child who are hungry and lost. I don't think we have to be rigid in holding to the law. We must consider justice and mercy, and mix it with common sense."

Instead of inspiring a stately philosophical discussion of justice, her fine words merely sparked accusations that some people along the West Track had aided the invading army in exchange for coin or certain expensive trade goods, or that other people had made such accusations not because they were true but to impugn the reputation of market rivals who were innocent of wrongdoing.

The old woman who had first greeted them said angrily, "In the old days we'd have held such charges for an assizes and the Guardians would have come and seen the truth of the matter. But now the cloaks have been stolen by lilu, so these disputes fester because there's none we can trust to judge."

A company of riders approached, hooves heavy on the road. Soon Anji walked under the arch into the courtyard, attended by local militia officers. Mai spotted the infant comfortably in the arms of Chief Esigu, who was in command of the eastern militia. The locals made a place for Anji on the benches, and he listened to their complaints about the disarray of the local assizes and their inability to resolve disputes with people from outside Candra Crossing's environs. What was to be done about the refugees from the north who were placing such a burden on the town? Why couldn't the reeves fly people all the way to Olossi?

He politely refused to discuss security and militia matters and deferred the other questions to Mai.

"It seems to me," Mai said at last, "that you're most frustrated that your voices and concerns aren't being heard. Perhaps a greater council can be chosen from among the local districts of Olo'osson and meet in company with Olossi's council. The question of assizes is a serious one. To rely on the old ways when they no longer function is like rebuilding a house without first making sure your foundation is solid."

Anji cut through the murmur of commentary following this speech by rising. "I beg your indulgence." He nodded around the benches. "I've a wish to stroll up to the beacon tower with my wife before the sun sets."

They fell over themselves to graciously retreat so the captain and his wife could enjoy what all described as a particularly fine view of the river and town, especially now that the rain had moved off and the sun was shining. After, Mai nursed Atani, and she and Anji, in company with Chief Tuvi and a cadre of soldiers, made their way through the late-afternoon bustle of town to the stone path that led up Candra Hill. Chief Tuvi carried Atani; Anji walked ahead with Mai up the steep stairs.

"You understand," he said when they were halfway up, out of earshot of the guards in front and behind, "that if you wish to see your uncle Hari again, I cannot discuss militia matters in your hearing. If he is a spy for Lord Radas, he can learn what you know."

"I do not believe he is Lord Radas's ally. Anyway, I doubt it is so easy even for a Guardian to know all that lies in a person's mind and heart. It must be more like searching for a child's doll lost in a field of ripe wheat."

"Perhaps, but I cannot take the chance."

"Then I accept the condition. I would rather visit Uncle Hari. Must I avoid all councils altogether? I would be sorry if that were so."

"Not at all. You do well with these local councils. They do not feel intimidated by you, and yet they respect you because of your wealth, your trade connections, and your ability to listen. It makes sense for you to push to create a wider regional council, one that can later act in concert with the militia. Since you are accompanying me on this circuit, it would be useful for you to broach the idea in every place we stop, even in the humblest village."

"Olossi's council will not like the idea of a regional council. They consider themselves to be the only regional council that matters, surely."

"Is that not an excellent reason to encourage a regional council? To put brakes, as a caravan master might say, on those inclined to throw down their weight?"

They had reached the top of the hill. She paused to catch her breath. Stones from the fallen walls had been used to repair the beacon tower. The men on duty had already lined up for inspection; they were all local men, disciplined in the Qin manner but very open with their smiles and greetings toward Mai.

Anji gestured for her to follow him. Together, they climbed the stairs of the tower and stood beside covered stacks of kindling and logs. The view of the flowing river and the town spread along West Track was splendid; the light cast a mellow fire over courtyards, paths, orchards, and rooftops. Wind danced through the flags marking the river crossing. Below, the local guardsmen admired the baby, who was in a chortling expansive mood, quite the charmer as the young men competed to make him smile and laugh.

"Why did you bring me along?" she asked, leaning on the railing as he crouched to examine the stacked wood.

He did not look up. "It's good for the people of Olo'osson to see my son, and to negotiate with the merchant who is my wife. Otherwise, they see me only as an outlander."

". . . One who intimidates them?" She studied him, easy to do when he was not looking at her. His topknot was neatly tied up; he had shed his armor and wore only a padded silk coat with the black silk tabard belted over it. He was not a handsome man, precisely; for simple beauty he could not compete with Reeve Joss or the many handsome young Hundred men with their ready smiles and easy way of displaying muscled physiques. He had a different quality; he was the wind that bends trees, the river that cuts the earth with its fluid strength, the inexorable sand that buries stone.

He caught her staring and did not smile, as if he was unsure of what she might be thinking, *how* she might be looking at him. Then she smiled, and he softened, rising to take her hand and stand beside her at the wall, a gesture of intimacy in which he rarely indulged in a public space.

"Are you content?" he asked.

She laughed. "An odd question, coming from you, Anji!"

"Yet you haven't answered it."

Was his tone dark, or was he teasing her? When she remembered the look on his face at the docks in Dast Olo, she wondered if she really understood him or only thought she did. The eastern reaches of West Track faded into shadows as the sun touched the western horizon. He waited, the pressure of his fingers light on her hand, as the shadows drew long and the men below laughed and joked. Several began to sing a prayer to the dusk, and others joined in.

"Look to the horizon! A voice calls.
Shadow Gate rises. Night is come."

When the prayer was finished, she replied. "My father would never have asked his wives that question, nor would their answers have concerned him. Why do you care if I am content?"

He released her hand to lean on his elbows on the wall, watching the child, safe in Tuvi's arms. "Are you?"

"As a merchant, I must now point out that you have negotiated me into a corner. If I say 'yes,' it may seem my belated agreement stems not from genuine feeling but from expediency. To say 'no' is unthinkable, whether or not it might be true. What am I to say to the man who has freed me from an unhappy household and a life of tedious drudgery as a wife married into the Gandi-li sheepherders' clan, ridden with me for months through desert and foreign lands defying storm and assassins, worked in concert with me to create a new home in a very fine land where we can hope to prosper, and given me in addition a handsome, good-natured infant son? If I were to say that it's as if I am living one of the storytelling songs I used to listen to and sing, you would laugh at me. You did before!"

"I never did."

She placed a hand over his, claiming him. "You did." She leaned in and quickly kissed him, although anyone who happened to be looking up would see.

"Mai!" He drew back hastily.

"I couldn't help myself."

His eyes flared as his hand tightened on hers. He whistled sharply; Tuvi looked up, then gestured to the escort to make ready.

"Have you seen all you wished to see from this pleasant vista?" Mai asked innocently.

He tugged gently, but firmly, on her hand. Hu! She knew that look and felt her own cheeks flush in response.

"Remind me never to negotiate with you, Mai. On this field, I am not your match."

She laughed and allowed herself, this time, to be led.

*   *   *

MARIT LEFT THE shore of the Salt Sea on the western edge of the Hundred and traveled east-southeast. Sardia, Farhal, upper Haldia fell away beneath and behind her as the moon waxed and waned in its full cycle of twenty-four days. The paths of air concealed her, so she rode low to the ground and measured the army's occupation. The land lay in a kind of enforced quiescence. In her time as a reeve she had seen children stand in such stillness, heads bowed, hoping to avoid a beating from angry parents by avoiding being noticed. Stillness never helped, not when the fault lay not with them but with those who had the strength and reach to abuse them. Along major roads or outside town gates rose cleansing posts, always under guard, a warning and threat to those who might consider rebellion.

If she stopped to free the hanged from the posts, she would reveal her presence; she knew the news would eventually reach one of the cloaks she was trying to avoid. If she did not stop . . .

The hells!

She stopped each time, and commanded the guards to release those of the condemned who weren't yet dead. She told the guards that cleansing was meant to refine the heart and that those who had been hanged from the poles were now cleansed, that you did not have to be dead to be cleansed.

Not as she was dead, her old life ripped away, lost forever.

Because she was thinking of Joss, she journeyed across the mouth of the vale of Iliyat to spend a night up on the Liya Pass, at Candle Rock, the last place she and he had embraced the Devourer. Twenty-one years ago.

Candle Rock was too stony to harbor trees; a few hardy tea willows grew out of deep cracks where water pooled in the rainy season, and spiny starflowers flourished on the steep northern slope. She came to earth on the summit of the rock and released Warning. The mare flew off toward Ammadit's Tit, but, like Jothinin and Kirit, Marit avoided the altars; her footsteps on the labyrinth would alert any cloak who, at the same time, stood on any other altar anywhere in the Hundred.

Walking down to the craggy overhang where she had stacked firewood when she'd come here over a month ago, she observed the land in the drowsy light of a cloudless late afternoon. The Liya Pass ran from the northern slopes of the vale of Iliyat over the Liya Hills into Herelia. The road ran below the cliff face, empty of traffic. As she crossed from sunlight to shade under the overhang, she stopped short at the sight of stacked firewood and kindling braced between unsplit logs. Someone had come here after her last visit weeks ago.

A hatchet, a wedge, and a sledgehammer had been laid across logs. The old axe she had used was gone. The oldest wood had been moved to the front and freshly cut wood stacked behind in alternating pairs exactly the way Joss had always stacked wood. Outside, a trail of dust led to bands of starflower where the remains of wood too punky to burn had been dumped. Down in the hollow where reeves jessed their eagles to one of several rings hammered into the rock, the dirt had been recently raked.

She drew her sword. She listened, but heard only the pee-wit of a fly catcher and the whine of the wind. When she had stopped here weeks ago, the patrol station had looked abandoned. Why had reeves abandoned it, and why had they come back? What in the hells *were* the reeves doing these days? She was twenty years out of touch.

It was getting dark. Wind died as the sun set.

She sheathed her sword and toiled back up the slope to the overhang. After collecting an armload of wood and kindling, she trudged to the summit. Joss was not the only person in the Hundred who stacked wood in that manner. It was just that she was thinking of him. She grinned, remembering how they'd kissed by this very fire pit. The dry season was creeping in on the last kiss of the Whisper Rains, and though it wasn't yet cold, she appreciated the fire as a friendly companion. It was funny how after only a few days in company with Jothinin and Kirit she sorely missed them, the envoy more than the girl, for there was no denying that the girl was not quite right. It wasn't just the way she looked, although that was disturbing enough. It was the way she acted.

As her gaze skipped around the circle of white rocks, she noticed a crevice gaping within the curving wall of stones opposite her, a pair of flat stones stacked within.

She grabbed a stick out of the fire and beat it on the ground until the flames died. With this tool, she poked into the crevice to make sure no creeping stingers dwelt within. Then she reached in for the stones. The one on top had been painted white on one side and black on the other; the white had caught her eye. The stone beneath was also painted in white and black, but on one side as a Sickle or Embers Moon and on the other as a Lamp or Basket Moon, just past the half. Reeves often left each other stones painted with the phases of the moon as a way to arrange meetings. So she and Joss had communicated. At Candle Rock, more than once.

When the pulse races, the world can grow hazy. At length her breathing steadied, and she smiled wryly. She had not yet let him go. No shame in that. Folk would hold on in their memory to what they had lost. In time, the attachment would fade, as attachments did. Even if twenty-one years had passed in the world, to her the wound was still fresh. Anyway, Joss was in the south, marshal over Argent Hall. Every reeve left such messages.

She considered the clear sky, lighter in the west and purpling in the east as the first bright stars penetrated the veil of daylight. The waxing Sickle Moon lingered in the west. The moon would lamp to the full in about ten days.

Was it time to talk to the reeves? Or was it only Joss she trusted? All the events that had transpired before her awakening, while she lingered on the threshold between death and life, were not even dreams to her; they were a hall devoid of light, a place in which she was blind.

Aui! She and Jothinin and Kirit were not alone in fighting the cloaks. They had to cast a net of alliance, because they would assuredly never succeed alone. She found another flat stone and stacked it beneath the others, leaving the white surface facing up: *Meet at the full moon.*

20

THE PRISON IN which he was being held, Shai reflected, had the pleasing symmetry of a well-tended garden. It was walled on all sides, and the cells were tiny barracks rooms, each with a barred and locked door that swung on hinges rather than sliding, and on the opposite side up very high there was a long slit of a window, too narrow to squeeze through. His window overlooked another garden within whose greenery folk sometimes walked, conversing or arguing; occasionally, he overheard the sounds of a man and woman having sex. He preferred the arguments, because the other forced him to remember that time with Eridit. Yet memory—a thorough consideration of the events that had led him here—helped him endure.

He had a bucket to eliminate in, porridge to eat, and watered-down cordial to drink. Day after day he had nothing to do except eat and sleep, so he trained his body in a fierce discipline, running in place until a trance gripped him, grasping the rim of the window and pulling his weight up and easing it down over and over until sweat made his fingers slick. Once a day at dusk he—and only he of all the prisoners—was allowed into the courtyard with its raked gravel and pots of blue and white flowers whose fragrance was the greatest pleasure of his day. There, he was allowed to bathe by pouring buckets of cold water over his head while the guards made jokes and the hirelings who hauled water from some cistern elsewhere said nothing.

Late one night the bar at his door was removed, and the door opened. An attractive woman entered, carrying a lamp and wearing a taloos of such sheer silk you could see the dark circles of her nipples through the wrapping. Four guards waited outside, making wagers on how quickly he'd succumb and how long he'd last.

"I just had to see your body myself," she said. "Strip."

"What are you going to do, beat me if I don't? You can't kill me, because the Guardian wants me alive."

She shifted ground, baring the curve of a breast but not venturing too close. "You must be terribly lonely here."

"Neh. There's plenty of prisoners more miserable than I am whose moans and cries I hear every day."

"You might hear me moan and cry, if you wished. I can see you're aroused."

"Sheh!" For shame. "You're like a demon, feeding on suffering."

She slapped him, and he caught her wrist and held it motionless, despite her twisting, to show her how strong he was. Panicking, she screamed, and the guards ran in with spears. Before they hit him, he shoved her away, into their advance.

"Perhaps the body is aroused, but the mind is disgusted. Beat me for refusing, if you must, but then I'll tell the Guardian. Do you want the cloak's scrutiny?"

"Maybe the cloak doesn't care what's done with the condemned before they die," said the woman as she recovered her composure, surrounded by the guards.

"Maybe not. I'm willing to find out. Are you?"

After that, they left him alone and no longer made jokes when he was allowed his nightly freedom in the courtyard. Something had happened to him that he didn't entirely understand. It was as if seeing the demon wearing the shell of Hari had strangled the last vestiges of the young man Shai had once been, the seventh of seven sons, least and superfluous, who had spent his youth remaining silent, keeping out of the way, and doing what he was told. The only one of his brothers he'd loved was lost to him; he'd likely never see his beloved niece Mai again; Zubaidit had walked alone into the army without him. Even Tohon and the children he'd helped save—presumably now safe—were as far away as if death had severed them one from the other.

So be it. He had a task to accomplish.

He was not a clerk or priest to know how to mark the passing of days, but the rains fell less frequently, and the pots of blue and white flowers withered and were replaced with pots of a mellow golden bloom. Occasionally new prisoners were brought in, some weeping, some protesting, some silent; he heard their voices but he never saw them nor could they communicate. The cell to Shai's right remained empty; the chamber to his left was the gardener's storeroom with all its tools. If he could only get in there he might acquire a weapon, but they'd stripped him when they'd first captured him, taken everything—his clothes and boots and knife and even Hari's wolf's-head belt buckle. They'd given him a flimsy kilt and vest to wear and, strangely, left him both wolf's-head rings. Besides that reminder of the Mei clan, all he possessed was mind and muscle.

He knew when Night came because of the way the voices of the guards changed. Many of the prisoners were taken away and never returned. At dusk, his door was opened. They herded him onto the porch. Out in the courtyard, a carpet had been laid over the gravel and a low table placed on it. A person was seated at that table, hard to see in the gloom.

"Strip," said the sergeant in charge.

After he stripped out of the kilt and vest, they gave him new clothing, exactly the same, and led him to the table. A pillow waited; he settled cross-legged on its plush opulence opposite the woman wearing the cloak of Night. Her hands were clasped and resting on the table beside a sheet of rice paper, a writing brush, and an inkstone. A lantern had been hooked to a post driven in the ground to her right, its light illuminating her pleasant expression and a lacquered tray with a wooden cup and a ceramic pot.

"Will you drink?" she asked. "It's a late harvest tea, sweetened with rice-flower-grain."

"Do you intend to poison me?"

"You're too valuable to poison. You're my hostage for Harishil's compliance."

The tea had a remarkable aroma that made his mouth water after so long on an unvaried diet. "I'll drink," he said, wondering if he could move fast enough to grab the lantern and bash in her head before the archers standing at a remove could kill him.

She smiled, as if guessing his thoughts, then poured. She, too, was sitting on a pillow, and beneath the pillow, sticking out on either side, lay a spear. His breathing quickened. She pushed the filled cup to his side of the table.

He lunged over the table, slamming her back and rolling to one side as he grabbed the spear's haft and yanked it free—

If thunder had shock rather than sound, it might lay a man flat.

Evidently, he blacked out.

When he came to, he was lying flat on his back with three spears—not the one he'd grabbed for—pressing into his chest. His right hand was in a hot flame of agony, and his mouth was as dry as if he'd not tasted liquid for days. His head throbbed.

"Let him up," she said kindly.

The spears withdrew. He winced as he sat up. Grainy spots of light spun and flickered in his vision, and yet there sat the cloak on her pillow with the table arranged in exactly the same tidy way as if nothing had happened. Only a spot of moisture on the gravel betrayed where the cup had spilled. How long had he been out? The moon had not yet risen for him to mark time's passage by its height in the sky.

"As you have just discovered, not even one who is veiled to my sight can hold a Guardian's staff," she said in her mild voice, lifting the pot. "Tea?"

He drank three cups in quick succession, and the spots faded and the pain ebbed, although his hand still hurt.

"What do you want? If I am meant as a hostage to force Hari's obedience, why talk to me at all?"

" 'One who is an outlander may save them.' Do you know the phrase?"

"It's from the tale of the Guardians. As a terrible war ravages the Hundred, an orphaned girl begs the gods for peace. The gods raise the Guardians out of a sacred pool and give them gifts and command them to establish justice in the land. But then after all that there is a prophecy that one among the Guardians will betray the others. And one of the gods tells the orphaned girl that an outlander will save them."

She gestured, and a servant crept forward, gaze averted, and took away the tray. The soldiers, at their remove, remained watchful, every gaze fixed on Shai.

"Over the generations," she said, "it has become commonly understood that this phrase refers to the land and its people, but in truth, it refers to the Guardians themselves. One who is an outlander may save the Guardians. That is why I need Harishil's cooperation to eliminate those who threaten the rest of us."

"Threaten you? Your army is the one that abuses and rapes children. That strings people up on poles. Attacks cities, burns villages—shall I go on?"

He meant to make her angry, but her calm was unshakable. "Certainly you are a young man who speaks boldly. What you are actually thinking, of course, I cannot know, because you are veiled to my sight. By any chance, are you a seventh son?"

The question startled him, not least because of its accuracy. "Why?"

"Not all the gods-cursed demons are seventh sons or seventh daughters, but many are."

"I'm not a demon!"

She went on as if he had not spoken. "Born from the same woman's womb, such a child will see and hear ghosts. Sired by the same father on different women, such a child will only hear or only see. So it is written in temple archives, and so I have ascertained in my time. I was just wondering if it might be true among outlanders as well."

Was Anji a seventh son, Shai wondered? It was not a question he'd likely ever get a chance to ask. Nor was he inclined to answer any question she asked about him, or Anji. Yet he must keep her talking, to see what he could learn.

"How can you know the phrase about the outlander refers to the Guardians, and not to the land and its people? How can we even know the tale is true as told, and not altered over time as folk forget old words and make up new ones?"

Her smile troubled him because it hid so much. "Some of us can know perfectly well what was meant, young man."

"No one can know, unless they were there themselves!"

She looked away from him, as if hiding her gaze, and yet she was simply beckoning to a servant to bring a new tray, with tea and sweet bean cakes. Hu! Seeing them, his mouth watered. He was so sick of porridge. But he kept his hands on his thighs, refusing to grab.

"Yet Harishil is not the only outlander. Here you are. What is your name, Shai?" She shook her head at his reaction. "Surely you must realize that old woman in the woods, knowing your name, would have revealed it to me. What do you want? What is your desire?"

To kill you.

"Wealth? Sex? Land? Better food? Children and a wife? Power to rule others?"

"I want my brother back, and then I want to go home." But it was a lie, because Hari had been eaten by a demon, and Shai could no longer imagine a life in Kartu Town.

"Harishil and the cloak are now one creature. A Guardian."

"Hari only came to the Hundred a few years ago. He can't have worn that cloak always. Someone must have worn it before him. So if a cloak can pass from one person to another, then Hari can be released."

"Then he will be dead."

"Hari is already a ghost. The only difference is whether or not he is your slave."

Her expression hardened. He drew back, suddenly afraid although she made no move or signal. The tightening of her eyes was threat enough. "It is easy for you to pass judgment on what you do not understand. Harishil was given the gift of a second chance at living, a chance to repair and restore what had gone wrong in his life before. It is no simple thing to leave that opportunity behind. What of those who sacrificed to bring justice? Who gave everything, risked everything, to help others? Are they, having made one or two small mistakes as Guardians, meant to be destroyed by other Guardians too self-righteous to be merciful? Must I, who am responsible for the greatest act of justice known in the Hundred, stand passively as others judge me? As others call *me* corrupted? I will not give up my life—"

"You don't have a life to give up," cried Shai. "You're dead. All of you are ghosts. You just tell yourself you're alive. But it's a lie. Everything you do is a lie."

She rose, and he saw in her an ancient power so twisted by fear it had become the opposite of what it was meant to be.

"Do you know to whom you are speaking? I am not to be spoken to with such disrespect."

"No, I don't know who you are, or what is your name is, or why I should care."

"I can have my soldiers kill you."

"But you can't kill me yourself, because I'm veiled. That's how it is, isn't it? You can't kill me, and I can lie to you. How that must rankle." What power words had! With each stab of sharp words, he felt her anger grow. "Yet if you have me killed, then you have no hold over Hari. And you need him, don't you? Him, or someone like him, a cloak you can control and corrupt. That's what Bevard is, isn't it? And Yordenas and Radas. You discovered their weakness, and you corrupted them. But Hari isn't proving so easy to corrupt, is he? Part of him is weak, but the part that is my beloved brother is strong, and he's fighting you."

He'd overreached; he felt her anger swallowed as the stillness that follows a cessation of blustery wind, and he tensed, waiting for a blow. She swept up the brush, paper, and inkstone and tucked them in a sleeve. She extricated the spear from beneath the pillow on which she'd been seated.

"You are correct," she said softly, "that Harishil can be released from the cloak if he proves unreliable. It has happened to others before him."

"Five to kill one, isn't that right? Without Hari, you're still one short."

"So he may have told you. So he may believe. But there are other ways. Maybe you will be next, Shai. What would you do, if you were to awaken as a Guardian? Were you to stand on the threshold between death and life, what would you choose?"

He rose, and the soldiers stiffened, raising their weapons, but he opened his hands to show himself unarmed. As he was, except with words. "I would do what is right."

Her smile twisted condescendingly. "So do we all say, at first, thinking we know what is right, and that what is right is easily known. It is easy to pray in ignorance and innocence that peace return to the land—" An expression chased across her face, fleeting, frightened, and quickly controlled. "—but to have to live for generation after generation with what you have yourself called forth, and the burden and struggle it entails, to see corruption strike and be helpless against its rot, again and again and again, that is not so easy, is it? Not when you are the one who will be blamed."

Skin prickling, uneasy and indeed in some manner revolted, Shai took a step away, and she flinched, as if his disgust actually hurt her.

"Who are you?" he asked.

She gestured to the soldiers. "Take him back to his cell. There he will remain until I—or the gods—free him."

* * *

"THIS IS TO be my new home?"

From the porch of Mai's house in the Barrens, Miravia surveyed the town of Astafero sprawled down the slope below them. Mai held her hand, enjoying Miravia's unadorned pleasure as her friend scanned the vista with its staggering mountain peaks in the west and the green-blue waters of the Olo'o Sea shimmering in the early morning light out of the east.

"It is a dry and dusty place, nothing special," said Mai. "I spent many lonely hours here. The market is small."

She glanced through open doors into the audience chamber where Anji sat listening to Chief Deze give a report. Tuvi was standing behind Anji, holding Atani—at any gathering of senior Qin officers, the baby was passed from one soldier to the next—and there were other officers, most Qin but two local men were in attendance as well as the Naya Hall submarshal and her chief reeves, Etad and Miyara.

"Maybe it is not allowed to go to the market," Miravia added, accustomed to disappointment, "because you were attacked by red hounds from the empire."

"That was months ago. Now the militia guards the roads, and the Hieros's spies watch everywhere else."

"I should like to be a spy, only I suppose my looks would betray me. Like Eliar's betray him." She sighed abruptly, releasing Mai's hand as she stared toward the mountains. "What do you suppose has happened to—" She coughed, shoulders tense. "There was another person who went south, wasn't there?"

Mai put an arm around her. "Keshad? I hope he's a good spy. He's a precise accountant and a good merchant. But very emotional. He is deeply attached—"

"To a woman?" Miravia's voice was sharp as she stepped out of Mai's embrace and into the sun; the light flooded her flawless skin and brush-tip eyes.

"His sister. Like you and Eliar." Mai forced a smile. She did not want to speak of Eliar, who had traded away his sister's happiness for a chance to play at spying. On such a glorious day, it was easier to signal to Chief Tuvi, who handed Atani over to Chief Deze, where the baby settled comfortably. Anji's gaze flicked to Tuvi as the chief nodded, and Anji's right hand shifted. It had taken her months to learn to see the small signals the Qin used among themselves.

Tuvi walked up. "Mistress?"

"We want to go down into the market, Chief. It is likely to be safe, is it not?"

"Safe enough, Mistress."

"Will the officers be wanting tea?"

Tuvi looked surprised, then gestured toward the chamber. "Did you not already order Sheyshi in with the cups? For there she sits."

"I did not!"

Yet the young woman was seated in the shadows behind Anji. A tray with tea bowls and a ceramic pot sat next to her, but by the way her head was sagging forward, Mai guessed she was dozing off, no doubt bored by the lengthy reports concerning the spacing and timing of patrols along the network of roads and paths in Olo'osson.

"How odd," added Mai. "Priya must have told her—"

"Priya went to the baths."

"Of course she did, at dawn. Hu! Perhaps Sheyshi thought of bringing the tea herself!"

She and Tuvi laughed at this absurd notion as they started walking down the hill, paced by their escort, but Miravia was not amused.

"Is it not wrong to belittle her? Besides that, why should any slave show initiative when they take no benefit from their labors?" She glanced at Mai and flushed deeply. "Begging your pardon, Mai. I do not mean—"

Mai took her hand. "I value your friendship because you are honest. Do not change merely to spare my feelings. I know you disapprove of slavery. That you wish I did not keep slaves in my own house."

"Certainly you treat your slaves with more consideration than many do, Mistress." Tuvi kept pace beside them with one hand tucked around his sword hilt and the other hanging at his side, his posture relaxed although Mai knew he was always alert, eyes and senses attuned to potential dangers.

"You gave me shelter, Mai. I don't mean to slap you in the face for it."

"Neh, let's get it out in the open now you live with us. You must see every day that Priya, O'eki, and Sheyshi are slaves."

"Not to mention the many debt slaves working off their debts here in the settlement," added Tuvi with that typical Qin instinct for going for the throat. He nodded politely at Miravia. "It is all very well to hold such views, just as it is all very well to chant prayers in the temples, but when we walk through the world we walk through things as they are. I had an older brother who became a priest of the Merciful One. I was a small boy. Once a year I would ride with my mother and sisters to visit him. How I admired him and the handsome temple buildings! He even learned to read the holy script, ring the bells, and chant the holy words. Then war came. He and his brother priests were cut down in the hall and the gold ornaments and silk vestments taken by soldiers. So I thought after that, that it was better to be a soldier."

"Did he not pray to the Qin gods?" Miravia asked. "Did he turn his back on the faith of his own people?"

"We Qin are not like you other folk. Our ancestors quarrel, and we are involved in the quarrels since we are their children. Besides that, the heavens watch over us. But that does not mean another holy one cannot walk on the earth. The Merciful One walks in some hearts and not in others. Yet a prayer does not stop a man, or a woman, from becoming a slave. Priya could tell you that. She is a wise woman. And like my older brother, she can read."

"Among my people, all children are taught to read. Isn't that better?"

"Yet you chose to flee your own people rather than remain among them in the marriage they had chosen for you," he replied. "So maybe you did not like that life so much among your own people who do not approve of slavery. Is it not to a form of slavery you compared the betrothal? If you believe the men of your people treat their women as slaves, then how can you condemn other people for keeping slaves or owning a debt that must be worked off by labor?"

"That I chose to flee—at a great cost to me—losing my family—never to see my dear brothers and mother again—has nothing to do with my statement that slavery is always wrong! You mistake the general for the particular, Chief Tuvi."

He smiled. "Maybe I do. But I don't understand how the Ri Amarah can insist that slavery is always wrong and then keep their women closed away behind walls. My mother and sisters would never have put up with that!"

"If the world is not as it is meant to be, then we must work to correct it." She turned with passion to Mai, grasping her arm. "You must dislike hearing us argue!"

"Was that an argument?" asked Tuvi, his pace not faltering.

The four soldiers kept an even distance at all four points. As they passed the thatched roof of the council square, six council members chatting over a morning tea rose to greet Mai.

"Verea! Well come. That you are here makes the day bright."

"Will you preside over an assizes before you leave again, verea?"

"You have not come alone, verea?"

"No, indeed," she replied, greeting each one by name. "Here is my sister, Miravia.

She will be running my household in Astafero." Mai studied their expressions as they eyed Miravia's face; they clearly knew what she was, rumor having traveled ahead. "If there is ever any question that needs my attention when I am in Olossi, that for some unlikely reason you cannot solve yourselves although I cannot imagine why that would be so, then you must bring the question to Miravia's attention. She will write a message which can be flown to Olossi by a reeve. She has my complete trust."

"Ah! Eh! Very good!" They revised their expectations, smiled more warmly.

Tuvi settled back as Mai stepped into the shade with the women. She asked after their businesses and their families. Mistress Sarana had married a Qin soldier and was noticeably pregnant; it wasn't so many months, really, since the first marriages had been blessed at the gods' altars. Maybe that rice had been nibbled on early! But wasn't that the way folk did go about things here, casual about sex in a way inconceivable to any woman in Kartu Town? Yet when she thought of how Anji had slapped her, her cheek still burned.

"Verea?"

"Just wondering how your daughter is, Mistress," she said to Behara, now head of Astafero's council. "I hear she ate Chief Deze's rice!"

"She did, and we hope there will be fruit soon, but too early to tell, eh? Anyway, he's been posted to West Track, so she'll live here for now and he comes to visit as often as he can."

That was the way things worked in Astafero. Some of the newly married women chose to migrate to new towns to follow their husbands on assignment. Others remained at the settlement with families growing as kinfolk who were struggling to eat came to live where there was work and food to be had. Miravia watched and listened, not saying a word.

When Mai extricated herself from the conversation, they walked down into the market with its familiar dried fish smell. There were new shops set up in crude storefronts with canvas walls and older shops newly refurbished with brick. They sold cloth, banners, harness, tools, dishes and serving utensils of everyday quality, storage chests of precious wood, baskets, bedding, mats, and spices and bean paste shipped or carted in from elsewhere. Miravia trailed behind as Mai chatted with every person she knew and met new people, because folk were coming to Astafero as people did where there was security in an insecure world. Yet Miravia did shyly smile at people who, despite being taken aback by her features, politely engaged her in the casual talk of the marketplace. At length, they worked their way down to the main gate. Mai surveyed the further sprawl of brickyards, smithies, fish racks, workshops, and the green patches of burgeoning fields watered from the underground channels still being dug. But she did not suggest venturing past the gate's shadow.

"The Ri Amarah have lived in the Hundred for four generations, and you not even two years, but you are treated as a cousin while my people are still seen as outlanders," said Miravia in a low voice. "I want to be part of the Hundred, Mai. Not an outlander all my life."

Tuvi had climbed the ladder to the parapet and was speaking to the soldier in charge of gate duty; the two men were pointing—quite rudely! how she would ever cure the Qin of finger pointing she did not know!—at some object or movement much farther out.

Mai took a deep breath. "*If* you were to marry Tuvi—"

Miravia pushed a sandal into the dirt, digging a hole.

"Not now, I mean! No hurry!"

"It's too early," Miravia muttered, cheeks scalded red although it wasn't hot.

"Of course!" Mai took her hand, tucked it into the crook of her own elbow, and indicated the market. "Best I go back to nurse Atani. Do you want to stay in the market?"

As easily as Miravia had taken to walking in public with her face exposed after so many years locked behind walls and veils, she was not ready to brave the market alone. Her smile was wan as her flush faded. "I'll go back with you." She clutched Mai more tightly. "Without you, I would be in Nessumara now. That you gave me shelter . . . I can never repay you."

Tears slipped down Mai's cheeks, but she never minded these swells of pure emotion, which like the wind off the mountains came as if from the heavens, a blessing from the Merciful One. "This is not a matter of exchange. We are sisters. I would no more be here without you than I would be without my husband."

"Mai!"

"You don't need to thank me any more than I thank you for welcoming me into your heart when I first came to Olossi, when I was alone and without a sister."

Miravia choked down her sniffles under broken laughter. "Now we will fall upon each other wailing and moaning."

Then they laughed so hard Chief Tuvi looked puzzled as he climbed down the ladder. But he did not react as a love-lorn man would; he neither sighed nor smiled to see their laughter. If she meant to coax this match into existence, she would have to work carefully.

"Let's go up," he said instead, brow wrinkled. "The captain will be wondering what became of you."

21

AT THE BASE of Liya Pass lay the town of Stragglewood, so called for the way the woodland was cut in strips and spurs into the hills where folk had taken the easy routes to collect and transport wood. The town was a way station for trade over the Liya Pass, which connected the region of Herelia to the main road leading southeast to Toskala along the Ili Cutoff.

Approaching on the road at dawn, Marit surveyed markedly tidier surroundings than those she recalled from the last time she had come through, twenty-one years ago. Every field boasted recently erected boundary stones. Young orchards were laid out in ranks spaced so evenly she guessed they had been paced out by the same person. She passed ruined foundations marking where poor clans' hovels had been demolished. A livestock fence ringed the garden plots, and compounds like a tannery, lumberyard, and byres whose stench and noise were kept outside the town. An imposing inner palisade circled the actual town buildings; at its gate a pair of middle-aged men stood on a platform that allowed them a view of both fields and forecourt.

Their gazes, briefly met, betrayed minds dismayed to see a cloak riding up to their town in a month in which an assizes court was not scheduled. A very bad omen. They shielded their faces behind hands.

"Holy One." The shaven-headed elder spoke through his hands. "Forgive us. We had no word or expectation of your coming. The assizes is not readied for your pleasure."

For my pleasure?

Warning snorted, tossing her head.

"What awaits me at the assizes?" she asked, cautious in her choice of words but sure she must speak boldly if she meant to continue the ruse.

Beyond the gate, people gathered in the forecourt, the squeak of leather rubbing, a rattling cough, a capacious yawn.

A man called out. "Heya, Tarbi! It's past time to open the gates and let us out to our labors, eh?"

The shaven-headed man climbed out of sight. Hands fumbled at chains; bars scraped; the gates were pulled open. In the forecourt stood at least fifty folk carrying hoes, spades, axes, and other implements. More were walking up. Seeing her, half the folk dropped to their knees as if they'd been felled by a sledgehammer. All raised hands to shield their faces. It was a practiced response the obeisance of which chilled her more than the cursed dawn wind. She turned Warning in a sweep that sent folk scuttling away from her.

"Finish with your duties," she said to Tarbi. "Then escort me to the assizes."

"You are gracious, Holy One." He unhooked a basket from under the eaves. Every farmer and woodsman, carter and tanner, elder and child filed past to hand him a pair of discs strung on leather straps. He examined them, tossed one in the basket, and returned the other to its bearer, who then slung it around the neck and hurried out the gate, careful never to look Marit's way.

When the first rush was past, Tarbi called down the other guard to take charge. He walked ahead; she led the mare. Children fled into their houses. Women flinched away, shielding their faces in the gesture Marit was beginning to loathe.

"Are there bandits hereabouts, that you lock your town gates at night?"

"Of course not, Holy One. The land is at peace."

Stragglewood had a central square fronted on two sides by capacious clan compounds ostentatiously renovated. Along the northern front of the square ran a long, low building that she remembered as the council hall. She was shown into its courtyard. The traditional elders' benches had been removed. A colonnade opened into an open hall whose elders' benches had been removed in favor of a chair built to outsize proportions and raised on a dais with a pair of smaller chairs set below to either side as obsequious attendants.

"Where are the assizes?"

"They are here, Holy One. We captured a gods-cursed demon. She's confined in a cell along with unclean ones awaiting judgment. She and two of the unclean ones will be sent to Wedrewe for cleansing when the chain comes through at the Lamp Moon."

"You've confined a gods-touched person?"

"According to the statutes."

"The law? Aui! And what in the hells are 'unclean ones'?"

"The criminals, Holy One."

She clamped lips closed over a furious reply and took a few deep breaths. The rafters of the hall seemed ominous; she did not want to walk under a roof where shadows spilled over the floor like the pooling of blood. "Where are the elders' benches?"

"Removed, according to the statutes, Holy One."

"Who judges the cases, then?"

His head remained stolidly, stubbornly, bowed. "You'll want to discuss these matters with the clerk, Holy One. I am only in charge of the gate passage." His fear trembled on the air, as delicate and complex as a spider's web. "We are always posted in pairs at the gate, Holy One. Hodard may come under suspicion if he remains there too long alone."

"Under suspicion of what? Allowing someone out without taking their token?"

As soon as the words left her mouth, she regretted them. For that was precisely what was going on: no one could enter or leave town without the act being marked. The tokens and palisade had nothing to do with protecting the town from bandits.

Tarbi's gaze skipped over her face so quickly she caught only a glance of a memory: a sobbing woman being flogged in the town square as prosperous-looking clans-folk shouted questions at her, "where has he fled to? where has he gone?"

Yet his thoughts were as clear as speech: *How is it she does not know this? It is exactly as we were warned! An impostor will come.*

He wrenched his gaze to the dirt.

She'd betrayed her ignorance. "Fetch the clerk."

With a haste that betrayed his eagerness to flee, he scrambled onto the porch and kicked off his sandals, calling out as he slid open a door. "Osya! Come quickly!"

Marit dropped Warning's reins and walked after him, pausing with one foot on the ground and the other braced on the lower of the two steps. A body appeared in the gate. She turned, but it was only a little child come to stare at the winged horse. Its open mouth and wide eyes, all wonder and excitement, made her smile. Then it caught sight of her, and it dropped so quickly to its knees, head bowed and hands raised in an obscene imitation of the adults' gestures, that she felt mocked. It bolted away into the square without a word.

Feet scraped along plank flooring. She overheard their voices because her hearing was so uncannily keen.

"Why aren't you at your post, Tarbi? You'll be flogged."

"Keep your voice down. There's come one of the impostors we were warned to watch for."

"There's never been such a sighting. Sky-blue, mist-silver, earth-clay, bone-white. Those are the ones we're to look for, neh?"

"Bone-white the cloak she wears. Send Peri to Wedrewe, as we were commanded."

"This is a bad omen! What if the lords cleanse the entire town, thinking us corrupted? We've followed all the statutes. It's not our fault!"

"Send Peri to the gate after me and I'll get him mounts and send him on his way.

Meanwhile, flatter and favor the cloak, persuade her to bide here as long as possible. There's a reward if she's delivered to the Lady. We'll prosper, you and me."

Marit stepped away from the porch as she heard footsteps approaching. She walked Warning over to a watering trough set under the shade of an open roof. Over in this corner, she smelled sour sweat and the ripe stench of human waste; a woman was sobbing softly. A man's raspy voice croaked out a whisper, "Shut up, will you, you bitch? If you'd just slept with Master Forren like he asked, you wouldn't be stuck in here. At least you're not being sent to Wedrewe to be cleansed, eh? What do you have to complain about?"

"Holy One." Tarbi hurried out into the courtyard, so flushed with fear and nervous hope that he smelled as ripe as the manure. "The clerk is coming."

"Best you return to your posting," she said before he could babble on.

"Thank you, Holy One."

He ran out. Not long after, a burly woman emerged from the hall with a very young man in tow, him with head bowed so deep Marit wondered he did not ram the top of his head into every pillar. He slunk out the gate as the clerk came forward with face shielded by her hands.

"Holy One. How may I serve you?"

Marit wanted to ask where Wedrewe was, but she had already roused their suspicions. "There is a woman here, imprisoned for not having sex with Master Forren. I heard of the matter and have come to adjudicate."

The clerk, visibly startled, forgot herself enough to glance look into Marit's face.

Master Forren hadn't any right to try to force the girl to bed him. Just because he's the richest man in town, and connected to them who built Wedrewe, he thinks he can have what he wants. Things like this never happened before Ushara's temple was shut down.

She threw an arm over her eyes, and groaned.

"I'll take those keys!" Marit yanked them out of the woman's fingers and crossed into a narrow courtyard that ran between the back of the building and a high wall. The cells were a row of twelve cages set against the wall, with no roof to shelter the prisoners from the rain and no ditch or gutter to sluice away their waste whose stench clawed into her throat. She halted on the edge of the porch, surveying a sludgy waste baked to a paste under the sun. She did not want to step into that.

The prisoners roused. Two stared boldly; five hid their faces. One woman was sobbing, crammed into a cage with an even thinner girl lying unhealthily still beside her. The last prisoner huddled in the farthest cage, back to Marit, unmoving, possibly dead.

The first man whose gaze she met had a steady stare; she tumbled into a morass as filled with muck as the ground beneath and around the cages. *He holds a stick with which he is beating beating beating in the head of an old man all for the scant string of vey lying in a heap on the rain-soaked earth.*

"That one is a murderer," Marit said.

Osya cowered on the threshold. "So he is, Holy One. He's not from here. He came as a laborer walking the roads. You may wonder, for it is not permitted to walk the roads without a token, but he carried a token so we gave him work repairing the palisade.

Then he murdered old Hemar for a mere twenty vey to drink with, and so we come to discover he had stolen the token months ago. That's the holy truth, Holy One." With her body hunched over in fear, she resembled a crabbed old crone rather than a stoutly healthy woman.

That he was guilty was evident. "What of the others?"

The clerk trembled as she indicated each one in turn.

This woman had cheated in weighing rice—

"I did it, Holy One," the woman gasped. "Please forgive me. My children were hungry. Now they've been sold away as debt slaves to pay for my crime."

This man had stolen two bolts of cloth from the town warehouse, claiming it rightfully belonged to him and had earlier been purloined by the town's militia captain at a checkpoint between Stragglewood and Yestal.

"It's a lie, what I said before. I was so fearful when they caught me, for fear they'd cleanse me right there, that I said anything that came to mind. I'll never steal again, I swear it."

Two young women had gotten a visiting merchant drunk and robbed his purse.

"We never did any such thing, Holy One. We let him buy drinks for us, because we hadn't any coin, so maybe we was taking advantage. But he claimed we'd robbed him, and we never touched his purse! And when they brought us up in front of Master Forren, then he said he'd dismiss the charges if I had sex with him. Have you ever heard of such a thing?"

"And you refused?"

"Of course I refused! He's a gods-rotted pig, meaning no offense to pigs. But we're poor folk, our people, no one to speak for us in council. We've been locked in here a year or more and Stara is so ill, you see how she can't even stand any longer. Now she's going to die, just because I wouldn't have sex with him! They won't let our kinfolk in to see us." It was all true, and no one in town had done a cursed thing to stop it.

An old man, too weak to raise his head, was a beggar.

"Why is he here?" Marit demanded. "Can't his clan take care of him?"

"He's got no clan."

"No one can have no clan."

"None who will claim him."

A young woman in the far cage pushed up to sit as she looked over her shoulder. It was difficult to tell her age because her face was smeared with muck, but she met Marit's gaze with her own wide brown one. And that was all it was: a look passed between two women. Her heart and mind were veiled to Marit's third eye and second heart. After all these months, the blank wall of a gaze hit hard.

"She's a gods-cursed demon, Holy One," said Osya.

"You put her in a *cage*?" Marit's hands tightened over the keys until the pain bit her and she remembered where she was.

The caged woman watched with the resigned calm of a person who has already given herself up for dead. Her stare was as even as sunlight on a clear day, almost brutal in its intensity.

"According to the statutes. We sent word to Wedrewe last month that we'd captured one, for we're required to alert the arkhons about any gods-cursed or outlanders."

"What do the authorities in Wedrewe do with the gods-touched and outlanders?"

"I suppose they judge them at the assizes, Holy One. As required by the statutes."

In the cage beside her, a burly man called, "I'm not afraid to be judged! They're the ones who should fear, for they have condemned me to the cleansing just to get what is mine."

"He's a liar," said Osya in a shaking voice. "He killed a man."

But he wasn't a liar. He met Marit's gaze willingly. He was not pure of heart; he had a temper, easily roused, and he'd gotten into his share of fistfights after an evening of drinking, and he had slapped his wife and been slapped by her in turn, a turbulent pair who didn't like each other much. But he worked hard, and he'd discovered an unexpected vein of iron in a shallow drift up in the hills on which he'd placed a claim according to the law. Forren had set four men including his own nephew to ambush him on the trail and it wasn't his cursed fault that he'd killed the nephew, who everyone knew was a clumsy foul-tempered lunk. He'd been defending his own life and his legal claim.

"He killed a man, it's true," said Marit. "But why aren't the men who ambushed him being held for assault and conspiracy?"

"He attacked them, unprovoked," said Osya. "It was pure spite on his part, him with his short temper."

The man stared accusingly. He was ready to be ill-used. He would never get a fair hearing.

She handed the keys to Osya. "Let him free. He's telling the truth."

He grinned, baring teeth. "Nay, I'll take the punishment, for otherwise the town council will take their revenge on my clan, and there'll be nothing I can do to spare my kinfolk. Knowing one Guardian heard and acknowledged the truth is enough for me. As for these poor lasses—" He indicated the sobbing young woman. "You can be sure she never said one word to encourage that asstard Forren, but the piss-pot would have her just to prove he can have what he wants, and leave her and her cousin to rot to death when she had the belly to say no to him. Hear me, Holy One. Maybe it's true we have fewer small troubles than before, but why is there no justice when those who hold the reins in this town do as they wish and get legal rulings out of Wedrewe to support them? They enforce the statutes among the rest of us, but hold themselves above because they were appointed by the arkhons out of Wedrewe."

Marit turned to Osya. "Is the town council appointed, not elected? Do they enforce the law on others and ignore it themselves?"

She hid behind her hands. "I just record the hearings and the deeds and the legal rulings set by the council according to the statutes of the holy one."

"You're a clerk of Sapanasu?"

"The Lantern's temple is closed, Holy One. That happened the year after I served my apprenticeship, twelve years ago now."

The words rasped out of Marit before she could bite them back. "Temples are closed? What have you become?"

"We are at peace, Holy One," whispered the clerk. "We are a peaceful place."

Marit sucked in a grunt as pain racked her torso. But the spasm passed, and she recognized not physical pain but the horror of knowing she had walked into a situation she had no power to alter. Maybe she could execute Master Forren or his cronies on the town council for their crimes, but she had no clear idea how her Guardian's staff—the sword she carried—sealed justice if she could not actually stab a person with it. Anyhow, if she condemned Lord Radas's justice, done at his whim, how could she justify her own?

Because you can see the truth.

Yet truth is not so easy to discern. Emotion twists memory; folk convince themselves of what they want to be true. They hide behind layers of self-deceit, not all of which are easily penetrated even by one who possesses a second heart and a third eye.

She did not trust herself to so casually wield the power of life and death over others while remaining convinced she was right. She did not trust anyone who did.

"Osya. Bring road tokens, enough for all who are prisoner here to depart unmolested. Then release all the prisoners except for the one who murdered the old man. Do not try to pass off false tokens as true ones, for I'll know the difference. After the prisoners have walked free, ring the town's summoning bell."

It was all she could do, and in the end the angry young man who had lost his claim chose to depart, helping the young woman carry her sick cousin. He alone thanked her; the rest fled without a word.

After they were gone, Marit led Warning into the main square, where she mounted and waited as the bell rang once, twice, and thrice. Folk approached in twos and threes in a stuttering stumble, fearful of her presence in a way that disturbed her so mightily she could not look at it squarely for it would make her consider what the Guardians had become in their eyes: not guardians of justice but "holy ones" who demanded obeisance.

It was foul. Obscene.

It was easy to recognize the members of the town council, replete in fine clothing and shiny ornament. They strutted until they marked her bone-white cloak; then they cowered with heads bowed. When she drew her sword, the assembly trembled like leaves battered in a storm.

"Look at me," she said, indicating each member of the council.

Amazingly, they first glanced toward the tallest man among them, who was also the most sleek, well-cared-for, and puffed up.

"Look at me, or be known as criminals because you fear my gaze."

She might have enjoyed the thrill of anger assuaged by their cringing fear and abject obedience now that they faced her sword, whose blade can cut death out of life, but she did not want to think she had anything in common with people such as this.

"First you, Master Forren."

"I am entitled—!"

Such a rush of self-important impatience frothed in his mind: He had done nothing wrong! The girl had encouraged him with her simpering glances and coy refusals. She was a cheap piece of rubbish, cadging drinks off visiting merchants and begging for a rich man to toss her a few vey. Was it wrong of him to demand something in return? As for the man who had murdered his nephew! He had claimed mineral rights that properly belonged to Forren; the town was given to him in its entirety to oversee in the name of the holy one's arkhons out of Wedrewe. How could Forren be blamed for exercising the rights given to him?

Who was this cloak to say nay to him? She might be unclean herself!

It is not easy to shame those who are sure of their own shamelessness.

He spoke the truth, but so twisted in his own mind it was no longer a meaningful truth; he could not see the difference.

Marit had never been as stunned in her life, not even at the moment of her death, when the dagger plunged up under her ribs. All that she, as a reeve, had flown for, had worked for, had believed in: justice, the assizes court, the temples and their offerings, truth. In this man's mind, hers was the dream and the lie, and his was the reality: The land was peaceful under the supervision of the holy ones and their arkhons at Wedrewe. His prosperity was all that mattered.

"You are not entitled by the law as written on Law Rock," she answered him.

"The old ways brought disruption and crime! We are better served by our new statutes."

"Some are better served, while many are served ill. Enough!" He shut up, as she meant him to do. Yet she had no power where folk did not recognize her authority. Fortunately, ironically, she could still lie. "I will return here in a month's time to stand again over your assizes. Act justly, and you will have no reason to fear me."

She sheathed her sword and urged Warning up. Wings spread, the mare jolted into a trot, found the paths of air, and galloped into the sky as the crowd ducked. Anger and despair smothered her, and then she clawed free. She could not overturn all that had gone wrong. She had to do one thing at a time, within the tiny sphere she could control. As she flew past the inner palisade she began to look for the lad named Peri.

She spotted him on the road running northeast. At each town where an inn boasted stables, he displayed a token that bought him a meal, a rest, and a horse; it was an efficient system, and he always got good mounts. He rode on oblivious of her presence. Folk on the ground might feel the tremor of her passage much as they felt the bluster and pressure of wind, but as long as she remained in the air their eye was not drawn to her; the movement of Warning's wings did not alert them.

She followed him north, over the Liya Pass, into Herelia.

22

"DO YOU LIKE flying?" The reeve, Miyara, shouted to be heard above the bluster of the wind.

Mai laughed, nervously, it was true, but also because the journey was so astounding. The sea lay behind them. The sun rode aloft. The land looked so different a place from up here. The steep ravines and ridges had a beauty that a person struggling to cross on foot could never see. The mountains spread in majesty into the southwest, and from the height, Mai saw how many more peaks marched away into an unknown distance. Clouds made turbulent pools of gray in the blue sky where they had caught on summits. A strange pattern glimmered on a saddle-backed ridge, but it was only a trick of the light on bare rock.

Mai recognized the steep-sided valley carved into high slopes and the stark cliff where the land plunged away into a mighty ravine. Water spilled down the cliff face, the air broken by rainbows, and mist teased Mai's feet as they battled against a current of air and banked in over thick forest to land in the clearing.

The glade was empty but for the two platforms, canvas walls tied down tight now that no one lived here. Miyara helped Mai unhook herself and the big wicker chest she'd brought. As soon as Anji and the baby were free of the young reeve, Siras, the two reeves signaled and left, the eagles' huge wings casting shadows over the downy grass. Mai lugged the wicker chest over to the smaller platform.

"You're sure the reeves have no idea Hari might be hiding here?" Mai asked as Anji strolled up, his hand on Atani's black hair. The baby was awake, watchful, content.

"Only Miyara, because she led him here." Anji scanned the clearing for signs of movement. "I've asked the reeves to stay out of the valley for the time being. I told them we must make privately all the necessary holy offerings in thanks for the boy's safe delivery to ensure he is not contaminated by demons."

"That's not how the Merciful One is worshiped, in private, shutting out others."

"They don't know that. Mai, it's necessary to keep your uncle a secret, isn't it? Besides Miyara, only Tuvi, Sengel, Toughid, and Priya know."

"Sheyshi was asleep. I didn't even tell Miravia."

"No one must know, not if we are to keep him safe. You understand the cloaks can see into our thoughts—"

"Into mine, and theirs. Not into yours."

"You make my argument for me." He untied the web of straps and cloth that had bound Atani against his chest and handed the baby to her. "We'll come up every month on Wakened Ox, that being the day of his birth according to the calendar kept by the clerks of Sapanasu, a reasonable time to make a thanksgiving offering."

"Three months today," said Mai with a satisfied sigh as she bound sling and plump baby against her hip.

"Although in truth just over four passages of the moon have gone by. The calendar here makes little sense to me. Why shouldn't each new moon begin a new month, as it does among the Qin? That's the simplest—"

"Anji." She touched his arm. "What if he's not here?"

Anji shrugged. "We'll perform the offering we told the reeves we came to perform. If he chooses to reveal himself, we'll know he has listened to your wise advice. If not, it is out of our hands."

He hoisted the wicker chest to one shoulder and began walking. His sword swayed at his hip; he had a knife tucked into each boot. She had her own pair of knives, bound at her back where they would not get in her way. She wrapped a shawl tightly around her shoulders as they passed from sunny glade onto shadowed path. The season of flowers and fruit had faded, but a few flowers lingered. She paused along the half-overgrown trail to cut stems and blooms and sprays until she had a respectable offering bouquet. Atani reached with his free hand for the bright colors. Anji paused, listening, but only birds sang, insects whirred, foliage rustled beneath unseen scrabbling claws.

They reached the waterfall and pool, the ruins at peace in the cold air. A tremulous wind spun leaves over the rippling water. The flow of water did not pound so hard; the rim of the water's edge was low, exposing a rocky shelf. Anji deposited the wicker chest on a remnant wall as she walked along the ledge into the womb of the cave behind. The curtain of falling wall had thinned enough that she needed no light to see the altar and a recent offering of flowers, petals scattered by animals and wind. Someone had been here, not long ago.

Yet the living guardians of the cave, whose shimmering blue threads had graced Atani's birth, were nowhere in evidence. Had they *died*?

She shuddered, stroking Atani's soft hair. As frightened as she had been at first, she had come to feel their presence in this holy place was linked to his well-being. In the songs she had grown up singing, such a child would be blessed by hidden spirits and gifted a spectacular destiny, or a brave death, depending on the story's end. Now, she felt unprotected as she knelt before the altar stone and its humble carven image of the Merciful One, as she laid her offering of flowers and chanted the prayers for thanksgiving. Anji came up behind her as she finished. But for the falling water, silence surrounded them. Sunlight winked on the dark mirror of the pool. A twig floated like a boat on the waters of eternity.

"Mai?"

That was Hari's voice!

She jumped up, but Anji stopped her from rushing outside. He indicated the baby. At first, she did not understand his intent; then she did.

"Uncle Hari, is that you?" she called as she unwound the cloth and transferred the infant to his father with a quick kiss to his unclouded forehead. Anji took him firmly, protectively. Mai hurried outside.

A man stood in the shadow of the cliff looking exactly like her beloved Uncle Hari except for his weary expression and the terrible cloak draped around him, worse than chains for being of such a beautiful weave. She looked him straight in the eye, and the tumult of her own thoughts and worries spilled so fast and hard that she stumbled as though she had been slapped.

"He hit you!" Hari cried. "Just as your father used to—"

"No, it's nothing like that."

Hari withdrew his reaching hand as if he were poison. "Tell me he treats you well."

She found her footing and walked over to the wicker chest. "I am perfectly well! There was a day's misunderstanding, it's true, but you must not think—I am my own mistress, here. I am Anji's wife, of course, but I am not only that." She fumbled with the cords, fixing her gaze on this task so she would not look at his troubled eyes. Why was her heart racing so? What was she afraid of? "Sit with me, Uncle Hari. I'll brew tea. There's a fire pit here that we became accustomed to using. Here is kindling and a flint."

Abruptly, she understood her fear, and tears began to fall. "I was so afraid you would not be here!"

Blessed be the holy one for the mercy of simple tasks, for it was possible to lay a fire and get it burning while you wept.

He sank down on the wall, not close enough to touch. "Where else am I welcome, Mai? You are the only home I have."

She wiped her running nose with the back of a hand. "Look at me! Just like Ti, a spouting teakettle, neh?"

"Do you miss Kartu Town?" he asked softly.

Everything she needed was in the chest: a tripod to angle over the fire from which to hang the little kettle in which to boil water, bowls to drink from, a straining spoon, the tea leaves blended by Miravia from different varieties. She need only dip water from the sparkling cold pool where its last ripples lapped the rocks.

"I miss Ti. And Mei—my twin! How it pains me I will never see him again! But no, Uncle. I don't miss Kartu Town. If I never went back there I would be sorry not to see my brother and sister-cousin, whom I love, but otherwise I am content here." She looked up, feeling he needed the reassurance of seeing that she spoke the truth. Yet this time there was a gentle sweetness in the exchange, as if her openness lessened the assault of his gaze. Maybe it was fear that hurt you most; maybe those who caused the most pain to others sought that fear and fed on it.

His smile faded as he looked away. "You have always had the gift of being content, Mai. It is a more precious treasure than gold or silk."

She fussed with the kettle, the firewood, the straining spoon, but in the end she must speak the question she most needed an answer to.

"Have you decided anything, Uncle?" At his ominous silence, she hurried on. "You need decide nothing, of course. You can just rest here. Tell me of your day. Or of some beautiful place in the Hundred you have seen. Or we can talk of anything you wish—the tea, if you like, or the weather, or this fine silk I am wearing, for I will have you know that I have more silk now than we ever had in the Mei clan, so much I must force my hirelings to wear it to their festivals since there is no real purpose in hoarding silk if you do not mean to display its beauty!"

On she chattered, just as she had learned to do selling produce in the market, setting people at ease. It was no easy thing to sit for hours in the market, on slow days and busy days and all the days in between. Folk did love to talk, and talking did pass the time, and for those who were too shy or weary or beset by cares to have anything to say, talking made them feel welcome despite their silence.

She poured hot water and watched it darken as the leaves steeped.

"Did you come alone?" he asked.

His words surprised her. She had thought the cloaks could sense people with their third eye and second heart. "No, Anji came with me. He is praying at the altar." She called, "Anji! Here is tea."

He emerged from the cave, his expression carefully polite. The two men eyed each other warily as Anji sat.

"Where is Shai?" Hari asked abruptly, watching Anji. "Has there been news of him?"

Mai looked away.

"Your news is the last news we have had of him," said Anji. "I will come to you with such news as soon as I have it. If I know where to find you."

Hari's wicked smile flashed, but there was a sharpness Mai recognized as bitterness. "So am I trapped here, waiting to hear."

Mai handed him a cup of hot tea, and he blew on the steaming liquid to cool it.

"Do you know what I miss most?" he added. "Companions. I am alone because I have been created to be alone. I cannot drink and gossip and boast with friends as I was accustomed to do. I am forever cut off from casual intercourse with people. So naturally that is what I miss more than anything."

His tone made her heart twist with pity. "You always have a home with us, Uncle."

Hari studied Anji, who had loosened the baby's wrap to soothe him as Atani started up with a mild fuss. "Tell me, Captain Anji, did you marry my beloved niece Mai merely for her beauty? Or did you know what a treasure you had found?"

Anji met his gaze squarely with a polite smile that told nothing and hid everything. "Naturally any answer I give within the hearing of my wife will have to be cut out of a cloth that will satisfy her. Let me just say she was bold enough to overcharge me at the market while all the other merchants fell over themselves to give away their wares. I admired her for that as much as I certainly admired her beauty. Will that answer content you, Uncle Hari?"

"I suppose it must. For like Shai, you are veiled to me."

Anji hoisted the baby to rest on his shoulder, never shifting his own gaze from Hari's. "There are many ways to judge the intent of those you face."

Hari laughed as he violently flung the dregs of the tea bowl to the earth. "Maybe I was just never a careful observer. It is easy to grow accustomed to living off one's glib tongue and pleasant manners. A young man may be reckless because he wants to impress his friends and in doing so overlook every good warning telling him not to act in such a rash way. Then he may find himself an exile, caught in a cage not of his own devising. Were you ever like that, Captain? Reckless? Rash? Leaping in with both feet onto ground you'd not measured beforehand?"

Anji glanced at Mai and slid the quieting Atani into the crook of his elbow, rocking him gently. "No," he said calmly, "I don't suppose I ever was like that."

*   *   *

"UNCLE, I KNOW we don't go to drink at the altars because the other cloaks might be walking the labyrinth, and then they would know where we are. But the horses go. What will happen to us if we don't drink?"

For several weeks Jothinin and Kirit had been running sweeps in widening circles out from the altar known as Crags, high in the mountain range called Heaven's Ridge that stretched along the northwestern reaches of the Hundred. Earlier in the day they had made camp at the edge of a pine grove in an isolated mountain valley, its grass not yet whitened by the dry season cold, and released the horses.

"If we don't drink, we age. Very slowly, it's true." He wrapped his cloak more tightly, shivering, although she seemed unaware of the chill wind cutting through their clothes. "When I awakened, I was a rather younger man than you see me now. I traded my youth to hide from my enemies."

"I don't like hiding." Kirit fed sticks into the fire with the intense concentration with which she approached every task, her serious face rarely smiling and yet never quite frowning. "Did the people who were grazing sheep here this morning see us coming and run away?"

"How can you know people were grazing sheep here this morning?"

"Uncle! If you look at the sheep droppings, they're still—"

"I need no description! I grew up in the city. I don't know sheep except to eat lamb on festival days."

"You'd be warmer if you wore wool clothing."

"Too hot for the delta! We scorned it as shepherds' and woodsmen's rustic garb. Nice for durable bags and blankets, but—"

"Uncle." Her tone altered as she slipped her bow out of its quiver and stood, an arrow fitted to the string. Seeing and Telling were flying back from the distant altar, and a Guardian on a winged horse was following them. Had they been careless? Or was it inevitable they'd be hunted down?

"Move back into the trees, Kirit."

She did not move. "I saw him before. On the rock with the others where they tried to kill Marit. He's one of the corrupted ones. I'll shoot him, like I did those soldiers. Do you remember when I did that by the sea, uncle? You told Marit we can't wield blades against the children of the Hundred. But once an arrow leaves my bow, it's not in my hand, is it? So maybe I can kill him. I'm a very good shot."

The hells! Was this what he wanted?

Seeing and Telling cantered to earth. A man wearing the cloak of Leaves rode onto the grass, reining aside his horse to look them over. Kirit nocked her arrow and took aim, a terrible sight indeed with her pale complexion and deadly blue eyes. She did not release. The cloak was clever enough to stay out of range.

"I'll go talk to him," said Jothinin.

"You can't talk to a demon," said Kirit.

"He's a Guardian. Or he ought to be." With staff in hand, he paced through grass that brushed his knees, his cloak rippling atop the stalks. Seeing passed him, trotting toward Kirit, but Telling swung around, ears flat, as if wondering where he was going.

The man watched Kirit more than Jothinin.

"Greetings of the dusk, ver," Jothinin called.

"I never saw you before," said the man. "You're the cloak of Sky. Night's been looking for you. Do you want to join us?"

"Neh, I don't suppose I do wish to join Night. But you're welcome to ride with us. You might find our company more congenial, if you take my meaning."

The man licked nervously at his lips. He had the slick palms of a merchant always sure he is about to lose a good deal. His gaze flickered erratically toward Kirit in a way that disturbed Jothinin. "That girl, she's very young. And an outlander."

"Older than she looks. She says she's met you before."

"Do you know where the cloak of Death is?"

"If I did, you can be sure I'd not tell you. My friend, you must know that I know what the situation is. What have you to say to me?" He scanned the horizon for signs of movement. Away to the west, he spotted three eagles, gliding in such high spirals that he could not tell if they were wild, or jessed with a scouting reeve.

"We could set a place to meet and talk further."

"Where you might set up any kind of ambush. I see you have your staff." He indicated the green sapling wand stuck in the man's belt.

The man's startlement brightened his face, and he grinned as abruptly as a child who unexpectedly answers a question correctly at school. "You must still be Jothinin, to know which staff I carry! Foolish Jothinin, so Night told us, although no one's seen you for generations. She was sure you had given up long ago and released your cloak. She's been seeking Sky. Now here you are. I've found you. I've done it right!" His pleasure in this triumph was disconcertingly childish.

Kirit whistled sharply, and Jothinin's senses prickled at her warning. Foolish

Jothinin, indeed! The cloak of Leaves rode alone now, but if he was searching for other cloaks he likely had soldiers nearby. If Marit and her allies were clever enough to figure out how to use other people to kill a cloak, then certainly Night had done so long ago. Indeed, now that he considered the matter, it was the only possible way Night could have taken control of the Guardians' council and kept replacing newly awakened cloaks until she found ones she could corrupt.

How had he been so blind?

"Tell her to stand back!" cried the man, and then he reined around and galloped away.

Jothinin strode briskly to where Kirit had halted, having taken a few paces away from the woods. She tracked his flight with her nocked arrow.

"Kirit, keep your bow ready in case he has soldiers close by. I'm going to pack up our gear and saddles the horses. We'll be departing immediately."

"Uncle," she said without shifting her gaze off the cloak of Leaves, "did you know there's another person in the woods, watching us?"

He jerked as if he'd been struck, then bent back to tying up the kettle and bedrolls onto the back of Telling's saddle as if nothing were amiss. "More than one? His soldiers?"

"Just one. Its heart does not whisper to me. Do you see that snake a few paces behind me? It might strike." Her tone changed. "There he goes."

The cloak of Leaves vanished over the nearest hill, in the direction of the unseen Crags. The sun set behind the high peaks in the west, its light across the meadow gilding the grass to a glossy gold in a last, tender kiss before nightfall. Jothinin, turning back, caught a slithering movement across the dark soil as a snake—easily as long as his outstretched arms—lifted its hooded head.

"Kirit," he said softly, "do not move even a finger. That's a very poisonous snake, and I can't be sure it's not simply a snake." She was a courageous girl; she did not move, not even to look around at the threat hissing behind her.

He cupped hands at his mouth and called. "If it is you, Eyasad, why do you hide from us? You've no call to frighten the girl. I'll chop that cursed snake in two, I swear it. She's innocent, even if I am not."

The snake's hiss abated and it settled, not moving away but its hood vanishing.

"Kirit," he said, "step away slowly, and saddle the horses."

"I won't leave you, uncle," she said, her voice cracking.

"I'm not asking you to. But we must be ready to flee if cloak of Leaves returns with soldiers. Move now, very slowly."

She slid her feet along the soil, and he sidestepped until he stood between her and the snake, which raised its head with an exploratory hiss.

"Eyasad," he continued, "listen to me. You were first to see the danger. You were right, and we were not just wrong but foolish and blind. Night has indeed corrupted four of the other cloaks. Having therefore control over five staffs, she may destroy the four who remain. She has turned Sun, Leaf, and Blood although there remains a question about Twilight's loyalties. We seek him. If we can assure ourselves he will turn to our side and walk the true path of the Guardians, and if you will join us . . . then we are five."

"You are two, Jothinin. Not five."

The pines clustered beneath a rockier spur of ground along an elongated hollow where richer soil had washed down over the ages to create a welcoming bed for deep roots. He did not see her because the gloom hid everything except the shadowy pillars marking the trees.

"I am one. Kirit is two, who wears the cloak of Mist. The cloak of Death seeks Twilight even now, to win him over. If you ally with us, we'll be five. I beg you, show yourself."

"A cloak in the hands of an outlander! No wonder it is so degraded, considering what a useless piece of chaff Ashaya was, easily led as well as stupid."

Her voice was thinner than he recalled it, remembering her hearty laugh and robust singing. "You're as blunt as ever, Eyasad. How I feared your tongue set on accounting my flaws!"

"You will have at your tiresome jokes all day if I do not stop you. Where is Death Cloak, if she is your ally? For I will tell you, Night pursued him who wore the Death Cloak above all of us, knowing him most likely to find a way to turn her strength against her and destroy her. What happened to him I do not know. I think she captured him, and destroyed him, and that this Death Cloak you speak of, once a reeve, is merely another creature of Night. Why should she not fool you, as easily as you are to be fooled? What a cursed idiot you are, Jothinin! Flying in here in broad daylight, so lacking in common sense that you did not see the shepherds who, seeing you, fled to warn me. Have you any idea what you've wrought?"

"Neh, but I expect I am about to hear."

From back by the horses, Kirit hissed, rather like the cobra, and to his surprise, the snake crawled away into the darkness, lost among the bracken as Eyasad spoke bitter words.

"For generations I have labored to build a haven for folk to live free of the corruption of the Guardians. Now I am betrayed. I must move all my people lest they be discovered and slaughtered. Yet where will they be safe, eh? Is any place safe from the Guardians?"

"The land will become safe if we make it safe by restoring the Guardians' council!"

"Do we execute the other Guardians at our whim just as Night did? And thereby become like her?"

"Do we stand passively aside and let her destroy us?"

"Either way, she has already won."

"What would you have us do?" he cried.

"It is better to do nothing."

"To do nothing when you see a man being killed, if you could act to stop it, is the same as standing among those who kill him."

"To do nothing is to refuse to participate in what is already corrupted."

"We are commanded to act!"

"Strange words, heard from you, foolish Jothinin, who was once nothing more than a gossip and games-player, a trifle among men, not worthy of comment except in the manner of your death."

"I am not the man I once was. I have changed."

"Grown older, anyhow. Once you had a youthful face."

"Aged, I grant you, over the long years, because I have avoided the altars to avoid Night and her allies. Eyasad, I beg you—"

"I am done with the Guardians' council. If we were betrayed once, then we can be so again. Why should there be Guardians at all, if they can be corrupted?"

Kirit padded up beside him, the bow held in her competent hands. Her voice emerged more strongly than he had ever heard it. "It is wrong not to act when there is suffering. Why do you reject us?"

"Because you have brought my enemies down upon me. Sheh! All that I have built, in ruins! Because of you! What can I do now? Who can aid me?"

"If we work together—"

"Enough! I am quit of you. Do not seek me out again."

During their conversation, night had swallowed them. Too late, he called light and plunged into the pine woods, but for all that he searched, he found no trace of Eyasad's passing. When he returned to the ashes of the fire, Kirit had the horses ready.

"Has Night corrupted her?" Kirit asked, her face ghostly above the light she had called from her hand to guide him back.

"Only if despair is corruption."

"I lived once in despair," Kirit said softly. "When I lived there, I was not a person and not a demon. I was a ghost. Maybe she is a ghost, too."

"Eiya!" He smiled gently. "Maybe. Yet she speaks of people she has built a haven for. She may reject us, but she still acts as a Guardian."

"What if she's right about the Guardians? Why should any of us, you and me, look into the hearts of others? Isn't it like violating them?" She spoke the words so calmly that he winced, thinking of what she had endured in the long months she had been a slave.

"Not if we act for justice."

Her gaze pinned him because she had no guile, nothing but the memory of pain whose hot grasp she had escaped. "If they do not give permission, then does it matter for what reason it is done?"

The light of the gleaming stars looked angry tonight, or maybe it was only the prickle of his own heart, stabbed by doubts.

"Uncle, for a long time, I could not fight and I didn't know how to die. That was worse than dying. So I don't fear death. If we are truly Guardians, then we must risk our lives to help those who are fighting the demons. You already said so! To do nothing when you see people being killed, when you could act to stop it, is the same as if you are killing them yourself."

He did not answer. He had no answer.

"So you see," she went on inexorably, "Marit is the one who is right. If the cloak of Earth will not help us, we have to use the other plan."

23

NORTH OF THE Liya Hills lay the plain of Herelia, its fertile fields fed by the River Vessi and its tributaries. Marit didn't know Herelia well; it hadn't been in her patrol territory. Its two major towns were Malinna and Laripa; its port city Dast Elia. At the base of the Liya Pass Road, the messenger turned in the direction of Laripa, riding through well-tended countryside as Marit kept pace above.

Two days later, on a bright and pleasant morning, they approached a town still under construction on the banks of the River Vessi. She raced ahead; at his lagging pace, he would not reach Wedrewe until midday. She flew a circuit over the town's layers: outermost, a swath of woodland clearly off-limits to felling where a hunting party crashed in pursuit of game, horns blatting; deep within the forest cover pits had been dug and filled over with loose soil, although from the height it was difficult to figure what they were for. At the woodland edge stood a perimeter fence and guard towers enclosing fields and orchards and corrals and gardens and tanning yards and smithies. On a backwater shore, rafts of logs lashed together were being beached and hauled up to lumberyards. A second wall ringed districts of humble row houses, its access funneled through guard gates. The third wall marked out open ground where company upon company of men drilled. Barracks and storehouses ran in ranks along the outside of the fourth and innermost wall, within which lay spacious grounds and gardens that resembled the temples of the gods and yet showed no allegiance to any. This vast inner compound was square, like Kotaru's forts, approached through triple-linteled gates as were Ilu's temples. It was roofed with green slate to reflect the Witherer's fecundity, and boasted handsome private gardens as in Ushara's realm. The symmetry of the buildings reflected Sapanasu's orderliness, and a young Ladytree, Atiratu's refuge, had been planted beside each of the four gates. In the center of all lay a walled garden surrounded by covered porch on all sides whose open ground was neatly raked around a flat-topped boulder—like those sacred to Hasibal, the Formless One—half buried in the ground.

She saw not a single temple or even a humble roofed altar. There was no Sorrowing Tower to lay the dead, and no Assizes Tower for justice, but there were watchtowers in plenty.

The inner compound hummed with the buzz of steady work being carried on beneath tiled roofs: the brush of scribes writing, the clacking of beads on counting racks, the beat of a stamp pressing metal for coins or medallions. Now and again a person garbed in a fine silk jacket or taloos made his or her way from one building to another, or passed a token to the guards at a gate in order to descend into the outer rings of the city. Wagons moved goods into storehouses whose roofs were still being tiled. In one of the private gardens, straddling a bench, a man and a woman were engaged in strenuous sex. In another, a pair of men moved stones on a checkerboard, at their ease under an awning while out in the sun slaves made sticks of incense.

In the deserted central garden, she brought Warning down. The mare's hooves stirred up the neatly raked lines in the gravel. She dismounted and led the horse over to and up onto one of the four long porches that faced the courtyard. Standing at the mare's head, she embraced the beauty of the humble garden as she inhaled the scent of late-blooming sweet-gold.

A whiff of fetid air brushed her nose. A whisper hissed and faded. She was not alone.

On three sides the porches were lined with barred doors built with hinges like smaller models of the hinged double gate in the northeast corner. Marit paced the length of the porch. Behind every hinged door was confined one, sometimes two, people: sleeping, weeping, moaning, muttering disjointed words, some mute with a despair that stung like poison on her skin. This was no meditative court, remarkable for its exquisite tranquillity. It was a prison.

At the end of porch lay a storeroom with racks of shelves. She grabbed a rake and erased hoof- and footprints until Warning gave a snort that cut through her crazed fit. What in the hells was she doing? Best just to get out of here. She raked her way back to the porch anyway. As she was hanging the rake back up on its pegs she heard voices and the thump of a door. The storeroom was large enough to accommodate Warning, and the mare ducked into the space willingly, as into a stall. Windows cut under the eaves allowed light and air to enter; she could count the shelves and the gardening tools and the other implements; there were many knives, lovingly polished and cradled on silk, and bundles of short staffs. *Reeve batons.* Ten bundles, at least. How in the hells did they have a hundred or more reeve batons?

"Who are you?" A man's muffled voice came from the adjoining cell. "You're not one of the guards."

Aui! "I'm—eh—a gardener."

"You aren't. There's a horse with you, yet the gates didn't open."

"Are you a prisoner?"

"I am. There are forty-three prisoners being held here, maybe more. The cells opposite are for criminals. To the left are rebels. This wing is meant for those accused of being gods-touched, which they call cursed, but they killed two some days ago and there's been none brought in since. Now they've an overflow of other folk stuck on this side."

"And what are you? A criminal, a rebel, or gods-touched? You've an odd way of speaking, ver."

"I'm an outlander. Who are you, with your horse who can enter a courtyard through closed gates? Who hides her horse in a storeroom, and rakes away the tracks she's left on the gravel?"

The big gates ground open. The prisoner ceased speaking as feet tramped in, marching in unison, and ceased their march with the clap of a command.

"Bring out the condemned," said a woman.

Warning nipped at Marit's sleeve. She, too, knew that voice: it was the cloak of Night.

Bolts clicked; bars scraped; doors bumped open. Gibbering and weeping and begging rose to a tumult as folk were dragged into the courtyard. Then, as the last door was shut, a fearful silence fell. Through a gap under the eaves behind her, she heard the huffing and puffing of that cursed man and woman having at the Devourer in the adjoining garden, in mocking counterrhythm to the ragged breathing of the prisoners.

"You are brought before me, who are condemned," said Night. More fool Marit for venturing into the center of the pit. "The punishment for your crime is cleansing."

A wail rose among the prisoners: "Please just kill me quickly I beg you!" "I'm innocent! I never did it!" "She murdered my brother for his coin and laid the blame on me!"

"Enough! All is known to me already."

"Then you know I didn't do it!" shouted a man. "Your gods-rotted cronies laid claim to our clan's land and sent me here to die because I wouldn't shut up and lie down and take it. And you let it happen. You're a lilu, a cursed—" He grunted. His voice ceased.

She continued speaking without any change of tone. "Without order, there can be no justice. Those who foment trouble disturb what is orderly. They cannot be allowed to damage the peace the rest have so laboriously constructed. Yet I am inclined to mercy, when mercy has been earned. Bring forward these to the stone of judgment."

She spoke five names, none of which meant anything to Marit, but one at a time Marit heard sobbing, the crunch of footsteps on gravel, and after the cessation of movement a sudden burning cut shivered the air as if the wind had been sliced with a fearsome blade. Spirit shaved from body. The Spirit Gate unfolds, and the departing spirit passes beneath to the other side.

Night had wielded her staff and killed them.

"The rest must be cleansed as an example. Transfer them to Malinna for execution."

"You're as corrupt as those who serve you!" shouted the man who had cursed her before. "The orphaned girl would weep, seeing what had become of the Guardians she begged the gods to raise!"

"Kill him," said Night in a deadly quiet voice. "Let him be bathed in his own blood in exchange for his crude words."

The killing was swift: the salt of the man's blood released into the air by a blade's cut. In the adjoining cell, the outlander slammed foot or shoulder into the wall, as in anger, and it seemed the entire building shuddered. Warning bobbed her head. A feather glimmered in the air, and Marit caught it before it touched the ground; she tucked its length inside her jacket.

Eihi! How then the others begged for such a merciful, swift release. How they debased themselves with frantic words and desperate pleas. Marit burned with humiliation, because she could do nothing as they were hauled away to whatever transport wagons awaited them. How useless the power the gods had conferred on her. All for nothing! Cloak of Night could not execute her without five staffs, but what if she ordered her servants to stab Marit and remove her cloak? She had almost certainly destroyed other cloaks in exactly that way. The cloak of Night was old beyond measure and so corrupt that she appeared sweet to the eye and kind to the ear. It seemed unlikely to Marit that she knew anything about cloaks that Night had not already considered.

"What of those accused of being gods-cursed, Holy One? We've brought in eleven since you were here last—" Running footsteps interrupted the officer. "The hells! You know better than to burst in—"

"Let the messenger approach, Captain Tomash. What is your name?"

"Peri, Holy One," he said in a voice choked with fear. "Sent from Stragglewood with all urgency. The guards let me through when I explained—"

"Look at me."

Feet shifted on gravel. A man coughed uneasily. The lad sobbed once, then was silent.

Night spoke. "We must march to Stragglewood at once. Captain Tomash, make ready your company. The impostor wearing the cloak of Death has walked into their town and demanded to preside over their assizes. Can the news I received at dawn be a coincidence?"

"What news is that, Holy One?"

"Ah. I had not yet told you that I may send you and an entire cohort to High Haldia?"

"High Haldia is a cursed long way, Holy One."

"So it is, but I need someone sensible and competent to lead an extended hunt. At dawn, Lord Bevard informed me he has seen and spoken to two cloaks in Heaven's Reach. One of them is Sky! Long thought lost, and yet now in company with the renegade outlander demon who has stolen the cloak of Mist. Crags is perhaps months' journey on earth, and they'll already be running, yet does it not seem to you, Captain, that suddenly the whole lies within our grasp? Lord Radas also communicated with me at dawn. The traitors in Nessumara will be dealt with as soon as agents infiltrate the city. Meanwhile, his cohorts are bringing lower Haldia and Istria under our complete control as we take direct action against the reeves. Steward Kallonin, when will the other cohorts requested by Lord Radas be ready to march south?"

"The Thirteenth Cohort has already marched, lady. On the usual route."

"Send a messenger after them. Have them march instead through the Haya Gap. They can take what supplies they need as they march."

"Yes, lady. The Fourteenth is in the field enduring their final initiation run. They will be ready to depart in one month. The Fifteenth will follow perhaps three months from now."

"So long?"

"We learned with the disastrous expedition to Olo'osson that poorly trained troops are no better than untrained rabble. After the Fifteenth marches out, we must wait to see who among the new recruits survives the first phase. It would be useful if we could recruit from among those in Haldia and Istria who may be persuaded to join us. We continue to hear reports of a foreign captain training a significant militia in Olo'osson."

"He is being dealt with. Are there any other reports I need hear before I depart for Stragglewood?"

"More depredations in the orchards, lady. We've flogged and caged suspects—"

"None I interrogated knew anything of the matter."

"So it seems. No one knows who is stealing fruit, and in truth, lady, it seems a paltry crime."

"Such small crimes, let go, turn into large ones. Find the culprits and cleanse them on Wedrewe's posts. Anything else?"

The steward cleared his throat uncomfortably. "We've received an unsubstantiated report from the port of Lower Amatya that a reeve and eagle have been sighted over the Elia Sea. What is your command?"

"This is unwonted news," she said in the tone of a woman who is not pleased to hear unwonted news, and the poor messenger—who had nothing to do with this distressing news—sobbed as if he'd been struck. "There should be no more reeves in the far north. I must consider before I take action on the other fronts, but in this case, detach a cadre—no, a full company—of experienced men to investigate. Sail all the way to the Eagle's Claws, if necessary."

"That is a month's hard journey or more, lady. Dangerous, and on treacherous seas. As I know from having taken the journey before."

"You promised me there were no survivors. Go back and finish what you've left undone, Kallonin. Leave at once."

"It is understood, lady," he said in a flat tone that could not disguise his horror at the assignment.

Captain Tomash laughed. "Suddenly High Haldia and Heaven's Reach don't seem so cursed far away, eh, Kal?"

"Bastard," muttered the steward, but he, too, laughed, in the way of friendly rivals jesting with each other. "Lady, I'll leave at once and travel night and day to Dast Elia, where I'll hire a ship. It's my mistake. I'll rectify it. Have you other orders?"

"None, for now."

"When can Steward Hefar expect your return, lady? It's four days' journey each way over the Liya Pass to Stragglewood, I believe—"

"He can expect me when I arrive. Captain Tomash, I'll meet up with your company at dusk. Expect to march all night."

The sigh and flutter of wings fell heavily as Night departed.

"The hells," said the steward. "We're in for it, eh? Eagle's Claws! Heaven's Reach!"

"Shut your complaining," said the captain with another laugh. "We've got the soldiers and the coin, never forget that."

"I never do. Heya! Men! Get moving!"

The guards dispersed with heavy steps. Quiet settled. An insect buzzed.

A hand scratched at the wall, and the outlander whispered. "You're that cursed cloak, aren't you? If you've come to preside over the assizes, you're too cursed late."

"Why weren't you taken out to be judged?"

"I'm a hostage."

"An outlander hostage! For whose good behavior?"

"My brother's," he said bitterly.

She cracked the door and peered through. The courtyard was empty but for six corpses. Five sprawled on the gravel, seemingly untouched; they'd been killed by Night's staff. The sixth, collapsed atop the rock, was splashed by blood. Could a Guardian execute a man with her Guardian's staff on a whim, just because she wanted to, or only if that man was *actually guilty* of the crime he was accused of? Had the cloak of Night spared these five from the agony of the cleansing to be merciful? Or had the others been sent to be cleansed because they were not guilty of a crime she could execute them for?

The double gate was pushed open by a man dressed in humble laborer's garb. A cart creaked in, pulled by a second man walking between the shafts. Both men had the debt mark tattooed by their left eye: slaves, not hirelings. They slung the bodies into the cart like so much firewood.

"She was merciful, eh? Six spared from the cleansing. You have to rake, Erdi?"

"Neh, I'm not assigned that duty today, nor washing off the rock. I'm hells glad about that, eh, for that one sure bled. Look, we've got blood all over. I don't want it drying on my kilt. It's the only clothes I got."

"Let's take a wash now. Corpses'll wait, eh?"

They grabbed up buckets from the end of the porch and trotted out the gates. Marit was out the door as soon as they were gone. The cell doors weren't locked, only barred. She shifted the heavy bar and shoved the door open. He emerged at once, holding a vest and a blanket in one hand. He pulled the door shut, set the bar in place, glanced at the winged horse nosing out of the storeroom, then turned to confront Marit.

"The hells!" she said, retreating a step in shock. "You look a cursed lot like an outlander named Hari. Could he be your brother?"

His body was lean and strong and, since he wore only a kilt, there was a lot of body to admire. But it was his stare—so intense she might have thought him half crazed—that disturbed her most, until she realized he was gods-touched. Veiled to her sight.

"Death's cloak," he said. "You're the one called Marit, aren't you? It's because of you the others don't trust Hari. What did he do? Seduce you?"

She grinned. "Neh, nothing like that. I seduced him." He almost grinned, but his was a serious face to go with that gods-rotted powerful body. "Aui! Listen. There's no Sorrowing Tower in this town, which means they must take the dead beyond the walls. Hide under those corpses. The slaves will haul you out the gates. It's the best I can do."

He reached for her arm, but before touching her he fisted his hand and tapped his chest. He wore two rings, with matching sigils. "If you gave Hari even a moment's breath of happiness, then I thank you for it. Beware of Night. She'll kill you, if she catches you. How she'll do it I don't know, but she has a way."

Hari's brother! Who knew where his loyalties lay?

"My thanks for the warning," she said. "Now, go."

Except for the blood, it wasn't so bad getting him hidden in the wagon. Wings unfurled, Warning waited. Marit grimaced at the blood on her hands. It had gotten over everything. Aui! Never mind it. She dashed back into the storeroom and grabbed three knives and two batons. One baton and two knives she shoved under, into his hands. The other knife and baton she kept, to remind her that a reeve and eagle had been sighted over the Elia Sea.

The cloak wanted her steward to go all the way to the Eagle's Claws to find and kill that reeve. So be it. Marit would get there first.

SHE MOVED OUT cautiously, flying low, but saw no sign of the other Guardian. The lovers were, amazingly, still at it: such stamina! Neh, it was a different man at work on the same woman. Anyhow, both were oblivious of what had transpired so close beside them. Eihi!

Wedrewe's people worked on, all oblivious, or perhaps all too aware of how quickly death could strike.

In an outer courtyard, the chain of prisoners was being shoved into tiny cages on wagons and locked in. Knowing herself a fool, she circled low until she saw the wagon with its corpses clear the perimeter fence and head into the woods. After that, she flew to the Vessi Road and followed it downstream until she spotted the prison wagons. Herelia was well-settled country but nevertheless there were stretches of road with no habitation in sight. She bided her time for several mey. In the late afternoon she clattered to earth on an isolated stretch of road with broken woodland and meadows on one side and denser growth blocking her view of the river. The prison wagons rolled into sight, and their sergeant called his men to a halt as she rode toward him and caught his surprised gaze with her own.

He is a killer. He has killed men.

"What is your name?" she asked. His cadre hid their faces behind open hands.

"Bolen," he said, the word squeezed from him by the strength of her gaze.

He spoke truth, which brightens you. His name, given to him by his mother, linked him to the Four Mothers, and deep within his essence which is body and spirit together, she saw, felt, heard, tasted, the thread that binds spirit and body into one creature. Easy enough, for her, to sever them, now that she saw their misty substance. She drew her sword. The soldiers cowered. The prisoners moaned. It was so easy, after all! She could cut away his life, send his spirit through the Spirit Gate. He was a killer. He had killed. She did not even have to touch him with her sword, only cut the threads that spun his shame and his wrongdoing into the pure air.

He hid his face.

"Release the prisoners," she said.

"Better you execute me with a clean death, lady," he said hoarsely, "than I face punishment by cleansing for disobeying my orders."

"Then it would be better for you not to serve unjust masters. These prisoners who face cleansing are assuredly not guilty or else they, too, would have been granted the mercy of a clean death at the hands of a Guardian."

"They serve as examples because of their stubbornness, lady."

"Release them."

He stammered out the order, and his cadre fell over themselves to pull the pins on the cages.

The prisoners hesitated. Then one man pushed free of his confines, scrambling off the wagon, and tugged out two comrades. These three dragged out the others, all but one older man who refused to bolt.

"Run," she said.

They ran, some into the brush toward the river and others into the woodland.

"You've done them and their clans no favors," whispered the sergeant, "nor me and my cadre, neither. Those who follow orders don't get hurt."

She was a fool, showing herself like this. Even if the prisoners survived, how were they to make their way through a Herelia that was in a way a vast prison? How was

Hari's brother to do so? But she could not live with herself if she did nothing, even if what little she did was not enough.

*   *   *

SLAVES DRIVING A wagonload of corpses weren't deemed suspicious in We-drewe. At each gate, after an exchange of words, they rolled on. Shai breathed through the blanket that pressed over his mouth and nose. He kept his eyes shut and listened. Eventually, the roadbed changed from rumbling pavement to squeaky dirt, and despite the stiffening weight of the bodies, Shai felt the softening presence of trees. As the slaves chattered away about a tournament of hooks-and-ropes played last month and still in dispute, Shai wriggled backward out from under the dead ones and rolled off the back of the wagon onto a woodland path. The wagon trundled on. They didn't even look back as he scrambled into the nearest brush and lay still, leaves flashing above him. The noise of the wagon's passage faded.

Hu! That had been the easy part.

He pulled on the vest, cut off a strip of the wool blanket to belt his knives and the reeve baton, and tied the blanket like a cloak at his shoulders. Then he considered the sun. When he'd been marched from Toskala's hinterlands to Wedrewe, a journey of nineteen days, he'd kept track of their general direction. Ignoring the drying stains and unpleasant smells on his skin and clothing, he began walking southwest, roughly parallel to the track. Twice he crossed streams, drinking before moving on, and he found late season berries he'd seen mixed in with his porridge in the prison, easy to gather and tie up in a corner of his blanket. Were those triangular green leaves edible? Yes, he'd seen the children eating them.

At dusk he reached the end of the woodland and stood looking over tidy farm-land where lanterns bobbed as folk hurried home. He sank to a crouch. As he scooped mashed berries, he considered the fields and the likelihood of barking dogs. Could he cross safely at night? Steal food, or even just a leather bottle to carry water?

A cough.

Before he even realized he'd been careless, they dropped down on either side of him with teeth bared in something that might have been meant to resemble a wel-coming grin or a fierce menacing scowl. He grabbed a knife, and the female knocked him flat so fast, pinning him, that he began to laugh because he was exhausted and hungry and his feet were scraped and bleeding and he stank of corpse and he was stuck out in the middle of enemy territory with scant chance of reaching anyone he might call an ally.

So what in the hells were two wildings doing here?

The male gestured with its hands, tale telling as vivid as speaking: a cloak flowed from its shoulders; folk hid their eyes; Shai did not hide his eyes; the cloaked one kills those who do not hide their eyes.

"Hu!" whispered Shai. "Did you follow me all that way? To get revenge? I didn't betray them. I had no idea your friends were going to be attacked. Or that poor gods-touched girl would be murdered just for being veiled. Please help me get to a reeve hall. That's all I ask—"

The male impatiently tapped its own chest, the female's shoulder, and finally indicated Shai: *Us. You. Together.*

Far in the distance, a horn's voice rose and faded.

Hurry.

24

THE NORTH IS a bitter world. Beyond the confines of the deep waters of the Elia Sea, a long spout of a bay connected to the northern ocean by a narrow strait, the coastline crawled north mey after dreary mey, violent ocean waves crashing at the base of rugged cliffs. In the pockets of shelter where safe anchorage might be found on a scrap of pebbled beach, fishing villages clung to the coast. Marit had never before seen houses in which folk nursed a hearth fire inside the same structure in which they slept, but the rock cottages breathed smoke as might any living body. Truly, it was as cold as the hells. She never stopped shivering. Who would want to live in this bleak landscape?

By the time she reached a wide oval peninsula the moon had blossomed to full and withered away. Here the land was rich in farm plots turned golden with harvest stubble. A pair of linked hills, steep enough to be called mountains, rose out of the peninsula's central rise; at their peaks glinted twin altars whose view thereby spanned the coast, one facing north and one south. Was this "the Egg" described in the tales? She'd heard of the place but had never set foot here.

She landed in an isolated cove on the northern shore and released Warning. The craving for the altar's elixir made Marit lick parched lips, but she resolutely took the last swig of musty souring wine and walked along the sandy shore looking for a fresh stream. Sea wrack littered the sand; a tree trunk had washed up many years ago and was now a haven to numerous tough plants. Pine wood grew beyond the high-water line.

"Heya! Honored Guardian!" A stout woman strode out of the wood, waving a length of cloth to catch her attention. "Greetings of the day!" The woman lifted both hands, palms open, to touch her forehead as a sign of respect before she extended her hands in welcome. She was smiling, her thoughts an unself-conscious tumult of astonishment, joy, and an old grievance over—Aui!—something to do with a pig. "I'm called Fothino. Please, walk with me to the village. We will be honored to host you for the assizes."

Marit sensed no danger. Of course, she'd sensed no danger on the day she'd been murdered. And yet she could not bear to live forever in suspicion of humankind.

"You honor me, verea."

The woman's smile brightened. "If you will be waiting just one breath so we may gather our things . . ." She walked briskly back into the trees and shouted in a strong voice. "Ridarya! Malilhit!"

Marit followed cautiously. The woman had two adolescent daughters who prettily offered the same formal greeting. Like their mother, they wore not taloos but long jackets of rough hemp thread closed with a sash and apron and, beneath all, a length of cloth wrapped to cover the legs.

"Finish you up quick now," scolded their mother.

They promptly set to whispering as they finished scraping resin into a barrel.

"She doesn't look different than anyone else."

"How could any ordinary person capture and ride a winged horse?"

The pine trees were being tapped, streaks of pale raw resin running down the wounded bark over a tin lip and into pots. The woman gathered up her cutting tools, wrapped them in burlap, and slung them over her back. "Girls! Run you ahead and tell the village of our good fortune. Let there be a proper greeting."

The girls raced away, barefoot despite the cold weather. Marit accompanied Fothino at a more sedate pace on a path winding through the woods.

"It seems peaceful here," Marit said.

"Eiya! Peaceful is as peaceful does. We're a quiet place far from anywhere else, I grant you. But folk will quarrel and bicker. Me no less than anyone, I tell you honestly, Guardian." The words she spoke were recognizable but accented, making her a bit difficult to understand. "I sent my good son all the way to Rulla Village just last year to live with his young wife's family just because he and me, we quarreled so much after my good husband's spirit departed through the gate. Girls are easier to raise, neh?"

"I don't know."

"Neh, forgive me if I've asked what I should not."

"Ask me anything you wish."

"Well, then, I will so. With your permission."

"You have it."

"According to the records kept in Sapanasu's temple, a Guardian invokes an assizes every seven years. Yet we've seen no Guardian for ever so many years, not since my mother was a child. Folk they pretty much thought we'd never see a Guardian ever again."

"That wasn't precisely a question. How far back do the records of your Lantern's temple go?"

"I wouldn't know, me being apprenticed to the Witherer in my time. But my lad, the older boy, the one who died, he was a Lantern clerk for three years. He one time told me the records in the temple went back to the very first day folk built the temple here. So it surely is very very old."

"Very old, indeed. I'm sorry to hear of your misfortune, losing the child."

Her stride continued unchecked. "He was a good peaceful boy. But I'm fortunate, even so. I've birthed nine children and only lost three, and two of those before their first moon's turning. So really, the gods have blessed me, nay?"

They passed a row of squat charcoal kilns built of earth and stone, empty and cold. Goats chewed at brambles grown around the brick. "There was a dispute over the ownership of these kilns," added Fothino, sliding so smoothly into this new subject that it seemed of equal importance to the death of her children, and in the life of the village, no doubt it was.

"Was it resolved?"

"Nay. Now we buy from Mussa Village, so it costs us more. It would be good if we could get these kilns running, but no one wants to open the dispute. There was a killing done over it."

"A killing!"

"A man died up on Curling Beach who was one of them arguing over kiln rights. Maybe he drowned, or maybe he was hexed, or maybe he was stealing from the trade offering left for the merlings—that's what I think he was doing, for he was a sneaking sort of man. That was four years back. Those two clans involved barely speak to each other to this day."

"A trade offering left for the merlings?" Marit had heard of this ancient custom in tales. "Do you folk still make such offerings?"

"Don't all folk do so? How can the proper balance be held, if the trade offerings aren't made to the other children of the Mothers? We share with each other, just as it says in the tales."

The woods gave way to sheep pasture and orchard. "How often do you see outsiders?"

"Outsiders? Like outlanders? A fishing boat or two, every year, from up north-away. They are very ugly people, skin like a white-fish's underbelly and—although I admit it is difficult to believe—some have red hair."

"Red hair?"

"Like flames."

Marit shook her head, unable to envision red hair. "What of folk from the Hundred?"

"There's a regular trader what comes in from High Point off Little Amartya once a year. Sometimes fisherfolk bide over here in a storm."

"You're well cut off."

"Are we? From what?"

They approached on a path through neat garden strips, the sturdy long houses rising beyond. The whole village had turned out, frail elders, wriggling little ones, restless youth, and stolid mature women and men. Singing and gesturing in a talking line, they chanted the familiar closing scene from the tale of the Silk Slippers in which the innocent girl is welcomed at long last to her home.

> come in, come in, we welcome you with garlands
> come in, come in, at long last you return
> food and wine we will bring you
> sit with us, for we have been waiting
> come in, come in

A girl child and boy child were urged forward with a bucket of water and juniper soap so she could wash face and hands. A second pair offered a ladle of fresh water to rinse her mouth. A third presented her with a garland of aromatic maile. The porch of the most prosperous family in the village—they were proud to tell her they were blacksmiths who worked metal for most of the peninsula—had been hastily garlanded with kuka nut and myrtle wreaths. A low eating table and pillow had been set out where she sat. An elderly man ceremonially wiped out a drinking bowl of fine white ceramic, small enough to cup in her hand, a piece of exceptional beauty in such an isolated village. A woman carried in a vessel of heated rice wine, and some rice cakes arranged on a wooden platter. A different woman, head shaved in the manner of the Lantern's clerks, murmured over these offerings a blessing so ancient

Marit had never heard it outside of tales: *Let the breath of the Mothers enter. Let the breath of the Mothers invest all things.* Had she walked into the past, through an unseen gate? The master blacksmith himself knelt humbly and poured out the wine. He stepped back.

"Let me not sit alone," Marit said.

Aui! Everyone crowded forward; the frail elders were brought up onto the porch and helped to sit on frayed pillows brought by children racing away to other houses to fetch extra; children and youth hunkered down in a crouch, arms hooked over knees; the others stood or sat or crouched according to their wish. But she must drink and eat alone, regardless, their gazes intent on her in a way startling to her after all this time with folk avoiding her gaze. She was careful to look no person straight in the eye, and yet their fascination did not overwhelm her. Not that they were innocent; far from it! But they did not fear her. It was fear that made the intimacy of the exchange so invasive and horrible.

Their silence lasted as long as the rice cakes.

"Honored Guardian," said the clerk, "we have sent runners to the other villages. Do you wish to visit each village separately, or meet at some central place? If I could recommend the Lantern's temple in Mulla—"

"Nay," objected the blacksmith, "the Devourer's temple is more appropriate."

"Only because your cousin is hieros there," said the clerk.

"Begging your pardon, honored Guardian," said Fothino. "What is your wish?"

"I have to go," said Marit, surprised by their assumption that she had come on purpose to preside over an assizes. Yet why not? They knew no other story here, where they saw one trading vessel every year and, perhaps, a few flame-headed barbarians. Here came a Guardian, so naturally she would preside over an assizes.

"I have to go," she continued, "in another day. Best call for the assizes tomorrow at a location folk can easily walk or ride to."

"Begging your pardon, Guardian," said Fothino, "but the folk from Rulla Village will take an entire day to walk even to Hasibal's stone. Can you not preside for two days at the assizes?"

They watched so expectantly and with so much hope.

A company from Wedrewe must march overland to the port of Dast Elia before sailing up the length of the Elia Sea and along a coast known for its rocky dangers and intemperate seas.

"Two days." She could say nothing else.

LONG INTO THE night the villagers chanted and danced, and golden mead and an amber ale with the essence of pears flowed as freely as if it were festival time.

WARNING RETURNED TO her at dawn, an event that silenced the merrymaking. Leading the horse, she walked with the entire village singing and clapping in procession along a path that wound inland through woodland. Before midday, they arrived in a meadow partway up the slope of the northern peak. In this vale of the Formless One dwelt an ancient stone sacred to Hasibal; flowers had been left as offerings on its flat water-pocked surface: a pair of fresh wreaths, withering bouquets, a desiccated necklace of blooms almost ground to dust.

She knew nothing about the rituals attendant on a Guardian assizes, but here the priests could recite the forms from memory. According to the gathered priests, the Guardian's seating place must face south in the morning and north in the afternoon; those who came to watch must stand at a distance; those who brought their cases must enter in groups and wait their turn at specific stations according to the nature of their complaint and whether they were accuser or accused. For the aged, pillows to sit on under shade; for young people come in from distant villages who could expect to meet and mingle with other young folk, a discreetly blind eye turned to the usual activities of youth. A makeshift market sprang up under the shadow of the wood.

No offerings of any kind were allowed, to avoid the appearance of bribery, and every village was expected to contribute food and drink in proportion to the number of people attending from that village. Folk must eat! For herself, she sipped at juice and ale, nibbled at flat bread, white pears, and a fish stewed with barley and some spices for which she had no name.

A pig had broken into a garden one too many times, destroying several crops of tubers, and the gardener had finally in a rage killed it and eaten it. The owner wanted damages paid; the gardener blamed the owner for not penning the pig properly after multiple warnings and demanded damages equal to her loss of crops. Five years had passed in which the dispute curdled on like a sour taste.

"What would content you?" In the face of her piercing gaze they agreed it was foolish not to have settled the matter much sooner: a piglet delivered to the owner in recompense for the lost meat; a stout pen built by the owner to avoid another incident, together with two baskets of pears, fifty tey of barley, and a bundle of sourwort leaves in exchange for the produce lost.

The placement of boundary stones must be reconsidered. Accusations of theft years old, suspicion still festering. Two bolts of good dyed linen cloth filched a mere ten days ago. Inheritance squabbles were the worst; she knew that already from her years as a reeve. One group dragged on its self-serving arguments for so long she lost her temper and let them know in detail the scope of their manifold faults. How they then scrambled to seek a grudging solution, having lost face so nakedly before the entire assembly!

Night came on, and torches were lit, and still they came, patiently waiting their turn, more folk straggling in from distant villages to set up awnings as they accepted a place in line. Yet she did not tire. The pleas and arguments, even at their worst, were like nourishment.

A man was accused of hexing a fatal illness onto a woman's three children; he had become outcast and yet he was innocent of the deed.

"There's an old feud here," Marit said as torches crackled, "that you are all covering up. I want the truth."

The truth can be ugly. It was at last revealed that the woman knew who had poisoned her children: her husband had done it himself, because he knew that another man had fathered two of them and he did not want the shame and dishonor revealed as they grew into their adult faces. But his clan was powerful and wealthy—by local standards—and she was afraid to accuse him and yet must accuse someone—a man of no wealth and no connections—lest she herself be condemned.

"I wish I was dead with my little ones," she sobbed.

So on through the night, so many grievances smoldering over the years and decades that folk did want, no matter the cost, to bring into the light. Marit wondered if the truth would ever be known about the man dead in the surf at Curling Beach. Maybe he was best left dead, his dying a mystery. Is this one of the truths that Guardians must learn? That the truth does not always bring closure?

Yet folk will go on with life, as a new day will dawn.

"But I don't want to marry him!" exclaimed the young woman, a strapping, beautiful creature with such an immense weight of self-satisfaction that it was like swallowing honey laced with garlic. "I want to marry his brother."

"His brother does not want to marry you," observed Marit, who did not even need to call for the brother's testimony. He was a handsome lad, one she would have liked to have tumbled when she was younger, but his embarrassment was apparent. "He was a kalos at the temple, not a suitor. He slept with you in the courtyard of the Devourer."

"Yes! Oh! Yes!" She gazed adoringly at the hapless youth. He looked away, helplessly, toward his disgusted family.

"Lust does not make a marriage." Yet she thought of Joss as she spoke the words. Had it been only lust she'd nurtured for Joss? They had spoken of bearing a child together. That was cursed serious, especially for reeves who served the gods and the Hundred; they didn't expect a normal life. "Daughter, you think too well of yourself. Refuse to marry the young man offered to you and have your clan look elsewhere. That is your right. But do not pretend that the worship shared in the Devourer's temple is meant to be carried outside the temple walls. The gods recognize that we are human in our greed and our lust and our joy and our striving, in the ways in which we fight and hate and nurture and love, in the ways we tend our fields with hard work or steal that which belongs to others when we know it is wrong. The laws of the Hundred allow us to live in harmony when otherwise all around us might fall into chaos and conflict. Marriage is for the clan. Desire belongs in the Merciless One's precincts, not in the village street."

The young woman burst into flamboyant sobbing, aware of how fetching she looked in her misery. Her doting friends led her away.

"Make the marriage, or do not," said Marit to the clans. "But I advise you to make your decision quickly. Seal the agreement, or make a clean break and go your ways without blame. This is a small matter. Don't let it fester until it becomes a big one."

In the end it took three days to get through all the cases people were willing to bring before her. In the afternoon of the third day Warning paced up to the rock and dipped her head, and Marit said to the assembly, "Now I must go."

They offered their thanks and, as they would with a reeve, a bundle of provisions for her trouble. She wanted nothing else, nor did she expect it. They had given her their trust; there was no better gift.

She and Warning rode into the sky as the gathering watched her depart. Down to the shore they flew. Was that a pod of merlings skimming the ocean's surface just beyond Curling Beach, where the waves formed tunnels? Was that smoke coming from caves along the northern shore just beyond the the thin ridge that connected the peninsula to the mainland? Did an outpost of delvings make their home in these far reaches, as Fothino had implied?

It was as if she had entered the Hundred at long last and now must leave it to return to lands where rot had wormed its way deep into the heart of what had once been solid.

Our thanks to you, Guardian.

For days onward these words sustained her.

25

YOU COULD KNOW a lot about the wildings' moods from their ears. As they walked along a deer track through one of the thick stands of woodland where Shai now felt safest, Brah's ears rose, flicked, and lowered halfway. Sis—Shai had started calling them Brah and Sis, names which amused them—was up in the trees, unseen, but she hooted softly. Brah brushed an ear with a hand, to say, "Do you hear?"

Shai did hear a sound like a murmur vibrating through the soles of his feet: They were coming to a big river.

They had trekked for over a month, first creeping and crawling through cultivated Herelia, stealing fruit from orchards and forgotten radishes from last season's gardens, and later hiking through forested hills until they reached what Shai figured was the Haldian plain. Twice, in the hills, they'd been caught out by local woodsmen, but both times he'd managed to drop to the dirt before being spotted while the presence of a wilding caused the folk to stammer formal greetings and back away.

Brah tapped Shai's shoulder in the gesture that meant: *Move.*

After a while, they halted at the woodland's edge and looked over cleared fields to a well-maintained road and, beyond it, a swift-flowing river. The current looked plenty strong and it seemed deep, too, cut by powerful waters with a hard blue tinge. Beyond the river lay more woodland, changing color as the afternoon shadows deepened, yet this wall of greenery made him uneasy: It was like seeing foothills and sensing that behind them lay mountains as mighty as the Spires, a wilderness impossible for humankind to penetrate.

Sis dropped out of the trees with a fearsome display of incisors. Her hands moved through gestures so fast that Brah flicked his ears in dismissal as if to say: "No use, he can't understand you."

But Shai did understand. "Is that your home?"

Brah snorted and punched him on the shoulder—*hard.* Shai had to take a step back to absorb the blow, but he grinned. Among the Qin soldiers, he had learned that you only slugged your friends; your enemies you went after with a sword.

Sis tapped his arm three times: *Alert.* He checked for branches, the position of his feet, anything that might make a sound—all in an eyeblink—before dropping behind a screen of foliage just as six soldiers strode into view on the road, spears ready, swords in sheaths. Two were archers. They marched on upstream, vanishing as the afternoon shadows lengthened.

Now.

They raced across the open field, scrambled up and over the raised roadbed and down the other side through the dry stubble of a harvested rice field. As they sprinted through the grassy verge to the steep bank, a shout of alarm cut the air. Sis splashed through the swirling shallows, hands underwater as if feeling along the rocks.

A horn's call shrilled. Shouts clamored.

Sis whooped and beckoned, then plunged in as Brah dragged Shai over. Beneath the water, attached to the rock facing, was a chain. He grabbed hold and took a step, was at once in over his head, the current tearing at his body with an intensity and power as shocking as the cold of the water. His knives and baton were torn loose as he went under.

Merciful One protect me!

He came up coughing and hauled himself along the chain, kicking to keep his head above water. Twice perhaps he heard a horn's call but it was difficult to be sure with the river thundering in his ears. The blanket tangled in his arms and for a moment he thought it was going to choke him; then the current slackened and he found a toehold and clambered up the far bank, heaving. An arrow skittered over the churning surface and was borne downstream. The soldiers had returned, running toward the chain; the two archers knelt, the better to make their mark.

Brah was thrashing in the shallows and abruptly a dull snake slithered away into the current: the wilding had released the end of the chain. He climbed up beside Shai, the two wildings *laughing* as a pair of arrows plunked into the nearby shallows and the archers bent their strings for a new volley.

Sis whooped a warning. Downstream, a dozen men with swords drawn were running toward them on *this* side of the river along a cart track. Brah and Sis broke into a run, Shai at their heels, as the soldiers pursued. The trees here had been harvested, replanted, pruned, coppiced—managed by human hands. They leaped over old stumps, crashed through tangles of woody shrubs.

A snap of breaking branch whipped Shai's head around; a body slammed into him, and he fell hard with weight atop him: that sour breath was definitely human. He shoved up with a hip, braced an arm within the gap that opened, and flipped the bastard; backhanded him with a ringed fist so hard the man grunted and went limp. Shai wrested a spear out of his hands, spun just in time to knock away a spear thrust from another soldier. Spears and staffs were poor weapons to bandy about in undergrowth. He charged, and tripped the man while catching him under the chin with an elbow strike, knocking his head back. The idiot went down hard. He hadn't even unsheathed his short sword. Shai grabbed the sword, sliced the belt, and tugged belt and sheath off the unconscious man. Then he ran, still gripping the spear in his other hand; he wasn't sure where to go, only that he must go deeper in and find a better place to hide. The wildings had vanished, and the villagers in this part of the world had done a hells lot of wood management because the woodland breaks went on and on, never quite giving him enough cover to risk a halt to catch his breath. Soon his lungs were heaving and his legs as heavy as if filled with water from the river crossing. At least his feet were by now as tough as leather.

Racing footsteps rattled through the undergrowth behind him. He cast a look back: three, at least, were gaining on him. A form hurtled out of the air and smashed into the leading soldier, the impact carrying both bodies into a tangle of vegetation. The second soldier was knocked sideways as the bare feet of the other wilding crashed into the man's shoulder. Sis somersaulted in midair, like an acrobat, and landed upright a short distance away. Shai feinted with the sword as the third man hesitated, not sure which target to strike. Shai darted inside the reach of the man's spear and struck him a hard backhand, sword hilt to temple. The man collapsed.

Whoop! Whoop!

The wildings danced out of the foliage and slapped him on the back, coughing with laughter. It was all a game to them.

An arrow rattled through leaves and bounced harmlessly on the earth. The male scooped it up and snapped it in half, still coughing laughter as the female's ears flicked straight up. Men advanced through gaps in the managed forest.

"Where do we go?" Shai cried.

Another arrow tumbled closer, an archer getting his measure.

The male slapped Shai on the shoulder and lit out running. Shai bolted, following him, but at least twenty soldiers were swinging in to cut him off. The burn in his chest as he ran sucked away his air. A whistle fluted on the wind. Ahead rose a curtain of thorns like the end of his hopes.

Yet Brah's pace did not flag. It was not a solid wall of thorns but rather a lacework growing over ancient trees whose vast limbs traced the contours of the ground like a massive fence on which brambles twined. They ducked under a limb and skipped over a skirt of knobbled roots.

Behind, a man shouted. "Heya! Weron! Come back! No man is permitted to cross into the wild—!"

"I've got them!" shouted a voice so close that Shai dropped to his knees, thinking it the only way to avoid death.

He rolled, but bumped against a tree as a soldier loomed with a triumphant grin, sword raised for the strike. A smear of movement flashed in the air. The man took two steps and convulsed. He was dead before he hit the ground. Seen through the lacework of the brambles and the fence of limbs, the other soldiers stumbled to a halt.

Shai had not rammed up against a tree but rather a pole decorated with a skull. In the clearing beyond the fence of thorns, each of a dozen such poles boasted a grisly head, most skulls affixed with rope but two were fresher, the eyes eaten away but sinews still making a semblance of a memory of a face. Eight wildings dropped into the clearing. The light was changing rapidly as twilight settled. The sergeant gave an order, and the soldiers fled back the way they had come.

The wildings looked him over, blinking to turn their eyes from colored facets to jet black. He glanced up at the skull. Its jawbone was missing; he spotted, in the gloom, a span of white cradled within the cushion of a fern.

Kartu Town seemed very far away right now.

Slowly, he set down sword and spear and raised his hands, palms open and empty.

No man is permitted to cross into the Wild. He had broken the boundaries, just as his scouting party had in the Lend, only this time he had no Eridit to entertain them with a chanted tale and no horses to lose in exchange for food or his life.

One of the newcomers picked up the spear and broke the stout staff over its knee, keeping the iron point and tossing the sword to a companion. Then it gestured to Shai: *This way. Come.*

As night fell, he followed them into the Wild.

*   *   *

TEN DAYS MORE it took Marit, flying into the cold and empty north. She had seen the Eagle's Claws once, at the end of her first year as a reeve when with a more experienced reeve she had flown a circuit of the Hundred so she might learn the breadth and length of the land she had sworn an oath to protect. She was not sure what she was looking for in this wild rocky outpost where forest-covered spines of land dug like talons into the windswept sea. She flew north into the Claws as dense forest gave way to sparser pine woods with an underlayer of rhododendron and myrtle. There were no villages, no goats, no shepherds or fisherman ranging, nothing but wind and waves and a lonely emptiness like the weight of a heart which knows itself to be alone without clan or hall.

Naturally the thread of smoke near the tip of the southernmost talon caught her attention. Along the ridges and cliffs rested huge nests, torn by wind and weather, evidence that the great eagles had nested here in the past. A cluster of ruins emerged, the clear imprint of an old reeve outpost, smaller than a hall but larger than a way station like Candle Rock. Training grounds and landing spaces had been cleared, grown over by a layer of rattle grass. Rubble marked old cotes and outbuildings, but the crude rock hall's thatched roof was in good repair. An odd white growth stubbled the nearby brush and rocky fissures.

In a hollow tucked away in a tiny bay below the compound, a crude stone hut sheltered against the cliff. A fire burned in a pit ringed with stones, and skewered meat raised tongues of flame where grease dropped. An eagle dove into view so suddenly she yelped in alarm and then laughed as the raptor swung up hard and thumped down on a rocky outcropping. Aui! How she missed Flirt!

A young man unhooked from the harness and dropped awkwardly to the ground, steadying a covered basket. He paused to scan sea and shore, looking past her as she approached. Satisfied, he released the eagle's jesses and bounded down stone steps to the cottage with the grace of a careless mountain goat. The eagle launched, found an updraft, and rose fast into the sky, ignoring Marit and Warning.

She backtracked to the ruins of the outpost and landed. A byre had been repaired with freshly cut wood, one post listing. Wind whined through the gaping doors of the rock longhouse, the kind of hall northern barbarians lived in, without proper doors and windows or even a porch. She left Warning with reins to the ground and approached the door, slowing as the musty scent of its interior assailed her.

A human leg bone gleamed in the entrance.

The wind's chill cut her as she retreated to quarter the area, seeing with new eyes the odd white growth strewn through the brush.

Human bones aplenty, arms, legs, ribs, skulls, the fluttering remains of sashes and the ribbons of belts, if not much in the way of scraps of actual clothing. But other bones, too: tumbled columns of vertebrae, huge sternums big enough to shelter under, and talons whose strength was bleached by sun and scoured clean by rain and wind. Tangles of old harness, its leather more resilient than flesh.

Hundreds of humans and eagles had been slaughtered here.

If the earth had dropped out from under her feet, she might have better known how to react: by flailing and shrieking. She stumbled back to the training ground and halted there, rocking with eyes shut until a keening wail burst from her throat.

A scuff of foot alerted her to a figure leaping behind the corner of the stone long-house. She bolted after him, and although he was young and lean and knew the ground, she caught him, grabbed the back of his jacket, and yanked him to a halt so hard his feet went forward while his body slammed back. He rolled, kicking and grunting, and she flipped him and sat atop his chest. He'd braided his long hair neatly, and his face was scrubbed clean and his chin shaven, cuts healing in two places where he'd scraped too hard. His eyes were wide with fright as he gaped up at her.

She took in the weight of his memories like a hammer to the head: a poor fishing clan's superfluous son, restless enough to range into dangerous waters and plucked from the stormy wreck of his sinking boat by reeves. The reeves were in exile, they'd told him, fled to the uttermost north and gone into hiding from implacable enemies whose name they did not share. He'd been too awed by the huge eagles and their fearless handlers to ask questions. What right did he have to do so, anyway? They'd taken him in and treated him well, that was enough, wasn't it? His fishing helped feed the hall, and he'd worked around the place in exchange for his keep. Once a month a ship came, its hold filled with sheep or cattle, because the Eagle's Claws did not nourish enough big prey to feed so many eagles. And one month he'd been out fishing beyond the point a day after the ship's arrival, when he heard shouting, screaming, the sharp calls of frantic eagles.

"I didn't know what to do," he stuttered, choking on sobs. "I was afraid to come in. After it got quiet, the ship sailed. I came back to find them dead."

He'd seen the corpses of clansmen washed ashore after losing their boats; he'd seen elders pass over to the other side, hands limp atop frail chests; he'd seen infants washed gray by death. But he'd never seen anything like this butchery, a brutal attack by people who had lured the eagles to their death by feeding them poisoned meat and killing any who did not succumb.

"Even after they were dead they hacked them up, like they hated them. How can you hate something so beautiful?"

He flung a hand over his eyes.

She felt the wings of an eagle swell in the air and heard a raptor thump down behind her. Its shadow fell over her. She moved very deliberately, remembering the time an eagle's talons had ripped into her, and shifted to sit off to one side. No threat. The hem of her cloak flickered on the ground as the wind picked up.

"Do you know who it was who killed them?" she asked in the voice she'd used as a reeve to question people who had just faced a violent death or sudden fatal accident in their clan.

"I don't know." He was telling the truth. He was just a village kid, way out of his depth.

"Where did these reeves come from?"

"They called themselves Horn Hall. They made a couple other outposts, in other ruins. But those others got killed, too. I went to every place. They're all dead!"

His voice raised to an edge of hysteria. He'd been living on the brink for a long time.

"They can't have all been killed. How could anyone manage it?"

"They killed the eagles first!" he cried with the frustrated disgust of youth, unable to penetrate the obliteratingly stubborn blindness of elders. "They brought good meat for all that time and got them into the habit of feeding it out in a certain way. And then they just did it."

Who had the means and the motive? Who might think that, by killing the eagles first, they would not only kill reeves but ruin the eagles' ability to reproduce, thereby destroying the reeve halls forever. "Did you ever see another person wearing a cloak like mine? A cloak like the sun, or night?"

The lad's sobs washed over her like a wild wind, but she could not succumb to panic, to rage, to despair.

"Listen! How long ago did this happen?"

He sucked down a few gulps and steadied himself. He'd grown up with women scolding him with sharp words; he knew how to listen and answer when listening and answering was preferable to a smack. "M-Maybe a year ago. It was the dry season. Just like now."

The eagle's shadow slid off her, as though it had decided she was no threat, and the raptor bent over its reeve, head twisting first to this side and then the other as it examined the young man. It was a young bird, still changing color, as inexperienced and naive as he was. Satisfied he was not injured, it moved off to the center of the parade ground, tail feathers swiping the ground.

"I'm called Marit. What's your name?"

The manners taught him by his aunts and grandmothers ruled him. "I'm Badinen, honored aunt."

An old-fashioned name, in keeping with this gods-forsaken isolated wilderness. "Where did this eagle come from?"

"I don't know."

"How does it happen that she jessed you?"

"I couldn't bear to leave even after they were dead. She just flew out of the sky one day. She'd been left behind, like me, I guess. We've been together ever since. I fish. There's plenty of game for one eagle."

She asked more questions, but he knew nothing of the world beyond his humble fishing village south of here. In truth, he was hard to understand, even after the assizes had accustomed her to the northern way of talking.

"Clan Hall must be told that an entire reeve hall fled here and was betrayed and massacred."

"What is Clan Hall?" He sat up cautiously, glancing toward his eagle, who had opened her wings to sun. "I know the tales. Clan Hall isn't one of the six reeve halls."

"They are the seventh hall. They supervise the other six halls."

"That's not in the tales. Maybe they're the ones who did the murder. If my reeves trusted them, they'd have gone there, wouldn't they?"

It was a good question. Why hadn't Horn Hall gone for help to Clan Hall? Why flee here?

"Anyhow," he added, "if we leave here, them ones who killed the rest might see us and kill us, too."

"You've already been seen. They're already coming for you. I came to warn you."

He frowned, a simple lad forced to comprehend twisted minds. "You might be luring me away to kill me. Best I stay where I know the land. I have hiding spots. No one will find me."

"I found you."

"I swore I'd watch over this place, for it's their Sorrowing Tower, isn't it? The gods have scoured them clean. Their spirits have passed the gate. I'm the watchman. It's a holy obligation. I have to stay, and you can't make me go. Why should I trust you, anyhow?"

She rose. Why should he trust anyone? Yet the folk at that assizes had trusted her, because they still trusted the old ways. As he might.

"Badinen, have you not yet recognized what I am? I am a Guardian. I've come to take you where you need to go, for the sake of those who died."

*   *   *

THE VAST FOREST known as the Wild breathed with a hidden heart. Born and raised in the desert, Shai choked on the thick green canopy that surrounded him. Vines tangled on every trail, and even so the deer tracks were the only way to get around if you were stuck walking, as he was, scraping his way through branches, leaves, ferns, and the trailing threads of barbed vine the wildings jokingly called "oo!-aa!" He wiped his brow clean of the moisture that dripped from leaves above, then thrust the tip of his staff into a curtain of dangling vines as thick as a woman's arms. His probe rousted no snakes or stinging wasps or biting lizards.

He wiped his brow again, more from nerves than moisture. Had they actually lost track of him this time?

With the staff angled to part a way, he plunged forward through the ropy vines, their smell as cloying as rotting pears. The vines began writhing along his back, and one leaped as might living creature and looped once twice thrice around his shoulders until he was trapped.

Whoop! Whoop!

Chortling and hooting, Brah and Sis slithered down from above and slapped Shai on the ass as they untangled him. Resigned, he allowed them to escort him back the way he had come.

Today's attempt to flee had ended, as usual, in failure.

They were so cursed good-natured about it.

They chattered in their way, oo aa ee ai eh, gesturing with their hands, and he could no more fathom what it all meant than understand the forest's complex net of life.

Go home, he signed to Brah. *I want go home.*

You wait, Brah replied in that patient way he had, like talking down to a child. *More come. We talk.*

They drank from a stream, hands cupped in the cold water. They threw stones at a gourd-fruit dangling high above although either of the wildings could have shimmied up the trunk and fetched it, but Shai's aim was getting cursed good, almost as good as theirs, and when his cast stone brought it down, they whooped and shoved him to show what a good job he'd done. Sis slipped her flute out of its sheath on her back and, as they walked on, played a tune that ran like water, as an afternoon breeze rolled through the high canopy and the blue sky flashed in and out of view as branches swayed. Birds fluttered in the canopy; butterflies flared bright colors; insects hummed and lizards chirred as they leaped from bole to bole. His left shoulder still bore a scar from his first encounter with one of the lizards, and he had been stung by wasps several times. As for snakes, those he'd only seen lying in a stupor at the wilding village, glands being pumped for the milky liquid the wildings used to poison their darts.

The wildings placed no fetters on Shai. The forest imprisoned him more effectively than chains.

They came to the margin of a rocky hollow deep in the breathing heart of the Wild where the stately crowns of grandmother trees rose above the cliffs. Home was a complex structure of nets and roofs and platforms strung together throughout the hollow's glades that it seemed the wildings were constantly constructing and reconstructing.

In the third glade, he had shaped a platform in the crook of a tree using deadwood lashed together with rope. He hadn't any privacy, of course. He set his staff against the crossbeam he'd wedged in place for a ladder and scrambled up. A swarm of young ones followed. They brought scrips and scraps of deadfall—never greenwood—for him to carve with the fine iron knife they'd given him to replace the ones he'd lost. Everyone wanted a figure. As he began carving, the children settled respectfully to watch and a few elders with coats going silver dropped in. With ears flattened in greeting, they gestured to ask permission to sit while he worked. He could carve for the rest of his life and not satisfy them.

It was odd to be treated something like family and something like a hostage and something like a captive. He'd been all these things, but he wasn't sure what he was to them, nor could he figure who the "more" were who were coming. As for the message he so desperately needed to get to Anji, it was certainly too late to prevent Hari tracking down the captain, yet he had much to report about Wedrewe and the Guardians. Day after day he fretted over the ambush in which the rebels had been killed. Had Hari betrayed them in a selfish and vain attempt to save Shai, or had he meant all along to betray Shai? Had Marit freed him for Hari's sake, or his own? Where had she gone afterward? He wished there'd been time for her to seduce him!

Smiling, he sat, shaping a horse with the stocky frame of the Qin horses, creatures with little beauty but immeasurable toughness. The wildings had the gift of stillness and patience, just as he did, and the afternoon passed as he shaped the muzzle and flanks with particular care, recalling the horses he had ridden when he had traveled with Captain Anji's troop from Kartu Town into the Mariha princedoms and thence over the border along the northwestern borderlands of the Sirniakan Empire and over the high Kandaran Pass into the Hundred.

So much had happened in the Hundred that it was difficult to recall his colorless life in Kartu Town. How had Vali and Judit and the other children fared, the ones he'd struggled to save? Would he see Tohon again? Was Zubaidit still alive? Was Mai happy? How strange it was to think of her in a peaceful house with a doting husband, given how Father Mei and his married brothers had treated their wives. Had she birthed a healthy baby?

Without warning, the wildings leaped into the trees. He set down the carving in its nest of wood flakes. The clearing lay half in shadow stretching from the west over cropped ground cover of springy dense leaves and tussocks of grass. A pair of redbirds scratching for insects on a sparse patch took wing. Not a single wilding was in sight.

He rose, knife in hand, and abruptly two older wildings dropped out of the trees and pulled him firmly behind a shield of leaves. A winged horse cantered down out of the sky as if following a track visible only to its eyes and solid only under its hooves. The cloak, a rust-orange-brown color, rippled in the lazy wind, and where it parted it revealed a woman so very old Shai was amazed she had the strength to ride. Yet when she dismounted, she moved with remarkable agility for one so aged. She wore a thick brown-colored neck piece wrapped at her shoulders. The horse furled its wings and moved away.

As the shadows overtook her, the colors within her cloak changed subtly, turning deeper and richer in hue. She sketched the subtle gestures known to the wildings. These gestures, Shai thought, were those copied in less complex form in the tale-telling of the Hundred. What she spoke with her hands was far too complicated for him to follow, but a trio of elderly silver-haired wildings ambled into the clearing and replied with an elaborate greeting. They did not bow their heads or avert their eyes. Like Shai, wildings could face a cloak directly.

Even the incessant forest voices had fallen silent, only the wind speaking. They finished by displaying their hands, palms open, and raising eyes toward the forest canopy. A sturdy basket dropped from one of the grandmother trees, and she nodded, acquiescing, and climbed into it. As she was pulled up, the wildings climbed so swiftly after her it was as if the foliage swallowed them.

The two wildings released him and sped away into the gloom as night-watch fires were lit under the trees in stone hearths. Shai cautiously stepped into the glade. The mare, now cropping at the grass, bore a faint gleam as if its coat were burnished with sparks. In the corner of his eye, he caught the suggestion of a glimmering path, a road in the air, a tracery visible because of the contrast between its misty light and the coming night. Footsteps whispered on the earth, and Brah padded up to stand beside him and pat him companionably on the arm: *Here I am.*

"She's a Guardian," said Shai, knowing Brah could understand every word Shai spoke, even if Shai could understand so little of the wildings.

Yes. The gesture was accompanied by a roll of the eyes as if to add: *Isn't that obvious?*

"Why has a Guardian come to the Wild? Why didn't they want her to see me?"

Brah mimed a knife drawn across a throat.

"Because cloak of Night and her allies kill the gods-touched?"

Brah gave a little jump, a silent whoop, as if after all this time Shai had finally shown signs of intelligence.

"They're afraid this one who came here will kill *me*?"

Brah shrugged, looking skyward. A conclave had taken life in the highest reaches of the nets, an assembly lit by the tapers woven out of wood litter and soaked in oil that were used around camp. The lights made constellations within the trees, and beyond them, as in a dark mirror, stars kindled. Shai glanced at Brah, who was shaped in some manner like humankind but in other ways was entirely unlike. He breathed as Shai breathed. He stared overhead at the lights of the conclave and at the spray of stars, just as Shai did. He licked his lips as though tasting the night.

"The Hundred is a strange place," said Shai in a low voice. "In Kartu Town, where I came from, folk would have named you wildings or the lendings as demons, but here it seems demons have a human face."

Brah indicated Shai and circled the oval of his face.

"A human face like mine?" said Shai. "Except I'm not a demon."

Brah nodded. *Yes. You.*

"I'm not a demon!"

Sis trotted out of the darkness and grabbed Shai's arm, swinging him around. A taper was descending from the canopy. A mature wilding appeared in its aura and indicated a basket. Brah and Sis, much subdued now, led Shai over and watched as he settled in. He was lifted, the basket swaying as it rose higher and higher until he wondered if he would reach the stars. Fortunately it was too dark for him to see the ground, but the night-watch fires were growing frighteningly small.

The basket lurched to a halt and strong wilding hands helped him clamber onto a net. His right foot slipped through the netting and he caught himself on his knees, gulping. There was nothing below him but air. He murmured a prayer to the Merciful One and slowly his racing heart calmed and he raised his eyes. The conclave flowed away along the net like a festival of lights. He crawled to get away from that horrifying edge before settling cross-legged. The wildings appeared as smudges against the canopy, but the old woman was clearly lit by tapers hung from even higher branches, as if they wanted to keep her well in sight.

Her voice, like her frame, was thin but her gaze was bright in the manner of a crow's. "Outlander, I journeyed a long way in desperate circumstances to ask my cousins the wildings for aid in finding a safe haven for innocent folk who are in danger. But they refuse to hear me or heed me. Instead, these cousins have accused me of coming to kill you. Is it true you witnessed a woman wearing a Guardian's cloak give the order for a demon to be killed?"

"A demon? I don't know about that, but I've seen a Guardian order the deaths of many people, most innocent and some criminals. As for the gods-touched, with my own eyes I saw her captain kill a young gods-touched woman named Navita. With my ears, trapped in a cell, I heard her order soldiers to kill others whose only crime in her eyes was in being gods-touched."

"So besides inflicting harm on humankind, this cloaked one has ordered the death of demons. Ones like you."

"I'm not a demon! Among my people, demons are—" The word in his grandmother's tongue, the old speech of Kartu Town that had been outlawed in favor of the trade speech Kartu's conquerors preferred, had no corresponding word: *evil*. "Demons are beings who are corrupt in their heart, in their flesh, in their spirit."

Her frown cut him. That quickly, he disliked her. "Outlanders have a perilous and imperfect understanding of the world, it is true. I suppose that is why the Four Mothers did their best to protect the Hundred against the flood of unwanted humanity that must continually wash in on the tide of years. Eight varieties of children were born to the Mothers: firelings, wildings, delvings, merlings, lendings, drag-onlings, demons, and humankind. Once they were equal in numbers, and each had their role to play in the life of the Hundred: humankind, with their busy hands; the merlings in the sea and the delvings in the stone; the lendings to walk the boundary between earth and sky, and the wildings to tend the net that binds the Hundred, all that lives and grows and changes. The firelings, who are the thread that binds spirit and flesh, the keepers of the Spirit Gate. The dragonlings have vanished and are seen no more, while demons are rarest of all. It's true demons are often born to humans, and like humans may be bold or timid, cruel or kind, silent or talkative, hungry or satiated. They even look like humans. But you are veiled to my Guardian's sight. Therefore you are a demon. Has no one told you?" Her smile mocked him.

He said nothing.

"Do you even know the tales of the Hundred, outlander?"

"One of Hasibal's pilgrims taught me a few refrains," he said, thinking of Eridit.

"Why do youths like you blush when thinking of sex?" she said with a snort.

His flush deepened as heat scalded his cheeks. "How did—?"

She was a sarcastic old woman, the worst kind. "Easy to know such signs when you have lived as long as I have. Listen, boy, the wildings recognize a demon when they see one."

"Is that why they rescued me?" He gestured more broadly, to show the conclave that he was addressing them, not the cloak. "Were Brah and Sis out looking for demons to rescue?"

He waited as the old woman talked in gestures to the conclave.

She laughed curtly. "It seems that, like many youthful ones, they ranged out to have a little fun. An adventure. Instead, they discovered humans up to worse trouble even than usual. And they discovered Guardians killing demons, which runs quite against what the gods intended. The justice of the Guardians was meant only for hu-mankind. That's why they brought you back. To save a cousin. They would have saved others, had they been able to do so. The elders tell me they are curious as to why you—an outlander—were spared when other demons were killed."

The stars burned, distant lamps illuminating the mercy of the Merciful One, which is infinite. The wildings moved closer, more of them coming into view within the aura of the tapers.

"My brother Harishil is a Guardian. He wears the cloak of Twilight. Night kept me as a hostage, because Hari does not cooperate with her as she wishes him to do. Otherwise, she would have killed me as she did the others. I came to the north to find him, and he tried to get me out of the camp of Lord Radas's army before one of the other cloaks caught me. He knew they were killing those who are veiled to their sight. Hari got me smuggled out. How the rebels who took me in got ambushed I don't know. I really don't. But Night and her soldiers caught me. They took me to Wedrewe. Brah and Sis found me there."

"How did you escape Wedrewe?"

"In the back of a wagon of corpses."

"They say you wish to go to a reeve hall. What will you do, if they convey you to a reeve hall? Where will you go? Back to the land you came from?"

He shook his head. "Kartu Town is no longer my home. Maybe that's the secret of demons, that they have no true home, always wandering."

She laughed. "Not so witless after all. Why do you want to go to the reeves? Where do you expect the reeves to take you?"

He folded his hands in his lap, thinking of the demon who had taken the form of Cornflower and murdered Qin soldiers. Thinking of angry Yordenas, and that pervert Bevard. Thinking of Lord Radas's poisonous voice, and Night's terrible, twisted heart. Even Hari, torn between honor and fear. "I cannot trust you, because you are a Guardian."

On her lap a snake raised its hooded head and hissed softly, but a rustling sounded among the branches as the wildings objected, and the snake subsided at the touch of her hand.

"You say so, to me? I, who am the last true Guardian?"

"That means nothing to me," said Shai. "I'm just an outlander. All I can judge is by what I have seen the cloaks do."

"Enough!" She spoke past Shai, addressing the conclave. "I came in respect and in humility, cousins, and now I am to be subjected to this outlander's insults? What do you want of me? I beg you, you who know the map of the Hundred better than any others can, all its forgotten caves and old ruins and secret glades and hidden valleys, grant me at least this much, that you tell me of some haven where the people I have sheltered can live in peace."

"No one can hope to live in peace," cried Shai, "until Lord Radas's cruel army and the cloak of Night's twisted plans are defeated! Hide if you wish. But in the end, if you do nothing, they will find you anyway. And then there will be no one left to turn to."

The ears of the elder wildings flicked high and flattened low, a sign of displeasure, but he plunged on.

"I must leave the Wild. I did not betray the rebels, nor will I ever betray the wildings, because they saved me and have shown me hospitality. But I must go to join those who fight Lord Radas's army. To say more would be to betray their secrets. Put me on the road to a reeve hall, or a port, any place not overrun by Lord Radas's army. All of this I have said already, a hundred times. What else must I say?"

She watched the elders, then spoke. "Where did Lord Radas's army come from?"

Startled, he tugged on an ear. "I truly don't know. That all happened long before I came to the Hundred. There's a camp in Walshow. Isn't that in the north? And the town called Wedrewe, in Herelia. That's some kind of headquarters."

"The wildings have never before involved themselves in human quarrels. Why should they start now?"

"If they don't wish to, they can let me go and go back to guarding their boundaries! Maybe that will protect them for now. But in the end, it's like hiding your eyes while the sand of the desert engulfs you. That you refuse to look doesn't drive away the storm."

All at once he was seized by such frustration that he feared he would leap off the netting just to relieve the pressure. He groped in the pouch Sis had woven for him, and withdrew a small block of deadwood, caressing it and listening to what it told him. Its glossy grain shimmered in the tapers' light. He unsheathed his knife and began to carve, revealing a horse's muzzle as the conclave watched in a kind of silence. They weren't voicing sounds, but they were speaking with their hands in the most ancient language of the Hundred, the one he did not know.

"How old are you, Holy One?" he asked. "You look older than the cloak of Night. Is she also one of the first—the true—Guardians?"

"How can she be, if I am the last of the true Guardians?"

"She told me she was responsible for the greatest act of justice known in the Hundred." He shaved down the slope of a long, elegant neck. "I may only be an outlander, who knows the tales poorly, but isn't the tale of the Guardians the most important tale sung in the Hundred?"

"According to humans."

"It's humans I've walked among, demon that I am. And in the tale of the Guardians, isn't it the orphaned girl who prays for peace to return to the land? Isn't she the one the gods listened to?"

The tapers illuminated the Guardian's aged face and bitter smile. " 'In the times to come the most beloved among the guardians will betray her companions.' Only we did not realize then, that those of us first raised as Guardians would not remain Guardians forever. That some would grow weary and ask to be released, that one might become corrupt and need to be removed. That new faces—new guardians— would rise wrapped in the cloaks. And when she whose pleas the gods heard and responded to became a Guardian in her turn—for did she not offer her life for the sake of justice?—how could any of us have supposed she was the one who would in the end betray us?"

"Night is that girl? The very orphaned girl from the tale?"

Wind rattled in the branches. The wildings listened intently, as if by listening they spun yet more detail onto the map of the Hundred, the unfolding tale of the land. The cloak of Earth did not speak, and for the first time Shai felt pity for her, because although she was veiled to him, as he was veiled to her, her expression spoke as any face might: it seemed to him that it was an inconsolable grief mixed with furious regret that stilled her tongue. To be betrayed by the one we have loved best is the worst pain.

"There's a way to kill her and the others, isn't there?" he asked softly as an elaborate fold of feathered wings came to life beneath his knife. "To take their cloak and pass it to a new person. Not the Guardian council, five to remove one, but a different way. A way no one is supposed to know."

A sigh fell like wind through the wildings.

"Tell me what it is," said Shai, "and then maybe I—or others like me—can stop these cloaks from killing demons and innocents. And if that's what the wildings want, that demons no longer get killed, then perhaps in exchange they'll tell you what you need to know, about a haven for your people."

She bowed her head. Many among the wilding conclave flicked their ears, but whether to show approval or hostility he could not tell.

Without looking at him, speaking into the darkness and the silent stars, she said, "There is a way."

26

MAI BIDED HER time and made her plans, and early in the Month of the Horse when Anji returned flushed with pride over a successful negotiation with the lendings for breeding stock, she struck.

"I would have liked to travel to the Lend with you, Anji," she said in the privacy of their innermost courtyard as she poured tea and flirted with him. He was freshly bathed, wearing a silk robe and soft slippers and lounging on pillows. "I am shocked beyond measure that you bargained such a poor deal."

"You mean when their headwoman offered ten horses in exchange for Tohon, I should have taken the horses?"

She laughed. "Did that really happen?"

"They remembered and valued him from their last encounter. But you would have approved. I said ten mares wasn't nearly enough, and they wouldn't go any higher."

"I suppose you did as well as you could. I would have held out for one horse in exchange for each lethra of oil of naya."

"No doubt you would have. I knew I was overmatched the moment she started negotiations by offering for Tohon."

"Then why didn't you take me? You've taken me on a circuit of Olo'osson now."

"I control Olo'osson. I cannot take my troops into the Lend without violating border rights, and I will not risk you and Atani out in such territory with no proper protection. I do not know what manner of creatures the lendings are."

"Except that they value men like Tohon."

"Yes. It was better to pay a worse price and not take the risk that they would value *you*."

He was in a good mood. The sun was shining over blooming troughs of gold butter-bright and blue heaven's-kiss; her favorite white and blue falling-water tumbled out of pots hung from the eaves of the little gazebo under whose shade they rested.

"It's almost around again to Wakened Ox. Time for our monthly trip to Astafero."

"You are eager to see Miravia," he said, humoring her.

"I have been thinking, Anji." She sipped at her tea, composing herself. "Since our circuit of Olo'osson back in the Ibex and Fox Months, I've been in correspondence with many village and town councils. I attend Olossi's council meetings every week. The question that most troubles people is the situation in the north. Naturally people fear the Star of Life army will return to Olo'osson."

He nodded.

"But the question of the assizes also troubles people. Two generations ago the Guardians presided over the assizes—"

"So folk say. Whether the tales are true, we cannot know."

"The Lantern's hierophants have shown me records held in Sapanasu's temple recording assizes a hundred and more years ago. They were presided over by Guardians."

"Or folk calling themselves Guardians, pretending to a tradition they believed was inherited from even more ancient times. Maybe it's true; maybe it isn't."

"Yes, exactly," she said, more tartly than she meant to, "but they believe it, and they are not content with the manner in which their assizes are now conducted. Should reeves preside, or are they only meant to patrol and bring in people accused of committing crimes? Should councils preside, or may they be disposed to judge according to what benefits those with the most wealth and power?"

He set down the cup, his expression as smooth as the balmy sky, untroubled by cloud or wind. The cool weather of the early dry season was passing off and it was getting hotter each day heading into the last season of the year, Furnace Sky.

"Where are you going with this, Mai?"

She went on in her market voice. "We have seen Uncle Hari twice, the first time in the Fox Month and last month as well. I am encouraged that he has not fled. But he is restless and discontented—"

"So demons must be, because of their essential nature."

"What folk in the Hundred call a demon and what you call a demon is not the same thing."

"You may call a demon any other name you wish, but it is still a demon."

"That is not what I meant." She rapped him lightly on the back of the hand, a piece of flirtatious scolding that made him smile and twine his fingers between hers. "Be serious, Anji. Please listen to me. I would say Hari despises himself. No one should have to live with such despair eating away inside them. Especially not my beloved Uncle Hari! Anyhow, even if you wish to consider him a demon, is it not better to give him a reason to want to be part of what we have built rather than merely wanting to avoid the cloaks he hates and fears? Will I not get a better price for the peaches I am offering for sale if the customer has a hankering for such fruit, rather than feeling forced to haggle where he does not—"

Anji laughed, and she blushed, seeing he had conceived a more intimate interpretation of her words. "I am not convinced that is a good comparison, whatever it was you meant to make of it," he said. "But you are right. It is better to act out of desire than fear. What are you thinking?"

ON THIS, HER third visit to Uncle Hari in the valley, she waited until she had hot tea poured and cups set on a tray, all the while chattering about the various councils of Olo'osson large and small as if this conversation were merely a way to pass a quiet afternoon. They sat, as before, in the ruins sprawled alongside the pool and waterfall. The cave and its altar remained dark and dry; no threads glimmered on the sloped roof, and no dark shapes roiled beneath the pool's murky waters.

They were alone in the upper vale: she, Uncle Hari, and Anji with the baby in his lap. Chief Tuvi stood below, where the path emerged out of the tangle, while Sengel and Toughid waited out of sight. Five reeves had dropped them off with an offering chest, none the wiser, and departed with orders to return a hand's span before sunset.

"You want me to preside over an assizes?" Hari asked.

She flushed. She had not yet spoken of her plan, although naturally it sat forefront of her thoughts.

"I know," he said, "that you were waiting to broach the subject until you had soothed me with gossip and tea, but you cannot conceal your plans from me. What use would I be at an assizes? Have I ever shown the least sign of wisdom in conducting my own wasted life?"

"Do this one time as a favor for me, Uncle. I beg you. Just one time. And then, afterward—"

"Stop!" he cried, laughing in the old remembered way, with his big grin and crinkled eyes. "You will slay me, Mai. I can refuse you nothing when you stare at me with that hopeful face. You want to make a song of it all." He looked toward the wash of water as it rained into the pool. "I once wanted to make a song of it all. You see how it worked out."

"The tale is not yet finished, Uncle. That is the mistake you are making, if you don't mind my saying so. You've closed the gate, but you can open it again. There are other paths—"

"Aiee!" He laughed again and this time, remarkably, looked at Anji. "Is she always this persistent?"

Anji smiled.

"One time," said Hari to Mai. "Because you asked."

"I have it all arranged," she said, although emotion tangled in her market voice, making it hard to speak. "You need only arrive at the council square just before sunset tomorrow, Uncle."

"They won't know I'm coming," he said, and she dreaded the way his voice softened, as if he were changing his mind.

"You'll come to Astafero and preside over the assizes, just like the tales say it happened in the old days. You'll see. Please—"

"No tears! Just this one time." He rose without drinking his tea and began to pace. "What am I to do? What am I to say?"

"Say as little as possible," said Anji.

"Let them speak," added Mai. "There will be a clerk of Sapanasu, to record the proceedings, and an envoy of Ilu, one of Kotaru's ordinands, a mendicant sworn to Atiratu, a diakonos serving Taru, and a kalos from Ushara's temple in Olossi." She glanced at Anji, who betrayed by no flicker any discomfort at this mention of the Devourer's temple. "There must be representatives of each of the seven gods at an assizes. Except for the pilgrims of Hasibal, because the Formless One has neither temples nor priests."

"You know the Hundred well, Mai."

"I'm just saying you need only listen and hear. Others know the law. But in the case of certain intractable cases, you'll know the truth."

THE NEXT DAY—the auspicious day known as Transcendent Snake—passed slowly. In the afternoon, after a draft of calming tea and water to cool her face, feet, and hands, Mai walked down to the council benches. Would he come? Or would he turn away?

The council speaker called the council to order. The first business was a continuing discussion of certification in the market. What authority determined which goods could be certified as best-quality, good-quality, everyday-quality? Should shoddy work be forced off the market, or fined? What if a competitor brought a charge of shoddy work merely to cut into another's sales? In Olossi, the council controlled certification, but in Astafero, no standards had yet been set. People had settled here from villages and towns all over Olo'osson, and naturally they did not always agree.

As the debate dragged on, Anji without fuss or announcement walked up with Sengel and Toughid to stand at the back in the last hand's-breadth of shade. A few people noted him, but the discussion flowed on regardless. His gaze wandered. He tipped back his head, following an object moving in the sky.

"Heya!" cried a youth loitering near Chief Tuvi's guardsmen. "What is that?"

A rider on a winged horse cantered to earth. Mai rose, heart pounding, as the assembly fell into a dead silence. Hari hesitated, looking—she thought—ready to fly away. What must she say, to draw him in without betraying her knowledge of him? He did not particularly resemble her except in coloring, but might people wonder anyway? Or would they not see past his winged horse and Guardian's cloak?

A faltering voice trembled through the first lines of a song, and other voices joined in.

come in, come in, we welcome you with garlands
come in, come in, at long last you return

The noodle seller, Behara, beckoned to her daughter and sent her running down into town. The six priests rose in consternation, and finally the hierophant extended open hands.

"Holy One," she said, but faltered, washed bloodless and unable to speak further.

"Make a space for the holy Guardian!" snapped the Lady's mendicant. "For as it says in the tale, face south in the morning and north in the afternoon. Isn't that how it goes?"

At first no one moved. Then, awkwardly, one man and another woman and more cleared a bench and backed away. Hari dismounted, and the horse furled its wings. A child came running up from town in company with Behara's elder daughter, and the little one—not more than seven or eight—without the slightest self-consciousness pattered forward with a garland draped over one arm and raised it as an offering. The garland was a little withered, truly, and where it had come from in *this* season Mai could not imagine.

Hari stared at it until the child said in a clear, carrying, and somewhat exasperated voice, "You're supposed to *take* it. It's an offering, Holy One!"

Hari's grin blazed. He bent low so the child could drape the garland over his head, then he walked down to the cleared bench, the child trotting behind. The silence within the assembly was so intense that Mai realized her nails were biting into her palms. She opened her hands and sat, to avoid notice.

"And stop pinching your big sister when no one is looking, just to get her into trouble," Hari said to the child, who chortled wickedly and bolted into the crowd.

Behara actually laughed, although it was her own grandson so accused. She stood. "Holy One, I pray you, sit down. Why are you come?" If she was nervous, she hid it well.

"I am a Guardian," he said as he let his gaze pass once over the assembly. Startled gazes flicked up, or down; a man gasped out a word; a woman chuckled; another sobbed into her hands. "Is this not an assizes?"

He sat.

Everyone looked toward the six priests, who were conferring in frantic whispers. No one knew what to do!

"Bring cases forward," said Behara impatiently.

"But there is a proper form—" cried the hierophant.

"Never mind the cursed proper forms," said Behara. "How are we to remember a ritual no one here alive has ever witnessed? We'll discuss the certification issue next council meeting. Aren't there other disputes to be brought forward today?"

It took some effort to force the first set of disputants to present themselves before a cloaked man with his outlander face and ominous Guardian's eyes.

A flock of sheep had been deliberately stampeded, and several lost. The man who owned the flock said those who had scared the beasts had stolen them. Not so, said the accused young debt slave, although he blushed and stammered as he spoke. He'd done no such thing; he'd been out walking and only fallen into the way of the scattering sheep and tried his best to round them up as a courtesy, only to be accused of theft!

Hari scratched his chin, looking—Mai thought—surprised as he examined each witness in turn. He indicated the men who owned the flock. "You *believe* the sheep were deliberately stampeded, that is true enough, you do believe it. You lost five of your flock, and that is also true. Maybe it is true the flock was deliberately set upon by people bent on mischief and maybe it is not, but there are no witnesses, so we can't know. However, this young man's story is also true."

"Then what was he doing out there, a debt slave like him?" demanded one of the owners.

Hari laughed. "What do you suppose a young man like that was doing, out away from town? The same thing I would have been doing at his age, had a lass as lively as the one he's thinking of made the same offer to me!"

As men smirked and women chortled, the owners blundered on indignantly. "But then why didn't he say—?"

There were a hundred reasons folk might not say: maybe she was married already; or she was ashamed of her lust for a lowly debt slave; or he was skiving off work and avoiding a beating. Aui! Who could blame a young man for doing what the young liked to do, eh?

"But what about our missing sheep?"

Hari's expression made Mai, who knew him so well, want to snort with laughter. "Can it be you have only taken up sheep-herding this year? No wonder! You need to hire an experienced drover, ver. Someone who knows sheep. I admit it will cut into your profit, but until you understand the ways of sheep you will find yourself in trouble again and again. I speak as a man who knows sheep. Is there another case?"

Indeed, there was. Underweight strings of vey were being passed off in the marketplace, but no one knew where they had come from. Hari surveyed the crowd with seeming absentmindedness as one merchant after the next approached to display the string they'd been shorted. He stopped a woman in midsentence with a raised hand, his gaze fastening on a face half hidden in the crowd. His eyes narrowed. Folk murmured anxiously.

"They're coming from the same people who are weighting their wheat flour with chalk dust," he said.

His words were answered by a flurry of sharp movement in the crowd as a man and woman tried to bolt. No one had suspected. They'd thought the flat bread tasted gritty because everything tasted of grit here. Anyhow, most folk were accustomed to nai porridge and rice, coming from waterfed lands; the drylands wheat and millet were a new taste. What punishment was to be meted out for such a crime?

Hari looked right at Mai, and she needed no second heart and third eye to see the plea in his expression. She broke in. "Olossi's market has a code for such violations that we may follow until Astafero codifies its own market laws. Surely it is the Guardian's business to determine the truth, and the council's business to determine the fine."

Hari's tense posture relaxed. Folk agreed that she had the right of it. The sun set over the mountains. A pair of youths lit lamps, the oil of naya so pure it blazed. The light shimmered in the twilight glamor of Hari's long cloak, whose fabric blended into the fall of night and yet caught the final fading measures of day. The way he sat so still quieted the assembly; they were nervous, but not precisely fearful. They watched him, but did not cower. His mouth wore a lopsided smile that was also half a frown.

He said, "What of this other matter that concerns you, Mistress Behara?"

The words startled the noodle seller, but she rose to address Guardian and assembly both. A gang of youths trying to extort protection money had been caught by the militia and now there was a dispute over what punishment should be meted out. The lads were hauled up before Hari, where they stammered out defiant declarations of innocence.

Hari made a cutting gesture with a hand that stopped them short. "Don't lie to me!" The young men wept as Hari's gaze staked them. Frown deepening, he released them and spoke to the assembly. "You have a more serious problem. These louts are an advance force from a criminal organization that was driven out of Haldia by the war. It's trying to move its operations into Olossi."

Folk gave way to let Anji through to the front. "I beg your permission to deal with this matter personally," he said to the council. "That such organizations operate in Olo'osson is not acceptable. I'll take custody of these men. With the help of the Hieros and her agents in Olossi, we'll track this back to its source and put an end to it."

The council looked to Hari, but Hari shrugged. "I've determined the truth. It's up to you to determine the fine." He rose abruptly. The assembly rose hastily, touching hands to foreheads as a gesture of respect. "I am done for this day."

He strode to his waiting horse, his cloak blending with the fall of night.

"Holy One," called the hierophant after him. "Will you preside again over our assizes?"

He half turned back with a smile as sweet as honey cakes. He beckoned, and Mai hesitated, sure he should not be singling her out, but she could not refuse him or the look that suffused him. She paced out the distance between them, not wanting to seem intimate with a holy Guardian who all presumed she did not and could not already know. Before she could speak to scold him for calling her, he was already talking, words tumbling.

"Is this really what the Guardians used to do?"

"So it says in the tales, Holy One."

He put a hand to his head as if reeling from a blow. "They lied to me. They've twisted and stained all of it, haven't they? It's not corrupt and ugly at all. Difficult, maybe. Unpleasant at times I am sure. But it's not at all what I expected—" He swallowed, and blinked hard. "I need time to think."

"No one will find you in the valley. Only we know you are there."

"I might do something useful for once, after all the useless idiocy I've had a hand in." He flashed a smile that warmed her, then turned away, mounted the horse, and rode into the twilight. Behind, folk broke into such a flood of talk and exclamation that it drowned her. Voices began a song: *Wait and be patient, because the gods will answer. Let the heavens bring their voice down to the land.*

"Mai?" Anji ghosted up beside her, a hand on his sword's hilt.

She grasped his wrist. "He sees there is another life, not just the terrible cruelty Lord Radas wields." She wiped away tears. A glimmer rose in the sky, briefly marking the track of Hari's flight, and vanished. "He's come back to us."

He had no time to answer as others swarmed up: Mistress Behara and council members and the priests. "What did he say to you, verea?"

She was borne back into the assembly, stammering a half truth that none of them could discern from her flushed face and awkward words. No one seemed to find it strange he had singled her out, and anyway they weren't really listening. They were spinning their own tale: after so many long years, a Guardian had returned, and where there was one then there must be other true Guardians, not gods-cursed demons like those in the north. By restoring justice in Olo'osson, the people here had merited a sign of favor from the gods. The overthrow of the corrupt council in Olossi last year; the recruitment of an expanded militia; the establishment of a regional council; the new settlement in the Barrens; the change of authority in the reeve hall, placing the best person in command even if she was a fawkner, not a reeve. All this they had done and must continue to do.

Anji walked with Sengel and Toughid and a pair of young soldiers bearing lamps up to investigate the place where the horse had trotted to earth. Their black tabards made them fade into the growing darkness as they studied the dirt for signs of the winged mare's passage and Hari's footprints. Astafero sang. Anji frowned.

*   *   *

AFTER THE SEVENTH bell had rung its closing, the temple of the Merciless One lay quiet on its island on the estuarine delta where the River Olo poured into the Olo'o Sea. Lanterns burned at Banner Pier, appearing from the air as small as fireflies.

As Jothinin and Kirit cantered to earth, a pair of youths came running with the stout batons in hand that would allow them to beat off unwelcome intruders. They pulled up in astonishment as they took in the horses' wings and the perilous cloaks. As they recognized Kirit's demon-pale hair.

"I remember you, Holy One," said the younger lad. "I'm called Kass. This is Rodi. You came and took the ghost girl away last year." He glanced at Kirit, who was scanning the shoreline and rock gardens for danger.

Her head whipped around. "I'm called Kirit."

The lads leaped back, so comically surprised to hear a voice that Jothinin laughed. He dismounted, so as not to sit so imposingly above them, but he did not approach any closer.

"Be obedient sons, and announce us to the Hieros."

Their frowns delighted him, torn as they were between obligations. "She's entertaining a guest, Holy One. She'll rip off our heads if we disturb her."

"I do not doubt it," Jothinin said, recalling the Hieros: obdurate and exacting but also courageous and honest. "But even the Hieros must have in reserve a means by which she can be summoned in an emergency. We came here first to be polite, son. We could have flown straight in to the inner courts." He smiled as he spoke.

"I'll go." Kass raced away into the compound.

The other lad stood with gaze cast down. Kirit scouted down the shore. Jothinin folded his hands and waited. The sleepy purl of the river's backwater meander through reeds flowed in counterpoint to the deeper voice of the main channel, always strong. A nightjar clicked. Abruptly, Rodi yawned, then mumbled an apology as if the act of yawning might be deemed an insult.

How Jothinin hated standing around in silence when there was someone to talk to! "A fine night, is it not? A little cool, though, don't you think?"

The lad shivered. If he had a voice, he could not bring himself to use it.

Jothinin sighed. "When I was a lad your age, I had already served my year's apprenticeship to Ilu, the Herald—"

"But you're a Guardian!" the youth blurted. "The gods made you as you are. You were never young. Unless it's true what they say, that the Guardians were eaten by lilu who took the form of Guardians to lure us into trusting them—"

With a pair of flying gallops, Kirit headed in their direction. The youth shrieked and bolted, vanishing through a gap in the fence as Kirit pulled up beside Jothinin.

"You frightened him," he observed, torn between rue and amusement.

"He frightened himself." She tilted her head back. "Here they come."

Ah! Voices heard faintly a-wing on the night's breeze as footsteps crunched on a graveled path.

The woman's firm voice Jothinin recognized as that of the Hieros. "I would prefer any such encounter as this to take place before the entire council, and especially with Captain Anji in attendance, but I cannot ask a Guardian to return at my convenience."

"I'll stand in Captain Anji's stead, Jara," the male replied in a pleasant voice, easy and calm. "All that is said here and now, he will hear exactly as it was spoken. But if what the lad says is true, the Guardian has brought the ghost girl. I saw that demon kill forty northern soldiers with nothing more than sorcery and a mirror. Not to mention the three Qin soldiers she killed before that. What if she has come here to kill *me*?"

The Hieros's airy laugh made the man chuckle. "What you Qin call a demon, we'd more likely call a lilu. With such magic, you'd think she would have killed you already if she'd meant to. Yet from from what I heard, the ghost girl killed three soldiers who had forced sex on her when she was a slave to the captain's wife's uncle. No other of the Qin were harmed."

"True enough. She even went after Shai that time, but she did not kill him. If that's the case, then I'm safe. But whether they are Guardians or demons, the cloaked ones possess magic. It is always prudent to assume they might be our enemy."

"Trust my judgment, Tohon. I met this envoy of Ilu before, and it seemed to me he was what he said he was. A holy Guardian whose duty is to serve justice, and the Hundred."

Their footsteps changed as they crossed to a surface more grit than gravel. The Hieros emerged from the darkness, her anklet bells tinkling so softly that the river's song had drowned their voice. An outlander walked beside her, a man of mature years Jothinin had seen months before in the company of the Qin soldiers as they rode over the Kandaran Pass when the Qin company had first entered the Hundred as hired caravan guards. Jothinin found the way they were ever so slightly canted toward each other to be very endearing.

Kirit said, in a low voice, "That Qin I do not know. He was not in the captain's troop when we left Kartu Town."

"Hush, Kirit," he murmured, more sharply than he intended.

The pair halted. The old woman had a tiny frame but a large presence. The outlander had a sinewy strength in his stocky frame of the kind that has been earned over a long and vigorous life. He had the manners of a cautious man, regarding the two Guardians sidelong.

The Hieros touched her fingers to her forehead, as in prayer. "Holy One. Greetings of the night." Deliberately, she looked at him.

He had learned over the years how to protect himself against the onslaught. In the early years, he had avoided looking folk in the face because every look, every meeting, was like a hammer to the head. But a Guardian could not fulfill his duty if every assizes was a brutal pounding. He had learned to filter thoughts and feelings as through a net, capturing those silvery fish he needed and letting the rest slip away. Every person hides within himself grievances and cruelties, but many are simply trying their best, sometimes failing and sometimes succeeding. Most folk were like nai porridge, a little bland and even boring while perhaps sweetened with a dollop of honey or spiced with the sting of eye-watering hot peppers.

The Hieros did not fear him. Her faith in the gods' laws was strong, and she had made hard choices that caused suffering to others, but she was not ashamed of her life or her tenure as hieros over this temple, her prominent place in the hierarchy of Olo'osson's temples and guilds and councils.

"What do you want from the temple?" she asked, because for her the temple always came first. There had been a girl, once, named Jarayinya—an old-fashioned name taken from the Tale of Patience—but that carefree girl had been swallowed up long ago by the All-Consuming Devourer. "When we met before, you told me that the war for the soul of the Guardians has already begun."

He nodded. "We are at war, Holy One. Now we are in need of allies. I am as you see me a humble man, an envoy of Ilu in appearance and a Guardian in truth. This young woman is an outlander, and yet she is also a Guardian. There is one other Guardian we count as an ally. That makes three."

"There are nine Guardians, Holy One. Every child knows that."

"Among the Guardians some have become corrupted. She who wears the cloak of Night rules them. Three obey her without question: Sun, Leaf, and Blood. One, a man wearing a cloak like to the twilight sky, obeys her but with reluctance. We'd take kindly to news of him, in the hopes of making him our ally."

"I have seen no Guardians but you two." She was speaking truth.

"So she's not a demon, then?" the outlander asked, indicating Kirit. "The spirit of an angry dead girl?"

"She is a Guardian," said Jothinin, "as am I."

"I have seen you before, ver," admitted Tohon. "You walked over the Kandaran Pass when we did. But you were trampled in Dast Korumbos during the bandit attack. I thought sure you were dead then."

Jothinin ignored his words. "Have you seen or heard tell of other Guardians?"

The outlander looked up. A glancing blow, that glimpse: he was an honorable man, loyal, cautious, and too deep to scan easily. He was far too deep to be easily led astray.

"I heard of one wearing a green cloak, a very bad man who did unspeakable things," he said as a spark of entirely unexpected anger flashed in his otherwise guarded gaze; so might a father swell with outrage at an attack upon a beloved son. Upon *Shai.* "Where he went I do not know. Marshal Joss spoke of seeing a death-cloaked woman in his dreams. Before the attack on Olossi our soldiers shot a cloaked rider on the West Track. We're told demons command the northern army, Lord Radas among them." He was telling the truth.

Jothinin raised both hands, palms out. "Let me tell you a story. My nose is itching. Many whispers have tickled my ears. The Guardians are not single spirits who have existed in all this time in the same vessel since the day the gods raised them at Indiyabu. The cloaks carry the authority and power granted by the gods. But the individuals who wear the cloaks change."

"How can this be?" demanded the Hieros. "Guardians can't die."

The outlander tugged on his ear, saying nothing.

"The cloak leaves a person when his tenure on this earth comes to an end, and awakens a new vessel. Any who inherit the cloak were ones who died fighting for justice, and are therefore granted a chance to restore peace."

"Then you *are* demons!" said Tohon.

"Neh, I think not. Maybe we are ghosts, of a kind. Solid enough. Able to laugh and to cry, to eat, to piss if we drink too much."

"But if Guardians can't die," the Hieros said, "then how can the cloak pass from one vessel to another?"

"Within the Guardian council, there has always have been a mechanism to guard against the shadow of corruption. Five cloaks, acting in unanimity, can execute one."

The Hieros laughed curtly, quick to see the flaw.

"Indeed," Jothinin said with a wry smile, "if a Guardian is canny enough and persuasive enough, she may corrupt enough of the council to make it party to her will. As the cloak of Night has done."

The Hieros snorted, her mood darkening with skepticism. "So this is your Guardians' war? You seek a majority of five, to destroy the others. What is to stop you, then, from becoming corrupt in your turn? From taking over this army that is ravaging the north?"

The question startled him. "Nothing but my own heart, Holy One."

"Why come to us? There seems little we can do that we have not already done: raise an army to safeguard ourselves, send out scouts, build up stocks of oil of naya, expand the safe zone so folk may plant crops when the rains come. You can be sure we do not wish to fall under the northern army's brutal yoke. You need only look at me, Guardian, to know I speak the truth. So what else can we possibly do?"

For once he stumbled, at a loss for words. He could not force words past a leaden tongue.

Kirit rode forward. "In my tribe," she said in her hoarse outlander's voice, "every person works. All work together, each at her own tasks. So must we work together, to bring peace." She frowned at Jothinin, as if scolding him.

The Hieros and the Qin solder waited as the lamps hissed and the river flowed.

The night wind's weary sigh spurred Jothinin on, despite his misgivings. "We come to offer you a weapon. I will tell you how to kill a Guardian and release its cloak to a new awakening."

27

ALTHOUGH IT WASN'T quite dark, a fire burned at Candle Rock as Marit approached from the north. The hells! She had expected the rock to be deserted, and yet hadn't she also prepared the way by shifting the message stones? It was two days off the full moon. She might have known some reeve would be waiting, as reeves did, loyal comrades who would risk their lives to aid one of their own. Her eyes watered, maybe only because of the stinging wind.

She'd left Badinen and his eagle riding a high current while she dropped down to scout out a safe landing place; they'd been traveling for many, many days, and every evening she and Warning landed first as a precaution. They pulled up sharply as the man sitting beside the fire leaped to his feet.

"Marit!"

Why did it have to be him?

Careful not to meet his astonished gaze, she dismounted and slapped Warning on the flank to send her off to the altar at Ammadit's Tit for sustenance.

"Are you a ghost or a lilu?" he demanded.

"I'm a Guardian, Joss."

He sat down hard on the ring of stones as if all the breath had been slugged out of him. "You can't be Marit. Not truly."

"Truly I am," she snapped.

"Marit died!" His head rose, and for a horrible moment she looked into him, all his shame and fury and reckless rule-breaking to make the gods say they were sorry, only of course he had caused her death by violating the altar on Ammadit's Tit just because he was too young and stupid to think something so awful could come of breaking the boundaries. And all the drinking and sex in all the twenty-one years after her death had not made his shame and fury go away; only the years themselves had muted his grief and anger, as years will do. By then, of course, he'd gotten into the habit of drinking and devouring—

She looked away before he did. "It wasn't your gods-rotted fault! You're being cursed absorbed in yourself to think it was!"

"Ouch." He chuckled weakly. "I suppose I deserved that."

She strode over to the ring of stones and sat down opposite, the fire between them. "You really don't believe I'm Marit, do you?"

"You look cursed like her and sound cursed like," he replied, careful not to look directly at her. "The way the message rocks were left reminded me of you. Maybe that's why I've come out here for the last three Lamp Moons, because I kept thinking of you and—Eihi!—"

Impossible not to think of the last time they had met on Candle Rock. He was startlingly older, but the cut of his shoulders and the curve of his neck hadn't changed. He still had a good smell, clean sweat washed with the bracing perfume of the juniper soap he must still receive from kinfolk at his home village.

"It's difficult for me to imagine how you could be her," he went on in a lower voice. "Maybe you're a Guardian. Maybe you're a gods-cursed ghost who stole a Guardian's cloak, like those ones who lead that cursed army. Some even call them demons. But I think it's most likely you're a lilu sent to tempt me."

The comment sucked the breath right out of her. "Do I tempt you still?"

He laughed harshly as he turned his head to look into the night. The hells! He was a cursed good-looking man with a strong profile, a lean, fit body, his arms bare in a sleeveless leather vest. The angular tattoos marking him as a child of the Fire mother hadn't changed, covering his right arm and ringing both wrists. His hair was no longer cropped quite so close against his skull; if it was going to silver, she saw no trace of fine pale lines in the changing light.

The moment was broken as Badinen and Sisit thumped down in the open space away from the fire, a graceful pair despite their lack of training. She jumped up as Joss rose, a hand on his baton as he gestured a "well-come-in-peace."

To Marit's surprise, the lad answered the gesture with the formal reply. He unhooked from the harness and, as Sisit looked around the outcrop, ventured forward.

"Ye Guardian sath she will dun brang meh teh ye Clan Hall. Ya one reeve?"

Joss blinked, then glanced toward Marit and wiggled his left hand, and she realized he was having trouble understanding the youth's thick dialect.

"I found this young man in the north, on the Eagle's Claws," she said. "I'm bringing him to Clan Hall for training. There's no soft way to say this, so I'll say it hard: Horn Hall has been slaughtered."

He didn't react, as if her own speech had become impenetrable. "Horn Hall has been missing for the last year. The hall abandoned, every reeve and eagle gone."

"For whatever the hells reason, they fled to the Eagle's Claws and set up outposts there. Someone poisoned the eagles and thereby the reeves and killed everyone else. It's one rocky Sorrowing Tower, bones strewn everywhere. It happened a year ago, maybe."

He reeled, swaying on his feet. "Give me a moment. Here, lad—" He spoke each word deliberately, shock scraping through his tone. "What is your name? I am called Joss."

"Badinen. An thas ya, I call ya Sisit."

"Slow down. She will need to be jessed and set for the night. My eagle Scar bides here also. Two eagles who are strangers may fight over territory. Do you understand?"

It was clear the lad understood Joss far better than Joss understood him, no doubt from his year serving the Horn Hall reeves. Marit felt Joss's relief as he took Badinen off to show him to the hollow where Candle Rock dipped into a natural bowl. Sometimes you could only absorb the worst news or endure pain and apprehension by engaging in the most ordinary of daily tasks.

Marit sat by the fire, watching the flames twist and dance. Now and again she fed a log to the fire. After it grew dark, Joss still did not return, but she heard as on the wind the genial crawl of a long conversation between him and the lad. She could not quite hear the words and did not want particularly to listen, but the tenor of their speech surprised her. The youth had never grown easy with her, despite their many days journey across the north together, but Joss was a kind of person he was familiar with and accustomed to obeying; anyway, the gods knew that Joss was an easy man to like when he set himself to be charming.

Aui!

The full moon crept up the span of the heavens. She could make out individual trees on the slopes of nearby hills. Atop Ammadit's Tit a glimmer winked, dazzled, and faded. Warning was up there, drinking from the altar's pool. She licked her lips, remembering its taste, and sighed.

Joss came walking up the path alone and halted a short distance away. She pretended he was not there. It was too difficult to know that he walked the earth and she could never touch him. Let him go.

"Is it part of the sorcery of the Guardians that causes you to appear to us as one we love, the one we yearn for and know is lost?" He spoke quietly, as if to the wind and the night. "For years I looked for you. Well, not for you but for your remains, so I could rest you properly on a Sorrowing Tower and say the prayers and make the offerings. It was like half of my own spirit had gone away with you, and I was caught as an angry ghost unable to leave or stay. We found Flirt so mutilated I couldn't imagine how any one could hate the eagles so much. I knew you were dead, therefore. But we never found your body. For years it was like a talon digging into my belly, that maybe they'd buried you, the worst thing they could think of doing. I broke the boundaries time and again trying to find some gods-rotted answer but in the end there wasn't an answer."

He tipped his head, listening to a faint melody. Down in the hollow, Badinen was singing a song about the big fish that got away. From the rhythmic scratch accompanying his singing, he was raking the dirt, a task that would take him a good long time.

Joss sighed. "But there is an answer, the one that's been staring at me all along. It all started here, in the Liya Pass, twenty-one years ago. That time when we stumbled across the beginnings of this Star of Life army. Only I mistook them for common bandits. They're the ones who killed you. Worse, they got away with it and maybe that's what made them so bold, seeing we were unable to stop them. Village by village we retreated over the years. We didn't fight because we thought the people did not want us in Herelia and then later in Iliyat and then later in other valleys and villages. When they refused to have us reeves stand at their assizes, we thought it was because they distrusted us or had come to hate us, maybe because of the actions of a few useless strutting reeves who abused their authority. But it's so obvious now. Of course there were some among the villagers who hated the reeves. There always have been, but that's not why things changed. Of course there were some who liked the new order, if it meant they could have what they wanted for the taking, because some folk are that way. But what if the rest were simply being coerced? Eiya! Not that such a thing didn't occur to some among us at the time, but it came on so cursed slow, a rot eating into the beams and posts while all the time you think the house remains sound and then it collapses around you and buries you. Eiya! Marit, you have no idea how badly I have missed you all these years."

Even Guardians can weep. They can grieve for what is lost.

"Marit—" Gaze averted, he walked toward her with a hand extended.

"Don't touch me, Joss."

He jerked to a halt as if slapped.

"Neh, you don't understand. I'm still the Marit who loves you, but I'm something else now, too. What folk are, what they're thinking, what they're feeling—it's all laid open to me now, like flayed skin."

He let his hand drop to his side.

She pushed on recklessly. "The Guardians are not pure gods-touched vessels given the form of humans. They're just people, like you and me, given a second life. Those who die seeking justice for others may be awakened by a cloak to become Guardians. The other cloaks aren't lilu or gods-cursed demons, they're just people who have succumbed to the worst in themselves, and who have twisted the power the gods granted them to serve their own corrupt ends."

"Why would the gods give cloaks to humankind if they could be so easily corrupted and used in the service of such monstrous goals?"

"Surely the question isn't whether it was wrong to begin with, but what is to be done about it now."

He shifted impatiently, his gaze still averted. "But it has to matter! We have to figure out why this gift from the gods was corrupted, and stop it from happening again. What has happened in the land to poison it? Maybe these troubles are only a reflection of our own selves. The marshal of Bronze Hall says we've betrayed the gods by forgetting the old ways, the traditional forms."

She considered the assizes she had so recently presided over, and a hollow weariness sank into her heart. "Maybe. But we can't cling to the old ways just because they're the old ways. Maybe that's the puzzle we're meant to solve, the mystery whose heart we must seek. Maybe this is a challenge, to discover how to walk forward from where we are now. Joss!" Yet she looked away, because it hurt to look at what she had lost. "You know as well as I do that if we don't stop this army, they'll infest the entire land and we'll all pass under the Shadow Gate."

"I know." He stared fixedly at the ground.

"Take Badinen to Clan Hall so he can tell his story, and get training. Then before you return to your duties in Argent Hall, you've got to convince the commander at Clan Hall that the reeves must unite in finding new ways to fight."

The smile that pulled at his mouth was wry and mocking in a way the young Joss she'd loved had never been, because he had always been straightforward and passionate and outward-moving. That had been a great part of his charm.

"That's easily done," he said as he looked up.

His eyes caught her: the reckless, bold, and sometimes furiously brooding young man had been tempered, beaten, burned, and yet emerged with the deepest part of him intact. The part she had fallen into love with, even if she had called it only desire. The part that was willing to rebel in the face of injustice even if meant standing alone. The part that was bold and crazy enough to try anything, however unexpected or difficult.

"*You* are Commander of Clan Hall!" she cried, gaping at him.

He closed the gap between them and grasped her wrist. Gods help her, she fell into him in the remembered way that had once come so easily, the way her arms embraced his torso and her hands crept up his muscular back; the way he held her close with one arm just below her shoulders and the other bracing her hips against his. His kiss was the same, at first tender and tentative and then abruptly passionate and searching.

In those first moments, her eyes squeezed shut, it was merely a glorious kiss. Aui! How she had missed this!

Then it hit.

The contact so intimate, so intense, released on her a flood. She was devoured again and again in the guise of different women—so cursed many!—and one young woman so blazingly and immediately vivid that his desire for *Zubaidit* was a knife in Marit's own longing heart; all his grief and anger poured over her, stupid petty disputes like stings, raging arguments, devouring thirst that no amount of rice wine could slave; yet also she was slaked by the calming friendships he treasured among the other reeves whose affection for him was balm, and yet this comradely affection more than anything made her ache for what she could never again share—

She broke away, blindly groping for a path out of her gods-rotted loneliness. "Don't touch me!" Grief felled her; she sank to her knees.

He knelt beside her but did not touch. "Ah the hells, Marit. I wasn't sure—Aui!—but now— No one else can kiss like that."

Laughter choked her sobs, or maybe laughter and tears were the same thing. "You sure as hells tried enough women to find out."

"Marit—"

"Neh, you have nothing to apologize for. Sheh! You thought I was dead. And even if I weren't, I hope I would never be the kind of person who was jealous of the Merciless One. Let it go, Joss."

After all these years, he could not. "Do you still love me, Marit?"

She wiped her face. "I love the memory of the love we shared then. How can I know if I love you now? I'm not so naive, nor should you be. I'm a Guardian. I have my duty, and you have yours. Please tell me you understand." She did not look at him. She did not want to know if he was lying or telling the truth.

He rose and paced away, his back to the fire. "What must I do?"

She rested on her hands until she was no longer shaking. Then she rose and wiped her face a final time, organized her thoughts as she would when, as a reeve, she was reporting to her marshal. "This is what I have seen. First, Herelia is poisoned. That is where they've built their stronghold. Wedrewe is a stranglehold gripping the throats of every person who lives within the cloak of their power. Wherever they extend their control, they choke until those they rule are grateful merely to be living. Second, I have come to see that in the days long ago the reeves were organized differently than they are now. They ranged more widely, and spread their perches into more outposts. They weren't all gathered into a few halls."

"Then why do the tales speak of six reeve halls?"

"The tales speak of 'the fifteen towns' of the Hundred, but that does not mean there are only fifteen towns today. A reeve hall might have meant something different in the tales. We say it is an actual place, but maybe it used to mean—oh—an allegiance, or a breeding line of eagles."

"Family groupings," he said, musing. "It's true, I'm trying to implement new patrol protocols, even methods of fighting in concert with our allies. But not all the reeve halls will join me. I've got to be cautious in how I approach them."

"Don't wait too long to act. A newly trained cohort has already marched from Herelia to join the main army. Another will march within the month, and a third in three months. Fifteen cohorts they have in number."

"*Fifteen?*"

"They will train more, whether with willing recruits or unwilling ones. These are the people who hang prisoners from poles. Surely you've seen—"

"I know what we face! We have Olo'osson's support. There's an outlander captain named Anji who is training an army, and he's very good. But how can we defeat an army that boasts fifteen cohorts of fighting men and is commanded by Guardians, none of whom we can stand against?"

"What if I told you there was a way to separate a Guardian from the cloak, to release that cloak to find a new vessel? Maybe a cleaner spirit, one who has not crossed the Shadow Gate."

He became still, as if holding his breath; it seemed the wind itself ceased. "Are you saying I could kill you?"

"Yes. If you could take me by surprise, render me senseless so you could separate the cloak from my body. Or if I let you because I was desperate enough to welcome oblivion."

"Are you that desperate, Marit?"

She could hear how badly he wanted her to answer no. He wanted her to be alive for his own sake as much as for hers. Yet she must consider dispassionately. She must delve into her own heart, her own spirit. Aui! How strongly that heart beat; how powerfully that spirit flamed!

"No. I'm not that desperate. I don't want oblivion." Her voice trembled with the the ferocity of her desire, unexamined until now. "I want to be alive. Even in such times, in these days, in this situation, I want to walk and breathe—" She shut her eyes, wondering if he would take the moment to draw his sword and run her through. "Great Lady. Therefore I am already corrupt."

Words spoken months ago by the woman who wore the cloak of Night, on the first occasion Marit had encountered her, sounded ominous and revealing now.

"*In the end even death can be defeated.*"

Could it be that simple?

All thinking, speaking creatures—the eight children of the Four Mothers— expected to die. But what if certain individuals were thrust out of death back into life? If the cloaks held a dead spirit in this world in order to serve them by measuring truth to exact justice, might that spirit, grasping its second chance at life, fear more than anything having to let go and cross the threshold of the Spirit Gate into darkness and oblivion?

Did the cloak of Night fear the second death so greatly that she had corrupted the council of the Guardians and now allowed this vile army to trample and destroy land and village and lives just to protect herself? Could anyone be that selfish?

"What you offer is more of a burden than a gift," said Joss softly.

She understood where her duty lay. She was a Guardian. She had to serve the land.

She spoke toward the distant tower of Ammadit's Tit, where the end of their days together had begun. "Maybe so, Joss. But war has come. The tale has changed. Let me tell you how to kill a Guardian."

PART FIVE: WEAPONS

28

"WE'RE BACK IN the Hundred at last," said Keshad to Eliar.

At the side of the road stood a white post. The name of the road, *West Spur*, was carved below the top in the old writing, and a single groove marked the first mey of the road. A wayfarer's lamp could be fixed to the post at night or in a storm. Today, although cold, was quiet, not even very windy. The caravan had climbed through snowfall on the southern side of the pass as the seasonal rains began their cycle; here on the northern side, they walked into the dry season.

But they hadn't left the worst tempest behind.

She approached on horseback. Her headdress glimmered with enough gold and gems to tempt the most cautious bandit. Why the old woman must flaunt her wealth Kesh could not imagine, but he supposed the five hundred Qin soldiers who accompanied them would slaughter importunate thieves.

With ten stolid Qin soldiers in escort, she reined in beside Keshad. Over the weeks, she had adapted her dialect of the trade speech to mimic Kesh and Eliar's by insisting they instruct her—and her chief eunuchs—every night. "This is the border gate, is it not? I will speak to the captain in charge."

"Your Excellency," said Kesh quickly, "of course you shall speak to the captain in charge. Please offer to me a moment's generosity and allow me to present our party and its purpose to the officer before you convey your requests."

Captain Anji had her eyes: handsome, dark, and cutting. "You fear I will offend some minor functionary, who will then refuse us entry simply to spite any woman who speaks bluntly to him."

"Maybe that is how it works in the empire, Your Excellency, but I assure you that in the Hundred, women speak as bluntly as men. Let me first explain why he should admit five hundred outlander soldiers. Unless you would prefer to send the military escort back to the empire and proceed with only the wagons."

"Not at all! My old friend and ally Commander Beje sent these troops to me as a gift."

"Naturally, Your Excellency, you can then imagine—"

"You need not repeat yourself!"

"I beg your pardon, Your Excellency."

"You do not." She was not angry, merely speaking exactly as she thought. "However, you are right. I have endured the distrust meted out to a foreigner for all of my adult years. As you are a son of this land, you are correct to remind me it will be no different here."

He glanced at Eliar, but the Silver was stalwartly staring up at a rugged mountain peak just off to the east, its bare summit surrounded on all sides of cliffs. Was that a

wink of light on the high peak's icy summit? Surely not; the sun was concealed behind clouds.

"Eliar, call the party to a halt in sight of the gate but at a prudent distance. I'll go
ahead."

Without waiting for Eliar's reply, he urged his mount forward. Behind, brakes
screamed as wagons hit the incline. Kesh approached the wall. Armed men watched
from the parapet as the caravan lumbered to a halt. Kesh rode across the big ditch
on the same plank bridge he'd used every time he'd come back from the south. He
hoisted his travel sack with his permission chits, ledger, and tax tokens.

"I'm Keshad, riding under the direction of Captain Anji of the Olossi militia. I
request to speak with the captain in charge."

The guardsmen were staring at the party behind him, and Kesh turned in his
saddle, abruptly seeing from their perspective: this was no caravan but a significant
military force with remounts, supply wagons, grooms, servants, and slaves. Why
should they even be allowed into the Hundred?

"Master Keshad?" Kesh looked up at a Qin soldier. "I'm Chief Deze. I know of
your mission. These Qin soldiers fly Commander Beje's banner together with that of
Anji's clan." He eyed the caravan without even the flicker of a smile. "Someone
wanted to make sure you arrived safely."

The white mountain peaks of the Spires loomed behind them, a seemingly impenetrable barrier between the Hundred and the empire. It was a fence Kesh would
never again cross, not if he wanted to stay alive. "I don't think my safety was of concern. This troop escorts Captain Anji's mother."

Some might call the Qin callous and hardened for their lack of emotion, but Kesh
was pretty sure they had simply learned in a hard school to mask their feelings behind impassivity. Chief Deze's astonishment flashed brightly as he leaned on the
parapet. Then he barked an order and vanished. Shortly, a big basket was swung
over the lip of the parapet, and Deze climbed in and was lowered down. He sprang
out of the basket and, after hurrying over to Keshad, grabbed his arm in a powerful
grip to tug him out onto the plank bridge. Adders writhed and hissed in the ditch
below, provoked by the movement. As the planks shifted under Kesh's feet, he was
dizzied by an overwhelming sense that he was about to plunge into the pit and be
bitten to death.

"This means that Commander Beje—or his wife Cherfa—has been in contact
with the captain's mother all along," said Deze in a low voice. He rubbed his wisp of
a beard, a man whose thoughts were spinning new threads into the weave. "Take
your party to Old Fort and there take the road to Astafero."

"Astafero? Where's that?"

"The naya sinks. That's what folk now call the settlement out in the Barrens. Do
not go to Olossi."

"Why not?"

Chief Deze began to speak, stopped himself, and began again very like a man
who has changed his bargaining position in the middle of negotiation. "You can see
that a big force of outlanders will scare the Hundred folk."

Kesh had gotten used to the soldiers. He liked them. But they were cursed intimidating, if you took a step back from familiar faces and considered them as a group.

There was a reason the Hundred folk called them the black wolves for their black tabards and Captain Anji's black wolf banner. And honestly, it was difficult to imagine how Anji's mother would react to a delegation of Olossi merchants and clanheads traipsing out to greet her with all the flourish and babble so beloved of Hundred merchants.

"I'll do it. Do you want to greet her?"

"Hu! If the var's sister wants to speak to me, she'll call me to her." Having reached a decision, the chief moved with dispatch. The gates were opened; the caravan trundled through, and the beasts set to water. Anji's mother took her attendants to the camping field where her servants set up screens of cloth so her veiled women—she was the only female who rode—could emerge from their wagon hideaways where no one could see, or count them. Anyway, their heavy robes and veils made them appear all alike. Most of the wagons conveyed their luxuries.

One of the eunuchs emerged from behind the screens and set up a padded stool fringed with gold tassels. The old woman sat down with her back to the cloth as a slave fetched Chief Deze.

"The Qin are cursed odd," muttered Eliar as he and Kesh watched the man approach. "Look how he comes like a dog to her call."

"He's not being servile, just respectful. No dog would be given such a consideration." Kesh smirked at Eliar as a folding stool was brought so the chief could sit. The old woman proceeded to ask him questions, or so it appeared, because he did most of the talking and she did most of the listening.

The caravan waited until she dismissed the chief. Then the veiled women climbed back into the wagons; servants took down the screens; the wagons were rolled into line.

"Did you see the reeve go?" said Eliar as they took their usual places at the front.

"What reeve?"

"You didn't notice, did you?" Eliar's self-satisfied smile at having noticed what Kesh had overlooked was, like a point scored in hooks-and-ropes, an unspoken boast. "A reeve flew, with a passenger in harness. The chief has wasted no time in sending word forward. A lot of trouble for one old woman, don't you think? The sooner the old bitch gets back inside the women's quarters, the better."

"Aui! You Silvers! Captain Anji's got no 'women's quarters.'" The train started moving, local guardsman falling in as guides. "It's not 'a lot of trouble.' It's just the respect you would show any eminent elder."

Yet Kesh wondered.

*   *   *

"CLAN HALL DOESN'T have the means to house and train you," Joss said to Badinen as they stood on an eyrie at the southeastern tail of the Liya Hills. "I'm taking you to Copper Hall. That's where I trained as a young reeve."

Whether Masar would curse him or thank him for bringing in a novice whose speech was difficult to understand and whose eagle was also young and untrained he did not know. But he'd not yet made contact with Gold Hall in Teriayne where they likely housed other reeves with a northern way of talking. Masar he could impose on. The old marshal owed him that much.

The lad was staring at the astonishing vista: not, mind you, at the cultivated plain, but at the vast forest spreading southward. He asked a question which Joss puzzled out as "What is that?"

"That's the Wild."

"The Wild? As in the wildings?"

"Indeed, wildings live there. It is forbidden for any human to enter its boundaries. Have you wildings up in the north?"

Yes, he did. He told an incomprehensible story about a tribe of wildings and a cliff and a valley and someone's child falling into a fell stream—or maybe a fallow field strewn with seed, hard to say—but his nonchalance in recounting the tale made Joss wonder what in the hells it was like growing up in the uttermost north where you might see a trading ship twice a year and now and again an outlander's fishing boat blown to shore in the storm season. He could barely imagine a place where all you knew of the Hundred were the tales handed down by your grandmother and the same everyday local faces. Which evidently included wildings.

"We won't fly over it today," Joss added, "but in your training you'll get a taste of how big it is. Come on."

They hooked in. Scar launched, and Sisit beat after, keeping her distance. She was very young, unsure of how to respond to another eagle except that she always kept her feathers up. Of course all eagles were hatched and raised in their early months in the distant mountainous wilderness of Heaven's Reach, but usually the fledglings returned to the halls with a parent in tow and learned to recognize their family group within the eagles. Within these groups the eagles could be remarkably cooperative. Outside them, training taught most to subdue their territoriality when in company with their reeves.

They sailed over the wide coastal plain. Farmers turned no earth; dug no ditches; trimmed no mulberries. No one was hauling water. No young shepherds guarded grazing flocks. When the first burned villages came into view, Joss knew he should have expected it, yet even so the sight shocked him. Lord Radas's army was spreading its blight.

Lord Radas, whom he might kill if Marit had told him the truth.

Yet thinking of Marit caused him to recall the way she had responded to his kiss.

The hells! He had to focus. With Nessumara under siege, the old Silver had ceased providing bags of nai and rice, and it had therefore become urgent to clear Law Rock of anyone not contributing to the defense. But because the town of Horn had refused to take in a single refugee, they had to haul the hapless refugees all the way to Candra Crossing from which staging area the refugees could slog the rest of the way to Olossi on roads made safe by Captain Anji's militia. It took a cursed long time to transport hundreds of people hundreds of mey, one at a time, but just seven days ago Nallo and Pil had lifted off with the last two. Now, at last, he might send messengers to the other halls to get their news and call for a council to coordinate plans. Meanwhile, Clan Hall's stores were running low, and it took too gods-rotted long to haul sacks from Candra Crossing. You couldn't feed a reeve hall, even a small one, one sack at a time.

Smoke billowed skyward in the distance. He tugged on the jesses to shift Scar's trajectory, and Badinen and Sisit followed. The lad handled the eagle cursed well for someone without a single day's training.

Seen from the sky, events unfold like tales: burning cottages and shouting farmers, bawling sheep and barking dogs heard intermittently as the wind changes. Folk fled a village; soldiers set torches to thatched roofs while others heaped wagons with sacks of rice and nai, cages of chickens, baskets of radish and rope. The villagers saw him; he knew by the way tiny figures hesitated, waved arms, then stumbled onward.

With the lad in tow, and him alone, he could not stop. What could he do for them beyond telling them to run and hide? He had the luxury to rage, on high, yet as always it seemed he could do nothing to stop injustice. For that was not the only village under attack along the coastal plain near his own birthplace. Smoke rose in bloated, expanding pools, dissipating as plumes reached the upper air. The watch beacons along the shore were on fire up and down the coast.

Had the army reached the town of Haya? Beyond it, to his childhood village?

The hells! Copper Hall's high bluff was surrounded by a full cohort. Incredibly, the army had brought up a fleet of fishing boats and coast-hugging trading ships that were roping in the skiffs and shore-boats used by Copper Hall's population to fish and collect kelp. The cohort had massed on the landward side to cut off retreat by foot, forcing thereby every eagle remaining in Copper Hall to take off from the training ground—no difficult feat, naturally, but those fawkners and assistants and slaves who had not already gotten out were trapped, so every eagle leaving was weighed down by a passenger.

An intelligent mind commanded the enemy. Archers launched volleys as each eagle banked up, vulnerable before it caught an updraft. Two eagles were already down. One lay lifeless, both reeve and passenger sprawled dead in the harness. The other was wounded, a wing trailing uselessly as it struggled to right itself on an injured leg. In its fury it dragged the harness, its reeve limp and unresponsive but the passenger fighting to get out of the tangle. Joss winced as arrows punctured the helpless eagle's flesh; blades flashed in sunlight as armed men closed in for the kill.

Another raptor was hit, but it kept climbing. Struggling. Listing. Tumbling into the sea as its reeve and passenger unhooked just in time to fall free into the rolling waters.

Blessed Ilu! How could this be happening?

He had taught Badinen four flag commands, the least you needed to know. Now he flagged: *Stay aloft.*

He sent Scar down the well-remembered landing path to the training ground just as a huge yammering shout rose from the gatehouse where soldiers had broken through. The raptor thumped down hard. Two eagles launched from the adjoining parade ground as Joss unhooked and dropped out of his harness .

Masar recognized Joss with a start of amazement, quickly controlled. "Can you take a passenger? What of that other eagle, the one with you?"

"He's freshly jessed and the eagle is still a fledgling. I can take two. Scar's strong enough."

"Strong enough, but you can't risk two. Arrow shot—they're so close now—"

Beyond the gate, guardsmen fought a hopeless rearguard to buy time, but the clash ended with a shout cut off in the midst of a word. Hammering shuddered on the closed gates that walled off the training ground. There were three eagles left, in addition to Scar, and seventeen fawkners, hirelings, and adolescent debt slaves watching with not one begging for passage despite the army killing their comrades outside.

"Masar! I can take two."

Masar's age already weighed on his shoulders; he seemed to wilt, his spirit burdened until it might break as he scanned those who remained.

"You two," Masar said, "and you three." The five he indicated were experienced fawkners, not the youngest by any means. Not the prettiest. That unfortunate distinction went to a young woman whose strained expression trembled, then firmed, as she realized—or perhaps she had already known—that she was to be left behind.

"Jenna," the marshal added, "take the rest to my cote and hide in the cellar. They'll burn everything, but you can wait it out as long as they don't find you. We'll send sweeps and pick up the survivors as we can."

"Yes, Grandfather." She turned to the others. "Move!"

"Masar!" Joss cried as the girl led her companions away. "You can't possibly be leaving—"

"We must save the experienced fawkners," said Masar. "You take Gerda and Eiko, they're the smallest."

Two small-boned women trotted up. They had the wiry toughness of fawkners who have survived many years caring for the raptors. Their expressions were fixed and bitter. Eiko carried a spare harness and leashes.

He weighed their builds, Eiko's height. "Eiko, you first and Gerda below," he said, knowing full well that the outermost person took the greatest risk of being hit. They nodded. They'd faced death before. He had often thought fawkners were the most courageous people he knew.

In silence the last reeves hooked in themselves first and the five fawkners after. One by one they flew, Masar lifting with his eagle Shy only as the gates came down. Up and up, with arrows flying. Gerda grunted, rocking in the harness. Scar's trajectory staggered momentarily; the raptor dipped, then caught a draft and pushed sloppily upward.

Two eagles were hit, their wings a broad target, but they labored on. One passenger shrieked, caught in the leg, his blood raining down over the compound as the enemy swarmed in. Torches were thrown onto thatched roofs of the outbuildings, while the gates of the big storehouses were thrown open. Copper Hall's guardsmen and hirelings lay scattered throughout the alleys and at walls and gates, having given their lives to allow others to escape.

Joss tugged on his jesses to get Scar turned north.

"Reeve," said Eiko, "Gerda's hit."

Unbelievably, he hadn't even noticed. No doubt he'd been too busy searching for sign of Masar's pretty granddaughter.

He reached past Eiko's torso and patted Gerda. His hand came away slick with blood. Impossibly, she had been hit in the throat, her life's blood pouring down her chest and legs. She hadn't made a sound, hadn't even kicked or thrashed, just crossed the Spirit Gate that quickly.

"She's dead," said Eiko. "I'll cut her loose."

"Eiya! Are you sure?"

"She's my good friend and comrade. I'm not about to cut her loose to settle an old score or save myself. She'd tell you to do it, to spare the eagle."

His breathing pinched, making it hard to force out words. "Do it."

She fished a knife from her vest and sliced the leashes. The body plummeted. He looked for Badinen because he could not bear to watch the impact. The lad trailed behind obediently. The hells knew what he was thinking now. If Eiko wept, she did so silently.

Lightened, Scar found a thermal and rose. Wind blustered against their ears. After a while Scar tipped out of the thermal and started the long sail to Clan Hall.

"If you don't mind my asking," said Eiko, "I don't know your name."

"I'm Joss."

"Joss?" The timbre of her voice changed.

"Yes, *that* Joss."

She snorted, finding a moment of humor in a grim day. "Aren't you the new commander at Clan Hall?"

"I am."

"Copper Hall in Nessumara is under siege and couldn't have taken us anyway. They've not had the room for a full complement for generations."

Each reeve hall housed by custom six hundred reeves, although at any given time many fewer were actually present in the halls: some eagles would be absent for their breeding season in Heaven's Reach; many would be out on patrol or, in more peaceful days, presiding over assizes. If what Marit said had been true, then in the days long ago reeves had spread themselves farther afield in outposts built to house family groups rather than the larger aggregations found in the halls.

"Copper Hall can't take you in," he agreed, "yet neither can Clan Hall. We can't even feed ourselves."

"What are we going to do?"

The land unrolled below, under siege or overwhelmed. Scar shifted, adjusting to the current, and Joss hitched his own position to accommodate the eagle's flight.

We will kill the Guardians.

Even to think it was like breaking the boundaries and violating the gods' law.

"We've lost, haven't we?" she said.

"We haven't lost." He wiped his eyes, but he only smeared the sticky remains of Gerda's blood on his face. "We're developing a new plan of attack. We'll set up outposts. Change our patrol tactics. We'll leave a contingent on Clan Hall. As long as we hold Law Rock, we can say we guard the law, can't we?"

"But where are *we* going to go?" she demanded.

It was so cursed obvious, death falling everywhere to remind him of what had been lost.

Horn Hall.

*   *   *

CAPTAIN ARRAS WALKED through the marshal's cote of Copper Hall pulling scrolls from cubbyholes and unrolling them to squint at the undecipherable writing before he tossed them on the low writing desk for a clerk to read. They would burn what was useless. In the marshal's sleeping chamber, an unlocked chest stored jackets, kilts, and sandals in different sizes. On top sat a basket of fruit, including a half-eaten plum hidden beneath two green globe-fruit, as if a child had taken a bite of the plum when he wasn't supposed to and decided he didn't like the taste. The storage cupboard contained five rolled up sleeping mats, old harness, a pair of cloth dolls, a basket of combs and brushes, two sun umbrellas, and several rain cloaks folded and stacked. It had mice, too; he heard scrabbling and then, as a board creaked under his weight, silence. He'd always imagined reeves lived more grandly, dining on rich folk's china with lacquered spoons and silk hangings to decorate their halls. These folk seemed pretty cursed lacking.

Sergeant Giyara clattered into the audience chamber. "Captain Arras?"

"Here I am." He stepped back into the main room.

The six subcaptains tramped in with boots on. Arras sat on the pillow behind the writing desk and pushed aside a bowl of half eaten nai porridge, now cold and congealed.

"Your reports?"

Over the past months he had trained them to give efficient and effective reports: all the information he needed but not more, delivered in a straightforward order.

Casualties. Eight eagles were definite kills, six bodies recovered and two lost in the bay. Eight reeves also dead, thereby. How many wounded eagles and reeves none knew for sure, but they'd done damage. On the ground, they'd collected seventy-eight corpses and one hundred twelve prisoners, adults who had been working as slaves, hirelings, and assistants at the reeve hall as well as thirty-seven additional folk who claimed to be fishers and farmers, refugees come to Copper Hall to beg for food.

Their own casualties were minimal: five dead, ten with serious injuries, and about thirty with wounds that would need a couple of days rest as long as they did not get infected.

"What are your orders concerning the prisoners?" Giyara asked.

"Let me consider," said Arras. "What about supplies?"

"Plenty of tools and weapons," said Subcaptain Orli, "but their supplies of leather and harness are cursed thin."

"What about food supplies?" Arras asked, for this was his major preoccupation these days. He could not feed additional slaves when it was difficult enough to feed his soldiers.

"We've done a sweep of the storehouses," said Subcaptain Piri. "Eight bags of rice and twelve of nai. Not enough to feed a hall with this many people for but another few days, eh?"

"Aui! The wine cellar's well stocked!" Subcaptain Eddon was the newest and youngest of the three subcaptains; he laughed recklessly now. "That new sergeant, Zubaidit—" Then he flushed and broke off.

Orli and Piri eyed Arras, searching for a flinch of satisfaction or shame at the name, but he'd promoted her based on performance, not favoritism. It wasn't as if he'd gotten any cursed benefit out of the deal beyond a decent cadre sergeant for that group of floundering misfits salvaged from the ruin of First Cohort.

"—found a cellar, here in the garden, and cursed if there weren't twenty casks of wine and cordial."

"Twenty casks!" Arras laughed. "I guess wine and cordial will keep your stomach warm when it's empty. Sergeant." He nodded at Giyara. "You're in charge of those personally. Hold out five for the senior command staff, but the rest will be rationed to the soldiers as their victory badge."

"Yes, Captain." None of the subcaptains protested; they knew Giyara couldn't be bribed. "What about the hall, Captain?"

"Burn it. As for the prisoners, those with a slave mark may be allowed to serve the cohort. As usual, watch for any who seem like potential recruits and for those who seem likely to cause mischief."

"And the other prisoners?"

Footsteps pattered up the steps. Giyara slid the screen a hand's-breadth open, a smile touching her lips as she flicked a gaze toward Arras. She shoved the door open to reveal Zubaidit, kitted out like the rest of the soldiers and sporting a sergeant's badge. The subcaptains glanced at her and then at Arras. Why everyone thought he and the young woman were having sex he could not figure, since he had never touched her.

"Captain Arras?" she asked, cool as you please for all that she had intruded on his command council. "A word with you?"

Eddon snorted.

Orli rolled his eyes and nudged Piri, who frowned. The other three subcaptains looked elsewhere.

Arras gestured for her to enter, and cursed if the others didn't simply take this as a dismissal.

Giyara, pausing on the threshold, spoke. "Captain?"

Probably he was a little flushed. He sent her off with a lift of his chin. Zubaidit slid the door closed with a foot and leaned against one of the load-bearing wooden pillars. She had a way of lounging while standing up that made you think of what she would be like lying down.

He let irritation show, instead of desire. "You've served ably enough to be promoted to sergeant very quickly given how few months ago you were a hostage. But you must know how it looks to the others, you walking in like this."

She looked the hells more comfortable than he felt, because she had that quality that did get him bothered. "Captain, what would you want in exchange for you doing something for me that would cause no harm to your soldiers or your command? A one-time thing."

"I'm the captain of this cohort. Why should I want anything?"

She smiled.

He rubbed his jaw because he had to move *something* to scratch the restless itch crawling through his body. "Without more information, it seems to me you're asking a cursed lot just on the belief that I'd like to devour you."

"Wouldn't you?"

"It demeans me—and you—to have sex if it just becomes a matter of coin or barter. Where I grew up, we had a proper respect for the Merciless One."

"Better to take coin, or barter, than be forced against your will, don't you think?"

"Forced? It's true some criminals and sick-minded folk might do such a thing, but that's what—" Then, sitting in the reeve hall which would soon be burned down, he heard his own words and stopped talking.

"That's what reeves and assizes are for?"

"Law courts will be set in place once the Hundred is under control."

"Meanwhile, soldiers will do as they please."

"What do you mean?"

"Surely you can't be so naive, Captain."

"I have expressly forbidden—"

She shrugged, the gesture as good as a slap, cutting him off. "Think so if you must. I had three men whipped until their backs bled because they forced themselves on village folk. I won't allow that under my command, and I made sure the rest knew what would happen to them if they tried it. Yet if soldiers can steal rice and nai and anything else they want from a cottage, why not sex as well? Who will stop them?"

"Those are First Cohort men, those in the cadre you were given to command!"

"I just thought you would want to know it's going on among your own troops."

"You're putting me off my guard because there's something else you want. What is it?"

"I can't tell you without you giving me your word you'll let me do what needs doing."

"I could give you my word and then change my mind."

"Not you, Captain. You're an honorable man."

He laughed, although the way she said the phrase stung him. "I'd say you were flattering me, but I don't think you flatter."

"A man who would do this favor for me would seemed cursed attractive in my eyes."

"Neh, you're still bribing me. Let me ask you a question, then. You served your apprenticeship in the Merciless One's temple."

"That's right."

"If you were a hierodule and I was a man come to the temple to worship, would you devour me?"

Her amused smile was an honest answer, enough to make him feel like he wasn't begging.

"I was a hierodule once," she added, "so I honor the Merciless One. Within the temple, the hierodule and the kalos are the equals of those who come to worship. Not their hirelings. Not their servants. Not their slaves. Not their conquest."

"Yet I've heard it said that of all those who serve the gods, those who serve the Merciless One are the most like slaves."

"At the temple, the hierodules and kalos choose as they please, and refuse as they wish. I admit, sometimes an unscrupulous hieros will pressure her apprentices to do what they might otherwise feel reluctant to do. However, such a hieros will find it hard to keep apprentices."

"What do you want?"

"I need to get something out of Copper Hall before you burn it. I'd like to get these items out untouched and unharmed."

"Wine? Jewels? Silk? Gold cheyt? I wondered where the reeves were hiding their wealth."

"Something a cursed lot more valuable to me." Her expression darkened in a way that surprised him, and he sat up, taking her presence far more seriously. "There's a chamber dug below this cote. I found about thirty youths, mostly debt slaves and hirelings. I hate to see children broken into slaves, Captain. And I truly despise seeing helpless young persons abused, as some will do, given the chance. I don't like to owe anything to anyone, but if you'll get them out no worse for what they've otherwise endured today, I'll be in your debt."

"They might be better off serving as slaves to this cohort than sent to wander the roads with the risk of falling afoul of a less merciful cohort."

"They might. It's a generous offer, but I don't think you can keep feeding more dependents."

He turned the bowl of cold nai halfway around just to do something. "I could have you executed for this conversation."

Her smile was cursed relaxed. "So you could."

"Aui! Does nothing fluster you?"

"Not much."

"Will it content you if I order all refugees and debt slaves released?"

"You'd have my thanks." Her smile offered more.

"I want nothing in exchange," he said curtly. "I'll have the refugees and debt slaves assembled here in the marshal's garden. Sneak the others in among them, and they'll all be escorted from the compound before we put it to the torch. You're dismissed."

"Captain." She slid the door open and went out.

He turned the bowl all the way round, then tapped it on the table's top as he frowned.

"Captain?" Giyara looked in.

"Did you hear all that?" he asked, because Giyara's expression reminded him of a darkness in Zubaidit's eyes.

"I did."

"What do you make of it?"

"She's a strange one. Yet she's right. No matter what you've proclaimed, there are soldiers who will force sex on captives. It's just wrong to steal what the Devourer offers. I hope most of your veterans would agree. You've got to come down hard on the First Cohort soldiers."

"The commanders of this army won't care one way or the other. Maybe those who order cleansings have no argument with other forms of torture. Where does that leave us, Giyara?"

She'd seen too much to make light of his concerns. Like him, she'd walked a hard road to get to this place. She was good at what she did. She trusted him, and he trusted her, because they'd set their boundaries and stuck to them. There were things a person simply refused to do, because they were shameful.

She knew what he meant without him having to explain himself. "We walk cautiously, Captain. And try not to attract much notice."

"These children Zubaidit found hiding— Eiya! That wasn't mice I heard!" She looked a question at him, but he waved a hand. "Never mind. Look over the prisoners. We'll release the refugees, and recruit or release those with debt marks and any young ones."

"And the hirelings and assistants from Copper Hall? Cleanse them?"

Someone had to take the blow. War was a hard business. It was idiotic to pretend otherwise. "No cleansings. Kill them, but make it clean and quick. When the compound burns, let it have a necklace of dead to remind the people hereabouts that the reeves, and those who support them, are going down to defeat."

*   *   *

STAGE BY STAGE, day by day, the caravan journeyed to Old Fort. The amount of local traffic on the road shocked Kesh. Men led donkeys piled high with firewood. Lads and lasses shepherded flocks in grassy clearings. Women walked—alone!—with baskets of mushrooms gathered from the forest, calling out a cheerful greeting to the soldiers. Now and again they saw an eagle and reeve overhead, patrolling. At every village they crossed a guard post with a barrier blocking the road while the escort sent with them from Dast Korumbos cleared their passage.

"I've never seen the roads so secure," said Kesh for the hundredth time. "You could send a cursed child walking from here to Dast Korumbos and not fear for its safety."

"All under the watchful eye of the Olo'osson militia," said Eliar.

"As long as they're protecting *me*." Kesh pushed forward to keep pace with the soldiers assigned them at the border. "Are the roads safe all the way north, even to Nessumara?"

They were local lads, clear-featured and well disciplined, wearing their black hair up in topknots to mimic the Qin. "Neh, things are cursed bad in the north," they said with serious looks.

Kesh bit back a grin to make it a grimace. "No one traveling up to trade in Nessumara and Toskala then, eh?"

They scoffed. "Tss! You'd be good as dead, you would. But we hear—" They bent closer, confidingly. "As soon as our army is ready to march, we'll do to them gods-rotted Stars of Life criminals, won't we?"

"Surely you will," agreed Kesh, surprised by the fervor in their expressions.

They descended toward a familiar hill, its ancient ruins overlooking the glittering expanse of the Olo'o Sea caught in the ruddy light of late afternoon. Old Fort's palisade gates were open. Folk worked in fields and orchards scattered all the way up to the upland highlands where the southern shore of the grassy Lend washed against the foothills. They labored in stinking butcheries and tanning yards, sawed and sledged in the big lumber yard by the water where ten ships were drawn up awaiting logs and planks. No sooner had their caravan rumbled in to the large encampment grounds then young and old alike swarmed them with wares to barter or sell, freshly roasted meat on skewers, kama juice, barsh. A pair of young women had set up a slip-fry stand and got to work as the newly arrived Qin solders stared.

In procession with her eunuchs, the captain's mother presented herself to the slip-fry girls. Kesh hurried over, Eliar at his heels.

"What are these items? In what manner are you cooking them? Is this typical in this country? What do you charge? Extra for use of a bowl?"

The girls did not know to be intimidated. Even the watching Qin soldiers did not frighten them, being, evidently, so common a sight in these days they were considered as unexceptional as passing sheep. "This is radish, verea, very crisp from my aunt's garden. Oil pressed from olives, verea, very healthy. For you, a special price because we've never seen a woman of your years come out of the south. We would never haggle with an auntie."

They then named an outrageous sum that made Kesh choke and even Eliar change color, a flush rising in his cheeks. The girls saw him, and they giggled and goggled at the young good-looking Silver in their midst, just as the newly arrived Qin soldiers stared at the girls, although without the lighthearted laughter.

The old woman speared Keshad with her gaze. "You will obtain a sample of local food so my people may taste what they can expect to eat. It smells awful."

She swept away with her attendants.

"The hells!" exclaimed the older slip-fry girl. "That was rude!"

Kesh distributed vey to the first dozen soldiers. "You pay this much and then return the bowl and leave," he said to them. "Make a line. That's how we do things here."

Mollified by paying customers, the girls got to work.

"This will be interesting," said Eliar in Kesh's ear.

"Did you ever believe otherwise? Now help me do as she asked. I don't know about you, but I don't want to have to stand before Captain Anji after she's filled his ear with complaints of our service."

"It must be twenty years since he's seen her. Didn't she send him away?"

"Yes, at the age of twelve, so he wouldn't be murdered in the imperial women's quarters you are so fond of. What's that to you?"

"That the Sirniakans are barbarians isn't my fault! I'm just remarking that it's not as if she raised him after that time. It's the age a boy leaves his mother's care and moves among men into a man's life. Why should he listen to her after all these years beyond the kindly respect any son must show a mother?"

You're an idiot. But Kesh held his tongue, thinking of Miravia. Maybe she had months ago been married off to the old goat, but perhaps there was time, since the roads north still weren't safe. Old goats died, and left the young goats behind. There was no telling what had happened while he was gone. He had to be patient.

"Heya! Heya!" The local guardsmen waved to get his attention.

A party of mounted men were riding up from the track that led west around the Olo'o Sea. The incoming troops were about one third Qin, the rest young local men who dressed and acted as if they wished they were Qin. Kesh was surprised to see Chief Deze at their head.

"Chief?" He hurried to meet them as the wiry soldier dismounted. "How are you come here so quickly? We left you at the border."

"The reeves gave me a lift. I'm traveling with you to Astafero."

"Is that where Captain Anji is?"

Chief Deze had a likable smile, and it slammed like a closed door on a question he had no intention of answering. "We'll resupply here and leave at dawn. I'll take charge now."

Never in his life had Keshad been happier to give up control.

29

"COMMANDER. INCOMING WITH PASSENGERS."

Joss stepped away from the stewards—one from Clan Hall and one from Copper Hall—who had almost come to blows over what should have been a cursed simple inventory of the harness rooms at Horn Hall.

"Kesta." He beckoned her into the dimly lit chamber, which like the marshal's cote got its best light before noon. "I'll let you help Tesya and Likard sort this out."

"Sort what out?" she asked suspiciously, examining their disgruntled faces.

"I didn't—" objected Tesya.

"She said—!" barked Likard.

"You have my full trust," said Joss as he hurried out. Kesta hissed a few choice words in the direction of his back. As he slipped out under the arched entrance hewn into the stone, he waggled a hand in an insulting gesture, but she had already turned away to scold the hapless stewards.

"Here we are, in the abandoned shell of a reeve hall whose eagles and reeves were massacred, and all you two can do is *argue over tack*?"

"If they were massacred," objected Tesya. "The commander heard the news from some gods-rotted ghost—"

"Neh," objected Likard, "that lad Badinen saw it all!"

Tesya snorted. "You can understand that fish boy? Anyway, my people *need* that tack. We lost everything—"

As Joss fled down the corridor, Kesta's voice rang. "Sit down and shut up!"

He would soothe ruffled feathers later. As a tactic it worked well to allow his most trusted reeves and fawkners to crack down on the ones who complained and bickered, while he could glide in later to coax the difficult temperaments back into good humor, but he was pretty sure it wasn't good strategy over the long haul.

Hirelings swept the eating hall, which was lit through shafts. He crossed the vast entry hall, flooded with brightness from a big hole gaping above. Hirelings hauled sacks of rice over their shoulders toward the kitchens. Three off-duty Clan Hall reeves were laughing with two Copper Hall reeves over a jest. Young Badinen watched their interaction with the expression of a neglected puppy hoping for attention. He'd been a pet of the Horn Hall reeves, Joss had worked out, but to the Clan and Copper Hall reeves he was just a novice no one had time to train. Something would have to be done about that.

Joss emerged through a high cave mouth onto an oval ledge as long and wide as Clan Hall's parade ground. All along the cliff wall were dotted perches and shallow eyries. He crossed the ledge to the rock wall that rimmed it. Squinting into the setting sun, he watched four eagles descend. Two landed on the parade ground at the top of the ridge, out of sight, while the other two thumped down not so far from him. Their passengers and reeves unhooked, and Captain Anji and Tohon joined him at the wall.

"I've come, as you requested," said Anji, gesturing toward the magnificent peak of holy Mount Aua some fifteen mey distant. "That's an impressive view."

Tohon peered over the wall, a significant drop of at least a hundred baton lengths to a slope slippery with scree that marked the base of the cliff. "Hu! That's a long way down!"

"There's no way up here except on the wing," said Joss. "This ridge is the final out-thrust of the Ossu Hills. It's all ravines and folds behind us. And we've got a perma-nent water source. And gardens atop the ridge."

"Easy to defend," remarked Anji, "and yet, according to the report your people brought me, these reeves are all dead."

"It seems they were specifically lured to an isolated peninsula in the far north called the Eagle's Claws. There, their eagles were poisoned, and the reeves died."

"Your source of information?"

"The surviving reeve's account strikes me as having the color of truth. He seems too unsophisticated to come up with such an elaborate tale and stick to it, and you can be sure I've run him over that ground many times. But this news didn't come from his lips alone. I heard it first from a Guardian."

"From a Guardian!" The captain crossed his arms over his chest.

"She brought news of region we call Herelia. There's a town called Wedrewe re-cently built to house an administrative center, where new cohorts are being trained. There, the masters of the army condemn prisoners and make an accounting of what they've won. It's walled, but not heavily fortified beyond the presence of so many troops."

"It's a place that might be attacked. Go on."

"Lord Radas may have as many as fifteen cohorts. And more recruits are being gathered, or forced into the ranks." Joss swiped a hand over his hair, recently shorn, its bristles like a warning prickle against his palm. He blew breath out between dry lips, and chose careful words, because he could not keep what Marit had told him to himself. "Captain Anji, I must speak to you in complete privacy, you and I alone, where none can possibly overhear us."

No flicker of surprise creased Anji's expression as Tohon tugged on an ear and, casually, as if he had seen something that interested him, moved about ten paces away along the wall. "This matter you and I must discuss in complete isolation. At a time no one suspects we are doing anything other than scouting."

"You already *know*?" cried Joss, the words so loud that half the people on the ledge turned to stare.

Anji laughed as if Joss had made a joke. "Who could fail to know that half the women in Olossi have come to the door of my compound asking if you will ever re-turn to Argent Hall? At least I may now tell them that you bide a little closer here at Horn Hall than when you made your nest in distant Toskala."

A flush burned all the way to Joss's ears. On the ledge, folk laughed.

"That must be Mount Aua," Anji went on as cool as you please, signaling to To-hon. "It's magnificent."

"Yes," stammered Joss. Had Anji come to know the terrible secret Marit had told him? She'd mentioned that she had allies. Or was it something else he meant to speak of? Yet it was easy to fall into the astonishing view of a gorgeous land and find his feet. "This time of year no clouds veil its peak. The Aua Gap is the wide saddle of land that lies between the mountain and us. West"—he nodded to the left—"lies

Olossi, south the golden Lend, and east"—to the right—"lies the road down onto the river plain, toward Toskala and Nessumara."

"There's the town of Horn." Tohon, returning in time to catch Joss's comments, indicated white-washed walls as tiny as a child's toy landscape and almost cut from their sight by the last spur of the Ossu Range.

Anji tracked the vista with his gaze. "Three roads meet here, under our eye: West Track from Olo'osson; East Track from distant Mar; and the Flats, out of Istria and Haldia, in the direction of Toskala. If I were a man wanting to stage my forces to move against Lord Radas, I'd start in Horn."

"My thinking as well," said Joss, following his lead, "which is why I asked you to come. However, the town of Horn has rejected my—ah—best attempts at persuading them that it's in their best interest to ally with us."

Anji considered the onion walls of the ancient town. "Send in my wife."

Joss laughed. "Truly, what man could resist her?"

Anji looked sharply at him, then walked along the length of the wall toward the steep stairway cut into the outer face of the escarpment that led from the ridgetop down to the ledge. Four figures were descending: Anji's two personal guardsmen, who attended him everywhere, and the two reeves who had ferried them here. Joss recognized one as young Siras, long limbs taut with excitement as he stared around.

"I was laughing because it's a clever plan," said Joss to Tohon, stung by Anji's seeming rebuke. "A man can't help admiring what is beautiful!"

"The captain frets over his wife but doesn't like folk to know he does." Tohon was leaning at his ease, elbows on the wall, as he surveyed the view. "He's not a man who likes his weaknesses known to others."

"Is she his weakness?"

"Maybe so, but he calls her his knife."

"His knife? That's a strange thing to call her."

"Not among the Qin. A man can be waylaid by demons wearing many guises. Lust for flesh or for gold, lack of discipline, disloyalty, reckless ambition, unchecked anger. A good woman is a man's knife. She protects him against demons. Don't you have the same saying here?"

Joss scratched behind an ear. "Well, truly, we don't. Maybe Mai can cut a path into the trust and hearts of the council of Horn."

"If anyone can, it would be her. A grand vista, if I must say so." He marked the eagles soaring on watch high above. "How's the lad doing, Commander? Is he a good reeve?"

Joss thought first of Badinen, floundering apart from his stormy northern seas and complaining of the heat. Then he realized that Tohon could not have met the young fisherman. "Do you mean Pil?"

Tohon nodded, shading his eyes to search the heavens for more eagles.

"He's a cursed solid young man. He's a good reeve, still inexperienced but he's really taken to his eagle and of course as you know he's a excellent soldier in ways we reeves haven't ever trained to be."

"Do the others—ah—accept him?"

"Because he's an outlander? So they do, but that's in large part because that foul-tempered Nallo has taken him under her wing."

"A woman?" Tohon rarely looked startled. His eyebrows raised, and his lips parted. "Are they lovers?"

"Pil and Nallo? I shouldn't think so. From what I've observed and heard in passing, neither are fashioned that way. It wouldn't matter anyway. It doesn't among the reeves."

"It's as well the eagle took him, if you understand me, Commander."

"I don't." Anji had met Sengel and Toughid at the base of the stairs and the three Qin stood where the wall met the towering cliff, gesturing at the spectacular vista as they conferred.

Tohon cleared his throat and tugged at an ear. "It's just that this fashioning you speak of, it doesn't happen among the Qin."

"Surely it's simply part of the nature of some folk."

"Not among the Qin. Maybe that's why the eagle took him."

"Ah," murmured Joss, tumbling at last: *Doesn't happen* meant *Better to say it doesn't happen than to admit it does.* "You outlanders have curious ways. For myself, I'm cursed glad to have a steady young reeve like Pil. We need him."

"He's a good lad," said Tohon. "Doesn't talk too much, which wears easily on his companions. Just like Shai." The shift of subject was so swift it reminded Joss of Scar altering his glide high in the heavens. Tohon's brows furrowed. "It would ease a man's mind to hear something, if there was word."

The glimmer of vulnerability took Joss by surprise. "Zubaidit I saw in Toskala, as you know. The Guardian I spoke to told me she'd freed an outlander prisoner in Wedrewe, but where he is now or if he got out of Herelia I couldn't say. It might have been Shai."

Tohon's smile was brief. "My thanks." He turned as Anji and his two guardsmen walked up with several curious reeves and fawkners trailing at a polite distance.

"With your permission, Commander Joss," said Anji, scrupulously formal and his voice pitched to be heard without him seeming to shout. "After we've looked around here, I have in mind—if you'll do the honors—to scout Lord Radas's army. I'd like to see for myself what we're up against. Talk to those folk who have a stake in the matter. Fly into Nessumara, if it's safe to do so. Scout Toskala and High Haldia. How much support can we get from the occupied population? If they truly chafe, they may be ready to bite back. What's needed is a coordinated plan with enough flexibility to adapt to changing local circumstances, a powerful lot of persuasion, and a cursed good chain of communication."

"My reeves can easily communicate over distance. Also, as you and I discussed before, we're trying out some new formations—strike forces, if you will."

Anji nodded. "They can plant soldiers and scouts behind enemy lines. Move diversionary troops, aid flank movements, and disrupt lines of supply. As archers, they could penetrate almost any fortification."

Joss grimaced. "You've thought this through beyond what I have. It goes against tradition for reeves to be used as soldiers."

"We can sit and wait, or we can act."

"Are you truly ready to lead an army against Lord Radas?"

"I have a son. I intend to see him grow to manhood." Anji indicated the grasslands to the south. "That's the kind of country the Qin inhabit. Yet when I went to the boundary of the Lend to bargain for horses, I was told humans were not allowed to walk in the grass."

"We can't break the boundaries. The Lend is forbidden to us. So is the great forest we call the Wild, in whose heart no human may walk. And the inner mountain fastnesses held by the delvings and protected by traps and magic. All the tales say humans once lived in those places. Now they no longer do."

"Things can be taken from us while we're not paying attention." Anji's smile bit like a sword cut. He gestured toward the high carved entrance into the caverns of Horn Hall. "Shall we go in?"

The eagles had cleared out, flying to perches where they could sun and preen. As Joss walked with Anji and his men across the ledge, Siras signaled with a flip of the hand.

"Go on in, Captain," Joss said. "I'll follow in a moment."

Anji looked at Joss, followed an unseen thread to Siras, smiled slightly, and nodded. With his men, he strolled into the first cavern, the soldiers staring around like curious children.

Joss hung back in the sun-swept plaza as Siras hurried over. "Greetings of the dusk, Siras. How is your eagle? Your training?"

The young man grinned. He didn't even need to say anything. But when his gaze shifted to the cave mouth and the huge vault within, his mouth turned down. "It's like this, Commander. Verena is marshal of Argent Hall—of course you know that."

The sun's glare was, at long last, triggering an ache in Joss's temples. Or maybe it was only the secret Marit had told him eating away at his heart. He nodded.

Siras went on. "She sent word to Arda at Naya Hall that the Qin have asked for reeves to be assigned as messengers and transport for the captain's use."

"Verena and I discussed it," agreed Joss, rubbing his brows.

"It seems because I served as your assistant for that time in Argent Hall, that the captain decided I was trustworthy. So he came to me five days ago—"

"Anji came to you?"

"He came to Naya Hall and asked me to fly him to Merciful Valley—"

"Merciful Valley?"

"That's what they're calling that valley up in the mountains where the captain's child was born. Mistress Mai placed an altar at the birthing place to her god, and no one could say her nay."

"No, I don't suppose they could. The Spires are the borderlands of the Hundred. I don't see why our gods would be jealous of an altar in such an isolated place. Go on."

"Afterward the captain said he'd like to keep the place off limits to reeves for the time being, until some holy thanksgiving boundary has passed. He's been going up once a month on Wakened Ox with his wife to make a thanksgiving offering. They take up a small chest, the kind you'd store expensive spices in or rich folk their jeweled combs and gold necklaces. Three months running. But this time the captain asked me to transport him up there alone."

"Alone?"

"That was the first puzzling thing, because you know he never travels anywhere without those two guards. He took up that same chest, only this time it was bound with an iron chain. He said he needed to make a father's private offering at the cave where his son was born."

"Go on."

"So I flew him there. At his request I left him and came back the next day to fetch him. He was wearing a different tunic and trousers. I only noticed because the ones he'd worn the day before were threadbare and patched, and these were newly sewn."

"It's possible he changed clothes to make his offering. Like we do for festival days. Is there anything else?"

"He didn't bring the chest back with him."

"Maybe it was part of the offering."

"What do you suppose the Qin use for offerings? I asked around. Reeves who were up in Merciful Valley before with the mistress said she takes flowers as offerings, just as folk should."

Joss thought of what Tohon had told him about the Qin habit of ridding themselves of imperfect children. Killing them. His cursed head was beginning to throb. "Any news of the child?"

"Atani?" His smile was innocent enough to charm a cadre of susceptible young women. "The market women in Astafero talk about him all the time. The mistress, she comes out to the big house in Astafero each month right around Wakened Ox and stays for a few days to confer with that Silver woman who runs her household there. If the Qin officers aren't carrying that child around as gentle as you please despite their grim faces and cold swords, then the house women haul him everywhere. How the market women do fuss over that baby!" His own expression was wistful, as if he missed a younger sibling from home.

"Odd news, indeed. My thanks for bringing it to me, Siras."

"Is there some trouble, Commander?"

"No. Why shouldn't a man make a private offering to thank the gods for the safe birth of a healthy child? If you see or hear aught else, bring it to me. I'm not just speaking of the Qin soldiers, mind you, but in a general sense. Olossi's council. What the market women are saying. Gossip among the militiamen. Rumblings among the hirelings. Whispers at the temple of the Merciless One."

The young man's eyes widened as he absorbed his new assignment. "Yes, Commander!" He grinned and hustled away, no doubt enamored of the idea of playing spy for the reeve halls.

What on earth did Joss think Siras might overhear, as guileless as the lad was? He walked into the shadowed cavern, his headache easing as soon as he was free of the sun's grasp. Yet the commander of the reeve halls was involved in a far greater enterprise than just simple patrol. The magnitude of what he'd taken on yawned before him like the gulf of air beyond a cliff face that drops away to jagged rock far below. Aui!

"Commander?" Captain Anji and his men were waiting.

Joss smiled crookedly and walked over to them.

Anji tapped Joss's forearm in a rare display of fellowship. "Why wait, Commander? Send a message to my wife now. Let her be brought at once by reeve to meet with Horn's council. If we move quickly, our enemy will be less likely to guess at our plans and prepare to fight us."

"You would risk her walking into a hostile city?"

Anji gestured to the emptied cavern, the shadowed ceiling, the dusty corridors. "If even the inhabitants of this unassailable hall could be killed—by treachery— then there will be no safe place in the Hundred until we make it one."

Joss grasped the captain's wrist, feeling the strength of Anji's arm beneath his hand. "Of course you are right. It begins here."

*   *   *

THE GATES OF Horn were huge, the height of six men or more. They were closed tight shut. Militiamen leaned over the parapets, arrows nocked. Mai had practiced speeches and phrases so many times that it was not in fact difficult to address Horn's closed gates. She had only to pitch her voice to be heard without sounding as if she were shouting.

"We are come as representatives of Olossi's council to meet with Horn's council in a place of your choosing, here at the gate or within your council hall. I am called Mai. Master Calon and I are merchants. This hierophant, Jodoni, comes at the behest of the temple council of Olo'osson. Please hear our words. We are come today to ask you to join with us in an alliance against the army who call themselves the Star of Life. They have overrun most of the lands along the River Istri. We beat back a second army at Olossi, as you may have heard, but you can be sure that if Nessumara falls, Horn will be next and after Horn, Olossi. Each city and town—every reeve hall—will fall as long as each attempts to stand separately. The only way to defeat this army and these demons posing as Guardians is to join together."

"Practiced words from a pretty girl," called a woman in a deep, powerful voice. Mai scanned the parapet but did not see her. "Are you one of Hasibal's pilgrims? We've learned that an actress, one of Hasibal's pilgrims, crept into our city in disguise months ago and spied on us. Why should we trust you?"

"Olossi did send scouts into the north. They had to discover if Horn supported the Star of Life army."

"We did not then nor did we ever!"

"Can you defeat the northern army if it marches against you in full force, fully fifteen cohorts?"

"Fifteen cohorts!"

A murmur of shocked voices drifted down from the wall. Wheels scraped, and the right-hand gate huffed open just far enough for a woman and a man to emerge. Both were dressed in formal council robes with sashes; the woman held the baton of a council "voice."

"I am Poro," said the woman, displaying the lacquered stick, "who speaks for the council. Seyon is the arkhon of Horn."

"We don't have arkhons in Olo'osson," said Master Calon, "but I understand an arkhon is leader of the council."

Seyon nodded but seemed uninclined to speak. He was short and slight and held about him a sense of chained energy.

The woman's emotions were all too evident, boiling right on the surface. "Fifteen cohorts?" She examined Mai as if Mai were a bolt of silk labeled as best quality but merely being everyday quality. "How can you know?"

"Reeves are excellent scouts."

"Reeves are not meant to *spy* for councils. They are meant to preside over assizes courts, to track down criminals, to maintain a proper distance from councils who might otherwise influence their judgments."

"What are they to do if the northern army overruns every city and town? If it burns the reeve halls? Then who will preside over the assizes? Not reeves. Not elected councils. Let me speak to your council and I will tell you what I know and what Olo'osson's council means to offer."

"It's said Olossi is raising an army, commanded by an outlander."

"Olo'osson has already been attacked by the northerners. We intend to protect ourselves, just as you do."

"Why not send this captain to negotiate with us, then?"

"Would you admit into your well-guarded city an armed man who is also an outlander?"

Poro laughed. "A not unreasonable point."

Seyon looked her up and down in a measuring way. "An armed man appears as a threat. So instead they send a beautiful young woman who spins words like golden thread. Who is more threatening, I ask you?" His smile took the sting out of the words; she knew she already had charmed him because she could see in his expression the look men got before they paid full price in the market even knowing they ought to bargain.

She met his gaze with a frankness that pleased him, seen in the crinkling of his eyes. "You have discovered our plot, ver. Forgive us the deception. But if we do not fight together, I assure you we cannot individually defeat fifteen cohorts and the lilu calling themselves Guardians who command them. If you cannot trust my report, we can send one of your trusted militia captains or council members north with a reeve to see for yourselves."

"Why should we trust any reeves when Horn Hall abandoned us last year? Their own marshal came to the council and advised us to surrender to the northerners rather than fight a losing battle. Then they left. That's why we locked ourselves away, not knowing who to trust."

"The reeves of Horn Hall were slaughtered, in the far north, at a place called the Eagle's Claws."

"The Eagle's Claws!" Poro bent to whisper in Seyon's ear, and he shook his head, a dour look darkening his face like a cloud over the sun. "It's spoken of in the tales. It's said that on some days in the season of Shiver Sky, the rain turns white. Does such a place truly exist?"

"One reeve survived the slaughter, and he can testify to the truth of what happened. I've more besides to tell you."

Seyon's long black hair was pulled back in a trifold braid. He fingered a braid in a thoughtful motion. "I say we let her speak."

Poro's face bore the irritable expression of a woman who hasn't been brought her expected cup of tea in the morning. "Whose idea was it to send you, verea?"

"The outlander captain of Olo'osson's militia."

"Perhaps he's wise enough to win a war that is clearly unwinnable. Enter, verea. The council will hear you."

Mai gestured toward her escort of soldiers, one of whom was Anji wearing an ordinary soldier's helmet.

"Let them wait here," added Poro. "To show you trust us."

Calon wheezed out a breath, his face sheened with sweat. Jodoni said nothing.
Mai smiled, even if it got a little hard to swallow. "Let the trust we offer you be the
trust you offer us, verea."

"So be it. Come."

Anji gave no order to stop her, nor did she look back.

The city of Horn was built against a spur of the Ossu Range. It had evidently begun as a citadel higher up and spread downward in walled layers, so the city descended in levels, each one separated from the next by gates. In midmorning, few
folk walked the streets, but the hammer and beat of their labors rang everywhere as
the party toiled upward on a wide stone staircase cut directly up the slope toward
towers rising at the highest point. A few kites circled above Sorrowing Tower. Here
in the Hundred they did not bury their dead but left their corpses out in the open air
until their flesh was devoured by beasts great and tiny. It seemed barbaric to her, a
last insult.

She had to set aside her revulsion. This was their land, and if she wanted to make
it hers, she must accept what she could and ignore the rest.

Seyon walked nimbly despite his seeming frailty. He chatted flirtatiously about
silk and, once she mentioned her own dealings in oils, about the many varieties of
oils used for cooking, cosmetics, light, perfume, healing, leatherwork, and wrestling.

"Naya oil of course is most difficult to come by, and thereby very expensive," he
added. "Yet it's well known it can heal certain skin conditions. We heard a story that
the army that attacked Olossi was driven off by pots of naya thrown on them and set
alight. That they burned to death."

She stumbled on the next step, clipping the stone rim, and he caught her under an
elbow and kept his hand there as she kept climbing, angry at her lapse. "The militia
and the reeves working in concert used naya to break the enemy," she said.

"I'd like a supply of naya, to be held in reserve to defend our walls."

She carefully let her arm slip out of his grasp. "I believe, ver, that you are opening
negotiations. Should that not wait until I stand before the entire council?"

He laughed, paused in his climbing although he was not at all out of breath, not
as she was. A tree cast a modicum of shade on the sun-drenched steps. He plucked
out of its dusty leaves a lush sunfruit.

"The last of the year," he said, presenting the yellow globe to Mai with a flourish.

Poro laughed. "Ever the flatterer," she said.

Master Calon raised an eyebrow. Jodoni shifted his writing box to the other arm
and said, in his scrape of a voice, "Is it much further?"

Was Seyon only humoring her? Yet she had risen to face challenges more daunt-
ing than talking sense into the intransigent and fearful council of Horn. She only
hoped they were not secretly in league with Lord Radas.

She tested the weight of the sunfruit in her hand. "Let us share both the sweet and
the bitter, ver."

As the others laughed, she peeled the fruit and handed out its slices, which they
ate as they climbed the last and steepest stairs, licking the juice from their fingers.

The council hall sat between Watch Tower and Assizes Tower. The squat stone Sorrowing Tower stood isolated up a lone path through a field of uncleared boulders, on a spur of ridge behind. A message pole stood on open space sufficient for a pair of eagles to land, but no red eagle banners were folded at its base; it looked abandoned. Overhead, about ten eagles seemed to hang in the air, and although she shaded her eyes and squinted, she could not make out if any were carrying passengers, soldiers primed to drop in fast if there was trouble.

The council hall had a tile roof and many pillars to carry the load, but no walls. From any spot within the spacious covered area, the view was so tremendous that Mai stared. She saw the distant peak of Mount Aua and the rolling gap of land between which flattened into the golden Lend to the southwest and fell away in hazy hill country to the east, dropping down toward the Istrian plain. Any movement on the roads that met below the city's gates was visible from the height. The inhabitants of Horn had closed their gates and watched the army out of the north march past, heading to Olossi. They'd done nothing.

How often did folk do nothing because they believed no action of theirs could deflect the inevitable? Had she not done so herself in Kartu Town? All her life she had grown up as the favored daughter of the Mei clan. She might observe untouched while others toiled and suffered; not that she had not worked hard, but even when her father had agreed to the Qin captain's marriage offer—one he naturally could not have refused in any case—she had been fortunate in the husband who had chosen her. Yet she had learned on their long journey and in the Hundred that she had the means and opportunity to aid those who stood "outside the gate." She could have done nothing. Instead, she had acted.

"Verea?"

She faced an assembly of forty-eight men and women, all considerably older than herself.

"The view is magnificent," she said with a smile that caused half of them to smile and the others to snort or frown with the impatience of people who, like certain customers in the market, have already decided before negotiating begins that you are out to cheat them. "Horn is well situated."

Half nodded, as if they were determined to be pleased by every word she spoke. The others sighed, tapped toes on the stone paving, nudged their companions; one old woman even rolled her eyes.

Mai gestured to Jodoni, and he opened his writing box. It was a capacious box, because clerks of Sapanasu carried all the tools of their trade with them. Instead of a brush or inkpot, he handed her a slender stick.

She stepped forward and offered the humble stick to the eye-rolling woman, who accepted it with an expression of skeptical bemusement. "If you will, verea, could you snap that stick in half?"

The old woman had a bit of Grandmother Mei's look to her, a complainer, but she also had a much cannier gaze. Grandmother Mei had never looked past her own desires, as if always gazing into her mirror rather than at the world beyond. With a grimace of satisfaction, she popped the stick in half.

Mai extended a hand, and Jodoni handed her a bundle of slender sticks tied together. Many chuckled as Mai raised the bundle.

"Can you break this so easily? It is only made up of flimsy sticks, just like that one."

"You've made your point," said the old woman, brandishing the two halves of the stick she had broken. "But haven't we already lost this war?"

Mai looked at each of them, forcing them to meet her gaze so they had to acknowledge her. "No. We haven't already lost. Listen! My nose is itching. Many whispers have tickled my ears. This is my tale."

They listened as she spoke, at length, describing what might be done: her speech contrived between her and Anji and Commander Joss spun a thread meant to convince without betraying too much of their purpose, in case traitors walked within Horn's council.

Afterward they questioned her at length, some hot, some cool, most doubtful, others with the troubled look of people who nourish hope but fear they are naïve for doing so. Calon and Jodoni gave answers when needed; they too had rehearsed their arguments and together agreed on a plan of attack.

"Why does Olossi only approach us now?" Seyon asked. "When we have all lost so much already? Why not before?"

"I myself and a consortium of merchants from Olossi attempted to send a party to Horn last year," said Calon, "but the roads weren't safe, as you must yourselves recall. The party was killed by bandits."

"Why now?" Mai continued. "Because now Olossi has acted to safeguard Olo'osson. But Olo'osson cannot stand alone. Only now are we strong enough to reach out for allies. It cannot have escaped any of you, sitting here on this hill with Aua Gap spread before you, that Horn provides an obvious assembly point for forces seeking to attack our enemy."

"Difficult to know if we can trust an outlander," said the eye-rolling old woman. "Yet it says in the tale that 'an outlander will save them.'"

The wind had picked up, a stiff blow rumbling over the high ridge and streaming across this height like a reminder of life's ceaseless disturbances.

"None of us can know what the future holds," said Mai. "All we can do is decide what actions we will take. Will we do nothing as the Star of Life attacks Nessumara and spreads yet farther, stage by stage? Or will we do something?" She bent her head in a gesture meant to fall halfway between respect and dismissal. "We'll leave you to discuss it among yourselves. Is there a place we might rest while you confer?"

That startled them!

"Of course! But if we have other questions—"

"If you have other questions," she said in her kindest voice, "I think you might consider running up the message banner. Then you can question those who would actually prosecute the war: the reeve commander and Olo'osson's captain."

They responded by coming to their feet in surprise and confusion. But Seyon called a hireling to escort her and her companions to a garden attached to the assizes hall built up against Assizes Tower. On the stony ground no vegetation grew except that planted in pots and troughs: miniature fruit trees barren at this season; a hedge of thorny heal-all dusted with purple blooms; ranks of bushy green growth waiting for the rains to flower again. Mai sank down on a stone bench, wiping her forehead as Calon sat beside her.

"Are you well, verea? You're pale and shaking."

Jodoni was speaking with the hireling, then walked over. "I've asked them to bring kama juice, verea."

She smiled weakly, feeling her energy ebb as if it had all been sucked out in a swollen rush. Her breasts felt heavy and were beginning to ache. It was well past time to feed Atani, and meanwhile the baby was safely ensconced with his aunt Miyara and Priya as nursemaid atop Horn Hall.

"Was it wise for you to dismiss them quite so abruptly?" Jodoni added.

"It makes them anxious, Holy One. Then they feel there is a sudden need to make a decision."

"Eiya! We'll discover soon enough."

Two women tattooed with debt marks carried in trays with a jar of kama juice, bitter this late in the season, and a platter of rice cakes and flat bread, nothing fancy but filling to one who was hungry. Mai was always hungry, although she carefully did not eat more than her fair share.

Master Calon wanted to rehash the meeting, going over every least question and gesture to squeeze from these hints any sense of the council's inclinations, but Mai pleaded weariness. Sipping the last juice from her cup, she wandered the angles of the garden's paths, her sandals crunching on stony earth, and found a secluded haven. The hedge screened off a smaller garden rimmed by a low rock wall that overlooked a ravine with scrub brush. Falls of rock made the steep slopes impassable. A trickle of water, not even enough to make spray, spilled from the height down into the cut. The sparse growth reminded her of Dezara Mountain behind Kartu Town, washing her with nostalgia not for home precisely but for the landscape that once was the only one she knew.

She knelt before the wide stone wall and loosened her taloos enough to ease the pressure in her breasts by milking a bit into the cup. She straightened her clothing with a quick look around. Raptors still spiraled far overhead. From this vantage, she could see only a sliver of the city, roofs and alleys pairing light and dark. She set the full cup on the flat stone and settled back onto her heels, pressing her hands to her chest as she prayed.

"I offer this nourishment at the feet of the Merciful One. Through the merit of offering may I walk the path of awakening. The body withers and disintegrates; what power we have now may be shorn from us tomorrow. Receive this offering with compassion. May the world prosper, and justice be served. Peace."

A whisper teased like wind through the tightly knit leaves of the hedge. Startled, she turned, hands touching her taloos, but it was safely pulled tight. Several women dressed humbly—hirelings and debt slaves—had gathered at the gap in the hedge. How long they had been watching Mai could not guess, but she composed her expression carefully as she rose.

"Forgive me if I was not meant to wander into this place, but it felt so peaceful."

There were at least eight women, ranging from a pair of girls younger than she was to an old woman supporting herself with a cane.

The old woman came forward. "Were you praying, verea?"

"I was."

"We never heard such prayers before, but we could understand most of them. Was that the Merciless One you were praying to? Were you a hierodule?"

She flushed. "I'm not that, nor was I praying to the Merciless One. I pray to the Merciful One, who gives us sanctuary."

"Is that an outlander god?" asked one of the girls.

"The Merciful One rests in all places. Anywhere folk suffer trouble or despair, or wish to celebrate joy and prosperity, they can seek refuge and peace with the Merciful One."

"They're saying you people come from Olo'osson to offer aid and protection."

"That's right." This was easier territory to negotiate. She smiled, and several smiled back at her. The younger girl skipped forward to touch her taloos, fingering the silk until the old woman rapped the girl's forearm with the tip of her cane.

"Don't be rude!"

"No matter," said Mai. "No harm in her being curious."

"It's very fine silk, verea," said the girl, who had a fresh tattoo at her left eye and an ugly rash like an infection spreading down from the mark, inflaming her face. She was newly sold into debt slavery, no doubt, but she had also the pinched cheeks and fragile wrists of a child who has never had enough to eat.

"So it is. It comes from the Sirniakan Empire."

"All the best silk comes from there," agreed her interlocutors. "But we've seen none here for years. The roads haven't been safe. Trade has died. Folk are hungry."

"If the Hundred joins in an alliance against this cruel army out of the north, then we can open the roads. Trade will flow. Merchants will haggle, and markets will spill over with wares from every town in the Hundred and even farther away, from the lands beyond. Folk won't have to sell themselves or their children into debt slavery—"

She stopped before she began prating on about there being food for everyone. Weren't there always children who were starving and folk passed for sale from one hand to the next?

The younger girl crept forward again, not without a furtive look toward the older woman and her cane. She extended a hand—clean enough—then withdrew, and Mai laughed and beckoned her closer to let her touch the best-quality cornflower-blue silk with its cunning embroideries worked in the same color thread into the fabric.

"Are you the outlander who has come to save us, verea?" asked the girl, eyes wide.

"Mai!"

The women melted back to make a path for Anji to stride into the garden. His gaze made quick work of its narrow confines, pinning each point where an assassin might hide and determining that they were not, at the moment, at risk.

"I didn't see you come in—!"

"The council raised the message flag," he said. "It seems you impressed them favorably enough that they agreed to meet with me and Commander Joss." His expression was so flat she understood he was very very pleased, and she could not restrain a smile of triumph, not for herself precisely, but for their cause. Or perhaps it was just for her personal victory, winning them over. She hardly knew.

"Calon and Jodoni lost track of you," he added with a frown as he studied her.

"I came here to pray. Then I was talking to these women."

He measured the company, acknowledging the older women with nods and ignoring the young ones, and indicated that Mai should accompany him. "We'll go back."

"Do you plan to fight them what have driven so many refugees out of Haldia and Istria, with such horrible tales they have to tell?" asked the old woman while the younger girls hid their eyes and one of the women with a fresh tattoo wept silently as at remembered pain.

"I plan to fight," said Anji.

His words made Mai's chest tight with despair, and fear, and pride. She followed him out and the others trailed after them, all but the youngest girl. Only when they entered the council square where Joss was already speaking passionately to the gathered council members and more folk besides coming up from the city to hear did she remember she had forgotten the cup.

30

THE CLOSER SHAI and his escort of a dozen wildings got to the edge of the deep Wild, the fewer trails offered passage. As he hacked at a vine wrapped stubbornly around his ankle, he heard frantic voices. A scream pierced the forest's veil. Shoving past a curtain of leaves, he stumbled down a wet-season gully sucked dry at this time of year. The gully offered a trail of a kind, and he splashed through isolated puddles, slipping twice along its slick pavement of damp leaves. Brah and Sis kept pace in the branches. The adult wildings had vanished.

The forest wasn't silent, which just made tracking more confounding: insects buzzed; birds chirred sweetly or squawked raucously; a larger animal cracked dead branches as it fled. He could never tell where the noises were coming from. Where the gully turned in a sudden bend, a bush had thrown tendrils across the depression. Shoving through this he slammed into the back of a man kneeling on the ground beside a child sprawled flat on its back.

The man toppled sideways with a yelp. Folk, unarmed and lugging only sacks and baskets and small children, huddled in a hollow sticky with the muddy remains of a wet season pond. At Shai's entrance, they shrieked. The surrounding canopy bent to dancing although the wind had not risen.

Shai leaped up, waving his arms. "Don't kill them! If you honor me, let me first speak to them!"

The man sobbed as his companions stared in horror at a sight behind Shai. He turned. The child had begun to leak blood from its nose and mouth; it twitched weakly, sucking for air, then was still.

Mist rose from the body. A shape congealed, casting around.

"What happened? That hurt!" Its cloudy gaze fixed on Shai. "You're an outlander! I never saw an outlander before!" He was sure the lad *smiled* as at a good joke, but abruptly its attention focused past him. "I see there—so bright!—" the ghost cried, and the boy fled through Spirit Gate, folding away into nothingness.

The trees ceased their movements. Had the wildings seen the ghost as well?

"Is that your child?" Shai asked.

"Neh." The man rubbed his forehead as if to wipe away blood or anger or dirt or grief. He had an ugly wound above his right ear, and his left arm ended in a stump wrapped with the bloody remains of a jacket. "He went by the name of Gelli. He was one of the children that came with us out of Copper Hall, but he had no family left. Said they were dead or scattered. No trouble at all, that boy. Even tempered and lively. He kept us smiling with his jokes and antics."

"Surely you know it is forbidden to cross the boundary of the Wild." He crouched beside the body. The boy's right hand bore a pair of purpling puncture wounds. "Snakebit!"

"It was dangling in those vines when the boy pushed around," said the man help-lessly. "Impossible to see, it being green like the vines. How was anyone to know a small creature could be so deadly?"

No wonder the darts of the wildings were so effective.

"Did you not see the poles with skulls set atop them?" Shai demanded.

They stared at him with the speechless intensity of folk who are hungry, thirsty, lost, and without hope except maybe for that given them by the antics of a lively boy now lying dead at their feet. Most were young, like the prisoners Shai had been held captive with, although these hadn't the battered, bruised, stunned look of the abused. These were merely starving, frightened, helpless refugees, swatting listlessly at bugs come to feast on warm bodies.

Finally, a very young and quite pretty woman stepped forward, clutching the hand of a boy no older than the lad who had died. She eyed him as warily as if he might be a snake about to strike. Not one seemed aware that they were surrounded by wildings.

"We're all that remains from those fled from Copper Hall," the girl said.

"Copper Hall? In Nessumara? Has the city been attacked?"

"That I don't know. I meant the other Copper Hall, the main reeve hall north of the city on the road to Haya. A cohort come and burnt the hall."

"Copper Hall is burned?" The simple words were so sharp a shock that he felt strangled.

Their tale spilled like rain: a cruel army rousting folk from their villages; farmers and villagers fleeing into the countryside and some coming to rest at the reeve hall where old Marshal Masar offered a haven. Then the reeve hall had been attacked and burned, eagles killed, the reeves fled. The old marshal had left behind his own grandchildren.

"He had to do it," said the young woman gravely as she blinked away tears, "because they could only carry one extra person each. If they didn't save the fawkners, who would care for the eagles? If there's none to care for the eagles, and the reeves die, then who will protect us?"

"The reeves haven't done a cursed lot of good protecting us, have they?" objected the man, waving a hand to clear away a cloud of gnats. "They saved themselves and left us behind to die."

"There was nothing else they could do!" cried the girl indignantly.

So many spoke Shai could not make out the speakers among the angry group.

"They could have fought against that cursed army, eh? Instead of flying up there out of reach and watching as the rest of us got hit over and over and over again!"

Houses burned. Captives taken. Men killed. Storehouses looted. Children and elderly dead of sickness and starvation.

"How are you come into the Wild?" he asked.

The girl took up the tale. "A sergeant discovered us hiding in the wine cellar and convinced the cohort captain to let us go. But after we traveled for some days, other soldiers harassed and chased us. They drove us in here. They killed them what would not go past the poles. We had no choice but to die at their hands, or hope to escape. We thought maybe we could walk a ways through the Wild and leave with none the wiser."

"That one sergeant," added the man with a weary kind of rage, "she did more than the cursed reeves ever did by hauling you children out of your hiding place and getting you out alive instead of giving you over to be slaughtered. Those poor cursed hirelings and assistants who got left behind were killed outright. Folk I knew well, every one of them. Think of it! It was that one sergeant, enemy as she was, who saved us. Not the gods-rotted reeves."

He had a debt mark at his left eye, easy to overlook because that part of his face had been scraped to bleeding.

"You'll not speak of my grandfather that way!" shouted the girl.

"Enough!" Shai glared until folk fell into an anxious silence. "There are wildings in the trees all around you, ready to kill you with darts soaked in snake venom like what killed that poor lad."

Some wept, shaken by fear. Others wore a look of glazed indifference, people pushed past their limit.

"Should we just lie down and die?" said the girl, her chin jutting in a desperate display of bravado. "If the wildings are so cursed deadly—if they even exist except in tales—then why haven't they killed *you*?"

Their despair made him reckless. "Because I'm not human. I'm a demon."

"I never heard that outlanders are demons. They're just people, like us, only they look funny."

"Hush, you idiot girl!" the man hissed.

Shai laughed. "What's your name?"

She slanted a look at him as if she had just discovered that he was a young man and she was a young woman, and things might go as they might go if things went. As he felt himself flush under her bold scrutiny, she smiled, flexing her power to disturb him. She knew men admired her, even as ragged and hungry and dirty as she was. Surely she'd not been assaulted and abused in the last weeks. She showed no fear, as if the thought of such a threat had never occurred to her. "I'm called Jenna. It's short for Jennayatha."

Someone sniggered. Others hissed. He was meant to understand the reference, but he did not.

"I'm an outlander. I don't know your tales, if you meant to convey some meaning by your name, verea. Tell me more about Copper Hall. What happened with the sergeant?"

The tale was neatly told, for the Hundred folk did know how to spin tales from any least event, and this was a story that could easily become woven into a true tale to be told to grandchildren should any of these survivors survive to dandle grandchildren on their laps. Barrels of wine and cordial had distracted the first lot of soldiers come to explore the cellar, but a sergeant had shined a lamp's light onto the faces of frightened children and withdrawn without betraying their presence. She had returned and marched them past ranks of corpses to join village refugees and hall slaves who were to be allowed to live while the rest were put to the sword. Each word was a blow to Shai's hopes. How was he to reach Olossi if he could not reach a reeve?

"That sergeant was a hierodule once," said the boy suddenly, speaking past his sister's grasp.

"A hierodule? What makes you say that?"

The lad looked around to make sure everyone was listening. "She said she was an acolyte of the Merciless One. That's how she knew there were times to show mercy and times to withhold it. No use killing children."

"That's what she said," his sister agreed, canting her hips as if to mimic the way the other woman had sauntered. "She had knives. And she ordered that lot around, didn't she? I liked her. Even if she was one of the cursed army."

Maybe it was the way he'd had of sensing a coming storm when he was up at the carpentry shop on Dezara Mountain. Maybe it was the way ghosts called to him. "Did she say her name?"

"She called herself Zubaidit," said Jenna. "But if I were marching in that gods-rotted army, I'd call myself something different than my real name, just for being ashamed!"

"Which cohort? Is there any way to identify it?"

"They had a banner . . . six crossed red staves on black cloth."

"That's right," the man agreed, and others nodded. "We saw those banners flying as they advanced. The soldiers what chased us into the Wild carried a banner with eight white nai blossoms on a green field. What will happen to us now, demon?"

"Can you return to your villages?"

Their laughter was harsh; their tears shamed him. "How can we go back? They have the weapons. We have nothing."

"Where did you last see the cohort with the six crossed staves?"

They spoke of landmarks, streams, a burned Ilu temple, the sea.

"Rest you here while I talk to the wildings. Don't try to run away. If you run, you'll be killed."

He batted at the leafy curtain with his walking staff, thinking of the green snake that had bitten the lad. When no snake twisted, he ducked through. Wildings blocked his way in the gully. Above, Brah and Sis swayed on branches, their grimaces of dismay easy to interpret.

One of the wildings, an older woman, gestured. *Must kill. Forbidden.*

"Listen to me, honored one." He, who had never spoken up in his long and dreary childhood, was learning how to speak. "They are not your enemy. They were forced to cross into the Wild. This war is your enemy. The Star of Life army is your enemy. The corrupt cloaks—the Guardians who walked under the Shadow Gate—are your enemy. Once they have burned villages and killed folk who respect the old ways, what is to stop them from pressing their attack into the Wild?"

Her hands spoke sharply. *We kill humans when they come across the boundary.*

"Maybe the first ones. But more will come. They will chop down and burn the forest. They are already breaking the boundaries elsewhere, killing the gods-touched who you call demons. By killing these villagers, you act as the army's allies. You bring your own death."

They talked with hoots and clicks, with hands shaping words too swiftly for Shai to make out transitions, and with their bodies: a shoulder might rise or a hip jut, an elbow swing and a knee bend. Folk in a council meeting could not speak so fast and say so much merely with words.

The day was cool, but his face was hot, and sweat greased the lids of his eyes as he blinked away stinging tears. The sight of these pathetic refugees had triggered the most terrible memories from those weeks when he had struggled to keep alive a cadre of children held captive by a cruel cohort of the Star of Life army. If he closed his eyes, Yudit and Vali's suffering was all he could see; yet with eyes open, he saw misery everywhere else.

The wildings stilled, and the oldest female stepped forward. *They go safe.*

"Thank you," he whispered, suddenly dizzy. Brah and Sis dropped out of the trees to shoulder him up so he could breathe.

You who see ghosts, where now do you go?

Among the Qin he had learned that in battle, adaptability is better than strength. As Tohon would say, strength can always be overcome, if you can find a way to do it. A man who can change course when needed has less chance of running into a wall. Think fast. Strike where there is an opening. Maybe he hadn't saved Anji from Hari, but he had other goals. His own fears and weaknesses were nothing against the promise of an act that could change everything.

"'A dart, a dart in my eye,'" he murmured; the memory of Captain Beron's ghost—speaking words only Shai could hear—was as powerful as a shout. "'How it stings.'"

He met each gaze, because the wildings respected the acknowledgment of the individual. "Copper Hall on the Haya road is burned. Nessumara is beyond my reach. It's unlikely I can make contact with the reeves. But I have another task. I'll find this cohort flying a banner with six crossed staves and give myself up to them, because they will be looking for gods-touched outlanders. I'll find Zubaidit. There's one thing I need from you."

Brah and Sis patted him on the shoulders, gesturing regretful farewells. He must go, and they must stay in the Wild that sheltered them.

What do you want, demon? the wildings asked.

"Darts, and a pair of blowguns, the smallest you have. And one other thing. I need snake venom."

* * *

IF ANJI WAS not the most patient man Joss had ever met, the reeve was not sure who was. For three long days, Horn's council wrangled. Everyone had a grievance; each council member had fears that had to be addressed; they all had unhelpful suggestions or urgently unreasonable demands.

Only three things made the three days bearable: they got to sit on benches in the shade of a tile roof, with a cool breeze blowing; the local cordial was exceptionally good; and Anji's calm demeanor never wavered, even as the interminable afternoon of the third day dragged on. The man could listen without breaking a sweat; without showing exasperation, without responding to the most inane or selfish complaints by snapping back a sharp retort; without slapping a hand to his forehead when people were being idiots.

From dawn until late into the night the commander of the reeve halls and the captain of Olo'osson's army sat in the council square, and not once did Anji raise his voice or interrupt.

Not that he needed to. Others raised their voices and interrupted; then the arguments would fragment into new and more complicated relationships, like clans marrying into festering disputes they'd not been warned about beforehand. Each time a new eruption occurred, Joss would grab for his cup of cordial while Anji's gaze would flicker toward Tohon, or Sengel, or Toughid. What passed in those unspoken exchanges Joss could not fathom: were they amused, irritated, indifferent? The scout and the two guardsmen remained as impassive as Anji, although now and again Tohon tugged on an ear.

Soon enough, Anji and Joss learned to milk that cow by falling into a rhythm between them, Joss's irritation balanced by Anji's reasonableness.

"We get refugees come begging every day," said the latest quibbler. "If we give a tey of rice, then they will keep coming back and living right in the dirt like animals, hoping for a handout. Yet if we turn them away then they steal from our gardens and orchards, so we must post guards at all hours. It's a cursed nuisance."

Joss swiped a hand back over his hair. "Amazing that they won't just crawl up into the hills and die so as to leave you in peace. Cursed impolite of them to want to live."

"We're already rationing our stores to our own folk! You want us to starve altogether?"

"It's a good point," said Anji in his steady voice, and every head turned his way. "If you starve yourself trying to feed every hungry mouth, then all will starve and none will survive. There's no sense in that. But starving folk will not lie down and die. Would you? If it was your children who were crying?"

"I'm not the one who ran from his home, who didn't fight, who planned badly and didn't take enough food with me, who—" The quibbler went on in this vein for a while until other people told him to hush.

Anji nodded into a silence others had carved. "To simply give away all your rice and nai solves nothing. But to do nothing, solves nothing. And it encourages refugees to steal."

"We could kill them if they won't go," said the quibbler enthusiastically.

Joss said, "We'll let you stab the babies first."

"Now, here, Commander—! What manner of man do you take me for?"

Joss had always really disliked selfish whiners like this prosperous man, who clearly had enough to eat and fine silks to wear. It was so easy to make them pop red with indignation, since they could think only of themselves. And it was anyway apparent by the way folk were smirking and rolling their eyes that this fellow wasn't liked. He gave an exaggerated sigh. "I can only judge you by your words and acts."

The man's eyes bulged as he opened his mouth to retort.

"If I may." Anji raised a hand with the orator's twist, one of the few gestures from the tales he had mastered. The quibbler sucked in hard and settled back. "The only way to remove the burden on Horn is to defeat the enemy and thereby make it possible for the refugees to return to their farms and feed themselves. They don't want to be refugees. They want to go home. But they can't."

Many among the council nodded. Onlookers standing in the back nudged each other, whispered, bobbed their heads in agreement.

The quibbler scratched his beard. "You're an outlander, Captain. Is that what you want? To go home?"

Anji's rare smile flashed. "Neh. My bridges are burned in the lands I came from, not of my choosing. I merely want to live peaceably here in the Hundred with my wife and infant son."

"And a cursed beautiful woman she is!" shouted a wag whose voice carried although his face was hidden in the crowd. "Bet you don't give her much peace."

Folk laughed.

Anji blinked; that was all. Sengel coughed. Tohon glanced at Joss, chin raising slightly. Was the captain annoyed? Or signaling an opening?

Joss lifted his cup of cordial. "I say, enough of this cursed nattering on. If Horn will join us in sealing an agreement to fight this cursed army, then the captain can sooner get back to his peaceable life which I am sure many of us envy him."

Anji rose. Their chortling and murmuring quieted as abruptly as if he had drawn his sword and sliced out a hundred tongues. "Surely every man and woman here is exhausted by living in such uncertainty. When do you think it will get better, if nothing is done?"

He scanned the assembly; no one ventured an opinion; their silence made his point for him.

"But it can get much much worse, and I assure you, it will. I have seen war. I've fought in war. It's nothing I want to see again. Peace is preferable, but you don't win peace by hiding from what troubles you. Do not think Horn's walls can withstand a determined assault if you have only a handful of ill-trained guardsmen to defend the walls. After three days of talking, you must know the choice is stark. Either you lose everything, while a few claw out a fragile truce with the brutal conquerors, or you fight, with allies at your side, and have a chance of restoring the life you want to live. There's been enough talking. You have to decide. What action this council takes is in your hands."

He walked out, pausing only long enough to make polite courtesies to the four most elderly councilors. Joss followed him through a dusky courtyard where lamplighters had begun their rounds. The two youths stared at the four Qin soldiers and the reeve.

Anji drove straight for a gap in a hedge. When Joss trotted after him, he found himself in a small private garden overlooking a ravine and one flank of the city falling away below. The three soldiers hung back by the entrance. Anji leaned on the low wall, frowning at the horizon. The sun's golden rim flashed as it slipped out of sight. The few smoky clouds were bathed in red, the sky darkening as twilight overtook them.

"That way lies Olossi," said Anji as Joss joined him at the wall.

"And Mai."

Anji's eyes narrowed. "Among the Qin, we do not boast of our wife's virtues in public. In the empire, we do not speak of women in public places at all."

"I might remind you that we are not in either of those places."

"True enough. Nor do I regret where I am now."

Joss was not sure what to make of the captain's strange mood or where to go with it. "You're a good negotiator, Anji. Better than I am."

"Do you think so? I thought we herded that flock together, even if you took the role of the dog, nipping at their heels until they moved in my direction."

Joss laughed. "That's one way to look at it. Neh, I meant that you told them what they wanted to hear in a way that encouraged them to seal the alliance we desire."

"Why would any man seal an alliance if it did not benefit him in some manner? It takes no brilliance to point out that we will both prosper if we work together."

"Yet some folk will consistently work against that which will help them, like turning their backs on the reeves. While others act in ways that benefit only themselves while harming others, even if another path is available that might allow both parties to benefit or at least not suffer."

"Maybe so." Anji spoke the words with the flat inflection that meant he was amused. He hitched up a leg and sat sideways on the wall, facing Joss. "You're a man who believes in the law, Commander."

"You are not?" Up here on the height the wind streamed steadily although with the twilight the rumble abated a bit.

"Certainly I believe laws are vital if we wish to live in peace. But I've lived in the empire, and among the Qin, and now I live in the Hundred. The laws here are not the same as the laws in the empire. Nor yet are they the same among the Mariha princedoms and caravan towns along the Golden Road, which the Qin army conquered. Still less are they similar to the laws enforced by the Qin var. What am I to think except that laws must change according to circumstance?"

"Maybe that is true in other lands, but here in the Hundred our laws were given to us by the gods."

"In the empire, the priests and nobles say the same."

"I'm sure they do. However, our laws are carved in stone, on Law Rock."

"By the gods' own hands?"

Joss was surprised that this comment both amused and irritated him. "No one knows."

"Is there no tale that relates the carving of Law Rock?"

"None say what hand cut words into stone, or if it even matters."

Anji nodded, standing again, as restless as Joss had ever seen him. Maybe he was more nervous about Horn council's deliberation than he cared to let on. "I'd like to see Law Rock."

"So you shall, because we'll go to Toskala, where we have stationed twenty reeves and one hundred and fifty firefighters and militiamen to guard the law."

"So you prove my point, Commander."

"Which point was that?"

"How quickly you forget my wisdom!" retorted Anji with a laugh. "Only this. You have kept men on Clan Hall to protect a physical object. But it is our deeds, or a council's actions, or the decisions reached at an assizes, through which the law takes a presence in our lives, is it not?"

"Without Law Rock, who decides what is justice? The army we fight has its own measure of what is justice."

"Do they? Maybe they just like having the power to enforce their will. If they were the ones without weapons and numbers, they would be asking for mercy."

"Then after all, you are saying there is a law we must all follow. One carved in stone, or present in the world whether we recognize it or not."

Anji gestured toward the city below. A few lamps bobbed in narrow streets; here and there a lantern hung to mark an entryway; otherwise, all was quiet, only the faintest buzz of living chatter betraying folk settling down to another uncertain night.

"I am saying that certain principles, applied effectively, tend to result in certain outcomes. A king who displeases his populace must either rule by force of arms and custom, or he must give way and change, or he must die. The governance which promotes a peaceful life for many is most likely to be pleasing, is it not?"

"We do not have a king in the Hundred."

"The Guardians did not rule in ancient days? Like kings?"

"The Guardians—" began Joss, thinking of the conversation they had not yet had about Guardians.

Anji shook his head, indicating the hedge.

"The Guardians did not rule," Joss said instead. "They presided at the assizes. They guarded justice. It was village arkhons and town councils, and in the north a few lords and chiefs, who ruled."

"It is exactly that splintering that has made you vulnerable."

"We have lived as the gods decreed. For a long time we lived with no wars or battles, so the tales tell us."

"So the tales tell you. But tales tell us only what those who compose those tales and who pass them down over many generations choose to record and remember. The Beltak priests of the empire bind the empire so that nothing will change. They use their spirit bowls and their prayers and their spies and red hounds and informers to build walls so no man can be other than what the priests tell him he is. Yet I wonder. Are the priests enforcing the god's will, or their own?"

Joss shook his head. "Can we blame the gods for our own weaknesses and faults?"

Anji again turned to stare west, as if he yearned for his absent wife. Mai had been taken by reeve back to Olossi two days ago. "I blame the gods for nothing," he said as night swept over them. His words weren't bitter or angry or joking. He said it as he might say *I wield my sword with my right hand*, a statement of fact.

"Are you not a believer, Captain? What gods do you worship? If I may ask."

Anji did not answer.

Folk bearing lamps crowded at the gap in the hedge. A decision had been reached. Horn's council had voted to ally with Olo'osson.

Anji glanced with a wry grin at Joss as he stood. "We'll feast and drink with Horn's council tonight in celebration, Commander. Tomorrow, we'll send a messenger to Mai and Tuvi in Olossi. It is time to mobilize the army. You and I will scout the ground ahead. I want to see with my own eyes what we're up against."

*   *   *

THE LAST TIME Kesh had walked on the shore of the Olo'o Sea in the Barrens, the wild lands had spread from the shoreline with its slicks and sinks all the way to the impregnable heights of the rugged mountains. Back then, a few tents had housed Captain Anji and his scouting party. Now they rode between fields of wheat, supplied with water from irrigation channels, and stands of pearl millet on the dryland slopes above. Sapling orchards had taken root. The shore was lined with racks of drying fish. Folk hauled buckets of dirt; shaped bricks; fertilized the dusty earth with nightsoil. Laborers toiled on scaffolding for a brick palisade that would soon surround the entire double hill of the primary settlement.

At the gate, Chief Deze sent the new Qin troop to the distant barracks. The remainder of their group and the wagons lumbered up the main market street. A noodle seller set down her ladle and gaped. A seamstress seated on a mat in the shade of her humble porch dropped her needle. Ten men with hands slick from bean curd raced out of the back garden of a shop to stare. Anji's mother stared right back, meeting each gaze in a way that made a few grin, a few step back, and a few look startled or ashamed.

Under an arcade with a walkway of raised bricks and a canvas roof, shopkeepers had set up stalls that sold ribbons and cordage, banners and flags, and bolts of cloth ranging from least to best quality. Now, many of the shopkeepers stood to get a look, and their customers turned to stare, ribbons and unrolled silk forgotten. A woman with hair bound back under a kerchief stepped out of the shadowed arcade into a corner of sunlight, leaning out to get a better look by bracing herself on a post.

Her movement caught Kesh's eye. But it was her face that arrested him.

Seen only once, but never forgotten because unforgettable: a handsome, serious, somewhat square face with full red lips and eyes like two brushstrokes. They were the most beautiful eyes, windows opening onto a treasure house filled with mystery and promise. Her features had seared him, a brand burned into his memory, a scar that would always mark him.

But she wasn't looking at him. Her expression tightened, and she pushed back from the pole and ducked into shadow.

Too late.

Eliar jerked his horse to a halt and flung himself out of the saddle. He leaped onto the raised brick porch and grabbed her arm.

"Eliar—" She tried to drag herself free.

"*What are you doing out here?*" he shouted as he shook her roughly.

The cavalcade rumbled to a halt as the captain's mother signaled, regarding this curiosity with a look that reminded Kesh abruptly of her son's powerful reserve: impossible to guess what she was thinking. Kesh dismounted, tossing his reins at the nearest soldier. He jumped up to the promenade and grabbed Eliar's turban at the base of the neck. The silk twisted cool and smooth under his fingers, best quality weave, very fine.

"Let her go," he said in a voice only Eliar and his sister could hear. "Or I'll rip this off right now. And we'll all know the the truth of whether you cursed Silvers have horns."

Eliar let go. Kesh released the turban's silk.

"Get out of my way," said Eliar, oblivious of multitudes who had swarmed over to stare at this delightful altercation between a Silver and a young woman everyone surely knew was an unveiled Silver woman walking in public as if she were no different from any other person there. "To find my sister in such a place, so exposed, is a clan matter. None of your business."

"To find a woman being roughly handled is a matter for all decent people to respond to," retorted Kesh.

"So say you, the slave master, selling women and men into servitude where they may be abused in any manner whether in public or private. You cant on so, but you are as bad as anyone."

"At least I do not drone on about abuses of slavery and then lock my women inside my house and yelp like a kicked dog when I find my sister enjoying the freedom of the market."

Eliar punched him. The fist landed in the curve between jaw and neck. Kesh toppled backward into a table stacked with twists of cordage. The stallkeeper shrieked as her wares scattered across the ground. Folk began yelling. Eliar's sister grabbed the table and righted it.

Shoulders heaving, Eliar glared at his sister. "How are you come here? Does the family know?"

Her face took on such an aspect of melancholy that it was as though all color had leached from the world despite the bright sun shining down upon them.

What she meant by that look Kesh could not fathom, but Eliar's mouth pinched.

"Eliar," she said, offering a hand in the gesture of greeting.

He turned his back on her and walked away, stumping past the cavalcade and up the avenue under the glare of the sun. She swayed as if ill. She did not call after him.

Kesh brushed at his jacket, straightening his sash. His tongue, like his sash, had twisted into a knot. His face was burning, and his hands were trembling.

"The hells!" cried the stallkeeper to the street at large. "Cursed Silver knocking everything over and then just walking off!"

Do something!

Kesh bent to rescue the scattered cordage, bumping into her as she knelt to do the same. Because her skin was lighter, it was easy to see the red of shame scalding her cheeks.

"He was wrong to say those things," Kesh said, the words pouring like the flood rains, "and to act toward you so rudely in a public street."

"You're Keshad." Her voice was barely audible. "The one who went south to the empire with Eliar."

His heart was pounding so loudly he thought the entire street must hear. "How can you know my name?"

"I saw you before." Her blush did not subside as she busied herself collecting the fallen cordage. "That day in the courtyard of Olossi. Maybe you don't recall it." She examined him until he could not breathe.

"Of course I remember!" He dropped to his knees, but she rose in the same moment and dumped an armful of gathered cordage on the stallkeeper's table.

"My apologies, verea," she said in her husky voice, its tones and timbre so sweet it was painful for Kesh to hear her speak just for all the longing he had carried with him in the months of travel. "If there is any damage to your merchandise, I will cover the cost."

"You did nothing wrong. You and your mistress are good customers, none better."

"I insist that if any of the merchandise is ruined, that we make compensation."

The stallkeeper's friends, gathering, jostled Keshad as they picked up the rest of the fallen cordage. "Neh, verea," they agreed, nodding and smiling at Miravia, "nothing but a bit of dirt. It was wrong of the Silver to shake you like that."

She thanked them and extricated herself from the crowd.

Kesh followed her down the steps of the arcade into the sun. "Eh, ah, maybe you need an escort up to where—ah—wherever are you living, verea?"

"I do not need to be rescued." She walked away down an alley.

Harness jingling reminded him of his obligations. He tripped over the stairs and bruised a knee, and a friendly passerby caught him by the elbow to steady him.

"You all right then, ver?" asked the man, a good-looking man with a pleasant smile and his long hair in a braid down his back. "Can I help you?"

"Do you know her?" Kesh asked wildly. What if he had lost her? After the way she had *stared* at him! "Where does she live?"

"The Silver girl? Lives up at the mistress's house. She manages things here now the mistress lives in Olossi. Talk has it she was thrown out of her family's house just for showing her face in a public street. It's hard to believe any clan could be so hardhearted, but they are Silvers and so there is no accounting for their outlander ways, is there?"

"Do you mean Mai? Captain Anji's wife?"

"Surely I do. Here, now. Your people are calling you. Where'd you folks come from?"

"South." It had to be obvious just by looking. "From the empire."

"Who is that old woman? She's got the look of those Qin soldiers about her, but truly, she reminds me of my eldest aunt, the one who cracked the whip." He grinned so engagingly that Kesh almost started talking, then recalled he was on a public street.

"My thanks for the hand, ver." Keshad shook free and trotted over to the cavalcade, where a Qin soldier held the reins both of his horse and the one Eliar had abandoned.

The captain's mother beckoned. "What was the meaning of that altercation? A lovers' quarrel?"

"No, exalted one. They are brother and sister." If rumor were true, if Miravia had been summarily exiled from her clan, what did that make her now? Not a widow. Surely not a wife.

"I see," said the old woman. "It is not Master Eliar who is the hopeful lover."

Her raptor's gaze was fixed on him. How deep her stare penetrated he could not be sure, but her claws were in him already.

She nodded. "Is your suit to be favored, or dismissed?"

He felt his skin gone clammy, and then a rush of heat.

"I have found you to be a sure-footed person on the whole, Master Keshad. So it must be you are uncertain of how your suit will be received either on the part of the young woman, or her family. Is there aid I can offer you?"

"*You*, exalted one? Offer me aid? Why?"

Her expression sharpened, as he had always imagined an eagle's might when it spots the flicker of movement that betrays its prey. "You have done me a service. I am a woman who settles her debts. Therefore, if you need my help, you need only ask." She raised a hand and the cavalcade resumed its upward progress. Folk stopped to stare at this remarkable sight while meanwhile she scanned the humble market street, the dusty lanes, and recently built brick houses; her gaze rose to the makeshift temples—the council square with benches set under thatched awnings—and the sprawling building on the height with a plank porch and canvas walls.

"A strangely modest palace for an emperor's son and var's nephew to bide." She glanced at the wagons behind her, her female attendants veiled behind curtained windows. "Is this the best the Hundred has allowed my son?"

"This is but a part of what he possesses, exalted one. Although I admit his exploits are chiefly military. It is his wife who negotiated for a substantial payment for services rendered and who included this valuable stretch of land, since it is here that king's oil can be harvested. They are partners in this venture."

"His wife? His wife was stolen by the western demons long ago."

"Perhaps that was another wife, exalted one. I speak of Mai. If you meet with the council here, they will speak so highly of her you might think they exaggerate. But I assure you, they do not. Although Captain Anji founded the settlement, it is surely through her efforts that the town has flourished."

"A local woman, is she? From a noble family in this region?"

"No, exalted one. It is not our way to have certain families set above others as it is in the empire. Anyway, she became the captain's wife before they arrived in the Hundred. I believe she is a merchant's daughter from the Golden Road, a place called Kartu Town."

"I never heard of such a place! One of those dreary little towns with nothing more than a well and a stable and a herd of sheep. In any case, my son cannot have married a merchant's daughter, although I suppose he might have taken one as a concubine. Is she here?"

"I believe she resides in Olossi."

"Go yourself and bring her to me, since Chief Deze seems determined to keep me out of the way until my son returns to offer a more fitting welcome. Bring her quickly, so I can take her measure."

"Take her measure? Anyone here will gladly give you her measure."

"Who is it you are in love with, Master Keshad? The blushing woman whose brother humiliated her in public? Or this other one?"

"She is Captain Anji's wife, exalted one."

"Yet would you take her, if she were offered to you?"

"She will not be offered to me! The captain is devoted to her, everyone knows that."

She pursed her lips. "These sentimental spoutings become tiresome. What man has ever held on to a concubine when he saw that his interests lay elsewhere? Because I like you, Master Keshad, I will give you the concubine and help you acquire this other female as well. Then you can have two wives. Or a wife and a concubine, however you wish it."

He choked, face burning. "I am not—"

"Are you not? Look how flushed you are!"

He swiped a hand over his sweating forehead. "Anyway, Mai is her own mistress. She is the administrator of their holdings and household, not him. She can't be bought or sold."

"Of course she can be! Only the price is negotiable."

"What are you saying, exalted one?"

"I am saying," she said with a glance toward the wagons ambling upward behind her, "I have plans for my son that do not include an inconvenient merchant's daughter."

31

HOME. HOME. HOME.

Mai had been gone from Olossi for only a few days, flown on eagle's wings to Horn and back again. In those few days so much had passed in Horn that to think of it dizzied her. But entering now through her courtyard gate she felt as if she had only stepped out of the compound walls to take a turn in Olossi's market streets before returning home to eat her dinner and go to her night's rest.

As Chief Tuvi escorted her in through the warehouse, voices faded to silence as people looked up. Factors hesitated, brushes were set down, vials of precious oil held forgotten in hands, people standing as still as if they had spotted a venomous snake near their feet. Tuvi shrugged with a frown of puzzlement. Priya wrapped the sleeping Atani more closely against her slender frame. When they reached the gate that led into the counting room, it opened at once, as if the folk inside had expected them. Tuvi stepped inside first, as he always did. He scanned the room, then gestured to Mai. After a glance at Priya and the baby, she followed.

O'eki stood in the center of the chamber with arms crossed, his big frame towering in the space. "Mistress!"

His gaze shifted to fix on the other person in the otherwise empty chamber, a young man with black and lovely hair curling loose as if blown in a whirlwind, his intense expression pinning her in the instant in which she recognized him.

"Keshad! You came back! You survived! What of Eliar?"

"Eliar is alive, not that I care for his well-being any longer. Mistress, where is the captain? Is he with you?"

"He's still in Horn." She shook her head. "What news, Keshad? By your face, it is momentous!"

"I've been sent to fetch the captain," he said, but he was a terrible liar; his gaze slid sideways, his eyelids flickered; his lips thinned as if he were squeezing back the truth.

She looked at O'eki, who shrugged. Standing, as always, in a position to block any move made against her, Chief Tuvi scratched at his straggle of a beard. Priya came in behind her and touched her elbow to reassure her. Atani smacked his lips.

"Best speak up, lad," said Chief Tuvi in a genial tone that would have milked blood from stone, if the stone were wise.

Voices broke into argument on the other side of the door that led into the house. The heavy door groaned, then slammed back, and Sheyshi stormed into the room with high color in her dusky cheeks.

"Mistress! You are come home! I was worried for you!" She seized Mai's free arm and clung to it, her breath sweet with mint tea and her fingers like claws digging into Mai's flesh. "I heard those two talking! That one!" Mercifully, she released Mai and pointed with her finger, tremblingly, at Keshad, who flinched at the rudeness. "I heard that one tell O'eki to keep a secret until the captain comes home."

"Keep what secret?"

Sheyshi heaved a passionate sigh. "There is trouble in the settlement for Mistress Miravia! And he won't tell you! Some important person is come, but I couldn't hear who. Now maybe your sister Miravia has trouble!"

"What important person, Keshad? Has Eliar threatened to take Miravia to Nessumara?" In her life maybe Mai had never spoken so sharply to anyone, but the events of recent months had spun a stronger thread in her, as tough as silk, as enduring as wool. *"Tell me!"*

He took a step back as if she had slapped him, then he wiped a hand over his face as if to brush away the pelting bruise of a cloudburst. The look he cast toward Sheyshi was bitter, even brutal, an ugly grimace that startled Mai. He could not control his feelings; he struggled to speak evenly as Chief Tuvi's placid gaze prodded him.

"There is much to tell, Mistress. The emperor, he who was the captain's half brother, is dead, killed in battle by his cousins."

Mai swayed. Priya caught her under the elbow, but she found her breath. O'eki stooped by his desk and rose to offer his writing pillow for her to sit, but she shook him off as Sheyshi wailed. "No, I'm all right. What does this mean for Anji?"

"The cousin has taken the throne and been anointed as emperor. But he is a peaceable man, seeking order, not war."

"Hu! Certainly it seems practical to him to want no more fighting now he has gained the imperial throne," said Tuvi with one those inscrutable smiles common to the Qin when they were amused by the ironies of life.

"Maybe so. I only met his gelded brother, who seemed—" The phrase spoken with a shudder. "—determined to achieve his ends. They have an offer for the captain."

Mai shook her head impatiently. "An offer? Of what kind?"

"Gelded?" said Tuvi. "Ah. He was cut. A eunuch cannot sit as emperor. Or var."

"They don't expect—!" Mai broke off as heat rose in her face.

Atani essayed a few gurgling sounds and reached for Mai from the wrap. Priya lifted him out of the cloth, and as Mai took his comforting weight in her arms she remembered that calmness served her better than anger and fright. "What is the offer, Keshad?"

"I don't know, verea. They sent an emissary. They sent the captain's mother. It's she who knows what they mean to offer him."

"The captain's *mother*?" said Tuvi under his breath, words she would not have heard if he had not been standing close enough that his shoulder brushed hers. "The var's sister? Is here in the Hundred? In Astafero? Hu!"

Sheyshi was staring at Kesh as if his words had hammered her, yet her gaze seemed fixed not on him but past him, as if she were seeing something else. Then her eyes flickered and she glanced at Mai and began to snivel. "I'm scared, Mistress. What if the red hounds come?"

"Hush, Sheyshi. Tuvi, if Anji's mother has come, I must greet her. Show her honor and respect. Can she not come here to Olossi?"

The Qin were not outwardly affectionate; they did not push and prod, except when soldiers wrestled and sparred in training exercises. In Kartu Town, folk kept a physical distance appropriate to their station and degree of relationship, and even within the Mei clan Mai had witnessed few displays of physical warmth and intimacy. One of the most startling aspects of the Hundred was the degree to which people casually touched other people, of either sex, in public spaces.

So when Tuvi now touched her hand, she was shocked enough that Atani startled, his little head tilting back to look first at her and then at the chief.

"Best she stay there and you stay here until the captain returns, Mistress," Tuvi said, but his sober expression cleared immediately and a smile softened his face as the baby squirmed and reached for him. Mai handed him over.

"She asked me if I would take you!" Keshad blurted.

"If you would take me where?"

"Take you as my wife. She has plans, verea, for her son, and they don't include you."

Tuvi's gaze was distant as he continued smiling absently at the cooing boy. These words did not surprise him, however much they confounded her. "Like I said, it's best if you do nothing until the captain returns, Mistress."

Mai stared at Keshad. "As *your* wife?"

Sheyshi sobbed and collapsed on the floor like a rag doll cast away by its indifferent owner. Merciful One! Could poor Sheyshi have been harboring an infatuation for Keshad all this time? And no one the wiser?

"Of course that's not what I want, not that I don't admire you, verea. But you must know—" His emotions galloped away and dragged him after. "You must know, verea, that I intend to marry Miravia. If she'll have me."

Sheyshi bawled.

"But you can't!" cried Mai. "I mean Miravia to marry Chief Tuvi! He's the only one who's worthy of her. And then she'll always stay with me. You can't have her, Keshad!"

"Who are *you* to order her life? Eliar repudiated her. In the market. In front of everyone. Will you do that, also, if she turns down Chief Tuvi in favor of me? No disrespect, Chief."

The chief studied the baby with brows furrowed.

"What makes you think she'll have you?" demanded Mai. "You, who traded in slaves for years!"

"I only did it to earn coin to buy my sister free."

"Miravia despises and rejects slavery."

"You keep slaves! She doesn't despise and reject you!"

Anji's *mother*! Blown in like a storm to overset everything. How could a woman who had never met her be speaking of handing Mai over to another man as if she were a slave purchased at the market? And yet hadn't Anji bought her from her father? That he treated her as a wife, not as a slave concubine, was only because he had chosen to do so. He could have used and then discarded her at any slave market during their long journey here. Why should Anji's mother—a woman of exalted birth, sister to the var who ruled over the Qin Empire and wife to the Sirniakan emperor himself—consider Mai to be any different from a slave? Any more than she was herself, a woman of far superior rank and blood, who had been discarded by the emperor when it was no longer politically useful for him to favor her?

"I will not be handed off to some other man!" cried Mai. "Meaning no disrespect to *you*, Master Keshad!" But the words were bitter, their bile a sour taste on her tongue.

Miravia was going to marry Tuvi. Mai had it all arranged and was just allowing time for Miravia's situation to settle. It was not acceptable for Miravia to marry this unpleasant young man with his handsome eyes and beautiful hair, exactly the kind of passionate features worn by the heroes in songs who snared so many luckless maidens. What if Miravia, so innocent, so unworldly, fell in love with his intense looks and rejected a steady, solid, intelligent, calm, and wise man like Tuvi just because he was old enough to be her father!

Yet how was Mai different from the rest if she managed Miravia's life, or Priya's life, or anyone's life but her own and her child's, merely to satisfy her own selfish desires? If she did not want to be so treated, then she must begin by refusing to inflict on those she had authority over what others had previously inflicted on them. What her father had dealt to her.

She turned to the big man. "O'eki, write up a manumission for all three of you. You, and Priya. And Sheyshi."

"Do you mean to turn me out?" Sheyshi sobbed. "Where will I go?"

"Of course I won't turn you out. If you want to stay, you can stay. It's just you won't be a slave. You'll be a hireling. You'll be paid coin, and if you want to work elsewhere, you can go elsewhere."

"I don't want to go elsewhere!" Sheyshi wailed, swaying back and forth like a tree whipped in a strong wind.

"You don't have to go anywhere," said Mai, expending her last store of even temper, she who had prided herself on her fathomless calm. Not for her Ti's storms or her twin Mei's sulks; she had held herself above Uncle Girish's tantrums and thoroughgoing nastiness, her father's controlling angers, her mother's jealousy and competitiveness, her aunt's scheming, and her grandmother's favoritism. And yet here they all surfaced in a swell of furious emotion that made her hands quiver and her shoulders shake.

Keshad will not get the better of me!

"Go on, O'eki!" she said harshly. "Do as I told you!"

With a shaking hand, O'eki moved paper on the desk and weighted its corners with stones. His brushstrokes were uneven, the calligraphy uncharacteristically sloppy, but he wrote the same text three times, a formulation familiar to him from his years as a slave in Kartu Town.

Tuvi dandled the baby with a thoughtful look on his face that might have meant anything. Surely he had guessed she meant him for Miravia, someone special only, but what he thought of her blurted confidence, the revelation of her most lovingly hoarded plans, she could not tell. Sheyshi's tears squeezed out through eyes pressed shut.

Priya said nothing, moved not. Keshad fumed. She'd stolen a march on him, hadn't she? Eiya! And now she was crying, but she let the tears flow. Tears were no reason to feel shame. Only dishonor shamed you.

O'eki lifted his brush as if to add another word but set it down on the brush stand instead.

"Mistress," he said in a trembling voice. "I am finished."

Sheyshi turned her face toward the wall, hiding herself.

Mai sank down beside O'eki. She plucked the brush from the stand, forefingers on the outside and small fingers on the back with the thumb to steady them. She touched the hairs to the inkstone and, ruthlessly, hearing only their breathing as her accompaniment, signed them with her formal name, Mai'ili daughter of Clan Mei, as Priya had taught her.

She signed Sheyshi's manumission. She signed O'eki's manumission. She signed Priya's manumission and pressed the seal over each one, to make them legal and binding before witnesses, work that the clerks of Sapanasu usually did but which those who could write could manage themselves without requiring the intervention of the temple.

The var's sister and the emperor's former favored queen, so grand and noble a woman, might consider Mai of Clan Mei so insignificant as to warrant no more consideration than a disposable slave, but Mai was no longer such an insignificant creature even if she had been so at one time. She had no need to ask anyone's permission to seal such an act. Hers to act and hers to seal because this was her household as much as Anji's and no woman like Grandmother Mei was going to totter in and think she could sell off Mai as though she were a helpless, propertyless daughter worth only as much coin as her beauty could be sold for. And she certainly wasn't going to let some handsome untested young man steal Miravia just because of his pretty eyes and reckless heart! She had a right to appeal to Miravia's affections, too.

"It's done."

Perhaps her tone had an angry edge. Perhaps she was shaking more than she realized, even if only one drop of ink stained the paper above her imperfectly brushed name. She wanted its lines to reflect the grace of proper calligraphy, to mirror the gravity of the occasion, but she was still learning, so it would have to do.

She set the brush on its stand. O'eki put a hand to his forehead.

Priya's fingers brushed her chest as if pain stabbed in her heart. "Free," she murmured as she leaned to the right as if trying to read the freshly inked letters. Without warning, she collapsed.

In her haste, Mai knocked the writing table askew, and before O'eki had even gotten to his feet she knelt beside Priya's limp form. "Priya? Priya!"

As faintly as the whisper of mice in the desert Priya spoke again one word. "Free."

Mai held her shoulders, keeping her head up. How slender she was! Not much weight to hold, and yet how generous in heart Priya had been all those years. She had served Mai faithfully, affectionately, warmly, loyally. Mai had never given her service a thought.

How blind she had been!

"Yes, you're free now, Priya. You and O'eki both. If I had understood . . ."

But she had not understood. Only now was the veil ripped from her eyes.

Priya rose to crouch at the table and touch the paper; paperweights shifted as she turned it so she could read. There is a flower in the desert that blooms only once in its life; it was as if Priya's expression took on that opening as her gaze scanned the words.

"Seren," said Tuvi in a voice startling for its eerie calm. "Take the baby."

The young soldier accepted the baby, although Atani's fabled equilibrium was, under this storm of emotion, beginning to dissolve into a fuss.

"As for you, Master Keshad," Tuvi continued, words all the more commanding for their even tenor and unimpeded flow, "having returned to this compound, you are back under my authority. You will tell me everything that transpired, in the south and on your return journey. Afterward you will bide here, confined and quiet and under my supervision, until the captain returns to interview you."

Keshad glared at Tuvi as at a rival in love. "What choice do I have?" he said with a dark frown that made his handsome eyes all the more intense.

Hadn't Miravia seen him that one time, in this very compound? Was it possible she had fallen in love with a face glimpsed across a courtyard, as lovers did in songs and tales?

Tuvi made no reply to Keshad's inane question. In his silence he exerted his authority.

Mai rose, tentatively brushing Priya's shoulder as if to test whether her beloved nursemaid recognized that she existed. Priya glanced up, eyes watery with tears, and touched the back of a hand to her own lips as if to say that she had, as yet, no words.

It was done. Mai could not regret it, no matter what happened next.

"I too must hear Keshad's tale," she said to Tuvi in her firmest voice, however weak it sounded to her ears.

He nodded. "As soon as the captain returns, you'll hear it all. Meanwhile, the young master wants feeding."

Atani strained toward her from Seren's solid arms. When she took him, he began to root against the silk of her taloos, trying to reach a nipple, while Keshad flushed and looked away. O'eki nodded at Mai with a faint smile, and gestured as if to say, "We'll come when we can." Priya was staring at the words that freed her. Sheyshi still stood with her back to them, so it was impossible to imagine what she was thinking. For how many years had the young woman lived as a slave in the Mariha princedoms? How had she come into Commander Beje's household? Was it possible that Sheyshi, simpleminded as she was, did not truly remember? That this household was the only one that meant anything to her? Or was Mai foolish to think anyone did not dream of what they had lost?

"Sheyshi, of course you can stay in this household if you wish it," Mai said again, although Sheyshi did not answer.

"Mistress, isn't that baby hungry?" said the chief.

She took comfort in the baby's fussing. Thanks be to the Merciful One for hungry babies, who soothe troubled minds through their uncomplicated need. When all else roils, refuge can be found in simple tasks. For she had to be honest with herself.

It wasn't losing Miravia she feared most. What if the empire's troubles reached up out of the south to devour Anji?

*   *   *

KIRIT WAS ARGUING with him again, annoying girl. For days Jothinin had dragged her from one makeshift campsite to the next along the western shore of the Olo'o Sea, whose isolation protected them. She stayed with him because the girl she had been had always moved with the tribe. She obeyed because she was accustomed to accepting the command of her elders. Today, she was rebelling.

"If we have allies," she said, flinging stones into the water, "then we should fight at their side!"

"Guardians do not fight," he said for the hundredth time. "Anyhow, Kirit, we have placed a weapon in their hands that can be turned against us."

"But they can't be our allies if they would turn against us! Why are you afraid?"

It was getting cursed hot as the season of Furnace Sky took hold, and here on the western shore of the Barrens there was no shade The ground beneath his feet had baked as hard as brick; a skin of salt left where wet season pools had evaporated crackled as he walked closer to the girl.

"It is better for us to stand back and let events follow the course they will. Afterward we can come forward and restore the assizes."

"'Foolish Jothinin, light-minded Jothinin'?" she sang. She didn't have the cadence right, and her voice cracked on the melody, as though she were not accustomed to singing. "Marit said you stood up and spoke out, even though you got killed for it. So what would have happened if you had hid then?"

"I'd be resting peacefully beyond the Spirit Gate, where I wouldn't be getting lectured by a girl who knows a hells lot less than she thinks she does!"

She glared at him with her demon-blue eyes, quite disconcerting in their cold fury. She opened a hand to let stones fall. "I am angry at you, uncle. I am going north to find Marit. She will listen to me."

When had he ever been able to stop a stubborn-minded girl from acting foolishly? That was the problem with tales; they didn't tell the truth but rather what people wanted to be true. Listeners did want the lustful farmer to get to sleep with the man she desired; they wanted the lad and lass forced to marry by warring clans to discover they could live in a peaceable house. They wanted a death that made you weep, and a joke that made you laugh. They wanted the carter's barking dog to be smarter than the greedy merchants who were trying to cheat the carter of his hire.

Everyone loved the tale of the Silk Slippers, in which he had played so striking a role. He *had* stood up in protest when the bandits had come to take her away, but the gods knew what an arrogant pain that girl had been, not the sweet innocent portrayed in the tale but rather a self-absorbed, demanding, vain spoiled brat who spent most of her time talking about whether people were paying enough attention to her. Her unpleasant personality hadn't made her cause any less just. But it was why no one else had made the effort to protect her. No one had liked her. He had only spoken because it was the right thing to do.

The wind blew hot and dry off the mountains.

"Kirit, what if they kill you?"

"I'm already dead, uncle. I want to fight."

"Let's say I agree," he said hastily. "We'll seek Marit together and decide what to do next."

She considered with that funny little frown creasing her pale lips and pallid face. "We saw many troops gathering on the Olo Plain. Now we see also ships hauling soldiers east across the sea to Olossi. We could ride with them!"

"As Sun Cloak rides with his army? Don't you see, Kirit? That would make people fearful. They must not believe Olo'osson's army is the same as Radas's army. Led by shadow-corrupted cloaks."

Tongues of water lapped the shore, the water faintly slicked with oil of naya. They were north of the new settlement, north of the most plentiful naya sinks, but cracks bubbled here and there beneath the waters. Its flavor coated his lips.

"I fear what we have unleashed," he said.

"You fear everything, uncle," she said with a flash of emotion he could not interpret: anger, maybe, or scorn. Or maybe she was just worried about him. Was that too much to ask? "I want to hunt down the other Guardians. Even if I can't kill them, maybe I can lead them to those who can kill them."

Her words alarmed him badly, but he smiled in the inane way he had perfected. "Perhaps you're right. Let's go search out some sunfruit, and then we'll fly to the high salt sea to meet Marit."

"It's not the end of the year yet, is it? Will Marit be there?"

"It's soon to become Wolf Month. Then there is only Rat Month, and after that the Ghost Festival welcoming a new year. Then it will be the Year of the Blue Horse, when we can hope for a secure, orderly, and tranquil year."

She agreed to go with him to the high valley she had discovered after her final awakening, the hidden valley where sunfruit grew in abundance. Yet when they flew in between the high mountain cliffs, they found that since the last time they had been here, others had claimed it. In a clearing hacked out of the trees, two neat structures had been built, simple but pleasant shelters raised on posts and walled and roofed with sturdy canvas. No one bided there, but closed chests and sealed pots and tidy cupboards told a tale of people who might come back at any time.

"I feel we're being watched," he said as he stared around the clearing. Telling nosed through the high grass by the trees.

Kirit had ridden ahead, following a path into the trees. He led Telling after her. It was cool up here in the mountain valley; the air was bracing, and a taste like the feel of a thunderstorm snapped on his lips. He shuddered at each least rustle and stir within the trees, but he saw no one. Birds fluttered in the branches and, once, a small sleek hairy pig scuttled across the path in front of him and raced away into the brush. The noise of its passage faded as he emerged onto open ground, a sprawl of ancient ruins beside a pool fed by a waterfall spraying down the side of a sheer cliff.

There was something odd about the water in the pool, something that hurt his eyes, like knives stabbing him, more pain than light. Even Kirit reined her mare away, wincing and shading her eyes.

"When we came before there weren't people here," she said. "But now they've made their mark and claimed it. Look! There's an altar in the cave. An offering of flowers, like they would offer to the Merciful One in Kartu Town where I was a slave."

There was a chain in the water, hard to see if you didn't have a Guardian's vision. It ran from the shallows into the deep black depths beyond his sight. Chains bound things.

"Something's happened here," he said. "Something bad. Best we leave quickly."

Kirit rubbed her eyes, looking as disturbed as he felt. "Marit will know what to do."

He was relieved, thinking of Marit's competence, her decisive nature, her clear-eyed vision, her blunt words. "We'll leave Olo'osson. It really is best for the army to march without us. If Marit thinks otherwise, we'll discuss it when we meet her."

He paused at the edge of the clearing as Kirit rode up behind him. The high peaks darkened as the sun set behind them, washing their outlines in a hazy purple-red whose echoes rippled in the pool where the falls disturbed the deep water. He shuddered and turned away, mounting his horse, making ready to ride. Kirit rode up close beside him, as uneasy as he was.

"Anyhow," he added as Telling unfurled her wings, "we can tell her we've accomplished our part of the plan. Just as we said we'd do."

*   *   *

ANJI HAD FLOWN enough that he had become comfortable both with the harness and with the height, with his feet dangling, with his safety held entirely in the hands of another man. Joss wasn't sure he could give up control so thoroughly; he was too accustomed to having his hands on the jess. But perhaps Anji, trained as a soldier, had long ago learned that his survival depended on the loyalty of his men. Who was the wiser, in that case?

"There!" shouted Anji, pointing so rudely with his finger that Joss flinched, and in the same instant—either because he caught the lapse or because he was that quick reacting—the captain curled his hand into a fist. He'd seen a ledge tucked high up on the rock-bound slope of Mount Aua.

"We can't go there," said Joss. "Guardian altars are forbidden."

"Who forbids them?"

"We're not allowed to break the boundaries by walking in the holy places the gods made for Guardians."

"Haven't the Guardians already been corrupted when demons stole their cloaks? Anyway, Joss, I have a vague memory that I was once told in passing by a person whose name I do not recall that when you were young you broke the boundaries many times. You got expelled from your first reeve hall because you dared to walk on Guardian altars? Can that be true?"

Joss laughed bitterly. "I'm wiser now. Perhaps."

"Ignorance weakens us," said Anji as the wind thrumbled in their ears and a glitter woke on the distant ledge like a promise.

If they only knew how the Guardians had become corrupted. For if one Guardian had become corrupted, why not all? He refused to believe it, not about Marit.

"The altars do not like our kind. They'll cast us out and try to throw us to our death."

"Are these altars alive? As the sands in the bone desert along the Golden Road are alive, inhabited by demons?"

"They are forbidden. The gods guard them. Nor will Scar be of any aid. You'll see."

Mount Aua towered above the Aua Gap, its peak capped with snow after the rains and oftentimes scalded to a balding patch as the heat built later in the dry season. Many tales of the Hundred met or mentioned Mount Aua; songs praised the mountain's strength and watchfulness. Folk did not cut trees on its lower slopes, and its crown seemed to graze the heavens, although Joss had once flown right over the ragged summit, gulping dizzily at thin air. The ledge was scored into the mountain's side about two-thirds of the way up. As Joss and Scar tested the currents and tried several routes to move in close without getting too buffeted by the winds swirling around the peak, Anji canted his body this way and that to get a better look.

"These altars, are they sited to give the Guardians an exceptional vista from which to observe the movements of people in the land? Or to give them a safe haven which few—beyond eagles and determined climbers—could ever hope to reach?"

"Hold on," said Joss.

He flagged the rest of their flight—six eagles in all—to stay in a holding pattern; then he gave Scar the signal for descent. They hit an eddy, dropped, rose, and finally he maneuvered a reluctant Scar in to the wide ledge. The eagle landed, spread his wings in protest, and chirped vociferously.

"Unhook . . . now," said Joss, and the two men dropped together, Joss shielding Anji from the eagle's irritation, but as soon as the men's weight vanished, the eagle folded his wings, tucked his head, and settled into the strange stupor that afflicted him on the altars.

"He's quiet," observed Anji as they paced away from the eagle, an arm's length from the sheer edge. "Hu! We're high up. I feel dizzy."

"Going so high so fast you may get light-headed."

The ledge ran like a divot scored out of an otherwise evenly sloped incline, and its inner edge was lost in the shadowy depths of a low-hanging cave cut into the rock. Up here, the wind really tore; no tree or bush or pile of boulders offered shelter, nothing but that cave, and between the cleft and the rim lay a glimmering pattern etched into the rock.

"Is that sorcery?" asked Anji. "Or a vein of crystal or gems grown into the rock?"

"It's a Guardian's labyrinth. The labyrinth guards the altar, which you can only reach by walking the maze. But anyone who attempts to walk the maze will be cast aside by the gods' protective magic before he can reach their sacred hollow. As I should know, having survived the attempt more than once."

Anji's eyes narrowed as he examined Joss, but he seemed also to be suppressing a smile. "In your reckless youth?"

Joss chuckled. "That's the answer I'll give if pressed."

"So if I try to walk that path, I'll risk being cast out and thrown to my death? What if I don't walk the maze? What if I just cut straight across the ledge to that cave behind, to see what's inside there?"

Joss slipped his flying hood back to drape along his neck and brushed a hand along his hair. "I doubt this is the time to find out, given we've just enlisted the recalcitrant council of Horn in our grand plan to defeat the Star of Life and its commanders. Perhaps you think otherwise?"

Anji laughed, studying the altar. "Prudence dictates caution. And yet . . ." The wind pulled a few strands of hair from his tightly coiled topknot; it tugged at the hem of his black tabard, and shinnied through his sleeves, catching in the coils of leather that bound his forearms, and the supple gloves encasing his hands.

What was the quality in Anji that drew the eye?

Anji was relentless, that was it. He kept after the tasks he meant to finish; he did not let up. People had a way of knowing who could be trusted to bring the sheep home and who might get weary of the shepherding and leave the flock out in the far pasture while bringing home excuses instead.

Anji smiled almost as if he guessed what Joss was thinking. He nodded toward the glittering path. "Do you suppose Guardians can overhear us when we stand here?"

"Cursed if I know. I wouldn't want to take the chance that they can."

"See you that open ground above and to the right? If we fly there we'll be able to speak in private and keep our eye on this altar at the same time."

They hooked back in and flew to a high open slope on the massive mountain, above the tree line, so high up that the air tasted as thin as four-finger gruel.

"We're as private as we're ever likely to be," said Anji when they had walked away from Scar. He glanced up, marking three eagles; the others were patrolling out of their sight. "What is it you wanted to tell me?"

"I thought by the way you looked at me at Horn Hall that you knew!"

"I know that when a man like you asks to speak privately, then I must heed him."

The ledge was partially visible off to the right. The labyrinth's glimmer had a pulsating rhythm buried beneath the surface glitter but present as a heart's beat in the body of a man. Had the gods poured the life's blood of the land into the altars? Threaded it with the land's spirit? Was that how new Guardians were born out of death, because the land—its spirit and blood—flowed through their hearts and into their flesh?

"We've got to talk about the Guardians, Anji."

Anji nodded. "Yes. Go on."

"Lord Radas and his allies have become corrupted and now use the magic of the cloaks for corrupt and selfish ends."

"They're demons, as I've been saying."

Joss shook his head impatiently. "Maybe that's true of the demons of your land. Here, demons are just one of the eight children, often wearing a human face but with their own ways and their own concerns. Just as wildings and lendings and delvings have. Anji, listen. The Guardians are not single spirits who have existed for all this time in the same vessel since the day the gods raised them at Indiyabu. The cloaks carry the authority and sorcery granted by the gods. But the individuals who wear the cloaks change. Humans who died serving justice are raised by a cloak to become a Guardian. But some among the Guardians crossed under the Shadow Gate and became corrupt. It's those Guardians we fight. Not the others."

"What others?" asked Anji, studying Joss's face intently.

"There are Guardians who oppose Lord Radas and his ally, a woman who wears the cloak of Night. Some among the Guardian council are not corrupt, and they seek to—" There was no way to put this except bluntly. "They seek to kill the corrupt Guardians in order that new individuals can wear the cloaks and become Guardians in truth."

"Let's say it's true there are those wearing Guardian cloaks who wish to kill Lord

Radas and his allies. How can we know they are not themselves corrupt and plan to take over the Guardians' council and Lord Radas's army for themselves? And even if they are not yet corrupt, how can we know they will not fall into the shadow in time? If one can be corrupted, then all can."

"The Guardians walked the Hundred for generation after generation, establishing justice, presiding over the assizes. It was only one who became corrupt and then worked to corrupt others, so once we kill her and her allies, the Guardians' council can return to the path of justice."

"I thought," said Anji so softly it was difficult to hear him over the wind, "that Guardians could not be killed."

A man did not have to be a Guardian to understand certain expressions.

"You do know," said Joss. "You've discovered there is a way—a dangerous way—for us to kill a Guardian."

"Two cloaks came to the Hieros in Olossi. Tohon happened to be there, visiting her, so he was present and heard everything they said, which he told to me. He described them as a man dressed as an envoy of Ilu whom you and I saw dying at Dast Korumbos, and the demon girl—who I know died in the desert along the Golden Road on our journey here—who has taken the shape of Shai's slave girl. She killed three of my soldiers. Later, she single-handedly killed a cadre of enemy soldiers. Does that make you inclined to trust or distrust them, Joss?"

"I'm sorry about your soldiers, although it's odd she killed only three if she meant to kill all of you. As for the other, that envoy tried to help when the village was attacked. I'd call that the act of an ally. So these two came to tell the Hieros there is a way to kill Guardians?"

"They seemed willing to trust the Hieros with this information. How did you find out?"

Joss had never spoken of the dreams of Marit that had haunted him over the years. She was his secret, his hidden desire, his heart's ease. "I was very young," he began haltingly.

"The storytellers in the market would make a song of it."

Heat scalded Joss's cheeks. "What does that mean?"

"Only that I've heard this tale before, although you may not recall telling it to me. You were young, and there was a woman, the best woman in all the world. It was Mai who mentioned the song. She is fond of market songs."

No doubt many are sung to her beauty.

Almost the words popped out of his mouth, but he thought better of it. "Marit was the first woman I ever truly loved," he said instead, "and I suppose the last one as well."

"And she appeared to you, wearing a cloak. Demons appear in the guise of those we most love. That makes us vulnerable to their lies."

"Your outlander notions about demons do not hold here in the Hundred. It truly was Marit. She is no lilu who set a trap to snare me."

"Beware wanting her to be something she may not be. One of those she claims to be in alliance with is known to be a demon!" Anger flashed in the captain's expression, and its strength made Joss cursed uncomfortable. "No creature has blue eyes like that ghost girl, none except demons!"

Joss raised both hands, in the gesture of soothing. "Heya! It's understandable you would distrust a woman who killed three of your men. But as you said, we met that envoy of Ilu before. I sensed no corruption in his person."

Anji's mouth flattened. His voice was coiled tight but very even. "How can we sense their corruption? Demons hide what they are behind a mask that makes them appear as human. These who wear the cloaks wield considerable power. They will always be a danger to us."

"Marit fights with us, for justice! She's not our enemy!" The memory of Marit—the feel of her skin under his hands, for there had been nothing inhuman about the flesh Joss had too briefly touched—overwhelmed him. She was as unattainable as she had ever been all those long years he had thought her dead. He had to turn his face into the wind so it could obliterate his tears. All along he had been carrying sorrow with him, a heavier burden than he had ever cared to understand.

Anji unleashed his riding whip and began drawing it through his fingers. "Perhaps they may be telling the truth," he said, although the admission sounded grudging. "Can you find Marit again? If I can speak to her we might learn more about Lord Radas, the cloak of Night, and the other cloaks who obey him. We can account for eight Guardians among these two factions, five opposed to three. That means one remains missing. Where is that one?"

"I don't know how to find Marit. She always found me."

Anji raised an eyebrow. "Can it be she still loves you, even though she is dead?"

The words made the air seem hot and the ground unsteady. Joss passed a hand over his eyes, and the world settled back into place. "She is a Guardian now. None of that matters. She and her allies offered us this weapon so we can fight, because they are Guardians who serve justice and the land."

Anji tapped his whip against a thigh. "If we sever the cloaks from Lord Radas and the other corrupted Guardians they command, it's likely we will cripple Lord Radas's army. Yet if we can sever these individuals from that which binds them to the land, then it seems their cloaks will be released to seek new Guardians. And then what? Will their greed for power not rise all over again? Don't you see the danger in that, Joss?"

"There's always danger. So can we all become corrupt. If that were an argument, then none of us would ever act. The gods raised the Guardians. That some have become corrupted doesn't mean all will be. Justice can be restored. We're obligated to serve justice and restore peace to the land."

"Of course." Anji's smile was rueful, his sigh deeply felt. "We speak of terrible things. You and I know how difficult the struggle to restore peace will be. What have we decided, Commander?"

"If only we'd known this before Zubaidit walked into the enemy's camp!" Aui! Now he must recall kissing Zubaidit! Would these gods-rotted memories of passionate women never cease troubling him? His groin stirred, and he unhooked his drinking pouch, unsealed it, and took a long swig of sweet cordial. "Captain?"

Anji accepted the offering, drinking deeply as well. Shadows drew a haze over the high slopes of Mount Aua; a streamer of wispy cloud trailed off the icy crown.

"If the corrupted Guardians discover what we know, they'll be put on their guard," added Joss. "So any person given this knowledge who confronts a Guardian must act immediately and succeed on their first attempt to sever them from the cloak. How likely is it that they can?"

"Only a person trained in the most exacting manner can be trusted. Can any of your reeves act no matter what the circumstance, even if they are themselves wounded or dying, and press forward to complete a task with no expectation of surviving the attempt?"

"Of course they can! They do all the time. You forget, Anji, we know full well that we die if our eagle dies. But as for killing a Guardian . . . it's hard to say if any would be willing to undertake an act that would seem blasphemous, as if striking at the gods. I'm not even sure I could bring myself to do it. What of your men?"

"Those of my soldiers I do not trust completely to be able to accomplish what I ask of them, do not still ride with me. Nevertheless, we must be cautious. If we could reach Zubaidit with this intelligence, she would act. Yet to attempt to reach her, if she's truly placed herself within Lord Radas's army, puts all at risk of discovery if the messenger is captured and interrogated by one of the cloaks."

"We are caught between too few knowing to manage the task, and so many knowing that we give away our plan."

"We walk a precarious path," agreed the captain. "Tell only those you trust to carry out the act. Let them be ready."

Joss laughed. "That's what I admire about you. When you decide to act, you don't hesitate."

Anji smiled briefly, as at a jest only he had heard. He gestured toward Scar. "Every day you hook yourself into the harness of a creature that could as easily eat you for its meal as tolerate your weight, for it would soar more easily without you. Is that not admirable?"

"No, for I'm doing my duty, as the gods decreed. Anyhow, Scar doesn't frighten me. The eagles know their duty better than we know ours. They can't be corrupted. They are as you see them. No mask. Nothing concealed. In that way they are more honest than we can ever be."

"More honest than we should be, maybe. Few people would truly be pleased, I think, to know what thoughts fly through the minds of their lovers and kinsmen and comrades."

"Maybe it would be like being flayed," Joss said, staring out over the vista and thinking of Marit: what she had become and how it isolated her. The woman he had loved still lived within her cloaked body; he knew that, because he had kissed her. But his touch had scorched her; it had told her too much, things she did not want to know. Maybe no one should know that much about another person. "Our masks protect us, don't they?" he said at last.

"So we must hope," said Anji.

PART SIX: CHOICES

32

NEKKAR WOKE BEFORE dawn and stretched to discover that, as always, Vassa had left his pallet without waking him. She returned to her clan's compound to take care of their needs first, as she must, but her presence lingered. As always, he smiled because their love was, even after all these years, a wellspring of unexpected joy.

Often enough, it was also his only smile of the day.

His stomach growled as he stowed the pallet and blanket in the cupboard. He dressed quickly, careful not to strain threadbare cloth. He kneeled on the pillow in front of his ostiary's desk, bent his head, and in the silence that held Toskala before first bell rang across the city, he prayed to Ilu the Herald, asking for strength to get through just this one day. As long as he had enough strength for *this* day, he could keep going.

And he had to keep going. So many people depended on him.

Two envoys, Seyra and Doni, waited for him on the porch. How they used to tease Doni for his plumpness! Now the young man's cheeks were hollow and his loose tunic and trousers accentuated how thin he'd gotten.

Seyra looked as frail as a wisp of straw. "Holy One. The night passed peacefully."

He nodded. "Thanks be to blessed Ilu for watching over us. Any disturbances?"

"Not that we heard or saw, Holy One."

The best he could now say of a new day was that no catastrophe had troubled the night. Two eagles spiraled aloft, so although many reeves and passengers had flown off Law Rock some days ago in a mass exodus, not all had abandoned them. That was something.

At the trough, an elderly envoy winched up a bucket of water from the well and poured it into the stone basin. The splash hit loudly in the hazy half-light. They washed, murmuring the cleansing prayer as the retiring night watch and the dawn-rising envoys joined them. Afterward, they walked as a group past rows of struggling vegetables being grown in the courtyard.

On the porch of the sanctuary they slipped out of their sandals. They sang the dawn prayers quietly so as not to waken the novices in the barracks next door. It was better to let the young ones sleep through the morning prayers than wake too early into the claws of hunger.

As his hands folded to close the last prayer, he bent his head to inhale a final breath of fragile peace. The matted floor cushioned his knees. His right shoulder ached. His left ankle twinged. His stomach gurgled. He raised his eyes to the dais, trying to quiet his mind. On the altar, in a latticed iron frame, sat a large nodule of polished turquoise veined with a spider's web pattern like a fireling's lost thread. Ilu's Eye was always watchful. He was surprised the occupiers had not stolen the precious stone along with everything else, but some at least still feared to rob the gods' altars.

That would come next. It was only a matter of time. With each step they took down the path of corruption, the next became easier.

The Star of Life army had occupied Toskala for almost six months.

With a sigh, he stood. He walked among the envoys and servants, commending them on their night's watch or reminding himself of their day's coming activities. The men must eat a scant bowl of porridge before they went out of the compound to work on building projects for the occupiers. Three times, now, young envoys had not returned, having been killed or imprisoned for what reason he could not fathom; he told them to keep their heads down and their mouths shut. Yet occupiers need have no reason as long as they held the sword and you held nothing. The males must go out so the females could remain inside or else risk multiple indignities. Therefore, the women gardened in the courtyard for such sparse gleanings as they could coax from its reluctant dirt, including the terig leaf they sold to the soldiers for a few paltry vey. All other work within the compound they accomplished as well, shut away within the walls. They raked the dirt into complex patterns, just to lend variety to their day. It was a cruel life to be so confined. Not one complained. No one within the temple had starved yet.

"Holy One, before you go out, please eat." Doni and Seyra waited with a steaming bowl of nai porridge.

They would plague him until he ate, or threaten him by refusing to eat until he did. So he ate. The nai was bland but filling; his mouth hungered for it, but his heart rebelled because so many in the city had no nai porridge to ease their belly's ache.

Trying to hide their relieved smiles, they hurried away with the empty bowl.

"Make sure you rest!" he called after them. "Tired eyes cannot see and tired ears cannot hear!"

The nai sat well in his belly. His legs felt stronger. It was time to go.

He tied an empty bag to his belt for the rations chits he would be issued and clasped his blue ostiary's cloak around his neck. Finally, he drank deeply of cool water from the ladle hanging at the well. At the gate, the men were lined up to leave. Today's gatekeepers—two tough young female envoys armed with staves and knives—shifted the bars. As the men passed, Nekkar touched each on the forehead with a blessing for safe return. When all had passed through, he nodded at the young women. Their expressions were as tight as drums, and they were weary.

"You're the last of the night watch?" he asked them.

"Yes, Holy One. There come our relief now."

He heard footsteps behind him. "Kellas did not return last night?"

"Neh, Holy One. Did you expect him so soon?"

"Neh, of course not." He couldn't expect Kellas back for two days at least. "I forgot. I shouldn't have mentioned it."

They wanted to ask where Kellas had gone but knew better than to inquire. Soldiers might come pounding on the gate with any purpose at all in mind, and the cloaks—should you be so unfortunate as to be forced to stand before one—could eat out your heart.

"Walk safely with the Herald, Holy One," they murmured.

Herald's staff in hand, he passed under the triple-linteled gate marking Ilu's holy precincts. At this time of day, men like his envoys and novices hurried in small groups to their assigned labor gangs, but otherwise the streets were empty. He checked the closed gates of the compounds. No white ribbons hung from any gate posts this morning, to mark a death inside. That was something.

At each gate he rang the bell and waited for a voice to query. "What news, Holy One?"

"The reeves still fly. Law Rock is still ours. What news inside?"

They might say, "All are alive, by the gods' mercy," or "Grandfather is refusing to eat so the young ones can have his portion," or "My cousin never came back from that gang they sent to fell trees, is there news, Holy One?"

Then he would go on.

Today's guards in Lele Square were too busy sucking on the harsh smoke of rolled-up terig leaf to acknowledge him, but they followed his progress with suspicious gazes as he circled the square to check the ribbons hung on gates. On the Red Clover merchant house hung a pair of ribbons, orange twined with white to mark a sickness, maybe a lung fever or a belly cramping; a single white ribbon marked a death in the adjoining compound, a clan of basket weavers. Otherwise, Lele Square had weathered another night.

An old woman draped in the undyed linen robe worn by Atiratu's mendicants limped along the eastern shadows of the square, leaning heavily on a stick.

One of the soldiers broke off from his companions and headed for her, skirting the public well. "Heya, old woman."

She halted to look, absorbing the insult.

"I have an itch on my cock. What do you have to cure it? Cursed girls must be wiping something on me, eh?"

Her gaze took in Nekkar's approach but she turned to answer the impatient soldier. "Truly, my nephew, if your tool is itching, then you must wash it every day with soap and a tincture of cloud-white oil, and you must not let it enter any woman or man's passage for one full turning of the moon. If it still itches afterward, wait another month."

"The hells! One full month! It doesn't itch that badly!"

"If you do nothing to rest it now it will turn red and develop sores, and then grow green with the Witherer's fungus. After that, I can't help you."

He yelped. For one sharp intake of breath, Nekkar thought the man meant to hit an elder, but he pushed brusquely past Nekkar and strode back to his fellows, who were laughing as the man's face darkened with embarrassment.

"Is that true?" Nekkar asked softly, careful not to look after the retreating soldier.

"Greetings of the day, Holy One," she said.

"Greetings of the day, Holy One. There's a sickness in the Red Clover compound."

"So have I come. There's a flux over in the masons' court alleys. Four children and one old uncle are dead. I fear their well has become fouled." She had a dagger's gaze, her mouth growing thin in an expression more like a stab than a smile. "As for the other, yes, it is true, except for the Witherer's fungus. The itching won't kill him, but if I can scare him into keeping his wick dry for one month, that's one less man sticking it where it isn't wanted, isn't it? I heard there's baskets for sale in Bell Quarter. Need you some?"

This news was unexpected, come sooner than he'd hoped. Kellas had been smuggled across the city in hopes of getting him up to Law Rock via the same route the southern spy Zubaidit had taken months ago, in a basket up a hidden cliff. Despite the strict curfew and restricted movement between quarters, Toskala's priests and clans and guilds had woven a network of communication across the city, although they dared not risk it often.

"No, not today, but I hope to buy a basket on the first day of Wolf Month, eh? What of you, Geerto?" He ostentatiously rubbed his right shoulder, as though he were asking her for advice.

She grasped his arm. "You've heard the rumor that the great flight of eagles some days ago, all double-laden, means that Clan Hall has abandoned Justice Square and Law Rock."

"That's why we sent Kellas, to find out—"

"Ah, of course." She made him raise his right hand high while she kept a hand cupped over his shoulder. "Anyway, yesterday the sergeant at Stone Quarter's gate told me the reeves had gone for good and that I could now go out to the brickyards."

"Eiya!" He dropped his hand. He had never stopped thinking of those three small children lost after Toskala's fall. No matter how often he asked, he was never allowed to go outside the city.

"I laid out five dead ones and sang the prayers of departing over their corpses."

He forced out the words, although they emerged with a vile taste. "Is it true they're burning the dead?"

She made a gesture to avert malign spirits. "There are fires, it is true, but I have not seen corpses placed on fire with my own eyes. If it is done, it is being done at night."

"What of the living?"

"Those able to work I am not allowed to speak to. The weak, ill, and dying are dragged out of the way. Not even under shelter, mind you. Left out in the sun." She swallowed several times, squeezed shut her eyes, and at length found enough breath to go on. "I got some honey water down the throats of three dying ones, enough to make their passage a little sweeter. I bound scrapes and cuts, and fed a strengthening tea to seventeen other children, although what good will come of that? All I have done is allow the poor things to be released to toil again."

"Better than dying."

"Is it?"

He bent his head, the sun already hot on his neck. They were entering the season of Furnace Sky, when the heat would become brutal and the suffering more intense.

"Yes, it is," he said at last. "We resist by living."

She touched his hand. "Thank you, Holy One. I had forgotten."

Her fatigue was evident in her drooping shoulders and in the creased lines alongside her mouth. "Never think you have forgotten, because every day you walk out to treat those who are ill is a day you have remembered."

"Heya!" shouted the soldiers. "You old folk! Get on, or go home."

They parted, she to her tasks and he to his. First, he made his way toward the market, pausing by Astarda's Arch. When the streets in either direction lay empty, he slipped into the old nook where, according to temple history, there had once stood an age-blackened statue of Kotaru the Thunderer. Five months ago he had arranged for a new statue to be placed there, crudely carved but with a compartment cunningly concealed in the Thunderer's right palm in the hinge where the god grasped his lightning's spear. He twisted open the compartment and fished out three rations chits, each one with three marks burned into the wood as a message: Nine provision wagons had entered Stone Quarter at dusk last night. There was something else rolling at the base of the hole: three glass beads and a single copper vey. The vey was new; he had no idea how to interpret it.

He held still in the nook as men passed, none glancing his way, then slipped out and fell into step behind them. The market, too, had changed in the last six months. The lack of chatter and laughter always struck him first, and after that the absence of the much-loved smells of oily slip-fry stands and steaming noodle water. The only foodstuffs for sale were dry goods and garden produce being sold out of four permanent stalls guarded by soldiers and presided over by well-fed men who spoke too boisterously.

The other merchants seated cross-legged on blankets or on stools under canvas awnings were older folk, mostly men but also some elderly aunties and grandmothers. They offered goods for sale, but few were buying. He paced down the lane of ornament sellers, who had combs and ribbons and such luxuries that no one could afford any longer, until he marked a shallow basket heaped with glass beads like those he held cupped in a hand. The woman was, like him, of middle age, with her hair bound in cloth. She had a scar on one cheek and her left arm in a sling.

"I'm selling beads, not buying them, Holy One," she said in a pleasant voice.

He pressed the copper vey down beside the three beads.

She bent forward as if to examine the vey. "Last week," she murmured, "a work gang from Stone Quarter was sent out to fell trees. Now we hear the entire gang was pressed onto a barge and sent downriver to Nessumara."

"Who did you hear this from?"

"One lad jumped into the river and pretended to drown, but he was a strong swimmer. He's in hiding. Clerks made a list of every man in that gang, so if they find him, they'll cleanse him."

He rose. "Neh, verea, I can't afford that today. My apologies."

She lifted a hand in the merchant's gesture of acquiesence. "Tomorrow, then," she said in the typical way of the marketplace. "Go well with the Herald, Holy One."

There were lines at the four stalls selling rice and nai, and as Nekkar approached the nearest one he watched as an old man made his slow retreat with a covered basket so small it was difficult to believe he was buying for anyone other than himself.

"Ver, if you please, a word," said Nekkar to the old fellow, but when the man looked at him with a frightened expression, Nekkar waved him on.

Instead, he walked to the head of the line where a woman with her head and torso swathed in a shawl was trying to bargain with the bored merchant.

"Ver, maybe if you would take this bolt of wedding silk in trade—"

"For a tey of rice?"

"One tey?" Her shock registered in her drawn and weary face.

Nekkar stepped up beside her as the silent folk waiting in the lines pretended not to watch. "A fine piece of wedding silk, verea." He smiled at the merchant. "A tey of rice, ver. That would feed me today. This bolt of silk is worth twenty leya, surely."

"It's worth what I'll pay for it," retorted the merchant, adding, after a pause, "Holy One. Rice and nai are expensive. Those who can't afford to buy must wait for their rations chit like everyone else."

"You have a good supply of provisions today, ver." Nekkar indicated the sacks of rice and nai piled on wooden pallets. "Where are you purchasing?"

"Same as always. What's it to you?"

"Some have plenty, while others starve. If you bring those sacks as an offering down to the temple, I'll make sure to distribute them among the compounds."

"Tss! You'll just sell it yourself and pocket the profit."

But he faltered as Nekkar caught his gaze and stared him down.

"Think you so, ver? If you think so, say it louder to all these folk waiting here so I can be sure I'm being accused in public, and not in whispers."

But the man could not speak such a lie out loud. Maybe it was Nekkar's steady gaze, or the simmering anger of people forced to buy at outrageous prices; maybe it was the restless presence of soldiers loaned him by the sergeant in charge, big burly lads recruited from out of town.

"Give the woman twenty tey of rice for the silk, ver, and I'll go on."

"You'll go on," said the merchant, rising belligerently, "because otherwise I'll have these fellows escort you to the well and toss you in."

The murmur that spilled outward from this threat flowed quickly through the crowd, but quieted when the soldiers spun their staffs, looking for a bit of excitement.

"The gods judge, ver," replied Nekkar. "If you cheat others to enrich yourself, then you are already dead."

Yet words did not feed starving people. He walked with a heavy heart down Lumber Avenue to the rations warehouse on Terta Square, for his morning cup of tea with the sergeant in charge of Stone Quarter. This ritual took place on the porch, in full sight of the square. Laborers were adding on to the barracks yet again, hammering on the roof and sawing planks. A pair of older men hoisted buckets from the public well, while several anxious lads brought ladles of water around for the thirsty workers. In another time—how long ago it seemed now!—the well would have been surrounded by chatting women, and handsome girls would have commanded the ladles with a smile and a tart word, but they were all gone now, hiding in their compounds.

A young woman wrapped tightly in a best-quality silk taloos brought cups of steaming tea to the sergeant, who slapped her on her well-rounded bottom. Three other young women peeped at him from inside the sergeant's quarters. One he knew by sight, a girl from the masons' courts who had been forced weeping into the sergeant's rooms.

"We had some trouble over in the masons' courts last night, uncle," said the sergeant, smiling. The day looked good to him, and in truth he was easier to deal with than the last sergeant had been. For one thing, he pretended to a modicum of respect for Nekkar's authority. "Three young criminals throwing rocks at the patrol. If not reined in, these hotheads will disturb every peaceful night with their violence."

"Where are they now?" Nekkar had learned to keep his tone even so no feeling spilled.

"The one that fought had to be put down, like a frothing dog. The other two are in the pen out back. Maybe you can talk some sense into them before they're cleansed."

"Perhaps they might be whipped and given a sentence of labor in the brickyards. Lads will lose their temper."

"One of my men got a big cut on the head and a concussion from getting grazed by a brick. If I let that go, more will come out. They brought it on themselves."

The cup trembled in Nekkar's hands. The pretty girl in the expensive silk was clutching one of the porch pillars so hard her hand had whitened at the knuckles, but she had such a bland smile on her face that she looked stupid. He'd not seen her before, nor had she the familiar features of any of the local Stone Quarter families. "I'll speak to them, Sergeant. What of the rations chits for today?"

"We've got nothing for you today."

"Folk who don't eat, can't work."

"Folk who don't work, can't eat. No wagons came in yesterday, so there's nothing to distribute."

This blatant lie Nekkar let pass, even as he thought of the sacks of rice and nai in the market being offered at prices no one could afford. "Perhaps men might be allowed to work in groups in the fields, to prepare the ground for the rains. Each clan can grow rice for its own needs."

"Neh, I doubt Captain Parron will agree. He's got laborers on the fields already."

"Yet we are always short of food, Sergeant."

"There have been enough incidents outside the walls—fights, runaways, all manner of trouble—that the captain will not allow it, and you know he's in charge, not me."

"If folk are not allowed to plant fields, then what will there be to eat a year from now?"

The sergeant shrugged. "I'll be transferred on by then." He beckoned to the lass and, when she hurried over, pinched her behind and afterward handed her the cup. "Take this inside."

She hurried inside, not looking back.

"I haven't seen her before," said Nekkar cautiously.

"Good breasts and ass, but a bit of a stammering lackwit. Look how she forgot to take your cup. She's a village girl from upcountry Captain Parron was keeping, but he got in new girls last night and passed this one on to me. Tasty enough, eh?"

Nekkar thought of Seyra, of all the young female novices and envoys under his protection. He might have raged or wept but instead sipped at the dregs of his tea, the leavings like ashes in his mouth.

"I can't keep four women. I've had that girl Fala the longest. She's from around here, isn't she? I'll send her on to the barracks."

If the sergeant heard Fala's gasp from the shadows, he did not show it by expression or comment.

Nekkar felt his face burn with anger and fear, but he kept his voice calm. "Fala is from the masons' court. I'd wager you could make those mason clans whose lads are giving you trouble a bargain. Let the girl go back home, and they'll rope in those stone throwers. Keep things quiet there."

The sergeant scratched the stubble on his head. Like most of the army, he kept his hair trimmed short against lice. "I'll think on it, but there's been some complaints at the barracks for want of recreation, so I need to shift new hierodules in there."

For all that Nekkar bound his tongue every gods-rotted day, that he paced out the pattern of his days with deliberate speed so as not to attract unwanted attention, this was too cursed much. "*Hierodules!* Hierodules serve the Merciless One of their own will! They are not forced onto men's pallets!"

Anger creased the sergeant's mouth, and he drew the whip he carried from the belt and smacked it so hard against the nearest pillar that Nekkar flinched. Then the man laughed, and he whistled three short notes, and the girl Fala came hurrying out like a dog called to heel. She crouched, head lowered, shoulders trembling.

"Yes, Master," she said, the words so soft Nekkar barely heard them. That the sergeant made her address him as slave to master only made it worse.

"You've a hankering to be a hierodule, don't you, lass?" said the sergeant with a grin, gaze flashing to Nekkar.

Hers flashed to the ostiary as well, her eyes black with desperation.

"Look at me!" He pressed the whip against her cheek.

She raised her chin, tears winding down her dark cheeks. "Yes, ver. I apprenticed to the Witherer, but I always wanted to be a hierodule."

"Well, then, take your things and get over there, report to the barracks."

She tried to rise, but her legs would not lift her.

Nekkar rose, cup clenched in his right hand. "Truly, Sergeant, let the girl go home. She's done enough, surely, served you for three months by my reckoning."

The sergeant drew his whip along Fala's neck. She was a pretty girl, alas for her in these times; her clan always made the proper offerings; she'd been betrothed to a young man from Flag Quarter, but Nekkar did not know if he still lived.

"Surely I can do that," said the sergeant with a smile lingering on his arrogant face, "but I need another girl in the barracks lest my soldiers grow restless. So if you'll send along one of those young novices you keep gated up in the temple, that lass—or lad—can take the place of this one. As soon as you send her, Fala can go home."

For the space of a breath, for the space of a bell, a day, a year, Nekkar lost sight and hearing, every sensation except the stink of failure and the rotting sweetness of a pain he could not describe or touch but could only taste like vomit on his tongue.

The sergeant laughed heartily, and Nekkar had to squeeze his walking staff with both hands to stop himself from slamming its haft into the man's face. His weak ankle shifted, and he tottered sideways. The poor girl had to steady him.

"Forgive me, Holy One," she whispered as he swayed.

For what she thought she was apologizing he could not fathom. As if his distress was her fault! What manner of holy one was he? She had endured for months while he had kept his novices and envoys protected behind the temple walls. And yet how could he throw any one of them to the beasts to be ripped and rended?

"The gods are cursed useless now, aren't they, Holy One?" sneered the sergeant.

Was it true? Had the gods abandoned them? Was this a test?

Neh. It was not true. The people of Toskala were not trapped by the gods' indifference but by human action.

"You speak lightly, Sergeant, because it is not a woman of your clan who will be abused every night by multiple men, none of whom will come to her with the respect and awe due to an acolyte of the Devourer. When Ushara's temples closed their gates to your soldiers, you knew then that the gods did not approve of what you did."

"And what happened to Ushara's temples, eh? We broke down the gates and took what we wanted. They should not have refused us."

"What you do is wrong. You know it, and I know it. You present me now with a terrible choice not because you want me to make a choice but because you want me to suffer for having to make the choice. Therefore, it is no choice you offer me. It is not my responsibility, but yours."

The sergeant's expression had grown tight in a way Nekkar knew presaged danger, but he could not stop speaking. "Please allow Fala to return to her clan. If the provision wagons have come in, let rations chits be distributed. I ask you, by the agreement made when the army first occupied the city, to remember that the people of Toskala must eat in order to work. Please allow me to take chits representing a fair portion of rice and nai, and I will distribute them to the clans and compounds in Stone Quarter as I've been doing for almost six months now."

"Get out, before I whip you," growled the sergeant. "Fala, get your things and go to the barracks. Neh, leave the silks. You'll not need them there. If you're still here after I've finished my morning meal, I'll whip you."

"Let her come with me," said Nekkar.

The whip's snap laid open his cheek.

Fala screamed and stumbled away into the interior. The women who had been watching from within scattered like mice.

Nekkar let the blood drip as he hobbled away, his bad ankle wobbling, while the sergeant shouted angrily at his women and his slaves and his attendants. No whip, no arrow, no spear followed the ostiary to the gate that opened into the courtyard in back, but the cursing, laughing guards refused to let him in to check on the lads imprisoned in the pens.

With such dignity as he could gather, he set off on his usual resting day round, only today he had to tell each compound expecting a rations chit that today there would be nothing and that he did not know when the next rations chits would be available. He did not tell them that the sergeant was hoarding all the provisions and handing them out to a few select merchants to sell at inflated prices.

Folk certainly saw his bleeding cheek and marked the whip's slash, but none asked. He was glad of that, because had they asked he would have to tell them the truth: He was whipped because he could not spare a young woman from abuse, a grandfather from starving, young men from being enslaved to the army or cleansed on the post, rice and nai from being stolen, children from dying in the brickyards.

He walked his round as always. Today, empty-handed.

He returned before the curfew to the temple, and Vassa cleaned the dried blood off the cut but did not ask him how he had come by it. He counted his people, and on this evening every single one came home, all except Kellas. He led the dusk prayers, then sat on his porch as the night bell tolled.

"What humiliations is Fala enduring?" he asked Vassa, who sat cross-legged beside him shaping a basket with her cunning hands. She needed no light to do this work, having woven all her life. If she did not keep her hands busy, she often said, she would go crazy. "Will Grandfather's spirit pass the gate tonight? What will happen to those sent south?"

"They have come to love cruelty because it feeds them," she said.

"Must I ask one of mine to go to the barracks and offer herself in place of Fala?"

Her handwork did not cease. "What makes you think they will honor the bargain? They may just take the other one as well, and then two will suffer."

"That is a story we tell ourselves. So we can sit here, and eat what we have, and listen to our young ones sleep at peace. Yet if we opened our ears, we would hear nothing but weeping."

"True, but it doesn't change the truth of what I say," said Vassa. "When people see you in the street, they discover their hearts are still strong. Thus they can endure another day."

Another day. Even another month. For how long before they succumbed to despair and obeyed while telling themselves it was for the best? Yet to voice such thoughts aloud was to start down that terrible path, so he kept silence.

33

CURSED ROCKS.

Nallo could not imagine a more idiotic training regimen, yet here she was flying sweeps with her new wing hauling a cursed basket of cursed rocks, each rock about the size of her fist. Poor Tumna took most of the strain, although the motion of banking or rising caused the basket to bump so heavily against Nallo's legs she was sure she'd end up mottled with bruises.

As if hauling a gods-rotted basket of rocks to lob at miscreants would do any good.

They flew out in wings of six: From her position she could see Warri and his eagle Dogkiller out on the right flank of the wing. She was next, flying at slightly higher elevation, and inside of her but lower flew Pil with Sweet in the second striker position. First striker, and head of the wing, was Peddonon with Jabi, flying yet lower beyond and in front of Pil. The third striker and left flank were Kanness with Lovely—a worse-tempered raptor than Tumna—and Orya with lazy Candle. The eagles tolerated each other—they had to, or no reeve hall could function—but Peddonon had had to try several different formations with the eighteen reeves left to him at Law Rock in order to send out wings whose eagles wouldn't take territorial swipes at one another. Even so, Tumna was cursed suspicious of Candle, enough that Nallo felt a tug whenever the raptor looked that way.

They had taken off from Law Rock midmorning and pushed south, practicing maneuvers and resting between times on powerful high thermals. That the land should look so peaceful astonished her. With the sun shining above, the river flowed like a spill of light away to their right. The variegated colors of the dry season gave the landscape an intense texture: fields stubbled with gold stalks not yet turned under; ponds fringed with a wrack of withered weeds and cracked dry soil where the waters had retreated; orchards and woodland seeping green. Dusty irrigation ditches and empty paths and minor roads netted the land, seeming almost to have some deeper pattern when seen from on high.

A whistle caught her ear. Pil was flagging with an orange cloth: *Alert! Follow close!* She tugged on the jesses, and Tumna, sighting an object on the ground, followed Sweet and Jabi. Nallo grabbed her own orange flag on its stick, thumping a knee against the basket while she was at it. Eihi! Pain throbbed, a lump blossoming beneath the skin.

This new formation was total rubbish, a cursed stupid plan.

Pil flagged with the orange and white stripe that meant: *Attack!*

The hells!

Tumna dropped, wings outstretched, and they sailed over woodland broken with clearings, unturned fields, and distant villages in the midst of rings of cultivated land. When she saw what Peddonon was aiming for, her heart seemed to rise up into her throat so she could not breathe. A heavily loaded cart pulled by two dray beasts was being coaxed across the ford of a substantial stream, a tributary river that wound toward the River Istri, now out of sight to the west. The dray beasts had decided they would rather wallow in the water, because they were trying to pull off the gravel bar that sliced partway across the ford and on into deeper waters where they could relax. One soldier was whipping the dray master; two others were whipping the animals. Another pointed at the eagles, alerting his fellows. There were too many to attack, twenty at least.

Yet Peddonon cut low, Kanness approaching from behind. Pil climbed, circling back.

Were they really going to try to hit this cadre?

Peddonon swooped over the ford as the dray beasts took advantage of the soldiers' distraction to pull hard for the wallow. The wagon began to slide off the gravel bar.

Peddonon upended his basket. Two arrows flashed upward through the hail of stones. Unlike the rocks, the spent arrows fell harmlessly back to earth.

Splashes, shouts, and the panicked blundering bellows of the dray beasts marked the impact of the first volley. Kanness came right behind, dumping his basket. A stone struck a dray beast right on the head, and the animal staggered violently, snapping its yokes as it collapsed to its knees. The cart yawed, tipped, teetered; the ox toppled, and the second, still bellowing, thrashed to try to break free and keep its head above as the cart tumbled over and into the deeper water.

Nallo had overshot. She tugged so hard on the jesses that Tumna objected with an outraged chuff, but the raptor had her hunting blood up; she banked sharply, returning for the kill.

The dray master was chest deep in water, trying to free the beasts. One soldier floated facedown in the water as Orya's basket, cut loose, spun earthward in the wake of a spent volley of rocks. Another man fled toward the far shore, his bow arm dangling limply, his weapon lost as he tried to drag his sword free with the other.

A group of captives cowered on the road, roped together, unable to move. The soldiers bolted back the way they had come, heading for the safety of a copse several hundred paces away. Nallo released her basket, but she had cursed totally misjudged their speed and her angle and distance and the entire gods-rotted pummel of stones rained uselessly on dirt.

They tucked their heads and kept sprinting. None saw Pil and Sweet stooping from above, or Peddonon and Kanness coming in at an angle.

Sweet struck with such breathtaking precision that Nallo shouted. The talons gripped, plunging right into a man's torso as he screamed. Then the raptor, beating its wings, rose; none of the soldiers even attempted an attack. They were too stunned. Pil, turning in his harness, released first one arrow, then another, and a third and fourth in quick succession as Sweet rose. Two arrows hit their mark. Sweet released her prey.

Kanness's Lovely struck, talons raised and wings battering, as if she was taking a deer. The men scattered, one uselessly flinging a spear in the direction of the eagle's tail feathers. Peddonon slammed a javelin into the back of the bold spearman as Jabi grazed another man, missing the strike and pulling up hard as Peddonon released his grip on his javelin. One soldier had the presence of mind to nock an arrow to his bow.

Nallo had overshot again. She passed over the ford. The captives struggled at their bonds, and the dray master out in the current had grabbed a dead man's sword and cut free one beast. He was now diving in and out of the tangle to try to save the other while the prisoners shouted at him to come cut them loose instead while they still had a chance to run.

Warri and Orya remained aloft, and that cursed idiot Warri hadn't even released his stones, which when you thought about it described him very well.

The hells!

Two soldiers ran up a path on the far side of the ford. Seeing her, they scrambled for the nearest bushes, any scant cover that might protect them.

She felt Tumna's attention like a burst of fire in her own body, a powerful spear of hunting hunger. Eihi! She hadn't cut the basket free; the cursed thing was in her way, but Tumna was already diving. She grabbed one of the four thin javelins stowed in a quiver to her right; no time to fumble for a knife and cut the basket loose.

How did she ever get to be such a gods-rotted slack-minded lackwit?

One man dove sideways into a crackling mass of thornberry.

Tumna struck the other.

Her wings flared; she thumped down so hard that Nallo pitched sideways and slammed into the raptor's body, then stubbed her foot on the hard dirt, but Tumna's powerful talons pinned them—and the soldier—to the earth. He twitched. He didn't yet know he was dead. He croaked, struggling to get free, and Nallo plunged her javelin into his back, right where she thought the heart must be. He sagged and went slack.

A howl. A roar. Behind her, the other soldier attacked.

In the instant, she thought: *He'll kill me from behind. How do I fight?*

All her lessons and training scattered like dross.

Tumna was faster than either of them.

She struck in one movement, piercing the man through the chest as Nallo drew up her legs and dangled in the harness watching a man die an arm's length from her face. He looked like a rabbit caught out in the field, too stunned to understand what was happening. His mouth opened and shut as if he had forgotten what he meant to say. Bubbles of blood beaded at his nostrils, sucked in and out. She grabbed her knife, unhooked the harness, and dropped into a crouch beside him. His gaze did not follow her movement, but Tumna squawked irritably.

"Hush!" Nallo snapped. "Do what you want with him."

She ducked out from under the raptor's wings and circled around to the other man, who amazingly was not yet dead. Somehow, he was trying to pull himself up the path. She got a foot under his body and shoved him over. She bent, grasped his chin, and held it back to get a full curve. Then she cut deep to sever the windpipe, the foodpipe, and the blood vessels in one strong stroke, as she'd learned to do growing up among goat herders in the Soha Hills.

Battle wasn't much different from slaughtering goats, when you thought of it that way. You killed when you had to, not for any joy you took in it.

Tumna shook the other man loose. She bent her head and nudged him.

"Heya!" shouted Nallo.

By now the cursed basket was half crushed. She cut the gods-rotted thing free, wiped her knife's blade such as she could in two swipes on the weaving, then shoved the blade back in its sheath. Pulling her reeve's baton, she approached Tumna brandishing it as the training regimen had taught her, as if anyone believed eagles actually feared the little stick of a baton that the reeves used to "train" and "control" the huge raptors. Tumna, anyway, was perfectly able and willing to rip off the head of her reeve, if her reeve annoyed her. But Nallo had been told time and again that it were better for a reeve to sacrifice herself than to allow her eagle to feast on human flesh.

Yet Tumna was only playing; she wasn't hungry, or inclined to eat; she rolled the body around and gave up, impatient with the corpse's lack of activity. It was only fun when they tried to escape.

"Aui!" muttered Nallo, hot and cold at once.

She heard folk calling, "Cut us loose, you gods-rotted—"

A dray beast bellowed. A man cursed.

She would have run down to slap some order into them, but Peddonnon had been clear in his instructions: Do not stay on the ground.

Flight gave the reeves their advantage; on the ground, they were easy to kill.

She whistled, and Tumna stretched her wings, looking around as if hoping for more entertaining hunting. Nallo ducked under the shadow of her wingspan and hooked in.

"Up!"

Up.

The eagle's majestic strength carried her. The unbelievable sight of the skirmish unfolded beneath her: the dray master had finally gotten both animals out of the water and was helping the captives free themselves. Some had plunged into the water to recover weapons or gear; trails of red spun out in the water, marking dead soldiers in the current. Three women were coming up the path in Nallo's direction, and

Nallo gestured to them, waving an arm to indicate where they should look for the fallen.

Shouts and cheers and the stamping of feet on earth sent her on her way, just as an audience showed its approval at the Festival contests. She was grinning as Tumna slipped into a weak thermal and got some lift. She couldn't really shout across the gap between eagles, but she found her place in the formation easily enough.

Peddonon flagged a "follow me," and they continued south toward the delta, an intense green shivering mass of vegetation ahead. Kanness was laughing as he banked into place; not that she could quite make out the lineaments of his face, but he was a hearty laugher; she knew him well enough by now to recognize how his torso and head looked when he was full-on guffawing.

She didn't feel like laughing, precisely, but it was so cursed good to know they'd finally inflicted some damage. After all the months of feeling like useless observers.

Why in the hells hadn't the reeves done this earlier?

We're not helpless any longer.

That cursed Commander Joss and his gods-rotted outlander ally had been right. Imagine that.

A month ago, the enemy had been dispersed across the plain of Istria and the lower reaches of Haldia, stretching to the Haya Gap, pillaging, burning, and generally causing havoc. Now it seemed everyone was marching toward Nessumara. Barges moved downriver, laden with slaves or building materials. Gangs worked in the western forests, felling logs, which were lashed into huge rafts and floated toward Skerru.

As they flew downriver after the skirmish, she observed with new eyes. That gang of men being marched under guard downroad was not vulnerable because they were guarded by too many soldiers for one wing to attack. Yet there, several mey from the river in heavily wooded hills, a half cadre of men hauling wagons was too far away from foot-based relief to call for help; a single wing could scatter them, and two wings working in concert—if such a thing could be managed—could obliterate them before their company came to their rescue.

Her hands itched, eager to pull Tumna's jesses, to go on the hunt. To strike a blow.

When the wing passed over the town of Skerru, she saw people like ants boiling, all hard at work building what looked like rafts. Something big was up, for sure.

She, Pil, Kanness, and Peddonon set down on Copper Hall's islet while Orya and Warri remained aloft. Three fawkners hustled over to greet them, a cursed sight friendlier than they had been the first time Nallo had landed here.

"What news?" the first cried as they clustered around Peddonon. "We're in the hells of trouble here."

"You must have seen!" blurted the second. "That gods-rotted army is building walkways to cross the marsh and swamp."

"The hells!" cried the third, looking at Nallo. "You've got blood all over your leathers."

Drying streaks splattered her vest and trousers. Flakes shed from her hands. A spot on her chin itched, and when she raised a hand to rub at it, the fawkners flinched as if they thought she was about to hit them.

"We've been in a skirmish." Peddonon gestured to get their attention. "I need to see the marshal at once."

"You're in luck," said the first fawkner. "They're in council now, with the commander and that outlander captain."

"Joss? Is here in Nessumara?"

"Just came in last night—"

"The hells! Kanness, you stay with the fawkners. Nallo, Pil, come with me."

The fawkners blurted out a protest but a glance from Peddonon, and the menace of his big frame, silenced them. Nallo and Pil trotted obediently after him as he made his way through the compound to the marshal's cote, a pretty cottage surrounded by a garden on the landward side and with a wooden pier jutting out onto a wide channel. Two low-slung boats had been tied to the pier. A girl, ten or twelve years of age and quite thin, was set to watch them. Two elderly reeves sat on the porch, mending harness. When they saw Peddonon they clambered to their feet. One tapped the sliding door and went inside the cote while the other blocked the stairs.

"I'm here to see Commander Joss," said Peddonon.

"You're Peddo, right? Where's your eagle perched?"

"I'm Peddonon, sergeant in charge of the contingent stationed at Law Rock. If the commander's here, he'll want to speak to me. If Captain Anji is here, he'll want to hear about the skirmish we just fought."

"Skirmish?"

The old man's gaze fixed on Nallo, taking in the blood. "Aui! What happened?"

"I'll give my report to—"

The door slid open, and the other old reeve indicated that Peddonon should go in.

He paused on the porch to take off his boots, nodding at Nallo. "Go wash yourself off."

"Where?" she demanded.

He waved a hand, but she wasn't sure if he meant the garden, or the pier, or the barracks. The door slapped shut behind him, and the old reeves stared so rudely! She grabbed Pil and walked to the pier. The heat was beginning to rise, already muggy and steamy here in the delta; in another few weeks it would become unbearable. She swatted at gnats attracted to her sweat, but they only returned, like that cursed army: swarms that would eat them alive if they could manage it.

"Abandoned again with the usual disregard important louts show for their underlings," she muttered. "Not one word of praise for our victory."

"Any decent fighting unit would have made quick work of our clumsy attack," said Pil. "The eagles are huge targets. We need better tactics, and much more training."

"Thank you," she said as she stamped out onto the pier, Pil following with more caution. The girl turned to stare at them. "Now I'll just shove you into the water, if you don't mind, so you can feel what it's like to have water dumped over your excitement at finally having done something right!"

Pil didn't like water; it had been hard enough to get him to bathe in the way Hundred folk did.

"I didn't mean it," she added, hating that stiff-faced expression he got.

"You were brave," he said. "You didn't hesitate."

She laughed. "That's praise coming from you, I suppose, with your fancy Qin ways."

The brown water flowed so sluggishly you couldn't quite see the current's ripple. A pair of boats eased downstream, one tied on behind the other, an older woman steering the forward craft. The woman glanced their way casually and then, startled, looked more closely at Pil.

"Heya! Auntie! Look where you're going!" A pair of young men called out jocularly to the older woman. She favored them with a long look, and whistled provocatively, and they laughed in reply. The men, rowing cargo upstream, were stripped down to loincloths, their muscular backs rippling as they stroked.

Nallo nudged Pil, but he was already looking in that pretending-not-to-look way he still had, as if admiring were shameful.

The girl ran her toes along one of the long lines, staring sidelong at Pil much as he was watching the passing rowers. "Why's he wear his hair all funny like that? Why isn't it short like a proper reeve? He's an outlander. So why's he wear reeve leathers?"

"I'm sure you're a smart girl," said Nallo. "If he come in here jessed to an eagle and wears reeve leathers, what do you suppose he is? Anyway, let me ask you a question. Why does this water stink so much?"

"It doesn't! You've got blood on you. All dried and flaking off. Yuck."

"It does! It smells like rotting fish and rubbish. Yuck."

"I never asked you!"

"Yes, but you had plenty to say about my friend here, and you never asked him, just talked to me like he wasn't even there."

"Outlanders can't talk proper speech, everyone knows that. If he could, why doesn't he say anything?"

"I have nothing to say," said Pil softly. The girl, hearing him speak, shrieked and danced away to the end of the pier. He grinned, more sweetly than Nallo ever did.

The male rowers had vanished past a point of land piled high with piers and warehouses and the auntie floated out of sight under a narrow arched bridge that stretched between Copper Hall's islet and a spur of land that held what looked like a council square behind a screen of mulberry trees. The channel lay empty but for a leafless branch swirling aimlessly like a dead snake in the brown water.

The girl sidled a few steps closer. "Folk say we're all likely to die," she ventured, still staring at Pil. "Not so much by starving, 'cause we got fields all over the islands, but 'cause that army, they coming back."

"This city is well defended by the river," said Pil. "Only on two roads can an army march in across the wetlands. Likely the army will build paths and rafts. But your soldiers have weapons, boats, archers. You know the land. All this you can fight with."

"We dun't really have soldiers," said the girl. "My brother got hisself killt. He was on Veyslip Island with the militia that held off the main attack on the east causeway. So he's a hero, but he's still dead. I dun't see how we can fight them again. My clan tried to get us out in a boat but it cost too much. At least we live here in the hall, and get nai every day for our labor. Why do you fight them?" she said to Pil. "You being an outlander, I mean."

He fingered his neat topknot. The clubbed hair bound around with thin leather strips had not a strand out of place. "I am a reeve."

"Heya!" Peddonon appeared on the porch. "You two!"

Nallo rolled her eyes. "He's changed now that he's been put in charge on Law Rock. Whew! High and mighty!"

Pil looked away.

"You got something going on there, eh?"

The girl snickered.

Pil's stance took on the rigidity that told her she'd gone too far.

"You can't hear me?" Peddonon bellowed.

"Eiya! I'm sorry. And an idiot." She slapped Pil hard on the shoulder, and he relaxed. "Let's go."

She trotted toward the cote, Pil's steps sounding behind her. Commander Joss and Captain Anji emerged onto the porch, chattering away like her brothers when they would go on about the most precise details of the cursed goats.

The outlander had an engaging voice, his accent more pleasing than difficult. "That huge old forest—the Wild, you call it—would be a perfect refuge for skirmishers. We could drop them in behind enemy lines to maintain a running disruption, and they could retreat into the forest when they got into trouble."

"No human can enter the Wild, and live. It's forbidden to go in there."

"What if we could speak to these wildings and ask them to allow our soldiers refuge? Just for the duration of the war? If they can think and communicate, then it is possible to negotiate with them."

"Had much luck trading for horses with the lendings?" asked Joss with a laugh.

The captain winced, then grinned. "It was my own fault. I did not listen to good advice. But if the wildings are people, like to us, then it is merely a matter of coming to understand what they need and how we can offer that to them in return for what we need. Then both they and we benefit, to our mutual advantage."

The tip-tap of a cane preceded the appearance of the marshal. He was old, weary, and stoop-shouldered, shaking his head as he appeared in the open doors as if disagreeing with Anji's statement. His evident weakness made the contrast between the three men even greater: Commander Joss's excessive handsomeness could not disguise his barely leashed energy, striking in a man who had counted a full forty years; the outlander captain had a quieter but more forceful charisma, a deadly wolf lying patiently in wait for the right moment to kill.

The captain addressed the marshal as if resuming a conversation broken off inside. "Marshal Masar, I know there is not time to properly train strike forces as efficient, disciplined units, but there is enough time to use them wisely. Reeves can carry soldiers and put them down behind enemy lines. We can sow confusion, pick off stragglers at little risk to ourselves. Create trouble. Draw off their attention while meanwhile I march the army up from Olo'osson. The key is to keep their gaze fixed elsewhere so they don't see us coming."

"It goes against all tradition," objected the old marshal.

Commander Joss's eyes widened as he noticed the blood on Nallo's leathers. "Masar, if we are all dead, then how will our traditions have served us? The ones who command the Star of Life army have cleansed tradition from their ranks. We need not kill tradition to fight them, but we must change to survive. Do you want Nessumara, and this branch of Copper Hall, to fall to the army? To suffer what High Haldia and Toskala have suffered?"

The outlander captain raised a hand. His gaze skimmed over Nallo and Pil in a way that made her stand up straighter; Pil said nothing, his gaze lowered as if he were ashamed, although what in the hells he would have to feel ashamed of Nallo could not imagine.

The captain lowered the hand and tapped his own chest. "Listen. I can move my army quickly. They're trained for exactly such a contingency. But I desperately need *your* support, and your support in particular, Marshal Masar, before I lay my plan before Nessumara's council tonight." He paused, brushing the back of a hand along his beard, his gestures neat and graceful. "We *must strike* while the people of Nessumara and Toskala and High Haldia and the entire countryside along the immense length of the River Istri still possess the will to resist. We must strike before they begin to prefer *any* form of peace, however onerous, to continued suffering."

The marshal dropped his gaze like a man beaten in hooks-and-ropes. An agony of sorrow shuttered his eyes. Abruptly, Commander Joss touched him on the arm in a manner meant to comfort.

"There was nothing you could have done," Joss said. "Do not blame yourself when the blame must rest on those who forced the choice on you."

"Why do you people hesitate?" Nallo cried, the words pouring out before she knew she meant to say them. "Do you think you're the only one who's lost a kinsman? Don't you understand I'm standing here today because that cursed army killed my husband and orphaned my helpless stepchildren? Maybe it wouldn't have happened if there had been reeve wings fighting along West Track. I would rather fight and kill these gods-rotted bastards than sit around on my clean bench and moan about tradition while folk are being slaughtered, women assaulted, villages burned, children enslaved. But who am I to know? Just a cursed hill girl, born to goat herders, married against my will to a kind man who treated me decently despite my bad temper. I'd be dead if it weren't for the Qin." The marshal was actually cringing, but that didn't make her feel the least stirring of shame for yelling at the sodden old fool. She fixed her glare on the captain, who watched her with unsettling interest. "My thanks to your men."

"Reeve Nallo, isn't it?" the captain said. "Yours is the daughter—she must be your stepdaughter, for you're not old enough to have birthed her—who turned down my good chief's marriage offer in favor of a mere tailman." He laughed, looking at the commander. "Bring Reeve Nallo to the council meeting. She'll argue our case convincingly."

"Because she's right," whispered the old marshal. "How many more must perish while we hang on to what is already dead?" With an effort he mastered himself, pushing up on his cane to regain some of the stature years and grief had taken from him. Behind that seamed visage trembled a younger man, the body and strength he had once worn: upright, pious, fair, or believing himself to be. "We believed the past could protect us. We believe that if we serve justice, then all will be well. But it isn't true, is it? Without order, there can be no justice. If the stubborn fools on Nessumara's council do not listen, then they deserve to have their beautiful city pillaged and burned and their corpses tossed into the channels to feed the fish!"

"Eiya!" began Joss. "I grieve with you, Marshal, knowing your sorrow at losing your grandchildren and family, but surely you cannot wish upon others what you have suffered."

"It is natural to be angry," said the captain. "But let me admit that I have taken part in the sack of cities." His tone was so thoughtful and calm it was impossible for Nallo to imagine him engaged in any such horror, yet on he spoke, not making light, but making sense. "I do not think even so that the folk in those places deserved what befell them. They were merely unfortunate enough to be there. If any should suffer, it should be their leaders, and yet too often those who rule can buy their way out of worse grief while those who live ordinary lives receive the full blast of the storm. How do you think I got my beautiful wife? I saw her in the market one day, and because I could, I took her. That she proved to be much more than even I had imagined is not to my credit, but to hers."

A horn's sad voice raised in a long plaint, and faded.

"That's the call to council," said the old marshal.

*   *   *

NESSUMARA'S COUNCIL WAS divided: Surrender and beg for protected status. Buy off the army with coin and supplies. Fight, despite not having enough men to defend the city after so many had been killed in the first battle nor an experienced commander to lead them.

It was pretty cursed obvious, thought Joss, that their arguing rose as much from the strain of a months-long siege as from any significant differences of opinion. They quieted respectfully when Marshal Masar braced himself on his cane to speak.

"The army has been spread out over Istria and Lower Haldia for weeks, but now they're joining forces and marching on Nessumara. You're cut off from the countryside, which itself has been pillaged and burned. While the delta protects you to the south and the swamp forest to the north, the eastern marshland is very dry. Lord Radas's cohorts don't need the causeway to advance from the east. This army has raised fifteen full cohorts. They are turning on you now and they mean to fight until they win."

His words fell hard; afterward, all sat in silence. Lamps hissed, a familiar and almost comforting sound. The council speaker carried an infant in a sling at her hip, its sleeping face illuminated by a pool of light. She took the speaking stick from Masar and offered it to Anji. "Sobering words, Marshal. How can anyone defeat fifteen cohorts, Captain?"

"I will not fight a pitched battle unless I can win it," said Anji in his cool voice, the one people listened to because they mistook it for that of a man who harbors no strong emotion. "There are many ways to win a campaign. If you sit here, you will starve even if you aren't overrun. Those of you who have ships can flee, as long as you are not caught and thrown into the sea. But in the end, the shores you run to will be overrun in their turn. A commander who can raise fifteen cohorts will raise more. He will take your sons as soldiers and your daughters to serve those soldiers—"

As voices swelled, people angrily protesting, the baby woke and began to fuss.

Anji crossed to the council speaker and offered to take the child, a pleasing baby of about the same age as Atani. After a hesitation, she handed over the infant. Anji had a deft arm, and as he paced, the little one quieted and, likewise, the assembly fell silent, watching him calm the baby.

He kept pacing, his tone incongruously pleasant and his aspect, with the babe in arms, so harmonious that his words fell like rocks dropped from a clear blue sky. "I ask you to hear me out. The Hundred is not like the rest of the world. Let this army overtake you, and you will discover you have far less control over your lives than you had before. Your sons will be forced to join as soldiers, or be killed. Your daughters will be raped. Your temples will be burned. Your coin and your children and your possessions and food stores will be stolen. You will be their slaves, because they will hold the sword. They are commanded by cloaks—whether demons or corrupted Guardians—who cut right into your heart. Who can kill you with a word. Is that what you want? As long as a single one of those cloaks walks on this earth, they have the power to raise another cadre, another company, another cohort. Another army."

He shifted the now happy baby to his other arm so he could hold the speaking stick like a sword. "Or do you want to fight? Because the only army that can defeat them now is an alliance of all those remaining who do not want to suffer under their rule."

The baby babbled in cheerful reply to Anji's brutal words. Was the man brilliant, or did he simply miss his son?

Joss scanned the assembly; this tidy speech had frightened the council more than the very events and consequences they had seen with their own eyes. People were strange that way. They pretended their bags of rice and bins of nai flour weren't almost empty, sang tales to wish away the news of spoiled harvests or a trade ship gone missing. And then the storm would hit, and they weren't prepared.

Yet was he any different? Sometimes he felt he was hooked into harness but held no jess, at the mercy of winds and wings, so far above he could watch the land unfolding beneath and yet never be touched by it. Until a baby's babbling set into relief the harsh reality of the situation.

He rose. He'd been quiet all evening, and Anji stepped back to give him the speaker's stick. "Listen, I know a few of you remember me from when I was a young reeve stationed at Copper Hall on the Haya shore."

Some cursed woman in the back benches whistled admiringly, and folk did chuckle, but this time he did not blush. It was good they remembered him. It gave him a weapon.

"I was known as a reckless young man. I lost a woman I loved, another reeve." *Who is a Guardian now, having died to protect you gods-rotted fools.* Yet after Anji's talk of cloaks and corruption, he must speak circumspectly. "She was killed twenty-one years ago, and I am pretty cursed sure she was killed by men under the command of Lord Radas. Why do I tell you this? Because I got in a hells lot of trouble when I was a young reeve. I broke boundaries, I flew to Guardian altars looking for answers, and in the end I was disciplined and sent to Clan Hall. In the end, I told myself my elders were right, that I was walking where I wasn't meant to go. But now I ask myself: What if we had understood what was going on sooner? If we'd made more effort to figure out why Herelia and Vess kicked out the reeve patrols. If we'd paid more attention to villages who cut themselves off from the assizes. If we had bothered to notice that young men were vanishing, that the settlements around Walshow were growing. If we hadn't avoided it then, maybe we wouldn't be in this terrible situation now. Do we keep avoiding the truth? Or is it time to accept that this is no tale, this is no chance event. Like the orphan girl in the Tale of the Guardians, we cannot live in the world we grew up in. We have to ask the gods for the strength to change things. It is time to go to Indiyabu, as the orphaned girl did. Maybe you say, Indiyabu is just a tale, a place long since lost to humankind. But it is also a place in our hearts, a place where we find the courage to do what we must."

Suddenly the air seemed too thick to breathe. His skin burned, and his hands and forehead went clammy. "How long must this talk go on and on when we don't have a choice?" he demanded, and heard that he had spoken aloud what he'd meant only for his thoughts.

Anji handed the baby back to its grandmother and pulled his riding whip from his belt, pulling its length through his hand like a man impatient to ride. "Honored council members, I cannot wait while you chew through all your fears and hopes and suspicions. At dawn, Commander Joss and I leave to continue our scouting. Then he'll return to his hall and I to the army. This is a dire situation. We are weak, and they are strong, but their strength is also their weakness because they do not believe anyone can fight them, much less defeat them. If we go our separate ways, then in the end, we will all fall into the shadow. But if we act together—" He raised his riding crop, slashed it once for emphasis in the air, its hiss cutting into their fears. "—we can triumph. I have said every word that I can say. To go on discussing it is to pretend words will win this war. Some wars, words can win. Not this one."

He gestured. Sengel and Toughid turned to make sure the path was clear. To Joss's surprise, Masar tottered after him to show which course of action he favored. So Joss rose as well. Nessumara's council members called after him in desperate voices to stay, to talk more, and it was Nallo, who had been standing in silent attendance through the meeting, who spoke.

"Go ahead and talk yourselves to death," she snapped, a parting shot as they walked out. "Just send someone to let us know when you've all expired so we'll know we can finally get something done."

BEFORE DAWN THE council sent a messenger to Copper Hall: Nessumara would ally with Olo'osson. Joss saw something he'd have sworn he would never see: Anji severed his faithful guard Sengel—Joss had actually never seen Anji without Sengel standing within sight—and left him in charge of Nessumara's defenses.

The hells.

It was like that instant when your eagle shifted, and you knew he was about to dive: the fight was on.

A WANING GIBBOUS moon shone over the promontory of Law Rock. The River Istri streamed south, a ribbon glistening under the pearlescent light. A lantern winked on the river, but although Joss scanned the darkness, he did not see it again.

"What do you think of our outlander captain?" Peddonon asked. "He strikes me as a cautious man. He keeps his guard close. Yet the Qin seem to haul around some odd notions, and hold to them pretty rigidly."

"They're disciplined," said Joss. "It's an admirable quality. That Anji is cautious makes me think better of him. If he were rash, I would think him likely to leap into a clash he could not win just out of recklessness. But he's got something to lose, should he fall and die. An infant son, and a cursed beautiful young wife."

"So everyone says," said Peddonon with a smile, "although I'm not the right man to admire her. Of more interest to me is that folk say she's a cursed clever merchant, who drives a brutal bargain. I'd say she shares that quality with her husband."

Joss leaned against the polished wood railing that surrounded the thatched-roof shelter built over the upright slab of rock—the actual stele on which the law was carved—whose base was buried in a trough filled with packed earth. Lamps hung from each corner of the shelter, although these days only one of the four was lit. It burned all night, of course. No matter how little oil they had, one lamp must always burn at Law Rock.

"Sometimes we only look at the surface of things, forgetting what substance lies beneath."

"Poor Joss. Women whistling at you again?"

"Eh, it'll take a better insult than that to hurt me. Since when can a Fox's nip harm a handsome Ox?"

"Since the Ox got too slow to move out of the way. If you need a walking stick, just let me know. I'm a fair hand at carving."

"That's one word for it, so I hear."

"Aui!" The younger reeve laughed. "A hit!"

"I've stored up a lot more insults in my very long and very old time. You'll never defeat me that way." Yet his mood clipped his smile. He tried to read the words bitten out of the rock, but one lamp did not provide enough illumination. "I'm just thinking about the law, and about Guardians."

"The captain calls these cloaks demons, but what you say makes more sense, that they're corrupted. Although the hells what sense there is to be made of Guardians becoming corrupted I could not say. I just don't know what to think."

"What if Guardians could be killed?" Joss asked, keeping his tone flat.

"They can't be. Anyway, I'd say that would be a cursed thing to do, wouldn't you?"

"What is this Star of Life army, if not cursed? Could you kill a Guardian, Peddo, if there was a way to do it? If it meant saving others?"

Peddonon glanced around. The shadowed figures of two firefighters stood at the guardpost on the farthest spur of the promontory, too far away to overhear. Behind, on Justice Square, a lamp burned to mark the entrance of the reeve compound; there was another at the barracks porch and a third at the warehouse entrance where two militiamen stood guard. Law Rock's defenders now consisted of eighteen reeves and two cadres of fighters, and most of them were loitering outside the council hall. At dusk, they had hauled up an ostiary and four other holy priests in the basket at the hidden cliffside so that these dignitaries from occupied Toskala could meet with Anji. The priests, the captain, the commander, and the rest had talked for quite some time, until Anji had called for a break in the proceedings so folk could stretch their legs, drink, and pee. Joss had taken the chance to contemplate Law Rock.

"That's a cursed odd question," mused Peddonon. "I can't say—it's hard to even imagine—it would be like burning a temple, wouldn't it? What makes you even think of it?"

As Anji had said, they could not tell anyone unless they were absolutely sure that person would act immediately and succeed on his first attempt. So Joss let it go. "Lord Radas wears a cloak and commands the Star of Life army. He's no holy Guardian, not judged by his actions. So how do we defeat him?"

"In alliance, just like Captain Anji says." He gestured toward Justice Square. Lanterns swayed where Anji, in company with the priests, walked back from the balcony overlooking the occupied city. "Do those soldiers who attend Anji ever sleep?"

"I wouldn't know. I was cursed surprised when he left Sengel at Nessumara. I would have been less surprised had he cut off a hand and given it orders to coordinate the delta militia. That's Toughid to his right. Tohon, the other fellow, is one of the solidest men I have ever met."

"A bit old for me, but good-looking in that outlander way."

"Don't you ever stop?"

"Not until I cross the Spirit Gate," said Peddonon with a grin. "And, I pray, not even then."

They began to walk back, sticking to a path that cut between strips of raised garden. The earth filling the troughs had looked pale in daylight, more grit than soil, but they were cutting it with night soil and leavings from the kitchens to strengthen it in the weeks before the rains.

"I never thought I'd see gardens up here," said Joss.

"There's a lot of things I never thought I would see. Toskala under curfew. Folk being worked to death. Gates closed and people starving. Hauling folk in secret up by the basket to pass messages to and from the city." With a harsh laugh, maybe covering anger, Peddonon punched him on the shoulder, and cursed if the blow didn't rock him. "That was cursed funny when we hauled up the basket just after dusk and out hopped a scrawny old ostiary instead of a comforting armful of hierodule. I thought you were like to weep from disappointment."

"Old! I don't think that ostiary is much older than I am!"

"Your vanity will kill you one day, Joss." They converged on the stone ramp that led up into the council hall just as Anji's party arrived. Peddonon offered a final murmured comment. "It's Ostiary Nekkar's approval we need."

So it was, Joss reflected as they greeted the folk who had spilled out along the ramp to take a few breaths of clean air as the night filtered away into the twilight before dawn. Anji was chatting with the ostiary. The holy man was not particularly old, but he walked with a stiff limp like an elder. Moreover, he was astoundingly thin, with wrists so frail one might think to snap them in two. Yet he had a presence like the promontory itself, a massive rock that wind and water and years had not defeated, only weathered.

The other priests who had been hauled up by basket in the ostiary's wake bent their attention to Nekkar. He was the one they touched, as if to assure themselves he had substance and was not a ghost. He listened more than he talked, and he listened well, not staring directly at people but cocking his head to one side as if to let the words pour more easily into his ear. He lifted a hand now and again to punctuate a point the other speaker had made.

Anji waved Joss over. "Ostiary Nekkar met Zubaidit. She pulled him out of a heap of rubbish, did you know that?"

Joss was pretty sure Anji was teasing him, having seen Joss and Zubaidit together. "Zubaidit came up in that same basket. That was months ago."

"Where is Zubaidit now?" asked the ostiary with a gentle smile.

Anji shook his head. "We cannot say."

"Ah!" The ostiary nodded. In company with the other holy ones, he made his way up the ramp.

As everyone flowed up into the hall, Joss held back. The night was so very quiet. In the days before, you could hear the night market in Bell Quarter churning until dawn, singing, voices and laughter soaring in the currents of air that swirled around the promontory. But now Toskala lay utterly silent, its people afraid to sing, to speak, even to stir.

"An interesting net these priests have cast over the city, eh, Commander?" Tohon fell in beside Joss as they ascended, their feet clapping softly on stone. "I asked the holy one how they smuggled him from his quarter to the basket in another quarter if all the gates between quarters are closed and guarded. Over the months, they have woven a net on which information and even people can be passed. An interesting way to get around the occupation. But after hearing his description, I can see ways it could be improved."

"Is there anything the Qin cannot improve?" said Joss with a laugh.

Tohon chuckled, but he did not reply. They entered the council hall, where a wealth of lamps burned. As Joss looked around the faces of those gathered—reeves, militiamen, and the handful of priests brought up to meet with the outlander—he knew the decision had already been made. Ostiary Nekkar sat beside Captain Anji and offered him with his own hands a cup of rice wine. The ostiary smiled with careful grace as the captain took a sip and returned the rest, a gesture like a physical echo of the bowl of rice offered by a woman to the man she agrees to marry. Nekkar took also a single sip, and passed the cup to the other priests. There was not much in it; enough for them to swallow, and then it was gone.

Nekkar looked around the council hall to catch every gaze. His was a pleasant voice, easy to listen to, but like silk rope strained taut by an immense weight, it held simply because it was so strong. "I agreed to the perilous journey here because so many suffer under the yoke of an enemy who has weapons while we have nothing.

You four, representative of the other quarters, have taken this dangerous path as well. I came to give this record to the reeves."

He drew out of his sleeve a scroll. "On this scroll, clerks have recorded the name and clan of every hostage known to have been taken south to Nessumara with the army. They have added the names of folk who are missing, and those enslaved or perhaps killed by the army during the occupation. We ask the reeves to look for these people. Perhaps all we can hope for is to hear confirmation of their deaths, so the families do not have to live never knowing."

He held out the scroll as if unsure who should take it.

Joss stepped forward. "As commander standing over the reeve halls, I accept this responsibility. We'll have copies made and distributed to every reeve hall and reeve station and to those in Sapanasu's temples who can safely take charge of this information."

Nekkar's expression bore a measure of calm that soothed without mock hope. "For so many months, we in Toskala did nothing, out of fear for the hostages. But we have come to understand that it was false choice offered to us. Our lack of action will not save them, nor will it save those taken into servitude yesterday, today, and tomorrow. Now we are offered a chance to fight. Let us ally with Olo'osson's army and the reeve halls. Let us accept their leadership in this matter. That is what I recommend."

Anji's nod, to Joss, was a simple gesture and a plain statement: *We have what we need.*

*   *   *

TODAY WAS A day like any other day for a spy skulking behind enemy lines. Shai hid in a tangle of evergreen hedge as soldiers marched down a path skirting fields. A village lay in the distance, but not a thread of smoke or a single barking dog or laughing child gave evidence that someone might be living there.

The company flew a banner marked with four white flowers on blue cloth: they were not the soldiers he was looking for. Two wagons were heaped with stores, ten ragged slaves trudging between. Three young women and a lad sat atop the wagons, chattering, looking far better fed than the captives. The soldiers looked complacent, their talk drifting on the breeze.

"Eh, I'm hoping there'll be a sight better pickings once we've taken Nessumara, eh?"

"Shoulda gone in all the way the first time. Don't know why those cowards pulled out like that, couldn't even keep it up! Now all the valuables are likely hidden away or shipped out. Less for us, eh?"

When they passed out of sight, Shai dragged himself out of the prickly branches and made a halfhearted effort at dusting himself off. He was so scratched up he thought his skin might forever after be hatched with white scars. It was slow work, moving through the countryside looking for one cohort in particular while not getting caught in the meantime and knowing you might never find them regardless.

Yet perseverance was no hardship. The wildings had loaded him down with strips of dried meat mashed together with dried berries; these provisions, while not tasty, had sustained him for many days as he had crept west and south toward the sea. Yesterday he had run out. Today he was hungry and still had seen no sign of a banner with six crossed red staves on black cloth.

He slogged through grass, sedge, and bush parallel to the road, wondering if he could scavenge supper in the nearest village. Movement flashed among the houses. He froze behind the partial concealment of a fence of saplings. Soldiers hustled through the village, breaking down doors, tipping carts. Shai counted maybe half a cadre, perhaps outliers of the company.

A dog barked frantically, then bolted out of a cottage. Soldiers gave chase, pelting rocks at its hindquarters. It yipped and scrambled on, limping. But an archer lined up on the poor animal and shot it once, and then twice, as the creature howled in pain, trying to drag itself off, but they would not let it go. They were enjoying their cruelty too much.

Merciful One!

He scanned the fields as the dog's agony stretched on—until his gaze was caught by a shadow shuddering over the untilled earth. An object hurtled out of the sky. It cracked open before it struck, spilling a cloud of black dust over the men who had converged on the wounded dog. The soldiers began to sneeze. A man thudded to his knees with an arrow in his back. Stones thundered onto the ground all around, and two men went down. The archer raised his bow, sighting, but cried out and bolted.

An eagle hooked him in its massive talons and rose as the man screamed and thrashed. The reeve hooked into the harness stuck him repeatedly with a javelin— panicked, Shai thought—before the eagle released him and his body smacked on earth beside the still-struggling dog.

The chase was on. The cadre ran, some taking to the road, some seeking cover; all too stupid to stand and fight. A company of Qin would have coolly stood their ground and darkened the sky with their arrows; the attack of the reeves was crude, effective only because it was unexpected.

As unexpected as a huff of air behind him. He jumped, stumbled as he turned, and found himself flat on his butt staring up at a fierce-looking eagle and a young reeve dangling an arm's length off the ground, feet braced on a bar.

"You're a cursed outlander!" cried the reeve. "What're you doing out here?"

"Not giving away my position," snapped Shai. "Or could you perhaps have dropped your flags on me to make sure the enemy knows I'm here?"

"You're that gods-rotted outlander we're meant to be looking for, aren't you? Chayi? Shayi?"

The eagle was huge. Its talons or hooked beak could tear him to pieces in a heartbeat. A stark scream from away down the road suggested that one of the soldiers had just met such a fate.

"Who wants to know?" he asked, flexing his muscles, brandishing the knife and staff the wildings had gifted him.

The young man laughed appreciatively. "Eh, that was badly started. I'm called Rayish. We've orders to bring you to Copper Hall in Nessumara."

"Not my orders. Leave me here, or tell me where to find an enemy cohort flying a banner with six crossed red staves on black cloth."

To Shai's surprise, the reeve spat. "That lot! That's the gods-rotted cohort that burned Copper Hall on the Haya shore."

"The very ones I seek." Heat swelled in his heart, although he could not tell if fear or excitement made his pulse swim in his ears. "I have a mission at the service of the militia and council and temples of Olossi."

The reeve scratched his head. Hu! He had a straggle of black hair pulled back in a clumsy approximation of a Qin topknot.

"When did you reeves start skirmishing?" Shai added, which brought a bright grin from the young man.

"New tactics from the commander. About cursed time, if you ask me."

"The commander?"

"Commander Joss of Clan Hall, and that outlander captain from the south. Those two are our commanders. Didn't you know that?"

Shai hid his surprise behind his usual baffle of impassivity. "I've been in hiding a long time."

An eagle swooped past, the reeve flagging them, and Rayish swore. "Hook in. We'll find this cohort, and I'll drop you behind their lines. Will that help?"

"The hells, it will!" Shai laughed. His new best comrade laughed. They were after all two young men fighting on the same side and eager to get their blows in.

The eagle launched right at him. Shai threw himself flat, but the eagle wasn't after *him*. With a high-pitched call, it struck so hard Shai felt the impact in his bones. A male voice screamed, the noise as horrible as the dog's agonized yips. Rayish cursed, dangling over a soldier punctured by the eagle's talons. Two more enemy soldiers were racing up behind.

Shai leaped up and plunged past the eagle's outstretched wings, heedless of the fierce beak. He caught both men unawares because they were fixed on the reeve and the eagle and their dying comrade. The raptor shook the man loose and struck at a second as Shai cut inside, thrust with his spear, and punched it into the third man's shoulder. He ducked out of the way of a flailing blow from the soldier's sword and kicked the man's knees out from behind him. As the soldier dropped, Shai grabbed his shoulder and slashed his throat. Hu! Not deep enough; he had to saw a second time. Blood gushed everywhere; piss stank where the dying men had voided; a cry raked the air so awful the sound made him wince, but his man was already dead and the raptor put its prey out of his misery.

"Aui!" Rayish retched right over the bloody mess as Shai got up, very very slowly, and stepped back as the eagle slewed its massive head around to take a good long look at Shai.

He displayed knife and spear. "I'm your cursed ally. Not your cursed dinner."

The eagle shook itself free and waddled backward out of the slick mess it had made, so awkward Shai had to wipe his eyes as laughter choked him.

Rayish spat, averting his eyes from the corpses. "Eihi! Feh! Gah!" He wiped his mouth with the back of a hand. "Hurry! We're vulnerable on the ground."

"I'm coming," said Shai. "Find me that cohort, and you'll have my thanks."

"You have my and Pretty's thanks already," said the reeve. "That third one might have got us."

That third one had ceased twitching and gushing although Pretty's two victims still spasmed. A misty extrusion twisted from the eyes and nostrils of the man Shai had killed, swirling in the streaks and pools of his blood until it took on a man-shaped form that rose to confront Shai.

"The hells! What hit me? Eihi! That cursed eagle! They said to watch, but I didn't believe—Bedi? Oyard? Can you hear me?" Hollow eyes fixed on Shai. "What are you, that you stare at me so? Are you one of those gods-cursed demons they warned us about?"

"Get over here! I have to leave." Rayish's shouts blended with the voice of the ghost.

"Am I *dead*?" The ghost sobbed. "They promised if we believed and served that we would escape death, if we wore the Star of Life it would shield us—"

Shai dodged away from the twisting mouth and insubstantial groping hands. The raptor's fierce talons and beak were as nothing, compared to a ghost's cry or the sight of what he had himself wrought: slicing a man out of life and into death.

Rayish hooked him in, shaking and laughing. "We did it! Gods-rotted rubbish, that's what they are now! Finally!"

A whistle shrilled by Shai's ear, and the beat of the eagle's wings shattered the ghostly mist into oblivion as they rose into the wind.

* * *

FROM TOSKALA, JOSS and Anji's scouting party flew north, intending to sweep past High Haldia and up beyond Seven and the Steps to the spectacular mountain-top fastness of Gold Hall. Anji wanted a look at the mountainous spine of Heaven's Reach, maybe even as far as the isolated valley of Walshow. The one place they were careful to avoid was Herelia, although they spoke of it often, mulling over the report Joss had heard from Marit.

So the council at Gold Hall went.

"Fifteen cohorts?" Marshal Lorenon demanded, looking at Joss. He had not once addressed Joss as "Commander." "And more in training? Do you know how many soldiers that is?"

He was a man of middle age but not in good health, and although his querulous tone never eased, he addressed his remarks to Joss and Anji equally, not showing any prejudice toward the outlander captain. On the whole, Joss thought him relieved to have someone to talk to who had an air of competency. His senior reeves sat in attendance and were as like to talk over him as to maintain silence. Discipline was breaking down in Gold Hall, and Joss thought the senior reeves tolerated Lorenon as marshal out of habit, or because they felt, by now, that they had lost the war and were only hanging on to the remnant that survived in their stronghold and in the few high mountain villages that supplied them with provisions and necessaries.

"Surely the Star of Life has recruited from the regions you patrol," said Anji. "Teriayne. The plateaus. The town of Seven and High Haldia. Young men do not like to feel they can be slapped around. In the end, even the responsible ones may feel it is better to march with those who have weapons than to cower with those who must bare their throats."

Listening reeves nodded, and ten different anecdotes poured out as they all talked over one another: a village arkhon had brought a complaint to the local assizes and was killed in the night on his pallet; lads had disappeared; trouble plagued the roads; gangs of armed men demanded coin from merchants to protect their market stalls against thievery. Men marched south in arrogant cadres, wearing a star hammered out of cheap tin as a necklace.

"It was never meant to be this way," said Marshal Lorenon when the passionate chatter subsided. "The laws bind all in equal measure. The Guardians were meant to put a stop to those who use swords or coin to abuse the vulnerable."

"The Guardians may have done so, in the years before," said Anji, "but those who command the Star of Life army now are corrupted. Whether demons or human, they have stolen the Guardian cloaks and twisted them to serve their own selfish ends. They have soldiers. They have swords. They have the means to look into your mind and your heart. They do not care how many people die, as long as they get what they want."

"So what in the hells is it they want?" Joss asked abruptly.

Anji shot him a glance, as if puzzled by Joss's puzzlement. "They want to rule. Maybe they even believe that the rule of a single strong arkhon or lord—what would be called the var among the Qin or a king or emperor in other lands—is a better and more stable rule than the tumult of a hundred towns and cities each ruling itself."

"Neh, the gods rule the Hundred," said Joss. "Their power resides in the temples. We each serve a year's apprentice to one of the gods, and some serve their entire lives, and thus we tie ourselves to the land. It is the gods' laws that govern us. As it says on Law Rock: 'On law shall the land be built.' Not on men, whether one man or many."

"Maybe so," objected Marshal Lorenon, "but right now, laws don't defeat swords. Can Olo'osson's militia really defeat fifteen cohorts, Captain?"

"Not alone," said Anji. It was a bit unnerving: the steady gaze, the square shoulders, the air of being in command that was not intimidating but rather *assured*. "In an alliance that spreads from Olossi to Nessumara to Gold Hall." He opened both palms in the storytelling gesture that invited listeners to make up their own minds. "Let me tell you how we can use wings of eagles to create strike forces. Combined with armed men, and stationed in small groups in high places that can't be reached by the enemy, these strike forces can pick off stragglers, assassinate sergeants and captains, sow confusion, and draw off their attention while I march an army up from Olo'osson."

"Aui!" said Marshal Lorenon. "I'd give my cursed sight to feel like I'm striking a blow for justice. After all this gods-rotted helpless, useless time."

He and his reeves leaned forward to hear more.

35

NORTHWEST THEY FLEW, spiraling up on the wild thermals that raged along a huge escarpment running hundreds of mey from middle Haldia all the way into the northern wilderness of Heaven's Ridge. This steep drop-off was known to the locals, unimaginatively enough, as the Cliffs, although the towering cliffs wore fancier names in the tales. Gold Hall's marshal had loaned them two reeves to guide them to Walshow. They flew first across the spectacular "steps" where the River Istri plunged in a series of stair-step falls from the Teriayne plateau down to the northernmost reach of the Haldian plain. After, they sailed north for half the morning along a spur of the great escarpment split with ravines and isolated valleys.

"Joss," shouted Anji, pointing in that cursed outlander way toward a teardrop-shaped valley with a lake near the center and woodland and meadows all glossy and green surrounding it, a lovely little haven. "Do you see? There's a cloak and a winged horse by the shore of the lake."

Scar had seen nothing, and at first Joss saw nothing, only sunlight winking on the exceptional cerulean waters like a captured piece of sky. Was that flash of white an outstretched wing, or a death-white cloak? He jessed the eagle around, flagging for the other reeves to stay back, and dropped for a closer look.

"The cloak's seen us," said Anji, gaze following movement. "The demon is running. Move off to the left. We'll follow it."

"What color—is—the cloak?" demanded Joss, finding it hard to breathe as he thought of Marit.

"Can't tell. It's flying north. It can't outpace us, can it? We're faster."

With Anji guiding, they tracked the cloak, Joss catching glimpses of a fluttering expanse of glimmering white. They banked away from the escarpment and over rugged foothills toward a substantial peak and three lesser ones known, the Gold Hall marshal had told him, as the Orator and Her Three Daughters. Looking ahead, Joss spotted a lake shining under the sun and spread all around it the dusty bones of overworked land leached to brown by the dry season. The town was a smear by the lake; impossible to say how many people lived there.

"This is Walshow!" cried Joss.

Anji, too, saw these things, but he twisted in the harness as they sailed past the daughter peaks. A voice sang among the spires, raised by the wind.

Anji said, urgently, "There! It's trying to escape us. It's dropping onto an altar. Do you see it? It's atop the smaller peak."

A gleam pulsed under the midday sun, the pattern circled by a ring of boulders atop the lowest of the four clustered peaks.

"Set down, Joss," said Anji in a cold, clear voice. "Set down *now*."

Joss's hands worked the jesses and Scar was turning before he quite realized he had done so. Before Joss could protest at being ordered about in such a way, Anji went on in a measured tone of exceptional intensity.

"We have to do it."

Because of Scar's swiftness and the angle of the currents, they came around so quickly that Scar pulled up over the boulders before Joss quite realized they had reached the altar. Was that a flash of wings at the center of the labyrinth? Did a ghostly figure walk the path, no more substantial than fog rising off the ground at dawn? He had seen a Guardian walk an altar once before, at Hammering Ford. Was this the same one, one of the army's commanders?

Before Scar actually touched ground, Anji unhooked and dropped, rolling side-ways out of the way. The eagle thumped down so hard that Joss swung in the har-ness, fumbling at the hooks as the captain jogged away toward the glittering entrance of the labyrinth. The hells! Joss dropped and stepped out from under Scar's shadow. The other reeves circled by the Orator, as if looking for him; as if the altar's magic concealed even the big eagle.

"Anji!" Joss shouted. "Don't walk the path!"

Anji did not walk the path. He strode *straight across* the open space as if the labyrinth did not bind his feet. It might not have been there at all. Yet when Joss ran after, with some crazy idea of supporting him or protecting Marit, he could not cross; what force held him back he could not name, only that it was like a wall, or a storm, or a woman's unyielding refusal.

Anji vanished into a swirl of mist pouring up out of the maze, and Joss stood there with one foot on the entrance and one off, shouting, but his words scattered into nothing. Was that a whisper that teased his ears from down the long, twisting path? He shut his mouth and listened.

"Who are you?" said a woman's voice. "How have you followed me?"

"Just come to offer my help, verea. Were you looking for something?"

"Eiya! You are another outlander demon! Veiled to my sight."

"I am no demon. I am a man, just like any other man."

"Obviously you are not a man, if you can walk here with no repercussions. What is your name? Why have you followed me?"

The pause before Anji's reply was measured by a sound like the exhalation of a sword being drawn. "Forgive me, verea. I mean no disrespect."

Scar took off abruptly, launching himself into the sky and abandoning Joss. The hells! His cursed flags were hooked into the harness, dangling beneath the raptor right where Joss could not possibly reach them now. The other eagles had flown out of sight behind the Orator. Neh, there was one, high overhead—

A light pulsed out of the labyrinth, followed by a blast like a sound so strong Joss felt it as a blow within his flesh that lifted him off his feet and flung him backward. He hit his head.

AND THEN HE AWAKENED.

"Joss."

An iron stake had impaled his head. He did not want to open his eyes, and yet he must.

"Joss!"

Not a stake, only a gods-cursed headache ripping open his eyes. He staggered up, shielding his vision from the hammer of the sun. Anji stood before him. The captain was not wearing his black tabard; he wore a quilted coat of silk whose color was as rich a blue as that cerulean lake they'd seen, soothing on the eyes. Joss cracked his lids a little more. Anji's right cheek was reddened, and he was favoring his left hand, its glove shredding to ash as though the fine leather had been singed. His black tabard was rolled up, his outer belt wrapped tightly around it end over end, looped and mazy, and fastened to loops in the quilted coat so the bundled tabard rode against Anji's hips. Blessed Ilu! The cursed fabric shifted and fluttered as if the wind had gotten inside it. Or his vision was blurring and distorting as the headache spiked.

Joss blinked away tears.

"Anji," he whispered hoarsely, surprised his voice worked.

"Call your eagle," said Anji, words bitten back with pain. "Let's get out of here."

"But—"

"Now."

Joss groped for his bone whistle, blew on it once, getting nothing because there was no air in his chest. He panted softly, then blew again. Scar banked sharply and descended. When the eagle thumped down, Joss ducked under and hooked in. With the familiarity of practice, Anji hooked into the secondary harness in front of him.

They rose on a thermal. Three eagles came into view, reeves frantically flagging. He fumbled at his all-clear flag and waved it. His headache had exploded into a knife of agony that made the air shimmer with bolts of light as he had a horrible feeling he was going to vomit right down Anji's back and over that expensive first-quality quilted silk coat.

Shutting his eyes calmed the queasiness.

"Anji," he said roughly, "you have to steer. Take the jesses. Neh, first, take the flag, the—ah, the hells—my head!—red and white gives up command of the flight to Vekess."

Anji did not hesitate. Joss hung there with his eyes squeezed shut, just surviving the buffeting winds and the interminable press and sway that made him wish for the first time since he'd been jessed that he had two feet on solid earth rather than hanging here far above the land at the mercy of the currents. Lights pulsed in his shuttered vision, patterns like the Guardians' labyrinth burned into the lids of his eyes. He flushed hot, and shivered cold, and it was possible he passed out and afterward came to.

He had broken the boundaries. Now he would be punished.

Yet both he and Anji lived.

He endured the pain of being alive, and in the end they fell, and he unhooked himself and collapsed. Scar brooded protectively over him as Joss faded in and out and his head throbbed and he threw up and, eventually, slept.

And woke.

A blanket had been thrown over him; it was night. A campfire burned to one side, a single figure sitting watchfully beside it, topknot silhouetted against the hazy aura of flame. Joss groaned, and the man came over to crouch beside him.

"Will you take some water?" Tohon asked. "Or cold nai porridge, if you can stomach it?"

"Where's Anji?" he asked, feeling the burn of his raw throat. "I'll take a sip of water."

The water was cool and went down easily. His face was sticky, his hands no better; his vest and shirt stank. Hadn't Zubaidit found him in such filthy conditions in a cell under Olossi's Assizes Tower, awaiting punishment? Where did these memories come from? He began to chuckle, then to laugh, and pressed a hand to his head and squinched shut his eyes.

"Commander?" asked Tohon in the gentlest voice imaginable. "Are you going to pass out again?"

"Just give me a moment. Where are we?"

Tohon explained in precise, measured words that they had perched for the night on a ridge-top haven used by reeves, with firewood and stores laid by. The Gold Hall reeves had returned home, so their party now consisted of Joss, Anji, Toughid, and Tohon, as well as Warri and Kanness from Clan Hall, who were carrying Toughid and Tohon, and Vekess, flying as an extra scout and second-in-command. At daybreak they would head south, hoping to make Horn Hall by the end of the day. By the time Tohon finished Joss had taken another few sips of water and felt he might live to see another dawn.

"Where is the captain?" he asked softly.

"If you would, Commander, let him sleep."

Joss rose unsteadily and cautiously walked around the fire, Tohon at his side. He had an uncomfortable feeling that the scout would run him through without hesitation were he to disturb the sleeping captain, but he had to look. Anji was lying on his side on a blanket. His topknot was disheveled, his quilted coat laid open beneath him to give a little padding. Beneath it he wore a light silk shift, rumpled around his torso. His face was at peace, his elbows bent and his hands tucked up below his chin. Both hands were wrapped in linen bandages; his cheek was bare but slick, rubbed with tonic to ease the blisters raised along his jaw. Resting by his knees was that odd bundle made of his black wolf's tabard, bound by belts and braid and even chains Joss recognized as the heavy gold necklaces normally worn by Toughid. The tabard was smothered in these bindings, and the weird way the fire's light flickered made it seem, as before, that the bundle contained a living creature struggling to get out.

Toughid slept—it was the first time Joss had ever seen the man asleep!—a sword's length from Anji, but his eyelids moved, snapped open, and he sat up with a knife drawn so fast that Joss stepped back and slammed into Tohon. Anji did not wake; he was truly exhausted. Toughid glanced at them, shrugged, and lay back down. The other two reeves slept elsewhere, and Joss paced out to the edge of the ridge where Vekess kept watch under a sliver of moon.

"Commander!" Vekess grasped Joss's arm. An edge of gray had lightened the night; dawn was coming. "Are you well? Eihi! You stink!"

"My thanks," said Joss with a laugh, feeling unaccountably better. "All the better to attract women, don't you think?"

"It might give the rest of us some hope, eh? If you don't mind my asking, Commander, what in the hells happened? We lost sight of you. Next thing, there was Scar flying aloft with neither you or the captain hooked in. Then he stooped and I swear to you there was a blinding flash of light, like the way sun reflects off water if the angle is just right. I caught sight of you on the smallest of the daughter peaks, and then you come aloft again, you sick as a dog and the captain with blistered hands and face like he'd fallen into a fire."

The gulf of air that opened before them seemed to billow and flow. Joss stepped away from the edge as queasiness roiled in his gut and a wave of dizziness swept his head.

"Best you sit down." Abruptly, Tohon appeared beside him.

Vekess and Tohon supported him to the campfire's lonely flare. Rosy light lined the east. Yellow-feathered elegants chirped; a morning red-cap sang.

He sat down hard, the earth's solidity remarkably settling. Anji woke and sat up, looking around to satisfy himself as to the nature of his surroundings. Toughid rose likewise and walked off to one side to take a piss. The sleeping reeves roused, went over to keep Toughid company, pissing off the edge of the ridge and laughing as they bantered.

Anji opened and closed his hands. Slowly, he got to his feet and walked over to Joss. "In what condition does dawn find you?" Anji asked.

"Reeking," said Joss.

"True enough," said Anji with a laugh. "You passed out yesterday. I wondered if you had taken a blow to the head."

"I'm not sure what happened."

Anji raised an eyebrow, and Tohon drew Vekess off.

"Did I dream it all?" demanded Joss.

Anji's face chased through one expression whose lineaments Joss could not fathom and settled on a different one, more confiding and the hells more serious, like when they come to tell you they've found your lover's eagle slaughtered and mutilated and would you please come to look yourself just to get a clear identification. Just to make sure it's the one they all are sure it must be.

"I killed one of the demons."

The words fell, but they had no impact. They were just words.

"I bundled the cloak in my tabard and bound it with every chain we have. I have imprisoned it, lest it escape to corrupt another."

Joss staggered to the rim, where the rock sliced down in rugged leaps and falls, hedged here and there with tough shrubby vegetation caught in cracks and tufts of sedge or thornberry laboring to survive in any scant crevice. From the ridge he surveyed the wide land called Haldia; the River Istri—not yet as tremendously wide as it would become farther downstream—churned along through a rugged gap where it spilled white through foaming rapids.

Anji's bandaged hands and blistered face spoke the words Joss could not say out loud. The outlander had taken a sword to the gift the gods had granted the Hundred.

"Male or female?" Joss cried suddenly. "What cloak? I must see it!"

"The cloth was more brown than orange, something of the color of clay soil. The demon appeared in the guise of a very old woman."

It was not Marit!

Yet that wasn't what should matter. They had broken the boundaries. Now they would be punished. Yet a dawn wind rose on the curve of the sun as it did every morning. Light spilled in the usual way over the rolling river, catching in the streaming waves, dazzling Joss's eyes until he realized those were tears. The world had not ended. The gods had not howled down and obliterated them.

"So it is done," he murmured. "We can never go back."

"We can never go back," echoed Anji.

"You must release the cloak to make a new Guardian. That is the gods' will."

Anji bore the daybreak without flinching. "I will, once our enemies are vanquished. As long as our enemies walk, they may corrupt any cloak newly come into power."

"How can we confine a Guardian's holy cloak?"

"In a chest wrapped with chains. Hidden away where it cannot be easily found." He turned away, speaking as he went. "Best we move quickly, Commander. We'll lose the element of surprise soon enough."

Joss spun, grabbing for Anji's arm. As Joss's hand darted out, Anji threw up an arm and slapped his hand away hard, then caught himself, took a step back, and deliberately relaxed. Toughid came running, pulled up to a walk, halted at a distance, a hand on his sword's hilt.

"My apologies," said Anji. "The hour is early. You startled me."

Joss shook off the ache in his hand and stepped in close. Anji did not react as Joss grasped the captain's forearm. He was taller than Anji, although the captain was sturdier. They'd both seen a lot of death, Joss supposed; they'd both trained in a hard school. Yet for the first time Joss wondered what would happen if they were forced to a fight.

A fight over what? Anji's beautiful wife? The hells!

"There is just one thing," Joss said, easing off the grip and stepping back to show he wasn't meaning to threaten. "Lord Radas, the cloak of Night, Blood, Leaf—and this other one you—" The word stuck in his throat, and after all he could not say *killed*. He swallowed. "Those alone are targets. The woman who wears the cloak of Death is not our enemy."

"Those who warned us cannot be our enemies, can they?" Anji's steady gaze never left Joss's face.

"No."

"Not unless they become corrupted by the sorcery that offers them so much power," added Anji.

Marit's own words—*I don't desire oblivion. Therefore I am already corrupt*—haunted Joss, not Anji's reddened face. Anji had done what must be done: Lord Radas and his allies must be stopped; there was no other way than the way the other Guardians had freely offered them, however impious it was. But what if the corruption, like a cholera spreading through a town, had already worked its shadow into those who did not yet know they were sick? What if corruption was inevitable?

WHEN THEY ARRIVED late that day to Horn Hall, weary, foul-smelling, and coaxing exhausted eagles to perches for a rest and a haunch of meat, a reeve out of Argent Hall was waiting with a message from Olossi. He did not even wait for them to come inside but bounded forward to offer the message to Anji.

Anji unrolled the scrap of paper to reveal a script Joss did not recognize. His eyes scanned the words swiftly. The flare of emotion was as edged as that of a sharp-set eagle so angry it cannot reason.

His expression smoothed to implacability as he studied the words again. His lips tightened. He glanced toward Toughid, who watched him with a gaze that took in every least reaction, measured and prepared to act at Anji's command. Secondarily, he glanced at Tohon, who was standing with Kesta at the ledge's grand wall, pointing toward the Lend at something Joss couldn't see. Anji glanced again over the message. He lifted a hand, signaling to Toughid, who ambled over while scooping his flint out of the pouch. He snapped sparks, coaxed a flare with a bit of dried moss, then applied the flame to the message. The paper caught, and Anji released it, fire consuming as it spun down. The white scraps Anji ground into the stone with the heel of his boot.

He turned to Joss, the bundle hanging at his back swaying with his movement. "I must return to Olossi at once. Ready your reeves. Keep the lines of communication open with our allies. Prepare a storeroom here with padding for oil of naya. We'll send the first vessels up via flights from Naya and Argent Halls. The army will march out of Olossi as soon as I reach there to give the command."

36

WITH ATANI BRACED on her hip, Mai watched Priya hoist a scant bundle of possessions across her narrow back.

The woman smiled gently. "I will come every day, Mistress, in time to say the dawn prayers with you," she said in the steady voice Mai had come to depend on. "It's just O'eki and I would like a little cottage of our own."

A hundred words wished to flood from Mai's tongue, but she held them back. Atani frowned thoughtfully at her, catching her mood.

Don't leave me.

You are the one I depend on.

What if you decide never to return?

She had to smile as Priya took her leave, departing through the garden gate, which Chief Tuvi closed and barred and latched behind her. He exchanged a few words with the guard on duty. In the fading light, he ambled over to Mai. He touched a finger to Atani's soft, dark cheek, offering with both hands to take him, but the baby turned his face into Mai's taloos and gripped his mother more tightly.

"He's afraid you'll take him away, too," muttered Mai.

Tuvi rubbed at the corner of an eye. He scuffed a boot on the gravel walkway. He took in a deep breath of the garden, still blooming because it was watered: the sweet haze of purple-thorn, now fading as the last flowers withered; the slightly bitter taste of tallowberry in its neatly trimmed ranks.

"You can hire a night nurse," he said. "Or purchase one."

"No one I can trust," said Mai. "I will bring Miravia back from Astafero."

He whistled softly, a falling note.

Was he blushing? "Do you like her, Chief?"

He sighed.

"Neh, never mind. I would never have said anything if all that hadn't happened, and that awful Keshad hadn't blurted out all those things, like he has only to wish something and it must be true. I don't like him!" She wiped her running nose with the back of her hand, and sniffed. Because Priya had gone.

"It's just down the street," said Tuvi. "A room in a block with a small courtyard. A hundred steps will bring her here."

"She's free to do as she wishes." It's just she hadn't thought Priya would desert her. For half of Mai's life, Priya had been a constant presence, the one comfort she could rely on.

"Mistress?" Sheyshi padded out into the garden, carrying a lamp. "Are you coming in? Did that wicked woman desert you?"

"She did not desert me, Sheyshi. You aren't to say so. Priya and O'eki have every right to set up their own household. I'm just fortunate they have agreed to continue in my employ, for I am sure I don't know—what I would do—without them—" The words choked her. Atani reared back to stare at her, looking perplexed.

"But Mistress—"

"Sheyshi," said Tuvi, his tone like a slap, "go inside now. We'll want to eat as soon as we come in."

Sheyshi fled, taking the lamp with her. If only Sheyshi had been the one to go, instead of Priya!

"Oh, Tuvi-lo." She let the tears flow, and after a while the tears were all shed and she pressed Atani's precious body against her as he patted at her wet cheeks with his chubby little hands and tasted the moisture that coated his tiny fingers. "I'm ready to go in. You won't leave me, will you?"

"Hu! A question not to be asked. Come, Mistress. Dinner awaits."

"I'm not hungry!"

"Of course you are."

How awful she was even to think of poor Sheyshi in that unpleasant way, because Sheyshi had nowhere to go and no one to go with. It wasn't her fault she so lacked charm and warmth that not one of the Qin soldiers—those who hadn't yet chosen wives from among local women—had expressed the least desire to consider Sheyshi, young as she was, for a wife.

"It's done," she murmured, "and done for the best."

"If you say so, Mistress."

"Priya has the right to desire freedom, just as you or I would." She shifted Atani to the other hip and crunched over the gravel to the porch. After mounting the steps, she kicked off her sandals and entered the lamp-lit audience chamber with its painted screens depicting rats dressed in human style and going about their daily lives: flying kites, throwing pottery on wheels, planting a rice field, rowing in a reed-choked channel of water while fishing.

A murmur of male voices caught her ear. Atani turned, caught by the same lilt, and her heart galloped ahead of her. She walked through the crane room, past the half-open door that looked onto the tiny altar room where Priya had promised to pray with her at dawn, and slid a closed door aside to step into the blazing lamplight of the dining chamber. Its doors were opened wide onto the innermost courtyard, her private sanctuary. On the porch stripping off his riding gloves stood Anji, attended by Toughid, Tohon, and a pair of Qin soldiers whose faces were hidden in shadow although she recognized Chief Deze by his thin frame.

"Anjihosh!" Chief Tuvi strode past Mai, across the matted floor, and out onto the porch. "You have surprised me!"

"Is that disapproval I hear?" said Anji with a laugh. He tapped Tuvi on the shoulder with the back of a hand, affectionately, but already he had looked past him, his gaze meeting Mai's with a look that stopped her in her tracks. His expression was unfathomable, intense, possessive. Disconcerting.

Heat rushed through her. "Anji," she said, her mouth dry and her cheeks flushed.

Atani strained away from her, arms reaching toward his father as he babbled *ba-dababa*.

Anji gestured, and Toughid took his riding whip and gloves. He hastily pried off his boots. In all his dust from his travels he crossed and in full sight of the men loitering on the porch he embraced her and kissed her full on the mouth, deeply, hotly, his body pressed against hers and already quite obviously aroused. Her own feelings spiked abruptly, but she could not forget the presence of his men. He abruptly pulled away and took the baby into his arms. And he laughed. His face was flushed and red; he had what appeared to be a burn along one cheek, blisters whitening along a reddened patch of skin in the early stages of healing.

"Anji! You're hurt. Your hands!"

His hands were wrapped in bandages of linen.

"It's nothing." His voice was hoarse as he examined her. He bent his head to kiss Atani not once but a dozen times, the baby chortling as he smacked his lips to kiss his father back.

"We'll eat," said Anji. "Bring Keshad."

"To the meal?" asked Tuvi, stepping into the dining chamber.

"I'll need a complete report from him. We depart for Astafero at dawn. Little enough time to learn what I must. I'll rest afterward." The look he turned on Mai did not promise rest.

"Sheyshi," she called, knowing her color was still high and that every man there could see it on her. The cursed girl wasn't there.

"Where is Priya?" Anji demanded impatiently.

She found words, clipped and short. "I have freed my slaves, Anji. Priya and O'eki have taken a household just down the street. They will not be here in the evenings, but have taken on a day hire with us."

Whatever passed in his thoughts he deliberately did not speak, so she could not tell if he was angry or bemused. "I see."

"I'll see what's happening in the kitchens. I thought Sheyshi—" To stumble over Sheyshi's dereliction of duty would only make Mai's householding abilities look suddenly suspect. Had Priya and O'eki done so much of the work that made the household run smoothly? Had she never noticed?

Where had that idiot girl gone?

Mai concealed her pounding heart and trembling hands by going to the side table and pouring water into the basin so Anji and his officers could wash before they ate. She poured too hard; water spattered along the polished wood. A droplet hung from the rounded corner, then separated and vanished into the mat. Exquisitely attuned as they were to Anji's mood, his officers washed hands and faces in silence, following the custom of the Hundred, while Mai tossed down additional pillows around the table so there was one for each man and, of course, for herself.

The men unbelted their tabards and quilted silk coats and tossed the gear back out onto the porch for tailmen to tend later. For some reason, Toughid carried a small traveling chest, no longer than his forearm and heavily chained, into the chamber and placed it against one wall. The others set their swords and knives beside their pillows and settled cross-legged around the table, Toughid joining them. There was, at least, tea to be poured, and enough cups. As they drank, she escaped out of the chamber and stumbled into Sheyshi, standing right behind the door with an empty tray in her hands, mouth slack and eyes unfocused as if listening.

"Sheyshi!"

She started so badly she dropped the tray. Mai caught it before it hit the floor, then grabbed Sheyshi's sleeve and tugged.

"I beg you, Sheyshi! Hurry!" She bit down her irritation, for the young woman could not help what she was. "Is the food ready?"

Sheyshi stammered as though a pack of amorous wolves were snapping at her heels. Mai composed herself as they hurried through the house, and when they reached the kitchens it was easy enough to calmly and smilingly designate portions and servers and return with a platter of dumplings as an appetizer.

She paused outside the closed doors of the dining chamber, tray in hand, leaning forward to listen. Inside, Anji was interrogating Keshad in that thorough way he had of uncovering each least detail, the one you thought wasn't important but which as it happened was the most important of all.

"How many soldiers?"

"I counted five hundred and thirty-seven."

"*All* Qin?"

"All."

"Do you know whose clan they serve?"

"They originally served under a Commander Beje."

"Ah. And the rest of the party?"

"There are forty-three males, all gelded, none Qin. I can't know about the women, as all go veiled except the exalted lady."

"How can you be sure that some among those who are veiled are not men?"

"Hiding in the company of women? Perhaps. It would surprise me, having traveled in the empire. The men would sooner kill themselves than stoop to being mistaken for women, and the women would be killed for mixing with men. A foul place, if you ask me."

"I did not ask. Numbers?"

Keshad did not sound the least cowed. "Of women? Hard to say. At least forty?"

"A household," remarked Anji in a tone that made Mai shudder.

Better to take action than stew in a brine of unexamined fear.

She pushed aside the door with her foot and entered briskly, setting down the tray. She washed, then murmured the ritual prayers to the Merciful One for the blessing of food, then seated herself on the pillow the Qin had carefully left for her at the central place at the table. The smell of sweat and horse was strong but not unpleasant. She offered dumplings and they fished them off the platter as Keshad, standing off to one side, shifted from foot to foot like a man whose skin itched but he could not scratch it.

"Master Keshad," said Mai, meaning to be polite but with an edge to her voice she could not disguise, "if you are hungry, please bring a pillow and join us."

"My thanks, verea," he said, answering curtness with equally clipped words, "but I will remain here."

Anji glanced at her. She shook her head minutely, and he snagged a second dumpling from the platter, wolfing it down. She was forcefully aware of his raised hand, his hips shifting as he changed position on the pillow; the way, when Atani grabbed onto his tunic with a chubby fist, he smiled at the baby and settled him on his left thigh within the crook of his left arm so he could eat more easily with his right. He glanced at her frequently, and there was a hungry sheen to him that made her feel he was holding himself in check by sheer will. No wonder the Hundred folk named their goddess Ushara, who presided over love, death, and desire: the Devourer.

Sheyshi led a train of four servers into the room. Mai served out soup and arranged platters, and herself ate. Atani sat contented on his father's lap and made a gruesome face when Anji got him to sip at the caul-petal soup and then coughed out the sip all over the best-quality silk of Anji's undertunic, which was an exceptional shade of heavenly blue. The officers laughed indulgently, and the baby looked all around the table, smiling at their attention, his little face very bright, and so as they ate he was passed from lap to lap, gurgling and babbling and being coaxed to try first another drop of soup or a lick of barsh or a bit of sweetened porridge or a flake of tender fish. Anji asked no more questions of Keshad. When they had eaten their fill he walked out to the porch with Tuvi while the officers dandled the baby. Keshad remained standing motionless, brooding, in his corner. Captain and chief consulted while Mai gathered up the platters and bowls and spoons and piled them neatly on trays. She called in Sheyshi, waiting right outside, to take them away.

"Sheyshi," said Anji, coming back in with the chief at his heels. "Call the other hirelings to take the trays. You may take charge of Atani, although I think his uncles wish to spoil him for a while longer this evening."

The uncles had the ability to chatter on right past this transparent speech. Keshad smirked, and even Sheyshi's gaze flashed from Mai to Anji and back to Mai. Heat scalded Mai's cheeks as she pretended she was rising of her own accord to walk to her husband. Anji hooked her elbow with a grasp of iron. Without a single word of parting he walked her out of the dining chamber and through rooms to the private chamber where none dared follow.

She shook her arm out of his grip. "I feel shamed! You summoned me just like a—a—"

He slapped the door shut behind them, swept her off the floor, and deposited her on the mattress, dropping down beside her.

"I have seen death," he murmured. "My death. Your death. Atani's. Any of us. As long as we live at the mercy of the cloaks who hold power over us, we are vulnerable. Mai." His voice scraped as though, like his face, it had been damaged, but it was only emotion that made it raw.

She gazed up, not that she could see him in the darkness, only the weight and shadow of him. So much of him she knew through physical touch, not through sight. She tasted tonight a quality in him she did not recognize, and yet his need—at this moment rough, aroused and desperate—was familiar to her. It called to her own, rising in part because she had missed him and in part because his sharp desire flattered her.

She captured his hands between her own. "How did you hurt yourself?"

"That is not a tale for this night, plum blossom. All in the course of battle. It will heal." He lowered his weight onto her and kissed her throat, her jaw, her lips; his breathing quickened.

"I'm afraid of what it means, that your mother has come."

"Not for this night, my heart," he whispered. "Tomorrow is time enough to face what will come." His voice took an edge, command rather than request. "Hush."

She knew then, right then, because it was betrayed by his tone and by the way he impatiently began to tug at her clothing and pull at his own quite heedlessly—he, who never hurried, who was always in control—that he too was afraid.

*   *   *

KESH WAS A merchant, and he knew better than to cede any bargaining advantage by showing too much eagerness too early in the process. So he waited through the interminable meal while the captain—quite uncharacteristically—looked ready to devour his wife right there in front of everyone and finally hauled her off while the officers pretended not to notice. Talk about poor market tactics!

The cursed baby did entertain the soldiers, it was true; for such a ruthless pack of wolves, they were as soft as porridge when it came to the child. The baby was very handsome and astonishingly good-natured, as long as he was the center of attention and being held, fed, pampered, and feted. Hard not to be content when your every need was fulfilled at the least hint of displeasure. He was a great deal like his father, Kesh decided; it was easy for Captain Anji to be so calm and even-tempered when the truth was everyone always did everything he wanted. Kesh had heard a rumor in the market that the captain had beaten his wife in public when he'd discovered her coming out of the temple of the Merciless One, and while folk in the market had argued whether such a scene was likely to have happened or ridiculous even to contemplate, Kesh believed it. Outlanders had peculiar ideas about what could be owned; he'd seen enough appalling behavior in the south to believe anything of them now.

So the trick was to figure out how to direct the captain's cosseted temper and Mai's resentment to his advantage, to win Miravia.

That Miravia remembered him, had bothered to learn his name, had given him hope. That she had scorned his kindness by refusing his aid troubled him. He could not interpret such behavior. He was accustomed to women who openly said what they wanted, or did not want.

"Keshad!" Chief Tuvi's voice cracked over him.

The hirelings were snuffing the lamps. While he had stood there brooding, the dining chamber had cleared, the officers had dispersed with their weapons and gear, and he'd been left like a lackwit in the shadows.

"We'll be departing early. Make sure you're ready."

Kesh furiously watched the man amble out of the chamber holding the last lamp, leaving Kesh in the cursed darkness. Did the chief wish to marry Miravia? Was he counting on Mai's support for his suit? Would Miravia choose loyalty to Mai over the impassioned pleading of one sorry man?

Aui! He had so little time to convince her he was worthy of her, although compared to Chief Tuvi he brought nothing to a marriage except his undying devotion. He'd stood on the auction block; he'd clutched his little sister to his side, devoted to her as well, but that devotion had not spared Zubaidit from being sold to the Merciless One's temple while he'd been dragged off to serve as a slave in Master Feden's household for twelve long years. Devotion was not porridge. You could not survive on it.

The compound was a large one, easily sleeping a hundred or more people. Kesh had been allotted a pallet in the warehouse along with two grooms and a man who swept and cleaned, but after persistent complaints about their snoring and farting, he had finally been given permission to install himself, his accounts book, and his coin chest in the counting room, like a night watchman. O'eki, Mai, and Chief Tuvi held the locks to the compound's wealth and accounts books; Kesh just rolled out a thin mattress at night and slept with his small coin chest as close beside him as he might one day hope to embrace a loving wife.

He retired there now, with a single lamp to accompany him. He knew to a vey how much he possessed, but he counted it again anyway. Two hundred and nine leya, and two cheyt. It was a substantial sum for a young man only one year removed from the debt slavery that had eaten his youth. Was it enough to set up as a merchant, rent rooms, feed the children that would result from their bed . . .

He wiped his brow, thinking of the way the captain had stared at his wife all through dinner. Whew! Arousal stirred in his body. Thinking of Miravia, he could not think. The thought of touching her was like a delirium. He sat with his hands caught in the strings of coin and tried to calm his breathing, but it was no good. He shut his eyes.

Voices yanked him awake from a slumped doze over the open chest. He banged down the lid just as the door to the counting room was opened from within the compound. Toughid came in first, a small chest hanging off his back like a quiver. He placed himself between Kesh and the captain, who entered with Chiefs Tuvi and Deze.

Anji wore an elaborate robe of best-quality green silk embroidered with sea creatures emerging from white silk thread wavelets. Kesh had never seen him without his hair neatly packed away in the Qin topknot; tonight it was merely tied back with a ribbon, hanging down his back. His hair was as thick and black and lovely as his wife's, and almost as long.

Kesh was as suddenly uncomfortable as if he had walked into the captain's private sleeping chamber to find him in bed with his wife.

"So," said Anji to Kesh, with his men looking on like executioners, "my mother has offered to give you my wife."

Anji was not armed, but the other three were; indeed, they looked as if they had slept in their clothes, if they had slept at all. Kesh had certainly not mentioned the matter, but his stupidity in blurting out the truth to Mai when they had been arguing over Miravia had tramped back to trip him up. Unless he could think very quickly indeed. Timidity would win him nothing now.

"Your mother insists you deserve a wife worthy of your consequence, as a man of elevated birth," Kesh said. "Son and brother of emperors, grandson and nephew of vars. That's what the Qin call their rulers, is it not? I suppose among you outlanders, who are eager to make such distinctions among families, you might care about such things. Here in the Hundred, of course, a person's suitability is measured by clan connections and the individual's own skills."

"You do not deny the offer was made?" asked Anji so easily that Kesh felt the knife already at his throat, although no one touched him.

"How can I deny it, when it is true? Her words surprised me as much as they do you, Captain."

"Her words do not surprise me at all."

That look might scorch walls! But the captain muted his anger as quickly as an incoming wave washes away a piece of sea wrack on a sandy shore: no longer in sight, it yet remains trapped in the watery expanse.

The time to bargain was upon him.

"Your mother is a formidable woman, Captain. Mai is a treasure that any man—any clan in Olossi—would be pleased to acquire as, I believe, you acquired her back in that dreary desert town that had nothing more than a well and a stable and a herd of sheep, and one very beautiful young woman selling fruit in the marketplace."

Chief Tuvi rested a hand on Anji's arm as the captain tensed, but Keshad kept talking.

"Indeed, your mother offered me both women—your wife, and Miravia. So tell me, Captain. It's a good offer. Why should I refuse it?"

"I'll kill you," said Anji as Tuvi actually took hold of the captain's arm.

Although Kesh was shaking, with the coin chest wedged against his knees as a most hideously inadequate shield against the captain's coiled fury, he knew he was about to win this negotiation. Because the one thing Anji had not said, which Kesh had indeed expected him to say, was that his mother had no say in the matter of disposing of his wife.

"Will you kill your mother, then, as well? She seemed most insistent that you could not remain married to—not that she recognized it as a marriage, mind you—an inconvenient merchant's daughter."

"Anjihosh," said Tuvi.

"Captain," said Toughid.

"My lord," said Chief Deze, "this man's blood is not worthy to stain these fine mats."

If the captain had been wearing a sword, Kesh figured he would be dead by now. But Anji wasn't, and he had enough pride not to grab for another man's weapon.

The flame hissed softly. Anji breathed harshly. Kesh barely breathed at all. Slowly, Chief Tuvi released his grip on the captain's arm.

Anji fisted his hands, as if to punch Kesh; opened them, as if wishing to strangle him; at last found a spot of stillness within which to slaughter Kesh with his stare. "What do you want, Keshad?"

Kesh glanced at Tuvi, but the chief remained impassive. "I want Miravia."

"Do you want to acquire her as you would a slave?" said Anji with a caustic laugh. "Would that make her come willingly to you, when you know she remains Ri Amarah in her thoughts and ritual, even though her family has abandoned her?"

Kesh indicated Tuvi. "I want no other claim put in my way."

Anji looked at the chief, but the chief shrugged. It wasn't negation; Tuvi had never said if he wanted, or did not want, the young woman; his gesture was a refusal to be roped in.

"If she eats my rice," Kesh went on, "then I want permission to leave Olo'osson. To ride elsewhere—"

"Into the teeth of the enemy?" said Anji. "Reckless, to be sure."

"There are other quiet valleys and market towns in the Hundred where we can make a peaceful life."

"Maybe there are now. But we're fighting a war. You cannot be sure those quiet market towns and valleys will remain quiet and unmolested. I have no doubt the soldiers of the enemy's army would be quite eager to plow Ri Amarah ground, for the novelty of it."

Kesh leaped up, charged past the chest, and lunged at Anji. His feet were kicked out from under him and he landed flat on his back with the wind knocked out of him, and Anji's hand wrapped around his throat and his knee dug into Kesh's chest. Kesh sucked air, but he didn't struggle.

The cursed man grinned, the more frightening because he hadn't loosed his grip on Kesh's throat. "You've got stones, I'll give you that. I take it this was your effort to negotiate from a position of weakness."

Anji knew exactly how much pressure he was applying to Kesh's throat and chest, as if he'd threatened, or even killed, men this way before.

"So you will listen to me now, Keshad. The only reason you are not dead is because I owe a debt to your sister."

Zubaidit!

"Yes, that's got you thinking at last, hasn't it?"

"Prol' . . . dead . . . now . . ."

"Perhaps. Obviously I have more confidence in your sister than you do. She has a rare gift. You ought not to value her so low. You ought to value her, in her own way, as highly as I value my wife. Listen very carefully, Master Keshad."

The mat pressed into his back. Anji's breath was sweetened with mint; his eyes were dark, and his black hair had slipped over his shoulder to brush against Keshad's shoulder as intimately as might a lover's.

"Mai belongs to me. Do not think to play this game, to go behind my back and make bargains with my mother. This is your only warning. I can kill you as easily as I breathe, and I will if you do anything to attempt to separate Mai from me. As for the other—who Miravia marries is no concern of mine, although Mai may have something to say about her wishes in the matter. It is with Mai you must negotiate, not with me, although I admit you might have preferred to negotiate with me knowing, as I am sure you do, that compared to my wife I do not know how to bargain at all. Indeed, Keshad, you might have learned this about me before you attempted it. I don't bargain, because I don't have to."

He let him go, rose to his feet, turned away.

He paused, then turned back. The finely embroidered hem of his best-quality robe brushed Kesh's body as if to remind Kesh that he himself wore everyday-quality linen, the most he dared afford.

"We leave from the harbor at midday. I expect you in attendance." He bared his teeth wolfishly, and Kesh shuddered. "You are still my slave, Keshad, until such time as your sister returns alive, or we have proof of her demise in the course of her mission."

"We might never know!"

"So we might," agreed Anji with a lazy smile. "You might wish to consider what that eventuality would mean to you."

He gestured, and with his officers left the counting room. Kesh heard him speaking as they went out the door. "Now, I will speak to O'eki and Priya. Given the situation, best if I go to them—"

Chief Tuvi shut the door and barred it from the far side without a parting glance. Kesh sat alone with his lamp and his coin. His heart burned, but his mind counted a colder price.

Anji would kill him; the man did not make idle threats. But if Anji was preemptively attacking Keshad to make sure he did not go behind Anji's back, surely that suggested that Anji feared his mother might manage to get her way despite Anji's wishes. In the light of the lamp, with his entire fortune contained in a chest that, like a heart's feelings, can be opened and perused by one who holds the key, Kesh saw better the shadows in the room. It was true he might negotiate with Anji's mother, betray Anji and Mai both, to gain Miravia.

Did he want to be that kind of man?

Miravia did not belong to him. Nor did he want her to, not in the way his labor had once belonged to Master Feden, or Zubaidit's body and spirit belonged to the temple she served.

He had made a story in his heart about their mutual passion, but it was only a story. He could not help desiring the face he had seen, the woman he had so briefly spoken with among the scattered cord and ribbon of the marketplace. Maybe it was only lust that drove him; maybe it was the lure of the forbidden; yet perhaps a true spark had leapt between them, promising a deeper bond.

Almost two years ago he had trudged over the Kandaran Pass north back into the Hundred in possession of a treasure to buy his sister's freedom from the temple. Things hadn't worked out the way he had planned. But he had said something one day, high in the mountains, while speaking with another traveler, a man who appeared to be an envoy of Ilu:

It matters what path a man takes as he walks through the world.

He finally comprehended what those words meant. Miravia was the one who would have to decide. She was the one he had to negotiate with.

*   *   *

IN THE BREATH of gray lightening just before dawn, Anji woke Mai. His hands knew her body very well, and he was determined to arouse her. He was always a careful lover, as if her pleasure mattered more to him than his own.

She captured his bandaged hands against her flesh. "Are you making up for last night?" She tried to make her voice light. "I received little enough pleasure from it, except perhaps to think it relieved you of some terrible anger or grief."

He had his eyes shut, savoring touch. "My apologies," he murmured, kissing her. "I was overwrought. I lost my head."

"That's not like you, Anji."

"No." He cracked an eye, measuring her. "Must we have this conversation right now? I was just beginning my attack. I have my strategy completely planned."

He hooked a knee between her legs, using his body's weight and strength to provoke her. At the feel of his body pressed against her, the familiar flash of desire flooded her. She could sense he knew in the way he shifted, in his smile, in the way he shut his eyes to savor her pretended resistance.

She remained stubbornly immobile. "What will happen now that your mother is in Astafero?"

He sighed heavily and opened his eyes, body relaxing. "That's done it. How can you possibly speak of such things in our bed, Mai?"

"Because we have privacy here, and therefore none of your officers are standing within a sword's length of you."

He looked away from her, toward the closed doors, and she released his hands, not that he couldn't have freed them at any time. At once, taking advantage, he rolled on top of her.

"Now, plum blossom. Listen carefully. We will travel together to Astafero, by ship."

"Not by eagle? You seem to be in haste."

"No, not by eagle, although events move quickly elsewhere and I do have need of haste. I need a full honor guard to attend me, to show proper consequence. I will present you to my mother. We will see what events have transpired—beyond the obvious startling news of my brother's death and my cousin's ascension to the imperial throne. I must know what has driven my mother north to the Hundred to find me."

"What if your cousin wishes to kill you, Anji? Isn't your claim to the imperial throne more legitimate than his?" Even to contemplate such a fate—Anji becoming emperor in that dreadful place!—made her want to weep.

He kissed her, as if to seal the thought away, unspoken and thereby rejected. "I do not wish to be emperor in Sirniaka. I am too much a son of the Qin to wish for that now. Nor would they want me, because I am no longer one of them." He had much of his weight resting on his arms as he addressed her. "But it cannot be ignored that my cousin may wish to have me killed. My mother would not for an instant be party to such a desire. But they may have sent agents with her to accomplish the task. Yet she will know that also, and be on the alert for it. She is no fool. Also, it seems she is accompanied by over five hundred Qin soldiers out of Commander Beje's command."

"Commander Beje! The one we met in Mariha." His first wife's father, who had thanked Anji for saving the clan's honor. "He's the one who saved your life by warning you that your own Qin uncle had agreed to have you killed, to seal a treaty with your Sirniakan half brother." Spoken aloud, the words fell like knives.

"So, you see, plum blossom, I have allies. We are not alone."

"But what of the war here, Anji? You were gone for days, scouting in the north, and I have heard not one word of what you saw and what you decided."

His gaze narrowed, as it did when dark thoughts troubled him. "War is coming. That's all I can say."

"Sengel did not come back with you. You've left him to prepare the way."

"You know how I trust him. Now. Have we discussed these matters in a satisfactory way, enough to put your fears to rest for the moment?"

"My fears to rest? Anji! We speak of assassins. Of a coming war!"

"Little enough time for pleasure in the face of these difficulties. May we continue?"

"No." She watched his surprise at her bald refusal, and in that brief startled release of his vigilance, she rolled him over so she was on top. She smiled, because what else could she do? He would ride away soon enough. She had him for so short a time. "But now we can."

THE BED WAS only a respite. He did not linger afterward. He washed and dressed, called for and dandled the baby on his lap while Mai, seated behind him, combed out his hair and twisted it up into its topknot, bound with gold silk ribbons, very festive. When she had finished and he was presentable, he left for the militia encampment with his officers. She nursed Atani and then, according to Anji's specifications, supervised packing up for a journey while Sheyshi fussed over which silks to bring and which to leave behind.

Priya and O'eki's arrival surprised her.

She kissed Priya, while O'eki went to supervise the closing down and sealing up of the counting room.

"I am leaving for Astafero." She dared not beg Priya to come with her, because she did not want to beg, and yet she could scarcely bear to go without her.

"The captain asked us to attend you," said Priya, indicating a traveling chest, two covered baskets, and a pair of scuffed old saddlebags stuffed to bursting.

Mai touched Priya's arm, shy of contact because she did not know how to treat a woman she had once called "slave." "Did he ask you, or command you?"

"I do not mind, plum blossom." Priya kissed her on the cheek with dry lips. "These last few days have been difficult for you."

"I have been selfish. If you do not wish to go—"

"We are going, Mistress. Let it be."

The harbor was busy, the town abuzz with messengers, gossip, commerce, and nervous anticipation: The army was on the move, leaving Olossi with a scant guard to protect itself should the worst happen and the attack into the north fail. The folk of Olo'osson were gambling, having offered up their young men, their horses, and significant supplies. They had only one chance.

"Should I have chosen a welcoming gift?" whispered Mai to Priya as they watched two low-slung cargo ships being laded with a remarkable amount of cloth and other fineries. Mai stroked Atani's back anxiously until the baby wriggled to show his discomfort, his dark eyes drawn down very like his father's when Anji was trying to hide annoyance. "I have to make a good impression. Why didn't Anji say something to me?"

"There the captain comes," said Priya, squeezing Mai's elbow.

Atani squirmed, hearing hooves, a sound he evidently associated with his father. He reached, spotting his father among a cadre of thirty-six riders. A cadre of foot soldiers marched behind.

The horses would be going with the army. Anji dismounted. He greeted Mai first, then kissed Atani and handed him to Chief Tuvi. He greeted Priya and O'eki with respect, acknowledged the others with a glance, even the silent Sheyshi. At Anji's look, Keshad actually took a step back, bumping into one of the hirelings, who muttered a curse. Many folk had gathered to watch, as Hundred folk commonly did, for any activity or interaction that occurred in public was meant to be watched, discussed, and commented upon.

"I forgot to bring a welcoming gift for your mother," Mai murmured.

"She would accept no such gift from you."

"How am I to greet and converse with a woman who has already tried to get rid of me?"

"Listen, Mai." He glanced back at Atani, content in Tuvi's arms, then bent his gaze toward her as they walked up the gang plank onto the deck. "She is my mother. She raised me. She saved my life at the cost of her own freedom. I owe her respect and obedience, as all Qin sons respect and honor their mothers. Anyhow, until I know what has brought her here, I can make no plan. You must follow my lead in this."

The same tension that had troubled his visage last night before he had devoured her settled heavily on him, making him seem a different person than the uncomplicated Qin captain who had plucked her out of the marketplace and carried her off to distant lands. But perhaps he had not changed at all. Perhaps this man had always been masked behind the other one, thickly chained like the little chest Toughid carried slung over his mount's hindquarters. Now and then this other man escaped, and however much she loved Anji, she was not sure she liked that piece of him very much.

* * *

SHAI TRACKED SIXTH Cohort for four days before he spotted Zubaidit. He was hiding in a stand of pipe-brush overlooking a stream, and cursed if she wasn't wearing a sergeant's stripes and leading the rearguard along the bank, striding along in that easy way she had. Her soldiers were quiet and disciplined, but they were also in a hurry. For four days Sixth Cohort had been marching toward Nessumara.

Shai pitched a stone into the water. The plop caught the patrol's attention. Then he ran the other way, across a weed-ridden field. He favored a leg, pretending to limp.

"Get him!" That was Zubaidit's voice. "Capture him alive."

Had she recognized him just from his back?

He stumbled on purpose, hoping to make the inevitable fall go more easily, but the soldiers hit him across the back with their staffs and piled on, grinding his face into a desiccated thistle. He inhaled bristles and grit.

"He's got a knife." They took his weapons.

He heard her voice. "Have you caught yourselves a gods-rotted outlander, lads? There's a cursed good reward for bringing in outlanders."

"Not fair," complained one of the men, "just because those three were close enough to grab him."

"I could take the whole cursed reward and forget about you lot. But I'll divide the reward and my bonus evenly between the entire cadre and give you three who tackled him a bit extra for your trouble. I'll take the knives and his staff meanwhile. Any complaints? No? Let him up."

The pressure on his back eased, and he spat out dirt. Cautiously, he rolled to sit.

Zubaidit wore soldier's garb and, around her neck, an eight-pointed star hammered out of tin, the mark of the army. Leaning on the staff they'd taken from him, she studied him, but the way she was looking at him made him cursed uneasy.

"Get rope," she said. "We don't want to lose him. Not with so much coin at stake."

"What do we do with him, Sergeant?" asked one of the men as he brushed dirt off his trousers.

"I'll search him for other weapons. Then we take him to Captain Arras. Hurry up! We're trailing behind, you cursed lagabouts. I could march faster when I was a wee toddler. There've been reeve patrols sighted in this area. A couple of cadres were hit by attacks."

"Wish I had an eagle." The youngest scanned the sky with a wistful look.

"So you'd wish, until it ripped your head off," said Bai with a laugh. "Here, give me the rope. Get ready to march out. You three, scout ahead."

She kneeled behind Shai and yanked his arms so hard up behind him that he grunted in pain. With his wrists tied tightly back, he sat there panting as she patted up his legs and torso.

"Cursed fool," she breathed into the back of his neck. "If you came deliberately, fist both hands."

He fisted both hands.

She grunted, like an echo of his pain. "Follow my lead."

She fastened a lead line to his rope shackles, fastened his belt and small pack over her back, and handed the lead to a soldier. "Six men on him at all times. Let's move."

As they marched, he in the middle of the cadre and she striding along close by, she commenced a running commentary. "Well built, isn't he? Are all outlanders so cursed well built, do you think? Look at those arms! Whew! He's got a cursed good chest under that shirt. Makes me miss my Devouring days, eh?"

"If you don't mind my saying so, Sergeant," said one of the three women who marched in the cadre, a fine-boned woman who carried a bow like she knew how to use it, "I thought the captain was after your ass."

"I'll tell you, Taria, the best piece of advice I'll ever give you, is never ever milk a man who sits in authority over you. Not unless you have no choice. And unless you like wielding the whip, don't milk one you have authority over. Slaves are different, of course."

"Why? You fancy this one? I can't say I think he's that cursed handsome, but— whew!—you're right about his arms. Why don't we strip off his shirt and look over the rest of him?"

Zubaidit grinned. "I wish we could sell him. But I suppose the cloaks will just take him away, since they're the ones who set the reward. Although what in the hells they want with outlanders I can't imagine."

On they strode, as the soldiers tossed suggestions back and forth, ranging from the mundane to the obscene. The odd thing was that this group was not any different from any gaggle of militiamen, mostly youngish men with a few older men and the three women, all archers and, by their similar features, probably related. Zubaidit threw in comments now and again, but she retained an air of separation very like the chiefs among the Qin. It was a strong cadre; they were alert; they looked out for each other; they kept up the pace. They were very little like the first cohort of Star of Life he'd met. These soldiers seemed human.

They paused at the fringe of a woodland copse beside a shallow pool ringed by mulberry trees and a pair of fallow diked fields. The cadre set up a perimeter using a pair of fallen logs as a line of protection, and the three archers headed out around the woodland with a trio of scouts flanking. Shai was allowed to take a piss, with Zubaidit holding the rope, just far enough away that, within sight of everyone but with their backs turned so no one could see their mouths moving, they could exchange a few words.

He did not hesitate. "I know how to kill Lord Radas. There are two precious vials of snake venom in the pouch. On a dart, the venom is deadly if it penetrates the skin. Even a cloak will fall if infected by the poison."

"Cloaks can't die."

"We have to strip the cloak off him while he's in a stupor."

"Can it be so simple?"

"Not if the cloak knows what you intend. Then it's impossible."

"Of course. They can always anticipate an attack." She swatted him, hard, across the back of the head, and spoke in a loud voice. "Aren't you finished? You're as slow as an ox!"

"And not as well hung!" shouted a soldier, as the others laughed.

"Has anyone checked?" asked another.

"Hush, now, you'll frighten off the game." Zubaidit tugged Shai back into the midst of the cadre, and he sank down and rested his forehead on bent knees, abruptly so tired he could not keep his eyes open. He'd shared the secret. She knew; she was still with him; they had their chance to complete the job.

May the Merciful One protect them!

He dozed, and was awakened when the hunting party returned with a half dozen birds and a plump yearling deer. At dusk they reached the cohort, which was settling for the night in a deserted village. The captain was a cautious man; he'd ringed the village with fires and a barrier hastily constructed out of boards torn from the cottages. They'd found a bag of nai flour to cook into porridge, enough for the entire cohort. Zubaidit's cadre fell to arguing over how much of their meat they had to share out among six hundred men, until she snapped at them to shut up. Then, with the three men who'd actually captured him, she sought out the captain.

He'd set up for the night in the council square, a roof over a square of benches screened on three sides by lattices grown with vines. He was sitting on a camp stool with his boots and armor off, relaxed in bare feet and loose jacket and trousers. Over the council hearth he roasted strips of meat on a metal rod over the fire. He rose as Zubaidit led Shai in.

All he said, after looking Shai up and down in the firelight, was a breath of a word. "Ah."

He sat again and bent his attention to the sizzling meat. They waited while the meat roasted, and afterward he pulled the strips onto a wooden platter and offered some both to Zubaidit and to Shai, although he did not offer to let them sit. Shai was so cursed hungry he burned his mouth by gulping down the meat while it was still too hot to chew.

The captain ate with the infuriating deliberateness of a man who is thinking hard and trying not to outpace himself. Zubaidit licked her fingers after; the captain watched her, realized he was watching, and looked away, right at Shai.

"Where'd you find this outlander, Sergeant?"

"Out lurking in the brush. I guess he panicked and started running. My men caught him. Here he is. I've told them they'll share out the reward. There was a reward, wasn't there? My cadre will be cursed irritated if they discover there isn't."

His lips thinned. Was he angry? "There is a generous reward." He rubbed a clean-shaven jaw. He reminded Shai of the Qin, a fit man who carried himself confidently. He looked again at Shai, and his frown deepened. "What in the hells am I to do with you?"

Zubaidit's eyebrows twitched; something in her expression made Shai uneasy, but he could not identify what it was. Was *she* uneasy?

"I thought you'd be glad of an outlander, Captain. Something to boast about at the next army council at Saltow. Or do you fear Commander Hetti will say *he* captured him and take the reward for himself? Isn't that what he always does?"

He cut another haunch of meat into slices and skewered them on the rod. "Why do you care, Sergeant?"

"I'm ambitious, Captain, just as you are. I'd rather be loyal to one who shows loyalty to those he commands than to one like Commander Hetti, who takes what others have done and uses it to raise himself up. I couldn't help but notice after the failed attack on Nessumara, that it was your proposals for prosecuting the war that Hetti adopted as if they were his own. The very things the army went out and did, which got you no credit. I don't mind saying I want the reward I've promised to my cadre, and I want a chance for a company command."

A female sergeant came forward with a kettle for tea and set it on a wire trivet over a bed of glowing coals raked off to one side. The captain glanced at her, an intimate look that reminded Shai of Anji's interactions with his chiefs. Her shrug was unfathomable to Shai, but the captain nodded.

"There are ways around Commander Hetti," he said. "So the question you and I must face, Sergeant, is do we really want a cloak to walk into our camp to claim this outlander, and meanwhile cut into our hearts and thoughts, as they will do. Are you willing to have your heart laid bare? Are you sure you will survive their scrutiny?"

"I have nothing to hide!"

"Maybe I do have something to hide," said the captain, gaze sliding smoothly to Shai.

Merciful One! Shai recognized him: this was the captain who had waited in attendance on Hari outside Toskala. He'd arranged for Shai to get smuggled out of camp.

He knew Shai knew; Shai knew he knew. But if he wasn't going to say anything, then Shai sure as the hells could keep his mouth shut. He had a job to do, whatever it meant for him in the end. A good soldier rides into battle without flinching. His comrades depended on him, and beyond all things, he must never let them down. That was the Qin way, and whatever else the Qin were—conquerors of the Golden Road and the Mariha princedoms—they had taken in and trained a hapless seventh son like Shai. He owed them something.

The captain shook his head with a sigh. "Unfortunately we can't rid ourselves of the outlander now. Everyone has seen him."

"Why would we want to rid ourselves of him when we have standing orders to bring in all outlanders and gods-touched—?"

"Never mind. We can send a message to Lord Commander Radas, sealed and for his clerk's eyes only. Be sure you have nothing to hide, Sergeant. For if you do, you'll be dead."

"I'll be dead anyway," she said with a Devouring smile that made the captain wince and then laugh ruefully. "We'll all be dead someday, Captain. Won't we?"

"The cloaks say otherwise," he said softly. "Don't you believe them, Sergeant?"

Bai's smile, in response, frightened Shai, for there was something implacable in it. Even the captain flung up his chin, looking startled, but her posture altered as she thrust out a hip in a provocative stance that reminded a man of how bodies might grapple. Shai broke out in a sweat, recalling his grappling with the actress Eridit in the rocks, months ago now, barely more than a dream. Yet what a dream!

"I serve where I am bidden," Bai said, the words like a promise.

The other sergeant's gaze tightened, watching this display. She nudged the captain.

"Don't," he said to Bai, "for we agreed there'd be none of that. As for the other, you're right. I don't like to think of Commander Hetti gathering to himself the harvest of what my cohort has sown, as he'll do if I don't act."

"I know what I want," agreed Zubaidit. "This outlander will help both of us get what we seek."

37

THE QIN TROOP arrived at the shore of the western Barrens after a two day journey over waters so smooth that even Anji had shown no sign of seasickness, although Mai had thrown up twice and given up on any food except nai porridge. A company of riders leading extra horses waited where the ships were dragged up onto the strand. Qin led the ranks and local men filled out the rest of the company, many of whom were growing out their hair to twist up in topknots.

This impressive cavalcade clad in black tabards provided their escort as they rode to the gates of Astafero. The dusty colors of the Barrens leached Mai's heart of courage, but she knew how to keep her expression placid and her hands from trembling. As long as Anji was beside her, she could face down anything.

Folk gathered at the gate; guards lined the wall walk, their spears adorned with rippling banners in the wind that blew down off the mountains. It was so hot that her mouth parched, making it difficult to swallow. Yet the bright colors worn by the local women pleased her eye, and the people who lined the main avenue leading up through town, waving banners and ribbons, sang a greeting. Their smiling faces and strong voices heartened her. Whatever Anji's mother might think of her, she had allies here.

At Anji's insistence, she rode beside him. He understood the protocols far better than she could; he had been raised in an imperial court until the age of twelve and afterward sent to his uncle's court as a prince, even if after all that he had ridden in the Qin army as a mere captain. And yet had he been a mere captain? Had she misunderstood his rank? Or had his uncle the var all along been suspicious of his nephew? Clearly, his uncle had been willing enough to rid himself of Anji, given the chance.

Had Commander Beje's only motivation been to repay the favor Anji had shown

Beje's clan by not dragging the clan's dishonor—his first wife's abandonment of him—through the var's court? Or did Beje covet other allegiances? Mai remembered old Widow Lae who had been hanged in Kartu Town for her treachery against the Qin. Where had her grandson gone? To whom had he been conveying her message?

Anji glanced at her; his hands were light on the reins, but his eyes were tight. She nodded coolly in return. He smiled, a flash that might have been loving encouragement, or anticipation of a cruel triumph as he forced his mother to accept a humble merchant's daughter as his wife. She looked ahead.

The porch wrapping around the big house had been extended, and whole sections around the side screened off with canvas. Even in the few weeks since Mai had last sailed to Astafero to see Miravia and to coax Uncle Hari out of the valley and down to the assizes that one time, the house had been changed: whitewashing on the walls, curtains screening the windows, pillars wrapped with elaborately painted but half finished floral scenes. In addition to all this other decoration, the big house had been festooned with banners in the Qin style, a rainbow of colors: bold scarlet, sun gold, heavenly blue, bone white, mist silver, festival orange, night black, rain-sodden green, and a sighing purple that reminded her of Uncle Hari when she had last seen him flying away from Astafero's assizes. How well the assizes had gone! She drew strength from the memory.

A figure was seated in an ornate chair placed on the high porch as if the entire settlement of Astafero had been built to display and enhance the seated person's authority.

"Be brave, plum blossom," murmured Anji. He carried Atani in a sling against his chest, the baby facing forward and looking around with his usual delighted expression, as if to say: all this! a parade for me! Not that Atani could possibly understand what was happening, or the import of this procession and what it suggested. When the Qin had taken over rule of Kartu Town, the city fathers and lords had processed to the fort in a show of humility. They had come to the Qin, not the other way around. So Anji approached his mother.

Attendants lined the plank walkway, sheltered from the sun by a new slate roof constructed over what had once been wings of canvas. Miravia stood on the lower steps, below the other attendants. Besides the kitchen women standing at the leftmost corner of the porch, Miravia was the only visible woman. Their gazes met across the gap, but Miravia did not descend to greet her. She glanced past Mai, searching for someone else, then self-consciously adjusted the scarf that bound her hair. Realizing what she was doing, she lowered her hand.

Anji signaled the troop to a halt, dismounted, and handed his reins to a groom. He beckoned to Mai. Tuvi dismounted and came to hold her horse. Swinging down, she paced as in a dream to Anji. He unwrapped the baby from his sling and handed him to Mai. To clasp the plump little fellow gave her courage. She had a piece of Anji that his mother did not.

They approached the porch and ascended past a silent Miravia.

The woman was seated in a lofty chair of bright blue silk embroidered with dragons in a darker blue thread; these intense colors set off her gold headdress and the gown with its draperies that flowed around her. She had a broad, bold face, no beauty but certainly handsome in the Qin way. She was not as old as Mai had thought she would be; her skin had a few wrinkles but no blemishes; her hands looked strong and capable, her shoulders were unbowed. She stared fiercely at her son—a man she had not seen for almost twenty years—and spared no glance for his wife and son.

Anji kneeled to touch her right slippered foot with his right hand, then brushed his fingers against his chest and his forehead before he looked up at her.

"Honored Mother." He did not grovel. His pride elevated him. Whatever his true feelings were, he kept them reined in.

No one spoke as the mother examined her son. If joy or memory or tears welled deep in that steel countenance, Mai could not perceive them. She took her time looking him over, much—Mai supposed—as Anji had carefully examined Atani when he had first held the little boy. Banners snapped; ribbons fluttered. Hooves shifted as horses grew restless. The sun blazed on Mai's back, but her body shielded Atani within its shade.

"You look well enough, my son. Not handsome, I am afraid. But you have grown up strong and fit." Nothing frail about her voice! Or her first line of attack, cutting straight for a vanity he did not, in fact, possess. "Possibly you're even competent, if the reports I have heard are true."

Mai was abruptly glad he had made no gesture commanding Mai to bow and scrape as he had done, for even fixed on her son, his mother's gaze had the biting remoteness of a desert adder's. Mai was pretty sure she could not bring herself to show obeisance to a woman who refused to show even one drop of affection for the son whose life she had saved years ago, a child she had not seen in twenty years. Yet she must be strong enough to welcome the woman's overtures, should they ever come.

"I am come from Sirniaka, Son. Your half brother Azadihosh is dead. I do not regret his death, or his family's slaughter, since it was his people who wished to kill you when they took pride of place in the palace. So do the gods work, in cutting the throats of those who forget that fate has a hand on every knife. Your cousins now hold the throne and its power. I am released from my prison and return to comfort you, Son. I do regret the many years we have been forced to live apart."

For all the sentiment of the words, her voice did not quiver. Still, incredibly, she managed not to look at Mai or the baby.

"Why did they let you go?" he asked. No pretty speeches; no joyful embraces. They got straight down to business. "Once a woman is brought into the emperor's palace, she is released only by death."

"Not even then," she said with a curt laugh, "for the white robes capture her spirit in their blessing bowls and confine it forever to the jar of misery that is all the afterlife they will permit women." Her smile held bitter victory. "Your cousins feared what might happen if they attempted to have me put down like a broken horse. My brother betrayed me when he sold me to the emperor in exchange for border trading rights, but he made sure the Sirni understood that my life and honor must never be tarnished. However, your cousins released me: to act as their emissary."

Her gaze flicked to Mai, like a blow: comprehensive, swift, and meant to make Mai flinch. Mai found her market smile and fixed it on like paint. The baby gurgled and reached one sweet little hand toward his father, babbling, "Baba. Baba."

"What business could my cousins have with me?" Anji asked as he smoothly took the baby out of Mai's arms and settled the silk-swaddled bottom on his upright thigh. He glanced down at the crowing infant. "Hush, sunflower," he said fondly.

Atani hushed, gazing raptly at his father.

The old woman's gaze tightened in exactly the way Anji's did when he was annoyed.

Mai felt her smile pinch toward a smirk, and she battled it back to the innocuously pleasant face she wore when men tried to grope her or women to cheat her. It was the face she had perfected through years of dealing with her hated Uncle Girish. Merciful One grant her open-heartedness! How could she have taken such a powerful and instantaneous dislike to a woman she did not even know?

The woman rose, and in rising displayed the smooth weave and magnificent embroidery of her gown. The silk was astoundingly rich and cunningly embroidered, a veritable treasure house of fabric. This was emperor's silk, not for the likes of a girl born to an insignificant sheep-herding clan in a dusty desert trading town.

"Your cousins are not unaware of the difficulty your existence poses to them. You have a legitimate claim to the imperial throne."

"Which I forswore by leaving the palace. By going into exile, I became as one dead to the imperial court."

"Dead to the court, but not dead in your physical form. The former is one style of death. The latter is more permanent. Naturally your cousin fears you may change your mind and choose to live. But your uncle, my brother, the var, might take it amiss if you were to die at the new emperor's hands."

"My uncle, the var, ordered me killed. Were you unaware of the bargain he made with Azadihosh?"

"I hear whispers, as must any woman in the palace who values the life of her son. My brother desired an easy path into the rich trade offered by the border towns. Your half brother Farazadihosh was desperate. He was newly come to the throne. He suspected his cousins meant to contest him, and he knew they commanded better and more numerous troops than he did. He sought an ally. Your uncle my brother sought advantage."

"And my life was the piece on the board my uncle was willing to sacrifice. Did that part of this tale escape you, Honored Mother?"

She brushed a hand over his head in an intimate manner, touching his topknot. "Of course it did not escape me. Do you think it was chance you survived?"

"Commander Beje gave me the opportunity to escape with my life."

"Did this surprise you?"

"It did, I admit it."

Her disapproval flowed hot like the sun. "It should not have. Your wife is Beje's daughter, a woman of suitable rank and noble lineage. I arranged the marriage myself through Beje's wife Cherfa when I sent you back to your uncle, the var, for safekeeping. Serpent and snake that he proved to be—my own brother! Hu! He had betrayed me beforehand by sending me to that terrible place. I should have expected nothing less from him. Naturally, in later years, when whispers reached my ears of my brother's further treachery, I turned to Cherfa again. She told Beje to aid you."

"I never saw Beje's wife, although he mentioned her," said Anji. "I will say that Commander Beje behaved in all ways honorably toward me."

"He is our ally. The soldiers he sent me are for you. He hands them over to your command."

"Mine? Hu!" He blew out breath between his teeth, swiped a finger along his beard as he considered this unexpected harvest. "Certainly I have no complaint of Commander Beje. However, I am no longer married to his daughter. She ran away into the west with a demon."

"Hu! I had not imagined Beje and Cherfa could sire a weak-minded female. Still, she may yet be alive."

"To me she is dead."

She brushed his topknot again and this time found a corner of wrapped ribbon a hair out of place and tweaked it to fall into line. "Too much pride is a weakness, An-jihosh."

"Call it what you wish. I was married to her at one time. Now she is dead." He hoisted Atani and, finally, rose; he was taller than his mother was but not enough for his height to intimidate.

His mother cut off his attack before he could pursue it further. "Come inside, An-jihosh. We will drink a proper greeting."

Her gesture commanded him to accompany her—into the house without taking off his boots! He could not refuse his mother, yet to walk with her forced Mai to walk behind.

Mai thought probably her ears were flaming red from anger, but she would not let her anger rule her. Miravia's clear gaze met hers. Mai gestured as the thought bloomed. Miravia mounted the steps to fall in beside her. Let Miravia stand for her allies, all the women and men in Astafero and Olo'osson who respected her as a woman of means.

Side by side, they walked behind Anji into the house that had once been hers and which was now transformed with all manner of fabrics and low couches and a slum-brous perfume of smoky incense that made her want to sneeze. Sirniakans evidently did not sit on pillows like civilized people. They raised themselves up on low couches, as if they could not be bothered to keep their floors clean by keeping peo-ple's dirt-laden shoes off the fine mats.

They tromped barbarically across the mats into an inner room whose doors lay open to receive light from the private central courtyard of the house. The doors to the outer audience chamber slapped shut behind them. In the courtyard, under the shade of the inner porches, sat about twenty women, from sweet-faced girls to wrin-kled crones. One quickly covered her face with a wing of pale blue silk shot through with silver cross threads. The others hid their mouths behind their hands and meas-ured Anji through sidelong, coy gazes.

He was the only man in the chamber.

Anji's mother seated herself and indicated that Anji must sit opposite on a couch facing both her and the courtyard. He remained standing until Mai reached him. He nodded toward the couch; when he sat, she sat beside him. Miravia slid in to kneel gracefully on the floor by Mai's legs, her back a solid comfort. She turned a little, and Atani smiled boldly at her and allowed himself to be passed into Miravia's arms.

Mai settled her now-empty hands in her lap, palms up and relaxed, in the manner of the Merciful One's bounty. She'd faced worse in Kartu Town's market, haggling over peaches. The women examined Mai more boldly than they had examined Anji. She did not flinch. Let them look! She knew her own worth.

Anji's mother clapped her hands. Slaves scurried out from whatever shadows they'd been skulking in to lay out cups and platters around a silver teapot. Out of this pot steaming hot water was drawn and poured into a ceramic blue teapot to rinse it, and the rinse water sluiced into a brass basin. Blackened leaves were sprinkled into the pot, water poured over them, and the teapot sealed with a lid. The aroma was powerful and very fine.

Two cups only, so finely wrought they seemed as thin as paper, sat on the low table.

Anji washed his hands out of the brass basin, his expression so collected Mai knew he was plotting as he wiped his hands dry. He grasped the teapot's handle, filled one cup a third of the way, the other to the full, and finished filling the first. After setting down the teapot, he picked up one cup with both hands and offered it to his mother. She took it, not hiding her smile, meant to announce her victory.

Anji picked up the second cup with both hands and offered it to Mai.

The attendants gasped, hiding faces behind veils of cloth or concealing hands.

Mai took the cup but kept on her placid market face as she met the older woman's steady gaze. So. Now they would stare in the manner of wolves waiting for one to submit to another. Mai would not look down. Neither would Anji's mother.

"Bring me a cup," said Anji, his tone so clipped it shocked Mai into looking at him.

A cup was brought. He poured for himself. He drank first, and then of course both women must hasten to drink as the women on the courtyard whispered, like leaves stirred by the rising wind off a coming storm. Anji drained his cup and set it down. His mother finished likewise, and Mai took a final swallow and set hers next to Anji's.

"You are being stubborn, Anjihosh," said his mother. "I see that has not changed."

"I came, obediently, as soon as I heard you had arrived in the Hundred, despite pressing events elsewhere that need my immediate attention. You are of course welcome to set up your own household here, if you do not wish to return to the empire or to the Qin. With what message do you come as an emissary from cousins I have never met, do not wish to meet, and who must by the custom and law of the empire seek my death?"

She folded her hands on the glorious silk of her gown. "I bring this message: Remain in exile, never to set foot in Sirniakan or Qin territory again, and they will not trouble you."

"Why should I believe they are willing to allow me live unmolested when there have been several attempts already on my life?"

"If the red hounds pursued you, it was by the directive of your brother Farazadihosh. Your cousins were too busy raising an army and fighting their war to trouble themselves with *you*."

"But now they do trouble themselves with me. The offer is too generous for me to believe it honestly meant. Surely you cannot believe they harbor no grievance against me, Honored Mother. Why is it you agreed to act as their emissary?"

"Because my first duty, my only obligation, is to keep you alive, Son. They know that. I know that. You know that. No other person will protect you as I have protected you and will—indeed *must*—protect you. Am I not correct, Anjihosh?"

He bowed his head. "You are correct."

"I assured myself that they meant what they said and that they were not attempting to betray you through my agency. Do you think I am a fool?"

These words were spat so sharply Mai winced, and although Anji's mother did not look at Mai, it was quite obvious by the way her mouth tightened that she had noticed Mai's reaction.

Anji held a breath longer than he ought, and expelled it as he gripped the teapot and poured a second round of tea into the cups. He did not wait for the women. He drained his cup and set it down hard on the table's polished grain.

"No more a fool than I am," he said.

"We shall see." She gestured, and the woman who had veiled herself at their entrance rose like a puppet and walked with graceless stiffness—the poor thing was either terrified or haughty—to stand at the foot of the couch on which Anji's mother reclined.

"Remain in exile, never to set foot in Sirniakan or Qin territory again, and they will not trouble you," Anji's mother repeated with a gloating satisfaction in her tone like that of a customer who feels she has gotten the better in a long tedious bargaining session. "The bargain to be sealed by a marriage between you and their sister."

The sister's eyes were all Mai could see; they were traced with a thick black line that emphasized their shape; her lashes were thick, her gaze exotic because it was all that existed of her. She might be beautiful; she might be plain. It was the mystery that excited.

"I have a wife," said Anji.

"You have a concubine, Anjihosh. And very pretty she is, as I am sure you wish me to mention. The child is yours, I collect. A handsome boy."

Her voice warmed as she deigned to examine Atani, who regarded her with the same equanimity as he regarded all people: he was sure they loved him. Hu! The woman could not be all horrid if she admired Atani.

"But a pretty girl of no rank or consequence is not the wife of a prince."

"Mai is my wife," said Anji.

"Furthermore," she went on as if he had not spoken, "you must marry in order to protect your life. My life. The life of your handsome son. Even the life of the pretty concubine is at stake."

The sword thrust home.

His eyes flared, as though he had taken a blade to the gut, and he sat back as swiftly as if he'd been hit and flung an arm out as though to shield Mai from the blow. He did not quite touch her; he had more control than that. Yet the gesture betrayed him.

His mother smiled tightly. "Keep your concubine if you wish. Beauty fades. Blood, however, never weakens. I will hold the baby now."

She extended her arms; the many gold bracelets she wore jangled along her sleeves, and they caught Atani's attention. The cursed baby went straight to her, as he went to everyone, and she seated him on her lap and let his damp bottom stain the magnificent silk and allowed him to wrap his chubby moist fingers around the baubles as though they were humble wood toys. She knew how to hold a child, and he was an easy child to hold. Anji relaxed his arm; his shoulders eased; he smiled.

The woman, behind her veil, watched him, and then she looked at Mai, and Mai looked at her. If there was a message in the other's gaze Mai could not interpret it. After a moment, the other woman looked away, and perhaps that shuttering came from anger, or shyness, or fear, or loneliness. What manner of woman was she, raised in a women's palace apart from men and confined within walls her entire life? As remarkable as Mai's journey had been from dusty Kartu Town through the desert and the empire into the glorious Hundred, how much farther in every other way this woman must have traveled.

Would the other woman demand that her exalted rank be acknowledged, or might they become as sisters? Rich men in Kartu Town kept two wives all the time; Mai's own father had taken a pair of sisters. It wasn't impossible; women learned to live together. What choice did they have? It was better to live in harmony than to fight over scraps.

Yet what was she thinking? She need accept no scraps. She had her own household. Her own coin.

Anji's mother was watching her while pretending to dandle the baby. So Mai smiled at her, very prettily; she had learned to smile in the marketplace and in the Mei clan, where tempers and tensions had trapped so many others.

But not her.

She had escaped.

"You will wish to wash and rest after your journey," said Anji's mother, handing the baby back to Miravia as to a servant. "I have set aside rooms for your use, Anji-hosh."

"I thank you," he said, rising and offering a hand to Mai so she must rise as well. Miravia clambered hastily to her feet, holding the baby. "I have urgent business to attend to at the militia encampment. There is a tent there set aside for my use. I will attend on you again." His gaze flicked to Mai, and his lips pulled up in that way he had when he was content with his victories. "In the morning."

He offered a formal gesture toward the veiled woman. "Cousin. My greetings." Then he switched to a language Mai did not know and spoke at more length, although the cadence of the words remained formal and not at all intimate.

The woman did not look at him as he spoke. When he was finished, she replied to the floor. She had a woman's voice, not astoundingly beautiful and not croaking or harsh; just a voice. Impossible to say what manner of person hid behind the veil of formality and distance. Maybe that was the advantage of such covering: if you were clever, you could hide the truth and do what you wished because no one could suspect your actual intentions, your secret heart.

Yet Uncle Hari could look straight into her heart, could he not? No veil would protect her then. Imagine what it would be like to have an ally who could always warn you of the hidden intentions of those who might wish you harm!

"Mai," said Anji softly.

She rested a hand on his forearm and looked first at Anji's cousin and then at his mother.

"Greetings of the day, verea," she said in the Hundred style. "Greetings of the day, Honored Mother."

The arrow struck home, an ambush, if you wished to call it so. But oddly, as Anji's mother's eyes narrowed, absorbing the hit, her lips quirked as though she were amused.

"Mai," repeated Anji.

Her ears were still flaming; she knew her color was high. She paced beside Anji as he led her out of the house whose construction *she* had overseen. *She* had boiled rice in those kitchens! *She* had strung canvas walls with her hirelings.

As they descended the steps, she muttered, "It is *my* house."

"You did well," said Anji. "Just think. Now you have another five hundred men to find wives for."

"Will these soldiers stay in the Hundred?"

"They're under my command, plum blossom. Of course they will stay." He strode up to Tuvi and clapped the chief on the back with a broad grin. "Five hundred Qin soldiers. Think of it, Chief. Allow me a moment to gloat. Hu! I think we can actually win this war."

Mai embraced Miravia. "I missed you," she whispered.

"Take me with you," murmured Miravia into her ear. "I beg you."

"Come, Mai," said Anji, taking the reins from his groom.

"Miravia will need a horse to ride," said Mai to Tuvi. Then she turned to Anji. "Will you marry your cousin? To keep the peace?"

He frowned. "One war at a time. I have battles to fight in the north that will not wait."

He mounted. Mai stepped into Tuvi's cupped hands and he hoisted her up into the saddle. The chief faced Miravia, whose blushes were easy to see. Was Tuvi also blushing? Did he care for her, or want to care for her, or was he simply overheated from the sun?

"I will take my son," said Anji.

The chief took the baby from Miravia. As everyone waited for Anji to wrap the child's sling around his torso and Tuvi to get the baby snugged in, that cursed Keshad emerged from the lines leading a horse.

"If you will," he said, his gods-rotted intense gaze fixed on Miravia as his color changed.

Miravia could barely look at him, but she accepted the reins and his help in mounting.

Chief Tuvi was still helping Anji with the baby, his back to them. Keshad slipped away into the lines. Miravia clumsily got the horse to move up beside Mai's mare. Anji signaled. The troop wheeled and, under the gaze of the Sirniakan slaves, headed down through town.

Anji was smiling, but Mai could not.

He had not said no.

38

THE DUSTY MILITIA encampment outside Astafero boiled with Qin soldiers, who wore tabards dyed a very dark blue. They were distinguishable from the black tabards favored by Anji's men only when the two garments were seen side by side. The captain and chiefs of the recently arrived Qin troop waited outside the three huge central tents together with the chiefs in charge of the training camp. The camp flew two cohort banners together with a Qin banner Keshad had not seen before: a crescent moon gleaming on a dark blue background the same color as the tunics. As Kesh dismounted and threw his reins to one of the waiting tailmen, Anji's banner, the black wolf, was being raised from the central pole to mark Anji's arrival.

The men clomped up onto the plank walkway that surrounded the three tents and, following Captain Anji's example, pulled off their boots before they entered. Mai's party followed: Mai holding Miravia's hand and smiling at something Miravia had said; Priya and O'eki with serious expressions as they talked; Sheyshi had a hand pressed to a cheek as if overtaken by a fit of shyness; three kitchen women who had worked for Mai in all the time Kesh had been in and out of the compound; two apprentice clerks of Sapanasu, who looked young and intimidated. By the time Keshad reached the walkway he was alone except for the ubiquitous guards, but those on duty recognized him and, after checking him for weapons, allowed him to pass.

His feet sank into carpet as he crossed an empty audience chamber furnished only with rugs, a bare expanse that could accommodate perhaps a hundred people sitting squashed together. Toughid sat cross-legged to one side on a rug, next to a small chest decorated with an elaborate brass clasp in the shape of a boar and wrapped in chains. He'd been hauling that cursed chest since Olossi, sleeping with it as though it were his wife. He looked half asleep now, callused hands relaxed on his thighs, a bead of sweat on his upper lip.

The heat simmering within the airless space made Kesh's neck prickle. Eight guards, each pair flanking a slit in the canvas, suffered at their stations with reddened faces. The military contingent had gathered in an adjoining tent, their voices buzzing. He hesitated, not sure where to go.

Chief Deze emerged from behind one of the curtains, Anji and Tuvi right behind him.

"—would have been prudent to leave her in Olossi rather than precipitate a battle you cannot win, Anjihosh," Tuvi was saying. "Not for your sake, mind you. I speak solely out of concern for Mai. It was a reckless, headstrong decision. You allowed your pride to over-master you. Do you really need to prove to anyone that you are no longer that twelve-year-old boy? Because by acting as you did, you have proven that you are. And furthermore—"

Anji's frown revealed his annoyance at the chief's scolding, but he made no effort to stop him nor did he disagree. However, when the chief saw Kesh, he clamped his lips shut. Reacting to the silence, Anji looked up. His gaze sharpened, fixing on Kesh.

"Captain?" asked Toughid, rising with a hand on his sword's hilt.

A wave of heat washed Kesh's torso. Like a rabbit hiding from a hawk, stillness might protect him. The guards perked up, their interest surely caught by the expectation of bloodshed.

Anji's smile was a fearful thing because that gods-rotted dimple made it so sweet. He seemed on the brink of laughter. "Master Keshad. Just the man I wanted to see. I need a ship filled with oil of naya, ready to depart at dawn for Argent Hall. Take Master O'eki and see to it. I recommend caution. Oil of naya is quite flammable."

"I understand oil of naya, like some men, is volatile if mishandled," said Keshad boldly.

Anji laughed. He gestured to Tuvi, and they crossed to the tent where the assembly waited. The cursed guards sighed, looking disappointed. Toughid sat, closed his eyes, and resumed his doze.

"I need to see Master O'eki," said Keshad. A guard twitched back one curtain.

He walked down a corridor between tents screened by hangings and past more guards into a separate tent. This space was much cooler because the inner walls and the flaps cut into the canvas roof had been rolled up to allow a breeze through. Pallets lay rolled up on one side, seating pillows heaped around them. Outside, a square of bare ground was shaded not by a canvas roof but by the high sides of other tents; here a hearth fire burned and the kitchen women had already set to work brewing khaif and pouring cordial. Mai was seated on a pillow on a plank porch, nursing the baby; Miravia sat beside her, whispering in her ear in an affectionate way that stabbed Kesh with envy. Would she ever lean against him so lovingly? Did she care about him at all?

Sheyshi, standing unremarked in a corner, was also staring, her eyes as unfocused as if she were—as she likely was—a bit lack-witted. Perhaps she, too, was jealous of the attention her mistress was receiving from the interloper. Sometimes slaves developed an infatuation with their masters, perhaps only to deflect the degradation of their own condition.

As sharply as if they had appeared out of the air to regard him with fear and reproach, he remembered the two girls he had sold to Master Calon, the young sisters who had clutched at each other for comfort. Calon had intended to train one as a jarya in expectation of gaining a greater price for her later. Had the other girl been sold to pay for her sister's training and upkeep? Where were those girls now?

Why should he even care? If he had not bought them in Mariha, someone else would have. A jarya's life and training was nothing to scorn. Certainly their lives would be better in the Hundred than they would have been in Mariha.

His lips were dry.

"Is Master O'eki here?" he croaked.

Miravia stiffened, without turning to look. After a moment's hesitation, Mai smiled in that pretty way she had that could as well kill a man as reassure him. The baby suckled noisily. Miravia acknowledged his presence with an awkward nod.

"Master Keshad?" O'eki emerged from yet another hidden chamber; this cursed place was full of little antechambers walled off by hangings and canvas and woven curtains. "Here I am."

Kesh kept trying not to stare at Miravia; he knew he was making a fool of himself, but she was so close and alive, and looking at him because she was free to do so. If she were free to look at him, then he was free to look at her. He ventured a smile, and knew at once how clumsy it must appear because Sheyshi snickered as Miravia flushed and looked away.

The hells!

"Master Keshad?" The big man loomed beside him. "How can I help you?"

"Er, ah, yes, we're to supervise the loading of a ship with oil of naya."

"Oil of naya?" asked Mai. The baby let go of the nipple and reared back to look at his mother, caught by her tone, which Kesh could not interpret. She quickly covered her exposed breast with her taloos. "Merciful One! To bring oil of naya again to battle. A cruel weapon. But effective."

"Better this way than drawn out long, Mistress," said O'eki with a slow shake of his head.

"It was just so awful to see," said Mai. "Never mind it. I'd rather win with oil of naya than lose by refraining. I'll come with you. I'd like to see how much oil has been stored up, and I want to check the accounts books. Sheyshi, could you bring me the sling?"

"I can carry the baby, Mistress." Sheyshi's wheedling tone made Keshad wince. Did he sound like that when he spoke to Miravia? Not that he had ever spoken to her except that one time in the market.

"I've been doing the accounts for the naya storehouses," said Miravia. "We've been shipping lots to Argent Hall for the last month. Just a few days ago two flights of reeves flew vessels out, although I wasn't told where they were headed."

"You've been my trusted eyes and ears here in Astafero for the last months." She kissed Miravia on the cheek. Kesh licked his lips, wishing they were his lips on that delicate skin. How envy stabbed! Was Mai taunting him on purpose? "Indeed, I can scarcely bear to be separated from you, now we are together again," she went on, and perhaps her gaze slid sidelong to pinion him, reminding him that he was the outsider. Or perhaps he was just imagining things.

As she wrapped Atani in the sling, the curtain was swept aside and Anji walked in accompanied by Tuvi. "Mai, you'll attend me."

Chief Tuvi looked up at the rippling ceiling and down again. "Captain? Did I not recommend prudence?"

"Tuvi-lo." Anji's tone ended the conversation. "Mai, I must absorb a full complement of Qin soldiers into my command. It is necessary for me to make them understand that you hold the position of my consort under Qin custom. For them to accept my command, as Commander Beje has ordered them to do, they must recognize and respect my chosen wife."

"Is this about your mother, Anji?" his chosen wife asked tartly.

Tuvi sighed gustily. "I recommend banking this fire rather than fanning it—"

"I haven't finished," said the captain, glancing once around the chamber, marking who was listening and who was absent. He raised a hand and pointed a finger at O'eki so rudely that Mai flinched and Miravia looked away. But he was just gesturing in the outlander style, making an emphatic point. "You understand me, Master O'eki? We spoke of this when I came to your house."

The big man inclined his head, but Kesh noted a difference in how he addressed the captain now. He was respectful, even cautious, but not subservient. "Priya and I both understand you."

"What is there to understand?" demanded Mai. "What aren't you telling me, Anji?"

Something in the look he gave her stopped her before she could go on with her questions and demands. Her lips thinned. Her gaze sparked.

Eihi!

Was she *angry*?

She raised her chin proudly, touched her hair as if to make sure the hair-sticks and combs were all in place, not that any man ever looked beyond her remarkable beauty to find fault in the details, and swept grandly off the porch and over to Anji's side. The baby wanted his father; he always did; but for once Anji did not cater to his infant whims. He led Mai, with the baby, to the curtain.

"Can't I go with you, Mistress?" sniveled Sheyshi.

Ignoring Sheyshi, Mai turned to Tuvi with a parting blow. "Tuvi-lo, please accompany Master O'eki, Master Keshad, and Miravia to the naya storehouses. I thank you."

Cursed woman!

Priya came out from the antechamber. "Ah, Sheyshi, just who I was looking for. There is no hand for mending as clever as yours, Sheyshi. You have the neatest stitch of anyone in the household. One of the master's robes has a tear right where a perfect butterfly is embroidered. Can you fix it?" She led Sheyshi away on this innocuous errand.

"Do we need the clerks?" asked the chief as O'eki fetched the accounts books. He indicated the young ones, who were sitting in the shade near the kitchen women and sipping cordial.

"I am competent to deal with the books," said Miravia. "I go the warehouses every day to discuss household requirements and cross-check the accounts books in Mai's name."

The chief nodded at her. Did his gaze linger? Did she look at him a moment longer than was entirely necessary?

They walked, Chief Tuvi at the van, Master O'eki and Miravia in the middle, and Kesh fuming at the rear, to the warehouse complex built adjacent to the militia encampment and ringed by the same earthen walls. A level road had been cleared from the complex down to the strand, to make it easy to move supplies up or the volatile oil of naya down. The warehouse factor's greeting made it clear Miravia was not only familiar to him but had ingratiated herself. He was a middle-aged man. Did he admire her, too?

His counting room sat in the center of the warehouse complex. He took books from a chained cabinet and escorted them to a pair of low storehouses dug into the earth so that, in case of accident, fire could not spread. Guards stood outside the double-chained and bolted gates, which the factor unlocked. They descended an earthen ramp to a musty dirt floor; a wide corridor extended into darkness. Each brick-walled storage chamber had a separate entrance off this corridor.

"Each vessel is numbered according to the storehouse, the chamber within the storehouse, and its place within that chamber," the factor was explaining to Tuvi, who carried a lantern in each hand. "Mistress Miravia and I crosscheck each week when we do a full accounting. We maintain a standing order with two Ri Amarah houses in Olossi, who take best-quality water white for medicinal purposes." He manfully did not look at Miravia as he said this, although they all knew what she was: her brushstroke eyes, lighter skin and square face betrayed her origins. "Otherwise, however, oil of naya is only conveyed to other militia encampments and to Argent Hall, by ship or via reeve flights. We control the naya trade, no one else. Mistress Miravia, will you mark off the vessels to be shipped?"

She took a lantern from Tuvi and moved into the first chamber.

"Chief, I would like to show you the locked vault where we keep the water white. We lost a single pot of water white two months ago to theft, so we've had to increase our security." The factor led O'eki and Tuvi into the gloom of the back aisles.

Tuvi's voice drifted back. "To theft? How can that be?"

Keshad drifted into the narrow chamber behind Miravia, who hung the lantern from a hook and began to mark a manifest as she logged the clay vessels. Such homely pots, to contain such treasure. The air was very close and the grit made him blink.

"Don't you worry the flame will light the oil and make everything burn?" he asked.

The scarf on her head could not contain her hair. Wisps trailed down the curve of her neck. Her profile, illuminated by the lantern's glow, had a glorious sheen; her eyelashes shadowed her dark eyes; her hand brushed steadily at the manifest.

"Why are you staring at me?" she said in a low voice, although she was not looking at him.

He had meant to be charming and patient, but what was the point?

"Because I love you."

Still she did not look! Perhaps her brushstroke stuttered; her hand, holding the ink bowl, might have trembled. "You can't love me. You don't know me. You must think you love me, and it must be some story you have told yourself about who I am that you love. But it can't be me."

"I saw you that day in the courtyard in Olossi and ever after I can only think of you."

Still writing, she licked her lips. The moisture made her lips glow, as kisses might. "That means you want to devour me, not that you love me. There's an easy way to slake that thirst, isn't there? When a pair of young people wish to devour each other but are already contracted to wed other people because of clan alliances? Then they go to the temple and slake their thirst there? There's a small temple dedicated to Ushara here. We could meet there—and then I could stop—" Ink spattered; she ceased writing.

He was shaking as he took a step toward her. "Then you could stop what?"

"I could stop thinking of you all the time!" She stoppered the inkpot, shoulders heaving.

"You love me!"

She turned, shoulders stiff and lips pressed together with anger. When she spoke, her words emerged like daggers as she glared at him. "I don't know you. I can't love you. Anyway, Mai wants me to marry Chief Tuvi. He's a good man. Why should you suppose I want to go off with you just because of wanting sex, and leave behind my dearest sister who is my only family?"

The lantern's flame made her skin gleam.

"I could be your family!"

"Just the two of us? And once the devouring urge is slaked, what is to keep two people together? Mai will always be my sister, because we are pledged in our hearts."

"So you think! My mother's sisters sold me and my little sister quickly enough when my mother and father died! They felt no sentimental obligation to their niece and nephew, although we were only twelve and ten, mere children, helpless to save ourselves."

Her mouth parted as she leaned toward him, genuinely shocked. "You were sold? As a slave?"

Like a good merchant, he sensed the weakness in her negotiating position and pursued it. "We were sold into debt slavery on the auction block in Gadria's Oval, which you might know is more commonly called Flesh Alley."

Now he had her sympathy! He saw it in her bold eyes and clear expression. In the way she paused before she replied, as if overwhelmed by pity at the thought of two weeping children. "Is it true, then, as I have heard, that you yourself sold captives into slavery? Young girls? And used the coin to buy yourself free?"

She might as well have slapped him! "People sell slaves or debt all the time!"

"That doesn't make it right."

"Only you Silvers say so!"

She was tall and magnificent in a taloos of dark silk, color impossible to distinguish in the dim light. "We are called Ri Amarah, Master Keshad. To call us Silvers is to insult our men and ignore our women, for the women do not wear the silver bracelets."

She was breathing as hard as if she'd been running, and she blinked multiple times, as if fighting tears or anger or some other mad impulse. "I don't like what you have done. You've selfishly traded in lives to benefit yourself, and without consideration of its effect on others."

"You think those girls would have lived a better life in Mariha? Here they can hope for a bit of respect."

"That's the story you tell yourself! If you say it enough, you may come to believe, and then you can sleep peacefully at night despite the harm you've caused others."

The voices of the men approached down the length of the storehouse.

"You Ri Amarah can't walk into the Hundred and tell us what our obligations are," he said in a furious whisper.

Her chin quivered angrily.

"But!" He ran a hand through his hair, trying to sort out thoughts and words. Her gaze fixed on the movement of his hand in his curls and her eyes widened with that glazed inward look women got when thinking of pleasure. "For you, Miravia, I pledge never to sell another slave, their body, their debt, their labor. Ever. Out of respect for you."

With a shaking hand she unhooked the lantern and, turning her back on him, spoke in so low a voice he was sure he had not heard right. "I will go to Ushara's temple tonight at the sixth bell."

She walked around him and out into the corridor, and he was too dizzy and his thoughts too scattered to move after her.

The factor stuck his head into the storeroom and said, "Master Keshad?"

"Yes! Yes, I am. Wagons."

"I'm sorry?"

The captain had assigned him a task! "We'll need wagons, with plenty of padding to cushion the vessels. I want to be done loading by nightfall so the ship is ready to depart at dawn, just as the captain has ordered."

I want to be done by nightfall. By sixth bell.

Only because he had years of experience separating his passions from the work he must do could he concentrate enough to supervise the bringing of wagons, the padding of wagons, the lading of wagons, the hauling of wagons down the long smooth road to the strand. A ship was already fitted with cradles for oil transport; its captain had hauled oil of naya, olive oil, and fish oil in plenty over the last months.

Down at the strand, other ships were being prepared for horse and troop transport. In the interests of time the entire Qin regiment was to be conveyed over the sea to Olossi despite their superstitious fear of water. But the weather was fair; the winds were mild; as the heat built, the days flattened into a monotony of predictable weather perfect for long journeys undertaken at speed over the gentle waters of the Olo'o Sea.

As dusk settled, Keshad trudged uphill with the last wagon to get a final load. The dray beasts were coated with the fine pale loess dust that covered everything in the Barrens. The carter, a voluble fellow, was discussing a recent hooks-and-ropes tournament held as part of the Breaking Ground Festival, in which a local group of laborers had defeated all comers, even several teams made up of young militiamen.

"Them Qin soldiers, they're taking to the game right enough," he opined, "but it'll take them a few more seasons before they can really get the nuance, neh? Did you see the new fields?"

"No," said Kesh, his attention attracted by a pair of men dressed in the Sirniakan style—flowing robes over loose pantaloons—who were striding out from the settlement. "What new fields?"

"It'll be ten years before we've really got irrigation enough to feed ourselves, but at the festival we harrowed five fields. Rice will be planted with the rains. Then we'll see how those irrigation channels work, eh? I tell you, best thing I done was to come out here and establish a branch clan of carters. I had my doubts, with the militia running things, but Mistress Mai made sure we have our own council."

"Was there any doubt you would not have your own council?"

"With all these soldiers, we might just have been run as part of the army, neh? Not that I resent them, mind you. Two years ago I thought my clan was done for. We had no work. The roads weren't safe. Now, we're prospering."

The Sirniakans were gaining, obviously in pursuit. Keshad swung his legs to the side and leaped off the slow-moving wagon. "Go ahead. Just one more load."

The man turned. "I don't trust those Sirniakans, I don't mind saying. The Qin, they're all right, but those others—Aui! Very odd birds, if you ask me."

"I'll head them off. I don't want them to know where we store the oil of naya, neh?"

He and the carter exchanged a friendly nod as the wagon moved on. Keshad waited on the road, cursed sure they were after him. They reached him at last, faces slick with sweat.

"Master Keshad?" asked the one holding the ebony baton that Keshad recognized as the symbol of the man's authority as a slave factor.

"I am Master Keshad. What do you require?"

"Your attendance, Master."

The prospect of being summoned to an interview with Anji's mother did not please him. He retained a visceral memory of Anji's hand clutching his throat; indeed, he could not stop himself from touching his throat with a hand. But he'd accomplished the task set him by the captain, so there was no use delaying the inevitable.

Unlike the carter and the laborers with whom he had worked all day, the Sirniakan slaves did not speak as they walked to the settlement gates and up along the market avenue. As night fell, the market arcades were shuttered. From behind curtains and closed compound doors lifted conversation, laughter, song; an argument; a baby's squall. A dog barked to mark their passage. Up they walked past a newly built Lantern's accounting house. The council square had been expanded to include the stone walls originally built to house Kotaru's temple, which had been rededicated in a larger space outside the settlement walls near the militia camp. A wooden gate with three lintels marked the domain of Ilu the Herald; it had not changed except for the addition of a thatched open shelter with cots where passing envoys could sleep. A flat boulder so deeply sunk in the earth that no one had bothered to excavate it offered a resting place for Hasibal, the Formless One; and in the fading light Kesh saw fresh offerings of flowers laid in a pattern that abruptly reminded him of the offerings Mai and her people made at the altar dedicated to their god, the Merciful One.

The two slaves climbed the steps and passed into the outer audience chamber without removing their outdoor shoes, but Kesh stopped and took off his boots.

"Hurry!" snapped the factor.

It was remarkably easy to channel his anger into overly polite words. "It's not our way to enter our homes shod in dirt, ver. Our mat makers pride themselves on their fine work. Why should we trample it as if it were no better than the street?"

He set his boots aside and ran a hand over his hair before entering behind the impatient factor. They crossed the matted floor on a trail smeared with dust tracked in from outside. The factor paused by the far doors and rang a hand bell. A door was slid opened; Kesh entered alone. Four low couches in the Sirniakan style had been placed in a square, a table set between them.

"Master Keshad." Anji's mother reclined on one couch. "Sit down."

He sat opposite and rested his hands on his thighs. Female voices whispered and giggled from behind curtains strung across one side of the room. Where slits parted, he glimpsed eyes, or cheeks, or gauzy veils stitched with shimmering thread.

"The ladies admire your beauty, Master Keshad. They're commenting on it."

"I beg your pardon, exalted lady," he said as more giggles assaulted him. His cheeks burned. With the force of will that had gotten him through twelve years of slavery, he refused to look again toward the curtains. "Your words startled me."

"Are you not commonly praised for your beauty?"

"No, exalted lady." He was unable to find a posture that did not make him uncomfortable. "Why have you summoned me?"

But he could already guess.

"We traveled a long road together, Master Keshad. I will therefore presume upon our acquaintance to forego the usual pleasantries and formal words and strike directly to the heart of the matter. I made an offer to you many days ago. What is your answer?"

There was more than one way to make trouble!

"I hope you will forgive my blunt speaking, exalted lady."

"I expect an honest answer."

The gods-rotted women hiding behind their cursed curtain were still whispering, the sound as irritating as the whine of a disaffected customer who has gotten the worse of the bargaining session through their own hapless negotiation.

"I must decline your most generous offer. I cannot take the captain's wife off your hands. I do not want to marry her."

"You need not marry her. You can take her as a concubine."

"I am hesitant to correct your observations, exalted lady, but believe me when I say she is a rich woman who is well respected among the councils of this region."

"She is very young!"

"Nevertheless. Most people credit her with convincing your son to fight the army that attacked Olossi last year. Also, the Olossi city council considers itself beholden to her for making it possible for them to overthrow the houses who ruled the council for many years solely to enrich themselves and their allies. Also, it seems she's been instrumental in supporting local councils and in creating a regional council in Olo'osson so all folk can have their voices heard."

She said nothing.

"And, to be blunter, exalted lady, your son will never allow another man to take her from him."

"I can direct my son."

"You can?"

"You doubt me?"

Keshad smoothed the fabric of his loose trousers over his legs, taking courage in the fine weave and reed green color; these were the best quality clothes he had ever owned. Yet her garb—the silk; the embroidery of gold thread; the headdress plated with gold rings and medallions—was as far above his rich merchant's fittings as his were above that of a beggar's tattered loincloth.

"I do not doubt you, exalted lady. But I must still decline your offer."

"You have given up on the other one? She's a clever girl, if reckless and possibly even inclined to disrespect. However, her accounting skills are good, she knows herb-craft, and she can even read and write. These are skills not to be scorned."

"I will win her over in my own time and in my own way."

"You can have two wives."

This was like talking to Zubaidit when she got going! "Exalted lady, please listen to my words. It is not what I want."

"But it is what *I* want. I can make it worth your while. Name your price."

Goaded, he laughed. "Exalted lady, your son will kill me if he ever learns that

I—or I suppose any man—has—well—Mai—" Aui! He was blushing. "Do you think he cannot?"

"I see." She might have been a statue examined from a distance, remote and unknowable. She clapped her hands three times, and a slave emerged from behind a curtain carrying a small sack, no bigger than a melon, in both hands. The slave offered the sack to Kesh.

"I beg your pardon, exalted lady. What is this?"

"Gold."

The slave released the sack. Kesh caught it; his arms tensed under its unexpected weight. "I can take no payment for an act I have refused to perform."

She smiled with real amusement, and for an instant he saw the personality that had captivated an emperor. Captain Anji's smile was more spontaneous. Hers was a weapon.

"This is not payment. It is not obligation. Nor is it a reward or a bribe. It is a gift. If it were anything otherwise, you would know. But I have the pleasure of making gifts exactly as I wish. I respect your honesty, Master Keshad. Now you may leave."

So he left, burdened with gold and with a sense that he had missed something important. As soon as he was out on the porch, as soon as he had pulled on his boots and began walking down through the quiet evening streets of Astafero where a man might perfectly well carry a bag of gold without fearing he would be robbed and killed, he saw away beyond the walls in the lowland plain a pair of torches marking Ushara's temple.

Sixth bell had not yet been rung.

39

THE BABY SPRAWLED naked in his cot, netting draped over to keep off mosks and flies and gnats, to discourage scorpions and snakes. Here in the Barrens the houses had to be elevated off the ground to keep away vermin, or else, as in Kartu Town, furniture must elevate the body away from the earth where poisonous creatures scuttled.

The commander's complex of tents had likewise been built up off the ground, canvas raised over raised plank flooring. Mai knelt behind Miravia, combing out her hair, which had a tendency to snarl. They were alone except for the sleeping baby.

"It's very irritating," said Mai, "that we cannot sleep in the house we raised but must push Chief Berkei out of his accustomed place to accommodate us. Not that the chief complained."

"You were invited to sleep in the house, were you not?"

"Anji was. In the suite of rooms set aside for his use just as if that woman had built and furnished the house and overseen the settlement. No doubt I was meant to sleep like a beggar on the steps."

"She's been kind to me. Not kind, precisely, but— Ouch!"

"Don't move! There, I got the tangle out. Hard to imagine her as *kind*."

"A poor choice of words. She has treated me with respect. She asked about you, but I pretended stupidity and told the other hirelings to do the same. I'm sure she did not believe us. She ordered me to take her shopping in the market and bargain for her. She seems to know no other way of talking to people except to command them. She talked a great deal about Keshad. He traveled with them all the way from the south. She seems to think he is a promising young man."

"Do her words stand in his favor, or against him?"

Miravia raised a hand to a cheek.

"You're blushing!" said Mai with a laugh, although she could not see Miravia's face.

"I don't think she speaks well of many people," said Miravia in a choked voice. "Oh, Mai, do you think of Anji every waking moment? When you close your eyes, do you see his face? Imagine his voice? Wish you might taste his lips? All the while knowing you are an utter fool for being obsessed?"

"No."

"No!" Miravia turned so quickly Mai lost hold of the comb, which remained trapped in her curls. "No?"

"Of course I think of him often. But I have other responsibilities, obligations, duties. Atani. My business interests. The household. I can't think of Anji all the time! I think of him enough! You are infatuated with Keshad. There's nothing wrong in that unless you lash yourself off a cliff for a man you don't know."

Miravia leaned back against her, and Mai wrapped her arms around her as Miravia spoke. "It's true you hear tales and songs telling of a glance seen across a street or looks exchanged in a garden that seal two hearts. How the arrow of a lilu hits its mark and makes the victim miserable for the rest of her days. I saw him that day, in your courtyard, that one time. Now I can't stop thinking of him."

"That isn't love, dearest," said Mai, as a pressure of annoyance built in her chest. "You can't love someone you don't know."

"Do you love Anji?"

"Of course I love Anji." She disentangled herself from Miravia and went back to combing her hair, because combing hair calmed her surging heart. "But I didn't love him when he plucked me out of the marketplace."

"You told me you did!"

"I was very frightened. So I had to believe it, didn't I? I had to sing the songs that allowed me to ride each day into unknown territory. Then, afterward, well . . ." Her hands ceased their stroking; she wrapped her fingers in Miravia's hair as she recalled the sweetness of Anji's lovemaking.

"You're blushing," said Miravia with a laugh, not needing to look at her to know that heat had flooded her skin. "Stop that! Your husband will return soon enough, a moth to your flame. Let me comb out your hair, or does he like to do that for you?"

They both began to snort and giggle, and Mai had to wipe her eyes and her running nose with a scrap of cloth. "Oh, hush," she said, "we'll wake Atani."

The curtain swayed, and a dark hand pressed it aside. Priya looked in, smiling. "Is all well? Have you awakened the baby?"

"No, thank you, Priya. All is well. Is there any signal of Anji's return?"

"No." She vanished behind the curtain.

"Where did he go?" asked Miravia, settling on her knees as Mai hitched up her taloos to her hips and sat cross-legged with her back to the other woman.

"I don't know. I sat through the entire afternoon at his side. He wanted me to tell the chiefs and sergeants about life in the Hundred and how I would help them find local wives and settle into local households once the war was over."

"Is he that sure we will win?"

"That's the story he must tell himself and others, isn't it? It's the tale I tell myself. They asked about the brothel, very shyly, I must admit, for they didn't wish to trouble me with such questions, but Anji told them that they must ask me everything even though he didn't expect *that* question! That's how he found out that since last time we were here, a temple to the Merciless One was dedicated and raised, at the order of Astafero's council! I thought he was going to ride down and burn it to the ground at that very instant. He said before he would permit no temple of Ushara in the settlement. He's still angry about—" She faltered, because she had never told Miravia about Anji hitting her. "—about me taking you to Ushara's temple in Olossi. But I turned his anger to my advantage, because he hadn't a word to say that he was willing to say in front of others. That allowed me to speak. I told the men about the local customs and that they must never offer coin in Ushara's garden and so on. You know all that better than I do. After all that, he calmed down, and the meeting was over at nightfall, right before you returned. Then an urgent message came from his mother."

Miravia pulled the hairsticks and combs out of Mai's hair and let it fall. "You shouldn't fight her."

"I don't want a battle. But what am I to do? Accept a place as his second, inferior wife?"

"You cannot ever be that to him!"

"I am a merchant's daughter. She is an emperor's sister." Hu! Now she was crying.

"It won't come to that. He loves you."

"As you love Keshad, perhaps?" she asked bitterly. "He loves my beauty, anyway. People do not marry for that kind of love. Their clans arrange a contract. Or a woman is purchased. Or two families seek an alliance. Or cousins pool their family fortune with a wedding. There are many reasons, but not that one. He would be a fool not to marry her and secure the benefits she brings to him. Anyway, if he does not marry her, his cousins will try to kill him."

"They may try to kill him no matter what he does or says. *She* might try to kill him, once she's in his bed. With a dagger she's hidden in her bosom!"

Mai sobbed, and Miravia embraced her, and then they both began to laugh because laughing was better than crying.

The sixth bell tolled across the settlement to mark the final descent into night.

Miravia shrieked and scrambled to her feet. "I have to go! I said I would meet him—!"

"No!"

"Yes!" How Miravia's face glowed at the thought of meeting a lover she ought not to have. "I thought, if I just devour him, then I'll have done it and I can think more clearly. And he'll have slaked his thirst, and he'll leave me alone and stop pestering me!"

"You go to the temple?"

"I go every week. I don't have to obey my family's strictures any longer. Why should I deny myself?"

To know that the women and men of the Hundred worshiped at Ushara's temple was one thing. To see Miravia making ready to leave with a reckless look in her eyes left Mai stammering. "B-But Chief Tuvi is a good man."

"Yes, he is a good man. What has that to do with anything?"

"I am hoping—you two could marry."

"He's as old as my father!"

"You were about to be married off to a man twice as old! That makes him half as young! He'll treat you kindly, and leave you alone to run your business affairs as I do mine. Then we'll always be together."

"Oh, Mai." Miravia bent to kiss her. "You're the one who sheltered me. Without you, and all you risked for me, I would be in Nessumara now in a cage. If you don't want me to go to Ushara's temple, I won't go."

Mai smiled ruefully as she snagged Miravia's scarf off the floor. She'd bought this scarf for Miravia months ago, admiring its beautiful color. The scarf was a gift of friendship, not an obligation to bind Miravia to Mai's wishes.

"Of course if you want to go, you must go. I will not rule you as I was ruled. Hold still." She tied it to conceal Miravia's hair, adding a pretty knot for flair. "Go on."

At the curtain, Miravia grinned. "Anyhow, Mai, who is to say I cannot meet a lover in the temple and marry a different man?" Then she was gone.

Mai stared at the curtain as it rippled and stilled. The lamps burned. The shadows lingered. Was she sad? Happy? Bewildered? Upset? She hardly knew what to think, and yet the memory of Miravia's deliriously hopeful expression made her smile.

Priya slipped into the chamber, crossed to her, touching her hand. "Plum blossom, are you well? So Miravia has gone off to meet the Devourer, has she?"

"Should I have dissuaded her, Priya? Keshad's rather unpleasant, but she thinks him handsome."

"I believe she acts wisely. The flame may burn hot and short, and then afterward even if there is pain at its death, it will be extinguished. Held apart, it will smolder for far longer than if it is allowed to consume the fuel of desire. Or they may find they truly care for each other."

"Two clanless people do not marry for love, Priya."

"What do you suppose O'eki and I did?"

When she had traveled with Anji and his soldiers across the desert and along the mountains and over the Kandaran Pass, almost every day had exposed a new vista whose unexpected contours surprised her, elated her, scared her, or made her look twice.

She stared at Priya, who stood exposed as a person whose depths she had never bothered to contemplate. "I never thought about you being married. It never seemed important because—"

The woman's gaze softened. "Because we were slaves. Yet we had no contracts, no property, no freedom to barter with, no clan to please, no family obligations because we were torn from our families. Because we were slaves. So we pleased ourselves. Your father could be a harsh master, but he was fair in his own way. He allowed us to marry, as long as we did our work and never let our association interfere with the household. He allowed O'eki to earn coin on the side with the hope of buying us free in time. Not every master in Kartu Town was as generous."

"I'm a fool," said Mai. "Forgive me, Priya. I never even looked. Or thought. Or wondered."

"You are no fool, plum blossom. You are young, and yet even so in your own way, wise enough to let Miravia go although I know you wish her to marry Chief Tuvi."

"Do you think Tuvi wants to marry her?"

"I think he wants to please you, Mistress. Or please the captain through pleasing you. Difficult to say. Perhaps both. He's an honest man. He goes to the temple now and again to please himself—"

"Chief Tuvi goes to Ushara's temple?"

Priya chuckled. "Does that surprise you?"

"Of course not. It's just— Aui! It's no business of mine."

"He has enough obligations within the household that I do not suppose he feels a desperate need to take on a wife and, later, children."

"But every man wants wives and children in order to be content!" She heard her own voice and laughed. She wiped her eyes and sighed. "I sound like my mother and aunt and all the other wives in the Mei compound. They must say so, mustn't they?" She swallowed. "Have you gone to Ushara's temple, Priya?"

Priya merely smiled, saying nothing, keeping her secrets.

"I'll never go," said Mai.

"No," agreed Priya. "Married to the captain, as you are, you will never go."

Hands clapped outside the entrance. O'eki stepped inside with such a look that Mai tensed. "Mistress," he said—and broke off.

Two burly men dressed in the southern style pushed past him, still wearing their *boots*. For an instant she saw one holding a long knife and the other a drawn sword; so had red hounds tried to kill her in a plain white room in the women's quarters of an unknown inn in an unnamed city in the empire.

She lunged for Atani's cot.

Priya tugged her to a halt. "Mai! Stop!"

The haze of her vision cleared. They weren't holding weapons: one held a scroll and brush and inkpot, the other a baton carved from ebony wood and inlaid with strips of gold, a factor's staff of authority.

Sheyshi rushed in behind them, took one look at Mai's unbound hair, and hurried over to the pillows to collect combs and hairsticks. "The mistress is not dressed to receive visitors!"

Words are no obstacle when the wind blows in. O'eki stepped to one side, holding the curtain back. Anji's mother strode into the room and halted, surveying the plain canvas walls, the scatter of pillows, the three small chests that contained Mai and Anji's traveling clothes and necessities, a tray with cups and pitcher and basin set to one side, the enamel pisspot set off to one side on the open porch, recently emptied and rinsed. She looked at O'eki, at Priya, even at Sheyshi.

Never let it be said the market had not taught Mai to think on her feet.

"Sheyshi, please offer a pillow for our guest," she said in the same gracious voice she would use when offering a tough customer a few almonds to nibble before getting down to serious bargaining.

"I see you are not dressed to receive visitors," said Anji's mother.

"At this time of night I am accustomed to receiving only my husband. Unfortunately he is not here to greet you."

"I am not come to speak to my son."

Sheyshi placed the best-quality pillow—embroidered in silver and red and gold thread with butterflies and bees—near Anji's mother.

"Am I to sit on the floor like a slave?"

"Honored Mother, it is the custom in the Hundred for all people to sit on pillows, on the floor, just as it is the custom here to do many things differently from what you and I may have been accustomed to in the places we lived before this."

"Do not condescend to me. You, a humble merchant's daughter, cannot in any way compare your circumstances to mine. Is there no stool? No camp chair? No captain's bench?"

Maybe there had been once, but these artifacts had vanished over the last year. Mai had a chair in the compound at Olossi, but she only used it when negotiating a particularly hard bargain. Some rich people liked couches in the Sirniakan style, but Mai preferred the ease of handsome furnishings that could be moved, changed, or put away quickly and with little effort.

"Now that we are come to live in the Hundred, Honored Mother," she went on stubbornly, with that same sweet voice, "we have found it easier to adopt the local ways rather than cling to our old ones."

"So say those who are weak-minded and lazy. Had I not clung to my Qin customs and ways in the long years I was trapped in the women's quarters of the imperial palace, I would be dead now. So would my son. A fact you should consider. I will not sit on the floor."

"Then you must stand, Honored Mother. My apologies."

She snorted. "Sweetly wielded. A knife coated with honey."

Mai let this pass. "May I offer you refreshment, Honored Mother? Khaif or tea can be brewed. There is also kama juice."

"What is your price?"

Mai smiled. Now they were walking on familiar ground. "I offer you refreshment as I would offer any guest refreshment, Honored Mother. This is not the market, that such drink would come with a price."

"Do not play this game with me. I am accustomed to female beauty. I have studied it over many years. Many beautiful girls and women inhabit the women's quarter in the imperial palace, some even more beautiful than you. But you are also intelligent, and more than that, you hold a piece of yourself aside. That is what lends savor to your beauty, although few men understand it is that quality they react to. I doubt my son understands it. He may believe it is merely your physical beauty and your intelligence he favors, but it is the particular quality of spirit which infatuates him so. He wishes to conquer all of you and knows instinctively that there remains yet a corner of your spirit which belongs to you only. How that must rankle him!"

Mai had learned to say nothing and show nothing long ago. Her market face had protected her many times. She found anger surging in her breast, and she pushed it aside. Later she could rage. Now, she waited.

"What is your price? Your own household? Coin? Gold? Fabric? Horses? Slaves? A handsome husband to replace this one?"

"You believe I am someone else, Honored Mother. I have my own household. I am rich, through my own efforts. I run things as I wish. I am content."

"Would you be as content if Anjihosh is murdered? They will come after him."

"They might come after him even if he marries the emperor's sister. Have you any reason to trust they will leave him alone in exchange for a marriage?"

"The marriage will show them he means to honor the agreement to remain in exile. The Hundred means nothing to the empire. There is nothing here they could possibly want."

"The giant eagles."

"Ah, the giant eagles and their reeves, which I have seen. Yet they are a curiosity, poorly deployed and without purpose. In the empire, the reeves would be slaves who served the throne, sent as messengers on the emperor's behalf or to strike at his enemies. It is Anjihosh the empire cares about, not the eagles or the paltry trade goods."

She took three steps toward Mai. Priya stepped forward as if to place her own body between the two women, but Mai put out a hand to restrain her. Anji's mother was only looking, studying Mai with a gaze not truly hostile but something Mai had no name for and no experience with. She herself measured fabric in the market with such a gaze, trying discern which would best suit her uses and which was not worth her time or coin. But you did not measure people as you measured goods in the marketplace.

Eihi! Of course folk did.

They did it all the time.

She folded her hands in front of her and said nothing, only returned that gaze without flinching.

Anji's mother nodded, a flicker of a smile flashing. Was that a dimple, like Anji's? It was already gone.

"You are more formidable even than I had supposed. Let us speak bluntly, then. Have you a price?"

"Let us speak bluntly, then. I do not have a price."

"Do you think it unreasonable of me to insist that my son make such an advantageous marriage?"

Obedience choked her. Duty choked her. Truth choked her. Powerful men commonly took two wives, multiple concubines. Clans made alliances for mutual benefit. In contracts, in business, love meant nothing.

"I see," said Anji's mother. "You understand perfectly well that it is not an unreasonable demand. But let us imagine that my son is too proud and stubborn to see you relegated to the status and rank of concubine, even if that is what you are in the eyes of any person born of noble blood and to high rank. Such distinctions often mean a great deal to the common people. Let us say that for a merchant's daughter, status as a concubine would be seen as lowering, shameful, even dishonorable. Would you therefore object to a position as his second wife, for certainly an emperor's sister must be designated his chief wife? There is no shame or disgrace in standing as the second wife to a prince."

Once she could have borne it in silence, let words wash over her and away. She had long ago determined to live life in her own way and on her own terms by holding a part of herself aside as a garden in which she could nurture a seedbed of personal, private happiness. In those days, she had been careful to hide her true feelings in order to never anger others, because if they were angry they might disturb the tranquil sanctuary she had so carefully constructed.

But now, it seemed, she no longer feared making other people angry. The girl she had been had passed through the Spirit Gate and become a woman whose voice she scarcely recognized as her lips opened and she spoke.

"You forget, verea, that in the Hundred Anji is not a prince. He is not an emperor's son, or an emperor's brother, or a var's nephew. Such titles mean nothing here. He is a militia captain, a man who works for coin just like everyone else. He is no greater or lesser than I am. If I walk first in his heart, why should I then agree to step back and become second?"

"To save his life. And the life of your handsome son."

Priya gasped. O'eki gave an inarticulate exclamation.

The ground lurched beneath Mai, or perhaps that was only her hammering heart and dizzied head as she stumbled to the cot and placed her body between the baby and his grandmother.

Who smiled, not unkindly. "Perhaps you now understand me. There is no abyss as fathomless as a mother's fear for her child. There is no beast who will fight more fiercely than a mother defending her child. So understand me in this. Anjihosh's son is as precious to me as Anjihosh himself. I am not the one you need fear in the matter of the boy."

"Then why do you threaten Atani?"

"I do not threaten Atanihosh. I am endeavoring to make you understand that with my aid and cooperation you can ensure the baby's survival."

"If I relinquish my place as Anji's wife."

"If you give way, as is proper, to a woman whose rank and birth lie far above your own. It would be best for you to leave the household entirely."

"Taking my son with me?"

The woman had the audacity to look startled. "Only Anjihosh and I can protect him!"

"Is this your argument? To abandon my son into the arms of a woman who speaks of his death?"

"Mistress," said Priya warningly.

"I will never leave him with you!"

She expected anger in response, but in her fury and fear she had forgotten the way the Qin veiled their faces with a bland expression that concealed any and every emotion.

"Do not cross me, pretty girl, because you will discover I have survived far worse in the palace than you can possibly imagine. I offer you two choices: I pay you handsomely to depart, and you may walk free to establish yourself as you wish and where you wish as long as it is not beside my son. Or you accept a place in his household as second wife, accepting the primacy of the princess and my authority to rule over any disputes such as may arise within the household."

"Mistress," said Priya urgently.

"No," said Mai.

Her breathing caught in her chest as she fought to expel the fury that rose like a haze. All she could feel was the pressure of the carpet's dense weave pressing up against her bare soles, and the faintly oily taste of air flavored by flames that consumed the reservoirs of lamps.

Voices rose angrily outside. The curtain was swept aside, and Anji strode into the room.

"Hu! Hot in here."

His voice pretended at evenness, but he was furious: his boots were still on, his gloves were still on. He never came into their intimate chamber dressed for riding; he had far better manners than that. He was tapping his riding whip against his thigh as though better that than a vicious slash across the face. . . .

"I received a message, Honored Mother, saying you had urgent trouble that warranted my immediate attention. Yet when I went up to the house, I was told to cool my heels while you were roused. Time passed as I waited with obedient patience. At length, I realized I had been outflanked. Now I am here."

Mai wanted desperately to call him over, to flaunt him standing beside her, supporting her, protecting the baby, but she did not move or speak. To call so obviously for his aid in front of his mother would betray weakness, and that of all things she refused to show.

"I am ready to depart," said his mother without the slightest hint of discomfort. "Yet if you will, might an attendant guide me to a private corner for I have some necessary business I must urgently complete before the walk back up to the house. If you will be so kind, Son."

Besides Mai, there were only two other females in the chamber, Priya with her disapproving frown and Sheyshi in the corner.

"You," said Anji's mother, pointing at Sheyshi.

Priya said, "Mistress, I will go—"

"I am not useless!" cried Sheyshi indignantly. "This way, verea."

"To a slave such as you," snapped Anji's mother, "I am addressed as 'Most High.' "

"Sheyshi is not a slave," said Mai.

But Sheyshi picked up a lamp and scuttled outside. Once both women were outside on the porch, Sheyshi shut the doors behind them.

Mai heard her speak in her clumsy way, "Here is the waste bucket, Most High."

"Not here, you stupid girl! A place with some privacy!"

Off they clattered into the depths of the inner courtyard.

"Out," said Anji to his mother's slaves, and they retreated so quickly Mai would have laughed, if she could have laughed. Chief Tuvi came in, looking as disheveled as if he'd been sleeping. Anji marked Priya and O'eki. "Tomorrow I depart by eagle for Olossi. The ships with the oil of naya and the new cohort of Qin soldiers will follow. As for you, plum blossom, my heart, my own, you will go to Merciful Valley. It is the only place I can know you will be safe from the dagger, or from poison. These are the preferred methods of the women's palace in Sirniaka. It's like a sport for these women. They have nothing else to do."

"She said that she would never harm Atani—"

"Of course my mother would never harm my son. You'll take Miravia."

"Keshad should go with O'eki back to Olossi to see to the business."

"That's fine. You only need your personal attendants. Chief Tuvi and your usual guards. Reeve Miyara and Siras—a few others—can fly in supplies. I'll assign a specific group, and the chief will have standing orders to kill anyone else who attempts to land. You will see no one until I have returned."

"But, Anji—"

"I can only fight one war at a time."

"Will you marry the emperor's sister?"

"You are my wife."

"Are you only saying that because you're angry at your mother?"

"No."

Chief Tuvi snorted, raising his gaze to the ceiling.

Anji shrugged. "Perhaps."

"Wouldn't it be prudent to seal a contract with your cousins?" Mai said. "To marry their sister?"

"I must fight this war in the north. And since I must fight, I must know you are safe. The rest can be discussed afterward."

Footsteps stamped outside. The distinctive sound of a slap, hand meeting cheek, cracked. One of the doors was wrenched sideways to slam against the frame. Sheyshi stood sniveling on the steps, a hand on her reddening cheek where the old bitch had struck her.

"What a stupid girl!" said Anji's mother as she swept in. "What useless doors!" She did not look at Mai. "You will escort me to my dwelling place, Son."

"I will let you make your own way within the considerable security of your impressive entourage to my wife's house in which you are temporarily lodged. If you must entertain yourself, I suggest you set yourself to discovering the extent and competence of the spies set in this town by the Hieros who sits in authority over the temple of the Merciless One. Surely you can outwit an elderly priestess from a land as provincial as you must believe this place to be."

He pushed the curtain aside with the riding whip and gestured. Head held high, his mother departed from the chamber; he followed her out.

Mai's face was burning, as if the scorching heat of Anji's tone had scalded her as well. It was better to move than to think. "Sheyshi, come inside. Here's some water to wash your face. Was she quite rude to you?" She wrung out a linen cloth and offered it to Sheyshi, even dabbed her cheeks as she sniffled.

"I'm sorry to cause you so much trouble, Mistress."

"Do not cry, Sheyshi. There is kama juice in the kitchens."

The curtain stirred. Anji had returned, this time without boots.

"Sheyshi," said Priya. "Let's go to the kitchens. Come along."

The chamber cleared, leaving Mai with Anji.

He had the ability to stand still, not restless at all; his self-control was impressive and a bit disconcerting. Had he ever worshiped at Ushara's temple? Somehow she could not see him relaxing in a garden that belonged to someone else. Probably she was just being naive.

"What are you thinking, Mai?" he asked in a low voice. "There is a piece of you that you always hold apart."

She licked dry lips, thinking of his mother's words.

Sheh! She would not let that woman's poison do harm!

"Tomorrow you will ride to war because you must, and I will hide, because you say I must."

"Mai—"

"I do not object to your concern. Atani and I will go, as you wish, to keep you easy in your heart so you can think only of the battle you must win." She approached him, and it was odd to note how he reacted with each step bringing her closer: his breathing quickened, his body tensed, he began to cant toward her. But he let her come to him. "Because you must win this battle. So."

She rested her palms against his chest and gazed into his eyes, which were measuring her, as always.

"Mai—"

She touched a finger to his lips, silencing him.

He might die. So might anyone die. No one could draw breath as they woke in the morning knowing for sure they would still be alive at day's end.

You could only know you were alive now, in this moment.

40

USHARA'S TEMPLE HAD not even a proper entrance court, just a high wall of rocks. The outer gates were canvas, and a youth sat cross-legged on a rough approximation of a rock bench illuminated by a lamp hanging from a tripod.

"Haven't seen you before," the youth said to Keshad in the rude way kalos and hierodules often had, as if the goddess chose them for their impertinent speaking. "We don't have a proper Heart Garden yet. Just so you know, the Hieros has come to detest you folk complaining about how things aren't so very nice out here."

"You're grumpy this evening. Did I offend you somehow?"

The youth grinned. "The Hieros has only been here for one month. You can't believe the things we've heard. Folk should be grateful we've been able to set up at all."

"Why is that?"

"Eh, the captain didn't want the the temple here at all when the verea was in residence. There was a rumor he's afraid the mistress will come find some pleasure while he's out fighting, but that can't be true. What man would begrudge his wife a little sex if he's off traveling all the time?"

"He's an outlander. They have different customs."

"Aui! Hard to believe. Anyway, the new Astafero council voted to establish a temple, so the Hieros in Olossi sent a kalos to stand as hieros."

"Can I go in?"

"The devouring urge is eating you badly, isn't it? Anyway, I know who you are."

"How can you know who I am?"

The youth grinned maddeningly and waved him inside as several Qin soldiers strolled up. Kesh pushed past the canvas entrance to avoid speaking to them. An elderly woman sat on one of a chain of rocks set up as benches in a square of ground that would perhaps one day harbor a garden with flowering shrubs and troughs of blooming yellow-bells or stardrops. Torches bound to iron posts flared.

"Don't you have pretty eyes?" she said wickedly. "If only I were younger."

Instead of gates, they had hung canvas to either side, these painted with the proper colors although in such dim illumination it was impossible to distinguish gold from silver except by the pattern: a round disk to mark the gold and a crescent to mark the silver.

At the entrance, the Qin soldiers were laughing at something the obnoxious gate-keeper had said, as jovial as you please in that calm way they had of never finding offense. He suddenly recalled the chief who had offered to take the Sirniakin palace concubine as a wife rather than see her killed. Would he have made the woman a good husband? Would he, like Anji, have threatened to kill a young man who had no designs on his wife purely for the unfortunate accident of having been made an offer for that wife he had no intention of accepting?

"No one will bite you," the elderly woman said with a laugh. "Unless that's how you like it."

He hurried to the men's side and rang the bell. The Qin soldiers came into the Heart Garden, but the old woman engaged them in conversation and like all the Qin they had very polite manners and therefore listened and responded dutifully as Kesh shifted, wondering how the hells long it was going to take and what if Miravia was already here waiting for him?

Away in town, the sixth bell rang its pattern, closing the day.

A young man twitched the curtain aside and looked Kesh up and down. He grinned in a friendly way, whistled sharply, then beckoned. They had done their best with the dusty environs. There was a cistern and a bathing tub, and several screens set back in the shadows for more private ablutions. Where normally a garden would sprawl with winding paths and hidden glades and ornamented private alcoves leading through the grounds to buildings set up in the back for those who preferred more traditional comforts, they'd thrown up a maze of canvas hanging from ropes strung between posts. It had a certain rustic charm.

Four women strolled out to look him over, one with a very sexy smile who was too old for him, one with a playful grin who seemed too young, and a pair more or less his own age, one thin and one plump.

The kalos draped an arm companionably over the shoulders of the youngest. "Good eyes," he said to the young one, who was perhaps seventeen, "but he won't be interested in you, dearest. Nor in you, grandmother," he added, with a grin at the older woman.

She said, sardonically, "Nor in you, peaches."

"I'm here to meet someone," interrupted Kesh.

They all laughed, but it was the kalos who replied. "You want to meet a lover, go find some dusty ravine for your assignation, like that idiot debt slave who got accused of stealing sheep when they were just trying to keep out of sight of her husband. The temple does not facilitate secret meetings."

"But she said to meet me here . . ." He trailed off, hearing how ridiculous he sounded.

The plump one looked bored by his evident idiocy and wandered off to twitch aside the curtain and peer through to look at the Qin laughing in the Heart Garden at the elderly woman's jokes.

"Which means she was telling you that she's not interested."

"But—"

"Aren't we always sure, when we're infatuated, that our interest is returned?" Was that *pity* in his gaze? Were these cursed people feeling *sorry* for him?

He grasped as at rice straw. "Maybe she doesn't know the laws. She's an outlander—not an outlander, precisely, a Silv—that is, she was but not now—" He stumbled to a halt, wondering if it was too late to save himself from utter humiliation.

Their expressions changed. Even the plump woman hurried back, having caught the end of this staggering speech.

"Oh!"

"Well!"

"You didn't say you were talking about Miravia!"

The hells! They looked sidelong at each other, sharing smiles. The plump one brushed a finger over her rosy lips. The kalos waggled his eyebrows as he shared a meaningful glance with the thin one. The older woman flashed that startlingly sexy smile again.

"You know her?" demanded Kesh.

"She comes to worship just like anyone," said the kalos appreciatively, "not that it's any business of yours. And not that it changes the law."

"It's possible she doesn't know," said the plump one, as if it mattered to her to help Miravia in any way she could. "He might be the one she was talking about. Those beautiful eyes. Not that it makes any difference."

"You'll have to go, ver," said the kalos sadly.

Kesh sure as the hells wasn't going to walk out of here without seeing Miravia unless it happened she had deliberately sent him on a fireling chase—the kind where you could not hope to catch what you were after—and he was cursed sure that a woman who stared at him the way she had stared at him was not pretending.

"Here, now," he said, the words flooding out as a scheme took shape in his mind. Zubaidit had nagged him months ago, and he had ignored her then. "I was sold into slavery at the age of twelve. My master never allowed me to serve my apprenticeship year even though it goes against the law to deny any youth that year. I want to serve as a kalos. Starting tonight."

A bell rang at the entrance.

The kalos grabbed Kesh by the elbow. "The Qin won't be wanting me. You and I are going to see the Hieros." As the hierodules admitted the Qin soldiers, the kalos tugged Kesh back into the Heart Garden.

"Trouble?" asked the elderly woman with an arched eyebrow.

"He says Miravia told him to meet her here for an assignation."

"I thought so," said the woman, clucking her tongue. "It was the eyes."

"Does everyone know Miravia's business?" he cried.

"She could have been a hierodule and served the Merciless One," said the woman with a chuckle that made him flush, "but she says she cannot take an apprenticeship because of her hidden god."

"This one says he wants to take an apprenticeship so he can serve Miravia!" laughed the kalos.

"Aui! The Hieros will sort this out."

The kalos led them through the canvas hanging—painted white—that sealed away the inner courtyard from whence the Hieros guided the temple. Behind the gate lay a featureless square of dirt faced on one side by a long stone building. A canvas awning was fixed over a porch constructed of paving stones set on a bed of sand. A man dozed in a sling chair, his behind almost scraping the stones while his feet and head were elevated. He startled awake as the kalos marched Keshad across the empty square.

"Why in the hells are you disturbing me, Dalon?"

"Holy One, my apologies." Dalon offered a disgracefully hasty gesture of respect that made it obvious this Hieros took a more casual authority over his underlings than the old bitch in Olossi. "You know the man Miravia thinks she's in love with—"

"The one with the beautiful eyes." The Hieros sat up, and cursed if Kesh didn't recognize him: a good-looking man with a pleasant smile and his long hair in a braid down his back. "Come closer."

Kesh stopped. "I saw you in the street, the day we first arrived here. You wanted me to tell you who we were and where we'd come from."

The Hieros raised a hand in an imperious gesture copied from the old bitch. "You may address me as 'Holy One.' Also, I meant it. Come closer."

Why the world was filled with people whose whims must be pleased Kesh did not know, but he walked to the edge of the flagstones, within the aura of lamplight.

"He says Miravia told him to meet her here," Dalon said. "Maybe she doesn't know private assignations aren't allowed. So he up and says he never served one of the gods, that he spent his youth as a debt slave and his master never let him. Claims he wants to serve his apprenticeship to Ushara starting tonight."

The Hieros grabbed his sandals, shook them before slipping them on, and rose. "It's a gods-rotted coincidence that you're Zubaidit's brother. Isn't it?"

Kesh gaped, left speechless.

The Hieros paced the length of the awning and returned. Zubaidit walked with the same deadly grace. "I trained Bai. I know all about her. Loyal Keshad." He smiled in a way that made Kesh very uneasy. "An unusual thing, I am sure, to think of devouring a Ri Amarah girl. Quite a feast to boast of later to your curious friends."

Kesh pinned shut his lips and glared.

The man's smile altered, growing sharper. "You're already under obligation—debt obligation—to the temple in Olossi. Not as kalos, more as a hostage although if you had asked me, which no one did, I would have said Zubaidit needed no hostage to seal her cooperation. She is the most loyal servant of the goddess I know, except for the old bitch."

"The Hieros?"

"Did you think I was speaking of someone else?"

Kesh grasped desperately for any advantage. "If Captain Anji finds out I'm speaking to you—"

The Hieros laughed again. "He'll what? Kill you? Try to kill me? He knows the temple has agents here. Indeed, he asked for them, which was polite of him considering we had them in place already. For him, we keep an eye on the settlement and all the newcomers. For ourselves, we keep an eye on the trade in oil of naya, on the training camps, on the reeve hall. On such very interesting developments as when you and the Silver youth returned from the south with a cohort of Qin troops and the captain's mother. Is it not odd that such an eminent individual was sent here instead of to Olossi? Peculiar, if you ask me. I'd love to know more. Give me information, and I'll let you meet Miravia here as often as she likes. But I can't take you as a kalos. You're not one of Ushara's apprentices. Too cursed passionate in the wrong way."

"You would trade Miravia's body for information?"

"She may reject you if she wishes, so I can promise you nothing from her. But I can have you thrown out so you have no chance even to speak to her. That's the offer I'm making. Talk to me, and I'll let you stay. What happens after that is up to her."

The scent of incense floated on the night breeze. A man and woman shared laughter. Water splashed, followed by a burst of cheerful play-shouting and shrieks.

"Dalon," said the Hieros in a mild voice that made Kesh stand straighter, "please go remind them we cannot take water for granted here as we can in Olossi."

The kalos trotted off.

Kesh's mind was already made up. He bore no grudge against one who bargained fairly, and he respected the other man's frankness and his swift, tough offer. "Must I stand? Or will you allow me to sit?"

"For you, ver, a sling chair so you can keep your feet off the ground." A sleepy man, rousted from the interior, carried out another sling chair, a table, and a tray with a pitcher of juice and cups. "We've got a cursed plague of scorpions out here and it's causing us all manner of trouble. One poor worshiper was stung right on his tool! Fortunately, the big ugly ones won't kill you, but he was cursed swollen for a good long time after. We've petitioned Astafero's council to rebuild in a different location, and we'll have to set the entire temple up off the ground, so we'll have to import posts and wood planking—very expensive, I'm sure."

"I heard the captain was dead set against a temple to the Merciful One being raised here in the settlement at all."

"The council voted to bring in the temple. It's not the captain's decision."

Kesh smirked. "You think he hasn't the power to stop it, if he wanted to?"

"An interesting statement. Why do you say so?"

"He's captain of the regional militia. It's more of an army now."

"Necessary to fight our enemy in the north," said the Hieros. "The temple works well with him. It's a mutually beneficial relationship."

"I don't trust him. He's willing to kill to get what he wants."

"Do you say so, to me? The Merciless One, the mistress of love, death, and desire, is also willing to kill."

"Don't say I didn't warn you."

"Warn me more. Talk."

Kesh talked. He told of his dispute with Anji; Anji's mother's peculiar offer; what he knew of the woman. His sojourn in the empire and what he had seen there.

The Hieros was an engaging listener, a bit of a flirt—naturally—and he knew how to look you in the face as you talked so you began to think you were the best storyteller who had ever drawn breath. He knew how to ask the questions that drew out the details whose unveiling revealed overlooked vistas and undiscovered crevices. Would the new Qin soldiers remain in the Hundred as well, marry, and settle down, or would they go back where they came from? And if they came from the south, would yet more follow? What other signs might Kesh have seen of the red hounds? Did he know anything of how they were organized? Was it true that in the empire even military cohorts were overseen by a Beltak priest? Why did Kesh carry one of their god's blessing bowls?

"I first went south when I was a slave. In the empire, a believing merchant is taxed at a lower rate than a nonbelieving foreigner. I built my first stake by carrying Beltak's bowl and keeping the difference for myself."

"Yet you're back in the Hundred now. Talking of serving a proper apprenticeship. Yet it's difficult to say which god you belong to."

"Bai said the same cursed thing to me, and it annoyed me just as much then as it does now."

"Yet you came to me asking to serve as a kalos. Was that insincerely meant?"

"A man may be sincere for different reasons than those expected of him, Holy One."

"An answer I can't fault you for."

Dalon trotted out of the gloom and bent to whisper in the Hieros's ear. The Hieros rose. "Will you come back, Keshad, and talk to me again?"

Keshad bolted up out of the chair so fast he knocked it over, and its clatter brought the other man out from the back with a staff in one hand. "Is Miravia asking for me?"

"You didn't answer my question."

Kesh wiped a hand across his suddenly clammy forehead. "You've been fair. Can I go?"

"Here's the thing, Keshad." One moment the Hieros was standing casually several safe paces away; the next he had moved so quickly and taken such a grip on Kesh's left arm, twisting it, that Kesh doubled over with a grating squeak that shamed him even as his shoulder and wrist flared hot with pain. "Don't think you've earned our trust just because Miravia is infatuated with your handsome eyes. Don't think you've earned our trust just because you're ready to sell any man on the block if it will bring you a few vey of advantage. If any of us ever discover you have mistreated her in any way, we'll beat the shit out of you and I personally know how to do it so as not to leave any visible marks and to cause you maximum suffering afterward. Is that understood?"

Kesh's eyes were watering. He braced a foot, and immediately his arm was tweaked so hard his vision hazed. "Yes!"

The Hieros released him.

He dropped, rubbing his shoulder. "Aui! What did I ever do to deserve that?"

"A question to which only you can provide the answer. Dalon, get him out of here."

Clenching his jaw, Kesh rose, shaking but determined. "I'd like tea and cups. Sweetened rice cakes, if you have any. Or bean cakes. On a platter."

The Hieros chuckled. "Would you now? I admire your stubbornness, Keshad. An undervalued trait. Dalon, bring him whatever he asks for, within reasonable bounds."

Whatever he asks for.

He ignored the pain in his shoulder as he followed Dalon into a barracks-like building flanking one side of the Hieros's courtyard. The courtyard stretched the length of the entire compound. A door led from the barracks into the women's garden, lively at this hour with laughter, conversation, and the sounds of one unfortunate who evidently had the habit of whooping loudly when she reached a climax. Most people were more discreet. Musicians were singing, accompanying themselves with drum, flute, and zither. Dalon led him to a tiny pavilion in a shadowed corner, hung a lantern from a hook, and left Kesh there alone.

There were pillows, a low table, a pitcher of wash water, a copper basin for washing. He washed his hands and face and poured the wash water into a decorative trough of snarling stardrops whose last flowers stubbornly bloomed although it was past their season. He knew how to be stubborn, how to get what he wanted no matter how long and how hard he had to work for it. He placed a pillow on each side of the table and scattered the rest so they did not clump all together, convenient for a quick tumble.

Dalon announced his return with a cough. He handed over a tray resplendent with a beautifully lacquered tea pot and matching cups, and two platters of delicacies: red bean cakes, yam dumplings, ginger rice cakes, raisins, and sliced mango.

Kesh set cups, platters, and teapot on the table and fussed with their arrangement, so engrossed in his task as his mind devised a plan that he was surprised when she spoke.

"Keshad?"

He started back, tumbling one of the empty teacups, and caught it as he straightened to face her. She was dressed simply, in an undyed linen taloos of fine weave, and wore no scarf, her lustrous hair tumbling over her shoulders like a fall of water. Eiya! He heard a distant voice singing of just such a sight: "Her hair, like the water, falls—"

He was terribly aroused, but he smiled as if he weren't lusting after her so badly it hurt. He knelt at the basin and washed hands and face again, this time with the proper prayers. She copied the movements but did not speak the prayer.

Lips parted, eyes bright as the lamp's sheen made them glisten, she turned to him, lifting a hand to touch his chest. "Keshad."

He scrambled to put the table between them, settled cross-legged—tremendously uncomfortable but determined to negotiate this with every cursed trick he knew—on one pillow and indicated the pillow opposite him.

"Look at these enticing foods the Hieros has had brought for us," he said.

Surprised, and cautious, she sat on the pillow with her legs folded to one side, leaning on her right hand, watching him. She had a way of dipping her chin and looking up through half-closed eyes that was likely to drive him to madness, but he was not to be swayed from his purpose. "What is this? I thought—"

She ceased speaking as he poured tea and, with the gesture known from the tale, offered her a cup. "I thought we could talk," he said.

"Talk?"

Certainly he wanted to devour her, right now, right here, but what would that gain him? She could come to the garden every night and have sex, with him or with some other person, as she wished. He must withhold himself until he had convinced her to want him for other reasons.

Watching him, she licked her lips.

Aui! This wasn't going to be easy. To hold her off, he had to make sure he distracted her thoroughly with the subjects that mattered more passionately to her than a night's devouring.

"We'll just talk." He was going to need a hells lot of cold water after this was over. "Tell me why slavery is wrong."

*   *   *

UNDER THE WEIGHT of a late-afternoon sun, the closed tent was sweltering. Arras sat with four other cohort captains on a bench; subcaptains stood in the back as Commander Hetti spoke. Here in Saltow, five cohorts and the command cohort had gathered for the new assault on Nessumara. Two cohorts had been deployed to the western side of the river to hold a defensive line during the upcoming attack. Three cohorts would make a coordinated attack from Skerru in the north, along the causeway that ran through the swamp.

Captain Deri of Eighth Cohort raised a hand. "Commander, the attack down the northern causeways five months ago was a disaster. Why repeat it? I understand it's meant to be a diversion for our attack over the dried-out wetlands here in the east, but isn't it a big risk to expose three full cohorts like that? Especially when we might strengthen our attack here?"

Arras caught his eye and gave him a nod. As unimaginative and overconfident as the command were, at least there were a few competent cohort captains.

"You're right it's a diversion," said Hetti, "but by placing three full cohorts at Skerru—and being able to draw on the two cohorts on the western shore for reinforcements—we can stop any of Nessumara's militia who break and try to run that direction. We've also spread a necklace of boats and ships in the bay. We've turned their delta fortress into a prison."

As Hetti went on, Captain Deri glanced at Arras and shrugged. It was a decent plan: advance at night with torches over wetlands mostly dried out here at the fiery end of the dry seasons; dig in before dawn, and if necessary light fires to raise smoke away from the main assault path as a smoke screen. If there was no resistance, keep moving forward until they reached the outer islands of the city.

From outside, a guard called, "The Lord Commander! Lord Yordenas!"

The tent flat was swept aside to admit a merciful gasp of a breeze, then slithered shut as two cloaks strode in. Every commander and captain fell to his knees, hands shielding eyes.

"Commander Hetti." Lord Radas had a pleasant voice, but it still made Arras's skin crawl to hear him speak. "Tonight our agents in the city will make targeted assassinations within Nessumara's council. They'll also kill Copper Hall's marshal. I'll be riding north to Skerru. Lord Yordenas will remain to oversee your forces. It's time to deploy. That is all. You're released to return to your cohorts. Which of you is Captain Arras?"

As the others rushed to exit the tent, Arras stepped aside on trembling legs, not looking up. "I am, my lord."

Lord Radas walked into an inner chamber more stifling than the first. Arras followed, sweat pouring. This might be it: a quick death, or a chance to move up. He halted, eyes screened behind a hand.

"You sent a message. Be quick. I must walk the Mire Pool Altar at dusk. What is it?"

"I've captured an outlander, my lord."

"Why did you not turn him over to Commander Hetti?"

"He is the outlander Lord Twilight was trying to hide, my lord. The one Night took prisoner. I don't know how he escaped. I thought you would want to see him personally. Also, I prefer to receive the credit rather than give it all away to Commander Hetti. Shall I bring him to you, my lord?"

"Twilight's brother, eh? Night wants him badly. Detail a detachment to remain here in Saltow until she arrives."

"Yes, my lord."

"Odd the outlander should turn up after escaping from Wedrewe," mused the cloak. "Look at me, Captain Arras."

The hells! He must look. Lord Radas's smile made him flinch; why in the hells had he listened to Lord Twilight? What could that cursed cloak ever do for him? The whole command structure was riddled with weak braggarts seeking preference—

"You think well of yourself, don't you, Captain Arras?"

He dared not look away, even as his heart was laid bare. Aui! Now he must think of Zubaidit, curse her!

Lord Radas looked bored as he gestured to let Arras know he was released. "Odd. You possess the power to force the woman to have sex, yet you refrain. You're a proud, ambitious man who thinks well of yourself and poorly of others. Do your part in taking Nessumara, prove yourself to me, and you may hope for advancement. I'll need a commander for the coming campaign against Olo'osson."

He bit down a grin of triumph. "Yes, my lord."

A man yelled a warning. The tent gave way. A big rock had plummeted to earth, carrying the canvas roof down with it, the frame collapsing as another rock struck and then a third, none atop him, thank the gods. But the weight of that collapsed fabric forced him to his knees. Lord Radas was cursing, and horns were blowing. Arras drew his knife and sawed at the canvas as the heat and heavy canvas began suffocating him.

Ai! Ai! He cut an opening and dragged himself through, began cutting where Lord Radas struggled. The cloak emerged in a fury; his gaze struck Arras so hard the captain fell backward with a shout of pain. So much anger, slapping back on him: *People are such imbeciles! I am the only one worthy to rule.*

Neh, these were not his thoughts. They were the cloak's.

A rock slammed down an arm's length from him, its impact shuddering through the ground. Men cried: "We're being attacked!"

He crawled over the writhing canvas as more rocks thumped down. They were being dropped by reeves. A subcommander had been hit, his head cracked open. Arras cut where men were trapped, freeing two, five, ten from beneath the fallen tent. One man was no longer breathing. Arras shouted for guards; he needed to return to his cohort. Were they holding discipline? What in the hells was going on?

A second flight flew overhead, dropping more rocks. A skirmish was spreading at the eastern edge of the camp, and then a flash of flame, and abruptly a thunderous sound like a storm crashing down, only the sky was cloudless. Horses were stampeding through camp.

Arras rounded up every soldier he could grab and formed a wedge as protection against the horses. Men who panicked and bolted were not so fortunate, tumbling under hooves.

Yet the flood poured away to become a trickle. Grooms dashed in pursuit. No third flight of reeves assaulted them. Arras ran to his cohort's encampment at the marsh edge of camp. His soldiers had held their ground against archery fire, but the assailants had melted away.

"Don't pursue," he ordered his subcaptains. "Hold position. You've done well."

He tracked down Zubaidit, who had held her cadre along a line of wagons that anchored one flank. One of her men had been grazed but was not otherwise hurt.

"What was that?" she asked. "A diversion?"

"Someone in Nessumara knows a thing about shaking up the enemy. You'll pick ten men and remain in Saltow with the prisoner when we move out."

"Will I? Why?"

"To turn him over to a cloak. Be patient, and you'll get your reward."

"Turn him over to Lord Radas? Is *he* here?"

Her words fell unheeded on his back. With Giyara and two runners in tow, he was already racing back to the command tent, wondering what Commander Hetti would say. Confusion boiled; tents had been smashed by falling rocks or trampled by frantic horses. Over by the horse lines, a fire was smoldering in hay. Sergeants called cadres to order; soldiers milled around casualties. Hirelings and grooms were out hunting horses. A chicken ran loose, and dogs barked, chasing it. Some idiot had dropped his sword.

At the collapsed command tent, a hurried council was in session.

Lord Radas beckoned to him. "Captain Arras. You kept your head about you when the tent collapsed. My thanks."

He kept his head down. "My apologies, Lord Commander. I went to check on my cohort. They held ranks, so I returned. There was archery fire on the perimeter, from attackers out in the wetlands. It was a coordinated attack—reeves, archers, horse lines—meant to frighten and bewilder us."

"These cursed reeves are getting out of hand," snapped Lord Yordenas.

"The reeves never worked in concert with the militia," said Radas. "When we first attacked Nessumara, their militia blocked the causeways, while the reeves only watched. In High Haldia, only the militia tried to hold the gates. The only time our forces have faced a coordinated attack was at Olossi. I want to know who is in charge of Nessumara's militia, and I want to be rid of him."

"Can you not see into the hearts and minds of all people, my lord?" asked Arras into the silence left by this bald statement. "If they have reeves who can scout, so can you scout out their plans. There is nothing they can keep hidden from us, were you to seek out the truth with your second heart and third eye."

"Yordenas," said Lord Radas, "you must fly into Nessumara and discover their plans."

"But—Lord Radas—!"

In that arrogant voice Arras heard the taint of fear.

Could Guardians *fear*? Yet hadn't Yordenas been injured in the first attack? Were the cloaks afraid to penetrate the heart of the enemy? Were they not as powerful as they seemed?

Lord Radas gestured with an arrow held like a speaker's baton. "They cannot see you until you touch the earth. Make them cower, and they will flinch. Execute any criminals who stand in your way. That will frighten the rest. You are a Guardian, and they must obey you. Move in fast, and move out fast. I must ride to Mire Pool Altar to give this and other news to Night. At dusk you will ride into the city. The information you return with will allow us to alter our attack so it is most effective. At High Haldia, Lord Twilight did not fear to ride into the city to scout out the positions of the militia. Can you not do what the outlander has already done?"

"Of course I can!"

Lord Radas turned to his military council. "Commander Hetti, the army must begin its push into the delta tonight. The dry ground favors our attack. We will reach the inner islands by tomorrow night if we push hard now. They will believe we are too frightened and bewildered to strike because they have thrown this insignificant diversion at us. Therefore, we will strike."

41

WHEN MAI AND her small party arrived in Merciful Valley, Toughid was waiting for them. He had been sent ahead, and now would be flown back to West Track to join the army and Captain Anji on the march. He spoke briefly to Tuvi but left with Reeve Siras before Mai had a chance to talk to him.

She drew Tuvi aside. "Did Anji send Toughid up here to warn my Uncle Hari that we would have to remain here for some time?"

Tuvi shook his head. "The captain did indeed send Toughid to scout the valley. To make sure no cloaks have come. To make sure no red hounds have found some treacherous path to this haven. It is possible that despite his lady mother's intelligence and sharp eye, one or two red hounds hid themselves within her party and got wind of this place."

"Or she welcomed them in herself!"

Astoundingly, he set two fingers on her wrist, the pressure causing her to go still. "Whatever else, Mistress, understand this. She will do nothing to harm her son, or his seed."

She clutched Atani against her breast. The wind murmured peacefully within the trees, and the birds had resumed their singing now that the big eagles had taken off. A deer paced into view and, as two Qin soldiers grabbed their bows, bolted back into the trees.

"If Toughid found no sign of intruders in the valley," he added, "then there are none."

"What of Uncle Hari?"

"Since he is a demon, he can surely hide himself so no human can find him."

They spent the rest of the day sweeping the floors and beating the dust out of the bedding and mats, setting a fire in the kitchen hearth, stowing rice and millet and foodstuffs as well as the small chests they had brought with clothing and spices and several of Priya's precious scrolls wrapped in silk and leather. As the afternoon shadows lengthened, Mai nursed Atani and afterward told Tuvi she would like to go up to the altar and make a dusk offering.

"Best you wait until morning, Mistress. I don't want you walking back at night, even with torches."

In matters of security, his command was Anji's command. It was not worth protesting. Let a few days pass in peace, and then she could negotiate for the daily prayers.

AT DAWN, ATANI'S hungry fussing woke her. She put him to the breast, his suck pulling an intense wash of pleasure through her body. Miravia slept restlessly beside her. Over in one dim corner, Sheyshi snored.

After Atani's demands were satisfied, Mai dressed, slipped on her sandals, and stepped down into the clearing. Priya was already up, seated on the porch cross-legged, watching the sky lighten. She smiled as Mai took in the high mountain cliffs and peaks that surrounded them, rock and snow so sharp in the clear air that it seemed an archer standing in this clearing might easily pierce their high majesty.

Their group was a small one: Miravia, Priya, and Sheyshi, of course; Chief Tuvi and twelve Qin soldiers, men Mai trusted. No one else.

Most of the soldiers were already up, hacking back jabi bushes, digging waste pits, repairing a corner of the barracks shelter. Two headed into the forest with bows and spears. She called Tuvi over, and with him beside her and a pair of sentries pacing behind, followed the stream down to the lip of the great ravine where water spilled into a vast gulf of air, its spray lost in the wind. A pair of rainbows shone so strongly the colors shimmered. Far below, to the east, the land tumbled out to become the barren plain that edged the distant Olo'o Sea, little more than a glimmer hazed out by the rising sun.

"It's so beautiful, isn't it?" she said as Atani cradled his head against her breast.

Tuvi said nothing, and when she looked at him, he was rubbing his chin as he examined specks in the sky. He wasn't admiring the beauty at all. He was searching for threats.

"I would like to go make an offering, Chief."

"Yes," he said at once. "But just you and Priya, Mistress."

"In case Uncle Hari comes out to greet us? I know we're the only ones besides you who can know."

He took the baby and together they walked back to the clearing. Sheyshi still slept, but Miravia had awakened; she'd slept poorly because of the strange noises and the brisk mountain air, nothing she was accustomed to.

Mai kissed her, laughing. "We'll be back soon enough. Then I'll show you the market."

"The market? What market?"

"The one we'll build with sticks, like a child's toy house. We can pretend we are bargaining!"

"You're horrible," cried Miravia. Then she saw the men digging. "Mai! Are you telling me I have to relieve myself in a ditch?"

Laughing, Mai bundled Atani up and set off with Priya and Tuvi, two soldiers walking rearguard. This late in the year, there were scant offerings to be found along the path, but just as they reached the top and she feared she would have to approach the altar empty-handed, she caught sight of a spray of white flowers off in the trees. She handed Atani to Priya, found a stout stick, and beat a path through to a massive knot of branches, the ground subsiding under a heap of leaves and disturbed ground. A few flowers still clung, bold white stars like the eyes of ghosts.

She shuddered, stepping away from the churned up ground as if it might erupt with a terrible demon. She snapped off a spray of flowers, careful not to take them all, and beat her way back to the path.

"Some animal's been digging back there," she said to Tuvi. "I never thought there were wolves or big cats here."

"We'll keep our eyes open," he said, moving on.

They came out of the tangled forest into the clearing with its ruins and waterfall. The falls' spill down the high cliffs was soft in this season. Instead of churning the water, it merely spread and rippled around the cliff. The broad pool had a dark, almost black sheen, like sheets of best-quality silk dyed to the color of a moonless night.

"Just let me see first," said Tuvi.

He walked through the maze of fallen walls and along the ledge past the thinned curtain of spray into the cave behind. Priya found a patch of shade by the high cliff wall and sat with the baby. The sentries waited at the path's opening, half hidden by the trees.

Mai walked to the water's edge. The fluid lapped the stone, its slight rise and fall like the pressure of breathing in and out. How strange the water appeared, not like water at all. Blood might appear so, somewhat viscous and, when she bent to brush her fingers along the surface, faintly warm to the touch. Not cold, as mountain water draining down from the icy peaks ought to be; as the pool had been during the rains. Its touch stung her fingers, and she winced and withdrew her hand.

"Mistress? You forget me!"

Aui! Here came Sheyshi, flapping and wailing as she ran in her graceless way past the sentries, who stepped back hastily to let her pass. Priya looked up and, horribly, did not move to come rescue Mai.

"You forgot me, Mistress! I want to pray, too." The young woman, tears streaking her face and a bit of snot running from her nose, hurried up to her, a hand clutching her right side as though she'd caught a stitch from running.

"You were asleep, Sheyshi. I thought it kindest to let you rest. We'll pray again at dusk—"

Sheyshi had a knife in her hand, slid out from the wrapping of the taloos she wore.

She had a knife in her hand.

"Even you, so kind as you believe you are," said Sheyshi in a voice Mai did not recognize; it was some other woman's voice, cold and hostile. "Even the captain, so clever as he thinks he is. You could only see the stupid slave I pretended to be."

It was not a sharp pain but more of a punch up under the ribs, hard and final. Like Anji's face when he'd seen her in Dast Olo coming off the boat from Ushara's temple. Strong and sudden, that blow. Hadn't he purchased her? Didn't she belong to him, and him alone?

I will not die.

Mai grabbed Sheyshi's arms and pushed. Pain flared as she jerked away, Sheyshi stumbled back, and Mai was free, blood pouring down the front of her taloos.

Sheyshi lunged. Mai staggered back, not dodging fast enough—she had no soldier's training—as the blade grazed her hip. She kicked and punched, connecting with Sheyshi's shoulder, then retreated into the shallows. The ledge of rock was slick under her feet, water curling up her legs as if to taste the blood leaking down her body. Sheyshi easily absorbed the blow by spinning as swiftly as a soldier, almost lovely as a desert cat is lovely, springing for the kill.

Priya's scream stabbed the air. "Mai!"

What if Sheyshi went next for the baby? She was mad.

Not mad. She knew exactly what she was doing.

Men's shouts rose, answering Priya. Footsteps pounded on the stony earth.

Sheyshi plunged forward, and Mai threw herself to one side; the knife scraped along her ribs, the sound vibrating through her flesh. The bright morning hazed dark.

No. No. No. She would not die.

She shoved Sheyshi with what remained of her strength, but the cursed woman only fell back a single step; she was possessed of a demon that infused her face and her eyes and heart; she was a monster concealed behind a human face, which had burst forth to eat its meal.

An arrow's flight hissed, and its head sprouted through Sheyshi's shoulder. She caught herself on a tumble of rocks, the knife still in her hand.

"Who are you?" gasped Mai, trying to escape through the shallows but her legs no longer worked.

"I am your death. So the captain's mother has ordered. So I, slave of the palace, obey."

The water was staining with skeins of pink being sucked into the black depths beyond. Chief Tuvi was running, but he was so slow. One more thrust of the knife would finish her. He would not get here in time. If she took a step back—

Her foot caught on a heavy chain, and her legs gave way. Where the ledge ended she fell into deep water. A splash became the swirl of her impact, a boiling sound in her ears as she sank hard and fast. Eyes open. Blood pumped out of her wounds like threads of life fraying.

Her sight and hearing scattered everywhere. Yet as from the mirror of the pool's thickened surface she saw through a rainbow's prism of colors onto the open space as Tuvi's sword flashed and Sheyshi went down. The two soldiers dropped beside the Mariha woman, one wrenching the knife out of her limp hand. Priya was clutching the baby, who had begun to wail.

Tuvi splashed into the shallow waters on the rock ledge. "Mai! Mai!"

A flare of light burst across the pool; he screamed in shocking pain as the water drove him out like fire scalding him. Yet it all took place so far away. Down and down she sank, she falling into death and her blood rising as toward the receding surface that was the unreachable sky as day bent its head and accepted the yoke of twilight and the victory of night.

She tried to grasp the chain. Two chains, after all, each attached far down in the well of the pool to a small chest heavily bound by yet more chains. Within each chest, a spirit woven more of will than consciousness struggled to break free just as she was struggling to break free of the pool. Only they were trapped, and she hadn't the strength.

She was dying.

Neh, she must claw upward. Fight for air. Open her mouth. A lungful of water choked her, yet she could not spit it out. Her hand tightened on the chain, the links biting into her palm.

I know you. A presence sang in her bones. *You and your young one, your child, released into the air as my children were born around you in the last storm season.*

"Who are you?" she said, if not precisely in words.

You have seeded another life, so soon. Its touch—like water—slipped inside her wounds, probing until Mai, too, recognized the spark that was another life—another child!—growing within her womb. *Go back, daughter. Go back to the air, where you belong. You cannot live with us in the storm.*

"I'm dying."

You are torn, but we can heal you.

"Who are you, Honored Mother?"

We are the womb of the firelings. In the words of the tongued ones, you call us Indiyabu, that which is aware and flowing through the land, the blood of the Hundred. Choose now, daughter. Let go, and pass the Spirit Gate in peace, or grasp hold, and accept the pain of healing.

The pain of life. Of truth.

Within the womb of the firelings, she could see, with a second heart and third eye that stand outside, the flesh that binds human existence. Two chests, cast deep because the holy waterfall and its fathomless pool had seemed a most excellent hiding place. Each confined a Guardian's cloak, severed from the body it had once sustained. One chest she had seen recently, in Toughid's possession; that chest imprisoned a cloak whose fabric rippled with the color of earth. Within the other, a cloak the color of twilight.

Uncle Hari was dead. Someone had killed him.

Someone who knew he was here.

The pain was already flowering: Anji had betrayed her and Hari both.

How could she bear it?

How could she not?

Anji was not the whole of her life.

I will live, she said.

She held on as pain engulfed her.

42

JOSS MET OLO'OSSON'S army a day's stage from Horn. The army had made remarkable time, marching eighty mey in eight days, and yet as they set up their night's encampment, the soldiers looked determined and eager, not exhausted. Anji sat under an awning on a cloth folding stool at a camp table on which a map was spread, its corners weighted by knives. Squares of rice paper and a clerk's writing paraphernalia had been pushed to one corner. He was receiving a delegation of local villagers who had brought in wagons loaded with supplies.

As Joss entered, Anji beckoned him over. "Bring a stool for the commander," he said, and another stool was unfolded.

Joss sat, looking around at the usual complement of Qin soldiers: Toughid was missing.

"We'll leave you with fifty lame and blown horses," Anji was saying to the villagers, "and we'll take the fifty you've gathered. With proper care, the animals we leave behind will recover, but you may lose a few. I can't guarantee you'll ever again see any of the horses we're taking."

"Say nothing of it, Captain," said their spokesman, an elderly fellow wearing a merchant's silk robe and sash. "It's a fair trade considering what you've done for us. A year ago we were hiding in the forest. We've thirty men wanting to join up and fight that cursed Star army."

Anji took a sip of steaming khaif and set down the cup next to a knife hilt. "I can't take untrained men right now, although men who wish to fight with the militia can join up at the training camp in Candra Crossing. However, if you've any experienced carters or grooms or smiths or harness makers, they can fall in with the infantry, which is marching about a day behind us. They'll have to keep up. Any who fall behind will be left to make their own way home, even once we're in enemy territory. Especially once we're in enemy territory."

It was understood that Anji was being not brutal but pragmatic. A baker presented him with a tray of sweet rice cakes and bean curd pastries, and there were other delicacies as well: mutton steeped in spices, a savory fish soup, venison, pickled radish, and nai bread sweetened with juice to cover its bitter aftertaste.

No rice.

Rice was a problem, as the villagers explained. Because of the trouble early in the rainy season, fields had been planted late and not as extensively as usual. There hadn't been enough people to replant and weed and thin; losses had been higher and productivity lower than normal. There would be hunger later in the year; some households were already resorting to eating woodland roots and se leaves to fill their bellies. If the war did not end soon, the coming year's planting would be at risk also. If they lost two crops in a row, there would be famine.

Anji listened, and ate, and shared out the food to every person who had reason to come in under the awning. Eventually, as twilight fell, the villagers were herded out.

Anji rose and paced once around the awning's edge before returning to his seat. "Joss. I just joined the army today. I was flown up in two stages from Astafero, with a stop in Olossi. What news from Clan Hall? How are things going?"

"The stockpile of naya is safe. Copper Hall reeves are conveying vessels into Nessumara at Chief Sengel's order. As for the enemy's troop positions—"

A young reeve with a limp and a dusty face came in escorted by soldiers. Besides her reeve's baton, short sword, and quiver, she carried a very small jeweler's chest bound with chains and clipped to her harness.

"Captain Anji?" she asked. "I'm Beiko, from Copper Hall. Chief Sengel sent me. He said to give this chest and this report into your keeping only." She unhooked the chest and handed it to him together with a folded and sealed square of rice paper. He gave the chest to Chief Deze, who slung it over his shoulder, no great weight.

Joss's heart raced, and his fingers went cold. He could not keep his eyes from the tiny chest, no matter how innocuous it appeared to others. What in the hells had happened in Nessumara?

"Ah." Anji rose, offered her his stool, and gestured for his soldiers to leave. Only Anji, Joss, and Chief Deze remained under the awning within earshot of the exhausted reeve. The reeve gulped down two cups of kama juice as Anji cut the seal and scanned a scribble of looping marks Joss could not possibly decipher, nothing like the ancient runes or the Lantern's familiar syllabary.

The hells! Could Sengel write, too?

Anji said to Deze, "Have Esigu tell the villagers that a cohort of five hundred Qin riders will be coming up after the infantry in a few days. I forgot to mention it before. I don't want them to be surprised." He nodded at the reeve. "My thanks, Reeve Beiko. You'll be shown to a pallet for the night. Take food and drink to refresh yourself. I'll have a message for you at daybreak."

"Yes, Captain." If she was curious about the contents of Sengel's message, she hid it well. A soldier led her off into the dusk.

Joss said, "What's in that chest, Captain?"

Anji's smile was like a fine steel blade. "To gain another cloak so soon is an unexpected advantage. They have no idea. Hu!" He handed the rice paper to Deze and pulled his whip from his belt, brandishing it with a flourish. "Events are progressing more quickly than we had hoped. Lord Radas's army has massed at Saltow. Sengel sent a diversionary attack to trouble them, nothing big, but they shook it off and began advancing into the wetlands—dried up this time of year—last night. During the night a cloak rode into Nessumara's council square, where Sengel holds his headquarters. Sengel had already uncovered a plot to assassinate the council members and Marshal Masar, so I suppose the cloak came to oversee the night's work. And to discover our plans, figuring everyone would fear him too much to act. But Sengel knew what to do—" He broke off. "Hu! No fears, Commander. Your face has gone gray! It was a man, wearing a cloak the color of spilt blood."

The hells!

Joss sank down onto the stool and, without thinking, took Anji's unfinished cup of khaif and downed it.

"Would you like some cordial?" asked the captain. "Rice wine?"

"No. Go on." His hands were shaking.

"That's all. Lord Radas has no reeves so he won't know how quickly we're moving up. That being the case—" He indicated the map of the Hundred, using his riding whip to point first at Horn Hall and then at Toskala. "—I'll need you to deploy your Clan Hall reeves to lift a strike force to Toskala. Once the battle is joined in Nessumara, a signal will be given from Law Rock to attack the garrison in Toskala. Do you have any questions?"

Joss bent close, lowering his voice. "I don't know who this cloak of Earth is. But if Blood is gone, then according to what Marit said, Lord Radas and Night no longer have the five they need to control the Guardians' council. It's enough, Anji. Let the Guardians sort out their own struggle, as the gods meant them to do. To go on with this is wrong. We've broken the boundaries."

"If we have, then so have the Guardians," said Anji, tapping the whip on the square that marked Nessumara and the tangle of lines that suggested the delta's web of water and land. "In truth, we're fortunate."

Joss sat back. "How can you say so?"

"They are poor leaders, these Guardians."

"They're not meant to be leaders! They're meant to be judges, to stand outside daily life, not to rule or command."

"How does that statement negate my point? This one called Night, eldest and most frightening, seems to have an ability to build armies but no interest in using them. Lord Radas seems interested in ruling but has relied on fear and intimidation and on the complete disorganization and lack of preparedness of the local militias. The enemy army sent against Olossi lost to our much smaller force because they expected to meet no resistance at all. From what accounts I have heard of the earlier assault on Nessumara, the enemy pulled back at the first sign of resistance. Yet you and I were told that Nessumara's militia was stretched to its limits and ready to collapse." He swept the whip to encompass the land, from north to south, east to west. "If Lord Radas's troops had pushed on into the delta five months ago, they would have conquered Nessumara. Obviously, the Hundred does not know how to fight wars."

"No, indeed," said Joss hoarsely as his face went hot, "and a fine thing that is, too. Why should we want to fight wars and live in tumult, when we might have peace?"

"You might have had peace once, but you don't have peace now. You see how vulnerable you have become. Do you suppose my cousins, knowing now that the Hundred exists beyond the Kandaran Pass and having their eyes drawn this way, might not covet your eagles? These guardian cloaks? Your rice fields? What other secrets hide in your forests and mountains and seas? Look at my map, see how much of it is blank. Who are these wildings and delvings and lendings and merlings? What are the firelings who embraced my son on the day of his birth? Do you even know what a rich land this is? Do you think that if the Sirniakans desire it, they will not march with many more than fifteen cohorts to take it from you and make you their slaves?"

"Commander!"

Joss looked up, but the man was speaking to Anji, not to Joss. A Qin soldier walked into the spill of lamplight under the awning.

"Toughid!" Anji met him with a grin. Forearms smacked together so hard Joss winced.

Toughid immediately noted the jeweler's chest slung over Deze's back. "Mai and the chief arrived safely in the valley. All is as you hoped. It's unlikely your mother can reach her there."

"Your mother?" demanded Joss. Why in the hells had he heard *no word* of this?

"Did I not mention that my mother has arrived in the Hundred? She was expelled from the women's palace by the new emperor."

"Your *mother*? She must be a formidable woman."

Anji shifted a knife on the map, the meaningless gesture of a man who needs to take his mind off uncomfortable thoughts. "Formidable, yes. And as difficult to please as I remember from my childhood."

The odd way Toughid had spoken scratched at Joss's uneasiness. "What has your mother to do with Mai's needing a safe place to shelter?"

For an instant, Anji looked as if he wanted to kill something. Joss reached for the hilt of his sword to fend off an attack. Guards stiffened; Toughid spoke a word in the Qin language.

Anji's expression eased into a bland smile. "Enough. A boy reacts this way. A man does not. Mai is safe. We march at dawn."

He sat, reaching for a square of rice paper and a writing brush. He poured a bit of water into the ink bowl to soften the ink, dipped the brush, and then paused with the brush poised above a untouched expanse of white.

"Hu! Joss, what other news have you?"

A bead of ink sank from the brush's tip, hanging—like unspoken words—from the delicate hairs. But it did not fall. After a moment, Joss wrenched his gaze away from the drop to find Anji watching him with the same patient, guarded gaze with which he treated everyone. That he might once have been a brash, impatient, emotional child seemed inconceivable.

"You've anticipated me," said Joss more brusquely than he intended. "Clan Hall's scouts returned yesterday late in the afternoon with the news that Lord Radas's army has massed around Nessumara. But that would have been before Chief Sengel's attack and the subsequent night attack, so it seems you have more recent information than I do."

Anji nodded. "Anything else?"

Joss pulled a scroll from his pack. "A formal accounting of Horn's provisioning preparations for the army."

"That can go to Chief Deze," said Anji. The bead dropped and splattered on the fresh paper. "There's a spare bedroll if you need it, in my tent. Or sit here beside me, if you wish. I'll be awake a while longer and would welcome your company. Can you fly Toughid to Law Rock in the morning after you've delivered the orders to Horn Hall? Toughid will be in charge of the attack in Toskala, when it's time."

Beyond the awning, the camp was quieting as men finished their chores and meals and settled down to sleep, to conserve their strength for the battle ahead. There was no singing, no carousing, no jokes, no drinking or gossip. Such discipline was impressive.

"Joss?"

"You're right, Anji. The Hundred never knew how to fight wars. My thanks for the offer of a bedroll. I have my own. Best I rest now. It will be a long day tomorrow."

Anji returned his attention to the paper, his hand assured as graceful letters flowed from the brush. Chief Deze sat in the other stool, the chest dangling along his back. Joss walked into the dark camp and its scattering of campfires to find a patch of ground on which to unroll his blanket and cloak. When he lay down to stare up at brilliant stars not yet joined by the waning quarter moon, his thoughts kept him awake for a long time.

They had broken the boundaries.

Now they would be punished.

*   *   *

KESHAD DELIVERED THE oil of naya to Argent Hall, as ordered. Because the ship was headed back for Astafero and there were no horses available and no reeves who had the leisure to haul a person as unimportant as he was, he headed for Olossi on foot. It was an easy path, a one-cart road raised on a berm over a flat plain, but a full day's walk.

He walked between dry fields awaiting the rains, the afternoon heat beating down over him, but he didn't mind it. He had a hat with a brim to shade his face and neck; he stripped down to his kilt, knotting his jacket and trousers and stuffing them into his pack. The heaviest thing was that cursed sack of gold the Qin princess had gifted him. Overhead, eagles and their reeves departed Argent Hall in staggered flights, hauling sealed ceramic pots containing oil of naya. Kesh trudged.

At twilight, he spotted lamps to the east on a path running parallel to his own. He hurried across a dusty fallow field and caught up to a train of wagoners rigged out with lanterns, driving supplies through the night to Olossi. They were all female, and happy to have a young man with such fine eyes and such a pleasant expanse of bare torso to admire since the young men in their villages had joined up with the militia months ago.

"You're not in the militia?" they asked him as they took a break to water and rub down their dray beasts.

He lounged against the foremost wagon, sipping juice their leader had offered. "I'm an agent for the command staff. I was on special assignment."

"Then why are you walking to Olossi, eh?"

"The army has requisitioned all the horses."

They knew it, for sure! And their dwindling rice stores were drawn down, too, with planting yet to come and it to be accomplished with a smaller workforce than normal due to so many lads and men gone with the army. But it was a small price to pay for not having to fear their villages would be burned like all those villages along West Track. They set off again, and their leader, a woman old enough to have girls of marriageable age, questioned Kesh closely about the Qin. Was it true they treated their wives and wives' clans well? Were there still soldiers looking to marry into local families?

"If you're truly interested, bring your offer to the captain's wife, to her compound in Olossi."

"They say she's a sharp bargainer. Got the better of the old council of Olossi. I don't know if I'd have the courage to face a woman like that. Have you met her?"

Kesh laughed, hoping the night hid his flush. "She'll treat you fairly. Or you can go to one of the training encampments where Qin soldiers are stationed."

"There's a camp near us with a few Qin in residence, training the others. They took their pick of well connected girls. Not that they were rude about it, mind you. They took what seemed best to them. Anyway, all that militia have marched. While here we sit, waiting."

"You're not waiting, verea. You're working."

She shifted the reins to move the dray beasts across a transition where the one-cart road merged onto a wider two-cart path on a massive berm that speared straight south over the plain. The waning quarter moon was rising in the east. In the wagon behind, young women were giggling as they talked.

"Work's a thing I'm accustomed to. Villages burned, refugees starving in the fields, roads unsafe—that's nothing I ever want to get accustomed to. I make my offerings to the gods and pray that our army defeats the enemy and brings peace. That would be worth plenty, neh?"

O'EKI HAD RETURNED to Olossi with the ships transporting the new Qin cohort and their horses. At the Qin compound in Olossi the big man welcomed Keshad with such a genuine smile that Kesh was taken aback. The chamber, large enough to house ten clerks, was silent, with only a single guard, a local man, standing at attention at the open door into the warehouse.

"Where are the other clerks?" Kesh asked after he'd covered his discomfort by washing his feet, hands, and face.

"Hu! I let them go because they weren't experienced enough. I keep the compound books myself. I hired the Haf Gi Ri house to keep track of the army's expenses and revenues."

"The Haf Gi Ri house? The Ri Amarah women?"

O'eki was cleaning his brushes and closing down his accounts for the day. Both doors were open in the accounts office, but no breeze blew through to cool them.

"In exchange for the contract, the Haf Gi Ri have undertaken to make no sales to anyone supplying the army. That way they can't enrich themselves on the side by cheating the books."

From the warehouse rose a genial exchange of greetings between locals. Indeed, there was not a single Qin soldier to be seen except for crippled Seren, who had command of the compound guard. A familiar figure clomped into the chamber from the warehouse, still laughing at a joke he'd left behind. Seeing Kesh, he coughed to silence. His silver bracelets, running three-quarters of the way up his arms, jangled as he stopped short. He had every bit of skin covered except hands and face, just like in Sirniaka.

"Eliar." Kesh rose.

"You're here!" said Eliar, with a flash of surprise before he looked away. He placed a bundle of accounts books on O'eki's writing desk. "I've brought today's accounting early. We've a festival tonight, and the women closed up the books early."

"Why are you surprised to see me?" asked Kesh. "I'm a hostage, you must have known I'd be dragged back here in time. In a way, I'm like your sister—"

Eliar turned his back on Kesh. "My sister is dead."

"Of course she's not dead—!"

"I'll thank you not to speak of her."

"You're the one who loses in that bargain. I see you have more bracelets, eh? Were you rewarded for your part in our southern expedition?"

Eliar tensed as he clenched a fist. "I'm getting married. The engagement's been sealed. My bride arrives any day now."

"How can she do that?"

"A female reeve will bring her. It's all been arranged."

"Just as your sister would have been hauled off to Nessumara— Wait! Which bride? The one they arranged for before? The one from Nessumara? The one they meant to trade Miravia for?"

Eliar lunged, fist cocked, but O'eki interposed his bulk between them. "I'll thank both of you pups not to bark. My thanks, Eliar. As always. Here's our book. I'll see you tomorrow."

There he stood with the immensity of a mountain, implacable and immovable, as Eliar grabbed the accounts book and left.

"So," muttered Kesh, "the Ri Amarah settle their problems by pretending they don't exist."

"I still hear barking," said O'eki. "I'm no longer a slave, Master Keshad. I'm factor here, with certain privileges. One of them is that I want you to shut up about this. It's a waste of my time, and I value the Ri Amarah, even if you do not."

Kesh bit back a retort.

O'eki smiled. "That's better."

"You're a cursed sight cleverer than anyone has ever thought you were, aren't you?" said Kesh.

"I'm a patient man. Now that I'm here, Master Keshad, I don't intend to lose what I've so unexpectedly gained, nor do I intend to suffer through two young men wrangling out of hurt pride and unmet lust. Do you understand me?"

But Kesh smiled. Lust was nothing. Lust passed. What he felt was not lust.

"I realize I am a hostage in this household," he said, "but with your permission I'd like the evening free to run a few errands."

"You're free to go. I'll be sending you back to Astafero in the morning by reeve to arrange for another consignment of oil of naya."

"Won't that clean out their stores?"

"The naya seeps will keep producing, won't they?"

"So they will. Why don't they lift it all out by eagle?"

"The eagles can only take two vessels at a time. There's still stock in Argent Hall to move, so why waste the reeves' time by making them lose two days flying to Astafero and back when we can ship in new supplies for them to carry once they've lifted the old?"

"You'd think the enemy might remember what was done to them at Olossi. Not that I was there, but I've heard the story a hundred times."

"Even if they know, what can they do?"

"I don't know. That's why I'm not a military man. I'll be ready to go at dawn."

In the hirelings' courtyard he washed, and dressed in a rumpled jacket and trousers. He didn't need to impress with his clothing and his looks. He wasn't a rich merchant. The gold from Anji's mother was like poison that he had to shed from his system.

He set out in the heat haze, keeping to the shady side of the streets. He stopped first at one of the Lantern's temples, and afterward made his way to Mistress Bettia's compound. The elderly doorman, a slave bought out of the south years ago, recognized Keshad and admitted him to the reception hall, a cozy chamber fitted with pillows, a decorative screen depicting famous actors from recent festivals, and doors slid open to display an inner courtyard ornamented with a fishpond and flowerpots.

He sat cross-legged on a pillow, watching the courtyard shadows consume the handsome pond and plants as the sun set. The inner door slapped open, and a slave entered, a young attractive woman carrying a tray with a pot and two tiny ceramic cups. A debt mark branded her face by her left eye; she was wearing a taloos so thinly woven that her body was half visible beneath, the kind of thing unpleasant masters made their massage girls wear when helping bored customers. She did not look at him, her face flushed with shame.

Mistress Bettia knew he and Nasia had been slaves together in Master Feden's household and it was almost certain she knew they had once been lovers. It was possible Nasia had even confessed to her mistress, or to one of the other household slaves, that she had cherished the hope that Keshad meant to buy her free, but of course he had ruthlessly abandoned her when he had a chance to free his sister from Ushara's temple.

Mistress Bettia entered the room, called for tea to be poured, and dimissed the slave.

"Whew! Such heat!" she said by way of opening the conversation, fanning her sweaty face. "You were gone a long time, Master Keshad. People thought you were dead."

"I'm not dead. I see you still have the slave you received from Master Feden."

"Nasia?" Her smile oozed a false surprise. "Not much use to me, I tell you. The Sirniakan couch I traded for her was of more use to me."

"How much?" he asked.

"How much?" Her trembling hand, lifting the cup, betrayed her greed. She licked her lips before she sipped. "Ten cheyt."

"That's the price for a good riding horse."

She laughed unkindly, setting down the cup. "You've not been in Olossi for some months, have you? A good riding horse costs five times that now that the army has requisitioned so many. I daresay you cannot purchase a riding horse in this city for any price."

Abruptly he was bored with haggling. "Ten cheyt it is. Sapanasu's clerks inform me that the going rate for Sirniakan dinns is four per cheyt. Here's your price."

He counted out forty gold dinns onto the tray and rose. "I'll wait outside. Send her and the bill of sale to me."

He walked out before she could find her voice. Out on the street, the doorman examined him with an odd expression, more frown than smile. Folk passed, making haste to get home as the light dwindled. Spiced meat was being roasted, and he licked his lips rather as Bettia had done, thinking she had caught the flavor of his weakness.

It was full dark before Nasia cautiously stepped onto the street. She handed him a hastily written bill of sale and moved out of the aura of the lamplight, hiding herself.

"I'm sorry about the pregnancy you carried and lost," he said in a low voice. He handed her ten dinns.

"I don't want your coin!"

"Shut up and just take it! This is your seed coin. You can start your own business, make a new life."

He could not see her expression in the darkness, but her voice was bitter. "I don't know how. I've been a slave since I was eight."

"Get yourself a Qin husband, then. After riding and training all day, they'd probably like a good strong pair of hands to massage their sore buttocks."

"An outlander?"

"They're all right. They're decent, honest men."

"That's more than I can say for you!"

"Say what you want about me, Nasia. I can't make amends for what can't be changed. Come at dawn to the Qin compound and you'll get your manumission, sealed and clear. You're free. What you make of it is up to you."

He tucked the bill of sale into his sleeve and walked off, not looking back. He walked to the night market and ate at a slip-fry stand, savoring the familiar spices and the inconsequential chatter. Then he made his way to Master Calon's compound, a new place rather higher on the hill in deference to Calon's newly elevated status in the city.

Master Calon received him not in his reception hall but in his private audience chamber, floridly decorated with layers of screens and paintings as if he felt obliged to display every ornament he owned. The effect made Kesh blink, even as lamplight softened the mismatched colors. Two expensive Sirniakan couches graced the chamber. Kesh sat on a pillow as Calon chuckled.

"Had enough of the empire, have you?"

"I have. Did you ever get a full accounting of my travels?"

"I wouldn't know. Together with Olossi's council and the Hieros, I met with Captain Anji before he left. I hear a rumor that a woman of exalted status resides in Astafero now, presumed to be his mother."

"It's true. A Qin princess, and formerly wife to the Sirniakan emperor, now deceased, the one who fathered Captain Anji."

Calon nodded thoughtfully. His grandfather had left the Sirniakan Empire as a young man and settled in Olossi, marrying into a local clan, but Calon's ancestry was still apparent in his prominent nose and the texture of his hair. He had the handsome coloring of the Hundred folk but his features weren't truly local. You could never look at him and not know he had ancestors who came from somewhere else.

"I'll make you a trade," said Kesh. "Sell back to me those two sisters I sold you, and I'll give you the same report I gave to Captain Anji, not a word left out. Name a fair price. I won't bargain."

"You're already bargaining," said Calon. "And it's a cursed hard bargain you're driving, too. I'd give a lot to have that information. But I sold away the younger sister to pay for the elder's training."

"Who bought her?"

Calon rang his bell, and a factor hurried in, a hireling by the look of him, eager to show he was doing a good job. "Bring my red book."

The book was brought. As he scanned the accounts, he spoke. "The older sister was coming along very well, with a pretty voice and a quick tongue. But her manner isn't fetching. She frowns and cries—"

"Did it ever occur to you she might miss her sister?"

Calon glanced up at him, mouth twisting as if he did not know whether to laugh or scold, then touched a line on the ledger. "Mountain Azalea clan. They run a lumber business."

Kesh rose. "I know where they are. Wait up for me, if you will, Master Calon. I'll return."

It was more difficult to get into Mountain Azalea's clan compound after dark, but in the end he shamelessly traded on Mai's name and wedged a foot between doors. An irritated older woman was sent out to interview him in the entrance courtyard, although he could see onto the porch of the reception hall that a lamp burned within, behind rice-paper screens.

"What do you want? Master Keshad, is it?"

"Yes. I'm recently returned from a trading expedition to the south, where I discovered some unexpected— Aui!—never mind that. I've just been to see Master Calon about the slave girls I sold him last year, and I understand he sold you the younger sister. How is the girl working out?"

She watched him as if he were a snake about to strike. "Why do you want to know?"

"It's nothing, I am sure. The trouble in Mariha . . . for sure it's most likely because of the tremendous heat down in those lands. That the problem happened with her sister doesn't mean it will be a problem for you."

Her eyes widened. "What problem?"

"Neh, nothing to concern yourself with. I was just asking if there had been any incidents, but if there haven't been—"

"What cursed manner of incidents?" she demanded, with a glance toward the shuttered reception hall.

"If there have been none, I see no reason to alarm you."

"We just bought her because she's young and likely to grow into something useful later. Right now she's mostly just an extra mouth to feed."

"I'm relieved to hear nothing is amiss and that none of the rest of you have suffered. I'll be going now. My pardon for disturbing you so late—"

"Neh, come inside, Master Keshad. Perhaps you'll take khaif and cakes and we can discuss the girl further. Really, these outlanders are a lot of trouble, aren't they?"

By one means and another he left the house with the girl, whose wan face turned several unpleasant shades as she recognized him, the man who had hauled her and her sister far from their distant homes and into the household of a master who had callously separated them. As he had once been separated from Zubaidit.

The hells.

But she went obediently enough. Young slaves learned to be obedient if they learned nothing else. She trotted beside him, for he practically ran all the way back to Master Calon's compound, impatient to be finished with the cursed business and hating her lifeless expression.

Calon had waited up, expectantly, with a tray of food and drink to greet their return. He chuckled as they entered.

"What demon has gotten into you, Keshad?" he asked.

The girl's color brightened; she looked around the room, straining as at an invisible leash. Calon rang the bell, and the door opened, and there stood her sister. The two girls wept and embraced until Calon told the factor to take them out and let them weep elsewhere, out of earshot.

"What do you want?" Calon said, when tranquillity had been restored and all they could hear was the clip-clap of a dray beast being led down the street just beyond the wall.

Kesh cleared the dishes off the tray and dumped the rest of the dinns on the lacquered surface. He hadn't counted them; he didn't want to know. Calon grunted, then put a hand to his chest as though he'd been struck.

"You always dealt fairly with me, Calon, so I'll trust you now. Here is the coin for their upkeep, and a stake for the elder sister toward her manumission. The rest she will have to earn herself. Here's the bill of sale for the younger. It will need to be sealed and signed off."

"Why are you doing this? You're the one who brought them over the mountains and sold them to me in the first place."

"I've had a change of heart." As he felt his burden lightened of all the tarnished gold gifted him by the Qin princess, of the females left behind in slavery so Bai could walk free, he knew it was true.

43

DRY SEASON IT might be, but Arras's cohort, given the right flank on the downstream end of the line, was able to move forward no more than about two mey during the night's advance. Despite torches blazing and no cursed reeves to plague them, they bogged down time and again in sludge-sucking hollows and spongy ankle-deep pools. One poor man had his leg bitten off by a kroke, which then slithered away into the darkness. The man died screaming. Shortly after, arrows flying out of the gloom drove the forward cadre into the protection of a hedge of thorny brush whose intertwined branches caught the missiles.

Arras came forward and waited a short space, tested an advance; no arrows flew. He personally led the reluctant cadre forward past the hollow where the beast had sheltered and the dead man sprawled. Marsh worms had already risen from the mire to sup on fresh blood.

"Where are my gods-rotted pioneers?" he shouted. "If you'd been out in front as you were supposed to be, testing the ground with spears and beating the brush, you wouldn't have been taken by surprise."

"What about the arrows, Captain?"

"Keep your shields up. Now, move out."

He took a stint at the front, searching for traps, hacking at tangles of thorny brush, shifting a rotting log into a ditch to fill in for better footing. That shamed the soldiers, and the men assigned to track forged out in front of him.

Soon after dawn, the first reeves passed overhead. None dropped rocks. Nor, in the mire, did he see any sign of skirmishers, not that it was easy to see within the tangle of growth. This was flat ground but dreadfully overgrown. The thorns were the worst, but there were also thick stands of pipe-brush and sprawling tangles of a shrub the locals called poison-kiss. Mosks followed them in clouds. Flies buzzed in ecstasy, drunk on sweat.

Five months ago this entire expanse of ground had been underwater, impassable. They moved forward step by cautious step, slow, hot, stinging, and nasty work, and the men were hard-pulled and short-tempered. So when one cadre cornered a kroke, not a very big one, he allowed them to delay the march to hack it into pieces. They took positions at midday on solid ground and rested under their shields. The sky was as blue as a demon's icy gaze and the heat was unrelenting. A few men fainted, but the rest held strong.

How the other cohorts were faring on the upstream side of the mire he did not know, but he found a knobby hillock and from that vantage thought he could see the causeway shimmering in the heat haze. Or perhaps he was just fooling himself, thinking he saw companies from what could be Eighth Cohort moving along the stone berm. Likely it was too far away to see, unless you were a cursed reeve harnessed up with your cursed eagle.

"Captain?" Giyara's face was red, but she moved easily in her boiled leather coat and quilted leggings. "The sun's easing. Best we move forward because at day's end we'll be staring straight into the sun for a bit, not able to see anything in front of us."

He signaled. The horns blatted, and the men began the next stage. They'd come about halfway. No doubt the commanders hadn't taken in account how slowly they would advance under these conditions. The commanders were accustomed to roads and paths, and never seemed to take into account that things might not go as they wished.

"You're thoughtful, Captain," Giyara said as they trudged behind the front line.

"I'd've been happier if we'd been allowed Eighth Cohort's position in the center. Captain Deri will do all right, though."

"Nice of you to say so."

"I respect competence." He swiped at mosks. His glove-encased hands were hot, but the thin leather gave him a better grip on his weapons. "If we're flanked," he added, "you'll go to the rear company and set up a defensive line."

"Do you think they're hoping to cut around behind us, Captain?"

"That's what I would do, if I were defending the city. When we reach the first open channels, we'll pull the pioneers back to reinforce the rearguard. Then if one of the other cohorts breaks as First Cohort did, we can send our reserve to rally them. Cursed if I'll retreat again. It also gives us the option of wheeling on the enemy, taking them from the back."

"If they attack."

"If I've thought through every contingency, I can act faster when the hells break loose, as they will. I worry that Lord Radas prepares himself only for victory. He's so used to people falling onto their faces before him he can't imagine anything else."

Her color heightened as if with a flash of heat. "Captain, if you'd keep your voice lower, I for one would appreciate it. This cohort is loyal to you but that doesn't mean there aren't men here who won't carry tales in exchange for the prospect of advancement. To be blunt, I'd rather not be cleansed for being under suspicion of harboring traitorous thoughts."

"Aui! My apologies."

Yet his mind would spin and weave as they slogged through ground increasingly difficult to push across, sinkholes and mud pits like ambushes laid across the mire. A better plan; better commanders; more disciplined men, soldiers honed to a peak of skill and loyalty. His cohort was all right; he trusted them to hold their ground because he'd trained them. It was the rest of the cursed army he didn't trust, and yet even to think that thought might get him killed, just for being honest about the army's glaring weaknesses. Aui!

"Keep moving," he called to a cadre of soldiers stymied by a slippery depression that in the wet season likely flowed with water. "Hack down the pipe-brush over there. Lay it down right across the mud. That's right. Excellent."

Onward, with the reeves watching from on high and, so far, no sign from the city hidden within the delta beyond that the Nessumarans meant to put up any further resistance.

*   *   *

AT DAWN, JOSS flew Toughid to Horn Hall and gave Kesta orders to delegate a reeve to convey Toughid, and an advance force, to Law Rock.

"Aui!" She glared at him. "We're undermanned. I've got an entire flight running messages up and down West Track for the captain already. To move one hundred soldiers from the army to Toskala will mean every reeve we have here must make the journey twice. It'll take three days at least. More if he decides he wants more lifted."

"I'll see if I can detach two flights from Copper Hall."

He glided down over Copper Hall in late afternoon, flagging for permission to land. Fawkners came running, one of them an old acquaintance who recognized Scar.

"Is Marshal Masar in his cote?" Joss asked.

"You haven't heard?" They wore expressions of grief-stricken pride. "You'll find the marshal in council square."

He crossed a bridge that linked the reeve hall to the council islet. A man dressed in reeve leathers trotted across the span toward Copper Hall, brushing past Joss without a word. Nessumara's council square was an entire islet, banked with a stone revetment. Its elaborate garden surrounded a tiled roof supported by carved wood pillars. The paving under the roof was famous, spoken of in tales, but Joss only remarked the older folks sitting tensely on benches in the copious shade. Clerks of Sapanasu were writing busily. A pair of aged men in militia sashes were talking to a young runner, a lean lass dressed in kilt and vest. As he approached, the lass gestured a respectful leave-taking and took off running toward the eastern bridge.

The elders looked up as Joss approached.

"Greetings of the day," said Joss.

The two men stared at him, making no welcoming gesture. Then one rose abruptly and smiled. Joss turned. Chief Sengel approached, accompanied by a stocky young man in a well-worn quilted militiaman's coat whose hands bore a farmer's calluses.

"Commander Joss! An unexpected visit." The hells. Joss offered a forearm; Sengel hit hard, and his grin flashed when Joss did not stagger or wince. "This is Laukas, freshly jessed."

"Is that right?" said Joss. "You're the first I've heard of in—well—months. You are well come to the reeves, comrade."

The young man did not smile. "I'm ready to fight," he said. His hair, Joss saw, had been pulled back but wasn't quite long enough to wrap in a ribboned topknot.

"What's your eagle's name? Maybe it's one I know."

Laukas glanced at Sengel, and the chief nodded. "Shy," said the young man. "Although she's actually pretty bold, so I guess you reeves—I mean, *we*—make a jest of their names?"

"But—" Joss stumbled over his words. "Shy is Masar's eagle."

"Wait here," said Sengel.

"Yes, Marshal." The young man stepped aside obediently.

"What in the hells?" demanded Joss.

Sengel walked with Joss out to the end of Council Pier where they could talk without being overheard. The channel was running low this deep in the dry season. A dead fish stank on a muddy lip of stone. The city had a tense anticipation of coiled rope just before it's flung. Boats moved purposefully, piled high with an assortment of debris and junk, branches, planks, wheels, a blackened spar. Older folk poled and rowed, accompanied by youths.

"A cloak came down in the night. We filled him full of arrows and javelins until he did fall and lie in a stupor. I'd spoken to Masar about the situation. He claimed the right to unclasp the cloak as payment for his family."

"He's an old, failing man!"

"Which is exactly why I let him do it. Don't you suppose that's how he wanted to die, knowing he'd struck a blow rather than wasting away on a pallet? Now what can I help you with? I don't have much time. The enemy's eastern line is more than halfway across the mire and we've not got everything in place yet. Do you bring a message from the captain?"

"Aui!" And yet, he could imagine Masar taking on one last battle. It was a proud way to go. "Listen. Can you spare a flight to move troops up from the army to Toskala?"

Sengel shrugged. "I can't, Commander. I've got three flights out today bringing in reinforcements to me. If you've just come from the army, you might have seen them."

Joss shook his head, rubbing his forehead. "I went by Horn Hall first."

Sengel looked closely at him. "What is it, Commander? Something troubling you?"

A horn rang in the distance. Drums rapped out a measure. Every soul seated under the council roof turned to stare eastward over a wide channel, although he could see nothing but the crowd of one- and two-story buildings that filled the neighboring isles. So much was hidden from him. He didn't know the streets and alleys of this city—not Nessumara, precisely, although its complex tangle of islets, islands, canals, river channels, backwaters, and mires was famous in tale and in truth—but this unfolding market of events whose paths were obscure to him.

"I just think it's cursed odd we reeves have become carters."

Sengel laughed in the easy Qin way. "Not at all. Reeves are soldiers, doing what needs done."

"Why'd the young man call you 'marshal'?"

Sengel began walking back to the shaded square where people waited impatiently for him. "A courtesy, nothing more. I'm in charge of Nessumara's defenses at the moment, and that includes the reeves. If there's nothing else, Commander, I have to go inspect the defenses. If you don't mind, could you walk Laukas over to Copper Hall? He hasn't even been issued reeve leathers or harness. It just happened this morning."

Laukas wasn't shy, precisely, but bitter.

"Who's marshal now?" Joss asked him as they crossed the bridge.

"Chief Sengel's acting as marshal. He's got everything in hand in Nessumara. Without him, it'd be like we were walking into a cursed ambush, wouldn't it? But now we have a hope of victory."

<h1 style="text-align:center">44</h1>

MIDMORNING, KESHAD WAS working in quiet amity beside O'eki, each man at his own writing desk, when the door into the compound slammed open. Keshad splattered ink over his neat column of accounts.

O'eki looked up more calmly. "Seren? What is it?"

The Qin soldier limped inside and a young reeve hurried in behind, his face so creased with worry that O'eki set his brush on its stand and rose.

"Reeve Siras has come from Merciful Valley," began Seren.

The reeve broke in over Seren's words. "You're to come immediately to Merciful Valley, Master O'eki. Chief Tuvi tells me to bring also Master Keshad."

"What's wrong?" demanded Keshad, throat tight.

The reeve wiped his brow. "Mistress Priya suggested you close down the warehouse until you return."

"Very well," said O'eki in a tone so flat Kesh was shocked to see how gray he had turned. "It will take me a short while to lock everything up. Seren, ask a hireling to collect a change of clothes and such necessities as we'll need."

The Qin soldier nodded and limped out, brows drawn down.

"What's happened, curse you!" demanded Keshad.

"Close up your books quickly, Kesh," snapped O'eki. "Grab anything you need. Make it fast."

The hells!

———

THEY LAUNCHED FROM Assizes Square. O'eki hooked in with Siras, and Kesh was handed over to Reeve Miyara, who looked as if she hadn't slept in a week.

"What happened?" he asked as she hooked him in.

"Anything the chief wants you to know, he'll tell you."

The earth lurched; the ground leaped away from under him as wings battered the air. He yelped, squeezing shut his eyes. She offered no word of encouragement, no friendly banter to ease the transition. After a while he cracked an eye only to find the land falling away so rapidly he felt sick to his stomach, so he clamped his eyes shut again.

"How do you get used to this?" he muttered. Her knee jabbed into his back. "Aui!"

He took the hint. If she didn't want to talk, then he wouldn't talk. But it was cursed hard to keep your eyes shut for so long, and the next time he opened them there was nothing but water beneath, swaying and glittering under a cloudless sky.

Better not to look. He lifted an arm to shield his eyes, but after a while his arm got tired, and then the other arm got tired, and eventually the steady rumble of the wind and the tense silence of his companion numbed him enough that he could regard the sea below with resigned terror. Just let Miravia be alive. As long as he held to that thought, he could endure.

They'd launched before noon and soon he had to piss, even though they'd warned him to relieve himself before flight. But there was nowhere to land except the south shore shining gold off to the left, and he sure as the hells wasn't going to ask her to detour just for him. They rose higher yet until the air stung in his chest and his eyes watered, and he started to shiver, but she said nothing and the eagle flew on, alternating gliding on strong winds and then beating for stretches. To cross the Olo'o Sea by ship took two days, or a long day and night, yet the waters quickly slid past as the day wore on. Late in the afternoon they passed above the hinterlands of Astafero, the settlement a smear of buildings far below, and sped straight for the magnificent Spires. The winds buffeted them, and he shuddered convulsively in a cold blast that swept off the high, forbidding peaks whose crowns glittered a blinding white.

They plummeted and he shrieked as the earth hurtled up. They hit and he fell hard to his knees as she unhooked him without warning. He knelt at a cliff's edge, the spray of a waterfall spanning the gulf of air. He crept away from the chasm, and the first time he tried to stand he could not. The reeve was shucking the harness from her eagle, releasing it, and by the time he got his feet under him she was walking in company with a Qin soldier into the trees. Another sentry waited at the path's edge, so he hurried after.

"Where's O'eki and the other—what was his name?" he called.

"Master O'eki is a heavier burden, and Siras hasn't as much experience to push his raptor so hard." She tossed the words over her shoulder and kept walking. He struggled past the sentry, who nodded at him but stayed where he was, waiting for the other reeve. Aui! He had to piss so badly that he staggered a few steps off the path, shook himself free of his trousers, and released.

Afterward, legs steadier, he loped through the forest and caught her up as she and her escort emerged into the clearing with its living shelters and storehouses and a herd of goats ransacking their way along the tree line.

Soldiers came running. Priya, sitting on the porch with the baby in her arms, looked up, then stood, her posture inexpressibly weary. She had cut off all her hair, shorn like a sheep every which way, and by the look on her face as she watched him stumble over the uneven ground toward her, he knew what had happened.

He should have understood. He had met the emperor's brother. He knew what manner of people the Sirniakans were. He knew what the captain's mother was. She had warned him.

"It can't be true," he said, stubbing his toes as he tried to take the steps in a single leap. "It can't be true. I could have saved her if I'd agreed to marry her. If I'd taken her away—"

Her voice was as colorless as undyed linen. "Chief Tuvi wishes to speak to you, Master Keshad."

He balanced on the porch's edge, heels bouncing over air. "Does he think *I* had something to do with it?"

Soldiers had fenced him in while he wasn't looking. These men had been sent to Merciful Valley to protect Mai's life, and they had failed.

"I'll go in," he said. They had all failed.

Priya nodded. The baby was suckling on a bottle sewn from a sheep's udder, content for the moment, eyes shut.

It was easier to shut your eyes, wasn't it? To pretend you didn't have to look at the horrible truth. He shed his sandals and pushed aside the canvas. The outer chamber was empty, two rolled-up pallets stowed out of the way, but a curtain was tied up to reveal the inner chamber. The canvas wall on the far side had also been tied up to allow in light and air. Miravia was sitting on a pillow beside a man reclining on a pallet, his legs covered by a length of silk and his torso belted into a silk jacket. She bent forward, setting a cup to Chief Tuvi's lips as she smiled and began to speak in response to something he had just evidently said.

She *smiled* at Tuvi!

Kesh's feet scuffing startled her. She spilled the liquid on Tuvi's chin as she jerked upright, head whipping around to stare. Her lips moved, forming his name. She had hacked off her hair, and what was left spiked in ragged clumps likely a badly mown hayfield. She was more beautiful in her grief than he had ever seen her, sorrow honing her spirit so its beauty stabbed like lightning.

The chief raised himself on an elbow, his gaze an arrow pinning Kesh. "Here you are," he said, his voice hoarse with pain. "Sit if you will, Master Keshad."

"You don't think I had anything to do with it!"

"To do with what?" asked the chief.

Miravia burst into tears and, sobbing, jumped to her feet and ducked out through the back flat onto the wraparound porch. When Kesh moved to go after her, Tuvi stopped him with a word.

"Sit."

Kesh sat, missing the pillow.

The chief pulled the silk off his legs. He wore a local kilt, and his skin, in the fading light, was revealed as a mass of welts and blisters.

"Bringing you here, did the reeves speak of what I told them to keep secret?" asked the chief as Kesh tried not to stare.

"No."

"Did the captain's mother ever speak to you of her plans?"

"I told Captain Anji everything! She offered to give me Miravia if I would take Mai as well. It was cursed obvious she wanted to be rid of Mai. What in the hells happened?"

"Sheyshi was her agent all along."

"Sheyshi? The slave? But she's . . . stupid. How could she be—?"

If you shut your eyes, you would not see what walked and talked right in front of you. Was anyone ever really as stupid as Sheyshi had constantly been?

"We saw what we expected to see." Tuvi grunted and lay back on the heap of pillows. "If you will, a sip of juice."

Kesh found the cup Miravia had set down before she had run off. How odd to feel compassion for his rival's pain. The man had never done him any harm, as far as he knew. After swallowing the juice, the chief breathed as his eyes watered.

At last, he sighed. "We were all taken in. She stabbed Mai by the pool. When Mai fell in, I tried to drag her body out but the pool's sorcery burned me. She sank into the depths."

"Are you saying you've no body?"

"I lost her. The demons—or maybe the gods of this place—took her." Tuvi raised a hand, welted with fine red scars, and covered his eyes as he wept.

He wept, as hardened a soldier as he was.

"That old bitch—!" cried Kesh.

"Sheh!" The Hundred word cut like an edged blade. *Shame!* "No man speaks so of the var's sister, a princess of the blood."

"She had Mai killed!"

"So it seems. Nevertheless, if you insult her again, I must kill you for the sake of the captain's honor. I admit, it is not the Qin way to make a stab in the dark, but when her brother condemned her to a life in the Sirniakan palace, it must be expected she would learn to live as the locals do in order to survive. So must we all. Mai's power was considerable. A threat to her, coming to this land as a stranger to a son who did not know her well and who never liked his uncle, her brother. The var is a hard man to please. Sheyshi must have been the princess's agent all along. The princess's relationship with Beje and Cherfa was closer than we ever imagined. They must have been in communication all those years. It was Beje who helped smuggle the young Anjihosh past the empire's border nineteen years ago. I was part of that effort, you know. I did not suspect Commander Beje might have been her agent still. Or perhaps he knew nothing, and she used Cherfa to place an agent into her son's troop. To protect him. It has only ever been her desire to protect her son."

Kesh had no answer to this. "What now, then, Tuvi?"

A soldier hung a lamp from a hook before retreating into the dusk.

"Tell me again, every word the emperor's brother said to you, every word the captain's mother spoke in your hearing."

So Kesh told his tale again, pausing at intervals to help the chief drink. When partway through it came time for the chief to relieve himself, two soldiers helped him beyond the porch to the pits. He could walk, with assistance, although the effort left him exhausted. Yet afterward, returning to the pallet, he indicated that Kesh must go on. After Kesh had related everything he could recall, the chief wiped his eyes.

"We should have suspected the slave," he said.

O'eki came in, eyes red from weeping. Priya walked beside him, carrying Atani, and Tuvi smiled as she settled the baby in the chief's embrace, the child so handsome and bright a face that a man might weep to think of what he had lost.

"If only I had agreed, I might have saved her," muttered Kesh.

Tuvi laughed, the sound raw. "Hu! You are no match for the captain's mother, Master Keshad. Mai was dead the instant Anjihosh said no to his mother." He handed the baby back to Priya, who took his look as a command and retreated with O'eki.

"One last thing, Master Keshad," said the chief, "and then I must sleep. The sooner I can travel, the sooner I can bring this news to the captain. Let me assure you, in case you do not understand me, that the reeves who fly in and out here obey me. I must inform the captain, none but me. None can know outside us until he knows. I'll kill you if there is any question that you might attempt—"

Kesh flung up his hands. "I want nothing! I have no plans!"

"You want something."

Ah.

There it stood, between them.

"Miravia," said the chief, "is a fine, well-mannered, and intelligent young woman, if not particularly handsome."

"Not handsome!" cried Kesh. "She's the most beautiful woman I have ever seen!"

"Nothing compared to that girl Avisha," continued the chief.

"Avisha! That spring-blooming flower, pretty for a season and then likely to wither? The hells! Are you *blind*?"

"The mistress wished me to marry her, because her family cast her out and Mai wanted to be sure that her dearest friend would always have the protection of a clan. It's a hard world for any person thrown without kin into the cruel battle of life, is it not?"

"As I know! I lived twelve years as a debt slave."

"And bought yourself free, which means you're an intelligent lad, if a reckless and irritating one. I will marry Miravia, Master Keshad, if that is what Miravia wishes. Because it's what Mai wanted. It would be the wise thing for Miravia to do. She'll never lack, as part of the captain's household."

"You forget there's a war."

"I don't forget it. But unlike you, the captain is not a reckless man. He has his plans laid well in place, a substantial army, and an additional five hundred Qin soldiers to back him up."

"Commander Beje's men!"

"No. These are men who would have been placed under Anjihosh's command had he been allowed to take his army on the eastern frontier of the Qin empire, but either way, it does not matter. We Qin who are soldiers fight for the man who commands us, and when we are sent elsewhere, there we fight. For Anjihosh now. In time, for his son."

"I thought you fought for the Hundred."

Tuvi gestured, and Kesh handed him the cup of juice. It was, in fact, difficult for Tuvi to grasp the cup with his burned hands, but the man was determined to recover enough to travel. To serve his captain. To do his duty. To fight.

"I will marry Miravia if that is what she wishes, and I'll treat her well. Although," he added thoughtfully, "the visits to that garden will have to stop. What a cursed wrongheaded thing that is! Hu!" He held out the empty cup, and Kesh took it. "But if she wants a different man, one who assures me she will not lack for any of the comforts and security Mai would have wanted her to have, then I will not raise my sword against that man, nor will I hold a grudge."

"Do you want more juice?" asked Kesh.

"No. I'll sleep now."

"Here. Let me help you with the pillows." Kesh settled the pillows so they braced the chief comfortably. "Do you want the silk over your legs?"

"No. The air cools the burns. Is that all you have to say?"

Kesh really looked at him, seeing a man of indeterminate years, forty or fifty, hard to say because the Qin hid their age so well with their weathered faces and easy smiles. An honest man, in his way, clear-eyed and clear-spoken. Brutal when he must be, but unexpectedly kind.

"You're a cursed road more generous than I could ever be, Chief Tuvi. She matters more to me than anything."

"I'm not generous, lad. Don't make the mistake of thinking so. I have a wife back in the grasslands, a good woman I'll never see again. It would be pleasant to have a wife again, if it falls out that way. Nevertheless, I'm a soldier, and my loyalty was given long ago and completely, as it must be. I'm Anjihosh's man. He is my life. Now, go on. I suppose you will find her by the pool. It's where she goes to mourn."

SHE HAD NOT taken a lamp, but he found her easily enough, kneeling beyond the waterfall and its ruins in the darkness of the cave where, so the tale had it, Atani had been born within a net of firelings. Kesh didn't believe the story, not precisely, because everyone knew firelings lived in storms, not in caves, but people would tell tales to fit what they wanted to believe. It made life easier.

"Miravia," he said.

She knelt before plaited wreaths heaped upon a stone slab meant to be an altar. There were no flowers; this wasn't a season for flowers. She didn't look up. She must have seen the light. She must have guessed it was him.

"If only I had—" she began through tears.

"Will blaming yourself bring her back?"

She said nothing, lips pressing tight in that stubborn way he was coming to adore. The overhang smelled faintly of wet season storms, a memory of thunder. Water pounded at their backs in a constantly shifting curtain. Where the pool's edge lapped at the rim of stone, right where the water fell and had gouged out the deeper pool, waves stirred and sighed as if trying to speak.

"Mai is gone," she whispered. "How can I endure it?"

Each step brought him closer until he knelt beside her, careful not to touch however desperately he wanted to stroke her arm, embrace her body, gentle the wreck of her hair. He set the lantern on the stone beside the wreaths; its light caught crystal in the ceiling and glimmered there as thoughts catch and brighten where there is love.

"It's too early to speak of such things," he began, "but I wanted to say—"

"Mai wants me to marry Chief Tuvi. He's a good man. It would make her happy."

"Is that what she wanted? I ask an honest question. I didn't know her, not truly. Did she truly want you to marry Tuvi, or is it just that she wanted you to be safe and protected, as she was?"

"She wasn't safe! They killed her!" The storm of weeping broke over her again, and she raged and bawled with a fierce anger that might have given the mountains pause, thinking they could match her in passionate outbursts. How had she lived all those years within such bindings as the Ri Amarah set on their women? Or did he just not understand them? Maybe they bred such women within their walls, and it was only that those outside their clans never saw them.

When the storm quieted, he spoke.

"Where did you lay out the body?"

"There was no body. She sank into the depths. When Chief Tuvi tried to wade in to grab her, he was burned. No one can touch the pool."

"Water can't burn."

"Chief Tuvi says demons took her. Priya and the reeves say it was the gods who took her. But Atani was born in the midst of a storm, with firelings aloft in the sky and a net of fiery blue threads aswarm in this cave. Mai thinks—thought—this valley is home to firelings. They must have a home, too, mustn't they? 'Delvings in the deep, merlings in the sea, wildings in the wood, lendings in the grass,' as it says in the tale. 'Humans in their villages, demons hidden among all.'"

"'And the firelings live in the storm,'" finished Keshad.

"Threads of blue fire. A pool of water whose touch makes the hair on your neck stand on end, just like the air snaps before lightning storms crash down. The firelings are the ones who took her. Maybe she's still alive—"

"Miravia! Don't cling to hopeless—"

"It's not hopeless! Corpses float, do they not? So where is hers? The water falling down off the mountains is water and yet . . ."

She strode to the curtain, stuck a hand in. Kesh copied her; bracingly cold water poured over his skin.

"Stick your hand in the pool!" Her stare challenged him.

At the lip worn by an eternity of water pounding away at the stone, he thrust his fingers into the dark pool. Yelped as the liquid crackled and stung. As the hair on the back of his neck prickled, rising. He fell back onto his rump, shaking his hand. "Eiyi!"

Her gaze devoured him. "There's sorcery here, Keshad. We can't know what truly happened. We have to be patient."

A love-struck man, in the tales, is usually portrayed as a figure of fun, bound to make a fool of himself time and again in his efforts to please the beloved one. He swallowed a retort and, without smiling, got to his feet opening and closing his hand although that did not make the stinging go away. She would know at once if he tried to humor her. If he lied.

"It's hard for me to believe," he said bluntly, "nor did I know her or love her as you did. I'm sorry for it, and I must admit I'm shocked, but I rode a long way with the captain's mother and honestly I'm not surprised."

"Captain Anji will repudiate his mother when he finds out!"

"Will he?"

"How could he not!"

Kesh thought about what Tuvi had said. "I don't presume to know how the captain will react. Meanwhile, I must assume Mai is dead. But if you want me to wait with you, I will."

Her gaze was fire, but he held against that searing blaze. At last, she reached; she grasped his hand in her warm fingers. The delirious dizzying joy made his heart pound and his eyes water.

"You're the only one who is listening to me," she breathed.

He thought his heart might actually stop for the brilliance of her eyes and the moist parting of her lips as she bent closer. She swayed, grief weighing her down like exhaustion. He embraced her. Aui! It went to his head like floodwaters, and he was grinning like an idiot even if fortunately she could not see his smile.

"As soon as he's well enough," she whispered, "Chief Tuvi means to have a reeve fly him to Captain Anji. He won't let anyone else tell the captain the news. He'll go—"

"And I'll stay."

She sighed against his shoulder. "They'll take Atani. Priya will go. She scarcely allows anyone else to hold him. They don't really need me. Among my people it's traditional to say mourning prayers for a year for a family member. A sister. Because—I don't know—I just think someone should stand guard here, just in case."

"They'll go, because they must. But if you stay, I'll stay."

The lamp burned. The night slumbered. The waterfall spilled, its voice speaking of high mountain escarpments from which white rain poured from the highest slopes into the lands below. She held him, saying nothing. For the first time in over twelve years, since the day he and Zubaidit had been orphaned and sold away by their disloyal kinfolk into debt slavery, Keshad was content.

*   *   *

JOSS REACHED LAW Rock on the wings of dusk. Toughid was drilling the eager young firefighters and reeves on the parade ground, but Joss did not watch; he walked to the promontory, leaned against the fence surrounding the stele, and murmured the well-known words carved on the rock although he couldn't actually read them.

On law shall the land be built.

Peddonon strolled up to lean beside him. A lamp burned at the southwest corner; the other three remained unlit.

After a while, Peddo said, "You're troubled, Joss. You haven't said a word."

"Do you trust me? You and Kesta?"

"That's the kind of question a lad comes out with just before he coaxes you into doing something idiotic."

"I've lost control of the halls. In truth, I never had it. Captain Anji and his chief, Sengel, command Copper Hall now. And you see how Chief Toughid has taken over our garrison up here."

The drilling men and a few women huffed and scrambled, hidden by darkness but easily heard as were Toughid's good-natured but relentless commands: "Drop! Ten spans left. Forward! Hu! Avoid the other. Feel the heat of their body. The kiss of their breath. Rise. Drop!"

Peddonon nodded. "I will say these Qin know how to fight wars."

"Here's my question: Do they know how to stop fighting them?"

Peddonon grunted. "Ask me that question a cursed bit later, will you? When folk aren't starving in Toskala, living in the woods because their farms have been burned, and fighting for their lives in Nessumara. We're fortunate the Qin are here, and on our side."

The marks chiseled into Law Rock had an uncanny sheen, as though gilded with a radiance that came not from human labor but from other powers. The faint blue tincture of the rock, touched by lamplight, reminded him of firelings, rarely glimpsed but never forgotten. Especially a cave thick with their presence and a naked woman giving birth within the shelter of rock, fire, water, and life-sustaining air.

"Why do you suppose we never see firelings in the dry season?" Joss asked.

"Eh? You're leaping too fast for me to keep up. Firelings live in storms. Everyone knows that. Merlings in the sea. Delvings in the deep earth. Lendings in the grass. Wildings in the wild wood. Whew! My grandmother drilled the counting songs into me, I'll tell you that."

"Where do humans live, then?"

"Humans in the villages and towns, and demons within us."

"Why do we have so little to do with the other children of the Hundred?"

"Don't they want it that way? I don't know. Truth to tell, Joss, I've never seen any, not even delvings. If it weren't for others who have, I'd tell you they're just tales." He extended a hand toward the stele, with its neat columns.

The law shall be set in stone, as the land rests on stone.
Here is the truth: The only companion who follows even after death, is justice.
The Guardians serve justice.

"A year ago," Peddo went on, "I would have told you the Guardians were just a tale, a story told at festival time. Maybe they are a grandmother's tale. Because I'm cursed sure that the cloaks who command that army are not truly Guardians. That's not justice. If we don't defeat them— Aui! We have to defeat them."

"So we do," murmured Joss.

Peddonon rested an arm companionably over his shoulders. "You sound tired, my friend."

"I need a drink and a pallet," admitted Joss. "Tomorrow I'll take two of your three flights down to Horn to help lift a strike force up here."

"We have fresh cordial, brought up from Horn Hall. Not bad, if a little astringent, late in the season berries, you know how they are."

"Neh. Tea, if there's any left." The offer reminded him of how Anji had so carelessly offered him cordial or rice wine last night. A more suspicious man might think the captain was attacking Joss where he was weakest—his notorious drinking habit—but surely that was just hurt injured pride. He'd never asked to be anything more in life than a reeve. That he'd been thrown into the marshal's seat had surprised him; his elevation to commander of the halls was not even accepted by the other halls, nor was there any reason it should be without a reeve council to vote. And there was unlikely to be a reeve council again until—unless—they defeated the enemy.

He could not stop thinking of the little jeweler's chest bound with chains.

"Peddo, it's possible to kill the cloaks."

Looking startled, Peddonon removed his arm. "You were talking about this before. But Guardians can't be killed."

"What if I told you otherwise? That there is a way, a dangerous way, to separate a cloak from the person wearing it. Would you be willing to risk your life and your spirit to do it? Even if such an act goes against the gods?"

The night wind breathed over them as Toughid's commands rose: "Drop! Rise!"

Peddonon listened for a moment before shaking his head. "Such knowledge would be a heavy burden. You'll have to tell Kesta. Yet if it's true, Joss, then what choice have those cloaks given us but to destroy them in order to save ourselves?"

45

IN THE LATE afternoon Sixth Cohort weathered a barrage of rocks dropped by successive flights of reeves. Huddling under tortoised shields as stones cracked wood or thudded into moist ground, Arras contemplated reeves. A smart commander could do a lot with reeves, if he had them on his side. If he wasn't obsessed with destroying them, as the cloaks were.

The attack ceased when the reeves emptied their baskets. He cautiously, stuck his head out from under the shields. "We'll stay under cover until dusk. Eat, drink, and sleep. At dusk we push the last distance, across the worst ground. By dawn at the latest we'll attack."

At dusk, drums beat up and down the line. It was hard going, the men in front probing in pairs, one man hoisting shield and lamp while the other probed with his spear for krokes, mud sucks, and mires. Men got stuck in mud sucks, but they'd learned to use poles and brush to lever out the victims; scouts tested for firmer routes; on they crawled, as the stars wheeled overhead and the Embers Moon rose. Twice they crossed shallow channels; as they waded, the soldiers joked to cover the fear of a kroke attack. Arras slopped through calf-deep water, squelching as he climbed onto dry ground.

"We're especially vulnerable crossing the channels" he said to Giyara as they paused on the far shore after the second crossing. The moon by now had climbed halfway up the sky. It was very late, and soon the dawn would make them a target again for the reeves. "Yet they don't attack."

She took a swig of water from a leather bottle and spat it out. "Maybe the reeves are all the attack they have."

"I wonder. Maybe they're luring us in. Maybe they're poorly led. Or undermanned."

"Maybe they're running away while the reeves cover their retreat."

He chuckled. "*That* hadn't occurred to me."

As they moved forward, as midges clouded his arms and the night breeze wafted the acrid scent of tarweed, he kept wondering. What was going on in Nessumara? The quarter moon reached zenith as the eastern sky paled toward dawn. Hummocks of earth and stands of spiky brush began to appear in silhouette against the flat landscape.

"Subcaptain Piri approaching," called a runner.

Piri appeared with an escort of two soldiers, one with a lamp and one with a spear and axe. "Captain, there's a canal ahead, proper brick sides and three narrow plank bridges with the planks pulled free and abandoned on the far side. I've already got men across and laying the planks back in."

"Either the defenders left in haste, or they're cursed stupid. Go on."

"Beyond the canal is an island with pasture and field. At the far side of the island stands a wall, mostly brush, broken wagons, boats, and rubbish thrown up between sheds and stables. It extends in either direction as far as I can see, maybe all along this front. They've erected platforms atop it, with archers. To reach the wall, we have to advance across all that open ground."

Arras nodded. "There's why they didn't attack us. Can we burn it? The smoke will shield us from the reeves, likewise."

"With the breeze out of the southwest, the smoke'll blow right back on us. Best we pull it down. I'll need a company of archers to check their archers. It's a hastily built wall. We can use hooks to tear it up. But I wouldn't march the cohort over the bridges until we're rid of those platforms. The open ground makes us cursed vulnerable."

Arras nodded to Giyara. "Detach a company of archers and shields. Piri, your company will open breaches in the wall. We'll attack in force once we've got an opening."

Piri and Giyara hurried off as the order passed down through the cohort and men settled under shields to rest and eat. Arras with his aides walked the shore of the canal. In the shade of a fisherman's rush-woven lean-to he surveyed the island beyond as the archers turtled their way onto the open ground and set up a steady fire from behind braced shields. Soon the platforms were cleared. Cadres pressed forward behind shields. More men scrambled up atop the platforms, but Sixth Cohort's archers had gotten their range and pinned them down as the cadres hacked and hooked where the makeshift wall looked most vulnerable.

"Captain! The lord commander!"

He stepped out from the shade as white wings floated to earth.

Lord Radas sat astride the winged horse in a swirl of sun-bright cloak. "Captain Arras! Why are you not advancing with your entire cohort?"

He ducked his face behind open hands. "Lord Commander. We deemed it more prudent to clear the platforms while providing cover to a few cadres cutting a breach rather than offer a wide target with my entire front line. In addition, I'll exhaust only a few cadres while attacking with a rested force—"

"Your orders were to advance. We must reach the center of Nessumara. I'll tolerate no more delays! I have personally flown over the city. This is the only defense. All my other cohorts have crossed the channel already and are attacking the wall. We must overwhelm them."

"Begging your pardon, Lord Commander, but there are two edges to war, subtlety and brutality. I think—"

"You think too much of yourself! How can you imagine you understand more than I do, who can fly above, who can see into your pathetic hearts, know your weakness, your crimes, your petty fragilities. Look at me!"

Arras winced. His aides, huddling in the lean-to's humble shade, groaned and gasped as if they had already been eviscerated.

"You fear me because I am more powerful than you are," said Lord Radas. "Because I can have you cleansed. You don't respect me. You think well of yourself but you do not understand how my plan plays out over the years. To you, it is all about today. I must consider tomorrow. Once we take Nessumara, we control the entire length of the River Istri. After the rains, we will strengthen our army with new recruits from Wedrewe, turn south, and destroy Olossi. Had we pushed forward the first time, months ago, we would have overwhelmed them. We will not make that mistake a second time. Now, move your cohort immediately. The cursed reeves will be out soon, but the day, and the victory, will belong to us. If Lord Blood visits your position, tell him to report to me at once."

His horse sprang into the air, and Arras dropped to the ooze as hooves flashed above his head. When he rose, hands and knees dripping with muck, he stared after the lord commander's progress until the wings were caught by sunlight and abruptly vanished from his sight. The hells!

"Captain?"

"Sergeant Giyara." He could speak, just barely, with an even voice as he tried to clap the muck off his gloves. "Get the men over the bridges and form up for a frontal attack."

Gods-cursed cloaks. As if he hadn't been the one who had argued against retreat in that first attack on Nessumara. Half his aides trotted away with the sergeant while he fumed on the canal's shore. The sun had risen high enough to spill its light over the canal's glossy waters. With Giyara in the van, troops began to funnel across the bridges. More enemy archers appeared on the wall platforms, but his archers kept up an efficient stream of fire.

Odd, really, how ephemeral that wall was, little more than planks and brush and hope. Surely they were not hinging their defense on it. He could not see Eighth Cohort much less the Eleventh and Ninth holding the right flank a mey upriver from his position, but he heard the murmur of distant shouting, men eager to get to fighting and looting. An eagle glided past above, the first he'd seen. Otherwise, the sky remained empty but for a dark haze towering along the northern horizon.

Have Lord Blood report to me at once. Didn't Lord Radas know where his subcommander, his brother cloak, was?

A round back rolled out of the water and vanished so quickly he wasn't sure if he'd truly seen it. A rainbow of colors skimmed the surface where light glittered. A water bird—not one he recognized—floated past the lean-to, preening viciously at its feathers like a dog with the mange. Odd that it ignored them, for surely folk in this part of the world hunted fowl just as they did everywhere else. Instead, it labored at its brilliant plumage, then lifted its beak as though struggling to swallow.

The hells. *Either the defenders left in haste, or they were cursed stupid.*

Or it was a trap.

He ran a hand through the water. It was strangely slimy to the touch. He sniffed a finger, licked it.

Oil.

"The hells!" His words startled his aides. "Call a full retreat. Get everyone off that island and form into marching order. We're moving back. Now."

"The lord commander gave the order—" one protested.

"This is a trap, and the lord commander is too stubborn, or too vain, to see it. He's cursed puffed up with his gods-rotted power. But I see it, and I won't allow my cohort to get caught in it. Do as I say, or stand aside."

They obeyed. They abandoned the wall, the island, and the bridges, and began a disciplined retreat across the ground they had so laboriously trudged over for the last two days. When men from the cadres who had been working on the breach reported that the debris was damp and slimy with oil, he sent a runner to the Eighth Cohort. Not in time.

They'd retreated not a quarter of a mey from the canal when flights of eagles swooped low, loosing arrows tipped with fire, and the land burst into flame. It was spectacular, really, easily seen across the flat landscape. The wall burst to become a ridge of fire, while flame skimmed along the canal like a coruscating snake racing along the ground. Bridges exploded into flame in sparkling yellows, whites, and blues like fireworks shot off at festival time.

The screams of the other cohorts, caught between the oil-soaked canal and the oil-soaked debris, chased his soldiers as they slogged across the mire to the causeway. Once up on the wide stone roadway, they marched unmolested and at double time toward Saltow. Away to the north, the haze was thickening, pillars rising into the sky. Something huge was burning. Had the defenders done what he'd not dared do: set fire to the land?

"Giyara," he said, as they strode along in the rearguard, "Lord Radas will have me cleansed for sure, but cursed if I'm going to sacrifice my soldiers for his ignorance. I'll do my best to protect the rest of you from his wrath. I'll face him alone."

"What do we do when we reach Saltow?" asked Giyara.

Behind, Eighth Cohort soldiers came running, entirely routed.

"Hells if I know. But I'd be cursed curious to know who planned this defense. For that's a man who knows how to fight."

*   *   *

NALLO HAD BEEN pacing or sitting restlessly all day, too nervous and eager to rest, although Pil had lounged on a bench with his eyes shut, a repose of calm that would have irritated her if she wasn't so fond of him. He was the brother she'd always wished she had, wasn't he? Not the braggarts and teasers who had ceaselessly bullied her time and again until, time and again, she lost her temper—no difficult task—and got in trouble with this uncle or that aunt, who never liked her much anyway, her being lanky and cranky and, as they always said, not worth the food she scraped from the bottom of the clan pot.

She was cast of them now.

She had a new clan, among the reeves.

An eagle appeared downriver. Flags flashed the signal—battle had been joined in Nessumara!—and the two flights of reeves atop Law Rock leaped to their harness. Up they spiraled as the fire bell clanged three times, and then twice, and last once, alerting their allies in Toskala. Heavy amphorae whacked her knees as she guided Tumna in a swing downriver over the sparkling current and back around toward the city below. Smoke already trailed up from a bright blue fire within the Ilu temple in Stone Quarter, and fireworks burst from a Thunderer's temple in Flag Quarter, and last from one temple in each of the other three quarters, according to the plan. The flight glided around the rock and over Toskala. Markets cleared as folk ran for their homes, but from the height she saw men and women forming up inside compounds with staves and shovels and hooks and work blades. Men pulled out wagons and carts. Then she was over the main garrison headquarters in Wolf Quarter. She cut the ropes that held one of the amphora. It plummeted, and shattered on the tile roof. She cut free the second, which crashed through the thatched roof of a shade awning in the courtyard, splattering soldiers come running to stare up.

Arrows tipped with flame flashed as Pil glided past on Sweet. Fire rippled down the roof tiles and caught in dry thatch. More arrows, unlit, struck among the soldiers, who scattered. Flame eddied along the packed dirt of the courtyard. More amphorae hit; then they passed over the gates to the tents and corrals of the garrisons, livestock herds and auxiliary encampment. She released the last two amphorae over the command tents. Pil shot, striking true. Flames stuttered and caught. The horses went wild.

The eagles swung wide. Coming around, she saw smoke and fire rising in the garrison strongholds. She headed back for Law Rock to pick up the second and last load of oil—mostly common cooking oil—while Pil and the other reeves who were decent archers spiraled low over the city in support of the locals streaming out of their compounds.

Toskala had risen.

*   *   *

NEKKAR SAT IN the shade of the porch on a thin pillow, teaching the apprentices the intricacies of the Tale of the Guardians, as it was chanted on the new moon. It was a good way to pass the time in the heat of a dry-season afternoon when everyone was exhausted from the months of occupation and weak from hunger. The young ones drooped; several dozed off and snorted awake as his voice startled them.

"When we speak of the orphaned girl who calls to the gods, we change the timbre of the chant to show respect for her courage and honor. The signs begin at chest height, close to the heart to show our connection to those who came before us, our ancestors. Then—" His own hands sketched the gestures. "—rise to show her courage and honor rising as she dares the dangerous path to Indiyabu. Her path is our path, for we must all rise in the quest for justice, we must brave the dangerous path because to stand aside and do nothing is a form of death. We turn our back on the gods when we turn our back on justice. We strive to show the same courage and honor that she displayed—"

The fire bell atop Law Rock clanged three times. He ceased speaking. Every apprentice looked up, eyes widening. The silence opened as hearts raced.

The fire bell rang twice. Envoys scurried into the courtyard, abandoning their daily tasks.

He rose, leaning on his cane, as a final clang resonated.

"Light the fire," he said.

Kellas leaped up from the porch with a pouch of copper salts and ran to the open hearth where wood had been laid days ago in expectation of this moment.

"Bring out the wagon. Your staves. You younger ones go into the sleeping quarters and remain there. As for the rest, it is time to rise with the courage and honor shown by the orphaned girl." He tested his ankle, found it firm enough for the purpose. An envoy brought him his staff, and he marched to the gates as fire caught in the hearth, blazing blue as smoke rose.

The lass up on the gate watch called down: "Fireworks from Kotaru's temple in Flag Quarter, Uncle Nekkar. Heya! The Lantern's temple in Bell Quarter has lit its fire. And Wolf! And Fifth! Look, Uncle! Look! The reeves are coming!"

"We march."

They had two cadres, trained in staff fighting, common to Ilu's Heralds who walked the roads and might have to beat off importunate wild dogs both canine and human. They pushed open the gates and emerged onto the empty street. Voices swelled as the city awakened from its imprisonment. In Lele Square they met a mixed group of folk, another two cadres.

"Holy One! How do we proceed?"

"Those with padded garments and weapons go to the front, behind the wagons and carts. The rest hold the line behind them. We must hold forces and not break. The soldiers will kill some of us, that is to be expected, but if we hold, we will overwhelm them."

As they headed down Lumber Avenue toward Terta Square, more folk joined them. It was a rash venture, peaceful folk as they were accustomed to being, and yet what choice did they have?

Aui! It was hot. Smoke rose in waves as the reeves targeted the garrison headquarters and the encampment outside the city gates. Horns blatted as Toskala's lazy garrison woke belatedly to the danger. From every street and alley, they poured into Terta Square pushing the wagons ahead of them. Soldiers were battling a fire on the roof of the Thirsty Saw, but the sergeant in charge called them to form up in a disciplined line. Arrows flew, hissing into the crowd. Men and women, lads and lasses, went down, and a young woman pushing a wagon crumpled as blood gushed from her throat. Her companions faltered.

"Push forward!" cried Nekkar, and the cry rose until it became a howl.

That was enough to spur them on.

The young men and women pushing carts and wagons broke into a run, and the vehicles crashed into the line. Soldiers fell beneath the wheels, while others scrambled to join their fellows, retreating toward the barracks. But the crowd was emboldened now; the months of curfew, of hunger, of humiliation had seared them; the young struck recklessly, pouring into the gaps within the army's lines, hitting the doors and windows, climbing the roofs to get over into the courtyard behind, so as to attack from the rear. His first cadre of envoys surged forward with the rest, but others held him as he tried to move forward.

"We need you here to command us. Stay back, Holy One."

Folk from all over Stone Quarter surrounded him, bearing planks and barrel lids for shields. A man five paces away, an arrow in his shoulder, toppled into the people behind him. The crowd lurched forward, then staggered back, then forward again, bodies pressed together, everyone caught in the crush. Weapons clashed and rang, but he couldn't see above the crowd. Far away, the fire bell clamored as reeves glided low over the city. A pot plunged out of the sky to break across the top of the barracks, and in its wake an arrow blazed down. Fire chased down the sides of the tile roof. A scream of triumph rose from some furious young person, hard to say if male or female, and the crowd broke forward until people were stumbling, trying to keep their balance lest they be trampled. Nekkar tripped over a body and hit his knees hard on the ground, bracing himself on a hand as he stared into the open eyes of the sergeant who had ruled Stone Quarter for the last months. He'd been wounded in the side, but he wasn't dead; he was awake and aware, and Nekkar felt obliged to speak a word of comfort, but before a single word escaped him a figure dressed in a ragged taloos dropped down beside him. Fala held a dagger in her hand, and she paused only long enough for the sergeant to see in her his death, and then she plunged the dagger into his chest once, and twice, and three times, and four times.

"Enough, niece!" Nekkar cried. "Enough!"

She looked up, hair falling over bruised shoulders; her cheeks were sunken. She was panting, licking her lips as blood leaked over her hands. "My thanks to you, Holy One. This is your doing, isn't it?"

"We found allies," he said.

Then she began to weep, and a pair of brothers or cousins shouted her name and pulled her away from the dead sergeant.

Others lifted Nekkar. "We've won, Holy One! To the gates!"

"Leave two cadres to make a sweep of the neighborhoods. There will be soldiers who escaped, desperate men who must be caught."

"Caught and killed!"

They marched to Toskala's gate, a roaring, singing mass, swarming out to the garrison encampment, which had already been subdued by a company of militiamen flown up from Horn. Already the uprising was losing cohesion as folk streamed toward the main road and its line of posts, to release the dead and dying who had been condemned to cleansing.

A pair of reeves landed hard in an open field, and a passenger unhooked and jogged across the field, heading straight for Nekkar.

"Holy One! I'm Chief Toughid. We met before." The outlander was a good-looking fellow, not very tall but hale and strong, a bit younger than Nekkar. Once you got accustomed to his accent, he was easy enough to understand. "Commander Anji's orders, Holy One, to speak to you first. I will order sweeps of the city to look for rogue soldiers. Also, we must set up a perimeter. Enemy soldiers from this region and from the lands down the river will attempt retreat. We must stop and kill as many as we can."

"What news from Nessumara?" asked Nekkar.

"Chief Sengel's trap was sprung at dawn. I tell you, Holy One, it is a poor commander who does not learn from his mistakes. The demon who commands the enemy did not anticipate that we might use oil of naya again. Hard to imagine such a creature can hope for victory. Good for us, though." He shaded his eyes against the late-afternoon sun as the giant eagles rose into the sky. A frown chased across his face as he examined one of the reeves; then he looked back at Nekkar. "What is it, Holy One?"

Nekkar had not realized how his fears and hopes were made plain on his face. Eiya! He was so weary, and yet elation lifted him. "I'd like to walk out to the brick-works, Sergeant. They were forcing children to make bricks, and I just wonder—"

I just wonder about those poor orphans.

But the words choked him. Across the encampment and from the city, people began to sing the famous "Prayer that lifts good news" from the Tale of Fortune.

This is a prayer that lifts good news.
An offering of fresh flowers in thanks.
This is a prayer whose seeds scatter.
Our voices honor you, who birthed us.

The chief whistled. Soldiers whose faces Nekkar did not recognize—Olossi men—converged to form a disciplined cadre awaiting orders. "Escort the holy one to the brickyards and wherever else he wants to go, and then bring him back to me. I'll be setting up an administrative center. Where do you recommend, Holy One?"

"Eh. Ah." He wiped moisture from his forehead and discovered, to his shock, that his hand came away smeared with blood. What a terrible day, for all its triumph. "Law Rock would be the proper place for an administrative center, as it's always been. That way no quarter feels slighted or honored. But the stairs will need to be cleared. That will take time."

The chief nodded. With a gesture, he sent the cadre off with Nekkar, with a special escort of two young Qin soldiers for the ostiary. Wagons had ground ruts into the ground, cracked in this season of dry soil. Folk from the city had already run before him to the yards seeking kinfolk enslaved to the work; the place was a hive of weeping and wailing as people found their lost ones or heard tales of death and despair. The Qin soldiers took in this scene without comment, sticking at his heels like dogs, quiet and respectful.

He trudged among ragged shelters, scraps of cloth fixed to broken planks to form caves against the sun. Thin children staggered in the heat, seeking a friendly face, but others remained in hiding. He would have missed them had they not recognized him, even after so many months.

"Holy One?"

The voice was little more than the brush of wind through delicate leaves. Under a grimy bit of canvas held down by the broken stubs of bricks a dusty skeletal hand lifted the cloth as a thin face peered out. A second body moved in the shallow pit the canvas covered.

Were these the same orphaned children he'd lost in the alley? Did it even matter?

"Come out now," he said in the voice he used to calm homesick young novices crying through their first month at the temple. "We're going to the temple. There'll be food and a bath and a pallet to sleep on."

"There's soldiers with you, Holy One. They look funny."

"They've come to set things right. Just like in the tale: 'and an outlander will save them.' "

The child crawled out, and after her—impossibly—the smaller and the smallest. All three had survived their months in the brickyard, although they were weak, emaciated, and covered with dirt and filth. The soldiers muttered to each other, and at first he thought they were disgusted and then he realized they were appalled, however little they revealed in their expressions. Such young men might well have younger siblings, lost to them now. Without hesitation they each picked up one of the smaller ones without regard to the reek and filth.

Nekkar took the hand of the eldest, a brave soul too weary and hungry to cry. "We're safe now."

"What if they come back?" whispered the child. "The bad ones."

Nekkar gestured to the Qin soldiers, who were gently cradling the littler ones. "We'll make sure it doesn't happen again. All will be well."

46

"SHAI!"

The whisper woke him. He sat up fast and was jerked hard against chains. The metal cuff had scraped raw the skin on one wrist.

It was dark within the cohort command tent, where Captain Arras held his cohort councils in the day on thin pillows and slept at night on a cot. The captain, of course, had marched out to attack Nessumara. The tent was empty. The canvas wall belled inward, and Shai shivered as if a ghost were embracing him, unseen but heard, trying to drag him away from life and past the Spirit Gate into death.

Words spilled outside. He recognized Zubaidit's voice, but her tone was stretched and anxious, quite unlike her. What was Zubaidit doing here?

Hu! She had joined the enemy's army in an effort to get close to the lord commander, and was now Shai's jailor. The entrance flap rippled, and she slid inside, the scent of her—leather and sweat and a fragrance he did not know but which sat sweetly on the tongue—rousing him.

"I'm awake," he murmured.

"A cloak's come," she whispered. "I've ordered Sergeant Fossad to bring the cloak here. We have to strike before she sees into my heart—"

Footsteps approached. Bai pressed a key into Shai's hand and lay down on the cot. As the tent flap was swept open and lantern light blinded him, Shai fit the key into the lock, clicked it over, then dropped it. He looked full into the gaze of Night. Her pleasantly unremarkable face creased in a kindly frown. So might a patient aunt survey the wreckage of the sticky buns invaded by a horde of lively and hungry boys: She can make more, but they hadn't asked permission.

"You got far," she said. "Where in the lands did you suppose you could find refuge?"

He twisted the cuffs off his wrists and rose with chains in his hands. "I find refuge in justice."

Bai rolled to stand with a sharp inhalation of breath. He knew she was setting hollow pipe to lips.

"A dart," he said, taking a step forward to draw Night's attention. "A dart in my eye. How it stings."

The cloak flinched, the barest movement; she swiped at her neck as at a midge. Shai leaped. In the instant before Shai slammed into the cloak, Fossad yelped and clapped a hand over his eye. Shai went down hard atop the woman, her cloak of night and stars billowing into the air. Where the fabric brushed his skin, his skin burned. He pressed the chains into her throat. She shoved, hands struggling for a grip on his vest, but the snake venom worked fast. Choking, she worked her mouth as if to breathe, to speak, to plead, to curse him. He locked his gaze on hers, but she was just a person staring at him, dark eyes in a dark face, no one to fear because she had no lackeys to command within this dark tent. Did terror burn in her gaze? Was she afraid of him? Do eyes speak, or do we only believe they do, pouring our own thoughts and interpretations into the gaze turned on us by another? We don't really want to know. For it is terrible to stand naked and without concealment.

A drop of blood beaded at her nostril, swelling out as air exhaled, sucked in as she fought for breath. For life.

I must not die. I cannot die. I will not die.

Yet all things die, in the end. Dead riverbeds wind a course across the desert; mountains shed in flakes and sediment their rock and soil. Grass withers, and new grows where the old has seeded the dust.

"It's time to pass onward," he said, "to cross the Spirit Gate. You've done enough here. Let go."

Her lips moved, but her breath was extinguished. No sound stirred the air, and yet he understood her.

I'll do anything. Just don't let me die.

"And so you have done anything," he said. "You did terrible things, and let terrible things be done. Go away now and leave us to build a peaceful life."

With a final burst of strength, she surged upward, the cloak wrapping him as to choke him, burning blistering cutting off his air and he saw

into her heart

the well that is fear which pierces from deepest earth to highest heaven, that eats your strength and leaves you hollow

the orphaned girl had bundled her courage and her heart like a pack to be borne and she had climbed the treacherous path to seek the gods in their high eyrie and there she had boldly walked into the water expecting to die but she had not died. The gods had brought forth the Guardians out of the pool of Indiyabu to walk the lands and establish justice, and the orphaned girl had gone on with her life in the ordinary way, and when the day of her death had come as it does in time to all creatures born out of the Four Mothers, she had been embraced by a cloak. For had she not offered her life in service of justice for the land?

Only the dead can be trusted, it said in the tale. But those who walk a second time may still fear death. Corruption and virtue wax and wane in the heart, and where fear feeds corruption, it consumes virtue until the heart is only a shell in which echoes its own voice speaking to its own self about its certain selfish concerns.

Hearing no voice but her own, she had betrayed not only her companions, the other Guardians, but the land and the legacy of her own tale.

Shai held on because he knew how to endure pain; because he was stubborn. Because he lived, and she had to die, again, to finally cross the threshold of the Spirit Gate.

The spark that burns within the eyes of the living faded. The cloak eddied and sagged. Blood trickled from her mouth as the poison killed her. She died.

"Shai!" Bai was standing by the entrance, sword raised as she flipped aside the flap to glance out. Fossad was dead, with blood leaking from mouth and nose and a smear of blood staining the eye that had taken the second dart. His startled ghost oozed from his body and reached for the lantern as though to light his way.

"Eiya!" cried the ghost. "My eye stings. What happened?"

"Hurry!" Shai said to him. "The Gate awaits you."

"Eh! I see the light!" Then his spirit was gone.

"The hells!" Bai cried, eyes flaring as she stared at Shai. She was so very alive that life radiated off her like threads of blue fire; she was as bright as the lantern, and only he, in the shadowed tent, was veiled and therefore opaque. "You're hells burned, Shai! All red. And look at the gods-rotted cloak!"

The ghost of the dead woman was pouring into the cloak, rather like the way the priests of Beltak had sucked the ghosts of dead men into their blessing bowls. The cloak would hold her ghost until its magic knit the body, and then she would live again. And again. And again.

"We've got to get this cloak off her body. Give me the gloves."

"The cursed cohort's returning," said Bai, but she leaped to the dead man's body and stripped his gloves, then tugged them on Shai's hands one at a time as he released his grip on the metal cuffs. He tossed them aside; they'd served their purpose. With gloved hands he grappled at the clasp, and the clasp *burned* into the leather; heat stung his palms, raising tears of pain. Hu! The cloak came undone, and he yanked it away so hard the body tumbled gracelessly, like rubbish. With a wordless wail, her ghost writhed out of the cloak into the body and *reached* for the cloth as if to insinuate herself back into the weave that had kept her alive for so terribly long. The cloak billowed wildly around him, humming as in a wild storm wind.

"We've got to bind it!" he cried.

"Release it to the wind!" said Bai.

"Her ghost will crawl back in if it touches the body. We have to keep them separate."

Bai grabbed a blanket folded neatly at the foot of the captain's cot. She ripped belts off Fossad and the dead woman. Shai wept as the bite of the cloak burned his hands, but he stepped on it, pressed it to earth, rolled the fabric inside the blanket; they folded it up and over and over again, pressed it tight and winched the belts over it and after that wrapped it in chains. How pain burned. The living were not meant to handle that which has the power to trap and succor ghosts.

A horn woke in the night. Shouts crashed like thunder.

"You betrayed me!" Her ghost swelled to fill the space like a storm of sand wailing out of the desert.

The tent flap was swept aside, and a lamp's steady glow cast gold over the interior as Bai stepped back with sword raised and Shai reeled, stumbled, and fell, his gaze hazing. The ghost reached into him but its substance passed right through his body; his heart was safe from her.

Then she was gone.

"The hells!" Captain Arras drew his sword in answer to Bai's guarded stance as he and his loyal sergeant stepped into the tent, she with lamp in hand and a hand on her knife. The entrance closed. Behind, a man called, "Captain Arras?"

"Tell the soldiers to set a doubled guard. Everyone else rest. We move out at dawn."

He scanned the scene. His mouth twitched, but he showed no other emotion and it was difficult anyway to trace the lineaments of a face slathered in muck. He did not lower his sword. "Sergeant Zubaidit. Can you explain this?"

"Fossad attacked this woman, Captain."

"The hells he did. That's one of the gods-rotted cloaks, the woman who wore the cloak of Night. The most fearsome of all. Yet now she lies here, just another cursed corpse like to the many that have been made today."

"Did we win?" Bai asked without blinking.

"We lost. I took my cohort and got out before we all got killed by soldiers who knew what they were cursed doing. Where is her cloak?"

His gaze caught on the bundle at Shai's knees, which had an odd way of shifting and bulging and receding as if the thing inside it were trying to find a way out. "Who in the hells are you, Zubaidit? A cursed spy, no doubt! An infiltrator. I should have seen it!"

The sergeant with him grunted.

"You warned me, Giyara," he added.

"Kill her," suggested the sergeant, not angrily but with resignation.

"You can kill me," Bai said coolly, "but you'll still take the blame from Lord Radas. You're the captain. Therefore you're responsible. Everyone knows you raised me up from hostage to soldier to sergeant."

"You're cursed calm about it. If I go down, you'll go with me."

"I'm prepared to die."

"I'm not!"

Her smile was thin. "That's the difference between us. But if that is your sole concern, I may be able to save you if you'll listen to me."

"What about my cohort? I won't sacrifice them to save myself."

"That you say so is the only reason I haven't killed you already. Believe me when I say, Captain, that you're a decent enough man, and good at your job. Do you love the cloaks? Has Lord Radas treated you well?"

"He didn't listen to me months ago when I urged him to push into Nessumara at the first attack, for I'm sure we could have broken the militia and taken the city without much trouble. He didn't listen to me this very dawn, when I warned him that something wasn't right. No doubt he's abandoned the cohorts who were killed this morning and flown away to the safety of his cohorts on the northern causeway. He's lost less than half his army, after all. He can still fight."

"Then choose new allies, Captain."

"And betray the old?" He looked at Shai, shaking his head. "Are you truly Lord

Twilight's brother? The resemblance is strong. Are you the outlander who will save us?"

"I need water," croaked Shai. His head was muzzy, and the pain was building.

"He's not the only outlander in this tale, Captain," said Zubaidit. "Lord Radas betrayed not just you personally but the Hundred itself. Time and again he has betrayed the cause of justice. Why do you aid him?"

"Because the gods command us to obey the judgment of the Guardians. Because with him, I could fight. Anyway, who can stand against the cloaks, who can see with their third eye and second heart, who defeat even death?"

"We can, and we did."

"Her cloak is gone," muttered the sergeant. "She looks no different than you or me. Just a dead body. Was it all lies? That the cloaks defeat all, even death?"

Bai's sharp smile made Shai shudder. Bai hadn't known if the cloaks could be killed, but she'd been willing to throw herself into the battle without thought for her own fate. Ought he to admire her ruthless purpose, or fear it?

"Now you see the truth of it," Bai said. "Join us."

"You might believe it's a tempting offer to a man like me," retorted the captain. "Especially since I'll have to immediately order you stripped and thoroughly searched, and all your gear confiscated and burned, to make sure you aren't carrying any hidden weapons. Weapons that can kill a cloak and Fossad, there. Then afterward tell me, you who have stood loyal to your commander, why should he trust me if I turn traitor to the one whose orders I obeyed before?"

Shai toppled forward, landing beside the bundle, the chains a finger's breadth from his nose. He smelled: the snap in the air before lightning strikes. He tasted: the flavor of a cloudburst, rain pounding on stone and muddying dirt. He felt: the cooling breath of a mountain wind on his blistered, reddened skin. He heard: Bai's words like the purl of cooling water over exposed rock.

"Let me tend to him. Shai never faltered. His courage is worthy of a song. As for the other, Captain Arras, I know a commander who can use your skills and the loyalty you would offer a commander who will treat you with the respect you deserve. I am his agent, following the orders of my Hieros, who together with the council of Olossi and the council of temples in Olo'osson has put their trust in him. Will you join us?"

"What surety can you offer me? What if we surrender, and your commander simply orders us executed?"

"If you want surety, I'll give you this."

"That's a blanket."

"Neh, Captain Arras. It's a blanket wrapped tightly around a Guardian's cloak. You can use it to buy a new life for you and your soldiers."

Arras's harsh laugh cracked against the fragile shell that bound Shai to consciousness. Splintering, he shattered, and fell into blessed darkness, where all wounds are healed.

47

OVER THE NIGHT, the reeves slept hard, and at dawn launched from the prow of Law Rock. All day Joss patrolled the skies above Toskala as Peddonon's two flights and the two flights flown in from Horn Hall harassed the routed garrison. They rained arrows down on desperate companies marching in ragged columns north toward High Haldia; they drove desperate men into ambuscades they had set up beforehand by lifting cadres of soldiers into position ahead of the fleeing soldiers. Their orders weren't to capture the enemy and bring them before the assizes to face judgment for their wrongdoing. Their orders were to kill.

They weren't the orders Joss had given. This wasn't justice, as the reeves were taught to serve justice. But as the reeves gathered on Law Rock late in the afternoon to seal their victory by breaking out the last of the hall's stores of cordial, even Peddonon was laughing with a grim sort of exaltation.

"Cursed hells-ridden bastards mown down like grass! Whew! Did you see that, Pil? When those militiamen caught them with their trousers down taking a—"

"Commander Joss!"

Joss left the gathering of whooping, drinking reeves and crossed Justice Square to meet a delegation from the city. They'd been winched up in the main baskets, now free to haul supplies and people up and down the rock.

"Chief Toughid." The chief offered a forearm for the traditional Qin bash, and Joss slammed him harder than he might have otherwise but he was still the one who winced. "Ostiary Nekkar." He had to be introduced to the other notables. "Is there to be a council? Might the city be better served to hold it below, where anyone who wishes can come and listen?"

The chief shook his head. "Too many voices will drown out the necessary orders."

Joss paced him into the council hall, the dusty benches of which betrayed it as the one building up on the rock that hadn't housed refugees over the long months of occupation. No one wanted to sleep in the place where so many people had been murdered on that long-ago Traitors' Night. Now voices rang with triumph as eighteen notables from the city in addition to Toughid and Joss settled on the benches. A number of the firefighters, reeves, and militiamen who had stuck it out atop the rock stood to listen, quieting as the ostiary rose.

The slender man nodded wearily, a fragile smile lighting his face. "Our thanks to Chief Toughid, and to the reeves. Yet the danger is not passed. We've driven out the garrison, but many survived to flee north while others ran south to join up with their brothers near Nessumara."

"A substantial number survive." Toughid's manner was brisk and unemotional. "We don't have a full accounting of the situation in Nessumara. We should hear midday tomorrow. However, the enemy has fifteen cohorts. Even if as many as five cohorts were disrupted in the last few days, that leaves ten cohorts unaccounted for."

"What do we do?" the council members demanded. Joss couldn't keep their names straight, making it seem as if they spoke with one voice. "There's not much oil of any kind left in the city."

Toughid nodded. "What advantage we have gained from oil of naya we cannot expect for the next phase of the campaign. In the morning I'll send a messenger—" He quite deliberately cleared his throat before starting again. "In the morning, Commander Joss will send a messenger to the main army to inform them of Toskala's rising. The soldiers lifted in will remain here to coordinate defensive measures. We must expect cadres and companies and even full cohorts to retreat from Nessumara past Toskala. Desperate men driven by fear are dangerous and unpredictable. I'll leave my best sergeant in charge of the defense. Place your militia under his command and use your reeves wisely, and you'll be able to hold the city."

"Where do you mean to go, Chief Toughid?" they demanded.

Joss sat on the end bench, shoulders braced against the stone wall and legs extended with feet crossed at the ankle. Not one person looked Joss's way. For all that the Qin soldier threw bones to the reeve commander, no one paid any attention to the faithful dog, not if he wasn't barking.

"For myself," said the chief, "I'll go on to Gold Hall. We've made an arrangement to launch an attack on High Haldia's garrison." He nodded at Joss. "Is there anything you'd like to add, Commander?"

Joss raised a hand in the gesture of agreement. "You have things well in hand, Chief Toughid. Our thanks to you and your men. However, the one consideration reeves must deal with before all others is the health of our eagles. If we push them past their strength, they'll grow sick and not easily recover. Our eagles need rest. I'll release a pair to lift you north to Gold Hall. We'll have to run short patrols here for as much as a week. No carting. No long flights. No raids. I'll carry the message myself to Captain Anji."

Toughid nodded, and the ostiary rubbed his chin thoughtfully, but the cursed council members would natter on like so many whining gnats. "We need flights to harass the enemy. How will we know what's going on if the eagles aren't flying? Those Qin soldiers keep riding and riding, never faltering—"

"If your horse or dray beast goes lame, then you can't ride or cart, can you, eh?" Joss said irritably. "And there's a cursed lot more horses and dray beasts than there are eagles. The reeves have been doing their part, and like all men and women can endure plenty, but the eagles are being pushed to their limits and I'm the one who has to protect them. That's all I have to say."

After the council ended, Toughid walked aside with him, carrying a lamp while Joss spun his baton through his fingers.

"You know my goal, Commander. Since we know there may be a demon in High Haldia, I must hunt him down and kill him if I can." Toughid's grin was as light as day. "Sengel got one. Can't let him have all the glory, can I?"

"I'll send Peddonon with you. He can nurse his eagle another few days. He's an experienced and trustworthy reeve."

They halted by the barrier blocking off the steps, Toughid wincing as at a bad smell. "Hu! If you don't mind, maybe one of the other ones. Vekess, perhaps. That Peddonon I hear is one of those—like Pil—you can see why it was for the best Pil was sent off to be a reeve."

"Why was it for the best?"

"It's not proper for men to behave that way. I'd prefer Vekess. He's steady."

Joss shook his head. "Chief Toughid, you've done well, and in truth we'd be in a cursed bad place without you Qin. I'll send you with Vekess if it's your request, but I feel obliged to say that you're in the Hundred now. Not in Qin country. How a man, or woman, worships the Devouring One has nothing to do with what manner of man he is. And I'll thank you to remember it."

The soldier nodded, his placid expression impossible to fathom. Was he offended? Understanding? Dismissive? Who in the hells could tell with these outlanders and their quick grins floating atop an implacable reserve?

"We'll have to clear this rockfall," Toughid said. "Difficult work but possible to manage if we work down through it a step at a time."

Laughter and singing swelled from the city below, where torches and tapers bobbed along the avenues and canals, a festival of lights as folk danced in the street. On the balcony, reeves and firefighters were jostling, joking, drinking, roistering. In the light of their last few lamps, Peddonon had pulled a knife and was waving it in front of Pil's face. The young Qin reeve was laughing, just like the rest of them, rather drunk and leaning casually in that way reeves had with a friendly arm around Nallo and a shoulder pressed companionably against one of the young firefighters.

"Heya! All that hair just gets in your way! You don't look like a proper reeve," the reeves were shouting as the firefighters egged Pil on.

Toughid's gaze narrowed as he watched.

Pil released his topknot, and his long black hair rippled down over his shoulders, chest, and back as women and men whistled appreciatively.

Peddonon stepped back, eyes wide and expression as startled as if he'd been slapped. Joss chuckled, having seen Peddonon through many a sudden infatuation. Pil was faster, though; he grabbed the knife out of Peddonon's hand and hacked off his beautiful hair as the others cheered and Peddonon pretended to mourn.

With a grunt, Toughid turned away. Walked away, pausing to call over his shoulder. "Commander, are you coming? I've maps to go over, more plans to consider."

Joss shook his head. "Neh. I'll meet with you at dawn, Chief. For now, I've a mind to celebrate. With my reeves."

"JOSS?"

He startled awake to find Peddonon jostling him in dawn's gloom. "Eh? What?"

Peddonon kept his voice low, as though he were trying not to wake someone else up. "You were talking in your sleep, Joss. You were saying her name again."

"Marit."

His frown swamped Joss with friendly disapproval. "Twenty years dead, and you've never let her go."

"What if I told you she was a Guardian now?"

"I'd wonder how much you drank last night."

Peddonon stepped back from the humble pallet unrolled on the mats of the sleeping chamber. One door was slid halfway open, and through the gap Joss saw a thin pallet stretched in front of the doors of the outer chamber. A naked man, his back to them, seemed to be asleep, sprawled on the pallet.

Peddonon grinned. He wore a kilt, hastily wrapped around his hips, but it was obvious by his sleepy eyes and mussed hair that he'd just woken up.

Joss mouthed, without voicing the words, "Is that Pil?"

Peddonon's grin widened.

"And yet I'm the one with the reputation," murmured Joss, groping for and finding his leathers. His mouth tasted sour and his stomach was curdling from too much cordial.

"Anyhow," Peddonon went on, "wouldn't that be a worse thing than her being dead? That she'd become a demon?"

"The Guardians aren't lilus, or demons, or any bad thing! Some may have become corrupted—"

"If some have, then how can we trust any of them? Ask yourself: Why do we need Guardians at all? With a militia to keep order, reeves to patrol the roads coordinated with guard stations on the ground, and reorganized assizes to oversee justice in the towns, we can do it ourselves. Cursed if I want cloaks creeping into my mind and heart like folk say they can do. When I was with the army yesterday I talked to some of the Qin soldiers, and they said—"

"They say whatever Anji tells them to say."

"Aui!" Peddonon retreated as if Joss's breath had driven him back. "Sheh! He might be an outlander, but where would we be if he hadn't agreed to put his life and his troops on the line for the Hundred, eh? Would else could have marched against Lord Radas and his army? We have hope, *at last*, for peace."

"The hells! I meant no criticism. It was just a statement. The Qin soldiers are loyal. Everyone knows that."

Movement stirred in the outer chamber as the young Qin reeve woke up. Maybe he had only been pretending to sleep. Peddonon slid shut the door to give Pil privacy, then grabbed up a cup from a tray sitting on the low table.

"You're sour this morning, Joss. Do you need cordial? Maybe a little rice wine?"

"At *dawn*?" Joss splashed water into the basin and scrubbed his face with a scrap of linen. *We have hope at last.* Was that uneasy worm curdling in his gut jealousy? Anger? Relief that he would not have to make decisions he wasn't entirely sure he was competent to make?

"Anyway," said Peddonon. "Pil cut off his topknot last night. Eventually the Qin will all become Hundred folk, like us.

"Peddo," he said to the water as it rippled to a standstill to form a dark mirror; his cursed handsome face stared back at him. How long had he let his vanity and charm carry him through life, soaked down with one cup of rice wine after the next? "I'm a good reeve, I think. I'm doing my best to be a good commander." He looked up.

Peddonon folded his arms. "What's this about?"

Joss wiped his face and pulled on his trousers. "The reeve halls are taking orders from Anji now. As if we're part of his militia. I see a danger in that."

"I see more danger in this cursed enemy that's rampaged across half the land! Are they defeated yet? Fifteen cohorts they've raised."

"Don't you see the danger in a man who breaks the boundaries, kills a Guardian, and then *binds her cloak* instead of releasing it to the gods?"

"Lord Radas broke the boundaries before we ever did! He had your lover's eagle killed, didn't he? We're only protecting ourselves. The hells, Joss! Can't we have this conversation when we have space to breathe? We're still at war!" He grabbed the linen towel out of Joss's hands and washed his face, swabbing down his chest and arms.

Joss fished his vest off the floor, taking a couple of calming breaths. "We *are* still at war. So I need to piss, and eat a bit of bland nai porridge, if there is any, before Scar and I head out." He grabbed his harness, his reeve's baton, his short sword, quiver, and empty provisions pouch. "You're staying here in charge of the rock. Your flights need rest. Vekess will convey the chief to Gold Hall."

They headed out to meet the day.

But late in the afternoon, after hunting along the wrong roads and down empty paths, Joss thought about Pil's topknot as he quartered Istria in search of Anji's army. The emptied countryside west of the River Istri was ragged with fields going to seed or never planted, harbingers of bare storehouses in the months to come. Hamlets and villages rose everywhere, and were everywhere abandoned. Where had the villagers fled to? Once he skimmed over woodland in whose depths he spotted canvas strung between trees, visible only because late in the dry season the foliage grew sparse. Later, he swooped low over a company of soldiers escorting a train of some forty wagons laden with sacks of rice or nai. They pointed at him as half their number readied bows, eager to have at him if he dropped into range. They were ready for a reeve attack. He swung wide to turn, heading west and north.

So was Anji's strategy to use the reeves already ineffective? Wouldn't it have been better for the reeves to stand aloof from the conflict so they might better administer justice? And yet, if Lord Radas's army won, what justice could anyone hope for? The mey flowed past below, offering no reply.

He caught sight of a trio of eagles spiraling up very high, and another trio west of them, gliding low as if following prey on the ground. Soon after, he caught sight of a cohort of mounted soldiers riding down a path leveled on a berm that cut through fields. He identified the horsemen as Qin, no doubt the group that had come up from Sirniaka recently. They'd made exceptional time, and as he turned again and pulled out in front of them he found, at last, the rearguard of Anji's army.

Horns blew and drums beat as the rearguard caught sight of the Qin cohort coming up behind. Joss and Scar skimmed low over an impressive mob of unsaddled horses, the army riding in disciplined ranks in staggered companies. Most of the young local militia men had grown out their hair to pull back in topknots. So who was becoming whom, eh? Pil was one Qin soldier. Here were hundreds of young Hundred men trying their best to look like their Qin sergeants and captains.

He set down in a clearing a short walk from the road. In this isolation he examined Scar's feathers, his bloom, his beak, his talons. The old bird was getting a bit sharp-set, so Joss checked his harness and when he found no raw skin or wearing, he released him to hunt, watching to see if there was any hitch in the motion of his wings as they beat upward to find the wind. The raptor looked well enough; he was tough and in his own way as even-tempered a raptor as Joss had ever met. A hunt and a rest would settle him.

As Joss was wrapping up his own harness in its sling, a cadre of horseman thundered into the clearing, a young Qin sergeant in the lead, his face vaguely familiar.

"Commander Joss?" He dismounted and trotted over. "I'm Sergeant Jagi. I've a horse, if you'd like to ride with us back to Commander Anji's headquarters."

"Jagi? Aren't you the one who married that girl Avisha?"

A brilliant smile flashed. A cursed man couldn't look any happier. "She ate my rice, that's right." Then he laughed and blushed, as if he'd just that moment understood there was another meaning to the phrase. "We're expecting a third—"

"A third child? But you can't have had two already, in less than a year, surely."

"We've the two older children, her young brother and sister. And a new one coming. We live out at Dast Welling. She's using her seed money to set up a business. She's very clever. Making healing drinks and such things to rub into sore wounds and—ah—" His knowledge of the finer points of Hundred lore failed him as he rushed headlong into his praise of his new wife. "She's very happy. Plenty to eat and a good house."

"The blessings of the gods on you, truly." Joss had to smile, because it was impossible not to respond to Jagi's joy. "I'll accept the mount, with thanks."

An adequate gelding was led forward.

After they'd ridden for a ways through the trees, Jagi said, "You've ridden before."

"Before I became a reeve, I rode messages as an apprentice to Ilu, the Herald." Before Scar. Before Marit. It was difficult to bring that youth into his mind. "It feels like a different lifetime. In another land."

And so it did, riding out of the open woodland to see the aftermath of a skirmish. The enemy cadre escorting wagons had been caught and killed to a man. Their archers hadn't protected them against a powerful ground attack. Now a sergeant was directing the accounting of the captured wagons and a trove of bows and arrows. Jagi's cadre rode past the corpses dragged off the path, young men hooting derisive comments about the equally young men whose bodies had been dumped. There was one corpse with a crooked nose, mouth caked with drying blood, and another with coarse black hair unraveled into a fan around his head. Joss had been young like that, once. Who was to say he might not have been talked into riding with the Star of Life army, not knowing better? Feeling angry, rebellious, hopeless, or just dragged along by friends?

"Commander?" asked Jagi.

"Do you suppose they were all killed fighting?" Joss asked.

"We've orders to kill every enemy soldier."

"What if they surrender?"

Jagi shrugged. "We can't guard prisoners. And we can't leave them behind our lines, can we?"

War was so simple, wasn't it? Much simpler than justice.

They reached an abandoned village on whose unsown fields the army was settling in for the night. In this hot dry weather, most men were simply resting with heads on a bedroll or stretched out on a thin blanket as a ground cloth, but an awning had been raised in the center of the camp.

Jagi took the horse and gestured toward the awning. "Commander Anji is there."

"My thanks, Sergeant."

The guards recognized him and made way. A pair of reeves were standing, giving a report, while Anji bent over a camp table with Chief Deze, Chief Esigu, and a hierophant with a shaven head whom Joss didn't recognize. With his whip, Anji was pointing to various places on the map as the reeves made their accounting. He looked up as Joss walked in under the pleasant shade.

"Commander Joss. We saw your eagle overhead a while ago. Sergeant Jagi found you."

"He did, indeed. You've made exceptional time. I saw a cohort of Qin soldiers reach your rearguard."

Anji was neatly clothed, his black tabard straight, no hair out of place, his top-knot bound with gold ribbon. "Yes. What news?"

"We're in control of Toskala."

The reeves gasped.

Anji nodded, as if it were the news he had been expecting all along. "Good. I'll get the details after I finish with these two." He picked up a rolled scrap of paper lying next to the maps and pulled it open to reveal the writing sacred to the Lantern: it was a message of some kind. "You'll be interested to know, Joss, that these two reeves killed messengers riding north from Skerru toward Toskala. Lord Radas sent a messenger north to Toskala ordering the garrison there to fall back to Nessumara to build up their forces. Naturally, he does not yet know that Toskala has fallen and its garrison is routed. Nor will he, if we keep intercepting his messengers." He handed the paper to the hierophant. "He mentions sending word to this place called Wedrewe, demanding reinforcements for a renewed assault on Nessumara. He's stubborn, I'll give him that. What interests me most is that the message is addressed to a Lord Bevard. He asks him if he knows the whereabouts of Lord Yordenas, and tells Bevard to fly personally to Nessumara to aid Radas in the next phase of the campaign."

Anji spoke openly of such grave matters, and yet it wasn't clear to Joss if the hierophant and the reeves understood the deeper meaning beneath the exchange.

He replied in kind, saying nothing and everything with a few innocuous words. "It must be the same Bevard Marit mentioned to me. If this Bevard is still in High Haldia, Chief Toughid may find him, for he's gone hunting with Gold Hall's reeves."

Anji nodded, then addressed the Copper Hall reeves. "Is there anything else?"

"That's all, Commander," said one. "Chief Sengel wants to know whether to specifically pursue the single cohort that retreated intact to Saltow."

Anji tapped the map with his whip, touching his own position first before pulling the tip to the thick line marking the River Istri. "We've a day's long march to Nessumara if we force march. It will surely take two days or more for this enemy cohort to reach Skerru from Saltow. As long as we know they are coming, we can adjust to meet them. For now, do nothing but observe. Our first concern is Radas's army in Skerru, which remains substantially intact since the burning of the forest cover drove them back but did not break them. One cohort has retreated from the west bank to join the others at Skerru. Jodoni will write a message detailing my plans. Go, get food and drink and rest. You'll fly out at dawn."

"Yes, Commander Anji." They gave Joss, the two chiefs, and the hierophant a polite nod, and took themselves off.

Joss surveyed the map, noting where fresh lines had been inked in. "You're filling in your maps as you march. Didn't we already send you copies of maps from Clan Hall?"

Anji examined the unrolled map with a thoughtful gaze. "You did, and my thanks as ever." He pushed a knife off one corner and peeled the upper map back to reveal more unrolled maps layered below. "But if you compare, you'll see the Clan Hall maps haven't been updated in years. By combining current observation and the older versions, I have accurate maps." He raised a hand, and an aide came forward to roll up the maps. "Let me call for food and drink. While we eat, give me your report. Will you fly out at dawn?"

"That's another thing we need to discuss." Joss took the stool offered and sat next to Anji at the table as trays were brought from nearby fires where rice and meat were being cooked. "Eagles are cursed rare creatures. If we overwork them, we will kill them. And we can't just purchase more from the lendings."

"If we go too easy, we might lose this war, which leaves us in an equally difficult situation, does it not? We must find a balance."

"I've released Scar to hunt. I don't expect him to return for at least a full day."

"Ah." Anji accepted a pair of cups, into which he poured rice wine, offering one to Joss before he raised his own. "Then you'll be traveling with the army for a day or two."

"So I will."

Anji's smile had a flash of warmth that surprised Joss. "I expect to you reeves things look different down here on earth. You'll ride beside me, Joss." His grin grew sharper, both jest and challenge. "If you can keep up."

THE ARMY ROSE before dawn and moved out in stages. The vanguard, and the reeve messengers, departed at first light; the second stage included Anji's command unit and plenty of spare horses.

"Did you buy every horse in Olo'osson?" Joss asked.

"Olo'osson supplied us with what we needed, just as villages and towns along the West Track supplied us with food and drink so we weren't slowed down by a baggage train."

They rode at a ground-eating pace, not so very fast but never slacking, and changed off horses twice.

"It's cursed odd to see so many men all in one place," Joss remarked as they rode along the curve of one of the many low hills sprouting in this part of Istria, where the land rose into a long ridgeline. Their route overlooked yet more untended fields stepped up the hillsides in terraces. No harvest had been brought in this year across much of Istria. Farmsteads and villages sat empty, no sign of life, everyone in hiding or fled. "Did no women volunteer to serve in the army?"

"War is men's business." Anji gestured to the Qin soldiers and the ranks of local men riding under their command. "Women have other work."

"Everyone suffers under war," said Joss, "so I should think it was women's business as well."

Anji shrugged. "It is better if women do not fight."

They rode with his usual aides and chiefs. Sometime in the night a new man had appeared, a Qin captain about Anji's age who was wearing very dusty clothes with unwashed hands and face. He'd been introduced to Joss as Targit, captain of the new Qin cohort. He seemed to continually be making jokes in the Qin language, at which the other Qin laughed heartily, but had spoken not one word in the trade language the Qin officers all knew which was so very like the language of the Hundred.

He looked up now with a sturdy laugh. "Hu! Women guard their tents and herds with a riding whip. Better they not have a sword, too."

Anji squinted at the sky, marking the flight of their reeve scouts, as the others laughed.

Joss pinned down his irritation and tried to speak in a cool voice. "I've been a reeve for over twenty years. Plenty of reeves are women. Maybe some of those above scouting for you are women. Should they not carry swords?"

"Maybe women should not be reeves," said Chief Deze. "A strange thing, do you not think?"

"How is it strange? The eagles jess reeves according to the gods' will. We don't make that choice for them, and I'm cursed sure that's a good thing, for then a marshal might raise his own son to be marshal whether the lad was a good commander."

"A man raised from childhood in the expectation of command will learn the proper lessons in his youth," said Anji. "Those lessons will make him a better commander than one who comes late to it, merely because of a chance act. How much more effective would reeves be if lads were raised around the eagles, knowing they would in time become reeves?"

"Had the gods wished it to be so, they would have made it so. But it is not what they wished. In the empire, I've heard the priests regulate behavior according to the rule of the southern god."

"Beltak, called Lord of Lords and King of Kings. But I ask you, Joss, do the priests follow the god's wishes, or their own? A priest might say anything, and how are we to know otherwise, if they alone can walk in the inner temple?"

"Priests can become corrupted, just as any man can. But surely a god must, in time, restore justice."

Anji laughed. "Do you believe so? Then you have more faith in the gods than I do."

"Do you not have faith in the gods?"

"Ought I to?"

"What do you believe in?"

Anji gestured to the army before and behind him, their ranks impressive for their discipline and number. Joss could not see, much less count, them all. "I believe in staying alive."

Drums beat down the line. Anji rose in his stirrups and shaded his eyes to look ahead. Men came alert, postures shifting as strung bows were fitted with arrows, swords were drawn, and spears readied. At a word from Anji, Captain Targit cantered off toward the rear. In the distance, Joss heard the clash of arms amidst variegated pitches of shouting and harsh screams, a clamor whose music might have been mistaken for the climax of a festival play if not for its brutal edge. He touched the hilt of his own short sword. Could he even ride a horse well enough to plunge into a battle? Give him a crowd of unruly malcontents to quell, or a stubborn village dispute to shout down, or a pair of angry combatants to whack into submission with his reeve's baton, and he knew exactly what to do.

But now they were moving and he was swept along. He was going to keep up because he was cursed if he was going to fall behind and be seen to be—the hells!—less

of a man. Hundred reeves were as good as any man or woman. Joss had always believed that. He had lived it for half his life. So he clung to the saddle and let his
mount—what in the hells was the gods-rotted animal's name?—follow along with
the rest as they pounded along the road.

Eagles flagged directions above, and cadres broke off to follow tracks that led
them away out of sight, converging on the unseen battle from several directions. Yet
by the time they reached the battleground, the skirmish was over and the vanguard
had already moved on. Men were stabbing each body to make sure it was dead,
stripping good weapons or armor off the corpses and tossing them into a heap to be
picked up later. Again, many bows and quivers stacked up; the enemy had been
ready for a reeve attack.

Anji surveyed the field. An eagle plummeted, and a horn called warning as horses
were pulled back to make an open space for the raptor to land. To Joss's surprise,
Kesta approached.

"Joss!" She looked at his horse. "What in the hells?"

"Scar's hunting. I thought to find you at Horn Hall supervising the reeves. Like I
told you. Best we not overwork the eagles—"

"Yeah, yeah." She waved a dismissive hand before addressing Anji. "Commander
Anji, there's two more enemy companies ahead, but you can send a cohort around
by a cart track and hit them from behind same time as you engage them from the
front. After that, there are a few scattered cadres trying to form up along the ridge,
but you've a clear shot at the bridge."

"The rope bridge at Halting Reach?" Joss demanded. "Wasn't that dismantled?"

"Reeves flew the main ropes into place this morning. Now they're building it out
at haste."

"Ah." Joss nodded at Anji. "You're going to reinforce Nessumara."

"No," said Anji.

A second reeve glided low, flagging to let Kesta know that she'd best move out because this one wanted to land and bring a message.

Anji said, "That's all, Reeve Kesta. You've got your orders."

She rapped Joss on the arm with her baton. "Heya, Joss, don't get into trouble. Are
you sure you know what you're doing?"

Someone in Anji's cadre chuckled, and Joss stiffened as Kesta, eyeing him,
stepped back. "I'll be going, then," she finished awkwardly. "I'll land at dusk to Copper Hall."

She launched, and the second reeve landed with a report from Chief Sengel.

They pushed on as the afternoon deepened. The air shimmered with heat. Men
rode without speaking, gazes bent toward the road ahead. The hills steepened. Once
again, Joss heard fighting, and again they poured over a slope into the teeth of a battle.
Long before Joss got anywhere near the front, the weight of their force pressed the enemy back and back to the rim of a high ridgeline that cut away into a ravine. Between
high walls, the powerful Istri River streamed south. The enemy broke, and those who
fled toward the ridge were forced to the cliffs until they had no recourse but to throw
themselves forward onto the swords of Anji's soldiers or backward off the cliff and into
wrathful current of the Istri. Men tumbled into the waters and were dragged down.

Where the road met the rim, heavy ropes spanned the gap in complicated curves.

Men out on the span were building out the bridge with planks and reinforcing anchor ropes. As skirmishing groups took off to pursue stragglers from the company they'd just defeated, the rest rubbed down and watered their horses, took a drink, or a piss, or a rest. It was night before Nessumara's defenders secured the last portion of the bridge and and winched it tight. Men and women crossed, hanging lanterns from hooks, and after them the chief engineer led across four dray beasts weighted with sacks of bricks to test the span. Fortunately, there was no wind.

After a consultation with Anji and his chiefs, the engineer sent her assistants back across with the beasts while she remained behind to direct the crossing. When the dray beasts had gotten two thirds across, the vanguard moved out in staggered cadres. Then it was the turn of Anji's command unit. They walked, while grooms led horses. Joss had crossed this span years ago, and the height didn't bother him although the sway did, the sense that the world did not hold firm beneath your feet.

Wasn't that a measure of these times? Weren't they all suspended above a chasm? The river rushed beneath so loud, its roar echoing and magnified, that no one, not even Anji, spoke one word on the long crossing.

Chief Sengel waited on the other side to greet Anji with a bash of forearms and personally escort him to a warehouse where food and drink waited. Joss got caught in the jostle and gave up trying to keep up with the command unit. Instead, he walked across Nessumara, crossing two bridges over dark canals until he reached the island where Copper Hall lay in slumbering quiet. The gates lay open, and a tired guard—an elderly man—recognizing his reeve leathers, waved him through.

Everyone was asleep except for fawkners busy in the lofts and debt slaves repairing harness and sharpening swords, but they brusquely sent him on his way. They had no time for any man, even one who called himself commander of the reeve halls. His legs were stiffening and his rear in agony before he tracked down Kesta, who had fallen asleep on a thin pallet in the third barracks he checked.

"The hells! Can't I get some rest? I've got to fly out at dawn, Joss."

"Is Arkest up to it?"

"She's close to her limit, it's true. But—"

"How can there be a but?"

"How can there not? There's room for you. Just take off your cursed boots and maybe wash your feet first."

There was a bench and table at one end of the barracks, but the lamp usually burning there had run dry. In darkness he washed face and hands and feet, and lay down beside Kesta, her familiar warmth as comforting as a sister's. They were both fire-born and thus forbidden; in truth, it was pleasant just to know you could be comrades. She flung an arm over his torso, and in her light embrace he fell hard and at once into sleep.

He dreamed.

Marit stands at the shore of the Salt Sea, a remote place he'd been only once. Her death's cloak billows in a wind he cannot feel. Beside her stands a slender man of mature years wearing the blue cloak of an envoy of Ilu; Joss has seen this man before, dying in Dast Korumbos, but he looks every bit alive now. Isn't there something uncanny, even wrong, in a man who can die and yet live on after? Who would ever choose to die, if given a chance to keep living?

Marit is speaking. "I searched for weeks around the valley where I met that young shepherd, the very place you yourself saw her. I even found the village the lad came from, but they told me—I saw in their minds—that they have not seen Earth for months. Not that they ever saw her much. It might not mean anything."

"I do not like it." The envoy glances over his shoulder.

A young woman is walking toward them, the wind pulling mist off her shoulders. With her pallid white face and pale grass hair and demon-blue eyes, she looks inhuman. What can it mean that the gods have cloaked an outlander, who cannot know what justice means in the Hundred? Have the gods abandoned them? Do they just not care? Or is there a deeper whisper here, a hint he cannot tease out?

Is his faith in the gods meaningless?

"Joss!"

He startled awake, sitting up so hard he slammed into Kesta.

"Aui!" She rubbed her chin, and he slapped a hand to his throbbing forehead. "You were muttering in your sleep. Why is it always Marit?"

"He killed her."

"We know the story—"

"He killed the cloak of Earth, the one she's looking for. But if Marit thinks she's an ally, then he killed a Guardian who is not our enemy."

"What in the hells are you babbling about?"

He scrambled up, wincing as his muscles screamed. "Where is Anji?"

"They marched out already. They took a short rest, food and drink, and kept going. Since you've not got Scar, I can give you a lift if you want to catch up to them. Best you eat before you go. No telling when you'll have a chance to eat again. Whew! I suppose we both stink. You look like the hells, I'll tell you."

He laughed. "That good, eh? They say the hells are filled with attractive women. We'll have to fight over them, you and me, eh?"

She slapped him on the chest as she stepped away. "There's a few who don't bend your way, thank the gods. Say, what news of Nallo?"

"What, that termagant? You've an interest there?"

"You might not see it, but she's cursed attractive. I like a woman who can rip off a man's head when he's being a gods-rotted idiot."

"She's given me the edge of her tongue, anyway, but not in the way I like it. I tell you, she scares me."

"Like I said, I like that woman." She grasped his wrist and tugged as he grabbed his gear and stumbled after. "You need some cordial to wake up, Joss?"

"At dawn?"

"It's what you always used to take."

"The hells I did!"

"Tell yourself what you must. Here." The barracks muster was abuzz with chatter, reeves and hirelings and fawkners drinking and eating in haste. A few women glanced twice, but nothing more than that. He ate and drank—the cordial did settle his stomach—and afterward relieved himself and washed in a trough half full of unpleasantly murky water, but the water was cool and the day was already sticky and hot. Kesta headed for the loft.

Joss stopped her. "Shouldn't we check in with the marshal?"

She shrugged. "There is no marshal. Chief Sengel gives the orders. Reeve Iyako acts as administrator. She's steady, and too old to fight. But we don't need clearance from her. I'll deliver you to the command unit and take my flight's orders from there." She waved to familiar faces waiting in the shade of a parade ground, next to lofts, and while she went in to talk to the fawkners, Joss greeted six reeves from Horn Hall, each one in a state of enflamed excitement at the prospect of impending action. Their talk poured like the river's current, a flood of noise that meant nothing to him. Any way you looked at it, it seemed that Horn Hall, Clan Hall, Copper Hall, and Gold Hall were treating Anji as their commander.

"Joss!"

Arkest waddled out into the empty parade ground, already harnessed. The raptor's feathers hadn't the bloom one liked to see in an eagle, but she wasn't obviously ailing.

"Best you rest her after today," he said as he paused beyond talon range to brandish his baton in the signal taught to eagles to recognize other reeves.

Kesta flashed him a look as good as a cut. "I'm not a fool, Joss. Hook in."

Up!

Arkest had a hitch in her flight that would have troubled him if he didn't know the bird was compensating for an injury taken in battle a year ago. She wasn't the fastest, but she was a smart bird and very experienced. They swung wide to the east so he could see the eastern approaches over the dried out wetlands where Chief Sengel's trap had lured in almost two thousand men, many to their deaths. The surface of the shallow channels had a rainbow gleam, slicked with the remains of oil. The foliage along the banks was charred, brightened by spots of untouched growth. Folk were dragging corpses off scorched ground and onto barges piled high with dead.

"They're hauling them down to the ocean and dumping them in!" shouted Kesta.

"The hells!" Yet what else could they do?

They sailed on along the empty stone earthwork of the eastern causeway until they came to Saltow. The town with its staging warehouses and many roads and paths lay as empty as if it had been abandoned, but folk peeped from behind shuttered windows. Here and there an adult scuttled down a back alley as if bearing contraband on a deadly mission. The enemy camp had been substantial; abandoned tents fluttered, several having collapsed into heaps. Dogs had dragged the corpse of a woman out beyond a tent's entrance while vultures watched warily, edging in.

It was easy to find the enemy, because reeves were tracking them, hanging lazily on the wind as the soldiers trudged on the main road in the heat below. Curiously, there were two distinct groups. One was hastening ahead in a disorganized hurry, flying the banners of three different cohorts, although there weren't enough soldiers to fill out two cohorts. They marched with no supply wagons, only wounded being bounced around in carts.

A stage behind the lead group marched a second cohort, this one in disciplined ranks under a single banner marked with six staves. They had supply wagons, extra dray beasts, horses, and sheep carefully herded in the center, and only four wagons with canvas shades that, presumably, sheltered their injured. One of the wagons was surrounded by the bristling spears of a cadre of guards, as folk might circle treasure or a valuable prisoner. Their captain, in his lime-whitened horsetails, shaded his eyes to watch them pass overhead. A sergeant marched to either side, both women by their shape although their faces were really too small to make out features.

"Kesta! The hells!"

"Quit jerking around, Joss. You'll pull poor Arkest—"

"That's Zubaidit! Wearing sergeant's colors and—"

"How can you possibly tell from this height?"

"I'd know that body anywhere!"

Kesta laughed. "You just might! If it's her, then she's turned traitor."

"Circle back!"

"No time, Joss. I've got to dump your weight. Arkest's tiring."

They swung west over the narrowing delta. Here in the northern reaches grew the forested swamp. A constant rain of leaves built up a thick underlayer beneath the trees, which got very dry when the rains died. A dirty haze hung over the swamp as they flew onward, wisps of smoke drifting upward. Now and then flares of red flashed where the canopy parted, fires smoldering.

"What happened?"

"Chief Sengel set fire to the forest along the causeway. The smoke drove back the cohorts attacking under cover of the forest canopy. It was the only way to hold them back until Commander Anji got here."

"But it's still burning."

The rising smoke made them cough. Animals teemed in the waters or on safe islands. Elsewhere, weakened trees had collapsed to open up the understory to the glare of the harsh sun. The stagnant backwaters were streaked with blackened branches and the bloating corpses of krokes and men.

"There!" Kesta pointed with her baton.

It was past midday, really hot now, and cursed if the army hadn't covered ten mey already, halfway to solid ground at Skerru. How could they maintain such a pace? For now, they had halted, strung out along the causeway over more than a mey, companies separated by gaps, men asleep under the shade of blankets, many dousing the horses and themselves with water hauled up from the swamp. The order of march had shifted. Now, Captain Targit's Qin cohort rode as the vanguard with a cadre of local scouts as escort. A cohort of local Hundred men led by Qin sergeants came behind them. After them came several companies of skirmishers and archers, and then the companies that had been in the vanguard followed by another cohort of mostly local Hundred-men. Anji's command unit now marched two units from the rear.

"Whoop!" shouted Kesta as they plunged.

They came to ground on the causeway in front of the command unit. Six guardsmen trotted out to set a barrier, and with polite smiles escorted Joss and Kesta into the shade of an awning strung up over the entire causeway with immense lengths of silk rope. Anji was in council, his chiefs seated on camp chairs while captains and sergeants stood behind them.

"Commander Joss!" Anji beckoned, smiling. "Cordial? Wine? There's kama juice. Mai's favorite." He frowned, the expression brief and disconcerting, then chuckled as the reeves walked in under the blessed shade. "I will say, Joss, I've seen you look better."

"So they tell me," said Joss, unaccountably stung, but Kesta laughed. She was drawn aside by Sengel while Anji offered Joss his own chair and took one relinquished by Deze.

"We lost you in Nessumara and couldn't wait," said Anji as they drank. "Do you mean to ride with us?"

"If you'll have me."

After Joss reported on what he and Kesta had seen that day, they talked for a while of inconsequential things. Anji asked about the swamp, the islands, the delta, and finally the old question about how Copper Hall had come to have two halls, one on the Haya shore and one in Nessumara, without becoming two separate named halls. He sounded like any merrily curious visitor come to a new town, happy to enjoy the fresh sights and local color. Others dozed, while a new shift of guards came on duty. Finally, Anji unrolled a blanket, lay down with his head resting on his rolled-up armor coat, and fell asleep so quickly that Joss was pretty sure it was between one breath and the next.

The heat weighed on him. Kesta had left. He slumped, dozing off, and startled awake just before he tipped off the chair. He'd meant to get Anji's assurance, yet again, that he would not attack the other cloaks. Yet the ghost girl had killed three of Anji's soldiers. Why wouldn't Anji want to kill her, too? If she rode with Marit, did that mean Marit could not be trusted?

But Anji slept, and he dared not wake him. A soldier offered him a blanket for the dusty ground, and he lay down but could not sleep.

Why did an army led by a Qin commander and Qin officers trouble him so? They were only a few hundred men. Even with the addition of a cohort of some five hundred new Qin soldiers, they amounted to less than a thousand. Lord Radas's horde was far larger and had done far more damage. The Qin had never harmed anyone except the enemy.

Except the Guardians.

Let it go. Now was not the time.

He slept, and did not dream, and was awakened by men rising. He drank and ate with the others, quickly and on his feet. Biting down a grimace, he swallowed the pain of mounting a good-natured gelding brought for him to ride. How efficiently the Qin had trained the grooms and tailmen who attended them! The forward companies had already started marching, so reeves reported; scouts rode up with their own reports.

"Where is Tohon?" Joss asked, riding beside Anji as the command unit set out.

"I sent him some days ago with a scouting force of reeves to find Wedrewe."

They rode through the last of the afternoon and into the swift dusk, twilight falling fast and hard. Soon night cloaked them. Local men trotted in shifts with lamps held high; wagons rolled in the gaps with lanterns swinging from their tailgates, beacons to guide their way.

They rode all cursed night except for one rest stop to changeover horses, and very late in the night, or so early that the first birds had begun to herald dawn with tentative songs, scouts rode in from the front with the expectant posture of men with stupendous news.

"The vanguard will be in visual range by dawn, Commander. We've killed eight pickets although some escaped."

"Is there any change in their fortifications?" Anji asked.

"Neh." These were local men, who knew the swamps and channels. "They've got shields set ten deep massed where the causeway opens onto the mainland. It's enough to press back any attack from the causeway, and it leaves them free to push forward at a moment's notice. They've figured out we're coming."

Anji said, to Joss, "They've dug some minor fortifications at the rear of their encampment. They're expecting skirmishing groups to come at them from behind. I expect they know that Nessumara doesn't have as many troops as they do, so the Nessumara militia could never risk a frontal assault down a confined corridor."

"Isn't it better to let the reeves lift troops over their heads and hit them from behind?"

Anji shrugged. "That's what they're expecting. That's why they have the fortifications at their rear. If you want to see, go forward with the scouts."

"My thanks. I'd like to go, if your scouts will have me."

Of course they would, if Anji said they must.

They were easygoing local men. Their way of talking fell smoothly on the ears of a man raised on the Haya shore, who had spent some time around Nessumara in his youth, although he'd never walked deep into the delta. Krokes and snakes did not appeal, and the smell of decaying vegetation overlaid with smoke and ash made his lungs hurt.

The scouts numbered sixteen; all walked with a stoop but so quickly that he struggled to keep up. He was sent off with a pair of older men. Forgi was short and stout and as graceful as a cat; Ussoken was about Joss's height, thin, and had such a dry wit that maybe it scorched the land more than fire. They both had spears with which they poked the ground, testing for hot spots. This far north, they informed him, they did not expect to find fire, because they had fired the forest about three mey south, luring the enemy in far enough that he had no choice but to retreat fast and furiously. But you never knew how far it might have spread, so it was best to be cautious.

"Krokes and snakes, too, I suppose," joked Joss. "Best to be cautious."

They chuckled. Krokes and snakes fled fire; they'd have departed for cooler waters. Still, they tested their ground and eyed eddying waters, just in case; he followed in their wake, careful to step exactly where they had also set their feet. They waited for him to catch up, then forged forward again. Forgi might warble like a bird; Ussoken might point, and Forgi would confirm with a nod, but whatever they acknowledged remained invisible to Joss. Once he glimpsed a ripple in a dark channel of water, but since the scouts ignored it, he assumed it was not dangerous.

Soon, they fell silent, and he asked no more questions. Every seed and dry leaf he brushed against adhered to his skin; although they came across no open swaths of fire, soot ran in streaks on his bare arms and powdered his leathers. A tiny five-pointed leaf fledged with hairlike spines stuck to his hands, and when he tried to wipe it away it left an inflamed patch of red. Forgi and Ussoken showed no sign of discomfort, although they too were smeared with ash.

Sloughs of water turned to isolated pools. Pine trees rose on dry islets. They were coming to the mainland. Abruptly, Joss realized he'd lost sight of Ussoken. A birdcall trilled within the trees. Forgi gestured for Joss to stand still. A muddy pool densely grown with reeds opened to one side, leaves from drooping branches skimming the surface of the water. Forgi moved sideways and, with a wicked big knife in hand, adjusted his body until it seemed he was part of the forest, almost fading before Joss's eyes.

The heavy foliage drowned distant sounds. They might have been alone in all the wide world.

Forgi let out a screech as he sprang toward the muddy shore of the pool. A figure Joss had not perceived rose out of the reeds, lifting a bow, but before the arrow could be launched Ussoken reared up behind the man. He grabbed the enemy scout's hair and yanked his head back, slit his throat so deep the head folded backward as the body convulsed. Ussoken shoved the body away and got out of the pool as it thrashed, a sure signal to wandering krokes. They moved on quickly, passing another freshly slain body, killed in a similar fashion. Flies swarmed on the open gash, their hum deafening. Eihi!

Yet Joss had seen worse things as a reeve. He knew what violence folk were capable of.

The ground began to rise and the foliage thinned, but now there were more thorns and entire thickets of those nasty five-pointed leaves. On the wind shuddered a drumbeat, a repetitive rhythm: five quick taps, three slow, five quick taps, two slow and a pause. Joss was glad to get the swamp out from under his feet but the scouts grew anxious, dropping to their bellies to crawl up a slope. Joss bellied up after them, arms red and scratched, although his leathers protected the rest of him.

"Whsst!" Forgi dragged Joss under cover of branches swollen with a profusion of yellow bells. The ground gave way, and Joss rolled onto his back, staring up through leaves and flowers. Sunlight flashed overhead, but wasn't it still morning?

Aui! A cloak circled over the camp as if he'd just come from scouting. His cloak glittered with the strength of the sun's fierce golden blaze. Forgi tapped his arm, but Joss kept staring, trying to follow the Guardian's path. How had this Guardian crossed into the shadows? What choice had he made? Must it happen in time to every Guardian?

Yet the Lady of Beasts had only said that one among the Guardians would betray her comrades. If Marit's story was true, Atiratu's prophecy had already come to pass, and an outlander *would* save them.

The drums beat, accelerating their punch, as Anji marched his army closer to battle. An answering clamor of drums rose like a challenge.

A man coughed. "Hsst! There he is!"

A spear jostled the branches. The hells! While he'd been lying here dreaming, a cadre of enemy scouts had rolled up and over the crest. Forgi was gone.

Joss spun sideways under the thicket and sprang up on the far side. Thorns ripped at him as he forced a way through brambles, leading with his baton. An arrow thwacked into stout vines. Others passed over his head as he bolted for the swamp.

"Got him!" A figure bowled into him, throwing them both to the ground.

Joss rolled up first, planting the length of the baton along the side of the man's head. He scrambled back as he shoved his baton into its leash and drew his short sword. The cursed enemy had gotten between him and the tangle of the swamp forest. He backed up the slope toward the crest. They were driving him into their encampment.

"Capture the reeve alive!" a man called, although Joss could not see him. "Lord Radas wants all reeves brought to him."

That gave him one advantage, then. He leaped to the left, stabbing, and the soldier he probed at stumbled aside, caught himself on his spear, and lunged. Joss skipped back, to stand backed up to the thorny bramble. A man was cutting through the vines. Upslope, men advanced. Aui! Eight—neh—nine men. A burly man wearing a sergeant's badge stepped into view.

"No use fighting us. That'll only get you killt. Come along with us, and you'll not be harmed."

Joss laughed. "Can you truly say so and expect me to believe it? Lord Radas's army has been killing reeves for twenty years, as I have reason to know. Even if you take me to him alive, so he can interrogate me, how can you expect me to believe he'll allow me to live afterward?"

The sergeant shrugged. "Agree to serve him, and he might let you live."

"We could use some cursed reeve scouts," shouted the man who'd knocked him over, wiping blood from his nose. "It's like we're cursed blind!"

"Enough!" The sergeant cut off a murmur of agreement with his roar. He raised his sword. "Surrender. Or we'll kill you now. It's really that easy a choice."

"It's never that easy a choice, ver. I've been a reeve for a long time. Folk may say things are simple, but they rarely are. Let me assure you of that. Better you let me go, or better yet, follow me into the swamp and save your own lives before this battle finds you all dead."

"This battle?"

They laughed heartily.

The sergeant nodded magnanimously at him. He was a reasonable man, his nod suggested, and reasonable men listened to each other. "You lot from Nessumara are on your last legs. The lord commander says so. You may have won a respite with your fires, but you've got thin forces on the ground. We've scouts who've told us you've got a cohort riding up the causeway, but when your militia hits our shields, they'll be crushed. And we've got two cohorts marching up from Saltow to join us, and another come in yesterday from over the river. It'll be all over for you lot in another day. We'll rule the north. So decide if you want to be among the winners or the losers. Tell you what, friend. I'll meet you in a fair fight, no weapons. I toss you, you come quietly. You toss me, you come quietly."

The men laughed.

Joss had a hells lot of experience as a reeve dragging out a tense confrontation until help arrived. You never knew when an extra mouthful of time might mean the difference between success and failure.

"I'll gladly spar with a big man like you, someone up to my weight. But I have to warn you, if I win, I'll have to arrest you all."

They were laughing, relaxing, because he seemed relaxed. Because he knew how to joke; he had the power of a glib tongue and a charming smile that worked equally well on men as on women. He unbuckled his gear, set his knife down next to his baton, and waited, hands at his sides, as the sergeant handed his weapons to a soldier. The big man approached, hands raised, bobbing a little, ready to take a punch.

Joss danced back, pretending to throw a punch or two, keeping his distance as the soldiers jeered and called him names. Dared him to close in. But he waited. And waited. For the flicker of the eyes, the moment when the other man's attention wavered. He ducked in and shifted sideways, got the man's beefy arm around and then up behind him, fingers back until the pain drove the big man to his knees with a shriek of surprised pain. He jammed his knee into his back and shoved him forward into the ground as the soldiers hesitated. They knew the law of fighting. There were a lot of awful things a man might do, but to violate that law seemed extreme. The sergeant slapped a hand on the dirt twice.

Joss had him. Now what in the hells was he going to do, with eight men brandishing spears and swords ready to stick him from all sides?

A vast shadow of wings rippled over the ground.

Joss laughed.

"And you lot can all go to the hells!" He flung himself sideways toward his discarded gear.

Scar struck. His talons pierced one man, and he knocked another aside with his cruel beak, then shook the first man free and onto the head of a third man. Joss freed his sword, whipped around, and lunged for the sergeant. The man thrust up his spear to catch the blow. Joss cut inside the sergeant's reach and stuck him through the abdomen, jerked his sword out, and spun to knock aside an attack from behind. Scar came down hard on a man who had panicked and started running. An archer fumbled with his bow as wounded men screamed.

The hells. Joss shifted his sword into his other hand, drew his knife, and in one smooth motion threw it; the blade flashed, then buried itself hilt-deep into the archer's belly. Scar fluffed his feathers and with uncanny speed pounced on the last soldier, who had been backing toward the safety of the thorns.

No time to ponder the vagaries of life. Joss sheathed his sword and clipped on his harness with the speed reeves trained for. Scar had turned his attention to the men who were thrashing, flexing his talons in the flesh of one and then another until they ceased crying out. The archer fell down and lay still, eyes open with terror, trying to play dead.

Joss brought his bone whistle to his lips and blew. "Scar," he said.

The bloody eagle swung his huge head to regard him. The raptor could rip his head off without effort, and yet Joss could never fear him. He trusted this bird. With his life.

Men shouted; they'd been spotted. Drums raced away over the trees. Joss hooked in to Scar's harness and tugged on the jess.

Up!

Arrows arced harmlessly as the land dropped away. The swamp passed under his feet. What a cursed mercy it was not to have to slog through that again. A reeve became used to flight. He jessed, and Scar swung wide and winged back over the enemy encampment.

A massive spur of ancient rock—Kroke's Ridge—split the river into two major channels, which then splintered into the vast web of the delta. The western channel, flowing against a western ridge, received the brunt of the current. The eastern channel, over the years, had been engineered into a net of channels, here bridged by two stone bridges and a series of ferries.

In the eastern lee of the ridge, on high ground bordered by the ridge on one side and the eastern channel—which would soon split into the hundred channels of the delta—stood the town of Skerru. Below the town lay the open staging ground, built up over generations, where the causeway emerged from the swamplands. It was a wide area where boats, barges, wagons brought over on the ferry, and pack-animal traffic could pay the delta toll and get permission to enter the causeway and move their goods down to Nessumara. It was easy to get across the river to Skerru, but Skerru controlled access to Nessumara just as Saltow, in the east, was gatekeeper of the eastern causeway. Rich clans lived here, and here on the open ground Lord Radas had settled his encampment, fortified by ditches and berms. Two cohorts were spread along the fortifications to defend against soldiers dropped behind the lines. After all, that's what Anji had done before.

Because the causeway was the only entrance to Nessumara, Radas had concentrated his best infantrymen there. An entire cohort braced in ranks, shields wrapped with dampened canvas against fire and oil. They were ready to hold, or to march; a second cohort backed them up. No Hundred militia could hope to penetrate this sturdy wall.

Qin cavalry, more than five hundred strong in even ranks, pounded down the causeway to the accompaniment of drums. Cantering, they transitioned in breathtaking unison into a gallop, an earth-thundering full-out run. Black wolves might bear down so upon their helpless prey. No soldier in the Hundred had ever faced anything like this.

They hit like a blacksmith's hammer.

The shields didn't hold, or waver, or even collapse. They simply disintegrated, like a fence of sticks stuck upright in the sand when a storm surge pours over them. A man stood upright in an eddy as horsemen cleared his fallen foes; untouched, he simply stood as one stunned, and then raised his sword too late as a passing rider cut him down.

They drove through the shields, a breaking wave. Through this narrow passage a second cohort galloped four abreast like a strong current cutting through weak soil. Ahead, the Qin cohort split like the delta channels into smaller cadres to make room for the soldiers coming up behind. They swung wide to hit the enemy's two forward cohorts from the flanks. Steel flashed. A horse went down, its rider tumbling to earth and yet somehow coming out on his feet, slashing as he rose. Shields pulled together, trying to hold. Out in the encampment, horns blew frantically, signaling a retreat, as the cadres who had been deployed for an attack from behind used ditches and berms to create barriers between them and the incoming horsemen. Out of the north, not yet visible to the people on the ground, flights of eagles were coming in, weighted with passengers to drop for a rear attack.

Joss tugged on the jesses, and Scar found an updraft skirling off Kroke's Ridge. He rose higher and higher yet, until the land seemed like child's vat of clay and all the people moving below toys whose lives and deaths fell away into insignificance compared with the sun's fierce eye and the sky's immense indifference. Clots of smoke still rose out of the delta. The fires set by the defenders had given Anji time to reach Nessumara, but how easily the measure might have turned back upon the defenders or burned all the way into the hundred isles of Nessumara!

And Joss thought: *Could I have ordered the forest set ablaze? Could I have set men on fire with oil of naya, knowing in what agony they would burn? Could I stand aside and order that all captured prisoners must be executed immediately, lest they slow down the progress of the army? Could I kill a Guardian? Or let another man do so, knowing the act would kill him?*

He could not shake the feeling that he—that everyone—stood at the edge of a precipice. Aui! Did he envy Anji? For his skill at command? For his evident intelligence and powerful ability to focus? For his beautiful, devoted wife? For the handsome child Joss would never have?

And yet why not? He wasn't too old to father a child. It wasn't too late to build a different life. He didn't have to be commander of the reeve halls; it wasn't as if the reeves seemed eager to accept him in that position. A simple reeve might hope to have a cottage to come home to with a spouse and children. Wasn't that what he had hoped for?

For it always came back to Marit, didn't it? To the ordinary life the likes he had dreamed of twenty years ago, when he had asked Marit if she would consider making a child together with him. Was that what he mourned more than anything? The life so many other humble people took for granted that had been ripped from him by a band of criminals up on the Liya Pass? And how was he therefore any different from uncounted Hundred folk whose lives had been destroyed and lands laid waste by Lord Radas's cruel army?

Out of the east, just beyond the eastern channels, horns cried and banners waved. The reserves from Saltow had reached Skerru. Lord Radas had reinforcements. Zubaidit, marching with the enemy, didn't know they were about to smash into Anji's army.

One way or the other, she'd be killed. He sure as the hells was not going to fly away to report to the hall while leaving another woman behind to die as he'd left Marit.

He jessed Scar hard, and they sailed over the eastern crossings, over the heads of the first Saltow contingent. The six staves cohort had gained ground and was now perhaps half a mey behind, closing the gap. He swooped recklessly low as, above, reeves flagged him desperately in warning. Below, the horse-tailed captain marked his approach, nudging Zubaidit.

Was the gods-rotted woman *insane*? A traitor? She said something to the captain, and cursed if a reeve flag didn't go up, signaling him to land: *Help needed!* Every reeve was obliged to answer the call. It was their duty.

Down.

They thumped hard, and Joss unhooked, dropped, and blew Scar's retreat. Scar launched without hesitation, leaving Joss to stand in front of an oncoming enemy cohort with his baton in hand, like a reeve facing down a riot single-handedly. There were worse ways to die. And Scar would be free to take a new reeve.

Yet the cohort halted in a display of discipline almost as impressive as Anji's Qin horsemen. Three people jogged out from the vanguard to meet him: the captain, accompanied by two women in sergeant's badges. The woman standing to the captain's right was past the first bloom of youth, tall for a woman and thick with a laborer's strength. Her eyes widened as she took in Joss; she shook her head with the twisted half frown of a woman who wants to laugh but isn't sure she ought to. She carried a stubby spear in her left hand and a short sword sheathed at her side. A long leather pouch was slung over her back.

The captain stopped a stone's toss away, rubbing his chin with the back of a hand as he examined Joss with a crooked half smile, as a man might not quite smile when he realizes he's lost a bet.

Bai sauntered forward, grinning that cursed grin that made Joss flush. "Reeve Joss. Come to my rescue."

"I'll expect a reward," said Joss, with a smile that stopped her in her tracks.

The other sergeant snorted.

The captain said, on a sharp sigh, "I see you two know each other."

"Not in that way, if not for lack of trying," said Zubaidit. "Don't be jealous."

"How can I be jealous for what I've never possessed? Reeve Joss, I'm called Arras, captain of Sixth Cohort. This is Sergeant Giyara. So tell me, reeve, why would you come down from your safe haven in the sky to parley with the captain of an army whose men you know are eager to kill reeves?"

These were cursed interesting currents, truly.

Joss turned his smile on Sergeant Giyara, who smirked in the way of a woman who was immune to his charm but enjoyed watching the effort. "The first time Zubaidit and I met, she tried to kill me. So I suppose I feel I still have the advantage. Tell me, Captain, are you marching into battle?"

"We're marching to meet up with Lord Radas, as ordered. What battle?"

Joss indicated the hazy sky. "That's dust, churned up by fire and battle. Captain Anji has broken Lord Radas's army."

"So you might claim. If I join up with the other Saltow contingent, we can flank the enemy and drive him back."

"You might, although I doubt it. Toskala is fallen to an uprising. Reeves from Gold Hall ought to be falling on the garrison in High Haldia today. Your side has lost, even if the limbs still function. You can retreat with your men and lose the war another day, or you can surrender."

"I can kill you at this moment," said the captain, not in an angry way, just pointing it out as a comment between friends.

"You haven't killed me. And I think you won't. I've given you fair warning, because Zubaidit marches beside you. Let me take her and go."

"She's our hostage," said the captain.

"Cursed spy," said Giyara without much heat, eyeing Zubaidit sidelong. Without looking at the other sergeant, Bai smiled provocatively, and Joss's ears flamed. Had she had sex with the other woman? Was that her game? The hells!

"For a man of your experience," said Bai in a voice whose purr made him think she'd seen into his mind as easily as might a cloak, "you're as innocent as the sky is blue in the dry season, Reeve Joss. I need to tell you that my brave comrade Shai killed the woman who wore the cloak of Night. He rests in one of those invalid wagons, badly hurt. I have to stay with him. Tohon would never forgive me if I let him die."

Joss's heart went cold; his limbs seemed paralyzed; his mouth went dry.

"Did you release her cloak to the gods, as is fitting?" he croaked.

"I gave it to Captain Arras."

The captain didn't even glance at Sergeant Giyara, who stood loyally beside him with a pouch slung across her back. An innocent burden, to the naked eye.

"I beg you," Joss said to Bai, "release it."

Captain Arras shook his head. "You comprehend my dilemma, Reeve Joss. I'm torn between my old commander and the prospect of a new one. A traitor has earned a short life, don't you think? I need a cursed valuable treasure to bargain with, and while the life of that young outlander we're hauling along in the wagons seems useful, I don't think it's enough."

Joss glanced at Bai and lifted his chin. A quickly drawn sword, and a pair of lunges, would take care of the captain and sergeant; they could release the cloak. Then he realized she wasn't armed.

Arras laughed. "I like you, reeve. You think the way I do. She agreed to walk unarmed. I've a Guardian's cloak and a veiled outlander to bargain with." Horns blatted in the distance, a call to arms. "Now, if you'll excuse us, we've got a battle to fight. Best you move aside, and let us march."

They were almost seven hundred men. He was one reeve, not quite ready to die pointlessly. He stood aside, and let them march.

48

ARRAS CLIMBED UP into a wagon's bed to address his soldiers, who were straining eagerly for news. They had heard the horns' cries from ahead. They'd watched the captain's conference with the reeve.

"I've brought you this far," Arras called. "You may have wondered why we retreated from the attack on Nessumara. You may have wondered why we did not march out in company with the Saltow survivors. Why we left our camp slaves behind in Saltow rather than bring them with us." He surveyed the assembled cohort but saw no man or woman there who looked angry or suspicious. They trusted him.

"As your captain, I have always put your welfare first. Maybe you think I'm a generous man, a merchant who gives out rice cakes to children just to see them smile." That caught and released a few chuckles. "Maybe you think it's occurred to me that I can't be a captain without a cohort to command, and so it should. What is a captain, except a man with soldiers to lead? What is a commander, even a lord commander, except one who holds the reins of an army? So I ask you, if a commander proves again and again through his actions that he is no wise commander, ought a captain to follow him even into disaster? If a captain places the welfare of his loyal men above all things, shouldn't he pause rather than leap blindly? If a captain who wants his men to stay alive, to fight again, to earn a decent reward, sees that those who give orders don't know what they're doing and are leading their army into a mire, isn't he required to change his path?"

He had their full attention.

"Who will feed us if we burn down all the villages, trample every field, and drive away the farmers? Most of you hail from such villages. Have you ever wondered what in the hells we're doing? What end it serves? Does it serve your families and clans? Does it serve us? For what reward are we fighting?"

They had settled into a stillness like that of children listening to the most ancient of tales, bound as by the sorcery of the storyteller. So far, it was working. Even his subcaptains, for whom this was not entirely a surprise, were nodding.

"I'll tell you, I'm tired of this. This isn't fighting. A soldier ought not to be proud of bullying the helpless. Of stringing up men and women from poles just to watch them suffer. I don't fear a fight. You know that, who served with me in High Haldia. Nor do I fear death more than any other. A fighting man always takes a chance with death. But there are better commanders to serve. And I know where they are. Right up ahead, as that reeve has given me to know. Lord Radas's army is not invincible. They're losing now. Toskala has thrown off its garrison. High Haldia's garrison will go down likewise. An army from Olossi has marched all the way here, and it's them who fight out there, them who have a leader who knows how to deploy his forces and take charge."

These revelations shocked them. They muttered restlessly, and he raised a hand to call for silence. They quieted at once.

"How can it have happened, you wonder? That we who have fifteen or more cohorts are struggling now? We're struggling because of poor command. Squandered units. Terrible planning. Because of arrogance and ignorance and blindness and pride. Yet aren't we trapped where we stand? Aren't we caged by our past choices? Neh, it's never too late to take a chance on a new path. Everything we do is subject to a thousand chances. So I'm asking you, if you trust my judgment, take a chance with me now."

They cheered. Not one hesitated or turned away.

He climbed down off the wagon.

To Giyara he said, "Give Zubaidit her weapons."

To the subcaptains he said, "Form up your companies in attack order. We'll go broad, one, two, and three across the front, four and five flanking, and six at the center back as reserve, Piri, so you keep your eyes open. I'll stand with you in the command unit."

He looked over the troop as they fell into marching order, each soldier knowing the comrades at whose shoulder he stood. He had trained them well; they knew their business.

"Shall we?" he said to Giyara, and to his subcaptains, who were gathered around him.

He was answered with an emphatic "yes." They, too, felt the sting of a hundred small slights and niggling doubts; he wasn't the only one who was ambitious, who felt he'd not received the reward he'd earned or a full measure of credit for his labors.

He gestured, and the Sixth Cohort banner was raised and lowered. The horns called the advance, and the drums set the pace. They marched out double-time, and soon the clamor of battle filled their ears, drowning out the sound of the river. The rearguard of the other Saltow contingent, massing at the ferries and bridges to cross, saw them coming and raised a cheer.

Arras signaled, the banner rose twice to pass the command. The pace quickened.

Again he signaled, and again the banner rose. The beat hammered faster, and the cohort shifted into a trot. From across the river, horses pounded, men shouted, steel clashed.

He raised a hand and the banner raised and lowered a final time as they closed with the now-bewildered Saltow units. The drums, like his heart, raced. He'd made his choice. There was no going back.

His front line broke into their charge.

*   *   *

JOSS HAD TO admire the way in which Captain Arras and his cohort smashed their former comrades. They hit them from the rear and took them apart while the other soldiers were still trying to figure out what was going on and who had attacked them. It was brutal but effective, worthy of Anji's Qin, if you wanted to look at it that way. From on high, he watched as the Sixth Cohort took control of the ferries and bridges. They cut down soldiers fleeing in retreat across those crossings toward what looked like the safe harbor of one of their own. On the other side of the river, Anji's rear units had reached the battleground and were advancing step by step, clearing all opposition. The open ground between Skerru's livestock palisade and the causeway was littered with the dead and the dying, with Olo'osson and Nessumaran militiamen stalking the wounded to drag free their comrades and finish off their enemies. Meanwhile, the forward units pressed the remnants toward the river. Many dismounted to harry the enemy on foot, while riders swept around the flanks to cut off men trying to escape into the swamp. Arrows flew with deadly grace. Skerru's gates remained resolutely closed, although some desperate men tried to scale the palisade and were driven off with poles and pitchforks wielded by Skerru's frightened populace.

As the army disintegrated, losing cohesion, the slaughter began. Here and there, soldiers threw down their arms and tried to surrender, but in the frenzy they were cut down anyway. Men threw themselves into the river, carried away on the current.

Anji's command unit rode through the carnage to consider the crossing arrayed on the other side. Captain Arras had managed to winch all the ferries over to his side of the river, leaving only the two bridges to protect. His cohort had fallen back to open ground away from the corpses of their dead comrades and shifted into marching order, ready to retreat in ranks and at speed. But they weren't moving.

A single figure sauntered out over the main stone bridge. She halted about two-thirds of the way across. To Joss's surprise, Anji rode out onto the span with six Qin solders in attendance. He dismounted, and he and Zubaidit conferred. She stepped away from Anji to wave a strip of cloth. At this signal Arras left the lines, also alone. Driving a wagon in which lay a man much cushioned by pillows and silk, he approached across the bridge.

Zubaidit looked up. Of course she had known all along that Joss was there. She waved the cloth again, a clear invitation. *Join the meeting.* Maybe even: *Meet me after.* Aui! A dangerous woman!

Setting down on the bridge was a risky and reckless maneuver. As a young man, he'd shown off in exactly such a way once or twice. He grinned, hands tightening on the jesses as he gauged the width of the span, the feel of the wind, and his angle of approach.

The sun's glamour flashed to the north, at the tip of the massive ridge that divided the river. Yet how could that be? The sun was high, although the shadow of Scar's wings protected him, and a heat haze combined with drifting smoke to obscure the landscape.

There was a Guardian's altar at Kroke's Ridge. He'd seen Lord Radas earlier. Where else would a Guardian go, but to an altar?

He hauled on the jesses. Reluctantly, the eagle's muscles bunching and easing behind Joss's back, Scar came around. Because he was looking, he caught sight of a second flash, like a signal sparking from a lamp. He followed that beacon down until he plunged toward a sun-swept treeless spine of rock where a winged mare ridden by a man swathed in a cloak the color of the noonday sun clattered to earth.

Lord Radas wore the cloak of Sun.

Lord Radas, at whose command Marit had died. At whose order Joss's dreams and hopes had come apart. And he was the least of it; he'd squandered some chances and made good use of others, but he'd not had his farm burned down around him, his husband murdered or wife raped, his children led away in chains to become slaves, his coin and storehouse ransacked, his body hung from a post until thirst and pain dragged him under.

Kesta and Peddonon were right. Lord Radas had broken the boundaries.

He tugged on the jesses and, obediently, Scar, with wings spread and talons pitched forward, dropped to land at one end of the spine of rock. Joss unhooked and hit two-footed. There wasn't much to see, a dusty level surface glittering under the hot sun. There was no cave, no boulders, no hollow, just a long flat ridgetop scattered with rocks and a ghost walking with a cloak like the sun shining its lamp in Joss's eyes. The heat and sun and smoke made his head ache, but cursed if he was going to let that stop him.

He drew his sword and ran forward to the entrance to the glimmering path that marked the Guardian's labyrinth, the track that led to the hidden altar, where it was forbidden for any but Guardians to walk. Anji had walked there, and lived to tell of it. Joss had survived its twists more than once, and this time, by the Herald, he'd have his revenge.

He put his right foot down, and then his left. The pavement on which he walked might have been the thinnest glaze of crystal, or it might have been the veins of the Earth Mother, cutting through stone into the depths of the obdurate earth. As he paced the measure, the air seemed to slowly rotate around him, and each time he shifted at an angle, a fresh landscape appeared as through an open window, glimpsed and, with each new step, left behind.

He knew these places!

Needle Spire, seen once beyond Storm Cape and never forgotten. A tumbled beacon, doubtless from the South Shore. Stone Tor in the midst of the Wild. An altar overlooking the Salt Sea in barren Heaven's Ridge. Mount Aua, where he and Anji had conferred. An unfamiliar village. Aui! The pinnacle where he had found Zubaidit and her brother.

There were one hundred and one altars sacred to the Guardians scattered across the land. And they were all empty except for a whisper that chased through his heart and rumbled like wind in his ears.

A man's voice made hard by selfishness. "Where are they all? Yordenas? Night? Bevard? Why do you not walk?"

Beneath, a different voice spun like song into the heart of the altar. *"Go to Indiyabu. Release me."*

Sinking deeper yet, as faint as a whisper, a woman spoke in a timbre oddly like Mai's voice: *"Anji betrayed me."*

He fought past the horrible whispers, for perhaps they were only the altar's third eye and second heart ripping his secret fears and angry hopes out of the thoughts and feelings he had struggled for years and months and days to conquer. He stumbled into a hollow as the sun burst in his face. Where his foot slammed into the ground, pain stabbed up through his sole, but he grasped hold of the billowing cloak with his free hand. The ground slammed sideways beneath his feet as the cloak pulled him back from the precipice. He stumbled backward into knee-deep water that burned through his leathers. A man knelt in the shallows with liquid pouring out of cupped hands that he lifted to his lips. He rose fast, straining against Joss's pull, his expression fierce with anger and pride and years of having his least whim obeyed instantaneously.

"Who are you?" he demanded, gaze striking like an eagle to grasp Joss in its talons. He extended a humble arrow as if to jab it into Joss's chest. "Look at me!"

Joss thrust his sword into the man's gut. He held on as water and cloak strangled him, fire on top of fire as blood poured down his arms. The man grunted softly. How easily his life drained away with his blood. How easy it was to kill. To be angry. To give up when the tide has turned against you; to give in to despair.

How much harder to build a life out of ruins or beyond the heartache of what has been torn from you.

The man's weight sagged onto Joss, and Joss slipped, and both fell. Joss gulped a lungful of air before the waters closed over them. Unlike his quarry, he was not taken by surprise. He groped with his gloves, just as Marit had told him to do, and unhooked the clasp and yanked the cloak free.

He drowned in blue fire so blinding it was like floundering in the heart of a gem. Voices thundered and snapped in his ears, too loud to be understood. Four Mothers extended their hands: she with skin as black as soot, her hair flashing gold with fire; she with skin the red-brown of clay, her hair short and spiky; she with skin dark as deep water and hair flowing in heavy coils like seaweed; she pale as the wind. Cursed if they weren't as attractive as any females he had ever seen, and they laughed to admire him, pleased with their own creation. *Let him be healed, for it would be a shame to lose such beauty, neh?*

The hells! Had it really come to this, after all these years? That he saw visions about his own gods-rotted good looks? Was he truly that vain?

The arrowhead grazed his forearm but did not stick. A hand clawed down his vest, but he twisted the wrist and shoved the grasping arm away. Then the creature who had called itself Lord Radas expelled a bubble of air and the body went limp. Joss broke the surface, gasping and choking, and stumbled up out of the pool hauling the sun-bright cloak behind him as he had once hauled fishing nets out of the sea. He folded it up in haste and weighted it under so many rocks it was hidden. A corpse floated in the pool, such a horrible desecration of an altar that he began to wade in to fetch it, but the touch of the water burned him and he skipped out, shouting in pain. He was wet through, yet his leathers were drying quickly under the sun's blast. He stripped off gloves shedding flakes of burned leather; beneath, his hands were chapped red but not damaged. Indeed, he'd come off more lightly than Anji had. He felt light-headed; his headache was gone; his mouth was dry, and his throat had a nagging rasp. He blinked back tears as he crouched in the hollow, in the heart of the holy altar, and watched the body floating in the pool. He watched for the rest of the day, and through the night, because Marit had told him that a cloak will heal the body it has chosen. Beyond all things, Radas must not be healed.

Dawn came at last, sun limning the eastern lowlands as distant horns called and the first bell rang in Skerru, although the town was impossible to see from here.

The flaccid corpse had nudged up at the lip of the pool, head down in the water. Joss carefully grasped the wet cloth of the man's first-quality silk jacket and heaved him up onto stone.

Lord Radas was dead.

He was dead, while Joss had survived.

It was not good enough. He wrestled the dead man out of his fine silk jacket, undershirt, belt and sash, and with these he wrapped the cloak of sun and stowed it in his pack. The corpse was beginning to stiffen. He dragged the body out of the labyrinth to find Scar slumbering on the rim of the height. He woke the raptor with a gentle tone from his bone whistle. After the bird had taken time to wake, to spread his wings to catch the sun, and to preen a few feathers, Joss hooked in. He harnessed in the corpse so it dangled before him, but the gods-rotted thing was by now so rigid it was difficult to handle.

He did not circle back to fly over Skerru or the battlefield, although he heard drums beating to mark an advance. He flew west, the dead man bumping against him all the way, until he spotted a deserted village. It was not that far a journey, in truth, for the entire countryside had been scoured and lay eerily silent.

They landed, and when he had unhooked the body, he could take a breath without gagging. He sought through farmers' sheds and porches until he found a shovel. In a woodland thicket he dug through the loamy earth, climbed down in the hole, and dug deeper yet, breaking the boundaries yet again, for all knew that to bury the dead was a calculated impiety. The dead are meant to rest on the high lattice of a Sorrowing Tower so they may be scoured by the four elements, as is fitting, leaving their spirits free to cross the Spirit Gate to the other side.

He scrambled out of the pit, shuddering, and shoved the body in. It tumbled in to make a ghastly sight with legs and arms stuck straight out, pointing rudely. He retched, bent over, yet nothing came up for he'd eaten nothing, only sipped at water. After the fit passed, he wiped his brow and began shoveling. Let Radas, once Lord of Iliyat, remain trapped beneath earth forevermore. Surely no Guardian's cloak could insinuate itself through the soil to revive him, nor he claw his way free. Surely he had sown enough injustice throughout the land that the gods would revoke their favor from him now and forever after.

He tossed the last shovelful of dirt and leaned on the shovel, sweat pouring off his bare back. He murmured prayers to the gods, not sure what was proper. *Let Ilu the Herald guide me, let Kotaru the Thunderer make my hand strong, let Sapanasu the Lantern reveal what I need to know, let Taru the Witherer ease that which pains me and let bloom my joy, let Atiratu the Lady of Beasts grant me wisdom, let Ushara the Devourer the Merciless One stoke my passion.*

He faltered, coming to Hasibal the Formless One. The midges were gathering in a fury. The only words he could think of were those he had heard chanted by Mai and her servant Priya to their foreign god, the Merciful One: *May the rains come at the proper time. May the harvest be abundant. May the world prosper, and justice be served.*

He returned to the familiar expanse of cultivated fields, orchards, ditches, and houses.

"Accept my prayers out of compassion," he said to the sky and to the earth, to the wind and to the waters of a pool lined with mulberry trees. He unfastened the bindings and shook out the silk jacket. Freed, the cloak of sun rippled like a living thing, billowing and beating into the air as the wind caught in the bright fabric and lofted it heavenward. Released to the gods.

"Peace," he whispered as it blew up and away over the trees, fading until he could no longer see it.

He laced his vest back on and trudged to the abandoned hamlet, where he restored the shovel to its place in a humble shed.

Scar was waiting, curious at his absence; he dipped his head to look at Joss first with one eye and then the other, as if a raptor's vision might see different aspects of a man's heart and spirit depending on which eye he was looking with.

"I'm content," Joss said to the eagle, and for once in his life, since that last day with Marit, he was. He spotted a damaged covert on Scar's tail, but only one, not enough to interfere with flight. He circled twice until he was satisfied there was nothing else amiss.

They launched, and he retraced his path east to the river. The afternoon sun gilded lonely pools. Narrow tracks wove through the landscape, and twice he glimpsed folk walking briskly toward unseen destinations, almost as if they were no longer afraid.

Late in the afternoon, the spiny ridge above Skerru hoved into view. Lanterns lit the town as if it were festival. The army had settled in for the night on the battlefield below the town, protected by the river on either side, although a huge herd of horses was grazing beyond the eastern crossing. A number of eagles were floating off in the distance, with no reeve dangling below. Out hunting.

Wagons were being unloaded, food prepared over campfires, horses watered and groomed and fed grain. Canvas had been set up in orderly units. The singing of victorious soldiers spun a joyful tune into the breeze.

The bodies of the enemy dead were being dumped in the river, swept away by the powerful current, carried away like so many petals torn from the flower necklaces worn at festival time; down to the sea with a single song sung over their departed spirits.

Yet what they had given, they had, in the end, received. The Four Mothers would take their bodies and turn and turn them until they became part of the land once again.

Four reeves, aloft as sentries, flagged him. He descended and was met by soldiers who kept a respectful distance from Scar as they looked Joss over with startled expressions.

"Commander Joss? The commander wishes to see you at once."

He slapped dirt from his hands and checked his vest and trousers, everything in place, quiver buckled tight, baton and sword swinging from his belt, his pack slung over a shoulder. Was there dirt on his face? Was that why everyone was staring?

An escort accompanied him through camp, folk turning to watch. Women, wagon drivers, stopped stock-still and stared; one whistled boldly as Joss blushed and the soldiers snickered. The command awning had sprouted wings, and a pair of curtained private chambers, but the central area looked the same as ever: a long low table, many camp stools, soldiers and reeves clustered in a meeting. Two rings of black-clad Qin guards eyed him with various expressions of dismay except for the one local man who looked him up and down with a smirk of appreciative interest.

He recognized Kesta from the back; she turned, having heard the murmur following him, and took a step back. "Joss! The hells!"

He stepped under the central awning as Anji rose from his camp stool. The captain cocked his head, eyes narrowing as he examined Joss with the expression of a man who has just conceived an intense distrust, but he said nothing as Kesta strode forward and grabbed Joss by the arm.

"The hells! You went missing, and I didn't know— So I came to report— But that hierodule said she'd seen you before the battle's end— I didn't know—" Tears streaked her face.

He was panting, sweating, dizzy.

"Aui!" Kesta's grip burned on his bare arm. "You look ten years younger, Joss, and twice as handsome. If that's possible, which I would have doubted. What happened to you?"

He and Anji's gazes had locked. It wasn't, Joss thought, that Anji was envious of him, or that he desired Joss's looks or charm for himself. It was that Anji was sure that a man as handsome and charming as Joss must lure away any beautiful woman who is offered such a choice. Therefore, let a woman—let Mai—not be allowed to face temptation, not as his first wife had been, coaxed away by a handsome outlander.

Yet how is it possible to fence in temptation unless one controls every road and gate?

"Joss!" Kesta shook him with an impatient grimace born of years of friendship. "Have your wits been addled?"

Joss blinked, and after all, Anji looked like an ordinary man, bemused but concerned.

"Bring drink, and food," the captain ordered, and men ran off as Chief Deze and Chief Esigu moved up to flank Anji as though they wondered if Joss meant to strike. "Do you need to sit, Joss? You look dazed."

"I killed Lord Radas."

The words sucked out the last of his strength. His legs gave out, and Kesta tugged him up before he hit the ground; an instant later, a stool appeared and he sat hard, sagging forward, head in hands. Trampled grass was crushed beneath his boots. The leather of his boots looked oddly mottled, charred and flaking, as though he had walked through fire. Why hadn't he been burned? Marit had told him that anyone who tried to take a cloak off a Guardian would suffer terrible agonies. Masar had died.

A cup of cordial was thrust into view, and he downed it, the sharp flavor slamming straight into his head.

"Can you repeat that?" asked Anji.

"I killed Lord Radas. The lord commander is dead."

Within the stunned silence, commonplace noises rolled on: horses whickering; a fire crackling; fat sizzling; a knife being sharpened *whsst whsst*; a woman's cheerful whistle as she wound down the old familiar tune, "Oh to clasp a man like *that* in my arms!"

A guardsman poured more cordial into Joss's cup, and the tinkle of falling liquid shook him out of his daze.

He looked at Kesta. "Is there a fawkner here? Scar needs tending, his harness shed for the night. I just—"

"I'll take care of it." She released him. "I was just afraid something had happened to you, Joss. If that's all—killed the gods-rotted demon, the enemy commander—the hells! Wait until I tell the other reeves!" Her grin was as bright as a lamp. She swatted him on the shoulder, spoke a courtesy to Anji and his chiefs, and strode away into the gathering dusk.

"Where did it happen?" asked Anji in a low voice. "Where is his cloak?"

"At an altar right where the Istri splits at Kroke's Ridge. As for his cloak—"

He met Anji's gaze again, but it was only a man like himself who looked back, worn by days of travel and given strength by the ferocity of his determination. What kind of man was Anji, really? A man who had killed a Guardian and bound its cloak in chains because he thought thereby that he was saving the Hundred from the rule of demons. But the Guardians weren't demons, not as Anji defined demons. They were just men and women, who might do the wrong thing believing it was the right one, or the right one hoping for the wrong; they might rise to the best in themselves or fall into what was worst in their hearts. You could not choke justice into existence. It had to live in the bones of the land.

"On law shall the land be built. I released the cloak to the gods."

Anji's eyes narrowed, a flicker of anger that flashed like a blade's edge. Then his expression smoothed, and he took a step back as two soldiers came forward, bearing trays that they set down on the camp table beside the unrolled maps.

"Eat with me," said Anji, and yet the words sounded more like a command than a request.

"I'd like to know," said Joss, hearing words pour out of his mouth as impelled by a lilu he hadn't known dwelt inside him, "if you have some objection to what I did, considering you may have had other ideas of what would best serve the Hundred."

"My concern is solely to win this war. Lord Radas's death aids us. Your courage and determination are to be praised, Commander Joss."

The appreciative murmur that greeted these words reminded Joss that he and Anji were not alone. No, indeed; Anji sat at council with many men—all men, an odd enough sight to Joss's eye. Chiefs Sengel, Deze, and Esigu sat closest to Anji, flanked by Captain Targit and two Qin chiefs unknown to Joss. Captain Arras was sitting at his ease among several militia captains, two wearing the kroke badges common in Nessumara and another wearing Skerru's forked lightning. Arras leaned over and whispered something, at which they grinned. There were other captains: a pair wearing badges from Horn and six bearded men most likely from Olo'osson. No reeves. No merchants or artisans. Not a single priest. All military men.

A tiny jeweler's chest, bound with chains, sat tucked between Arras's feet.

Anji set down his cup. "And if Lord Radas is truly dead, then we have a significant hope of victory." He broke off, his gaze catching on movement behind Joss.

Reeves approached, caught by the gatekeepers before they could come too close, but a stockier man striding in their wake pushed between them.

Joss leaped up with a grin. "Tohon!"

Sengel stepped forward on one side, Deze on the other, like shields. Tohon's gaze flicked from one to the other, assessing their movement and his risk, but his jaw had a determined jut that made Joss step aside, making space for him.

"Did you find Wedrewe?" Anji asked casually. Yet his own cursed chiefs subtly shifted position as if they had some notion that Tohon—Tohon!—might be a threat.

"I did. Commander, I hear you've found Shai. That he's grievously injured."

"We've recovered him. He lives. After you give your report—"

"I'll see him now," said Tohon in a friendly tone no man could possibly misunderstand. "My report can wait, if the lad is doing so poorly that, as I heard as I walked through camp, it's rumored he's like to die. Where is he?"

Sengel coughed as might a man reminding a comrade he's forgotten his manners, but Tohon's gaze was fixed on Anji and did not waver.

Anji gestured to one of the curtained chambers. "The hierodule is nursing him."

"That's something," muttered Tohon. He nodded a greeting at Joss, then looked again, as taken aback as a man might be to wake and discover his wife has become a kroke. "What happened to you?" The words were only a reflex. His brow creased; a frown darkened his expression as his thoughts scouted elsewhere. He walked to the curtains and vanished within. It had grown so silent under the awning that Joss heard the murmur of voices, male and female, as Tohon and Zubaidit greeted each other, but he could not make out what they were saying.

"Commander?" asked Sengel, so softly Joss heard the word only because he was standing next to Anji.

"We've no proof he's anything but Beje's man," replied Anji, equally softly. "Not my mother's. Not my uncle's. He's served faithfully enough. Let it be for now." He picked up his cup, gesturing to the captains. "Now. About our lines of supply. We must not strip what remains in the countryside and the towns lest the population starve. Our task is twofold. Obviously, we must hunt down and destroy the remnants of Lord Radas's army, any companies or captains who might dream of restoring the army. This could take months, or even years. But we cannot achieve these objectives if those we've fought to protect die. People are afraid to return to their villages. Supplies are low everywhere. Reserves are depleted. People cannot plant until the rains, and then must hope for an uneventful growing season while waiting for the crops to ripen."

"So you're saying we'll be eating a lot of se leaves?" asked one of the Olossi captains, and men chuckled.

" 'Better to live on sour se leaves than die with your hand in an empty rice bowl,' " Anji replied to approving laughter, having learned at least one common Hundred saying. "Even if all that goes well, which it will not, for you can be sure no battle plan survives contact with the enemy, then what about Wedrewe? Captain Arras?"

Arras rose. If some regarded him with suspicion, the rest waited to hear what he had to say. "Wedrewe is where all the orders came from, although I never went there myself. More cohorts will be training there, and I'm cursed sure all the coin and precious loot and best silks were sent there, so no doubt they guard a healthy treasury. There's also Walshow. That's where many cohorts were raised, including mine. It's isolated, hard to reach, and easy for folk to scatter into the wilderness and hide should they be attacked."

Arras kept a foot pressed against the jeweler's chest, keeping track of what was, after all, the prize that had earned him Anji's acceptance.

Anji was standing next to the table, his own boots blocking a gap where two small jeweler's chests bound by chains rested under the table. Joss's heart took a sudden lurch; he sank down on his stool as flashes of memory blinded and deafened him: the billowing cloak as bright as sunlight; Lord Radas's limp body; the way one arm, stuck in rigor, had seemed impossible to cover with dirt, fingers clutching for air as Joss had ruthlessly buried him.

"We cannot relax our vigilance," Anji was saying. "Only six of the demons have been killed, while three remain at large." He loosed a glance at Joss. "The cloak of Sun will rise to corrupt another man, who can take control of remnants of the army."

"Hold on," murmured Joss. "I only know of four." Anji had killed Earth; Masar had unclasped Blood; Shai and Zubaidit had killed Night and given the cloak to Arras. Joss had released Sun. "How did there get to be six? We agreed no hunting beyond those allied with Radas and Night."

Anji was in many ways an ordinary-looking man, if you surveyed what appeared on the surface: Of medium height and neither slender or stocky, he was strong with the fitness that comes from constant relentless movement. He had the broad cheekbones of his mother's people and the hooked nose common in the empire. But the land cannot be understood with so cursory an inspection. Nor could a man. Handsome eyes redeemed his face, but that was not what commanded the eye. His gaze was as bright as steel, and it penetrated not to your heart or mind, as the gaze of Guardians did, but to your gut, where you decided not just whether to trust this man but whether to place your life and welfare in his hands. He had powerful hands, not big but graceful and masterful, a man who held on to what he possessed and never let go.

Once Anji got hold of the Hundred, why should he let go? The Qin soldiers were conquerors, weren't they? That's what they trained from boyhood to be. Brutal. Effective. Relentless. Utterly reasonable, with those cheerful grins and easy laughs.

Anji's gaze narrowed as he studied Joss studying him. "I haven't finish briefing my captains," he said as Sengel took a step closer to Joss. "Did you have a report the officers need to hear, Commander?"

Maybe such thoughts were crazy, an artifact of walking the altar. Maybe Lord Radas's poison was corrupting his mind. Maybe he was just exhausted after two days without sleep. "I need to talk to you privately. After your council. For now, I'd welcome a chance to rest."

"Sengel will show you to where the reeves are camping," said Anji.

Sengel smiled that easy Qin smile and walked away with Joss as if they were old comrades accustomed to walking out in company.

"You did well in Nessumara," said Joss.

"I did what needed doing," remarked Sengel.

"There are three chests under the awning. Wasn't one already taken to Olossi?"

"Toughid died in High Haldia getting the cloak off a demon calling himself Lord Bevard."

"Toughid!" It was impossible to grasp that Toughid, with whom he'd so recently argued—as much as you could argue with the Qin, who receded before disagreement until you realized you had nothing to push against—was *dead*.

Sengel's stride betrayed no weakness. His expression betrayed no sentiment. "The chest arrived midday soon after our victory. Here are your reeves, including the ones who brought the chest." He gestured toward an encampment set up within the boundary of a shallow ditch and berm, dug in haste by Lord Radas's soldiers. "I'll return to Captain Anji."

"One question, Chief Sengel."

"What's that?"

"Whyever would you think Tohon could be your enemy?"

The man blinked, taken by surprise. "Tohon?"

"Just because a man expresses a desire to look in on a badly injured comrade before he gives a report doesn't mean he's not a loyal soldier."

Sengel brushed a hand over his creased brow, and Joss realized the man was likely exhausted, held under a taut rein. "Commander Joss, with all respect, you do not understand the factions within the Qin. Nor are we likely to explain them. For we're not in Qin lands anymore, are we?"

"Are we?" Joss asked sharply.

At once, he was sorry he had spoken so recklessly. Sengel smiled with a grace and speed that was frightening. How could you tell if a man was sincere when he could smile like that no matter what you said to him?

"I'll leave you with your reeves," Sengel said. "Commander Anji will come by later to offer thanks for their good work. And to let you know what needs doing tomorrow."

With that, he walked away.

Lord Bevard, wearing the cloak of Leaf. That still only made five.

Joss scrambled down to a makeshift encampment where about forty off-duty reeves had set up awnings. They were a mix of people he knew and others he did not, mingling with the comfortable familiarity of folk who did the same work and knew the man or woman standing beside them would understand their complaints.

"Joss! The hells! What happened to you?" Peddonon strode forward with a big grin. "You look like a gods-rotted lilu come to lure us to our deaths, although in a most pleasurable manner, I am sure. Die with a smile on your face, that's what I say."

Reeves slapped him on the back or embraced him, as they chose. Even sharp-tongued Nallo looked not displeased to see him. She might even have looked startled.

"Cordial for the man who killed that gods-rotted lilu, Lord Radas," called Peddonon.

Cheers and whoops rose. Reeves he didn't know grasped his arm. One attractive young woman offered a juicy kiss, which made everyone shout with laughter.

"The hells!" laughed Joss, pulling away as he felt the stirring of an all too familiar arousal. "Cordial for everyone."

But as they filled their cups from a barrel, he frowned. Looking around, he discovered a small chest—not one bound with chains but simply a chest in which a man or woman might store coin or jewelry or spices—cast aside in one of the ditches. Spoils of war. He hoisted it up and slapped it down on the ground under the shade of one of the awnings.

"Heya, all of you! Sit down!"

They weren't as disciplined as Anji's troops. They grabbed cordial and passed around a basket of whiteheart, whose ripe shells could be pried apart for the fragrant, sweet flesh within. Sucking down the juice and licking grimy fingers, they shouldered aside their friends with jokes and roughhousing and settled cross-legged on shared blankets or slapped hindquarters straight on the churned-up dirt. They were all dusty, stained, sweaty, and smelling of days without a decent bath. They were reeves, and that was a reeve's life.

"You lot have a reek about you," he said, to general laughter, "which means you've been out serving justice again. I've got a nose for it."

"How did you get to be so cursed handsome?" shouted one wag, a male.

A woman called, "Sleep with me tonight, eh? I've a friend in Copper Hall might join us."

Joss grinned. "I'll tell you my secret if you'll quiet down a moment and listen. For listen you must. We all must listen."

His tone caught them. They were weary, but feeling their victory in their bones, and the combination opened a path from their ears into their hearts.

"We are fortunate, jessed as we are. It's a hard life, truly. In a way, you leave your family behind, even if you can always drop in on them. I won't tell you that the reeves become your new clan, for it's a tired old saying, isn't it? Yet here we are. We're camping together, eating together, drinking together. We know who we are, whether we're from Clan Hall, Horn Hall, Copper Hall."

"I'm up from Naya Hall," called the attractive young woman who had kissed him. "Don't you recall me, Commander Joss? I saw you bathing that one time, naked but for the kilt and with it being wet and all, it didn't hide much. As I recall, you had quite an audience."

Peddonon whistled; folk would laugh, and yet he was used to the admiration; he knew how to throw it in his favor.

"I'd happily toss a bucketful of cold water over my head again if I can just get people to quiet down and listen." They were finally settling, the heat and the sure knowledge of a hard-fought fight that had ended in victory relaxing them as the sun sank toward the horizon. Soon dusk would come and, exhausted, they would sleep. Strike while the chance is upon you.

"The reeves have served the Hundred, as we always have. Today we've been part of a victory over an army whose cruelties have scarred the north. But let's not lose sight of what happens after victory."

"We haven't won yet!" called one of the Copper Hall reeves. "Commander Anji says as long as the enemy poses a threat, we must keep pursuing them! We must keep fighting!"

Joss shook his head. "Are we meant to be just another cohort in the army? Or to be reeves?"

"What does that matter as long as there are remnants of the army running and hiding?" objected the young man as his companions nodded to support him. "There are cohorts still training in this place called Wedrewe, up in Herelia. I saw them."

"Wedrewe must be dealt with," Joss agreed, "but I want you to think a moment about the remnants of the Star of Life army. Who are they, really? Yesterday I fought hand-to-hand a sergeant in Lord Radas's army."

"Who won?" called the Naya Hall lass.

"Do you even need to ask?" They laughed, and he waved them to silence. "He reminded me of certain men in the village where I grew up. It's easy for a man to set a foot on the wrong path, to walk crooked out of anger or grief or greed. Those men are like dogs lost in the woods. But they aren't our enemy. They're our brothers and cousins. In different circumstances, they might have been ourselves. We made them because we didn't pay attention while the world fell apart around us. Some can be lured back and make restitution, rebuild a life, and some just can't. But those who can't are criminals. They should be treated as the criminals they are. They should be arrested and brought before the assizes to answer for their crimes. The assizes is the rightful place for these matters, not a single commander. For think of what a powerfully dangerous thing it would be if one man can pass judgment according to the strength of his will? Isn't that exactly what Lord Radas was doing? Isn't that exactly what the corrupted cloaks did, who hammered stars out of tin and gave them to their followers to wear? Do we want to become like them? Or do we want to restore justice? Maybe to make some changes—yes—" He nodded at the Copper Hall reeves who seemed about to object again. "Yes, we need a new halls council—"

"With you sitting over us all as commander, no doubt," accused one of the Copper Hall reeves, a curly-haired youth with a scar on his chin and, evidently, a chip on his shoulder. "I've heard stories of you and the trouble you got into back when you were my age."

Joss grinned. "You haven't heard half of it, then!" The lad ventured an answering grin, piqued by curiosity. But Joss sobered. "Listen, I don't care about being commander of the reeve halls. The reeve halls must call a council no matter what. They must debate what changes to institute, how to reconstitute the assizes here in the north, how to rebuild the halls and train the many new reeves. How to repair the damage left by the slaughter of Horn Hall's reeves." They were absolutely silent, every one of them, intent on his words. "Every hall must send representatives to meet. It's this council that will elect a new commander. Of course we must be vigilant. We must be vigilant on behalf of the law, for we must never allow the law to be corrupted by those who might claim to—"

He broke off, sensing movement to his left.

Anji stood on the berm, flanked by Sengel and Deze. How long had he been listening?

Seeing Joss had noticed him, Anji walked in among the reeves with the confidence of a man who knows his place. They rose to greet him, and he moved through the group speaking to each individual, maybe asking to see a baton or spinning an arrow through his fingers as he listened to an impassioned tale whose sketched gestures told of a skirmish. He gathered smiles and nods and flushed, excited expressions in return for his attention.

Joss settled beside Peddonon. "Where's Pil?"

Dear Peddonon. He blushed a lover's blush, and it made him look fresh and sweet. "I left all my flights resting at Law Rock according to your orders, including Pil. But I wanted Nallo to give a personal report to Commander Anji, which she did. She was there when Chief Toughid was killed by the demon. I came with her to make my own assessment of the situation. To ask after you. Things are quiet in Toskala. Ostiary Nekkar has the council well in hand."

Joss sheared off in search of Nallo. She stood to one side, watching the sun set. "Heya, Nallo."

"An impressive speech, Commander, even if you didn't get to finish it," she said tartly. She glanced at the Qin soldiers still chatting with reeves. She had fire enough to burn; she just hadn't learned how to use it, as blacksmiths did, to forge something more powerful out of the raw and malleable earth. "I listened to every word. I'm thinking about it."

"Joss!" Anji strolled over, marked Nallo, and nodded gravely. "Reeve Nallo. We spoke earlier. Is there anything else you need?"

"I've done my duty, Commander. I'll keep doing it."

He raised an eyebrow, hearing an edge in her words that might imply the woman disliked him. But it was difficult to tell with Nallo, because she always sounded like that. Then Anji turned to Joss. "I thought you'd want to hear Tohon's report on Wedrewe. Shai is sleeping, and Tohon sees no need to wake him. Will you accompany me? We can talk on the way."

His smile was a beacon. Aui! Joss liked this man; he liked him very well. But he no longer trusted him.

"Of course I want to hear Tohon's report. I've never met a more skilled scout."

"He was a rare gift from Commander Beje," agreed Anji.

"Who is Commander Beje?"

"A Qin officer of princely birth, a good man. I was married to his daughter."

"Had you a first wife?" said Joss, startled by this confidence. "I didn't know." And had his first wife abandoned him in favor of a handsome outlander? Better not to ask.

Anji squinted into the sun drenched west toward eagles, although the light made it hard to tell if they were approaching or flying parallel to the river on patrol. "The past is dead to me."

The men scrambled up a berm and walked, using the height to survey the encampment as the light turned the amber that presaged dusk. Most men were already sleeping, exhausted from the days of forced march and the battle. Those who were still awake were scraping the last bits of rice or nai from big bowls. A pair of enterprising young women—where in the hells had they come from?—had set up a slip-fry stand, but it seemed they had sold all their food and were now just chatting merrily with a crowd of admirers.

A crew from Nessumara was still pitching corpses into the river, but the men from Anji's army who had been killed were being hauled aside and piled on wagons and carts so they could be conveyed to a Sorrowing Tower and given a proper ceremony. There weren't as many as Joss had expected; Radas's army had taken the brunt of the casualties.

"What do you Qin do with your dead, Anji?"

"If we're at war, we leave them. Once the spirit is fled, the body is only a husk. If in camp, the women have their own rites."

"And in the empire?"

"In the empire, the Beltak priests control all passages, birth, death, marriage, fealty between master and servant. They take a tithe at the market, and collect tolls on the roads and at every gate."

"A fence against every manner of temptation," said Joss more sharply than he intended.

"A knife," said Anji, "with which to protect themselves."

"A knife is a useful tool, but in the hands of a drunk man or one who minds only his own greed, it is a dangerous weapon."

"Therefore we keep knives out of the hands of those we cannot trust to wield them wisely."

"Six cloaks you said, Anji. But I count only five."

"Did I forget to mention? The cloak of Twilight is the sixth. Here we are."

The council of captains had been dismissed, and in its place Joss found himself alone among Qin officers, a single Olossi militia captain, and the hierophant Joss had seen before. The Lantern priest was holding a charcoal stick and tracing lines according to Tohon's directions: Here. No, to the right. Erase that bit. Yes, down that way.

Anji, Sengel, and Deze strolled up to the table as the guardsmen who had followed him around camp fell back to join the ring of guards. A soldier stood beside each stout pole that held up the awning, and two men guarded the curtained entrance off under the right-hand wing of the awning.

The men pressed up to the table, all but Sengel settling into stools as Tohon drank cordial.

Two reeves hurried up, escorted by guards. "Our apologies for keeping you waiting, Commander," said the curly-headed youth with a scar on his chin.

"If you three will report on your observations, we'll listen and ask questions." Anji offered the reeves stools and gave Tohon his whip to point with.

The reeves deferred to Tohon, offering asides only when he could not explain or had missed some typical local object or tree or landmark. They had flown above the Istri Walk to Toskala and thence along the Ili Cutoff and across the vale of Iliyat to the Liya Pass.

"That's Candle Rock," Joss said when they described a high sanctuary where they'd camped for the night. "You can see Ammadit's Tit from the rock. It's a Guardian's altar. And that abandoned compound you saw, on the way up? That was once a temple to Ushara, although it was popularly supposed that they trained assassins there. There was a woodsmen's encampment near there, although it's likely long since grown over. That's where Reeve Marit and her eagle Flirt were killed. Theirs are the first known deaths definitely linked to Lord Radas. I think it might have been the first cadre of his army."

The curtained entrance off to one side swayed, and a woman ducked out. Tohon smiled, making room for her, but she snagged a stool, walked around the table as if to peruse the map from all angles before she fetched up, quite as if by accident, next to Joss. She set down the stool and herself in it. Her hip pressed against his. She leaned over the low table, one of her breasts brushing his arm as she used the hilt of a knife to tap the spot on the map he'd just been discussing.

"The temple of Ushara was attacked and all its hierodules and kalos murdered." She straightened, setting the knife back to hold down a curling corner. "The many hieros across the land have never let any hierodule or kalos forget it, either. Didn't you ever hear the rest of the story, Reeve Joss? They found a young hierodule—barely fourteen—chained to a death willow and raped and abused, as if to spit on the generosity of the Devouring One. She was dead, a knife to the heart."

"I was one of those who found her corpse," said Joss so quietly that everyone looked at him. "Which is a moment I will never forget as long as I live. As you say, a knife to the heart."

The words had an odd effect on Anji, whose gaze had drifted past Joss toward a movement in camp beyond the awning. His expression tightened in a puzzled frown, then opened to a look of sheer violent falling helplessness as he recognized what he was looking at. He leaped to his feet, his stool tipping and falling behind him. He fisted a hand and for one breath Joss could have sworn Anji swayed as though he had taken a knife to the heart. Sengel caught his arm. Stepping sideways, shaking off Sengel, he strode around the table and out from under the awning. Joss twisted to see.

Out of the dusk settling its wings over the encampment limped Chief Tuvi carrying a bundle in his arms. Neh, no bundle but a living, squirming baby. Tuvi was carrying Anji's son.

Joss stood, intending to follow, but Chief Esigu blocked him. Sengel and Deze trotted up on either side of Anji as Anji halted in front of Tuvi and engulfed the baby in his arms. Tuvi's lips moved, speaking words Joss was too far away to hear.

Sengel and Deze grabbed Anji under the elbows, and Tuvi swept the child back. The two chiefs held their captain as his legs gave way.

Had the wind failed? For it seemed the entire camp was holding its breath, taking in the news with the captain, still supported by his senior officers.

Kesta and Peddonon jogged out of the dusk, circling wide around the knot of Qin, who stopped Peddonon at a distance but allowed Kesta to hurry up to the awning.

She grasped Joss's arm, pulling him aside. "Siras flew Chief Tuvi in from the Barrens. The captain's wife was murdered up the Spires, that place they call Merciful Valley."

"Murdered?" As well say the sky was green, or that folk preferred bread to rice given the choice. "Who would murder Mai?" Beautiful, clever Mai. *The Ox walks with feet of clay, but its heart leaps to the heavens where it seeks the soul which fulfills it.*

"One of her slaves stabbed her. Siras says she fell into the pool, and her body was lost in the depths beneath the falls. Maybe that makes sense to you." She caught him as he sat heavily, almost tipping over the stool.

Siras came running, but Qin soldiers halted him beside Peddonon as the chiefs steered Anji in under the awning and sat him down on his stool beside the camp table.

"How did she outflank me?" Anji asked, the question all the more wrenching for his even tone, like he was asking for a report on the weather.

"She had an agent in your midst all along, that slave named Sheyshi," said Tuvi. "None of us suspected. The girl played her part, and none of us suspected all that time."

"Commander Beje must have known."

"That Sheyshi was your mother's agent? It's likely. That your mother would strike through the slave? How could any Qin man guess? There was nothing you could have done, Anjihosh. The princess was caged in the women's palace for many years. She is far more skilled on this battlefield than you or I. She defeated you with a superior flanking movement."

"I should have known," said Anji as he reached for a knife that Chief Deze snatched up before Anji could touch it. Anji went on as if he had not noticed, hands splayed open on the careful detailed lines of the map. "I should have suspected. Mai is the sharpest knife a man could hope to possess. The biggest threat to my mother's power. I should have brought Mai with me, never let her leave my side—" His hands fisted. He bent as in a gust of wind, and his eyes lost focus. A sound more gasp than moan strangled in his throat.

The baby had begun to noisily fuss, wanting his father, and Tuvi thrust the angry child onto Anji's lap, anything to take that stunned blank expression off the captain's face.

Joss had known these feelings once. Nothing would make the killing blow easier to absorb; nothing could ease the searing pain. Only the baby, who demanded his father's attention by beginning to cry.

"What have you been feeding him?" asked Anji in a harsh, hoarse voice.

"Goat's milk and nai porridge," said Tuvi. Revealed in lantern light, his face and hands were netted with scars, as though he had plunged into a burning spider's web. He stood awkwardly, and when a soldier brought a stool, sat gingerly as if every movement was agony. Yet his his gaze was bent on his captain as Chief Deze sent soldiers to find goat's milk and nai porridge. Anji soothed the child by speaking in another language, the words flowing like a chant. His expression was scoured raw; his eyes flared white, like a spooked horse, and yet, every time he ceased speaking even for a moment, his jaw clenched as tight as if he were choking down a scream.

Kesta patted Joss's shoulder and jerked her chin toward the spot where Siras was confined between a pair of watchful soldiers. Joss stepped away from the table. Sengel glanced at him, nodding to acknowledge his leave-taking, but Anji did not look up nor did Tuvi register their departure. He hadn't looked at Joss once.

Siras was bouncing on his toes as Joss walked up with Kesta. "The hells, Commander! What happened to you? You look gods-rotted younger, or something."

The Qin soldiers delicately stepped away, one lifting a hand to show they were moving off now, no trouble.

"Keep walking," muttered Joss.

Soldiers approached the awning with bowls and bottles and by lamplight Anji bent over his son to coax food into the squalling visage as his chiefs gave orders for the night's sentries. The four reeves strode away, Kesta leading them toward the river's shore where they might hope to find some privacy.

"What in the hells happened?"

"The captain sent Mistress Mai and a few attendants and guards to Merciful Valley. To keep her safe while he went on campaign."

"From the red hounds? Those Sirniakan spies?"

Siras shrugged. "The rumor runs that the captain's mother had Mai killed."

"The hells! That's what Chief Tuvi implied. Why would his mother kill his wife?"

"She brought a Sirniakan princess from the empire. She wanted him to marry the outlander, but he refused."

"So she killed Mai? How in the hells would that serve to persuade her son to marry the woman she'd chosen for him? Aui! How can anyone understand outlanders? Is this what we have to hope for?"

"To hope for what?" asked Kesta.

"Not here," said Joss, lowering his voice. They walked awhile until they reached the low bluffs that ran along the western channel. It was impossible to penetrate the river's layers, the surface glitter, the streaming deeps, the muddied eddies where sticks washed up. This conflict was like the river. They thought they were fighting a single war, when in fact multiple wars were raging around and above and beneath their feet, unseen but nevertheless permeating the land until the Hundred overflowed with hostilities.

"Lord Radas is dead."

"Thanks to you," said Kesta.

He shrugged, shaking off the compliment. "Anji and his army have defeated major contingents of Lord Radas's army."

"Thanks be to the gods," said Peddonon with a fierce sigh.

"Meanwhile, there remain remnants of that army wandering in the countryside, an outpost at Walshow, and headquarters at Wedrewe in Herelia. Why can't Anji just take over the entire apparatus and stand as—what do the Qin call their ruler?— stand as *var* over the Hundred, with an army he trained and which is loyal to him to enforce his will."

The river's voice had the clarity his own lacked. The danger seemed so cursed obvious to him. How easy it was to cross under the gate of shadows, never knowing you passed the threshold of corruption until it was too late to turn back.

"Joss," said Kesta in the voice of an auntie who is about to tell you that the woman you're hankering after just isn't interested no matter how many smiles and songs and silk scarves you ply her with, "don't you think you're spinning a tale out of your own fears? Have you thought maybe you're a bit envious? I admit I've been startled by how quickly Commander Anji and his chiefs have taken to giving orders to the reeve halls, but hasn't it worked? Aren't we at the threshold of victory, after all the terrible things we've seen?"

"When in the hells," Joss demanded, "did everyone stop calling him 'Captain'? This isn't about being commander of the reeve halls. For sure I never wanted the position, and if we can ever get the reeve halls to meet in council, then I'll be glad to follow a new commander. But tell me this, Kesta." He grabbed a rock off the ground and pitched it toward the river, waiting until he heard, like an echo of his doubts, its hollow splash. "If the reeve halls met today in council, if Anji stood up before them with his eloquence and persuasiveness and his good-humored smiles, what makes you think they wouldn't elect *him*?"

49

SHAI WAS CONSCIOUS, and he was hurting, and his ears were filled with voices that nagged as stubbornly as young nieces and nephews wanting a ride on his broad shoulders.

How do I get home? Can you tell me?

I never wanted to march with the army. But it was cursed sweet to have my belly full every cursed day, eh? I don't feel hungry at all now.

Aui! It hurts! I'm scared!

Gods-rotted cowards, falling back like that. If only we'd listened to—

Ghosts plagued him, worse than a horde of nieces and nephews because there was nothing he could do for them. He wanted to shout "I can't help you!" but he had no throat, no tongue, no mouth. Sand had been poured over raw flesh and rubbed in until he was a single screaming wound.

Cursed if he would cry about it. Others had endured worse. This was only physical pain.

"Out!"

The voice rang strong, startling in its fury. The whispers snapped out, the ghosts fleeing as Shai took a breath, although even a simple breath hurt, scouring his lungs.

Yet he was still not alone. Two voices disturbed his peace.

"Now we talk, Captain Arras, here in this private place where no one will disturb us. Just you and me. I have a sword, and you have no weapon but your wits. Zubaidit served my army well, so as a favor to her I did not kill your soldiers or you immediately, although I could have. I have accepted the cloak you brought as an offering, and I'm appreciative that you have hauled this man Shai to my camp. I have allowed you to sit in my council and pretend to be my loyal officer. But you're not. You're a traitor."

"I would argue it was Lord Radas who betrayed me and the soldiers who served him."

"Go on."

"The truth, Commander, is that I joined up with Lord Radas's people because I was an ordinand of Kotaru who got into some trouble and I had no where else to go. I didn't kill anyone, mind you, nor abuse those weaker than me, as some men will do if they can get away with it. But those who commanded in Kotaru's temple didn't like my attitude, and I didn't like their incompetence. I sought scope for my talents. I served in Seven's militia for a while, and that worked out all right, they are decent people there, except I wasn't a local man and only local men got raised to positions of command. So then some men came recruiting, and what they promised sounded good to my ears. I came in as a sergeant and soon got rewarded with a company and later a cohort of my own. I had hopes of really doing something when we started our campaign. But as it turned out, Lord Radas was just as incompetent as my other commanders had been, in his own way. I suppose I thought a cloak who could rip out the hearts and minds of those who opposed him would be a better commander than ordinary fellows, but I guess after all that the magic a Guardian bears is meant only for the assizes, not the battlefield. The cursed cloak could look right into my heart, and steal my understanding of the tactics and strategy that would have worked best for the army, and still he made one bad decision after the next."

"Will you judge me incompetent in my turn, and seek a bolder and more intelligent commander?"

"Is there one?" The question was not meant to flatter.

"Here, in the Hundred? I doubt it." The answer was not a wishful boast. "But will you betray me in turn? People do it all the time, as I know to my cost."

"An impossible question, because I have to deny it to win your trust. So, listen, Commander. I'm willing to suffer under your suspicion until I prove myself. I've no ambition to rule a vast army. I just want a cursed command that means something. I want it to matter that my men are well trained, and that I usually know what I'm doing. That my sergeants and subcaptains are competent soldiers who can be rewarded with higher command, if such comes open. Do what you must to prove to yourself that I'll serve you. I'm patient. I'll do what I must."

The other man laughed, a bark of anger. "Until I give you an order you don't respect?"

"If you're the kind of commander I think you are, you'll never give me an order I don't respect."

"You think a lot of yourself, Captain Arras."

The man chuckled. "Someone must. I'll do what I can to make you think well of me. Even if you do kill me now, having decided I'm not trustworthy, I'd ask you to spare my soldiers. Let them serve you. They're disciplined and loyal. They never betrayed their captain, did they? I'd hate to see them suffer for my decision, as I and they have suffered from the idiot decisions of our former commanders."

"A captain is only as strong as his soldiers."

"I'll offer you one more thing. A piece of advice that comes with this small gift. Handle it carefully."

"A hollow pipe, thorns, and—this?—some milky liquid."

"Don't open that. In the Wild lives a snake called a two-stepper. That is its venom. If it pricks you, you have two steps before you're dead. This venom is deadly enough to kill a cloak. I knew a person like Zubaidit would be hiding weapons. Sergeant Giyara searched her thoroughly. If Zubaidit is *your* loyal servant, then you're well served. But if she's not yours, then I'd consider her a very dangerous weapon. Best you hope that the one who controls her doesn't decide to go after you."

"I appreciate your words, Captain Arras. They're wisely spoken. Even I can be outflanked." The speaker's voice rasped with such a ragged edge that Shai moaned as if the tone were scraping him where he was raw.

"Call Tohon. He's stirring. Captain Arras, be assured I have my own defenses and weapons. You may become one of them. Serve me ill, and you'll fall hard and fast and dead. Serve me well, and you'll find yourself rewarded." A clap shattered the air. "Let Tohon in. Captain Arras, you're dismissed."

Shai's hearing had become painfully acute. Boots scraped on dirt. A man was breathing swift and shallow as if he'd come running. A musty, dusty sweat of bracing familiarity breathed across Shai's nostrils, and he turned his head like a blind man rooting for treasure.

Was it truly Tohon?

"Here, now, son. Can you open your eyes? Raise a hand to show you hear me?" A touch as soft as wind brushed his fever-dampened hair. "If you don't mind, Captain Anji, would you hand me the bowl? My thanks."

Gentle fingers dabbed a cooling infusion onto his burning skin, starting on his face and working down his neck and onto his bare shoulders and chest.

"You treat him as tenderly as you would a son."

"I miss my sons and daughter. Whether they're dead or living now, which I can't know—except for the girl, of course, and the lad I know was killed in the wars—I miss them. A man likes to have a child around, as you must be well aware of at this moment, Captain Anji."

What cools at first touch may turn to a blaze of heat. Pain flared across his body as though he were being smothered in a cloak of fire. Someone drew a sword.

"Did Commander Beje and Lady Cherfa plan Mai's death all along in concert with my mother?"

"Put down the sword, Captain, or stab me in the back after I'm done here." The voice soothed, not wavering. Nor did the hands falter, spreading the healing infusion down Shai's raw, aching legs. "I'm Commander Beje's man, serving at his order. He ordered me to serve you, so I did. I'm a Qin soldier, Captain. Not a red hound or an agent of the Sirniakan women's palace. I'm not even a slave to Beje's wife Cherfa."

A sword hissed back into its sheath. "What did you know about Sheyshi?"

"Hu! If it's true what they say, she fooled us all, for I thought her the most lame-witted female I'd ever encountered. Although now I think about it, looking back over ground I already scouted, I missed what was obvious. She was always skulking around, wasn't she, pretending to drop things or forget what she was doing? She let us believe she was stupid, and that made us stupid, didn't it? Seeing the face without ever trying to look behind it. No, I didn't suspect her. But I suppose Commander Beje knew what she was and placed her in your troop at his wife's request."

"Why would he do that?"

"Surely you know, Captain, that Beje and Cherfa have been your mother's allies from a long way back. It's he who helped her get you out of the empire when you were twelve. It's she who gave you their daughter to wed, to give you status in court when your uncle the var meant to belittle you, even if it didn't work out with the woman in the end. It's he who warned you that your uncle was out to kill you, wasn't it? He—or his wife—intercepted a messenger out of one of those desert towns, some widow's grandson. They knew beforehand what your uncle intended. He had time to set his snare. He sent me to intercept you and guide you to him, so he could warn you. That he placed your mother's agent with your troop certainly couldn't have been to threaten *you*. All your mother the princess has ever done has been to protect you, her only son. The slave was just one more knife at your service."

Anji's breathing had gentled as a horse's might, being walked after a bruising gallop. The sting of fiery pain along Shai's skin lessened. He tried to open his eyes, but a sticky paste held them shut. He tried to move his fingers, but he couldn't feel his hands.

"She outflanked me," Anji whispered.

"What will you do now, Captain?"

"We're still fighting a war. Tomorrow, Tohon, I'll need you to—"

"With all respect, Captain," said the scout in a mild tone as cooling as the infusion he'd finished laying on, "I'll not be going anywhere, nor will this lad. I've arranged for a bed in Skerru so he doesn't have to be moved. He needs not to be moved, if he's going to live. I've given you my report. There's others who can scout for you—"

"All those reeves, you mean, who might yet fly off at a word from their handsome but rebellious commander just when I need them most. You're my best scout, Tohon."

"But I'm not your only scout, Captain. Now that Mistress Mai is dead, for which I truly grieve, for she was a fine woman, I am this young man's only family. Hu! There was something about an uncle, wasn't there? Uncle Hari?"

"No." Anji's reply was a knife in the heart. "There is no Uncle Hari. And Mai is gone." The word broke; the heart shattered; the world wept. "For her sake and in her memory, then. Stay with him and make sure he lives."

*   *   *

ZUBAIDIT WALKED BEYOND the ring of Qin guards to an open stretch of ground. The camp was held hostage under the uncertain grip of Commander Anji's temper. Would he break down and weep? Strike out in anger? How strong was his self-discipline? She'd never in fact met his wife, the woman whose beauty all praised and whose intelligence was manifest in how often she had outnegotiated her rivals and how quickly she had woven her husband's Qin soldiers into the intricate network of kinship and obligation that was clan life in the Hundred.

Bai had had a clan once, but they'd forfeited her loyalty when they'd sold her to the temple. How she had hated the old bitch who ruled in Ushara's garden, even while respecting the woman's devotion to the Merciless One. Yet walking away from the temple after Keshad had freed her, she had realized she could never walk away from the goddess. Once she accepted this, every decision became simple. Die in the service of the goddess? Of course, if it proved necessary. Live? Then she would do so, if that's what was needed.

After so many months trapped in a guise worthy of one of Hasibal's actors, Zubaidit embraced the prayers she had been so long denied because to pray would be to reveal the truth of what she was: one of Ushara's devourers, devoted to life, death, and desire, sent as assassin and spy into the enemy's camp. As lamps flickered among the shelters and campfires burned where a few soldiers still retold their stories of the day's fighting, she stamped the rhythm with her feet and sketched the story with hands as she sang.

> "*The Four Mothers raised the heavens and shaped the earth,*
> *and then they slumbered.*
> *and then they grew large.*
> *and then they gave birth.*
> *The seven gods are their children,*
> *who brought order into the world.*
> *who built the gates that order the world . . .*
> *and thus Shining Gate rose and Shadow Gate rose.*
> *Thus day and night gave order to the world.*
> *Look at the horizon! A voice calls.*
> *Shadow Gate rises.*
> *Night is come.*"

He approached through the darkness, footsteps quick on the earth. He was not the man she was waiting for, but he was the one she had been expecting.

"Captain Anji. Or is it Commander, now? That's what I hear folk calling you."

He dismissed this trivial banter with a curt wave. She wouldn't have thought this man had a temper, but she could see it in the creases of his narrowed gaze and in the way his mouth was shut as if he was holding back a scream of thwarted fury.

"We may have won a victory here," he said, "but the war is far from over. We've accounted for eight cohorts, but Lord Radas and the cloak of Night raised fifteen cohorts. Even if we win another battle or two, how many will be left skulking in the woodlands and the hills, starving and without cordial or rice wine to slake their thirst? Hungry, you see, without the least scrap of remorse or control? What of them? What if the cloak of Sun, so recklessly released by Reeve Joss, raises another demon? One with less arrogance and more cunning? More discipline and less vanity? How do we protect ourselves against such eventualities if we can't work together to make sure the cloaks are bound, so they cannot be used as weapons against us? If we who command the Hundred cannot even agree that the cloaked demons are our enemies?"

Overhead, the stars bloomed in profusion, like festival lamps. The churned earth was settling, but smoke from the forest fires tainted the air. A person might dart out her tongue, like the ginny lizards, and taste blood spilled in the past and blood yet to be spilled. She'd done her share of killing. As Ushara's servant, she would kill again if the goddess so demanded.

"Shai told me the cloak of Night sought outlanders and the gods-touched. She saw them as a threat to her power. Are you by any chance a seventh son?"

"I?" He sounded genuinely surprised. "Of my mother's bearing, certainly not. Of my father's siring, I couldn't say. I had one half brother older and four younger the year I made twelve. How many had been born, or died, before and after I cannot know. Why do you ask?"

"An outlander will save us. Are you that outlander, Commander Anji?"

"It is not my place to answer such a question."

She knew how to coax a man on. In the temple she'd helped along men afflicted by youth or age or hard luck or certain physical ailments that embarrassed them. This man was crippled by none of those things. She wondered idly if he had pleasured his young wife in the bed or merely taken what he desired. Not a question to ask now!

"You're surely correct in believing there remains more thunder and lightning and battering winds in store. Why have you approached me tonight? For unless you've come to worship the Devourer, I'm not sure why we're talking."

"Your Hieros and I have discussed at length that order serves the Hundred better than disruption. Order serves farmers, who must plant and tend. Order serves merchants, who desire safe roads and markets. Order serves the temples, who wish folk to have peace for prayer and tithing. The Hieros, and Olo'osson's council, agreed I must do what is necessary to restore order. The wrong choices now will have terrible repercussions. They already have had."

Now she saw where this was going.

"Commander, if you're not here to devour me, then I must assume you are here to ask me to kill someone. Your mother, perhaps?"

"My mother!" To catch him off his guard—when she knew as well as he did that out in the evening shadows his guards stood with bows at the ready—surprised her. "The woman who birthed me! Raised me! Taught me to ride. Rescued me from death at the cost of her own freedom. Why would I want my mother dead?" He shut his eyes, too choked to speak. Then he recovered, although his voice was hoarse. "She did what she thought was necessary."

"Obviously I've misunderstood. Anyhow, I can undertake no such commission unless the hieros of whatever temple I'm assigned to orders me to carry out an assassination."

"The Hieros in Olossi told me to do whatever I thought necessary, with whatever weapons I had at hand." He nodded at her. "You are a sword of finest steel, Zubaidit."

He wasn't a man who flattered. Even so, the comment made her uneasy.

He went on. "It is the danger the cloaked demons represent that will prove hardest to vanquish. Maybe there are some people who would interfere out of a sentimental attachment to an illusion—what you might call a lilu."

"A lilu? Speak plainly."

For the first time, he hesitated. "You have not heard that one of the cloaks appeared to Reeve Joss as a lilu in the guise of his old lover, a reeve who was murdered twenty years ago by men believed to be in the employ of Lord Radas?"

Handsome Joss! His name spoken in the same breath as the mention of an old lover, twenty years dead, no doubt the woman whose death, like best-quality silk, draped him with that aura of being one laugh away from tears, an aura whose reckless lure had caught many a woman. Anyhow, what demon would not choose to appear before Joss in a guise that might encourage him to a bout of devouring? She could take men or leave them—she'd been trained to hold herself detached—and yet there he walked, the only man who really tempted her. Thoughts of him plagued her like mosks, swarming, biting, impossible. He was provoking and annoying, and too convinced of his charm's ability to get him out of any situation. He drank too much, and his smile was a cursed yoke, dragging her into endless thoughts of what it would be like to have him close and hot and wild.

The hells!

Was it actually possible Joss was a threat to their hopes for peace in the Hundred? That he was in league with the remaining Guardians, all of whom were corrupt or bound to become corrupt, if Anji was right? Or could it be Anji was just a jealous man who wanted to rid himself of a rival as in an old and tedious tale? But if so, why would it matter now that his beautiful wife had been murdered by his own mother, whose crime he could so coldly forgive as necessity?

Necessity for whom?

"Is there a point to this?" she asked, hearing the irritation she ought to have strangled before its thorny hide crawled out in her words.

"You have a brother whose life you value, do you not?" he asked.

She'd been trained from an early age in a hard school to show no emotion that might betray her thoughts. The tremor that raced through her muscles, that sliced her heart and knotted in her gut, she subsumed, but even so it hit with such force that she shifted from one foot to the other to bleed off its power, and he tensed as if expecting an attack. In the shadows, soldiers tensed as well, their movements like a whisper of thunder on a still day.

Beware.

"Keshad is safe in your household. You assured me of this yesterday when we met on the bridge. Or is he dead, too, in the attack that killed Mai? Is that what you came to tell me?"

"He wasn't there. He's alive."

She had not wept for years. She'd forgotten how tears stung.

"I sent Mai to Merciful Valley to keep her safe," Anji continued. "We all want those we love to remain safe. Even a man as experienced as Reeve Joss wants to protect a demon because she appears to him as a woman he once—that he still—loves." He gestured sharply toward the flutter of the awning where lamps burned and Chief Tuvi walked back and forth with the baby asleep on his shoulder. Never letting go. Anji's grief emerged like a kroke from the murky waters of the swamp, ready to snap. "Just as I want to protect my son, who is all I have left of her."

The tears dried up. Her heart hardened as Anji's threat emerged. "A handsome baby, indeed. I don't think I've seen a more beautiful child."

The teeth of his anger closed; if a tone had color, his would have waxed bright with the shiny hard surface of a gemstone, brilliance without warmth. "I will not let anyone or anything stand in the way of making this land safe for him. So tell me, Zubaidit, how much do you love your brother? Who is confined in my custody. Enough to kill to keep him alive?"

50

COULDN'T A MAN get some sleep? Joss hadn't realized how exhausted he was until the first slug of cordial left him reeling. He might as well have downed ten cups as one, for the way his head spun. A kind soul found him a blanket, and he lay down in the midst of the camp, yet twice just as he'd dozed off some cursed reveler tripped over him, and then that flirting Naya Hall reeve had to drag a young Copper Hall reeve almost next to him and get noisy. Had these young people no respect for others? Couldn't they be bothered to seek out a little decent privacy?

Had he suddenly turned into an elder, rapping his cane on his porch and ranting at high-spirited children to get out of his orchard?

He hauled the blanket up to the berm and shook it out before lying down, on his back, to face the stars. There trundled the Carter and his Barking Dog, materializing to the southwest as the last glow faded. Low in the east, the Oxen trudged on their steady path, rising. There were always two, yoked together. How was it possible Mai was dead?

The Ox is always beautiful.

Peddonon sank down cross-legged beside him. "Do I smell tears?"

"She was a lovely woman, but I think that her physical features weren't her true beauty. If she talked to you, she talked to *you*, as if you were all that mattered to her in the wide world. I don't know how confused or frightened she might have been, to walk into the Hundred as an outlander, but she never faltered. She's the one who overthrew the Greater Houses in Olossi. That settlement in the Barrens flourished because of her, didn't it?"

"I wouldn't know. I'm sorry anyone with a kind heart is dead. If you're going to sleep out here, mind if I share your blanket? Kesta stole mine to go sneak off with Nallo, and even as filthy and sweaty as I am, I just don't want to lie smash on the ground."

Joss scooted over. "There's your half."

Instead of lying down, Peddonon stood. "The hells," he muttered, looking into the gloom. He snorted. Joss heard soft footfalls. "Looks like I'm the only one who's not going to get devoured tonight."

Joss sat up to see—the hells!—Zubaidit approaching along the berm with a blanket slung over one shoulder.

"There's a woman who plans ahead. I'll just take this." Peddonon grabbed Joss's blanket and yanked hard, toppling Joss sideways. "Greetings of the dusk, verea. I'm out of your way."

"Greetings of the night to you, ver," she shot back, as sweetly as the auntie to whom you've just brought a basket of fresh-picked duha berries. Peddonon laughed and walked off.

"Reminiscent of the first time we met," said Joss from the ground, noting how her kilt was rucked up to expose a hells lot of long legs. "Although certainly I'll be hoping for a different outcome."

He didn't ask why she had come. He knew. She knew. Bodies knew. There were some things you just had to get out of your system.

He stood, and that fast she had an arm around him and her hips shoved against his groin, offering a kiss that lasted so long and got so intense he only broke it off because he belatedly heard cheering and hooting coming from the reeve encampment a stone's toss away. She didn't ease off on her grip.

She spoke in a lover's whisper as she nuzzled his ear. "Captain Anji wants you dead."

He broke away as their audience whooped and laughed. She hitched the blanket higher and walked away along the berm with a twitch of that shapely ass, the motion as much a natural phenomenon like wind or rain as a thing he could actually see in the growing darkness.

"The hells!" he called after her. She kept walking. He pulled a hand over his hair, which was spiky with grime from all that digging. Was it only this morning he had buried Lord Radas's corpse deep in the earth? It seemed like a lifetime ago, an act that had severed him from the life he'd lived before. Aui! She had him hooked now, didn't she?

With a laugh, he caught up as she slipped down the side of the berm to open ground. He got an arm around her and reeled her in, and the sheer excitement almost overcame him, but he kissed her hard to relieve some of the heat and then pressed his lips to her ear.

"That's got me going more than the knife did," he murmured, his free hand sliding down to cup her buttocks. "You can't possibly ask me to believe you hope to lure me out and murder me by telling me you're luring me out to murder me."

"Obviously it's working." Then, a little louder, "Umm. Yes. Just like that." Her voice dropped again. "Can you swim?"

"Of course I can swim, I grew up on the ocean. What threat do I pose to Anji?"

She nuzzled his neck. "He wants to kill all the cloaks, and he thinks you don't want to."

"He agreed we need only kill those who were with the enemy—"

She tripped him, and down they went, the words knocked back into his throat by the impact. She was on top, sitting right across his hips, her hands splayed over his chest. She leaned closer and halted with her face a finger's breadth above his, their noses kissing, her warm breath tickling his lips. "A man can say anything. He threatened me, Joss. He told me that if I didn't do something about you and your infatuation with a lilu appearing in the guise of your long-dead lover—"

"Marit!"

She insinuated a finger through the fastenings of his vest and stroked his bare skin. "Is that her name?"

"Yes. Ah."

"A little louder, please." She ground her hips into his, her kilt wrinkling around her legs, and he really did groan aloud. How long had it been? Best not to consider that question. He had to listen hard to hear her whispering, as crazy as her words seemed here in the darkness out of sight of the other reeves. "Maybe he envies you your unfortunate good looks, or maybe he wants you out of the way because you're commander of the reeve halls."

"Did he threaten to kill you if you didn't kill me?"

"No. He threatened to kill my brother. Let me tell you something."

How could she talk this through so coolly while he ached everywhere? He crept a hand up her torso and traced the round curve of a breast beneath her tight vest. Her breath caught; her words faltered as she sucked in a sharp, delirious breath; he grinned.

But she mastered herself, bit his lower lip to break his hold on her, and went on in a murmur. "I love my brother, but I serve the Merciless One. The gods built the land on law. Maybe folk think there are agents among the hierodules and kalos who engage in unlawful activities, assassinating people for coin, for instance. But in truth every case brought before us is carefully considered and only undertaken if three different hieros from different temples agree that a significant breach of justice has occurred and no recourse seems likely through the assizes."

"That's still taking matters into your own hands, outside the assizes."

"I am their weapon, not a judge." She lay down flat atop him, and stretched out her legs. Her toes rubbed his boots. "To ask me to kill outside the proper channels, and by using a threat as coin, violates the precepts by which every servant of the Merciless One lives. As well force a hierodule to bed a man she despises. It's like a form of rape."

"What will happen to your brother if you don't kill me?"

Joss knew women's bodies pretty well; when he was with a woman, he was careful indeed to be with her only and entirely. So he felt her attention focus away from him, how the fire of her arousal banked, how her thoughts flew.

"I love Kesh, but I cannot betray the Merciless One to save him. Yet if the Hieros had personally commanded me to kill you for the same reason, I'd have done it, Joss. Don't think otherwise. I wonder: What if Captain Anji is right? Maybe the Hundred needed the cloaks a long time ago. But I've felt their power, I've had my heart laid open, and I'll never trust them now, even if they claim to be holy Guardians."

The stars bloomed like an echo of the campfires and lamps strewn around the encampment. The past was as unreachable as the stars, something we can gaze on but never touch.

"You're wrong about the Guardians," he said. "That some became corrupt doesn't mean all must. That some turned against justice doesn't mean all will. We're all susceptible in so many ways, but we don't all succumb. That Anji says so, doesn't make it true. Especially when it serves him to get rid of them."

"I'm thinking about it," she murmured. "I haven't made up my mind. Meanwhile, I have a plan. A strong swimmer can make it across the river. It'll be a steep climb up the western bank, but at dawn you can call your eagle. Fly me to Olossi, so I can give my report to the Hieros and warn Kesh, get him away to where Anji and his soldiers can't ever reach him."

"I thought you disliked her."

"She is Hieros. She serves Ushara faithfully. Anyhow, I'm bound to report to her."

"That current is cursed powerful. It would be crazy enough to try to swim across in daylight. At night, it's a death trap. Better you wait out the night with me here and I'll take you away in the morning on Scar. Anji can scarcely attack my reeves, can he? He's not fool enough to kill me in front of the entire army. I'll whistle Scar in at dawn, and we'll be out before he knows we're gone. Of course I'll fly you to Olossi.

Why not? I've always wondered what two people could manage while harnessed up in the air. Wouldn't you like to try?"

She laughed. "No one can see us here," she whispered. "*Now.*"

She flung wide the blanket and they rolled onto it, kissing and caressing as she worked him out of his leathers and he unfastened her thin vest, untied her kilt, and loosed her hair so it tumbled over her shoulders. Skin to skin, he thought he was likely to be obliterated out of sheer pleasure, the earth their bed, the river their song, the wind and stars their coverlet, desire blazing.

And they'd barely gotten started. He knew how to take his time. She knew how to make things last.

But there is an end. Afterward the cooling ardor had its own glories: the simple animal sense of satisfaction, a tincture of smugness as she nestles against you well pleased, the easing of your heartbeat as you're overtaken by smiling lassitude.

He sighed contentedly as he grinned. "If my murderer intends to take me off my guard, now would be the time."

She sat up and tied back her hair. "Best we go," she said in a brisk voice that might not have been moaning moments before in that terribly arousing and aroused way. "We shouldn't have, but—Aui!—I've been waiting to do that for a cursed long time." Yet she briskly untangled her clothes from his and shoved his leathers onto his chest, then dressed so quickly it was obvious she'd trained to have facility at these tasks in the dark. "We must go. He'll strike when you least expect it. Joss—"

"It's beyond reckless to try crossing that river at night." He sought and found a hip, his hand urging her closer. "We'll go back to camp, wait it out among the reeves. And then tomorrow—or again tonight, if you insist—"

She twisted out of his grasp and rose. "I'm going now. Come with me."

"You'll get to Olossi faster if you go with me at dawn. I admit, I have doubts about Anji, about the way he's taken control of so many aspects of this campaign. But we must take this discussion in front of the councils. Indeed, I have to. For if I seem to have run, bolted under cover of night, I'll lose what little authority I've worked to build. They'll call me a coward. I can't—I won't—do that to the reeve halls."

"You're a gods-rotted fool, Joss. Come with me now."

"Not until morning—"

She loped into the night so abruptly he didn't fancy leaping up and chasing stark naked after her. The hells! Yet she was a hierodule. An assassin. She wouldn't have warned him unless there was smoke signifying fire. Not unless there was a deeper plot afoot by the Hieros to set Joss against Anji for the temple's gain. What did Ushara's temple gain out of an alliance with Anji? The same things Anji gained: order, and control.

The hells. Joss wrestled with his thoughts as he fumbled with his leathers. His hands were clumsy, as if that bout of devouring had eaten his coordination. He shook out the blanket and stumbled back to the reeve camp, where Peddonon, asleep on the blanket he'd stolen from Joss, cracked an eye for long enough to squint at him in the light of the single sentry lantern, and mumble, "So does that bewildered expression mean you've just had the best sex of your life, or the worst?"

"My head hurts," said Joss, and Peddonon laughed, and they settled companionably down side by side. Joss fell so hard into the pit of sleep that he was startled when the sun's light flashed him to wakefulness. He was lying on his side, facing east, the sun a glare on his eyelids.

He sat up, rubbing his mess of hair. Most of the reeves were awake. The camp was moving, shrugging the sleep off its shoulders. He got up and dusted grass off his leathers, spotted Peddonon off in the distance laughing with some soldiers, found a place to take a piss. Shook out and rolled up her blanket. Aui! That had been something. Just to think of it—never mind. He fought down the intense physical memory that washed him, and gave serious consideration to running over to the river and plunging into the shallows just to cool down.

Had she really attempted a night crossing? Could she possibly have survived?

No use walking down trails that led nowhere. The army was getting ready to move out. It was time to act like the commander of the reeve halls. He set his bone whistle to his lips, blew Scar's signal, then waved to Peddonon and set off for the awning that sheltered the command unit. The guards let him through. Anji was awake, of course, hair in its neat topknot, tabard brushed clean, and holding his sleepy son as he conferred with his chiefs and captains.

He looked around, noting Joss's approach; there wasn't a cursed hint of surprise or consternation, nothing but a pleasant smile.

"Joss. Greetings of the dawn to you. We're just discussing the day's march. We've had a day to rest and resupply. Now we've got to begin a pursuit and patrol of the countryside and road between here and Toskala. I'll need the reeves to—"

"Commander Anji. I know you need the reeves. But as commander of the reeve halls, I need to be called in at the start of any council that concerns my reeves. Especially in the current situation, when so many reeves are dealing with eagles who have been pushed to their limit. Naturally, we've got to work together in order to deal with the remaining cohorts, but my reeves and eagles are stretched thin and now is not the time to break them."

Anji's gesture turned into a wave toward aides waiting to one side. "Bring cordial. Or juice if you'd prefer."

"Either is fine. My thanks."

"I wasn't aware," Anji continued reasonably, "that Copper Hall or Gold Hall had recognized you as commander of the reeve halls, even in a ceremonial position. I've received Copper Hall's sanction to deploy them as I see fit. But no matter. You're right to feel concern on behalf of the eagles. They're more valuable than men, are they not? Isn't it true that if a reeve dies, his eagle will simply choose a new reeve, but if an eagle dies, his reeve dies with him? Ah, here's the cordial. Will you be needing nai porridge? Rice? We've already eaten."

Joss was aware how he must look, having slept on the ground and done much else besides although surely none of these men could suspect. Captain Arras, looking Joss over, had a frown on his face that caused Joss to brush his stubbled jaw to make sure some telltale mark hadn't been left, but there was only a stray wisp of grass.

With his free hand, Anji poured from a ceramic pot into cups, took one for himself, and let the rest be passed around. Joss drank with the others. The baby dozed, his head on his father's shoulder. Anji wasn't wearing the Qin armor today but only a thick quilted coat under his tabard. Dark circles beneath his eyes made him look drained of life and spirit, but how could he not be? Just last night he'd heard that his beloved wife had been murdered.

Aui! Could it be the news had driven him insane enough to threaten Zubaidit? Was it likely a man in the first shock of grief could even conceive of such a convoluted plan? Had Zubaidit misunderstood Anji? Could she have made it up? But that made no sense either.

Anji *was* dangerous. Like fire, he had to be contained. But at the same time, he'd done more to save the Hundred than any other person except perhaps Mai. Wasn't she the person who had persuaded him to fight in the first place?

"We're weary, and snappish," said Joss. "As we get when we're exhausted. But Anji, someone who knows eagles and who does not fear to disagree with you to your face must always be on hand when it comes time to determine how the reeves will be deployed. Otherwise, more harm than good will come of it in the long run. Men can be pushed harder than eagles. And even men will break if pushed too hard."

"So they will," said Anji. "Perhaps you'd like to make an accounting of the reeves here as their eagles come in, and let me know what their status is so I know how many and at what distance I can deploy them."

His quick capitulation surprised Joss, but he knew better than to linger over such a trifling victory. He downed a second cup of cordial and took his leave to return to his reeves. Eagles were circling overhead, waiting to be flagged down. He jogged over to the encampment, reeves tidying up, rolling up blankets, tugging on harness. The young woman from Naya Hall whistled as Joss strode in. Many laughed, while others smirked. Jests were tossed; he let them fall untouched.

"Heya! You lot. I want to talk to each one of you and see how long you've been flying since you had a decent rest, since your eagle had a real hunt. Come on. One at a time."

When you used a decisive tone of voice, folk did tend to obey. Peddonon and Nallo he sent immediately back to Law Rock, for an easy day patrolling northward as long as it ended at Clan Hall and rest thereafter. Kesta and her flight he grounded for another entire day. The Copper Hall reeves were testier, their eagles already down and waiting to leave.

"But we want to patrol. We've gotten cursed good at raiding. We can kill off a couple of fleeing cadres. Commander Anji would—"

"I'm commander until a full council is called. You two go back to Copper Hall and let your fawkners make the judgment. She's got a croak coming on, can't you hear it? And he's been plucking his feathers. They need care, not more work. Also, you need to feed them up. Or do you want to kill them?"

They were young and feckless and eager, but that was the one threat that always worked. They slouched away to their eagles.

Peddonon gave Joss a swift hug, then slapped his ass. "Now they're marching. See you in Toskala, Joss?"

"Tonight or tomorrow, most likely. Get out of here."

He worked down through the other reeves from Horn Hall and Copper Hall plus the flight that had ferried oil of naya up from Olossi and afterward remained with the army.

"Your flight looks all right," he said to the leader of the Naya Hall contingent. "But

I want you to check in with the fawkners at Horn Hall before you go the rest of the way. I recommend you send a messenger to Argent Hall asking for three seven-reeve flights to be released up here and replaced each week in staggered order."

"That's more or less Marshal Verena's orders, Commander," said the saucy young reeve. "Our other flight is already out, meant to sit out the night—if not so appealingly as you or I did, I suppose—at Law Rock. They'll be coming downriver to meet up with the army. We expect two flights tomorrow or the next day, and then we've standing orders to return to Argent Hall."

"I knew Verena would make a cursed good marshal. All right, then. Go on."

Peddonon and Nallo had left. Spotting Scar, Joss flagged down the bird.

Kesta also slapped his ass. "Where *are* you going? Commander."

"Can you two not leave your cursed hands off me?" he said, laughing as he shoved her.

"From what I heard—just secondhand, mind you—that's not what you were saying last night. She finally devoured you, eh? That hierodule we met at Law Rock?"

"You should talk."

She laughed. "No one talks about me. That's the difference between us, eh?"

"Sheh. First I'm going to follow those two hotheaded Copper Hall reeves, make sure they go back to the hall. You know what gods-rotted idiots young men can be."

"Just *young* men?"

Scar thumped down, talons extended, wings high, in a whuffle of dust. The raptor had set down in an open space well away from the companies packing up and moving out in ranks. A company of mounted archers wearing the beards and colors of Olo'osson men led their horses past, heading for the bridge. Scar's presence always made horses restive.

Joss jogged forward with his gear, his baton out in case Scar found the movement of the army, however well controlled, too distracting. Fortunately there was a lot of space.

He gestured with the baton as he came in, paced slowly as Scar dipped his big head to greet him. There was a smear of blood on the eagle's beak, so he'd fed, and he had a bit of weight to his lumber. Copper Hall was far enough to go today. The old bird was getting tired.

Joss checked Scar's harness and then dragged his own from its bundle and found it all tangled. He was as cursed tired as the raptor, not thinking straight. He shook it out as Scar scraped restlessly at the dirt.

"Joss! Give me a lift to Copper Hall?"

He turned. The rising sun behind him, Anji approached Joss across the dusty field from the direction of the reeve encampment. He had the clipped, brisk stride of a man who knew where he was going. Two Qin guardsmen flanked him. Joss squinted, stepping to one side, shading his eyes. Qin riders, a hundred or more horsemen, clattered up in his wake, veering off to the left to avoid the Olo'osson company getting its horses calmed down. Which they would have a cursed easier time doing if they would just move off away from Scar.

"Heya! Anji!" At least he wasn't carrying the baby. "Slow down, stand back, and wait until I flag you in so Scar knows—"

Anji was coming in fast, too fast, hand on the hilt of his sword in the way the Qin often had, a posture of readiness but that looked a hells much too aggressive from the perspective of a weary old raptor. Scar opened his wings, tail fanning. As big as he was, when he flared he looked twice the size. And yet Anji picked up his pace. With the sun behind him, he was more undefined sharp movement than an actual familiar person who'd flown before with Scar.

"Stand back!" shouted Joss, fumbling with his harness.

Maybe it was the way Anji turned his body, the angle of his torso, the gesture visible like the taunting display of a competing eagle as he slipped his sword half out of its scabbard.

Scar struck toward the captain, accidentally knocking Joss over as he lunged talons forward. But the sun was in Scar's eyes, and the eagle was tired. Anji dove and rolled and by the time he was back up on his feet it was too late.

Men's shouts rolled like thunder, and the hissing rains fell. Only it wasn't rain. It was arrows. A hundred—or a thousand, for they fell so hard and so fast—flying in defense of the man who commanded them. Scar was on the ground defending his reeve. He didn't have a chance.

Therefore, neither did Joss.

The sun splintered into shards that pierced his eyes and his flesh. The world turned to gold. The sun rose as darkness devoured him.

51

TWENTY DAYS AFTER the battle at Skerru, Tohon told Shai that Mai was dead and then left him alone to weep. How could it have happened that he walked into danger but sweet, generous Mai was the one who died?

The next day, the Qin scout hired a wagon and supplies in Nessumara and found them a place in the first caravan headed over the plain of Istria to Horn. No one had much to sell; it was more the principle of the thing, brave souls wanting to test the new security on the roads. After all, a caravan had gone north to Toskala and returned without harm, although there'd been one scare with a cadre of scruffy men who, it had turned out, were farmers driven by starvation out of hiding. They hadn't even known that Lord Radas's army had been defeated at Skerru. Now, of course, those farmers as well as everyone else had regained their freedom to trade where they wanted and to move between markets and through open countryside once infested by bandits and scoured by an army whose soldiers wore a cheap star beaten out of tin whose leaders had promised them life but led them to death.

The Qin scout rode, switching off between a quartet of scruffy little steppe horses. Besides the four guards, only Tohon had horses. Half the Hundred, the merchants noted, had been cleaned out of riding horses for the army; these days, only soldiers rode, a fair exchange when you thought about it.

The driver was a taciturn woman old enough to be Shai's mother. She spoke only to complain about aches and pains or the weather, while handling the dray beasts with great ease and competence. Shai dozed on the pallet fitted into the bed of the wagon, under a canvas awning rigged up with rope to protect him from the baking sun. He wore a loose kilt and, when he had to, a vest; he healed best with his skin exposed to air. Each day in the morning he walked alongside the wagon for a while before resting; each day in the late afternoon he walked a little more. Tohon never once told him to be careful of overdoing it, although the driver often informed him that he was risking a relapse in this reckless way. More hair than wit! Not that he had much hair these days, that having been cropped down to his scalp.

"Eat a few more spoonfuls, son," Tohon said each night, the only time he nagged him.

Each night, he ate a little more than he had the night before. He listened to the merchants chatter, sing, laugh, swap stories of the months-long siege of Nessumara. Where were you during the first attack? It was a close thing, wasn't it? If they'd not stopped when they did, we'd have been overrun. Did you see what happened to the Green Sun clan, after it was discovered they'd tried to trade secrets to the invaders? Every individual including the children sold into debt slavery, and their compound and storehouses gifted to Chief Sengel, in thanks. Why, the Qin chief had even taken a local delta woman—connected to several wealthy clans both by kinship and through her business dealings—as his wife.

One of the merchants had a cousin named Forgi who had been one of the scouts who'd guided Commander Anji's army north along the causeway, and he regaled the caravan with the story of how his cousin had been saved by a flight of reeves who had killed an entire cadre of men about to stumble on his hiding place. Too bad about that one reeve who had died, eh? Women all over Haldia and Istria were surely weeping their hearts out, for everyone said he was that handsome. Still, even and maybe especially a handsome man could be curdling with bitterness and ambition inside, for hadn't he been trying to claim he was commander of the reeve halls, when everyone knew that it took a reeve council to elect a new commander? Why, they'd convened just a few days ago, hadn't they, right there at Copper Hall? Every reeve hall except Bronze Hall had sent representatives, and they'd elected Commander Anji to serve as their commander, which only made sense. So it was just fortunate Commander Anji hadn't been killed when that cursed eagle had tried to rip off his head.

The outlander had saved them. Not that there weren't still stories out of the countryside of desperate men ransacking villages, and rumors of cohorts fallen back to Wedrewe in Herelia, making ready for a new assault. Thank the gods for Commander Anji and the garrisons and reeve patrols he was setting in place in the cities and major towns and all along the roads. The Hundred—well, those parts safeguarded by the army—was a peaceful, orderly place again.

So it proved on the eight stages—eight days—from Nessumara to Horn. Riders patrolled the roads in "short" cadres of six and eight horsemen with an experienced man as sergeant, a pair of corporals who had served in the commander's army, and the rest of each group filled out by local men glad to have a chance to feel they were doing something to keep the peace. All along the route, men and women worn thin by months of scarcity prepared the fields against the rains, due to come any day now, if the gods were merciful. May the rains come at the proper time. May the harvest be abundant.

How odd to hear prayers chanted to the Merciful One woven into the conversation and chant of the locals. Did they even know where they came from?

"You're getting stronger," said Tohon approvingly as they wandered Horn's market with its scant pickings. "You're ready to ride."

They were buying supplies for the next leg of the journey. A young woman working a pair of slip-fry pans paused as the oil spit and the vegetables sizzled and gave Shai the once-over, a look torn between appreciation and pity. He hadn't known he could still blush.

An elderly man selling radish and nai—nothing special, but all he had on offer today—nodded as Tohon picked through the baskets. "You're one of those Qin, eh?"

"I am," Tohon agreed amiably. "Just taking the lad back to Olossi."

"I heard," said the old man, "from a merchant what come in yesterday from Nessumara I guess in the same caravan as you, that this lad was burned killing one of those gods-cursed cloaked lilus. Tell you what. I'll give you a sack of nai for nothing, as thanks. It'll be a touch bitter, as it's leftover from last season, but it'll feed you. The radish I have to sell, though, as I've a clan to feed just like anyone."

They filled up their wagon cheaply enough despite the high prices at the market. Everyone wanted to thank the Qin soldier and the young man scarred by burns by offering them a bit of this or that—prickle headed apples, caul petals for soup, rices cakes and bean curd, a sack of rice—for under market price. At a loss.

Mai would have been appalled.

"There now, son," said Tohon. "You can't help thinking about her. It will come and go, but it will never stop hurting."

"Do you still weep for your son and daughter and wife, Tohon?"

"I remember them every day, when I see some new thing I'd like to share. A bolt of red silk. A red-capped bird. The way pipewood sets up a rustle when the wind runs through it. There's no other sound like it. That Mount Aua, a fine bold peak, don't you think?" He'd learned to point with his elbow, indicating the distant mountain, tipped with white, towering and strong.

" 'Mount Aua, who is sentinel,' " murmured Shai, " 'We survive in his shelter.' Tohon, are you sure the children are safe?" He'd asked a hundred times, and yet he must ask again, always, because his heart ached so.

Tohon's answer was always the same, and delivered in the same patient tone. "I delivered them to Nessumara before the city fell under siege. I believe they were shipped to Zosteria to keep them out of enemy hands. Eridit and the two militiamen knew enough to take care of them. I think they were going to head to Mar. But sometimes, lad, you have to accept that you may never know."

"Is that how the Qin manage? Riding away from their families for years, or forever? Sending their sons away to war, and never knowing?"

Tohon had a firm grip, and he knew exactly where he could grasp Shai's arm without bruising tender skin. "You learn to ride on the path and keep your eyes open so you can see what is there, not what you wish were there." His gaze was level, and after a moment he smiled. "And then after all you might discover that what is there is what you wished for all along."

THEY SIGNED UP with a new caravan out of Horn, heading along the West Track to Olossi. Riding was harder—it chafed, and he had to wear trousers—but each day he rode for longer at a stretch. By the time they reached Olossi, he rode half the day and walked half the day and split wood every evening as the driver sat on a folding stool and watched, commenting on his form and likely chance of hurting himself, and how he could be more efficient if he altered the angle of his axe. When he got tired of hearing her criticisms, he altered the angle, and was surprised to discover she was right.

They passed through checkpoints and entered the inner city. At the gate of the Qin compound they were met by a woman with a debt mark at her left eye who told them cheerfully that, no, the Qin no longer owned this compound. It had been sold last month to Master Calon, who was her new master, a decent man for all that his grandfather had come up from Sirniaka.

Who had the authority to sell it? Everyone knew that the new mistress of the Qin household was the commander's mother, a formidable woman before whom the entire market quaked, known to be intimate with the Hieros and, indeed, every head priest of every temple in the city as well as having already secured a seat on the city council and gotten herself invited into the compounds of the Ri Amarah.

No one had any great affection for her. She wasn't the young mistress, the one who'd been killed by red hounds, agents of the southern empire whose eye was now turned north and whose reach was cruel and arbitrary, for truly why would anyone want to kill Mistress Mai, who had overthrown the corrupt Greater Houses and secured wives for the Qin soldiers and nurtured the new settlement of Astafero in the Barrens that supplied the city with oil of naya and a very good grade of wool? And who had been kind and generous while doing it, never a harsh word or a cutting remark either to your face or behind your back.

Be that as it may. The empire was a terrible threat, everyone understood that now, here so close to the Kandaran Pass. The murder of the commander's beloved young wife proved that, didn't it? As for the mother, all approved of her devotion to her grandson. The baby had been sent to Olossi with his nursemaid last month, hadn't he? While the commander was on campaign in the north, naturally he would entrust the little lad to family. The grandmother was devoted to her grandson. It was sweet to see her with him in the market, dandling the boy—for he was a beautiful and lively baby with whom everyone fell in love at first sight—while ruthlessly ordering around her slaves and hirelings and bickering with the market women in that imperious way she had, as if she thought the sun rose and set on her likes and dislikes . . .

"Our thanks, verea," said Tohon, steering a stunned Shai away from the gate. "We'll just find our own way, then."

Shai's head was whirling. He couldn't keep track of where they were going. As his feet slapped on stone, the impact jarred up through his bones to addle his thoughts yet more. But Tohon knew the twists and turns of the lanes and each rise and fall of hill, and so they climbed to the height, to a substantial compound sprawled next door to a compound whose walls flew the banners of a Ri Amarah clan. The Qin guards at the gate recognized Tohon, although they were not soldiers Shai knew; they were newcomers, from a cohort of Commander Beje's men sent north with the Qin princess and now likely to spend the rest of their days in the Hundred.

"We need cordial and juice," said Tohon to the guards, "and a place to sit in the shade."

"Better than that," said the young man, eyeing Shai's scars or his muscles, hard to say. Shai *was* showing a cursed lot of skin in his kilt and sleeveless vest. "We got word you arrived. Come this way."

He led them to the porch, where they took off their sandals, and thence deep into the house past several layers of sliding doors, each threshold guarded by more black-clad soldiers, until they came to a long, quiet chamber covered with woven mats and furnished with a single low table and a single pillow on which sat Anji. Chief Tuvi, kneeling behind him, was twisting up Anji's topknot and fixing it with a gold ribbon. A pair of Qin soldiers were standing to either side of three small chests bound by chains. Shai felt a sting on his skin, and he shuddered. He knew what was in those chests.

"Sit," said Anji without looking up.

Shai sat, trying not to remember how the cloak had smothered and burned him. He dared not shut his eyes, so he watched as Tuvi finished his task in silence. When the chief sat back, Tohon spoke.

"We'd be appreciative of a cup of cordial, or some juice, Commander. We just arrived after a long journey."

"So have I also just arrived," said Anji, rising, "although by reeve." He examined Shai without expression, then nodded. "I wasn't sure you would live, but I see Tohon has taken good care of you."

Shai could say nothing. Watching Anji, he could only think of Mai.

"Come with me," said Anji.

He led them into a courtyard guarded on one side by Qin soldiers and on the other by massive men of foreign mien, muscled like wrestlers, and as clean-shaven as Toskalan men. They entered a narrow antechamber. After a pause during which Shai heard female voices murmuring and the faint fragile kiss of a delicate porcelain cup touching to plate, doors with painted screens were slid open. The chamber beyond was a wide porch, its plank floor heaped with carpets, its far side open to a courtyard infested with fountains, ornamental pools, and dwarf trees carefully pruned. Its ends were hung with curtains which rippled as unseen people moved behind them. Eyes peered through gaps as Anji, Tuvi, Tohon, and Shai entered the room.

Two women sat facing over a low table. The elderly Hieros sat on a pillow, while the Qin princess reclined on an embroidered couch. The Hieros wore a simple taloos of best-quality burnt-orange silk, wrapped to expose her arms, thin and age-worn but still wiry with strength. The Qin princess wore robes that covered her from wrist to ankle to throat. She glittered with gold chains and a gold-knit headdress stabbing like a tower from her head.

"Ah, Anjihosh," she said. "You have come at last. Sit down."

No pillow was offered for the men with him.

Anji indicated that Shai should take the pillow. He remained standing while Shai, too exhausted to care how it looked, sank down to rest.

"This must be the uncle," continued Anji's mother, surveying Shai. "Hard to say if those scars will ever entirely go away. I suppose he was a good-looking young man once, although nothing like the niece."

"Anjihosh," said Tuvi quietly, like a rider calming a storm-maddened horse.

The Hieros lifted a porcelain cup and sipped, watching the interplay between mother and son. She set down the cup with a crooked smile. "A dark day, Commander Anji, when we heard about the murder of your devoted and beloved wife by red hounds out of the empire."

"The red hounds?" blurted Shai, seeing a flash of triumph in the Qin princess's eye. What had he to lose by speaking out? They could do nothing worse to him than had already been done. "You were the one who killed her!"

Anji's mother regarded him with amusement. "I? I did not stab her. The slave Sheyshi stabbed her. It is to be supposed—how else are we to explain it?—that she acted as an agent for the red hounds. Every son and grandson of Emperor Farutanihosh was under a death sentence. The boy's mother simply got in the way as she protected her child."

"So it is to be supposed," murmured Anji, like a spike of lightning as Tuvi rested a hand on the commander's forearm.

"It's a lie! A lie you have all agreed to tell to protect—!"

"Shai! Silence!"

Once, that tone from Anji would have silenced Shai, but no longer. "Is there to be no justice for Mai?"

But his cry rang in empty air, and *their* silence was his answer. He might as well have remained mute, for all the notice they took of him. Tohon laid a hand gently on his arm, that was all.

Anji turned away. In a hoarse voice, he said, "Where is my son?"

His mother clapped her hands. A slave slipped out from behind a curtain. "Fetch the boy."

The Hieros's gaze paused on Tohon as she accepted from him a nod, and moved again to Anji. "As folk are saying, Commander, the eyes of the south have turned this way. The empire now knows—and cares—we exist. Because of you."

"My apologies," he said, and the words sounded sincere enough. "I did not seek their attention."

"Yet you have it. I suppose if I could rid myself of you and your beautiful son and thereby end the problem, I would. But that would leave me with your Qin soldiers, and your Qin-trained militia, and enemy cohorts still at large in the north. They are still at large, are they not?"

"We have not yet marched into Herelia to take down their headquarters in Wedrewe. We have spent our efforts over the last month securing Istria and Haldia, the countryside, the towns, and the cities. I'm particularly concerned that every farmer can plant as soon as the rains come without fear he will be vulnerable to attack out in his fields. Starvation is a significant concern across the north, and it will only get worse. If folk cannot plant now, the situation will become catastrophic. As it is, it may take years for people to rebuild. Wedrewe, and the remnants gathered in Walshow, are a danger, but they can be dealt with later."

"I suppose they can," murmured the Hieros. "What do you want, Commander Anji?"

He had the grace to look startled. "Why, to raise my son in peace. A peace that will shelter all the people of the Hundred." His gaze sharpened. "Isn't it the same thing you have many times told me you want, Holy One?"

"Ah." She sketched a series of fluid movements with her left hand, in a language that would have meant something to the wildings and to any Hundred-raised folk. "And therein lies the tale, does it not? If you die, we are left as in the tale of the Guardians. 'Long ago, in the time of chaos, a bitter series of wars, feuds, and reprisals denuded the countryside and impoverished the lords and guildsmen and farmers and artisans of the Hundred.' This time, I fear, we cannot rely on the Guardians to establish justice."

"The assizes must be reopened," agreed Anji, "without the interference of demons. The roads must be safe, tolls and tithes and taxes fair. People want to eat. I could go on, but I won't. For all this, we need peace."

A slave entered, and behind him walked Priya, carrying a plump baby whose luminous face and brilliant smile brought as much radiance into the chamber as a hundred lamps. Shai could not help himself; he began to cry.

The baby spoke up in a piercingly sweet voice: "Dada! Dada!" He reached; he yearned.

Anji strode across the chamber and engulfed the baby, showering his black hair and dusky face with butterfly kisses that made the little lad chortle as he tried to purse his tiny lips in imitation. Priya looked away, bowing her head.

The Hieros watched, sipped her tea, and set down her cup. "So, Commander Anji, do you suppose you and your son can ever hope to live in peace? That you'll be safe from those who might wish to kill you?"

Anji glanced up, tucking the child into the curve of his left arm. "I rely on your support."

"And you have it, because I, too, have people I wish to protect." The Hieros's smile did not reassure, but it possessed the pinch of finality. She looked at the Qin princess and received from her a nod no less final. An agreement incubated, hatched, and thrived in that wordless exchange between two women who knew how to order the domains they ruled. "I am a weary and elderly woman. This trouble has harmed the Hundred grievously. We are not ready to fight another war while this one is not yet ended and the empire in the meantime shrugs a shoulder our way, wondering what mosk has stung its ear. Let it be stated, therefore, that we are allies."

"Let it be said," agreed Anji. "I have every respect for you, Holy One. I will work in concert with you and the temples. We seek the same goals."

"I suppose we do. Now, I am finished here for today." She rose with light grace to her feet, needing no aid, and paused by the door to look at Tohon.

"My apologies, Holy One," Tohon said regretfully. "I'm not at leisure at this time."

She nodded with careful neutrality, or rueful resignation. The doors slid shut behind her.

"Well, Mother," said Anji, "now you have what you want."

"Yes."

"Everything except my affection. Which you will never have."

She twitched out of the hands of a hovering slave a square of cloth so lushly embroidered with fine silver thread that it glittered. After patting her forehead, she handed it back and sat straight, tucking her feet sideways under her, her skirts heaped in ravines and ridges around her.

"I do not need your affection, Anjihosh. I only need you to survive. That is my victory. You will marry the emperor's sister to placate him. I have dulled the knives of the Hieros and her spies and assassins, and will mock into submission those on the council who voice doubts about any aspect of your enterprise. The rest you are already on your way to accomplishing. The Hundred is a fine inheritance for your son, don't you think?"

"Why would the emperor's sister allow Mai's son to live, after she bears a son of my siring?"

"Because I will command it done that way. Let Atani be her son, Anji. Let him call her 'Mother.' She is a biddable creature, and desperate to please. Let her bear daughters in plenty to dote on, and I will rid you of any inconvenient sons who might trouble the waters, for you and I can both see that Atani will shine brighter than any of them possibly could. There, it is settled."

Anji was, Shai saw, on the edge of tears. He was trembling. The baby, looking worried, patted his father's mouth.

With an effort of will that seemed to actually reverberate through the room as a lute's string vibrates, the more powerful for its lack of sound, Anji reined himself in. He buried the tears. He kissed the baby's palms, first one, then the other.

He said, "It is settled."

Tohon grunted, as though he'd been punched in the gut.

Carrying the boy, Anji turned his back on his mother and walked out of the chamber. Shai scrambled up to follow Tuvi and Tohon through the courtyard and into empty chambers furnished with nothing but the barest comforts, absent any of the wild, artful abandon with which Mai would have filled a house. Where were the taloos-wrapped rats flying kites, the first screen she had purchased in Olossi's market just because it had delighted her so? All trace of her was gone.

All except the baby.

Anji came to rest in the chamber with the three chests. He turned to Tuvi. "We'll fly at dawn to Merciful Valley," he said. He looked at Shai. "Not you, I think."

"Not me? Is there yet more you have to hide? Did you conspire with your mother to have Mai killed, and now fear I will speak to her ghost and she tell me the truth? Can it be true you have just told your mother that you'll marry the woman she killed Mai to force you to marry? I don't believe you wanted Mai dead. I think you loved her, as much as you can love anything. And even so—can it be true?—you'll allow the baby to grow up thinking your new wife is his mother, as if Mai never existed?"

"Anjihosh," said Tuvi in his hands-on-the-reins voice.

Anji had walked beyond anger. Indeed, Shai thought, he had walked beyond shame. He had walked beyond honor. He knew what he wanted and he knew how to get it; the ghost of another man, a man he might have been, faded behind him.

"It matters not," Anji said. "It's done. It's over."

Tohon said softly, "A man can be waylaid by demons wearing many guises. Maybe they cloak him with a lust for flesh or for gold, or with vanity or a lack of discipline or the scourge of disloyalty. Or maybe they cloak him with unchecked ambition. A good woman is a man's knife. She protects him against demons. And if he loses her, and does not honor her memory properly, I suppose he risks becoming a demon himself."

After the silence died to something more stifling, Anji spoke. "Are you finished, Tohon?"

"I am, Commander. I've said what I felt needed saying."

"Then you're dismissed."

"Yes, Commander. I suppose I am. Are you coming with me, Shai?"

Anji held the baby, the last piece of Mai existing on earth. The baby who would never know who his true mother was.

"I want to see where Mai was killed," said Shai raggedly. "That's all."

"Very well," said Anji. "That much I will offer you, for her sake."

So it was done. It was over.

THE REEVE FLIGHT, rising into the steep foothills over which towered the gods-touched mountains, left Shai speechless, not that words had ever come easily. Six reeves deposited six travelers in the valley midmorning and departed immediately, promising to return in the afternoon, as Anji requested.

Merciful Valley was aptly named. Its beauty softened grief, if grief can be softened by anything except time. A mist of cool rain kissed the trees and sang a lullaby over the grass, herald to weather brewing within the peaks.

In addition to a contingent of Qin guards stationed in the valley, two people remained here. One Shai vaguely remembered, an impetuous and irritating young man named Keshad who ignored Shai while he attempted to ingratiate himself to Anji while casting dagger glances at Chief Tuvi, although why anyone could dislike Tuvi, Shai could not figure. Tuvi was a decent man, solid, honest, and loyal.

The other inhabitant of the valley was kinder, a young woman whose grief for Mai was a comfort to Shai. In the humble audience chamber of the two room shelter, she offered hot bark tea to suit the chill in the air.

"The soldiers say you pray every day, Miravia," said Anji after he had handed the baby over to her. She kissed Atani's hair and unhooked the baubles hanging from her ears so he could clutch them in his chubby little hands.

"It's our tradition, among my people. After the death of a beloved relative, we pray each day for one year."

"To ease their passage to the other side, or to ease your own heart?" he asked between sips of steaming tea.

"Does it matter?" She wiped away tears.

Anji cast a sidelong glance at Keshad. "Miravia, I would be grateful if you would honor Mai's memory by remaining here for the entire year and praying each day. It would ease my grief, to know you watched by the place she died. I would remain here, but I'm called away. The campaign continues."

"Of course, Commander Anjihosh!" she cried.

"Keshad, I understand your sister has returned alive to the temple. Which means you are free to go."

"I heard," he said, with a grimace of relief that then shaded into irritation. "And also that she is staying as a hierodule in the temple. I don't know what the old bitch said to her—" But he broke off and looked at Miravia. All at once the young man's motives unfurled to Shai's gaze as a flower under the sun. "I prefer to stay here, if I may be permitted to."

Anji's answering smile troubled Shai. He looked exactly like a man who has just watched his bets in a wagering game fall into place.

"I think it can be allowed for you to remain here, if Miravia has no objection." But Anji glanced at Tuvi as Miravia blushed, and Tuvi shook his head, as if to answer for her. Anji rose. "I wish to pray at the altar and make an offering in Mai's memory. If you'll excuse me."

"Do you want me to go up to the waterfall with you, Captain?" Miravia asked.

"No. I'll go alone."

He did not go alone. He carried Atani, and Tuvi and two guardsmen—men who flanked Anji everywhere he went, just as Sengel and Toughid had once done—each carrying one of the small chests. Another pair of guards followed. Shai was allowed to walk behind them.

"I'll just come along with you," said Tohon, falling into step beside Shai.

"You think he's going to kill me, too? What benefit is there in that? I'm nothing to him."

"I'll just come along," said Tohon, patting him on the arm. "Hush, son. Don't tire yourself out. We've got a long way to go yet."

It was a hard, long hike for a young man recovering from such burns as he had sustained. Odd how Chief Tuvi did not labor as much, or seem as weak, although he bore ropy scars as if he'd been lashed by a fiery whip. The Qin forged ahead, while Shai, shadowed by Tohon, fell behind. Losing sight of the others, they trudged up a trail fenced in by thick walls of vegetation. The trail had been dampened by mist, but the dirt wasn't yet mud.

Into a clearing they walked. Beyond the ruins, a waterfall and pool churned as mist spattered the stones. Atani was chortling, reaching for the pool and babbling complaints when his father would not let him touch it. Distant thunder boomed in cloud-shrouded peaks. A dark shape roiled the depths. Blue fire like spikes of lightning snaked through the water and vanished as Atani laughed.

The Qin stood a few paces back from the lip, where waters rippled and sighed. There was no sign of the three little chests, as if they'd thrown them into the pool. Anji gripped the struggling baby more tightly and, leaving his guardsmen to wait, he crossed behind the curtain of water into the overhang behind.

But Shai could not move to follow him. For a ghost sat on one of the low walls, hands resting on thighs as he tracked Anji's departure. Looking back, his ghostly expression flickered with startlement as he rose.

"Hari!" breathed Shai.

Hari's essence looked exactly as Shai had seen Hari last, dressed in the local manner with loose trousers and a tunic tied at the hips, except he was a ghost, not truly substantial. His crooked smile hadn't changed at all, for he was angry at the world and laughing at himself for the futility of it.

"Hello, little brother. Hu! I hoped you would find me. How can it be you walk beside the man who killed me?"

Of course Anji hadn't wanted Shai to come here. He'd known there was a chance Hari's ghost might linger. He'd known Shai could hear as well as see ghosts. But Shai already knew enough to condemn Anji. This was just one more stab wound.

"How did he kill you, Hari?" he said past this fresh grief.

Anji's men looked at Shai, looked at each other, shrugged, and went back to waiting.

"He walked up here alone. I thought he was come to deliver a message from Mai, or check to see if I was alone before he allowed her to come up. He does guard her so, does he not? You'd think he actually loves her, which I suppose might even be possible for a Qin. Then before I knew what he was about he drew his sword and cut me down. He unclasped the cloak and tore it from me. It was easy to let it go, once a person with more determination than I had was willing to relieve me of it. I'm free, Shai. Spirit Gate calls me. But I can't cross. I need to warn Mai what manner of husband she has, that he would promise her one thing and then turn around and do the opposite. He's veiled, did you know? Like you. That's why I couldn't see it coming. Is Mai safe, Shai? Tell me she's safe."

Ghosts are caught in the moment of their death. They do not know past or future; they cannot feel the passing of days or years. That is their fate, and their misery.

Shai could not add to Hari's misery. Not now. After all, those who are veiled may lie to both cloaks and ghosts.

"Yes, Hari. She's safe."

"Don't weep for me, little brother. It's for the best. It's only that I worry about Mai." He laughed the familiar, mocking life. "Now you can take my bones home to our ancestors, can't you? If you can find my sorry remains. Not much to show for a life, is it? Yet Mai would poke and prod in that way she had, wouldn't she? Getting you to do more than you had any intention of doing. I had just started to hope I could learn what it truly meant to be a Guardian."

Tohon cupped a supporting hand under Shai's elbow. Anji emerged from the spray, the baby still squirming, quite the handful as he babbled as if to spirits in the air that no one else could see, batting and waving his hands. Anji's gaze caught on Hari's ghost, then tracked to Shai. He halted, waiting for Shai to speak.

What was there to say? Mai's father had told Shai to bring Mai home if Anji didn't treat her well, but what a pointless little speech it had been. Father Mei had only said it to make himself feel better, knowing he'd sold away the treasure of his house. The road that passes under Spirit Gate runs in only one direction. There is no going back.

"I need my brother's bones," said Shai.

Anji nodded. "I'll have my men dig up his remains."

Wind moaned along the cliffs. The waterfall wept its constant tears. The baby buried his sweet face against his father's neck.

"I'll take you home, Hari," Shai said, "if it's truly what you want." But already Hari's ghost was dissolving under the chill spray of falling water. He'd held on. He'd given warning. Too late.

"Ah, well," murmured Tohon. "Kartu Town is on the way, if we take the northern route."

"The way where?"

Anji and his men walked down through the ruins and vanished into the forest. Only Chief Tuvi glanced back.

"I thought . . ." Tohon tugged at an earlobe. He examined the lofty peaks as if seeking a lofty speech there. Abruptly his gaze fastened on something Shai did not see. He tracked it, lost it, shrugged. "You'll take his bones to Kartu Town. What about the mistress's bones?"

"There are no remains. Anyway, she doesn't belong to the clan. She was sold to the captain. Her bones belong to him."

"Indeed, they do. We'll go to Kartu Town, then."

"I don't want to return there." To think of being trapped again in the Mei clan made his stomach roil and his anger burn. "I can't, and I won't."

"No, of course not. You're not the lad you were then, are you?"

Yet his tone had changed. Cool, calm, collected Tohon sounded unsure. He fussed with his knife. He patted his hair as if he'd forgotten his cap, but he was wearing neither cap nor helmet today. His words fell diffidently.

"After you get your brother's bones settled, you're welcome to come home with me."

Shai staggered. When had he gotten so dizzy? He groped, found a broken wall, and sat. "Home with you?"

"I've been dismissed from Captain Anji's service. I'll have to report in to Commander Beje, but I've served with honor. It's time for me to go home to my youngest son's wife's tent and meet my grandchildren. Come with me, Shai. We'll find you a good woman to marry. She can be your knife, as you can be hers. You'll be my son, and I'll raise your children as my own."

Tohon watched him with dark eyes and a vulnerable smile. He'd been hit hard before, but he knew how to keep riding even if the path didn't open onto the vista he wished was there. That didn't make the question any easier to get out. "What do you say, Shai?"

Beneath the water's roar and the wind's cry, a voice as sweet as Mai's whispered: *Yes.*

Shai could say nothing, not with words. So he grasped Tohon's hand and then, unexpectedly, Tohon pulled him up and embraced him, as Shai had never once been embraced by his own father.

At length, Tohon pushed him gently back and looked him over with that same smile. "Hu! A long journey ahead of us, neh? Come on, son. Let's get what we need here, and go home."

PART SEVEN: GATES

52

KESHAD HATED DAWN most. At dawn, the first bell woke the city of Olossi. Its clangor jarred him out of the glorious oblivion of sleep and into the sickening realization that he was still enslaved by his debt, that he must rise as he did every day and labor under Master Feden's cruel yoke. Each morning, waking, the pain blossomed as brightly as it had the very first morning, when he'd been a child of twelve bewildered by having had his own kin push him and his younger sister up onto the auction block. The knot of anger never softened.

Now he woke and braced himself as memory flooded: *I am a slave, my sister is a slave, and this day will be no different from the days that came before.*

A warm, naked body stirred against his, and Miravia rolled over, her swelling belly pressed into his abdomen, and kissed him. "I thought you would never wake! Didn't you hear the rooster?"

He clutched her close, tears brimming, and buried his face in her thick hair. It was shoulder-length, still ragged at the ends where she had chopped it off seven months ago.

"Are you *crying*?" She brushed a finger along his cheeks before letting it tangle in his curls.

"Just a bad dream."

Beneath blankets and on a plush cotton-stuffed mattress raised on a pallet of wood, they made their cozy nest. He would have lingered here half the morning stroking her hair and caressing her skin, but after frowning at him, as if she wasn't sure he was telling her everything, she wriggled out of his grasp and rose. How glorious she was, all curves, and her smile in the dim sleeping chamber as she looked down on him was the most glorious curve of all. Her belly was growing each day.

If joy could kill you, he would be dead right now. He would have expired seven months ago, the first time they had kissed.

She poured water into the basin and washed, then deftly wrapped a taloos around her naked body. Pausing with a hand on the curtain that partitioned off the sleeping chamber, she swept her hair back from her face.

"I'm going up to the pool to pray," she said, as she did every morning at dawn.

The curtain slithered down behind her. Her footfalls tapped on the planks of the porch that wrapped the shelter. She exchanged a greeting with someone farther off, and moved away.

Canvas walls tied down between floor and roof beams blocked the wind, which moaned over the sturdy roof. A pair of chests lay closed, with clothes draped over them. A bowl of oil blended with mosk-chasing purple thorn had burned out during the night, leaving its lingering scent. He closed his eyes and luxuriated in the fading heat within the comfort he had made for them out of Miravia's grief. As he drifted between waking and dozing, he smiled, breathing in the scent of jasmine she always left behind. Maybe in the world beyond Merciful Valley she would have refused to eat his rice and chosen Chief Tuvi instead, out of loyalty to Mai, but Tuvi had left to serve Captain Anji, and Kesh had stayed. So the world beyond the valley didn't really matter, did it?

"Keshad? Aui! Come out here and help me, you cursed lag!"

He sighed. Rising, he wrapped a kilt around his hips and, shivering, pulled on a wool tunic over it. It was cursed cold up here in the mornings, with the season of rains fading. His toes ached as he yanked on a pair of the woven socks necessary up in the mountains. He hurried outside just so he could pull on his boots over his freezing feet.

Reeve Miyara was waiting at the steps, arms crossed, scanning the darkening clouds spilling out of the west on a driving wind. "We're in for another storm. You'd think the cursed storms would stop with the end of the Whisper Rains, eh? Do you think the firelings bring the storms here? For I've never seen so many firelings as I have in this place. It's like they've come to visit that Silver prayer ritual with Miravia. There were so many in the cave the day Mai gave birth to Atani. Maybe they've all come to visit the place she died."

"Surely they were here before you reeves ever discovered this valley and used it as a refuge." Kesh put out a hand. Was that a drop of rain? He'd heard no thunder.

"It's hard to think of firelings as being like us, as having a home, isn't it?"

If it rained, Miravia would run back home and strip off her soaked taloos, and . . . He smiled.

She laughed. "You're not truly listening, are you? You're wishing you were back in your bed. What is it about men that they get that idiotic look on their faces when they're getting good sex regularly?"

She was an honest, hardworking Lion fifteen years older than he was. He did not know her well; she visited once a month, an assignment mandated by Captain Anji. She arrived on Wakened Eagle with a sack of rice or nai and a pouch of salt and spices. More important, she came bearing an offering to be presented at the altar at dawn on Transcendent Deer, which was the day Mai, stabbed by her traitorous slave, had vanished into the pool. Then they would share a meal, while she and Miravia would reminisce about Olossi's markets and festivals or discuss flowers and herbs, a passion the two women shared. She usually left at dawn on the next day, Resting Crane, but today she seemed inclined to linger. Nor did he see her eagle.

"Why did you agree to the assignment?" he asked, emboldened by her joke. "Flying supplies for us? Visiting the cave?"

"I grieve for Mai. I didn't know her well, but I loved her, too. The Hundred was a different place, when she was still with us."

"What do you mean?"

By the way she took a step back and pinched her lips together, he realized she did not trust him. What in the hells had he ever done to earn her mistrust? He'd been loyal to Miravia. As bored as he often became isolated up here, he never for one breath regretted his choice to stay.

Miyara's distrust annoyed him. "I know you asked for the assignment, after Captain Anji asked for the valley to be set off limits until Miravia's year of mourning had passed. So he can send his offerings and observe the proper rituals, too. You and Reeve Siras are the only people we ever see."

Her frown passed swiftly, like dawn's rising. "If he's truly observing a year of mourning, then it seems strange he married again so quickly. But maybe it's all of a piece. Maybe Joss was right."

"He married again? When? Who?"

"Neh, think nothing of it. Outlanders have different ways." She licked her lips nervously and gestured toward the thatched roof that sheltered the kitchen. "Miravia put on the rice before she went up. I came over to ask you to help me choose among the turnips and radish, which you'd like me to harvest, it being your garden."

"The hells!" He tromped down the steps, and she stepped back, a hand curling around the reeve's baton that swung from her belt. He stopped short as his irritation sparked from a smolder to a flame. "You can't just let a remark like that flash like lightning and not think I'm going to jump! Married! It's true most folk wait a year, unless there are young children who need care and not enough aunties and uncles to—" He broke off, thinking of the infant child Tuvi had carried off with him. Surely that baby had plenty of uncles! "What else has been going on out there we don't know about? Why don't you and Siras tell us anything?"

"Do you ever ask a cursed thing about what is going on beyond this sheltered place?" she retorted. Her anger boiled up as suddenly as the thunder now rumbling out of the peaks almost as if it had been birthed by the force of her words. "Or wonder if we've been commanded to keep our mouths shut?"

"But— I—"

"Heya!" Her eyes widened as she looked past him. She broke into a run.

He turned. Miravia had stumbled into the clearing from the trail that led up to the waterfall; she was swaying, hands extended as a falling woman begs for help.

The hells!

He bolted, passing Miyara easily, and reached Miravia in time to catch her as her legs gave out. She was washed gray like a corpse, and breathing hard.

"My love! Ravia! What's happened? Are you hurt?"

Her mouth opened, but no words came out. In her stunned gaze he saw nothing but blank incomprehension, as if a lilu had sunk its claws into her heart and drained away all thought, leaving only emotion. But her body worked. She regained her feet, pulled away from him, and began running back up the trail. He had to follow, glancing back to assure himself that Miyara, armed with baton and sword, was jogging at his heels. A look of alarm erased the suspicion that had so recently scarred her expression. They wound up through the thickly perfumed trees, the late flowering bushes, the profusion of fruit. He bumped his head on a dangling sunfruit, which dropped to thud on the earth and tumble away into the undergrowth. So much lay hidden.

Commanded to keep our mouths shut.

"Ravia!" he called, but she kept running, passion the wings that carried her.

He was puffing and heaving by the time they burst out into the ruins. He stumbled to a halt as Miyara stopped beside him.

"The hells!" cried the reeve with the breath he could not take.

The waterfall, swollen with the last of the rains, pounded its fury into the pool. Water lapped to the brim, wavelets spilling along flat terraces of smooth stone. The cursed pool was writhing with blue threads like infant firelings pouring up from the depths. Miravia was staring not at the pool but at something else entirely.

A slight figure huddled on one of the low stone walls whose tumbled remains graced the ruins. Black hair plastered her neck and wove trails down the soaking wet silk of her bloodstained taloos. Her mouth was parted, and slowly, as if it hurt to move, she straightened and looked toward them.

Thunder boomed. It began to rain in a fierce, unexpected cloudburst.

Mai.

*   *   *

THEN SHE WOKE, coughing water out of her mouth. Only half aware of what she was doing, she dragged herself onto a shelf of rock and lay heaving until she could breathe again. Her chest hurt; pain squeezed her ribs with each sharp inhalation.

A woman screamed.

Hu! What if Tuvi hadn't gotten here yet and Sheyshi tried again? What if the slave had gone after the baby?

She pushed up through an agony of tight muscles, but instead of Sheyshi and Priya and the baby, Miravia was standing a stone's toss from her with hands shielding her cheeks and her mouth and eyes gone all round as though an awful demon was rising out of the pool behind Mai about to pounce. She actually turned to look, the feeling was so strong, maybe Sheyshi climbing out of the water with her knife, but there was no one, only a shimmering surface of blue threads she recognized as the newborn spirits born in the womb of the firelings and not yet strong enough to take flight into the storms.

How did she know that?

"Miravia!" she rasped, but Miravia was already gone, fleeing *flip flap flip flap*, her footsteps reverberating through the empty ruins as water poured over the high lip and roared into the pool. Spray moistened her face. She staggered to the path that led behind a curtain of falling water and into the overhang. Priya might have hidden Atani in here, but the overhang lay dim and empty but for the altar stone heaped with withered wreaths and flower necklaces and a fresh-blooming spray of plum blossoms. Out of season surely, she thought at random as she caught herself on the stone, trying not to topple over.

A ring sat on the stone. She stared at it a long time: a Mei clan wolf's-head ring, big enough to fit a man's finger. She'd given hers to Anji, but she knew who this one belonged to: It was Shai's ring. Left on the altar.

She snatched it up and stumbled outside, hand pressing into her stomach as a prickling pain spread across her midsection. Legs giving out, she sank onto the ruins of a low wall. Her flesh felt ragged beneath her probing fingers. The lips of the stab wound were still tender, felt through the wet silk of her taloos. Where had all that blood come from that soaked the silk? Why did it still hurt so much?

She had to go find Atani, but she didn't have the strength to rise. Just rest a little, and a little longer yet, and then strength would come. It must. She had to find Atani, and Priya, and O'eki. She had to warn Miravia. Sheyshi was a murderer, an agent long since planted into her household without anyone knowing. Not even Anji had known. She was sure of it.

Anji would never have acquiesced to her death. Or at least, not under these circumstances. He hated to lose, and he would never allow his mother to win. That was his weakness. Of course her beauty had attracted him in Kartu Town's market, but any Qin officer might admire beauty and even sample what could not be denied to him, and then ride on. Why hadn't she seen it before now? Perhaps he had been, as he claimed, amused or even impressed when she had tried to sell him almonds at a price twice market value. But now she wondered if it had irritated him as well. Folk feared the Qin. They were wise to do so. And here this slip of a girl from a dusty provincial trading town, a place of no possible importance in the wide world, had the gall to mock him by demanding such a price.

She could see the scene unfold with stark clarity. It was easy to see from this side of the knife that had plunged into her flesh, whose blade had wept her blood.

He had taken her, just like in the songs. The dashing, powerful officer. The humble fruit seller unable to say "no." Yet their hardships had bound them together; their journey had forced them to forge a partnership. They had been building something worthwhile, hadn't they? Didn't Anji truly love her? Hadn't he defied his mother on her behalf? Or had he only been irritated at having his will crossed?

Because Anji had betrayed her anyway, when it suited his purposes. He had promised to safeguard Hari but had killed him instead. Who else would Hari have trusted to come so close? Who else could have walked right up to him without Hari having the least idea what was about to happen?

Only Anji.

Thunder boomed. Rain hammered the clearing as if it meant to disintegrate her and sweep her fragments back into the pool whose healing touch had saved her. Saved her for what? For waking up to realize that she could not trust the man she loved?

So when she heard the clap of running feet followed by the intake of shocked breath followed by silence as the rain gave out as abruptly as it had washed through, it was hard to be frightened of what they might do to her. She'd already been stabbed in the heart and survived.

Miravia had returned, bringing with her Reeve Miyara, whose unsheathed sword and expression of stunned fear kindled a flame of indignation. What had she ever done to make people fear *her*? She was the one Sheyshi had tried to kill!

"Mistress Mai?"

"Master Keshad!" This was too much! Her sight wasn't clouded. He placed a hand intimately on Miravia's hip to shift the young woman behind him, but not before Mai realized that the bulge in Miravia's taloos wasn't the fabric twisted and pouching. "Miravia! Are you pregnant? By *him*?"

"Mai!" Miravia pushed past Keshad and flung herself at Mai, her body solid and warm and comforting as Mai hung onto her and she hung on to Mai, sobbing and hugging.

"Best get away from her," said the reeve into their blubbering reunion. "She must be a lilu, Miravia. Come to lure you to your death by taking the form of one you love."

Mai sat straight, releasing Miravia and wiping her nose. "I'm the one who was stabbed! How can I then be the lilu? Where is Atani? Where is Sheyshi? Shouldn't you be chasing after *her*?" She rose, and the reeve leaped back as if expecting Mai to smite her.

Keshad paced forward with hands extended in an annoying way meant to placate, as if he too thought she was a lilu and must be bribed. "Here, now. What do you want, lilu?"

"Miravia, you can't possibly believe I'm a lilu! Where is Atani?"

Miravia trembled as she brushed fingers over the sopping fabric of Mai's taloos. "Commander Anji took him, of course. He thought you were dead. Everyone thought you were dead, because you were stabbed and blood was everywhere and you sank into the pool and no one could reach you. Mai, sit down."

Mai sat, coughing as though there were more water in her lungs, but there wasn't, just a sick weight of dread. She spread a hand over her own belly, where she and Anji had seeded another life, although no one could possibly yet suspect. "Miravia, how are you come to be so obviously pregnant, when this morning you weren't pregnant at all?"

"Don't touch her!" cried the reeve.

Keshad sat down, so Mai was boxed between him and Miravia. "Careful, lilu. I have a knife and I'm not afraid to use it."

"Kesh! Don't you dare!" Miravia took Mai's hand and turned it over, opened her fingers, traced the lines that creased her palms, although in truth her hands were horribly wrinkled as they would be after being immersed in water for a long time. "Mai. Listen to me. Sheyshi stabbed you. Then the Qin killed her. It seems Sheyshi wasn't stupid at all but only playing a part. She was an agent for Anji's mother all along."

"Anji's *mother*! The old bitch! She warned me she wouldn't let me get in the way of her plans for Anji. When he finds out what she did—"

"Mai! Listen! He already knows. It's been seven months—two hundred and fifty-two days—"

"Two hundred and fifty-three," said Keshad.

"You think it's really Mai, don't you?" demanded Miyara, keeping her distance.

"Of course it's Mai," said Miravia as she stroked Mai's arm and smiled, her face as bright as the threads whose glow made the pool shimmer both on its visible surface and in its depths. "She's annoyed with me for getting pregnant by Kesh, because she wanted me to marry Chief Tuvi. No lilu would care about that. Anyway, isn't it obvious? The firelings saved her. They hid her away until they healed her. Just like in the tales."

She wept tears sweetened by joy, but Mai had heard a different melody in Miyara's voice, and she captured the reeve's gaze until, at last, Miyara shook her head with a twisted smile.

"I could believe it. I want to believe it. But Mai—"

"Tell me what you fear to tell me," said Mai. "I beg you."

"Think of what Anji will say when he finds out she's alive!" cried Miravia with happy abandon.

Miyara made an awning with a hand over her eyes, thinking. After a while, she looked up. "Maybe a bowl of rice and a cup of cordial first."

"No." She opened her hand, displaying the ring. "What does this mean?"

The reeve shrugged. "Your uncle Shai left that as an offering on the altar."

The Merciful One's touch might untwist the knot in your heart, dizzying you. "He's alive, then. He survived."

"He did. But he's gone, Mai. He left the Hundred with that scout, Tohon."

"Taking Hari's bones back to Kartu Town. Poor Shai. He'll hate it there. And I'll never see him again."

"He may have said something about a Kartu Town, but I think he was going on with Tohon, to wherever the Qin live. They were like father and son, if you know what I mean."

Ah. The words eased the ache a little, knowing that Shai had a hope of being happy. "And what about my son? Is Atani dead? Did that old bitch have him murdered, too, so the emperor's sister could marry Anji and make a treaty and fine fat children between them?"

"The child was taken away by his father," said Miyara. "Everyone knows Commander Anji dotes on the boy. But the rest is as you say, Mistress. His mother took over the running of his household. He married the Sirniakan woman."

Mai wiped beads of moisture from her face, her heart as cold as her chilled skin and damp hands. Anji had betrayed her.

"There's one thing I need to do first. Miravia, will you help me?"

"Of course."

"Wouldn't it be wise to ask what it is before you agree to it?" demanded Keshad, but Miravia cast him such a look that Mai would have smiled if she had remembered how.

She rose. "After that, I beg you, Miyara, please take me to my son. I'll never leave him in the clutches of those women."

BY STAGES.

First she sent Keshad out with Miyara to Astafero. Miyara returned with Siras and a brash young reeve named Ildiya so passionately infatuated with Siras that she would do anything he asked. Ildiya flew out with Miravia, while Mai followed with Miyara. Siras hauled the single heavy chest of the few but precious items worth taking away from Merciful Valley.

They flew to Naya Hall, now a training hall for all newly jessed reeves from across the Hundred. After a period of training, these novice reeves were assigned to one of forty-six secondary halls and outposts according to family groupings and flight assignments. It was a new system, devised by Commander Anji.

"Anji is commander of the reeve halls?" Mai demanded. "How can that be? What happened to Joss?"

So it was with the shattering news that Anji had also killed both Joss and his eagle thundering in her heart that Mai spent a miserable night in Astafero. The house built for her and Anji lay abandoned but for a few desert mice, chirping geckos, and two stout clothes chests shoved forgotten into a back storeroom. At dawn, having sent a message ahead asking Mistresss Behara to meet her, she walked down to Astafero's council square.

Several hundred people had gathered, and they wept, and touched her, and showed her the flower-bedecked altar they'd set up under a roofed shelter at Hasibal's stone.

"Do you want to pray to the Merciful One, Mistress?" Behara asked her. "Many of us do, remembering the prayers. How can it be you are alive? Everyone said you were murdered by the red hounds out of Sirniaka."

"Is that what they said?" And yet, how to explain what would only make them distrust her? "In truth, verea, I was sorely hurt and I suppose it was deemed better to set it about that I was dead than to risk a second attack."

Ah. Of course. This made perfect sense. Exactly the kind of wise decision Commander Anji would make to confound his enemies. They showed her the sprawling market, the burgeoning fields, the expanding docks, the steady expansion of the irrigation channels being dug mey by mey up into the hills. The garrison fort with its well-behaved soldiers.

No one feared attack from the empire. The commander had taken care of that even if he had had to marry that foreign woman who, it was said, no one ever saw. Those problems with bandits and renegades in previous years? Neh, not a problem at all any longer, at least not here in Olo'osson. Trade was brisk and profitable. Why, a woman walking alone could carry a precious vessel of water-white all the way from Astafero past Old Fort and to Horn, and not fear she'd be assaulted! The commander had taken care of that.

They prayed the prayers to the Merciful One at the altar of Hasibal every day, they told her, and their prayers had been answered.

They flew north in stages.

The second night they slept over in a village on West Track, a quiet town whose innkeeper welcomed them gravely. He proudly showed them a newly built dormitory set aside for traveling reeves and soldiers. A much smaller chamber was set aside for female reeves, with only two pallets folded up in the bedding cupboard.

He had no idea who Mai was, although he looked twice and then three times at Miravia and, when Kesh pointedly draped an arm around his wife's shoulders, smiled apologetically as he explained he'd recently been serving numbers of Ri Amarah men hastening to and from Toskala on business for the commander.

"I thought they kept their women— Never mind. My apologies, verea."

He invited them to dine in the main room of the inn and hurried off to the kitchen. The inn wasn't crowded but the locals were drinking, eyeing them with the satisfaction locals take in seeing outsiders look unsure of themselves. A pair of young men really looked Mai over, and then began arguing in low voices. The innkeeper and his wife brought their party cordial and a big pot of well-spiced barsh to share for their supper.

"How much?" asked Mai, preparing to bargain.

He looked surprised. "Eh, verea, any reeve or soldier or messenger receives free lodging and food. It's part of the tax, isn't it? The militia tithe." He grinned. "However, I'm only obligated to serve you a single cup of cordial. After that, you have to pay house prices."

"The militia tithe? What manner of tax is that?"

His smile softened, as if he'd just figured out she was as stupid as she was pretty. "So the army and the reeves can patrol, make sure we're not burned out of our villages, killed in our beds. I'm happy to feed them, seeing how peaceful things are now."

The young men sauntered up, swaggering with nervous bravado. "Velin here says he's seen you before, verea," said the one courageous enough to speak first. "He says he's sure he saw you in Olossi that one time he went there for festival. Aren't you one of Hasibal's players? They take in outlander slaves, sometimes, and train them up. Hard to see how a man could forget a face like yours. I'm Noresh, by the way. We'd be happy to buy you a cup, eh?"

She knew how to smile to make a man feel she regretted the necessity of discouraging his advances. "My apologies, ver. I'm on a mission with these reeves. Nothing I can speak of."

That impressed them. Out of misplaced pity, a scab she kept picking at, she told the innkeeper to pour them each a cup and handed over a few vey. They wandered away, flushed and whispering at their triumph, and kept glancing her way as they lingered over their cups as if to drag out the ecstasy. A woman brought out her lute and began accompanying herself on songs, the folk joining in on the chorus and the hand gestures. The music flowed so sweetly; thoughts might wander down these bright tuneful paths and let go of the shadows.

Until the woman began a new song, one whose response was answered raggedly by folk still eagerly learning it: how the outlander had saved them and been rewarded with the love of a young woman as beautiful as plum blossoms shimmering dew-laden at dawn, only to have her stolen away from him by a jealous lilu.

Mai, choked and unable to breathe evenly, excused herself and returned to the tiny room. Miravia followed her and lay down beside her on the pallet they would share for the night.

"Mai . . ."

"Neh, it's nothing. Nothing I understand. He betrayed me."

"He loved you!"

"Maybe he did, but now I wonder if this would have happened in the end no matter what? Demons stole me! That's one way to put it. But there's another story, a truer tale, isn't there? We sing the songs, and hear the tales, hoping they will have a happy ending—the bandit prince falls in love with the brickmaker's daughter and they live forever after in harmony—or at least a satisfyingly gruesome one in which everyone dies, but that is why they are tales, isn't it? Forever after in harmony, as long as I always did what Anji approved of. And then, when I did not . . ." She touched her cheek, the one he'd slapped.

"Folk do get angry with each other, Mai. Kesh can be so irritating, but I love him despite it, because of it, including it. If people can never be angry, then isn't that a way of lying?"

Mai smiled, remembering how she had thrown a cup at Anji, which he'd caught. Then she wept, and Miravia held her.

People travel onward by stages. Seven months is a stage, a chasm whose loss cannot be recovered, only bridged.

Late on the third afternoon they found shelter in an outpost atop a hill, a way fort overlooking the major road across Istria called the Flats. A cadre of soldiers was stationed in tent barracks set on raised plank floors. Their commander was a Qin officer attended by four Qin tailmen whom Mai did not recognize and who did not recognize her. The soldiers recognized Kesh's partnership with Miravia, and deemed Miyara too bored with their youth to flirt with, but Mai and Ildiya they marked as fair game despite Siras's obvious jealousy.

"Enough!" said Miyara finally after yet another tray of cordial had been brought and hopefully presented to the young women. "Have you louts no manners? We'd like to eat in peace."

"Neh, I was finished," said Mai, for the sweat and rowdy clamor and the presence of Qin soldiers made her stomach knot and her eyes fill with tears. Every man, even the local ones, wore a black tabard and his hair bound up in a topknot. "I'll just walk outside."

Kesh jerked as if he'd been kicked. "Ow!" he cried, flashing an indignant look at Miravia. She nodded toward Mai. "Ah. Well. I'll just walk out with you, verea. Keep you company. Guard you in case there are wolves prowling."

Every man there, even the Qin, watched them leave the eating porch, and avid gazes tracked them out along the ridge. They reached a platform sited for an excellent view of the road running below, the distant crown of Mount Aua to the west, and a nearer view of an oddly shaped ridge, slightly higher in elevation than their own, cut by a ledge whose stony surface glittered as the setting sun caught its length at just the right angle.

"I wish you would call me 'Mai,'" she said as she leaned on the railing, the wind battering against the clasps and sticks with which she armored her hair. "Miravia is my dearest friend. Maybe she is my only friend. Even Miyara can't tell me what has happened to Priya and O'eki, only that they went away with Anji. I hate to be called 'verea' by you, as though we're acquaintances in the market. I'm very angry she married you, but surely I can still think of you as my brother." She wiped a tear.

"Eiya! Why are you crying?"

"Just missing my twin."

"You have a *twin*! One as beautiful as you?"

She shot him a glance, and he blushed horribly, looking mortified, and she laughed for the first time since she had woken. "I have a twin, a brother. Maybe he grew into his looks. I hope so." Poor Mei. Always hounded by Grandmother and Father Mei and their mother and aunt. He was no silkworm to wind a cushion of silk to protect himself. He was a fragile leaf, subject to their storms. How was he faring? Could she send him a message across the vast distance, let her family know that she was alive? Would the family ever know the full story of what had happened to Hari?

"Did you ever look in the pool, Keshad? Did you ever see the chains?"

"What chains?"

"Never mind. Did Shai truly say nothing to you, that time he came up with Anji a month after—" She rubbed a hand over her vest, feeling the scar tissue along her ribs. "After Sheyshi stabbed me?"

"He never talked to me at all, and I admit I didn't talk to him. I was too cursed worried that Ravia would take it into her head to tell Chief Tuvi she would marry him, out of loyalty to you. So I didn't pay much attention to his troubles."

She rested a hand on his forearm, and he was so startled he jerked it away, then flushed again, and settled his arm back beside hers on the railing as if within the reach of a particularly fearsome snake, and endured her fingers resting lightly on his hand.

"You do love Miravia, don't you?" she asked.

He looked irritated. Then he flung back his head as the sun winked hard on that distant ledge. "I just remembered. The captain and his men brought three small jeweler's chests bound with chains. But they left without them. I thought they were offerings for the altar. He sent up flowers every month, plum blossoms if he could get them. But that doesn't explain why he left those good quality chests behind, does it? Indeed, they emptied a clothes chest from the barracks shelter and took it away with them, although I never knew—nor asked—what was in it, I was that glad to see them go without taking Ravia with them."

She changed the subject, stumbling over a momentary awkwardness by falling back on the one subject she never tired of. "Tell me again, how was the baby that last time you saw him, when Anji came to take him away?"

He had the same smile any Hundred man would have, thinking of a plump, healthy child. "An exceptionally beautiful child. He has such a chortling laugh, like everything amuses him! Very good natured."

Four soldiers tramped up behind them, laughing in a quite different way, shoving each other and showing off, making themselves big and noticeable as they crowded against the railing two on each side.

"Heya, verea! Like the view, eh?"

"It's a very fine view of the road. I suppose you keep an eye on travelers and caravans. Make sure no one comes to harm."

"We do oversee the roads, of course." They were young men, desperate to boast. "But that's not the chief reason we're here. We're black wolves, you know."

"Black wolves?"

"The army's elite. We're trained to hunt demons."

"You hunt demons?" She looked at Kesh, but he shrugged.

"See that Mount Aua? There's a demon cradle there, a place demons might try to shelter for a night, sip their demon nectar. And that ridge there—see how it glitters? That one, too. So we're posted here to keep an eye on them. There are other outposts like this one. Chief Chartai commands the entire black wolf cohort here in Istria. We're the second such cohort, you know. Just commissioned two months ago. See our banner?"

It flapped from a pole, two wolf's heads grinning in the breeze.

"We figured you maybe had a brother or husband who died in the service of the wolves, verea, seeing as you wear the ring."

She looked down at the wolf's-head ring, sigil of the Mei clan. The necklace had slipped out from the neck of her vest and Shai's ring dangled at the curve of her breasts, which they were staring at, as men would. It was the same head, the very same. They held up their hands to show they, too, wore wolf's-head rings.

Her throat tightened on words she did not want to say. She slipped the errant chain and its ring back beneath her vest and was at once sorry she'd done so, because they followed the movement of the ring as if with their own hands.

"What kind of demons are you hunting?"

"Any demons, really, traitors or bandits or murderers. But particularly cloaks, verea. Those ones who say they're Guardians but are really gods-rotted lilus waiting to corrupt us and lead the Hundred back into war." They preened, just like sunning eagles. "Only the black wolves are told the secret of how to kill demons. It's a dangerous job. We're not afraid."

But now she was. Fear snapped, a wolf who had just decided to eat her up.

The fourth day they ought to have made it all the way to Toskala, but Miyara was stricken as by a shuddering sickness, and then she wept while still aloft, and afterward they sailed down and came to rest in a pasture as sheep scattered. The buildings of a substantial town rose ahead. Farmers and herdsmen came running.

"Miyara, what is it? Are you ill?" Mai was dangling with her feet off the ground, kicking a little, wanting to stand on solid earth instead of being helpless.

"I'm scared, Mai, I don't mind saying. There's a thing I've never told you. About Joss. They say Scar went after Commander Anji. They say Joss was jealous that Commander Anji was doing a better job than Joss was commanding the reeves, so he tried to kill him."

"Joss? Reeve Joss? Are we talking about the same man?"

"The cursed handsome one."

"That's right. He's an Ox, just like me. I admit he was vain, but very charming! Yet I never met a man less ambitious to puff about his own importance and authority than Reeve Joss. I mean, he seemed like a man who'd been dragged into authority and didn't like it much."

"That's how I saw him, I admit. But others didn't. It's not what folk said afterward. I wasn't there. But let me tell you something and I beg you never to say I mentioned it. There's a contingent of reeves—not many, but people who were close to him—who flew to Bronze Hall down in Mar. You wouldn't know them, they'd just be names to you. They've never truly confided in me, but I've been thinking as each month passes that once I've discharged the obligation I made to ferry supplies up to Merciful Valley for the one year—a promise I made to Commander Anji on behalf of the boy, who is my nephew, if you'll recall—"

"I do recall it. I know what I owe you."

"Never mind that. It's nothing any Hundred woman wouldn't have done."

"What have you been thinking?"

"That I'd leave Argent Hall and fly to Bronze Hall. Siras is thinking of coming with me—and I suppose Ildiya will tag along with him. Anyhow, we just want to hear what they have to say. Bronze Hall's not a member of the reeve council. They never sent a representative to the council in which Commander Anji was elected as commander over the reeve halls. They're not subject to him."

"And what does Commander Anji think of that?" Mai asked tartly. "That one hall doesn't acknowledge his authority?"

"How could I know? I'm just a reeve in Argent Hall, far away from Law Rock. I know there's been plenty of fighting up in Herelia and Teriayne and the north. The war's not over yet. I'm sure Commander Anji is too busy to bother himself with sleepy Mar, way down on the southeastern coast."

"Let me down, I beg you, I have to pee."

Miyara unhooked them both, and they both went to pee in the woods. When they reemerged, the farmers were gawking from a distance at the eagle while the herdsmen and their barking dogs chivvied the sheep through a gap in the woods toward a safer clearing.

Mai was struggling with the trousers. "I hate these things. A taloos is so much easier to wear, much less pee in."

Miyara hauled out a flag and signaled Siras and Ildiya, who headed down.

"Tell you what, Mai," said Miyara. "Let's shelter here for the night. Then we'll reach Law Rock in the morning. Better in the morning than late in the afternoon, eh?"

"Why?"

She jerked the flags down and rolled them up tightly, hands tense. Her eyes had a faraway look, as a caravaner in the desert might eye a distant haze wondering if it is a killing sandstorm. "Better to have plenty of time to leave, don't you think? If things aren't so hospitable."

"Reeve! Verea!"

A man and a woman came jogging toward them along the road. "We saw you come down. And here are more of you! Surely you'll honor us by staying over. We're a humble town, but we've a garrison station newly built and still empty. You're welcome to stay there for the night. We'll feed you gladly."

It was impossible to say no to such an enthusiastic offer. The reeves shucked the harness from their eagles, seeing it was earlier in the day than they normally halted, and they accompanied the townsfolk along the road as the farmers gestured friendly greetings and went back to their resplendent fields, half grown in stagnant rectangles of water.

"Look at that growth! That's our second crop this season! I don't mind telling you, it was cursed lean pickings until the first crop was brought in. We all struggled to survive, and some of the children and elders and invalids did not, for all our stores were stolen by the demon army and some of our lads and lasses besides." The ancient road was an astonishing landmark, smoothly paved and massively built, raised up from the surrounding countryside and flanked on either side by tracks worn into the earth by generations of trudging feet. The town lay ahead, a half built palisade now abandoned; plenty of people were out in the fields and among the orchards. "But that's all settled now. Why, just three months ago a girl who'd gone missing fully ten months ago—given up for dead!—came riding home behind a Qin soldier. Very finely set up she was, too, for he'd taken it into his mind to eat her rice, and she'd been minded to finish the bowl he started. Her clan were nothing more than day laborers, and now they're the third richest in town. What do you think of that!"

The abandoned palisade had been fitted with gates, set open with iron bracings. Four posts had been erected to the left of the open gate.

Four posts, from which dangled the remains of men, strands of hair fluttering where flesh hadn't yet rotted away from the skulls, the tattered remnants of their clothing frayed and faded. So had the Qin hung out executed criminals in the sunblasted citadel square in Kartu Town after their armies had conquered the area.

Maybe she fainted. Maybe she just tripped on uneven pavement. Maybe she just forgot to breathe.

Then she was on her knees, shaking, hands over her face.

"Mai!" Miravia steadied her.

"Why are corpses hanging from posts?" She'd never forgotten Widow Lae. On the day of the widow's execution for treason and spying, every man, woman, and child of Kartu Town had been required to assemble in citadel square to watch. That had been the day Anji had first spoken to Mai's father. That had been the day he'd made it clear to a man who could not refuse him that he intended to have her for himself. Of course he'd never asked her. It would have been surprising if he had!

How could she ever have thought it was romantic?

And yet hadn't it been just as sweet and satisfying as one of her beloved songs? Up until the end, when he had killed Uncle Hari. When his mother had taken over Mai's household. When he'd married a woman he didn't know in capitulation to the very mother who had arranged the murder of the woman he loved.

And all for what?

For now she understood what she had been hoping for, in the last four days. The unspoken wish, the unexamined dream: that, upon seeing her, Anji would cast all the other aside, discard it without a second's thought, and embrace her. Just as it used to be.

"Them's the executed men, verea," their escort was saying. "So sorry if it upset you, if it came unexpected. But surely you have assizes down there south, too, don't you?"

"We do," said Miyara slowly, "but I never saw such posts as these. I heard that the Star army would cleanse people, hang them up by the arms until they died of pain and thirst. It gives me a sick feeling to look at these dead men and think of them suffering like that."

"The hells! I know the cleansing you're speaking of. We're not such savages. This was done all according to the law. The assizes came through, just like in the old days. Very fair, it was. Very orderly. Because we're so close to Toskala, we happened to host the commander himself just for the one day, a very impressive man with excellent manners. He come accompanied by judges, just like the Guardians of old with their law scrolls and each one wearing a tabard in a color that marked their specialty. You know, white for murder trials. Green for agricultural disputes. Gold for boundary disputes. Red for— Well, anyway! I don't mind telling you the local lads had captured twelve fugitives from the demon army who'd been hiding out in the woods. The commander interviewed each one personally, in front of witnesses. Two he deemed were just young fellows, led astray but salvageable, and those he sent on to a militia training camp in High Haldia. Two were auctioned right here into debt slavery, for a seven-year term. Four were sent for a three-year term of labor on public works in Toskala, very fair, mind you. These four, though—they were the senior men, and poison-mouthed fellows they were. The judges really had no choice but to condemn them—it has to be unanimous, you know. They got a quick execution, more merciful than what things they themselves done to innocents at their own confession, I'll tell you. Their corpses were hung up on these posts as a warning to them who might think of turning to the shadows, and as a reminder to the rest of us that justice was served."

SHE SLEPT POORLY. Maybe they all did, for they rose before dawn and left as soon as the eagles could be whistled down.

Not long after dawn they reached Toskala. The city filled up a wedge of ground between two rivers, the breadth of its packed buildings, avenues, alleys, compounds, walls, and outer districts where the dirty work of living was carried out sprawled northward along the banks. It was almost as big as the Mariha city she had glimpsed in the distance, right before they'd been detoured up to Commander Beje's villa where Anji had been given a reprieve from his death sentence.

A huge promontory of solid rock thrust up at the southern point, a spear dividing the two rivers. The Greater Istri glittered like hope under the morning sun; its tributary, almost as wide, streamed into the greater in a web of currents and countercurrents as complex as the yearning and anger interlaced in her own heart.

Miyara flagged them down over the huge rock, toward a reeve hall strung along the western cliff in a series of long barracks and open parade grounds. They landed in one of the parade grounds. After unhooking and handing her eagle over to the care of fawkners, Miyara led Mai aside to a tiny cottage set back in a small garden.

"Vekess is marshal here, isn't he?" she demanded of the elderly man sweeping the porch. "I need to speak to him immediately."

"He's out on patrol." He frowned at her brash approach, and then he saw Mai. He smiled, setting his broom to one side. "What's this? Where are you come from?" He looked up to see Keshad and Miravia hesitating in the alley, with Siras and Ildiya at their backs.

"I'm Reeve Miyara. I have brought messengers from Merciful Valley. I was hoping Marshal Vekess could tell us where Commander Anji is, and arrange for the messengers to meet with him."

"I'm Reeve Odash. Sit down. I'll send for someone from headquarters to speak to you."

"I beg you," said Mai, "but perhaps there's a place I might relieve myself. And change out of these dusty clothes?"

Of course there was, a tiny square garden shed nicely made with sliding doors on two sides and cupboards and shelves inside so neatly organized with shears and rakes and digging spades in four different sizes that it was a pleasure to admire their disciplined ranks. The old reeve, with a grandfatherly solicitude not without a touch of a wistful lust, carried in a copper basin, a pitcher of cool water, and a linen tower. Even so, she could only wash her face and hands and feet and, with Miravia's help, clasp and pin up her hair so it was tidy. Last, she succumbed to the vanity she had often pretended she did not possess. In Astafero, she had taken a first-quality taloos from the dusty storeroom. She shook out the cloth now. The intense blue green color mirrored the salty waters of the Olo'o Sea and was chased with faint silver threads outlining the foam and waves of a sea caressed by winds. She wrapped its silky glamor around her body as Miravia shook her head.

"How do I look? You're my mirror, Miravia."

Miravia's frown deepened. "Are you meaning to confront him, or seduce him?"

"Should I make my entrance in all my dust, in those unattractive trousers and vest? Looking like a—a—sheepherder?"

A hand patted one of the doors. "Mai?" Miyara was whispering as if she dared not let anyone know who was concealed within. "Can you come out? *Now?*"

A decisive step thumped on the porch and the door was slammed open to reveal a Qin soldier with sword drawn.

"Tuvi!" She grasped Miravia's arm, seeing the sword's ugly curve, the tip as deadly as an eagle's beak.

His other arm flashed out and he caught himself against the wall. He stared at her as at a monster. The sword wavered, drooped. He took a step back, and Miyara had to jump back down the step to avoid being shoved off by his movement.

"How can this be?" he said hoarsely.

"Chief Tuvi."

"What are you, that comes here wearing Mai's face and form?"

"I'm Mai, Tuvi-lo."

"You can't be Mai. She is dead. I saw her die. She vanished into the pool." He found his balance and held out a hand to display the ropy white scars across the skin. "I tried to pull her out, but the demons had already claimed you."

"No. That pool is the womb of the firelings. They healed me."

"Of course that is impossible," he said, "and it is foolish of you to claim it could be true. For then why do you only appear now? No person can breathe water. Only demons can. Therefore, you are a demon. Now you have come here with anger and a demon's mischief in your heart. What do you want?"

He shifted back one more step, enough to gesture toward people outside she could not see. "Sergeant! Hold the three reeves and that man Keshad under guard." He stepped into the chamber, raising his sword. "Miravia. Go outside."

She stepped in front of Mai. "No. This is truly Mai, Chief Tuvi. I know it."

"She is a demon, what the people here call a lilu. She has seduced you, Miravia. Even you."

"I want my son!" cried Mai.

"So after all it has come to this. The child was born in the midst of demons, and now they seek to claim him. Miravia, step aside. I don't want to harm you."

"No," said Miravia, but Mai shouldered her aside and placed herself in front, staring him down as she drowned in the death of her hopes.

"Kill me then, Tuvi-lo. I do not fear death. Not much, anyway. But tell me, if you please, if it is true these stories I hear. That Sheyshi was his mother's agent. That when he discovered who had me killed, he allowed his mother to take over the running of *my* household anyway! That he married the Sirniakan princess his mother brought for him. That his army is spread across the Hundred guarding every gate and road, just like the Qin army across the towns of the Golden Road? Paying taxes they call tithes. Hanging executed criminals from posts as a warning, just like you Qin did in Kartu Town in our citadel square after making us watch the executions. Is that all true?" The tears began to flood, but she had to speak. "Is Atani well? Is he thriving and healthy? Do they take good care of him? Did Priya and O'eki stay with him, or were they dismissed? And did Anji's mother or his new wife find you a good wife, Tuvi? Someone special only, as I would have?"

Mai had never set out to deliberately cause another person pain. She had never cut anyone, much less killed a man, but she saw the blow connect in the way he gasped as his eyes lost track of her briefly as the words stabbed home.

No. The women in charge of Anji's household had not found him someone special. Why should they? They didn't care about Tuvi personally. He was just another weapon at Anji's disposal.

He sheathed his sword. "Miravia, go with the others. You—what must I call you?"

"You know my name."

His mouth pinched closed as he refused to say it. "You will come with me. For after all, I find I cannot kill you, even knowing what you are. Let the captain decide."

Let the captain decide.

"Mai?"

"Do as he says." She kissed Miravia on each cheek, and they embraced tightly, for it might be the last time. "Be happy with Keshad."

She must go quickly lest she lose her composure. For it was composure she needed more than anything. She walked through the garden with Tuvi at her back, close enough to kill her swiftly should it come to that. Reeve Odash leaned on his broom, his face seamed with confusion, but he did not protest. Tuvi's escort of twelve men stared openly, as much delighted as startled to find Tuvi marshaling a beautiful young woman out of a garden shed. Two of the soldiers were Qin soldiers she knew, young men she'd traveled with. They gaped like fishes, but Tuvi's fist nudged her in the small of the back so she kept moving without a word even as he ordered them to run ahead and clear a path.

So it was that folk were ducking out of the way, hurrying into barracks, closing shutters, as Tuvi marched her through the alleys and training yards of the reeve hall. They passed under a gate guarded by two soldiers and along the verge of a cliff on a narrow trail paved with flagstones, past pools scratched into the stone, and thence to the very prow of Law Rock where the wind sang over the rushing waters. A humble thatched roof surrounded by a simple wood railing sheltered a dull stele, squat and wide, set in the earth, nothing much to look at except for the flower necklaces draped over its upright end. One had slipped off, the white flowers a blaze of brightness against the raked dirt.

Then they came around the point and walked up a flagstone path on the eastern rim that ended in a wall and a gate guarded, once again, by soldiers. She did not know these men, and they were definitely outlanders with smooth cheeks and eyes as hard as pebbles as they looked her over without lust but with a glint that warned her, too late, that they had recognized *her*.

"What is this, Chief Tuvi?" they asked. "Isn't this—?"

"Let me through," he said in the tone of a man who does not expect to be refused. They hesitated just long enough for his expression to kindle, and in that battle Mai saw the war within the household. Who ruled? Anji, or his mother?

They rapped a signal on the gate. It was opened, and Tuvi guided her along a narrow whitewashed corridor and past several slits behind which she heard voices speaking in a language she did not know. Twice, Tuvi paused to answer a question posed from an unseen interlocutor, and twice another gate was opened and they passed through into an identical blank corridor. The third gate opened onto a porch that overlooked a garden, its ornamental bushes severely pruned and its flowering shrubs exceptionally elegant in a sparse aesthetic she recognized as Anji's.

The blow took her like the knife up under the ribs. There he was, seated on a simple camp stool under a simple awning beside a low table, bent over what was almost certainly a set of maps while he talked with a pair of local men she did not know. One was a militia captain and the other an ostiary of Ilu, if one judged by the stripe on his blue cloak. He smiled in that familiar, beloved way in response to a comment by the ostiary, but perhaps the wind alerted him to the scuff of their feet as Tuvi touched her elbow to bring her to a halt under the shade of the porch. Perhaps the birds—for there were birds, a pair of red caps and several bright yellow bellies with their green banded wings—called a warning. He stiffened. He lifted his chin, as though scenting the air. He rose and slowly, almost hesitantly, turned.

Of course he knew her instantly. The air sang with his shock. The wind smothered its cry in the leaves. A petal spun lazily, drifting to earth.

Her breath caught on a sob.

There. It was done.

He spoke, although he was too far away for her to hear. The militia captain looked startled, squinting at her as if the sun was shining in his eyes, while the ostiary's posture suggested a more complicated wine fermented with equal parts rue, resignation, and compassionate amusement. They took themselves off, crunching away on a graveled path.

Anji picked up one of the knives holding down a corner of his maps. Then he came, his trim figure simply arrayed in a tunic of first-quality silk dyed a shade of red so bold it seemed garish, like a fabric someone with poor judgment had chosen for him just because it was gaudy.

She was shaking so hard she grasped at the thought, as trivial as it was. She needed something to hold on to as he mounted the steps onto the porch.

"That color does not suit you, Anji. It reminds me of the way young men boast to get attention. Subtle greens and blues are more elegant."

He passed Tuvi, handing him the knife, and put his hands on Mai's shoulders, holding her so he could examine her. The weight of his hands was familiar; his scent, laced with sweat and horse and the mild spice of khaif on his breath, made her want to wilt into his arms; his gaze devoured her.

"How can this be?" he murmured, hands hot on her shoulders and face flushed with that same driving heat.

Without another word he embraced her and kissed her, and although she had meant to say a hundred things to him, to negotiate, to name a higher price than the market value, she could say nothing. She clung to him. She twined her hands in his hair. She kissed him wildly. This was still her Anji.

"Anjihosh!" Tuvi's voice was the whip that separated them, and his the hand that wrenched Anji away from her. "She is a demon. You must see that."

Anji yanked his arm out of the chief's grasp. "Of course." He rested a hand so gently on the curve of her cheek that she sighed, feeling those cursed tears again. "Of course she must be."

Love is cruel. Could she do nothing but weep?

She stepped back out of reach of his hand. "Anji. Your mother had me stabbed."

"I know."

"I fell into the pool, but the firelings healed me."

"The firelings?"

"The pool is the womb of the firelings." She could not make sense of her surging feelings, one instant wanting to kiss him and the next to rage. "Why did you kill Uncle Hari? You promised him safety. You promised *me* you'd protect him."

He shrugged off the question. "The cloaks are all corrupted. It was necessary to save the Hundred."

"Then kill me, too. If you think I'm a lilu, isn't it necessary? Didn't your mother think it was necessary to rid herself of a rival? Just be quick about it, so I don't suffer more than I have already. Tuvi has a sword, and he's holding your knife."

"You are my knife, Mai. Even if you are a demon. So be it. I am helpless before you. Or maybe the firelings fell in love with you as any man must love you, and have healed you and sent you back to me, where you belong. That's all that matters, isn't it? Now you are here."

"Anjihosh—" said Tuvi.

"Give her the knife, Tuvi. If she wants to kill me, let her do it now."

"I don't want the knife!"

"What do you want, Mai?" He took her hand in his, turned it over, kissed her palm in a promise that made her flesh burn and her heart sing.

I want it to be what it was before.

"Papa! Papa!"

Anji let go of her hand. Out of the garden had come a procession, unseen and unheard until now. A lovely little child toddled forward on stout legs toward the porch, half ready to fall forward in his haste. Anji laughed and leaped down to the path to scoop up the toddler before the lad tumbled onto his face on the gravel. Tuvi made a sharp gesture, and the half-dozen persons halted dead still back by a hedge that screened the far porch from the eye of this one. There they waited obediently. All were women, drawing up cloth to cover their faces so Mai saw nothing but a distant glimpse of kohl-lined eyes and expensive silks in colors as garish as Anji's tunic.

Anji hopped back up on the porch, holding Atani with the ease of much practice. How sweet the baby was! How much he had grown! How dear and precious her beautiful boy had become! He was a darling, as sunny as day and with a brilliant chortling smile that vanished as soon as Mai extended her arms to take him. He flung himself against his father's shoulder to hide his face.

"He's shy," said Anji. "It's the age for it."

"Won't he come to me?" She touched Atani's back tentatively, that sweet flesh like balm to her aching heart, but Atani glanced up and, shrieking, squirmed against his father, anything to get away from her.

She recoiled, gulping down tears.

"Mistress," said Tuvi, his grimace one of sudden sympathy. "He doesn't know you. It's been too long."

"I know," she gasped.

That didn't make it hurt less.

One woman stepped away from the others, still holding cloth across her face, but a gesture from Tuvi stopped her on the path, where she was too far away to really know what was going on. Anji's expression clouded. A frown splintered his joy, and the child sobbed once and was silent.

"That woman is pregnant," said Mai.

"Yes." He descended and kneeled on the path, setting down the boy and speaking softly into his ear, then patting him on the rump. "Go to Mama," he said, giving the child a swift, affectionate kiss on each plump cheek. "Go now, Atanihosh. Hurry!"

The unfortunate stranger was forgotten. The boy set out with laughing determination. "Mama! Mama!" he cried, trundling down the path with his arms outstretched toward the other woman.

"I have to sit down," Mai whispered as her heart was ripped from her. It would have been better to be dead.

Tuvi reached for her, but Anji had already jumped back onto the porch and he caught her and held her as Atani was swept up into the arms of the woman he called "Mama" and whisked away behind the hedge.

"Mai," Anji whispered fiercely, holding her close, "don't leave me. Stay here with me. Don't faint. I've got it all worked out."

"Anjihosh," objected the chief. "Your mother—"

"She's got the treaty she wants. A grandson to raise. My wife will bear a child and we'll be fortunate if it is a girl. Why should I not take a second wife? I suppose it was inevitable. It was just too difficult to consider at the time, with the demons' army threatening the north. But now with the enemy army mostly hunted down and killed, there's no impediment—"

Mai shoved him off, slamming back into the wall, bracing herself against it. "None? Not after your mother tried to kill me when I wouldn't agree to become your second wife? When I refused to step aside and let her rule over my household, the one I built and nurtured and fed? Knowing she set her agent on me, Anji, you think I'll expose myself to her again?"

He shook his head impatiently. "Of course not. I can see it would be impossible for you to live under her suzerainty. But it is easy enough to set up another household, one that you hold authority over entirely. Some place close by, that a reeve can lift me to—"

"When you want sex? A second household? Close by? For your convenience? Do you expect me to agree to this?"

"The boy can visit you, Mai. I would bring him with me."

"Visit? My son can *live* with me!" she cried, seeing the trap as it was sprung, the bait her hunger for her baby, as desperate as she was to hold her child against her breast.

"Ah," he breathed. "The boy."

He glanced at Tuvi, at the eaves, at the hedge behind, and at the empty, silent garden. At his own hands. He wore her wolf's-head ring on his little finger, and it was this he stared at. She could practically see the thoughts chasing behind his eyes in currents and countercurrents, two rivers of desire colliding and mingling until, at last, his gaze hardened, even if the expression was tempered with regret.

"Neh. The boy belongs to *her* now. That was part of the agreement, that he believe she is his mother. It's the only way to ensure his safety. Surely, Mai, you can see that Atanihosh's survival must be our chief concern. A bitter price, but a necessary one. You and I will have other children. Many others, plum blossom."

He reached to embrace her. She extended a hand, palm out, to stop him.

The future, a bolt of shimmering first-quality silk, unrolled before her. An elaborate compound furnished just as she wished, with painted screens and embroidered pillows and a spacious counting room for her mercantile business fitted with drawers and cubbies and writing desks, and that irritating Keshad as her chief accountant. She would insist on living in a town, or preferably a city like Toskala with a substantial market, whose streets and alleys and stalls she and Miravia could browse at their leisure. She would become a woman of means, using the coin she had herself earned, nothing gifted to her, and no doubt she could demand a position on the council which naturally no council would deny her. And Anji, for a day or a week or a month at a time, in her bed. His kisses and his warm embrace.

She enduring the cage for the sake of the boy, as Anji's mother had done all those years locked up in the women's palace within the emperor's palace in the Sirniakan Empire. All that she was, having meaning only because of the precious boy and a powerful man's desire for her.

"That's your offer," she said, drawing down her market voice and her market face. "Now here is my counteroffer."

"Mai," he said softly, with a soft smile that cut as sharply as steel, "there is no counteroffer. There never was. Not since that day in Kartu's market."

The thing about Sheyshi stabbing her is that it had anticipated the pain yet to come. This pain, severing flesh and bone and blood, she must absorb without letting any trace of it show on her face. She must lock it away now and only later let the agony tear through her.

"No." She eased her hand away from his chest, not sure what she would do if he were to move in to kiss away her defenses, but the word was shield enough. His brows drew down; his gaze narrowed in that way it did when he felt thwarted. "I will not be your second wife, and have my son call another woman 'mother.' I want my son back and to be your partner, as we were before."

He laughed bitterly, his hand darting in to grasp strands of her hair that had fallen over her shoulder, to twist them between his fingers. "Oh, Mai, however much I might wish it, it's impossible. We've crossed under the gate. There is no going back."

She turned her head away, and he released her.

"This isn't about going back," she said. "But we can go forward on the path we were set on before. I had my business ventures, my warehouse. You were captain of Olossi's militia . . ."

She faltered.

He, who was now in all ways but in name the ruler of the Hundred. The Qin commander, accustomed to conquest.

To think she had mistaken him for the hero of the tale.

Flowers swayed as the wind danced through them. A high-pitched shriek of excitement rang: her child's voice. Then there was silence but for the rustling leaves and the mournful ripple of the awning. The unweighted corner of the map rose, as invisible fingers pried for secrets, and sagged down again.

Tuvi took her hand in his with the affection of an elderly uncle who has seen a great deal of the world and knows what to value. In his measured expression she saw the chief she had grown so very fond of. "Mistress, he will treat you well. Be sure of that."

"No."

Tuvi's smile was like the last spark of the sun before darkness swallowed day, more farewell than comfort. "A lilu would have said yes. If you leave now, Mistress, you can never return."

"If she leaves?" cried Anji. "She can't leave!"

The market was her territory. Here, she knew what to do. "I have coin enough to pay you in full what you paid to my father."

His was an anger chained and bound. "You are not my slave. I have never treated you as a slave. But you cannot leave, Mai. I will not allow you to go out into the world where some other man will claim you. Then I would have to kill him."

"And me? Would you have to kill me?" she asked sadly. "Neh, Tuvi-lo, stand aside, for it's better if I know the truth." With a sigh Tuvi took a step away, leaving Anji to face her.

He wanted to touch her—she could see it in his posture, his hands, his expression—but he refrained. "You know I could never harm you, plum blossom. I have never even raised my hand against you—except that one time. Mai, when I look at you I see all that is best in the world. Your beauty, your generosity, your intelligence, your honor. How can you expect me to step back and let that go?"

"Anji, there's something I must tell you." Because there is always a counteroffer. "When Sheyshi stabbed me, when I fell into the pool, I lay in a place which is caught between the life of the world and the Spirit Gate beyond. When I woke, I thought it was the same day, that only a few breaths had passed while I struggled to reach the surface. Do you understand me? Months passed for you, but for me—for my body— it was less than a pair of breaths."

She had taken him off guard.

"I'm pregnant, Anji." She couldn't lie outright. But he was vulnerable, and so she must strike. She need only speak a name, and he would presume the rest. "Joss."

The veil ripped asunder. She had one glimpse of sheer brutal throat-choking fury.

"Tuvi, give me your sword."

The chief coolly interposed his body between them. "No, Captain. You'll regret it later."

"Tuvi, give me your sword." He wasn't a man to grab at things. He expected to be obeyed.

"No, Anjihosh." Keeping his back to her, Tuvi said, "Mistress, return by the way we came to the reeve hall and don't ever come back."

"Tuvi, where are Priya and O'eki? Please tell them that I live, and that they should stay with Atani if they must, to care for him, but if they are at all unhappy, then they must—"

"I'll tell them. *Go.*"

She fumbled at and opened the door. Even then she thought perhaps Anji might call after her, might realize how ridiculous his suspicions were, might change his mind, might see a different path, the one she wished for rather than the one he had chosen, but after all, he did not.

53

THE NIGHT IS dark, and the sky is hazy, and a campfire is burning like a friendly beacon, three figures seated companionably if forlornly within its fragile aura. Folk like to tell tales and sing around campfires, especially if they are seated at the edge of an abyss as threads of fire flicker like lightning across the stone ledge on which they rest.

The brigands raged in,
they confronted the peaceful company seated at their dinner,
they demanded the girl be handed over to them.
All feared them. All looked away.
Except foolish Jothinin, light-minded Jothinin,
he was the only one who stood up to face them,
he was the only one who said, "No."

"And then what happened?" a woman asked with a rough-timbred, sexy laugh just exactly like Marit's, the laugh of a woman who is not afraid to see the humor in just about anything because she's learned that's one way to make sense of life. "I mean, truly what happened? Did you start talking on and on and on until—"

"Until they fled out of boredom? Until they expired for not having any air to breathe after I had used it all for my lengthy speech? No, indeed, that is not what happened, even if you think it must be. I'm deeply saddened and grievously wounded that you would even insinuate such a thing."

Marit laughed again.

"In the tale," said a third voice, "you cry aloud about the injustice. You gather crowds, who listen, who gain courage. The bandits cut you down for they fear to hear you speak the truth. And then the people rise up in noble anger and drive them away, and the girl—" Here her raspy childish voice took on a shine of intensely smug contentment. "—is saved and never troubled again."

The man sighed lengthily and with much effort in drawing out the exhalation to its last lingering wisp. "Well, now, I wish I could say it transpired all so neatly as you say, Kirit, but in truth—"

"The hells!" Joss sat up. "We're on a cursed Guardian's altar. We've broken the boundaries *again*—"

He tried to rub the haze out of his eyes, for there came Marit scrambling up from the fire and running toward him with a grin like a blaze of joy.

She dropped to her knees beside him. "Joss. Do you know who I am?"

For answer, he embraced her and then, because her body crushed against his body felt so cursed good, just as it ought, he kissed her. Oh, the kissing was good. He'd never forgotten the taste of her, and the way she had of—

Memories cascaded so hard and fast that he broke away and clapped his hands to his head as if he had the headache that afflicted him when he was drinking too much. Only his head didn't hurt at all.

"Aui!" She laughed. "That wasn't the greeting I was expecting. But I admit, it's the one I would have wished for."

He lowered his hands "You're dead, Marit. Twenty-one years dead. To think I could never let you go, for I tell you I missed you so badly and then would go on and on blaming myself for what wasn't truly my fault. Eiya! I'm remembering—" He pressed palms together, pinched himself, smoothed his hands down his thighs. He was wearing his reeve's leathers, although they were dusty in some spots and in others smeared with a stain that slid with an oily slime under his testing finger. "I hesitate to say this, but I have an odd memory that you are a ghost pretending to be a Guardian haunting my gods-rotted dreams and that I was . . . I was . . ." Yet it was all haze, a smeary, oily confusion of arrows flying and men shouting and one man—could that be himself?—desperately trying to shield his beloved companion. What in the hells?

She grasped his hand in one of hers. A death white cloak shivered at her shoulders: a demon's cloak.

Neh, not a demon's cloak. That had been someone else's word for them. That had been Anji's word.

"Joss, there's no easy way to say this. You're dead. I don't know how you were killed. Or how long ago it happened. But Jothinin and Kirit and I found you, and we've done our best to help you awaken."

"Awaken from what?"

"From death."

"Marit, no one awakens from death. You pass through the Spirit Gate and cross to the other side."

"Except for a few of us, a very few, who as it says in the tale must walk the lands to establish justice. If they can. A rather heavy 'if' in days like these. Or in any days, I suppose."

"You're talking about the Guardians."

"I am. And you are. Because you've been—well—you've been claimed by a cloak, Joss. Jessed, if you will. Don't take this the wrong way, but the cloak that's wearing you is the one that used to belong to Lord Radas. Not that that means anything, mind you. It's not the cloak that corrupts the Guardian. I don't believe that. I think it's something inside the person that weakens and breaks, so just because you're wearing the cloak of Sun doesn't mean you'll become corrupted as he did."

He felt its weight dragging like stone on his shoulders, and yet its power coursed through his body like a river's streaming current or the wind's blustery push or a flame's fiery snap. It draped over him, whispering against the stone on which he sat. An arrow was half hidden under the fabric. When he picked it up, it fit easily in his hand.

Across the ledge a glittering labyrinth flowered as if the arrow's touch on his skin had brought it to life: the maze that led to the altar and its hidden pool spread in patterns that winked and tempted. How easily he could walk it now! Those twists and turns ignited memories, banished the haze.

"Captain Anji killed me. Only he didn't really kill *me*. He didn't dare strike at *me*. That gods-rotted bastard. He had his soldiers kill—"

"Calm down, Joss. You're upsetting Scar. Here now, give me a kiss." She tipped his chin up and kissed him lightly once, twice, thrice, until he laughed and, behind her, that cursed envoy of Ilu—what was he doing here?—spoke.

"Yet again we have proven women believe sex solves everything."

"He was getting agitated!" retorted Marit, but she sat back on her heels and smiled in a way that made Joss's ears—and more—burn. "The hells, Joss. Not that you weren't a pleasant armful before, but you were just not this cursed handsome when you were young. What happened to you?"

He was working back through her words, spinning the arrow once around slowly. "What do you mean? I'm upsetting a scar?"

"Ah." She rose, walked back to the fire, and poured liquid from a leather bottle into a cup. Beyond her, three horses stood close together, heads and necks drooping, one with a hind hoof tipped up on the toe. A bulky feathery bulk sprouted from their shoulders and folded back along their flanks all the way to their croups.

"Those are winged horses," he said indignantly as she returned.

"Drink this."

It was a tart cordial, just the way he liked it, with real bite. And he was cursed thirsty all of a sudden. But he set down the cup.

"Let's say, just for the sake of argument, that I'm awake, and not dreaming or plowing my way through some manner of drunken stupor. Let's just say those are three winged horses. Let's say I'm wearing a Guardian's cloak, for I'm certainly wearing something like it. And that this arrow in my hand is somehow connected to the cloak of Sun. Let's say that you and these two individuals are also Guardians. I can't believe I just said all that."

Now he did knock back the cordial, and it seared his throat and made his eyes water in a most satisfactory way.

"Do you remember what Marshal Alard used to say, Marit? If you have to choose between what seems the most reasonable explanation, and what the cold, hard evidence reveals—"

"Go with the evidence," she finished.

"There you stand, wearing the cloak of Death. Him, the cloak of Sky, I suppose. And her—" The firelight must have been playing tricks on him, for she looked like a ghost, not like a person. "My apologies, verea. We've never met."

Marit tugged him up, biting her lower lip in that way she did with her eyes so inviting. She chuckled as he flushed. Eihi! Now he remembered what he had been doing not long before he'd died, and it hadn't been with Marit but rather with that gods-rotted magnificent hierodule Zubaidit, and it had been cursed energetic and tremendously wild and hot and—

"What are you thinking about?" she demanded, really laughing now. "Neh. Never mind. For I'm pretty sure I don't want to know. And now, thank the Lady, I don't have to." She led him by the hand over to the fire, where she introduced him to Jothinin and Kirit. The girl was a cursed odd-looking person, an outlander, ghastly pale with almost colorless eyes and hair like straw. Fortunately, she was quite young, likely not more than sixteen or eighteen, and treated him with the reserved deference due to an uncle never before met.

They had a nicely spiced porridge and several ripe sunfruit and mangoes, not that he was particularly hungry, and more of that wonderfully tart cordial. He had a curious idea that he didn't actually need to eat, but the act was comforting, and the food was tasty, and he had anyhow lived all his life eating in company. It would have seemed strange not to do so now.

Jothinin was a talker, just like the foolish Jothinin in the tale, but he had a pleasant voice and a great many entertaining tales to tell, many of which were a joke on himself. But at length even he fell silent as the fire sparked and popped, and Kirit, its keeper, gifted more wood to its flames.

"So let's say it's true, that I'm a Guardian," said Joss. "What does that mean? For here are four of us. Anji has the other five cloaks. He's bound them with chains into chests and I'm pretty sure he means to hold them. I admit, seeing what happened with Radas and Night, it's not entirely surprising Anji believes the cloaks dangerous and corrupting." Yet when he pulled the fabric of his Sun cloak through a hand, he felt no shadow, no dark seam cracking wide to eat out his heart and turn him into a lilu. Not that he couldn't crack. Not that every person wasn't vulnerable in some way. But it wasn't inevitable, as Anji had claimed.

"We weren't sure what happened to the other cloaks. But we're the ones responsible. For we—Jothinin and Kirit and I—told him what he needed to know to kill Guardians."

Kirit said, "But the bad ones are gone now. Isn't it better they're gone?"

"So there we lie, between the sea and the shore, just like in the tale." Marit turned to Joss. "What if it is better that they're gone? It seems the Hundred is settling into peace again. Folk can labor and live without the fear they had before. Because the outlander rules with his army. They rule the roads, the gates, the assizes, the markets. You see where I'm going with this. He's not a cruel master. Life prospers. The crops are good. The roads are safe. Children sleep in peace. But we daren't get close. His soldiers and his reeves are hunting us. Hunting Guardians. Now that he knows he can kill us, he means to rid the Hundred of Guardians. And what if he's right to do so? Who among us is free from the threat of corruption?"

Jothinin scratched his head. Kirit stared into the gulf of air, as if the night held answers.

"No one is," Joss answered. "Not us. Not Anji. Not any man or woman. What are you all looking at me like that for? It wasn't that cursed wise a comment."

Kirit's eyes had gone wide and she shrank down as if to curl herself into a ball. Jothinin shifted to place himself between the girl and the fire. Marit rose as the ground made an odd shushing sound behind him and a light tremor vibrated up through the stone into Joss's body. The horses woke, and one—two—three they spread their fine bright wings and galloped off the cursed ledge and into the night.

"Why are there only three horses, if there are four of us?" he asked.

"Aui! That was the other shock, the one we've been waiting to drop on you. Just stand slowly, and turn around."

He obeyed her, for he felt an odd monstrous presence looming behind him like the charged breath of a late season storm prickling his neck.

"No one truly understands the bond between eagle and reeve, what invisible leash jesses one to the other. We guessed you must have died because your eagle died. For

I am cursed sure living eagles don't fly at night and seek out Guardian altars, not as this one does."

The old raptor lowered his head to Joss's level, an uncanny glamour in those huge depthless eyes.

"How can this be?" Joss asked, as Scar offered a series of chirps in greeting.

"In a way," said Marit, "you died together."

Joss was left to wonder if it was he, or Scar, who had died fighting for justice. Or maybe after all it was the two of them in partnership, just as it had always been.

54

WHEN A PREGNANT widow and her household move into town, the event is certain to be talked about for days. When the widow is young and beautiful, the gossip will spread across weeks. And when she opens her own emporium that competes successfully with local warehouses and merchants who have lived for generations in the bustling port of Salya on Messalia Bay, then it is likely that rumor will mildew into the kind of antipathy that flourishes for months in shadowed corners and uncleaned cupboards.

And yet, stage by stage, week by week, month by month, it did not.

Mistress Karanna, the head of Seven Cups clan, was won over when the young widow advised her on the quality of silks and which hues were more appropriate to her particular complexion and personality. Master Dessottin of Merling's Gift clan discovered that the widow's married sister—not that anyone believed they were actually sisters—not only shared his obsessive interest in plant lore but actually knew how to play an obscure game of counters called "emperors and warriors" which he had long studied in equally obscure texts first encountered when he'd served his apprenticeship as a clerk of Sapanasu; that she beat him more often than not did not lessen his enjoyment of the matches. His influence brought round several local clans, one of which was doubly charmed when the married sister specifically requested a formidable aunt to attend the birth of her daughter because of the aunt's long experience in midwifery.

The farmers and artisans and laborers appreciated the widow's fair prices and willingness to dicker at length and to trade in kind, if that was all they had to offer. A few hired daughters and sons into her household, where they were fairly treated and well paid, although there were a few complaints about the widow's clerk, who had such an exacting eye for detail that he spared little patience for people who made even trivial mistakes.

The local secretive Ri Amarah household, after substantial initial resistance, made some manner of deal regarding import of certain hard-to-acquire precious oils. And when the Four Petals clan began to simmer with resentment, seeing their trade in oil cut into, the widow befriended their unmarriagable eldest daughter and within two months had helped them open up a promising negotiation with an upcountry sheepherder's clan that included the promise of an expansion of the wool trade.

Even the horribly crippled and notoriously solitary marshal of Bronze Hall began to fly in once a week with certain of his senior reeves to take tea on her spacious porch right out in public view, the only place in her compound she ever met with men.

So when after the course of seven moons the widow gave birth to a healthy baby girl, only two important holdouts remained: a branch of the White Leaf clan out of Arash, who were in any case only third-generation local with therefore the usual insecurities of newcomers, and the hieros at the local temple of Ushara.

The White Leaf clan was dispatched with a ruthlessness that had the town laughing for days: she simply asked the old widower, whose temper was infamous, to stand with Bronze Hall's marshal and a senior reeve named Peddonon as one of the uncles over the delicate newborn, whom the cranky old man certainly must hold. Wasn't she precious and darling even with her unmistakably outlander features? Who could say no to such a request, coming as it did from a young woman so very lovely who no longer, alas, possessed the extended family with which to comfort and influence the baby?

Three months passed. She made a thanksgiving offering at each of the temples, and laid flowers on Hasibal's stone together with prayers no one had heard before. But she did not make the traditional procession to the Devourer's temple. She never went there at all. The young man who assisted the head gardener got drunk one night and told a friend, who told a friend, who told her cousins, that he had once overheard the mistress say there were spies in the temple keeping an eye on her, which was a very odd sort of thing to say even for a beautiful and mysterious young widow with an air of tragedy cloaking her like first-quality silk.

Or so folk whispered, until the day the Qin soldiers rode into town.

It was clear she had been warned ahead of time, likely by the Bronze Hall reeves, because she appeared midmorning on her porch dressed in a rainwater-blue taloos of such exceptional silk that a girl passing by on the street actually went running to Seven Cups clan to fetch Mistress Karanna so she could see it for herself.

But Karanna no more dared approach than did anyone else when a cohort of black-clad soldiers—the very black wolves who, it was said, ruthlessly hunted down criminals and kept the peace in the Hundred, not that they'd seen any such soldiers down here in the isolated and peaceful backwater of Mar—rode into town, their horses filling the streets and their blank expressions frightening children. About a third of them were outlanders, solemn as herons, so easy astride their horses they might have been born in the saddle.

The commander at the head of the procession was also an outlander. He was magnificently dressed in a knee-length silk jacket sewn from silk of such a surpassingly delicate green, like sea foam under the evening sky, that Mistress Karanna actually wept. Or maybe she wept because he and all the soldiers were armed, and with his sword swinging at his side he climbed right up onto the porch as if no one could stop him from doing so, which no one could.

The widow made no courtesy, nor did she cower. She greeted him coolly, and anyone with eyes could see they knew each other.

This was not to be a happy meeting.

At first it seemed the point of contention was the baby, and that was a wonder, indeed, for anyone who had seen the infant—and most everyone in town had peeped into the emporium or porch over the last three months to take a look—must instantly recognize that the tiny face bore some resemblance to that of the Qin soldiers. Was her nose destined to grow to something like his? An unfortunate fate for a girl, perhaps, but when the widow allowed him to hold the child and examine it, which he did very carefully, one might begin to suspect she was not, after all, a widow. That he might in fact be the father of the precious darling. That the point of contention was not the child, although clearly there was something about the child which mattered deeply to him, but the woman herself.

Anyone with eyes or ears could see what kind of tale this was. Every variation on this song has been sung down the years. She retreats; he pursues. He desires; she refuses. A slave buys herself free, but the master cannot bear to let her go.

What then?

The siege lasted one full month.

He was a persuasive and extremely powerful man, a reasonable, intelligent man, who consulted with councils from villages and towns all over Mar, presided over assizes, and discussed certain efficiencies of reorganization that were proving successful in other regions of the Hundred. He examined the local varieties of wool and rice, seven times rode out hunting with local men, and once took a canoe to Bronze Hall to meet with its recalcitrant marshal, an expedition he did not repeat. All that besides the mornings or afternoons he spent dandling the baby while courting the woman, although it was noted that she never actually invited him to visit nor was he ever, for even one instant, alone with her behind closed doors.

By the end of the month many of the locals had come to cordially loathe his well-behaved and standoffish soldiers especially as dozens of local youths began to wear their hair up in topknots and certain local girls got over their shyness enough to flirt with an enthusiasm that their disgusted elders put down to the novelty of the soldiers and the heavy strings of coin they had to spread around. One Qin tailman fell so desperately in love with a chance-met local girl that he persuaded her to ride away with him when, at last, the commander had to admit defeat and leave. He had other regions to oversee, other councils to consult with, other assizes to administer.

"Other wives," the married sister was overheard to say tartly to her husband, "to impregnate."

The next day the hieros packed up and left with a dozen of her hierodules and kalos.

One month later a new and quite young hieros sauntered into town in company with a pair of middle-aged outlanders and their wagon.

"Do you think he'll come back, Priya?" Mai asked three days later as they sat on pillows and sipped tea on the porch. Dusk hovered but hadn't yet fallen. "I don't know if I could bear to go through that again. Do you know how badly I wanted to have sex with him?"

"Why didn't you?" asked Priya. The baby was asleep on her lap, snoring softly with a bit of congestion, feet and hands twitching with baby dreams.

Mai reached across the table to touch her hand. "Do you know, Priya, it wasn't until I came here that I realized that when I was Anji's wife, I was always under guard. Did you and O'eki choose a house yet? Maybe that cottage by the lake you were talking about? It was very, ah, scenic."

Priya laughed. "You are not a country girl, are you? Anyhow, there were too many mosks. We were thinking of something in town. There's a tiny compound just down this street and around the corner."

"I know the one! Perfectly respectable. Although it has no porch as fine as this one."

This porch wrapped the main house, which was set at exactly the right height and position to command a spectacular view over the bay, whose sunset-gilded waters were darkening fast as twilight rushed over them. A pleasant breeze blew up from the shore. The port-side neighborhoods down at the strand were lively as the night market set up, but here compounds were settling in for the night, a few people hurrying home with lantern in hand. Their street was empty except for a dog purposefully trotting along, as if leashed by someone they could not see. The dog loped out of sight. Song drifted up from the streets below.

Inside, Miravia shrieked with laughter, and Keshad swore angrily and, evidently, stomped out of the room.

"The poor lad is jealous because Miravia gets along so well with his sister," remarked Priya as Miravia and Zubaidit began giggling. "Imagine what it must be like to struggle for so long against seemingly insurmountable obstacles only to get exactly what you want."

"Ah." Mai shut her eyes.

"Oh, Mai, what a foolish thing for me to say."

"Neh, never mind it." She opened her eyes and drained her cup. "See. No tears. Anyway, Kesh didn't exactly get everything as he wished it. Zubaidit still serves the temple."

"I would say she serves the goddess. It may not be exactly the same thing. For I would call it very interesting indeed that she—of all people—has come here—of all places—just now—of all times."

Mai lifted the pot. "She told me she requested service at this temple so she could be near her brother. More tea, Priya?" She poured gracefully and lifted the lid to see how much was left and, after consideration, decided to let it be as it was. "I'm so glad you've come, and come to stay. Yet I think of Atani, left alone there."

"He's well taken care of. The women spoil him. Commander Anji loves the boy, Mai."

She watched the face of her sleeping daughter wistfully. "That will have to be enough, won't it?"

A rowdy group of twenty or thirty reeves surged into view, singing raucously but in remarkable harmony.

"Mai!" Peddonon stumbled on the lower step as he leaped onto the porch. "The hells! My knee!"

"You're drunk."

The baby, startled, woke and began to bawl lustily.

"I beg you, verea, let her uncle take her! She's crying because she misses me!"

Peddonon swept her out of Priya's lap and began to dance and sing along the porch as Mai winced, hoping he wouldn't topple off the edge, but in fact he wasn't drunk at all; he was just pretending as reeves tramped onto the porch and made a great deal of noise with a great swirl of currents during which Priya recovered the baby and Miravia brought out cordial and a tray of cups and Peddonon caught Mai's arm within the concealment of all the commotion and pulled her back through the house to the quiet courtyard and garden that, in the Mar style, ran the length of the back of the house.

"How a prim Ri Amarah woman like Miravia came to develop such a crude sense of humor I will never figure," said Zubaidit, stepping out of the shadows under a towering paradom bush.

Mai yelped, both hands slapped to her breast. "Eihi! You startled me, sneaking up like that."

"I like that rat screen in the public room," added Zubaidit, "but I feel I have seen it before."

"I used to own it, but it was sold away. I tracked it down specially and had it carted here."

"In fact," said Peddonon, "I had it wrapped in layers of canvas and flew it here. You were terrible gloomy, Mai. A man would weep to see it. We had to do something to lighten you. My wise grandmother always said that a sad woman gives birth to a fussy baby."

She stretched on tiptoes to kiss him on the cheek. "You're a terrible good man. Now why have you two sneaked me out here?"

"To admire your plantings." Zubaidit drew Mai into the heart of the garden in all its evening solemnity, although the reeves' chatter, laughter, and song rose overhead like so much heady wine. "Is that muzz? Proudhorn? Musk vine? Stardrops! You'd think you were planting a Devourer's garden here, Mai. Or thinking of one, anyway."

She flushed. "I like their scents. You know what my situation is."

"Well," said Zubaidit with a shrug, "he only specified men, didn't he? You're always welcome at Ushara's temple, whatever you choose. He'll hear nothing from me." She removed her hand as they reached the long, open stretch where dirt had been marked with flags and ribbons tied to and between sticks for the digging of an ornamental pool, meant to commence two months ago but suspended because of the siege. "Look there, Mai."

Three figures waited at the end of the garden, discernible by the glamour woven into the cloaks they wore.

Mai halted as her hands clenched. "Have you betrayed me?" she whispered.

"The hells!" Peddonon turned on the hieros. "I told you this was a bad idea to spring it on her without warning."

"There!" Zubaidit looked skyward.

A shadow covered the stars. A vast weight thumped down right in the middle of the open ground, crushing the carefully surveyed flags and ribbons. It was, Merciful One protect her, an eagle, even though she was sure eagles didn't fly at night. A lithe figure unhooked, dropped, and strolled forward, grinning.

"Greetings of the dusk, you cursed show-off," cried Peddonon, rushing forward. But he pulled up short before, tentatively, reaching out to grasp arms with the man as the others came forward.

Four Guardians. The last of their kind.

She recognized the envoy of Ilu leaning on his walking staff; his cheerful smile coaxed an answering smile from her even as he was careful not to look too hard into her face. She shied away from the girl who wore the face and body of the slave

Cornflower, who had killed Uncle Girish, three Qin soldiers, and, if the stories were true, an entire cadre of the enemy; a mirror hung from the girl's belt, an incongruity against her rough traveler's clothing.

It was the Guardian reeve's identity that shocked her. "Joss? I thought you were dead! I would never have said—"

He released Peddonon and grasped her hand as much to hold her off from the lamp-like shimmer of the cloak that swathed him. "You would never have said what?"

He looked into her face, raised to his.

"The hells! You told Anji *what*?"

"I didn't *say* so, I just let him assume you might be the father—"

"The hells!"

"It was the only way to get Anji to release me. It was just an idea I had, that you were the only man he really feared."

"Because he thought you would have wanted to sleep with me?" He clipped off the words, broke off the contact, smiled glancingly and heartbreakingly at Zubaidit, and turned to the woman wearing a death-white cloak as she walked up beside him, a sword sheathed at her side. "This is Marit."

Zubaidit said nothing, her gaze fixed on the shadowy net of an arbor of patience, still so young and sparse that its characteristic falls weren't yet long enough to dangle over the horizontal posts. She might have been smiling, but it was difficult to tell under evening's cloak.

"Well, this is more awkward than I had realized it would be," said Peddonon. "Do I babble to smooth over the unexpected undertow, or do we move straight to business? Straight to business it is, then. You may wonder, Mai, what brings us here tonight, or how it comes that four Guardians are walking in your garden."

"No," said Mai, taking his hand and smiling when he squeezed back, the pressure of his fingers warm and comforting. "I am honored to welcome four holy Guardians into my courtyard. Joss surprises me, and while it pleases me and heartens me to see him, I have to say, beautiful Ox you may be, but I think you're a little old for me."

Joss laughed, and Peddonon relaxed, and the woman called Marit smiled. Zubaidit bent her head and brushed at an eye as though flicking away a gnat.

"I'm surprised all four travel together, as vulnerable as they must be now anywhere they could be boxed in, trapped, and cut down. The black wolves are hunting you."

"We know," said Joss, rubbing his left shoulder. "We've made a few tactical errors. We've spent months searching out people we can trust."

"Like Peddonon and Zubaidit," she agreed. "Who in the end must have led you here. I expected one or more Guardians might eventually track me down to find out if I knew what Anji had done with the cloaks he took off the other five."

"He told you?" Joss demanded.

"Neh. He did not tell me. He could not, considering the first cloak he killed was my beloved Uncle Hari, who trusted him only because I had assured him that Anji could be trusted."

"We tracked the commander's movements eventually to Merciful Valley, but it's under heavy guard."

"I told you not to rush in," observed Marit with a tone of amused if critical intimacy that made Zubaidit wince and Mai suddenly wonder if Joss and Marit were lovers. Surely this could not be the very murdered reeve his heart had pined for all those years?

"It is," said Joss wryly, and Mai jerked her gaze away, realizing she had been staring at him.

He's tethered to one post, Anji had said scornfully when they had first heard the tale from Joss. Hu! And look how things had turned out for Anji, riding all the way across the Hundred to try to get her back.

Maybe the breeze shifted. Maybe the singing changed cadence, or one of the budding night candles opened to release its heart-easing scent. The night was still dark, but her mood unaccountably lightened. She had a life yet before her, and with the grace of the Merciful One it might be a long life. There were a hells lot of things you could do with a long life.

"Yes," she agreed. "It would make sense that Merciful Valley is heavily guarded. There are five chains hammered into stone just beneath the rim of the pool, under water. At the end of each chain, in the depths of the pool, lies a small jeweler's chest, wrapped in chains. It's easier to throw them in than to drag them out. During the season when the firelings are birthing, or if the ancient ones are wakened, the water burns you. But the rest of the time, it's just water.

"I admit, I love my silks, and such clasps and hairpins and other ornaments that go with them. When I was stabbed, no one thought to clean out my garments and such trivialities as I had brought with me to the valley. My things were just shoved into a cupboard and forgotten, as some of my clothes chests were forgotten in the compound in Astafero. So it was possible for me, with Miravia's help, to drag five small chests up from the deeps and hide them in one large chest, and toss five objects down into the depths in their place.

"I asked myself, if Anji truly wanted to rid the Hundred of the Guardians, why not throw the chests into the pool without a chain? Why not sail them out onto the ocean and dump them overboard weighted with rocks so no one could ever hope to retrieve them? Because he would never take the chance that they might not serve him as weapons later. Yes, I know where the cloaks are. They're right here, in my house."

A burst of laughter rose from the porch, and there was whooping and stomping in appreciation of some doubtless crude jest. But in the garden, it was silent.

Finally, Joss whistled softly.

"And an outlander will save them," he said with a smile so charming and bright and handsome she was glad he was too old for her because she might otherwise have been tempted.

"Zubaidit," she said softly, "come with me?"

They went inside to the dark house. Mai paused, after she'd slipped off her sandals, to light a lamp with which she illuminated their progress down a corridor to her private rooms.

"Are you crying, Zubaidit?" she asked as she slid the door aside. Priya was sitting comfortably beside the baby's cot in the darkness, and she nodded but did not leave the baby as the two women quietly walked past her and into a narrow storeroom with closed cupboards and shelves stacked with bolts of silk.

"A little." Swallowed tears made Zubaidit's voice hoarse. "It was cursed good sex,

I have to tell you, not that you really want to know, and it hurts to know that was the one and only time. He's a holy Guardian now. You can see he loves her. But I swore my oath to the goddess years ago. I know my path."

"Well," said Mai, "I'm sorry. Or not sorry. However you wish it." She kissed the other woman's cheek before turning to the second cupboard and opening it.

She had hidden the chests in plain sight, stacked among her other chests and fripperies. Easy to pull out, they had so little weight she could stack three in Zubaidit's arms and easily carry the other two. Such a small thing, to mean so much.

Peddonon and Joss were deep into a serious conversation, heads down, not touching but standing close together as Peddonon sounded irritated and Joss regretful, when Mai and Zubaidit returned. The men broke off as the women set the chests down on the ground. Mai went into the garden shed and returned with a wedge and a big hammer, which she handed to Peddonon.

He bit his lip. Then, with a set of neat blows, he shattered the locks. They watched her unwrap the chains and, one by one, open the chests.

Uncle Hari's cloak was first. She hadn't meant it that way, but it seemed appropriate. There was something unsettling in the way they slithered and twisted out of their cages, and yet their flare and flash caught at her heart like banners rumbling in a bright joyful wind. Twilight-sky; blood-red; earth-brown; seedling-green. Last rose night, sewn with stars fallen deep within a cradle of black, its corner brushing her hand with a shiver of memory. It's the ones who can't let go—of fear or anger, lust or greed, vanity or pride or power—who are most at risk of becoming corrupted.

Then they were gone, vanished into the darkness.

On their wings the Guardians took their leave. They were no longer truly part of that world where fussy babies slumber restlessly, and reeves sing bawdy tales on the porch, and a young woman contemplates her future, which after all looks like a series of gates, one after the next and no two alike. Hard to say what lies beyond each threshold.

We must be ready for anything.

ABOUT THE AUTHOR

KATE ELLIOTT is the author of more than a dozen novels, including those of the Crown of Stars series, the Novels of the Jaran, and, most recently, *Spirit Gate* and *Shadow Gate*, the first two novels of Crossroads. *King's Dragon*, the first novel in the Crown of Stars fantasy series, was a Nebula Award finalist; *The Golden Key* (co-written with Melanie Rawn and Jennifer Roberson) was a World Fantasy Award finalist; *Jaran* was named *Voya*'s Best Science Fiction, Fantasy, and Horror of 1992, and was a *Locus* recommended fantasy novel of 1992. Born in Iowa and raised in Oregon, she lives in Hawaii.